PENGUIN BOOKS
SEA OF POPPIES

Amitav Ghosh is one of the most widely known Indians writing in English today. Born in Calcutta in 1956, he studied in Delhi, Oxford and Egypt. He worked for the *Indian Express* newspaper in New Delhi and earned his doctorate at Oxford before he wrote his first novel, *The Circle of Reason*, which won the Prix Medicis Etranger Award. His other books include *The Shadow Lines* (Sahitya Akademi Award), *In an Antique Land*, *The Calcutta Chromosome* (Arthur C. Clarke Award), *Dancing in Cambodia and Other Essays*, *Countdown*, *The Glass Palace* (Grand Prize for Fiction at the Frankfurt International e-Book Awards), *The Imam and the Indian* and *The Hungry Tide* (Best Work in English Fiction, Hutch Crossword Book Award). Amitav Ghosh was also the winner of the 1999 Pushcart Prize, a leading literary award, for an essay that was published in the *Kenyon Review*, and in 2007 was awarded the Grinzane Cavour Prize in Turin, Italy.

He lives with his wife, Deborah Baker, and their children in Brooklyn, USA.

### Praise for the book

'The real strength of *Sea of Poppies* is that it is deeply and persuasively grounded in the great tradition of story-telling, which brings characters and situations alive and develops its themes without ever being cute, clever, wordy, or pretentious. This is the work of a man who knows he has a truly ripping yarn—the digressions swirl like eddies and crosscurrents within the main narrative stream—and is simply happy to tell it. For a deeply political novel, Ghosh adopts a tone of self-possession and restraint that highlights the triumph of the human condition in the face of extreme adversity...Ghosh has written several acclaimed novels before but *Sea of Poppies* is indisputably the finest and most enjoyable work from his pen yet. When the Ibis trilogy is written, it will be no surprise if it goes down as a classic, not just of Indian writing in English but of modern fiction.'—*The Hindu*

'Ghosh has deftly creat[ed] a web of beautifully interlocking stories and characters. [He has] abandoned the sophisticated literary experimentation that marked his superb early books...and is now channeling his creative energies into the skilful story-telling and pacey narrative development which made *The Glass Palace* such a wonderfully gripping tale. *Poppies* is a worthy successor to that book and is every bit as enthralling and as passionately written. For, like the opium that forms its subject, the narrative becomes increasingly powerful and addictive as it takes hold, and most readers will now be waiting anxiously for the two further instalments of the trilogy which Ghosh is working upon.'—William Dalrymple, *Outlook*

'If migration is the movement that animates history to the rhythm of the outcast's heartbeat, Amitav Ghosh is its most elegant choreographer. [A] richly textured, minutely researched novel [*Sea of Poppies*] chronicles the migratory movements in which we may find the first drafts of a million ancestral sagas. As you board the vessel, remember what the connoisseur of opium says elsewhere in the book: let not a wisp escape.'—*India Today*

'Ghosh is the most scholarly of fiction writers—an anthropologist with a deep interest in the convoluted histories of people and places.'—*Business Standard*

'Intoxicating stuff…Ordinary lives, extraordinary tales…[Ghosh] is a master at pitting stories of ordinary people against a historical swathe spanning generations and continents.'—*Financial Express*

'In *Sea of Poppies*, part one of the Ibis trilogy, Ghosh pulls off a most remarkable transformation. In a novel that hinges on transgressions and focuses on deep and often violent change (both personal and social), [he is] cast anew as a writer who can inform, edify, provoke and entertain. This is a barnstormer of a book. When it ends and you're done wiping your palms and your brow, you'll give thanks that it's only the first installment in a trilogy, which means there's more to come.'—*Time Out* (Mumbai)

'A grand narrative that gently reveals history…the strangers on the schooner [the *Ibis*] are not easily forgettable and could have you reaching for Book Two [of the trilogy], like an afeemkhor for abkari.'— *Indian Express*

'A good story told well.'—ibnlive.com

'*Sea of Poppies* is a meditation on colonialism in the guise of a novel, but such is the author's meticulousness in matters of research, and so firm is his grasp of the unexplored (at least in historical fiction) underbelly of the British empire, that his work ends up as a page-turner for anyone with a modicum of interest in India.'—*Mint*

'[Ghosh] doesn't let scholarship come in the way of storytelling…[this book is] a voyage of many charms.'—*Hindustan Times*

'*Sea of Poppies* is a consummate page-turner that unravels the notorious opium trade of the 19th century…The cloak-and-dagger machinations of virtually all the characters, the dramatic plots and escapes, the rapidly shifting locales and the almost implausible daredevilry sometimes displayed, make for a nail-biting experience.'—*DNA*

'*Sea of Poppies* is a stunning, page-turning adventure.'—*Mumbai Mirror*

'Amitav Ghosh is undoubtedly one of the finest storytellers of our time. *Sea of Poppies* confirms this reputation.'—*Mail Today*

'Ghosh has turned out a novel of somber brilliance, offering an amazing blend of sympathy and cynicism, irony and joviality…an enduring achievement written by a pure literary virtuoso…'—*Tribune*

'*Sea of Poppies* reasserts Amitav Ghosh's reputation as a master storyteller.'—*Statesman*

'*Sea of Poppies* is a novel of immense variety and scope.'—*Asian Age*

'[A] remarkably rich saga . . . which has plenty of action and adventure à la Dumas, but moments also of Tolstoyan penetration—and a drop or two of Dickensian sentiment.'—*The Observer* (London)

'India in the 1830s is wonderfully evoked—the smells, rituals and squalor . . . Coarseness and violence, cruelty and fatalism, are relieved with flashes of emotion and kindness. [*Sea of Poppies*] is no anti-colonial rant or didactic tableau but the story of men and women of all races and castes, cooped up on a voyage across the "Black Water" that strips them of dignity and ends in a storm . . . It is profoundly moving.'—*The Times* (London)

'[A] terrific novel . . . In bringing his troupe of characters to Calcutta . . . Ghosh provides the reader with all manner of stories, and equips himself with the personnel to man and navigate an old-fashioned literary three-decker . . . Yet for all its research, *Sea of Poppies* is full of the open air. It never, as the eighteenth century used to say, "smells of the lamp".'—*The Guardian*

'The seaboard sections rival those in Melville and Conrad, but the scenes ashore are equally gripping and one leaves this long page-turner wishing it could continue . . . *Sea of Poppies* is a tremendous novel . . . [The] "Ibis" trilogy will surely come to be regarded as one of the masterpieces of twenty-first-century fiction.'—*The Literary Review*

'Hugely entertaining . . . Glorious babel of a novel . . . Carried along by the sheer energy of the narrative, most readers will soon tune in to this marvelously inventive lingo . . . [*Sea of Poppies*] is utterly involving and piles on the tension until the very last page . . . The next volume cannot come too soon.'—*The Sunday Times* (London)

'Bedazzling . . . Amitav Ghosh's *Sea of Poppies*, the first volume in his "Ibis trilogy", revisits in new, breathtakingly detailed and compelling ways some of the concerns of his earlier novels . . . We [await] with eagerness the second volume of the trilogy.'—*The Independent*

'*Sea of Poppies* is bathed in rich vernacular . . . [It] is a thoroughly readable romp of a novel, filled with excellent set pieces, comic digressions (especially its comedies of manners), love interest, subterfuge and betrayal. We are left thirsty for more.'—*New Statesman*

'Epic . . . Each scene is boldly drawn, but it is the sheer energy and verve of Ghosh's storytelling that bind this ambitious medley.'—*The Daily Mail*

'Rich and panoramic, Amitav Ghosh's latest novel sees this Indian author on masterly form . . . *Sea of Poppies* is a sprawling adventure with a cast of hundreds and numerous intricate stories encompassing poverty and riches, despair and hope, and the long-fingered reach of the opium trade . . . Lustrous.'—*The Economist*

'The cast is marvelous and the plot majestically serpentine, but the real hero is the English language, which has rarely felt so alive and vibrant.'—*Publishers Weekly* (starred review)

'In vivid settings ranging from the hellish precincts of an enormous opium factory, to absurdly lavish upper-class households, to the *Ibis*' grim hold, Ghosh unfurls tales of betrayal and tyranny, revelation and transformation, while reveling in the mischievous inventiveness of a bawdy polyglot lingo favored by sailors on Eastern seas. With intimations of Dickens and Melville, Ghosh's vital saga encompasses suspense and satire, perverse cruelty and profound kindness, and the countless ways humans conceal desire and fear behind arrogance and brutality.'—*Booklist*

'Ghosh orchestrates his polyphonic saga with a composer's fine touch ... The density of settings, from rural India to teeming Calcutta to the Sudder Opium Factory, is historically convincing, and the author pays close attention to variations in speech ... Planned as the first of a trilogy, this astonishing, mesmerizing launch will be hard to top.'— *Kirkus Reviews* (starred review)

# Sea of Poppies

AMITAV GHOSH

**PENGUIN BOOKS**

PENGUIN BOOKS

Published by the Penguin Group

Penguin Books India Pvt. Ltd, 11 Community Centre, Panchsheel Park, New Delhi 110 017, India

Penguin Group (USA) Inc., 375 Hudson Street, New York, New York 10014, USA

Penguin Group (Canada), 90 Eglinton Avenue East, Suite 700, Toronto, Ontario, M4P 2Y3, Canada (a division of Pearson Penguin Canada Inc.)

Penguin Books Ltd, 80 Strand, London WC2R 0RL, England

Penguin Ireland, 25 St Stephen's Green, Dublin 2, Ireland (a division of Penguin Books Ltd)

Penguin Group (Australia), 250 Camberwell Road, Camberwell, Victoria 3124, Australia (a division of Pearson Australia Group Pty Ltd)

Penguin Group (NZ), 67 Apollo Drive, Rosedale, North Shore 0632, New Zealand (a division of Pearson New Zealand Ltd)

Penguin Group (South Africa) (Pty) Ltd, 24 Sturdee Avenue, Rosebank, Johannesburg 2196, South Africa

Penguin Books Ltd, Registered Offices: 80 Strand, London WC2R 0RL, England

First published in Viking by Penguin Books India 2008
Published in Penguin Books 2009

Copyright © Amitav Ghosh 2008

ISBN 9780143066156

For sale in India, Nepal, Bangladesh and Bhutan only

Typeset in Sabon by SURYA, New Delhi
Printed at Replika Press Pvt. Ltd.

To Nayan
*for his fifteenth*

part one

~

# Land

# one

~

The vision of a tall-masted ship, at sail on the ocean, came to Deeti on an otherwise ordinary day, but she knew instantly that the apparition was a sign of destiny for she had never seen such a vessel before, not even in a dream: how could she have, living as she did in northern Bihar, four hundred miles from the coast? Her village was so far inland that the sea seemed as distant as the netherworld: it was the chasm of darkness where the holy Ganga disappeared into the Kala-Pani, 'the Black Water'.

It happened at the end of winter, in a year when the poppies were strangely slow to shed their petals: for mile after mile, from Benares onwards, the Ganga seemed to be flowing between twin glaciers, both its banks being blanketed by thick drifts of white-petalled flowers. It was as if the snows of the high Himalayas had descended on the plains to await the arrival of Holi and its springtime profusion of colour.

The village in which Deeti lived was on the outskirts of the town of Ghazipur, some fifty miles east of Benares. Like all her neighbours, Deeti was preoccupied with the lateness of her poppy crop: that day, she rose early and went through the motions of her daily routine, laying out a freshly-washed dhoti and kameez for Hukam Singh, her husband, and preparing the rotis and achar he would eat at midday. Once his meal had been wrapped and packed, she broke off to pay a quick visit to her shrine room: later, after she'd bathed and changed, Deeti would do a proper puja, with flowers and offerings; now, being clothed still in her night-time sari, she merely stopped at the door, to join her hands in a brief genuflection.

Soon a squeaking wheel announced the arrival of the ox-cart that would take Hukam Singh to the factory where he worked, in Ghazipur, three miles away. Although not far, the distance was too great for Hukam Singh to cover on foot, for he had been wounded in the leg while serving as a sepoy in a British regiment. The disability was not so severe as to require crutches, however, and Hukam Singh was able to make his way to the cart without assistance. Deeti followed a step behind, carrying his food and water, handing the cloth-wrapped package to him after he had climbed in.

Kalua, the driver of the ox-cart, was a giant of a man, but he made no move to help his passenger and was careful to keep his face hidden from him: he was of the leather-workers' caste and Hukam Singh, as a high-caste Rajput, believed that the sight of his face would bode ill for the day ahead. Now, on climbing into the back of the cart, the former sepoy sat facing to the rear, with his bundle balanced on his lap, to prevent its coming into direct contact with any of the driver's belongings. Thus they would sit, driver and passenger, as the cart creaked along the road to Ghazipur—conversing amicably enough, but never exchanging glances.

Deeti, too, was careful to keep her face covered in the driver's presence: it was only when she went back inside, to wake Kabutri, her six-year-old daughter, that she allowed the ghungta of her sari to slip off her head. Kabutri was lying curled on her mat and Deeti knew, because of her quickly changing pouts and smiles, that she was deep in a dream: she was about to rouse her when she stopped her hand and stepped back. In her daughter's sleeping face, she could see the lineaments of her own likeness—the same full lips, rounded nose and upturned chin—except that in the child the lines were still clean and sharply drawn, whereas in herself they had grown smudged and indistinct. After seven years of marriage, Deeti was not much more than a child herself, but a few tendrils of white had already appeared in her thick black hair. The skin of her face, parched and darkened by the sun, had begun to flake and crack around the corners of her mouth and her eyes. Yet, despite the careworn commonplaceness of her appearance, there was one respect in which she stood out from the ordinary: she had light grey eyes, a feature that was unusual in that part of the country. Such was the colour—or perhaps colourlessness—of her eyes that they made her seem at once blind and all-seeing. This had the effect of unnerving the young, and of reinforcing their prejudices and superstitions to the point where they would sometimes shout taunts at her— *chudaliya, dainiya*—as if she were a witch: but Deeti had only to turn her eyes on them to make them scatter and run off. Although not above taking a little pleasure in her powers of discomfiture, Deeti was glad, for her daughter's sake, that this was one aspect of her appearance that she had not passed on— she delighted in Kabutri's dark eyes, which were as black as her shiny hair. Now, looking down on her daughter's dreaming face, Deeti smiled and decided that she wouldn't wake her after all: in three or four years the girl would be married and gone; there would be enough time for her to work when she was received into her husband's house; in her few remaining years at home she might as well rest.

With scarcely a pause for a mouthful of roti, Deeti stepped outside, on to the flat threshold of beaten earth that divided the mud-walled dwelling from the poppy fields beyond. By the light of the newly-risen sun, she saw, greatly to her relief, that some of her flowers had at last begun to shed their petals. On the adjacent field, her husband's younger brother, Chandan Singh, was already out with his eight-bladed nukha in hand. He was using the tool's tiny teeth to make notches on some of the bare pods—if the sap flowed freely overnight he would bring his family out tomorrow, to tap the field. The timing had to be exactly right because the priceless sap flowed only for a brief period in the plant's span of life: a day or two, this way or that, and the pods were of no more value than the blossoms of a weed.

Chandan Singh had seen her too and he was not a person who could let anyone pass by in silence. A slack-jawed youth with a brood of five children of his own, he never missed an opportunity to remind Deeti of her paucity of offspring. *Ka bhail*? he called out, licking a drop of fresh sap from the tip of his instrument. What's the matter? Working alone again? How long can you carry on like this? You need a son, to give you a helping hand. You're not barren, after all . . .

Being accustomed to her brother-in-law's ways, Deeti had no difficulty in ignoring his jibes: turning her back on him, she headed into her own field, carrying a wide wicker basket at her waist. Between the rows of flowers, the ground was carpeted in papery petals and she scooped them up in handfuls, dropping them into her basket. A week or two before, she would have taken care to creep sideways, so as not to disturb the flowers, but today she all but flounced as she went and was none too sorry when her swishing sari swept clusters of petals off the ripening pods. When the basket was full, she carried it back and emptied it next to the outdoor chula where she did most of her cooking. This part of the threshold was shaded by two enormous mango trees, which had just begun to sprout the dimples that would grow into the first buds of spring. Relieved to be out of the sun, Deeti squatted beside her oven and thrust an armload of firewood into last night's embers, which could still be seen glowing, deep inside the ashes.

Kabutri was awake now, and when she showed her face in the doorway, her mother was no longer in a mood to be indulgent. So late? she snapped. Where were you? *Kám-o-káj na hoi*? You think there's no work to be done?

Deeti gave her daughter the job of sweeping the poppy petals into a heap while she busied herself in stoking the fire and heating a heavy iron tawa. Once this griddle was heated through, she sprinkled a handful of petals on it and pressed them down with a bundled-up rag. Darkening as they toasted, the petals began to cling together so that in a minute or two they looked exactly like the round wheat-flour rotis Deeti had packed for her husband's midday meal. And 'roti' was indeed the name by which these poppy-petal wrappers were known although their purpose was entirely different from that of their namesake: they were to be sold to the Sudder Opium Factory,

*Amitav Ghosh*

in Ghazipur, where they would be used to line the earthenware containers in which opium was packed.

Kabutri, in the meanwhile, had kneaded some atta and rolled out a few real rotis. Deeti cooked them quickly, before poking out the fire: the rotis were put aside, to be eaten later with yesterday's leftovers—a dish of stale alu-posth, potatoes cooked in poppy-seed paste. Now, her mind turned to her shrine room again: with the hour of the noontime puja drawing close, it was time to go down to the river for a bath. After massaging poppy-seed oil into Kabutri's hair and her own, Deeti draped her spare sari over her shoulder and led her daughter towards the water, across the field.

The poppies ended at a sandbank that sloped gently down to the Ganga; warmed by the sun, the sand was hot enough to sting the soles of their bare feet. The burden of motherly decorum slipped suddenly off Deeti's bowed shoulders and she began to run after her daughter, who had skipped on ahead. A pace or two from the water's edge, they shouted an invocation to the river—*Jai Ganga Mayya ki . . .*—and gulped down a draught of air, before throwing themselves in.

They were both laughing when they came up again: it was the time of year when, after the initial shock of contact, the water soon reveals itself to be refreshingly cool. Although the full heat of summer was still several weeks away, the flow of the Ganga had already begun to dwindle. Turning in the direction of Benares, in the west, Deeti hoisted her daughter aloft, to pour out a handful of water as a tribute to the holy city. Along with the offering, a leaf flowed out of the child's cupped palms. They turned to watch as the river carried it downstream towards the ghats of Ghazipur.

The walls of Ghazipur's opium factory were partially obscured by mango and jackfruit trees but the British flag that flew on top of it was just visible above the foliage, as was the steeple of the church in which the factory's overseers prayed. At the factory's ghat on the Ganga, a one-masted pateli barge could be seen, flying the pennant of the English East India Company. It had brought in a shipment of *chalán* opium, from one of the Company's outlying sub-agencies, and was being unloaded by a long line of coolies.

Ma, said Kabutri, looking up at her mother, where is that boat going?

It was Kabutri's question that triggered Deeti's vision: her eyes suddenly conjured up a picture of an immense ship with two tall masts. Suspended from the masts were great sails of a dazzling shade of white. The prow of the ship tapered into a figurehead with a long bill, like a stork or a heron. There was a man in the background, standing near the bow, and although she could not see him clearly, she had a sense of a distinctive and unfamiliar presence.

Deeti knew that the vision was not materially present in front of her—as, for example, was the barge moored near the factory. She had never seen the sea, never left the district, never spoken any language but her native Bhojpuri, yet not for a moment did she doubt that the ship existed somewhere and was heading in her direction. The knowledge of this terrified her, for she had never set eyes on anything that remotely resembled this apparition, and had no idea what it might portend.

Kabutri knew that something unusual had happened, for she waited a minute or two before asking: Ma? What are you looking at? What have you seen?

Deeti's face was a mask of fear and foreboding as she said, in a shaky voice: Beti—I saw a jahaj—a ship.

Do you mean that boat over there?

No, beti: it was a ship like I've never seen before. It was like a great bird, with sails like wings and a long beak.

Casting a glance downriver, Kabutri said: Can you draw for me what you saw?

Deeti answered with a nod and they waded ashore. They changed quickly and filled a pitcher with water from the Ganga, for the puja room. When they were back at home, Deeti lit a lamp before leading Kabutri into the shrine. The room was dark, with soot-blackened walls, and it smelled strongly of oil and incense. There was a small altar inside, with statues of Shivji and Bhagwan Ganesh, and framed prints of

Ma Durga and Shri Krishna. But the room was a shrine not just to the gods but also to Deeti's personal pantheon, and it contained many tokens of her family and forebears—among them such relics as her dead father's wooden clogs, a necklace of rudraksha beads left to her by her mother, and faded imprints of her grandparents' feet, taken on their funeral pyres. The walls around the altar were devoted to pictures that Deeti had drawn herself, in outline, on papery poppy-petal discs: such were the charcoal portraits of two brothers and a sister, all of whom had died as children. A few living relatives were represented too, but only by diagrammatic images drawn on mango leaves—Deeti believed it to be bad luck to attempt overly realistic portraits of those who had yet to leave this earth. Thus her beloved older brother, Kesri Singh, was depicted by a few strokes that stood for his sepoy's rifle and his upturned moustache.

Now, on entering her puja room, Deeti picked up a green mango leaf, dipped a fingertip in a container of bright red sindoor and drew, with a few strokes, two wing-like triangles hanging suspended above a long curved shape that ended in a hooked bill. It could have been a bird in flight but Kabutri recognized it at once for what it was—an image of a two-masted vessel with unfurled sails. She was amazed that her mother had drawn the image as though she were representing a living being.

Are you going to put it in the puja room? she asked.

Yes, said Deeti.

The child could not understand why a ship should find a place in the family pantheon. But why? she said.

I don't know, said Deeti, for she too was puzzled by the sureness of her intuition: I just know that it must be there; and not just the ship, but also many of those who are in it; they too must be on the walls of our puja room.

But who are they? said the puzzled child.

I don't know yet, Deeti told her. But I will when I see them.

~

The carved head of a bird that held up the bowsprit of the *Ibis* was unusual enough to serve as proof, to those who needed it, that this was indeed the ship that Deeti saw while standing half-immersed in the waters of the Ganga. Later, even seasoned sailors would admit that her drawing was an uncannily evocative rendition of its subject, especially considering that it was made by someone who had never set eyes on a two-masted schooner— or, for that matter, any other deep-water vessel.

In time, among the legions who came to regard the *Ibis* as their ancestor, it was accepted that it was the river itself that had granted Deeti the vision: that the image of the *Ibis* had been transported upstream, like an electric current, the moment the vessel made contact with the sacred waters. This would mean that it happened in the second week of March 1838, for that was when the *Ibis* dropped anchor off Ganga-Sagar Island, where the holy river debouches into the Bay of Bengal. It was here, while the *Ibis* waited to take on a pilot to guide her to Calcutta, that Zachary Reid had his first look at India: what he saw was a dense thicket of mangroves, and a mudbank that appeared to be uninhabited until it disgorged its bumboats—a small flotilla of dinghies and canoes, all intent on peddling fruit, fish and vegetables to the newly arrived sailors.

Zachary Reid was of medium height and sturdy build, with skin the colour of old ivory and a mass of curly, lacquer-black hair that tumbled over his forehead and into his eyes. The pupils of his eyes were as dark as his hair, except that they were flecked with sparks of hazel: as a child, strangers were apt to say that a pair of twinklers like his could be sold as diamonds to a duchess (later, when it came time for him to be included in Deeti's shrine, much would be made of the brilliance of his gaze). Because he laughed easily and carried himself with a carefree lightness, people sometimes took him to be younger than he was, but Zachary was always quick to offer a correction: the son of a Maryland freedwoman, he took no small pride in the fact of knowing his precise age and the exact date of his birth. To those in error, he would point out that he was twenty, not a day less and not many more.

*Amitav Ghosh*

It was Zachary's habit to think, every day, of at least five things to praise, a practice that had been instilled by his mother as a necessary corrective for a tongue that sometimes sported too sharp an edge. Since his departure from America it was the *Ibis* herself that had figured most often in Zachary's daily tally of praiseworthy things. It was not that she was especially sleek or rakish in appearance: on the contrary, the *Ibis* was a schooner of old-fashioned appearance, neither lean, nor flush-decked like the clippers for which Baltimore was famous. She had a short quarter-deck, a risen fo'c'sle, with a fo'c'sle-deck between the bows, and a deckhouse amidships, that served as a galley and cabin for the bo'suns and stewards. With her cluttered main deck and her broad beam, the *Ibis* was sometimes taken for a schooner-rigged barque by old sailors: whether there was any truth to this Zachary did not know, but he never thought of her as anything other than the topsail schooner that she was when he first signed on to her crew. To his eye there was something unusually graceful about the *Ibis*'s yacht-like rigging, with her sails aligned along her length rather than across the line of her hull. He could see why, with her main- and head-sails standing fair, she might put someone in mind of a white-winged bird in flight: other tall-masted ships, with their stacked loads of square canvas, seemed almost ungainly in comparison.

One thing Zachary did know about the *Ibis* was that she had been built to serve as a 'blackbirder', for transporting slaves. This, indeed, was the reason why she had changed hands: in the years since the formal abolition of the slave trade, British and American naval vessels had taken to patrolling the West African coast in growing numbers, and the *Ibis* was not swift enough to be confident of outrunning them. As with many another slave-ship, the schooner's new owner had acquired her with an eye to fitting her for a different trade: the export of opium. In this instance the purchasers were a firm called Burnham Bros., a shipping company and trading house that had extensive interests in India and China.

The new owners' representatives had lost no time in calling

for the schooner to be dispatched to Calcutta, which was where the head of the house, Benjamin Brightwell Burnham, had his principal residence: the *Ibis* was to be refitted upon reaching her destination, and it was for this purpose that Zachary had been taken on. Zachary had spent eight years working in the Gardiner shipyard, at Fell's Point in Baltimore, and he was eminently well-qualified to supervise the outfitting of the old slave-ship: but as for sailing, he had no more knowledge of ships than any other shore-bound carpenter, this being his first time at sea. But Zachary had signed on with a mind to learning the sailor's trade, and he stepped on board with great eagerness, carrying a canvas ditty-bag that held little more than a change of clothes and a penny-whistle that his father had given him as a boy. The *Ibis* provided him with a quick, if stern schooling, the log of her voyage being a litany of troubles almost from the start. Mr Burnham was in such a hurry to get his new schooner to India that she had sailed short-handed from Baltimore, shipping a crew of nineteen, of whom nine were listed as 'Black', including Zachary. Despite being undermanned, her provisions were deficient, both in quality and quantity, and this had led to confrontations, between stewards and sailors, mates and fo'c'slemen. Then she hit heavy seas and her timbers were found to be weeping: it fell to Zachary to discover that the 'tween-deck, where the schooner's human cargo had been accommodated, was riddled with peepholes and air ducts, bored by generations of captive Africans. The *Ibis* was carrying a cargo of cotton, to defray the costs of the journey; after the inundation, the bales were drenched and had to be jettisoned.

Off the coast of Patagonia, foul weather forced a change in course, which had been plotted to take the *Ibis* across the Pacific and around Java Head. Instead, her sails were set for the Cape of Good Hope—with the result that she ran afoul of the weather again, and was becalmed a fortnight in the doldrums. With the crew on half-rations, eating maggoty hardtack and rotten beef, there was an outbreak of dysentery: before the wind picked up again, three men were dead and two of the black crewmen were in chains, for refusing the food that was put before them. With hands running short, Zachary had put aside his carpenter's tools and become a full-fledged foretopman, running up the ratlines to bend the topsail.

Then it happened that the second mate, who was a hard-horse, hated by every black man in the crew, fell overboard and drowned: everyone knew the fall to be no accident, but the tensions on the vessel had reached such a point that the ship's master, a sharp-tongued Boston Irishman, let the matter slip. Zachary was the only member of the crew to put in a bid when the dead man's effects were auctioned, thus coming into possession of a sextant and a trunk-load of clothes.

Soon, being neither of the quarter-deck nor of the fo'c'sle, Zachary became the link between the two parts of the ship, and was shouldering the duties of the second mate. He was not quite the novice now that he had been at the start of the voyage, but nor was he equal to his new responsibilities. His faltering efforts did nothing to improve morale and when the schooner put in to Cape Town the crew melted away overnight, to spread word of a hell-afloat with pinch-gut pay. The reputation of the *Ibis* was so damaged that not a single American or European, not even the worst rufflers and rum-gaggers, could be induced to sign on: the only seamen who would venture on her decks were lascars.

This was Zachary's first experience of this species of sailor. He had thought that lascars were a tribe or nation, like the Cherokee or Sioux: he discovered now that they came from places that were far apart, and had nothing in common, except the Indian Ocean; among them were Chinese and East Africans, Arabs and Malays, Bengalis and Goans, Tamils and Arakanese. They came in groups of ten or fifteen, each with a leader who spoke on their behalf. To break up these groups was impossible; they had to be taken together or not at all, and although they came cheap, they had their own ideas of how much work they would do and how many men would share each job—which seemed to mean that three or four lascars had to be hired for jobs that could well be done by a single able seaman. The

Captain declared them to be as lazy a bunch of niggers as he had ever seen, but to Zachary they appeared more ridiculous than anything else. Their costumes, to begin with: their feet were as naked as the day they were born, and many seemed to own no clothing other than a length of cambric to wind around their middle. Some paraded around in drawstringed knickers, while others wore sarongs that flapped around their scrawny legs like petticoats, so that at times the deck looked like the parlour of a honeyhouse. How could a man climb a mast in bare feet, swaddled in a length of cloth like a newborn child? No matter that they were as nimble as any seaman he'd ever seen—it still discomfited Zachary to see them in the rigging, hanging like monkeys on the ratlines: when their sarongs blew in the wind, he would avert his eyes for fear of what he might see if he looked up.

After several changes of mind, the skipper decided to engage a lascar company that was led by one Serang Ali. This was a personage of formidable appearance, with a face that would have earned the envy of Genghis Khan, being thin, long and narrow, with darting black eyes that sat restlessly upon rakishly-angled cheekbones. Two feathery strands of moustache drooped down to his chin, framing a mouth that was constantly in motion, its edges stained a bright, livid red: it was as if he were forever smacking his lips after drinking from the opened veins of a mare, like some bloodthirsty Tartar of the steppes. The discovery that the substance in his mouth was of vegetable origin came as no great reassurance to Zachary: once, when the serang spat a stream of blood-red juice over the rail, he noticed the water below coming alive with the thrashing of shark's fins. How harmless could this betel-stuff be if it could be mistaken for blood by a shark?

The prospect of journeying to India with this crew was so unappealing that the first mate disappeared too, taking himself off the ship in such a hurry that he left behind a bagful of clothes. When told that the mate was a gone-goose, the skipper growled: 'Cut his painter, has he? Don't blame him neither. I'd of walked my chalks too, if I'd'a been paid.'

The *Ibis*'s next port of call was to be the island of Mauritius, where they were to exchange a cargo of grain for a load of ebony and hardwood. Since no other sea-officer could be found before their departure, the schooner sailed with Zachary standing in for the first mate: thus it happened that in the course of a single voyage, by virtue of desertions and dead-tickets, he vaulted from the merest novice sailor to senior seaman, from carpenter to second-in-command, with a cabin of his own. His one regret about the move from fo'c'sle to cabin was that his beloved penny-whistle disappeared somewhere on the way and had to be given up for lost.

Before this, the skipper had instructed Zachary to eat his meals below—'not going to spill no colour on my table, even if it's just a pale shade of yaller.' But now, rather than dine alone, he insisted on having Zachary share the table in the cuddy, where they were waited on by a sizeable contingent of lascar ship's-boys—a scuttling company of launders and chuckeroos.

Once under sail, Zachary was forced to undergo yet another education, not so much in seamanship this time, as in the ways of the new crew. Instead of the usual sailors' games of cards and ablewhackets, there was the clicking of dice, with games of parcheesi unfolding on chequerboards of rope; the cheerful sound of sea-shanties yielded to tunes of a new kind, wild and discordant, and the very smell of the ship began to change, with the odour of spices creeping through the timbers. Having been put in charge of the ship's stores Zachary had to familiarize himself with a new set of provisions, bearing no resemblance to the accustomed hardtack and brined beef; he had to learn to say 'resum' instead of 'rations', and he had to wrap his tongue around words like 'dal', 'masala' and 'achar'. He had to get used to 'malum' instead of mate, 'serang' for bo'sun, 'tindal' for bosun's mate, and 'seacunny' for helmsman; he had to memorize a new shipboard vocabulary, which sounded a bit like English and yet not: the rigging became the 'ringeen', 'avast!' was 'bas!', and the cry of the middle-morning watch went from 'all's well' to 'alzbel'. The deck now became the 'tootuk' while the masts were 'dols'; a command became a 'hookum' and instead of starboard and larboard, fore and aft, he had to say 'jamna' and 'dawa', 'agil' and 'peechil'.

One thing that continued unchanged was the division of the crew into two watches, each led by a tindal. Most of the business of the ship fell to the two tindals, and little was seen of Serang Ali for the first two days. But on the third, Zachary came on deck at dawn to be greeted with a cheerful: 'Chin-chin Malum Zikri! You catchi chow-chow? Wat dam' t'ing hab got inside?'

Although startled at first, Zachary soon found himself speaking to the serang with an unaccustomed ease: it was as if his oddly patterned speech had unloosed his own tongue. 'Serang Ali, where you from?' he asked.

'Serang Ali blongi Rohingya—from Arakan-side.'

'And where'd you learn that kinda talk?'

'Afeem ship,' came the answer. 'China-side, Yankee gen'l'um allo tim tok so-fashion. Also Mich'man like Malum Zikri.'

'I ain no midshipman,' Zachary corrected him. 'Signed on as the ship's carpenter.'

'Nevva mind,' said the serang, in an indulgent, paternal way. 'Nevva mind: allo same-sem. Malum Zikri sun-sun become pukka gen'l'um. So tell no: catchi wife-o yet?'

'No.' Zachary laughed.''N'how bout you? Serang Ali catchi wife?'

'Serang Ali wife-o hab makee die,' came the answer. 'Go topside, to hebbin. By'mby, Serang Ali catchi nother piece wife . . .'

A week later, Serang Ali accosted Zachary again: 'Malum Zikri! Captin-bugger blongi poo-shoo-foo. He hab got plenty sick! Need one piece dokto. No can chow-chow tiffin. Allo tim do chheechhee, pee-pee. Plenty smelly in Captin cabin.'

Zachary took himself off to the Captain's stateroom and was told that there was nothing wrong: just a touch of the back-door trots—not the flux, for there was no sign of blood, no spotting in the mustard. 'I know how to take care o' meself:

*Amitav Ghosh*

not the first time I've had a run of the squitters and collywobbles.'

But soon the skipper was too weak to leave his cabin and Zachary was handed charge of the ship's log and the navigation charts. Having been schooled until the age of twelve, Zachary was able to write a slow but well-formed copperplate hand: the filling of the log-book posed no problem. Navigation was another matter: although he had learnt some arithmetic at the shipyard, he was not at ease with numbers. But over the course of the voyage, he had been at pains to watch the Captain and the first mate as they took their midday readings; at times he had even asked questions, which were answered, depending on the officers' moods, either with laconic explanations or with fists to his ear. Now using the Captain's watch, and a sextant inherited from the dead mate, he spent a good deal of time trying to calculate the ship's position. His first few attempts ended in panic, with his calculations placing the ship hundreds of miles off course. But on issuing a hookum for a change of course, he discovered that the actual steering of the ship had never been in his hands anyway.

'Malum Zikri think lascar-bugger no can do sail ship?' said Serang Ali indignantly. 'Lascar-bugger savvi too muchi sail ship, you look-see.'

Zachary protested that they were three hundred miles off course for Port Louis and was answered with an impatient retort: 'What for Malum Zikri make big dam bobbery'n so muchee bukbuk and big-big hookuming? Malum Zikri still learn-pijjin. No sabbi ship-pijjin. No can see Serang Ali too muchi smart-bugger inside? Takee ship Por'Lwee-side three days, look-see.'

Three days later, exactly as promised, the twisted hills of Mauritius appeared on the jamna bow, with Port Louis nestled in the bay below.

'I'll be dickswiggered!' said Zachary, in grudging admiration. 'Don't that just beat the Dutch? You sure that the right place?'

'What I tell you no? Serang Ali Number One sabbi ship-pijjin.'

Zachary was to learn later that Serang Ali had been steering his own course all along, using a method of navigation that combined dead reckoning—or 'tup ka shoomar' as he called it—with frequent readings of the stars.

The Captain was now too ill to leave the *Ibis*, so it fell to Zachary to conduct the shipowners' business on the island, which included the delivery of a letter to the owner of a plantation, some six miles from Port Louis. Zachary was making ready to go ashore with the letter when he was intercepted by Serang Ali, who looked him up and down in concern.

'Malum Zikri catch plenty trouble'n he go Por'Lwee like that.'

'Why? Don see nothin wrong.'

'Malum look-see.' Serang Ali stepped back and ran a critical eye over Zachary. 'What dam cloth hab got on?'

Zachary was dressed in his workaday clothes, canvas trowsers and the usual sailor's banyan—a loose-fitting tunic made, in this instance, of coarse and faded Osnaburg cloth. After weeks at sea his face was unshaven and his curly hair was grimy with grease, tar and salt. But none of this seemed untoward—he was just delivering a letter after all. He shrugged: 'So?'

'Malum Zikri go so-fashion to Por'Lwee, no come back,' said Serang Ali. 'Too muchi press gang in Por'Lwee. Plenty blackbirder wanchi catch one piece slave. Malum go be shanghaied, made slave; allo time floggin', beatin'. No good.'

This gave Zachary pause for thought: he went back to his cabin and looked more closely at the possessions he had accumulated as a result of the death and desertion of the two ships' mates. One of them had been something of a dandy and there were so many clothes in his trunk as to intimidate Zachary: what went with what? What was right for which time of day? It was one thing to look at these fine go-ashores on others, but to step into them was quite another matter.

Here again, Serang Ali came to Zachary's aid: it turned out that among the lascars there were many who boasted of skills

*Amitav Ghosh*

apart from sailoring—among them a kussab who had once worked as a 'dressboy' for a shipowner; a steward who was also a darzee and earned extra money by sewing and mending clothes; and a topas who had learnt barbering and served as the crew's balwar. Under Serang Ali's direction, the team went to work, rifling through Zachary's bags and trunks, picking out clothes, measuring, folding, snipping, cutting. While the tailor-steward and his chuckeroos busied themselves with inseams and cuffs, the barber-topas led Zachary to the lee scuppers and, with the aid of a couple of launders, subjected him to as thorough a scrubbing as he had ever had. Zachary offered no resistance until the topas produced a dark, perfumed liquid and made as if to pour it into his hair: 'Hey! What's that stuff?'

'Champi,' said the barber, making a rubbing motion with his hands. 'Champoo-ing too good . . .'

'Shampoo?' Zachary had never heard of this substance: loath as he was to allow it on his person, he gave in, and to his own surprise, he was not sorry afterwards, for his head had never felt so light nor his hair smelled so good.

In a couple of hours Zachary was looking at an almost unrecognizable image of himself in the mirror, clothed in a white linen shirt, riding breeches and a double-breasted summer paletot, with a white cravat knotted neatly around his neck. On his hair, trimmed, brushed and tied with a blue ribbon at the nape of his neck, sat a glossy black hat.There was nothing missing, so far as Zachary could see, but Serang Ali was still not satisfied: 'Sing-song no hab got?'

'What?'

'Clock.' The serang slipped his hand into his vest, as if to suggest that he was reaching for a fob.

The idea that he might be able to afford a watch made Zachary laugh. 'No,' he said. 'I ain got no watch.'

'Nebba mind. Malum Zikri wait one minute.'

Ushering the other lascars out of the cabin, the serang disappeared for a good ten minutes. When he came back, there was something hidden in the folds of his sarong. Shutting the door behind him, he undid his waist knot and handed Zachary a shining silver watch.

'Geekus crow!' Zachary's mouth fell open as he looked at the watch, sitting in his palm like a gleaming oyster: both its sides were covered with intricately filigreed designs, and its chain was made of three finely-chased silver strands. Flipping the cover open, he stared in amazement at the moving hands and clicking cogs.

'It's beautiful.' On the inner side of the cover, Zachary noticed, there was a name, engraved in small letters. He read it out loud: '"Adam T. Danby". Who was that? Did you know him, Serang Ali?'

The serang hesitated for a moment and then shook his head: 'No. No, sabbi. Bought clock in pawnshop, in Cape Town. Now blongi Zikri Malum's.'

'I can't take this from you, Serang Ali.'

'Is all right, Zikri Malum,' said the serang with one of his rare smiles. 'Is all right.'

Zachary was touched. 'Thank you, Serang Ali. Ain nobody never gave me nothin like this before.' He stood in front of the mirror, watch in hand, hat on head, and burst into laughter. 'Hey! They'll make me Mayor, for sure.'

Serang Ali nodded: 'Malum Zikri one big piece pukka sahib now. Allo propa. If planter-bugger coming catch, must do dumbcow.'

'Dumbcow?' said Zachary. 'What you talkin bout?'

'Must too muchi shout: planter-bugger, you go barnshoot sister. I one-piece pukka sahib, no can catch. You takee pistol in pocket; if bugger try shanghai, shoot in he face.'

Zachary pocketed a pistol and went nervously ashore—but almost from the moment he stepped on the quay he found himself being treated with unaccustomed deference. He went to a stable to hire a horse, and the French owner bowed and addressed him as 'milord' and couldn't do enough to please him. He rode out with a groom running behind him, to point the way.

The town was small, just a few blocks of houses that faded

away into a jumble of shacks, shanties and other hut-houses; beyond, the path wound through dense patches of forest and towering, tangled thickets of sugar-cane. The surrounding hills and crags were of strange, twisted shapes; they sat upon the plains like a bestiary of gargantuan animals that had been frozen in the act of trying to escape from the grip of the earth. From time to time, passing between fields of sugar-cane, he would come upon gangs of men who would put down their scythes to stare at him: the overseers would bow, raising their whips deferentially to their hats while the workers gazed in expressionless silence, making him glad of the weapon in his pocket. The plantation house came into view while he was still a long way off, through an avenue of trees with peeling, honey-coloured bark. He had expected a mansion, like those in the plantations of Delaware and Maryland, but in this house there were no grand pillars or gabled windows: it was a one-storeyed wood-framed bungalow, skirted by a deep veranda. The owner, Monsieur d'Epinay, was sitting on the veranda in his drawers and suspenders—Zachary thought nothing of this, and was taken aback when his host apologized for his state of undress, explaining, in halting English, that he had not expected to receive a gentleman at this time of day. Leaving his guest to be waited on by an African maidservant, M. d'Epinay went inside and emerged a half-hour later, fully dressed, and regaled Zachary with a meal of many courses, accompanied by fine wines.

It was with some reluctance that Zachary checked his watch and announced that it was time for him to leave. As they were walking out of the house, M. d'Epinay handed him a letter that was to be delivered to Mr Benjamin Burnham, in Calcutta.

'My canes are rotting in the field, Mr Reid,' said the planter. 'Tell Mr Burnham that I need men. Now that we may no longer have slaves in Mauritius, I must have coolies, or I am doomed. Put in a word for me, will you not?'

With his farewell handshake, M. d'Epinay offered a word of warning. 'Be careful, Mr Reid; keep your eyes open. The mountains around are filled with marrons and desperadoes and escaped slaves. A gentleman on his own must be careful. Make sure your gun is never far from your hands.'

Zachary trotted away from the plantation with a grin on his face and the word 'gentleman' ringing in his ears: there were clearly many advantages to being branded with this label—and more of these became apparent when he arrived at the dockside quarter of Port Louis. With nightfall, the narrow lanes around the Lascar Bazar had come alive with women, and the sight of Zachary, in his paletot and hat, had a galvanic effect on them: clothes became the newest addition to his list of praiseworthy things. Thanks to their magic, he, Zachary Reid, so often disregarded by the whores of Fell's Point, now had women hanging off his arms and elbows: he had their fingers in his hair, their hips pressing against his own, and their hands toying playfully with the horn buttons of his broadcloth trowsers. One of them, who called herself Madagascar Rose, was as pretty a girl as he had ever seen, with flowers behind her ears and painted red lips: dearly would he have loved, after ten months on a ship, to be dragged behind her door, to stick his nose between her jasmined breasts and to run his tongue over her vanilla lips—but suddenly there was Serang Ali, in his sarong, blocking the lane, his thin acquiline face compressed into a dagger of disapproval. At the sight of him, the Rose of Madagascar wilted and was gone.

'Malum Zikri no hab got dam brain inside?' demanded the serang, arms akimbo. 'Hab got water topside, in he head? What for wanchi flower-girl? He not big pukka sahib now?'

Zachary was in no mood for a lecture. 'Get knotted, Serang Ali! Can't nobody turn a sailor from a snatchwarren.'

'Why for Malum Zikri wanchi pay for jiggy-pijjin?' said the serang. 'Oc-to-puss no have see? Is too muchi happy fish.'

This had Zachary foundering. 'Octopus?' he said. 'What's that got to do with anything?'

'No hab see?' said Serang Ali. 'Mistoh Oc-toh-puss eight hand hab got. Make heself too muchi happy inside. Allo time smile. Why Malum not so-fashion do? Ten finger no hab got?'

*Amitav Ghosh*

It wasn't long before Zachary threw up his hands in resignation and allowed himself to be led away. All the way back to the ship, Serang Ali kept brushing dust off his clothes, fixing his cravat, straightening his hair. It was as if he had acquired a claim on him, in having aided in his transformation into a sahib; no matter how much Zachary cursed and slapped his hands, he would not stop: it was as if he had become an image of gentility, equipped with all that it took to find success in the world. It dawned on him that this was why Serang Ali had been so determined to keep him from bedding the girls in the bazar—his matings too would have to be arranged and supervised. Or so he thought.

The skipper, still ailing, was now desperate to get to Calcutta and wanted to weigh anchor as soon as possible. But when told of this, Serang Ali disagreed: 'Cap'tin-bugger plenty sick,' he said. 'If no catchi dokto, he makee die. Go topside too muchee quick.'

Zachary was ready to fetch a doctor, but the Captain would not let him. 'Not goin't'a have no shagbag of a leech fingerin me taffrail. Nothing wrong with me. Just the running scoots. I'll be better the minute we make sail.'

The next day the breeze freshened and the *Ibis* duly stood out to sea. The skipper managed to stagger out to the quarter-deck and declared himself to be all a-taunto but Serang Ali was of another opinion: 'Captin catchi Cop'ral-Forbes. Look-see— he tongue go black. Better Malum Zikri keep far from Captin.' Later, he handed Zachary a foul-smelling decoction of roots and herbs. 'Malum drinki he: no catchi sick. Cop'ral-Forbes— he one piece nasty bugger.' On the serang's advice Zachary also made a change of diet, switching from the usual sailor's menu of lobscouse, dandyfunk and chokedog, to a Laskari fare of karibat and kedgeree—spicy skillygales of rice, lentils and pickles, mixed on occasion with little bits of fish, fresh or dry. The tongue-searing tastes were difficult to get used to at first, but Zachary could tell the spices were doing him good, scouring his insides, and he soon grew to like the unfamiliar flavours.

Twelve days later, just as Serang Ali had predicted, the Captain was dead. This time there was no bidding for the dead man's effects: they were thrown overboard and the stateroom was washed and left open, to be cauterized by the salt air.

When the body was tipped into the sea it was Zachary who read from the Bible. He did it in a voice that was sonorous enough to earn a compliment from Serang Ali: 'Malum Zikri number-one joss-pijjin bugger. Church-song why no sing?'

'No can do,' said Zachary. 'Ain could never sing.'

'Nebba mind,' said Serang Ali. 'One-piece song-bugger hab got.' He beckoned to a tall, spidery ship's-boy called Rajoo. 'This launder blongi one-time Mission-boy. Joss-man hab learn him one-piece saam.'

'Psalm?' said Zachary, in surprise. 'Which one?'

As if in answer, the young lascar began to sing: ' "Why *do* the heathen so furious-*ly* rage together . . .?" '

In case the meaning of this had escaped Zachary, the serang considerately provided a translation. 'That mean,' he whispered into Zachary's ear, 'for what heathen-bugger makee so muchi bobbery? Other works no hab got?'

Zachary sighed: 'Guess that just about sums it all up.'

~

By the time the *Ibis* dropped anchor at the mouth of the Hooghly River, eleven months had passed since her departure from Baltimore, and the only remaining members of the schooner's original complement were Zachary and Crabbie, the vessel's ginger cat.

With Calcutta just two or three days away, Zachary would have been only too glad to get under weigh immediately. Several days went by while the fretful crew waited for a pilot to arrive. Zachary was asleep in his cabin, dressed in nothing but a sarong, when Serang Ali came to tell him that a bunder-boat had pulled alongside.

'Misto Dumbcow hab come.'

'Who's that?'

'Pilot. He too muchi dumbcowing,' said the serang. 'Listen.'

Cocking his head, Zachary caught the echo of a voice booming down the gangway: 'Damn my eyes if I ever saw such a caffle of barnshooting badmashes! A chowdering of your chutes is what you budzats need. What do you think you're doing, toying with your tatters and luffing your laurels while I stand here in the sun?'

Pulling on an undershirt and trowsers, Zachary stepped out to see a stout, irate Englishman pounding the deck with a Malacca cane. He was dressed in an extravagantly old-fashioned way, with his shirt-collar up on high, a coat that was cut away in the skirts, and a Belcher fogle around his waist. His face, with its bacony hue, its mutton-chop whiskers, beefy cheeks and liverish lips, looked as if it could have been assembled upon a butcher's counter. Behind him stood a small knot of porters and lascars, bearing an assortment of bowlas, portmanteaus and other baggage.

'Do none of you halalcores have any wit at all?' The veins stood out on the pilot's forehead as he shouted at the unbudging crew: 'Where's the mate? Has he been given the kubber that my bunder-boat has lagowed? Don't just stand there: jaw! Hop to it, before I give your ganders a taste of my lattee. Have you saying your bysmelas before you know it.'

'I do apologize, sir,' said Zachary, stepping forward. 'I'm sorry you had to wait.'

The pilot's eyes narrowed in disapproval as they took in Zachary's dishevelled clothes and bare feet. 'Caulk my dead lights, man!' he said. 'You've certainly let yourself go, haven't you? Won't do when you're the only sahib on board—not if you don't want to be borakpoked by your darkies.'

'Sorry, sir . . . just a bit discombobb'd.' Zachary stuck out his hand. 'I'm the second mate, Zachary Reid.'

'And I'm James Doughty,' said the newcomer, giving Zachary's hand a grudging shake. 'Formerly of the Bengal River Pilot Service; currently bespoke arkati and turnee for Burnham Bros. The Burra Sahib—Ben Burnham that is—asked me to take charge of the ship.' He waved airily at the lascar who was standing behind the wheel. 'That's my seacunny over there; knows exactly what to do—could take you up the Burrempooter with his eyes closed. What'd you say we leave the steering to that badmash and find ourselves a drop of loll-shrub?'

'Loll-shrub?' Zachary scratched his chin. 'I'm sorry, Mr Doughty, but I don't know what that is.'

'Claret, my boy,' the pilot said airily. 'Wouldn't happen to have a drop on board, would you? If not, a brandy-pawnee will do just as well.'

# two

~

Two days later, Deeti and her daughter were eating their midday meal when Chandan Singh stopped his ox-cart at their door. *Kabutri-ki-má*! he shouted, Listen: Hukam Singh has passed out, at the factory. They said you should go there and bring him home.

With that he gave his reins a snap and drove off hurriedly, impatient for his meal and his afternoon sleep: it was typical of him to offer no help.

A chill crept up Deeti's neck as she absorbed this: it was not that the news itself was totally unexpected—her husband had been ailing for some time and his collapse did not come entirely as a surprise. Rather, her foreboding sprang from a certainty that this turn of events was somehow connected with the ship she had seen; it was as if the very wind that was bearing it towards her had blown a draught up her spine.

Ma? said Kabutri. What shall we do? How will we bring him home?

We have to find Kalua and his ox-cart, Deeti said. *Chal*; come, let's go.

The hamlet of the Chamars, where Kalua lived, was a short walk away and he was sure to be home at this hour of the afternoon. The problem was that he would probably expect to be paid and she was hard put to think of something to offer him: she had no grain or fruit to spare, and as for money, there was not a dam's worth of cowrie-shells in the house. Having run through the alternatives, she realized that she had no option but to delve into the carved wooden chest in which her husband kept his supply of opium: the box was nominally locked, but Deeti knew where to find the key. On opening the lid, she was relieved to find inside several lumps of hard akbari opium, as well as a sizeable piece of soft chandu opium, still wrapped in poppy petals. Deciding on the hard opium, she cut off a lump the size of her thumbnail, and folded it into one of the wrappers she had made that morning. With the package tucked into the waist of her sari, she set off in the direction of Ghazipur, with Kabutri running ahead, skipping along the embankments that divided the poppy fields.

The sun was past its zenith now and a haze was dancing over the flowers, in the warmth of the afternoon. Deeti drew the ghungta of her sari over her face, but the old cotton, cheap and thin to begin with, was now so worn that she could see right through it: the faded fabric blurred the outlines of everything in view, tinting the edges of the plump poppy pods with a faintly crimson halo. As her steps lengthened, she saw that on some nearby fields, the crop was well in advance of her own: some of her neighbours had already nicked their pods and the white ooze of the sap could be seen congealing around the parallel incisions of the nukha. The sweet, heady odour of the bleeding pods had drawn swarms of insects, and the air was buzzing with bees, grasshoppers and wasps; many would get stuck in the ooze and tomorrow, when the sap turned colour, their bodies would merge into the black gum, becoming a welcome addition to the weight of the harvest. The sap seemed to have a pacifying effect even on the butterflies, which flapped their wings in oddly erratic patterns, as though they could not remember how to fly. One of these landed on the back of Kabutri's hand and would not take wing until it was thrown up in the air.

See how it's lost in dreams? Deeti said. That means the harvest will be good this year. Maybe we'll even be able to fix our roof.

She stopped to glance in the direction of their hut, which was just visible in the distance: it looked like a tiny raft, floating upon a river of poppies. The hut's roof was urgently in need of repairs, but in this age of flowers, thatch was not easy to come by: in the old days, the fields would be heavy with wheat in the winter, and after the spring harvest, the straw would be used to repair the damage of the year before. But now, with the sahibs forcing everyone to grow poppy, no one had thatch to spare—it had to be bought at the market, from people who lived in faraway villages, and the expense was such that people put off their repairs as long as they possibly could.

When Deeti was her daughter's age, things were different: poppies had been a luxury then, grown in small clusters between the fields that bore the main winter crops—wheat, masoor dal and vegetables. Her mother would send some of her poppy seeds to the oil-press, and the rest she would keep for the house, some for replanting, and some to cook with meat and vegetables. As for the sap, it was sieved of impurities and left to dry, until the sun turned it into hard akbari afeem; at that time, no one thought of producing the wet, treacly chandu opium that was made and packaged in the English factory, to be sent across the sea in boats.

In the old days, farmers would keep a little of their home-made opium for their families, to be used during illnesses, or at harvests and weddings; the rest they would sell to the local nobility, or to pykari merchants from Patna. Back then, a few clumps of poppy were enough to provide for a household's needs, leaving a little over, to be sold: no one was inclined to plant more because of all the work it took to grow poppies—fifteen ploughings of the land and every remaining clod to be broken by hand, with a dantoli; fences and bunds to be built; purchases of manure and constant watering; and after all that, the frenzy of the harvest, each bulb having to be individually nicked, drained and scraped. Such punishment was bearable when you had a patch or two of poppies—but what sane person would want to multiply these labours when there were better, more useful crops to grow, like wheat, dal, vegetables? But those toothsome winter crops were steadily shrinking in acreage: now the factory's appetite for opium seemed never to be sated. Come the cold weather, the English sahibs would allow little else to be planted; their agents would go from home to home, forcing cash advances on the farmers, making them sign *asámi* contracts. It was impossible to say no to them: if you refused they would leave their silver hidden in your house, or throw it through a window. It was no use telling the white magistrate that you hadn't accepted the money and your thumbprint was forged: he earned commissions on the opium and would never let you off. And, at the end of it, your earnings would come to no more than three-and-a-half sicca rupees, just about enough to pay off your advance.

Reaching down, Deeti snapped off a poppy pod and held it to her nose: the smell of the drying sap was like wet straw, vaguely reminiscent of the rich, earthy perfume of a newly thatched roof after a shower of rain. This year, if the harvest was good, she would put all the proceeds into the repairing of the roof—if she didn't, the rains would destroy whatever was left of it.

Do you know, she said to Kabutri, it's been seven years since our roof was last thatched?

The girl turned her dark, soft eyes towards her mother. Seven years? she said. But isn't that when you were married?

Deeti nodded and gave her daughter's hand a squeeze. Yes. It was . . .

The new thatch had been paid for by her own father, as a part of her dowry—although he could ill afford it, he had not begrudged the expense since Deeti was the last of his children to be married off. Her prospects had always been bedevilled by her stars, her fate being ruled by Saturn—Shani—a planet that exercised great power on those born under its influence, often bringing discord, unhappiness and disharmony. With this shadow darkening her future, Deeti's expectations had never been high: she knew that if she were ever to be married, it would probably be to a much older man, possibly an elderly widower who needed a new wife to nurse his brood. Hukam Singh, by comparison, had seemed a good prospect, not least because Deeti's own brother, Kesri Singh, had proposed the match. The two men had belonged to the same battalion and had served together in a couple of overseas campaigns; Deeti had her brother's word that her prospective husband's disability was a minor one. Also in his favour were his family's connections, the most notable of which consisted of an uncle who had risen to the rank of subedar in the East India Company's army: on his retirement from active duty this uncle had found a lucrative job with a merchant house in Calcutta, and had been instrumental in finding good posts for his relatives—it was he, for instance, who had procured a much-coveted job in the opium factory for Hukam Singh, the groom-to-be.

When the match advanced to the next stage, it became clear that it was this uncle who was the motive force behind the proposal. Not only did he lead the party that came to settle the details, he also did all the negotiating on the groom's behalf: indeed when the talks reached the point where Deeti had to be led in, to drop her ghungta, it was to the uncle rather than the groom that she had bared her face.

There was no denying that the uncle was an impressive figure of a man: his name was Subedar Bhyro Singh and he was in his mid-fifties, with luxuriant white moustaches that curled up to his earlobes. His complexion was bright and rosy, marred only by a scar across his left cheek, and his turban, which was as spotlessly white as his dhoti, was worn with a negligent arrogance that made him seem twice the size of other men of his height. His strength and vigour were evident as much in the bull-like girth of his neck, as in the surging contours of his stomach—for he was one of those men on whom a belly appears not as an unnecessary weight, but rather as a repository of force and vitality.

Such was the subedar's presence that the groom and his immediate family seemed pleasingly diffident in comparison, and this played no small part in earning Deeti's consent for the match. During the negotiations, she examined the visitors carefully, through a crack in a wall: she had not much cared for the mother, but nor had she felt any fear of her. For the younger brother she had conceived an immediate dislike—but he was just a weedy youth of no account, and she had assumed that he would be, at worst, a minor source of irritation. As for Hukam Singh, she had been favourably impressed by his soldierly bearing, which was, if anything, enhanced by his limp. What she had liked better still was his drowsy demeanour and slow manner of speech; he had seemed inoffensive, the kind of man who would go about his work without causing trouble, not the least desirable of qualities in a husband.

Through the ceremonies and afterwards, during the long journey upriver to her new home, Deeti had felt no apprehension. Sitting in the prow of the boat, with her wedding sari drawn over her face, she had experienced a pleasurable thrill when the women sang:

*Sakhiyā-ho, saiyā moré písé masála*
*Sakhiyā-ho, bará mítha lagé masála*

Oh friends, my love's a-grinding
Oh friends, how sweet is this spice!

The music had accompanied her as she was carried, in a palki, from the riverbank to the threshold of her new home; veiled in her sari, she had seen nothing of the house as she went to the garlanded marital bed, but her nostrils had been filled with the smell of fresh thatch. The songs had grown increasingly suggestive while she sat waiting for her husband, and her neck and shoulders had tightened in anticipation of the grip that would push her prone on the bed. Her sisters had said: Make it hard for him the first time or he'll give you no peace later; fight and scratch and don't let him touch your breasts.

*Ág mor lágal ba*
    *Aré sagaro badaniyá . . .*
*Tas-mas choli karái*
    *Barhalá jobanawá*

I'm on fire
    My body burns . . .
My choli strains
    Against my waking breasts . . .

When the door opened to admit Hukam Singh, she was sitting coiled on the bed, fully prepared for an assault.

But he surprised her: instead of parting her veil, he said, in a low, slurred voice: *Arré sunn!* Listen there: you don't have to curl yourself up, like a snake: turn to me, look.

Peeping warily through the folds of her sari, she saw that he was standing beside her with a carved wooden box in his hands. He placed the chest on the bed and pushed back the lid, to release a powerful, medicinal smell—an odour that was at once oily and earthy, sweet and cloying. She knew it to be the smell of opium, although she had never before encountered it in such a potent and concentrated form.

Look! He pointed to the interior of the box, which was divided into several compartments: See—do you know what's in here?

*Afeem naikhé?* she said. Isn't it opium?

Yes, but of different kinds. Look. His forefinger pointed first to a lump of common akbari, black in colour and hard in texture; then it passed on to a ball of madak, a gluey mixture of opium and tobacco: See; this is the cheap stuff that people smoke in chillums. Next, using both hands, he took out a small lump, still in its poppy-petal wrapper, and touched it to her palm, to show her how soft it was: This is what we make in the factory: chandu. You won't see it here, the sahibs send it across the sea, to Maha-Chin. It can't be eaten like akbari and it can't be smoked like madak.

What's done with it then? she asked.

*Dekheheba ka hoi?* You want to see?

She nodded and he rose to his feet and went to a shelf on the wall. Reaching up, he brought down a pipe that was as long as his arm. He held it in front of her, and she saw that it was made of bamboo, blackened and oily with use. There was a mouthpiece at one end, and in the middle of the tube there was a little bulb, made of clay, with a tiny pinhole on top. Holding the pipe reverentially in his hands, Hukam Singh explained that it came from a faraway place—Rakhine-desh in southern Burma. Pipes like this one were not to be found in

Ghazipur, or Benares, or even Bengal: they had to be brought in, from across the Black Water, and were too valuable to be toyed with.

From the carved box, he took a long needle, dipped its tip in the soft black chandu and roasted the droplet on the flame of a candle. When the opium began to sizzle and bubble, he put it on the pinhole of his pipe and took a deep draught of the smoke, through the mouthpiece. He sat with his eyes closed, while the white smoke drifted slowly out of his nostrils. When it was all gone, he ran his hands lovingly over the length of the bamboo tube.

You should know, he said at last, that this is my first wife. She's kept me alive since I was wounded: if it weren't for her I would not be here today. I would have died of pain, long ago.

It was when he said these words that Deeti understood what the future held: she remembered how, as children, she and her playmates had laughed at the afeemkhors of their village—the habitual opium-eaters, who sat always as if in a dream, staring at the sky with dull, dead eyes. Of all the possibilities she had thought of, this was one she had not allowed for: that she might be marrying an afeemkhor—an addict. But how could she have known? Hadn't her own brother assured her that Hukam Singh's injury was not serious?

Did my brother know? she asked, in a low voice.

About my pipe? He laughed. No; how could he? I only learnt to smoke after I was wounded and taken to the hospital barracks. The orderlies there were from the country we were in, Arakan, and when the pain kept us awake at night, they would bring us pipes and show us what to do.

It was useless, she knew, to be seized by regret now, on the very night when her fate had been wedded to his: it was as if the shade of Saturn had passed over her face, to remind her of her destiny. Quietly, so as not to rouse him from his trance, she reached under her veil to wipe her eyes. But her bangles tinkled and woke him; he picked up his needle again and held it over the flame. When the pipe was ready to be smoked, he

*Amitav Ghosh*

turned to her, smiling, and raised an eyebrow, as if to ask if she wanted to try it too. She nodded, thinking that if this smoke could take away the pain of a shattered bone then surely it would help in calming the disquiet in her heart. But when she reached for the pipe, he moved it quickly out of her reach, holding it to his chest: No—you won't know how! He took a mouthful of the smoke, placed his mouth on hers and breathed it into her body himself. Her head began to swim, but whether from the smoke or from the touch of his lips she could not tell. The fibres of her muscles began to soften and go slack; her body seemed to drain itself of tension and a sensation of the most delectable languor followed in its wake. Awash in well-being, she leant back against her pillow and then his mouth closed on hers again, filling her lungs with smoke and she felt herself slipping away from this world into another that was brighter, better, more fulfilling.

When she opened her eyes next morning there was a dull ache in her lower abdomen and a painful soreness between her legs. Her clothes were in disarray and she reached down to discover that her thighs were crusted with blood. Her husband was lying beside her, with the brass box in his arms, his clothes undisturbed. She shook him awake to ask: What happened? Was everything all right last night?

He nodded and gave her a drowsy smile. Yes, everything was as it should be, he said. You gave proof of your purity to my family. With heaven's blessing, your lap will soon be filled.

She would have liked to believe him, but looking at his enervated and listless limbs she found it hard to imagine that he had been capable of any great exertion the night before. She lay on her pillow trying to remember what had happened, but was unable to retrieve any memory of the latter part of the night.

Shortly afterwards, her mother-in-law appeared by her bedside; wreathed in smiles, she sprinkled blessings from a container of holy water, and murmured, in a tone of tender solicitude: Everything went exactly as it should, beti. What an auspicious start to your new life!

Her husband's uncle, Subedar Bhyro Singh, echoed these blessings and slipped a gold coin into her palm: Beti, your lap will soon be filled—you will have a thousand sons.

Despite these reassurances, Deeti could not shake off the conviction that something untoward had happened on her wedding night. But what could it have been?

Her suspicions deepened in the following weeks, when Hukam Singh showed no further interest in her, being usually in a state of torpid, opium-induced somnolence by the time he fell on his bed. Deeti tried a few stratagems to break him from the spell of his pipe, but all to no avail: it was pointless to withhold opium from a man who worked in the very factory where it was processed; and when she tried hiding his pipe, he quickly fashioned another. Nor did the effects of temporary deprivation make him desire her any more: on the contrary, it seemed only to make him angry and withdrawn. At length, Deeti was forced to conclude that he could never be a husband to her, in the full sense, either because his injury had rendered him incapable, or because opium had removed the inclination. But then her belly began to swell with the weight of a child and her suspicions acquired an added edge: who could have impregnated her if not her husband? What exactly had happened that night? When she tried to question her husband he spoke with pride about the consummation of their wedding—but the look in his eyes told her that he had no actual recollection of the event; that his memory of that night was probably an opium-induced dream, implanted by someone else. Was it possible then that her own stupor had also been arranged, by someone who knew of her husband's condition and had made a plan to conceal his impotence, in order to preserve the family's honour?

Deeti knew that her mother-in-law would stop at nothing where her sons were concerned: all she would have had to do was to ask Hukam Singh to share some of his opium with his new bride; an accomplice could have done the rest. Deeti could even imagine that the old woman had actually been present in the room, helping to roll back her sari and holding down her legs while the deed was done. As for who the accomplice was, Deeti would not allow herself to yield to her first suspicions: the identity of her child's father was too important a matter to be settled without further confirmation.

To confront her mother-in-law, Deeti knew, would serve no purpose: she would tell her nothing and spout many lies and soothing reassurances. Yet every day offered fresh proof of the old woman's complicity—in nothing more so than the look of proprietory satisfaction with which she watched over the progress of the pregnancy; it was as if the child were her own, growing in the receptacle of Deeti's body.

In the end, it was the old woman herself who provided Deeti with the impetus to act upon her suspicions. One day, while massaging Deeti's belly, she said: And after we've delivered this one, we must make sure there are more—many, many more.

It was this throwaway remark that revealed to Deeti that her mother-in-law had every intention of ensuring that whatever had happened on her wedding night would be repeated; that she would be drugged and held down, to be raped again by the unknown accomplice.

What was she to do? It rained hard that night and the whole house was filled with the smell of wet thatch. The grassy fragrance cleared Deeti's mind: think, she had to think, it was no use to weep and bemoan the influence of the planets. She thought of her husband and his torpid, drowsy gaze: how was it that his eyes were so different from his mother's? Why was his gaze so blank and hers, so sharp and cunning? The answer came to Deeti all of a sudden—of course, the difference lay in the wooden box.

Her husband was fast asleep, with drool trickling down his chin and an arm thrown over his box. Pulling gently, she freed the box from his grasp and prised the key out of his fingers. A ripe odour of earth and decay came wafting out when she opened the lid. Averting her face, she pared a few shavings from a cake of hard akbari opium. Slipping the pieces into the folds of her sari, she locked the box and replaced the key in her husband's hands: although he was fast asleep, his fingers closed greedily on this companion of his nights.

Next morning Deeti mixed a little trace of opium into her mother-in-law's sweetened milk. The old woman drank it thirstily and spent the rest of the morning lazing in the shade of a mango tree. Her contentment was enough to dispel whatever misgivings Deeti may have had: from that day on she began to slip traces of the drug into everything she served her mother-in-law; she sprinkled it on her achars, kneaded it into her dalpuris, fried it into her pakoras and dissolved it in her dal. In a very short time, the old woman grew quieter and more tranquil, her voice lost its harshness and her eyes became softer; she no longer took much interest in Deeti's pregnancy and spent more and more time lying in bed. When relatives came to visit, they always commented on how peaceful she looked—and she, for her part, never stinted in her praise of Deeti, her fond new daughter-in-law.

As for Deeti, the more she ministered the drug, the more she came to respect its potency: how frail a creature was a human being, to be tamed by such tiny doses of this substance! She saw now why the factory in Ghazipur was so diligently patrolled by the sahibs and their sepoys—for if a little bit of this gum could give her such power over the life, the character, the very soul of this elderly woman, then with more of it at her disposal, why should she not be able to seize kingdoms and control multitudes? And surely this could not be the only such substance upon the earth?

She began to pay closer attention to dais and ojhas, the travelling midwives and exorcists who occasionally passed through their village; she learnt to recognize plants like hemp and datura and would sometimes try little experiments, feeding extracts to her mother-in-law and observing the effects.

It was a decoction of datura that wrung the truth from the old woman, by sending her into a trance from which she never recovered. In her last days, when her mind was wandering she often referred to Deeti as 'Draupadi'; when asked why, she would murmur drowsily: Because the earth has never seen a

*Amitav Ghosh*

more virtuous woman than Draupadi, of the Mahabharata, wife to five brothers. It's a fortunate woman, a *saubhágyawati*, who bears the children of brothers for each other . . .

It was this allusion that confirmed Deeti's belief that the child in her belly had been fathered not by her husband, but by Chandan Singh, her leering, slack-jawed brother-in-law.

~

Two slow days on the silt-clogged river brought the *Ibis* to the Narrows at Hooghly Point, a few miles short of Calcutta. There, beset by squalls and sudden gusts of wind, she dropped anchor to await the incoming tide that would carry her to her destination early next morning. The city being only a short distance away, a messenger was dispatched on horseback, to alert Mr Benjamin Burnham to the schooner's impending arrival.

The *Ibis* wasn't the only vessel to seek shelter at the Narrows that afternoon: also moored there was a stately houseboat that belonged to the estate of Raskhali, a large landholding a half-day's journey away. Thus it happened that the approach of the *Ibis* was witnessed by Raja Neel Rattan Halder, the zemindar of Raskhali, who was on board the palatial barge with his eight-year-old son and a sizeable retinue of attendants. Also with him was his mistress, a once-famous dancer, known to the world by her stage-name, Elokeshi: the Raja was returning to Calcutta, where he lived, after a visit to his Raskhali estate.

The Halders of Raskhali were one of the oldest and most noted landed families of Bengal, and their boat was among the most luxurious to be seen on the river: the vessel was a brigantine-rigged pinnace-budgerow—an Anglicized version of the humbler Bengali bajra. A double-masted houseboat of capacious dimensions, the budgerow's hull was painted blue and grey, to match the Raskhali estate's livery, and the family's emblem—the stylized head of a tiger—was emblazoned on its prow and its sail. The main deck had six large staterooms, with Venetian windows and jillmilled blinds; it also boasted a grand, glittering reception chamber, a sheeshmahal, panelled with mirrors and fragments of crystals: used only on formal occasions, this cabin was large enough to stage dances and other entertainments. Although sumptuous meals were often served on the budgerow, the preparation of food was not permitted anywhere on the vessel. Though not Brahmins, the Halders were orthodox Hindus, zealous in the observance of upper-caste taboos and in following the usages of their class: to them, the defilements associated with the preparation of food were anathema. When at sail, the Halder budgerow always towed another, smaller boat in its wake, a pulwar; this second vessel served not only as a kitchen-tender, but also as a floating barracks for the small army of piyadas, paiks and other retainers who were always in attendance on the zemindar.

The top deck of the budgerow was an open gallery, ringed by a waist-high deck rail: it was a tradition among the Raskhali zemindars to use this space for flying kites. The sport was much beloved of the Halder menfolk, and as with other such favoured pursuits—for example, music and the cultivation of roses—they had added nuances and subtleties that elevated the flying of kites from a mere amusement to a form of connoisseurship. While common people cared only for how high their kites soared and how well they 'fought' with others, what mattered most to the Halders was the pattern of a kite's flight and whether or not it matched the precise shade and mood of the wind. Generations of landed leisure had allowed them to develop their own terminology for this aspect of the elements: in their vocabulary, a strong, steady breeze was 'neel', blue; a violent nor'easter was purple, and a listless puff was yellow.

The squalls that brought the *Ibis* to Hooghly Point were of none of these colours: they were winds of a kind which the Halders were accustomed to speak of as 'suqlat'—a shade of scarlet that they associated with sudden reversals of fortune. The Rajas of Raskhali were famously a line that put great trust in omens—and in this, as in most other matters, Neel Rattan

Halder was a devout upholder of inherited traditions: for over a year now, he had been pursued by bad news, and the sudden arrival of the *Ibis*, along with the changeable colour of the wind, seemed to him to be sure indications of a turn in his luck.

The present zemindar was himself named after the noblest of winds, the steady, blue breeze (years later, when it was time for him to enter Deeti's shrine, it was by a few strokes of this colour that she would make his likeness). Neel had but recently come into the title, having inherited it upon his father's death two years before: he was in his late twenties, and although well past his first youth, he retained the frail, etiolated frame of the sickly child he had once been. His long, thin-boned face had the pallor that comes from always being shielded from the full glare of the sun; in his limbs, too, there was a length and leanness that suggested the sinuosity of a shade-seeking plant. His complexion was such that his lips formed a sunburst of red on his face, their colour being highlighted by the thin moustache that bordered his mouth.

Like others of his ilk, Neel had been betrothed at birth to the daughter of another prominent landowning family; the marriage had been solemnized when he was twelve, but had resulted in only one living child—Neel's eight-year-old heir presumptive, Raj Rattan. Even more than others of their line, this boy delighted in the sport of kite-flying: it was at his insistence that Neel had ventured up to the budgerow's uppermost deck on the afternoon when the *Ibis* dropped anchor at the Narrows.

It was the shipowner's flag, on the mainmast of the *Ibis*, that caught the zemindar's attention: he knew the chequered pennant almost as well as the emblem of his own estate, his family's fortunes having long been dependent on the firm founded by Benjamin Burnham. Neel knew, at a glance, that the *Ibis* was a new acquisition: the terraces of his main residence in Calcutta, the Raskhali Rajbari, commanded an excellent view of the Hooghly River and he was familiar with most vessels that came regularly to the city. He was well aware that the Burnham fleet consisted mainly of locally made 'country boats'; of late he had noticed a few sleek American-built clipper-ships on the river, but he knew that none of them belonged to the Burnhams—the flags on their masts were of Jardine & Matheson, a rival firm. But the *Ibis* was no country boat: although not in the best of trim, it was evident that she was of excellent craftsmanship—such a vessel was not to be cheaply acquired. Neel's curiosity was piqued, for it seemed possible that the schooner's arrival might presage a reversal in his own fortunes.

Without unloosing his kite-string, Neel summoned his personal bearer, a tall, turbaned Benarasi called Parimal. Take a dinghy and row over to that ship, he said. Ask the serangs who the ship belongs to and how many officers are on board.

Huzoor.

With a gesture of acknowledgement, Parimal retreated down the ladder and soon afterwards, a slim paunchway pulled away from the Raskhali budgerow to nudge up alongside the *Ibis*. A scant half-hour later, Parimal returned to report that the ship belonged to Burnham-sahib, of Calcutta.

How many officers on board? Neel inquired.

Of hat-wearing topi-walas there are just two, said Parimal.

And who are they—the two sahibs?

One of them is a Mr Reid, from Number-Two-England, said Parimal. The other is a pilot from Calcutta, Doughty-sahib. Huzoor may remember him: in the old days he often used to come to the Raskhali Rajbari. He sends his salams.

Neel nodded, although he had no memory of the pilot. Handing his kite-string to a servant, he gestured to Parimal to follow him down to his stateroom, on the lower deck. There, after sharpening a quill, he picked up a sheet of paper, wrote a few lines and ran a handful of sand across the page. When the ink was dry, he handed the letter to Parimal. Here, he said, take this to the ship and deliver it personally to Doughty-sahib. Tell him the Raja is pleased to invite Mr Reid and himself to dine on the Raskhali budgerow. Come back quickly and let me know what they say.

*Amitav Ghosh*

Huzoor.

Parimal bowed again, and retreated backwards into the gangway, leaving Neel still seated at his desk. It was there that Elokeshi found him, a short while later, when she swept into the stateroom in a swirl of anklets and attar: he was sitting in a chair, his fingers steepled, lost in thought. With a gurgle of laughter, she clapped her hands over his eyes and cried: There you are—always alone! Wicked! Dushtu! Never any time for your Elokeshi.

Peeling her hands off his eyes, Neel turned to smile at her. Among the connoisseurs of Calcutta, Elokeshi was not considered a great beauty: her face was too round, the bridge of her nose too flat, and her lips too puffy to be pleasing to the conventional eye. Her hair, long, black and flowing, was her great asset, and she liked to wear it over her shoulders, with no bindings other than a few gold tassels. But it was not so much her looks as her spirit that had drawn Neel to her, the cast of her mind being as effervescent as his own was sombre: although many years his senior, and well versed in the ways of the world, her manner was as giggly and flirtatious as it had been when she'd first attracted notice as a dancer of sublimely light-footed tukras and tihais.

Now, flinging herself on the large four-poster bed in the centre of the stateroom, she parted her scarves and dupattas so that her pouting lips were laid bare, while the rest of her face remained covered. Ten days on this lumbering boat, she moaned, all alone, with nothing to do, and not once do you so much as look at me.

All alone—and what about them? Neel laughed and inclined his head in the direction of the doorway, where three girls were sitting crouched, watching their mistress.

Oh them . . . but they're just my little kanchanis!

Elokeshi giggled, covering her mouth: she was a creature of the city, addicted to the crowded bazars of Calcutta, and she had insisted on bringing along an entourage to keep her company on this unaccustomed expedition into the countryside; the three girls were at once maids, disciples, and apprentices, indispensable to the refinement of her arts. Now, at a gesture from their mistress's forefinger, the girls withdrew, shutting the door behind them. But even in retreat they did not stray far from their mistress: in order to prevent interruptions, they sat in a huddle in the gangway outside, rising from time to time to steal glances through the chinks in a jillmilled ventilation panel on the teakwood door.

Once the door was shut, Elokeshi divested herself of one of her long dupattas and floated it over Neel's head, snaring him in the cloth and pulling him to the bed. Come to me now, she said, pouting, you've been at that desk long enough. When Neel went to lie beside her, she pushed him back against a bank of pillows. Now tell me, she said, on the undulating note that was her voice of complaint: Why did you bring me all this way with you—so far from the city? You still haven't explained properly.

Amused by her affectation of naïveté, Neel smiled: In the seven years you've been with me, you'd never once seen Raskhali. Isn't it natural that I should want you to see my zemindary?

Just to see it? She tossed her head in a gesture of challenge, miming a dancer's enactment of the role of injured lover. Is that all?

What else? He rubbed a lock of her hair between his fingertips. Wasn't it enough to see the place? Didn't you like what you saw?

Of course I liked it, said Elokeshi; it was grand beyond anything I could imagine. Her gaze drifted away, as if in search of his colonnaded riverside mansion with its gardens and orchards. She whispered: So many people, so much land! It made me think: I'm such a small part of your life.

He put his hand under her chin and turned her face towards him. What's the matter Elokeshi? Tell me. What's on your mind?

I don't know how to tell you . . .

Now her fingers began to unbutton the ivory studs that ran slantwise across the chest of his kurta. She murmured: Do you know what my kanchanis said when they saw how large your zemindary was? They said: Elokeshi-di, you should ask the Raja for some land—don't you need a place where your relatives can live? After all you need some security for your old age.

Neel groaned in annoyance: Those girls of yours are always making trouble. I wish you would turn them out of your house.

They just look after me—that's all. Her fingers strayed into his chest hair, busying themselves in making tiny braids, as she whispered: There's nothing wrong with a raja giving land to the girls in his keep. Your father used to do it all the time. People say his women had only to ask to get whatever they wanted: shawls, jewellery, jobs for their relatives . . .

Yes, said Neel, with a wry smile: And those relatives would go on receiving salaries, even when they were caught embezzling from the estate.

You see, she said, running her fingertips over his lips. He was a man who knew the value of love.

Not like me—I know, he said. It was true that Neel's own style of living was, for a scion of the Halder family, almost frugal: he managed to get by with a single two-horse carriage and made do with a modest wing of the family mansion. Much less a voluptuary than his father, he had no mistress other than Elokeshi—but on her, he lavished his affections without stint, his relationship with his wife having never progressed beyond the conventional performance of his husbandly duties.

Don't you see, Elokeshi? Neel said, with a touch of sadness. To live like my father did costs money—more money than our estates could possibly provide.

Elokeshi was suddenly alert, her eyes keen with interest. What do you mean? Everyone always said your father was one of the richest men in the city.

Neel stiffened. Elokeshi—a pond needn't be deep to bear a lotus.

Elokeshi snatched back her hand and sat up. What are you trying to say? she demanded. Explain to me.

Neel knew he had said too much already, so he smiled and slipped his hand under her choli: It's nothing, Elokeshi.

There were times when he longed to tell her about the problems his father had left him with, but he knew her well enough to be aware that she would probably start making other arrangements if she learnt of the full extent of his difficulties. It was not that she was avaricious: on the contrary, for all her affectations, he knew that she had a strong sense of responsibility towards those who were dependent on her—just as Neel did himself. He regretted having let slip his words about his father, for it was premature to give her cause for alarm.

Let it be, Elokeshi. What does it matter?

No, tell me about it, said Elokeshi, pushing him back against the pillows. A well-wisher in Calcutta had warned her of financial trouble in the Raskhali zemindary: she had paid no heed at the time, but she sensed now that something was really awry and that she might have to re-examine her options.

Tell me, Elokeshi asked again: You've been so preoccupied these last few months—what's on your mind?

It's nothing you should worry about, Neel said—and it was certainly true, that no matter what happened, he would see to it that she was provided for: You and your girls and your house are all safe . . .

He was cut short by the voice of his bearer, Parimal, which suddenly made itself heard in the gangway, arguing furiously with the three girls: he was demanding to be let in, and they were adamantly holding him at bay.

Hastily pulling a sheet over Elokeshi, Neel called out to the girls: Let him in.

Parimal stepped in, keeping his eyes carefully averted from Elokeshi's covered form. Addressing Neel, he said: Huzoor, the sahibs on the ship said they would gladly come. They will be here soon after sunset.

Good, said Neel. But you'll have to take care of the bandobast, Parimal: I want the sahibs to be entertained as they would have been in my father's day.

This startled Parimal, who had never known his master to make such a request. But huzoor, how? he said: In such a short time? And with what?

We have simkin and *lál-sharáb*, don't we? Neel said. You know what needs to be done.

Elokeshi waited for the door to close before throwing off the covers. What's all this? she asked: Who's coming tonight? What's been arranged?

Neel laughed and pulled her head to his shoulder. You ask so many questions—*báp-ré-báp*! Enough for now . . .

~

The unexpected dinner invitation from the budgerow started Mr Doughty off on a journey of garrulous reminiscence. 'Oh my boy!' said the pilot to Zachary, as they stood leaning on the deck rail. 'The old Raja of Raskhali: I could tell you a story or two about him—Rascally-Roger I used to call him!' He laughed, thumping the deck with his cane. 'Now there was a lordly nigger if ever you saw one! Best kind of native—kept himself busy with his shrub and his nautch-girls and his tumashers. Wasn't a man in town who could put on a burra-khana like he did. Sheeshmull blazing with shammers and candles. Paltans of bearers and khidmutgars. Demijohns of French loll-shrub and carboys of iced simkin. And the karibat! In the old days the Rascally bobachee-connah was the best in the city. No fear of pishpash and cobbily-mash at the Rascally table. The dumbpokes and pillaus were good enough, but we old hands, we'd wait for the curry of cockup and the chitchky of pollock-saug. Oh he set a rankin table I can tell you—and mind you, supper was just the start: the real tumasher came later, in the nautch-connah. Now there was another chuckmuck sight for you! Rows of cursies for the sahibs and mems to sit on. Sittringies and tuckiers for the natives. The baboos puffing at their hubble-bubbles and the sahibs lighting their Sumatra buncuses. Cunchunees whirling and tickytaw boys beating their tobblers. Oh, that old loocher knew how to put on a nautch all right! He was a sly little shaytan too, the Rascally-Roger: if he saw you eyeing one of the pootlies, he'd send around a khidmutgar, bobbing and bowing, the picture of innocence. People would think you'd eaten one too many jellybees and needed to be shown to the cacatorium. But instead of the totteeconnah, off you'd go to a little hidden cumra, there to puckrow your dashy. Not a memsahib present any the wiser—and there you were, with your gobbler in a cunchunee's nether-whiskers, getting yourself a nice little taste of a blackberry-bush.' He breathed a nostalgic sigh. 'Oh they were grand old goll-mauls, those Rascally burrakhanas! No better place to get your tatters tickled.'

Zachary nodded, as if no word of this had escaped him. 'I take it you know him well then, Mr Doughty—our host of this evening?'

'Not him, so much as his father. This young fellow's no more like the old man than stink-wood is like mahogany.' The pilot grunted in disapproval. 'See, if there's one thing I can't abide it's a bookish native: his father was a man who knew how to keep his jibb where it belonged—wouldn't have been seen dead with a book. But this little chuckeroo gives himself all kinds of airs—a right strut-noddy if ever I saw one. It's not as if he's real nobility, mind: the Rascallys call themselves Rogers, but they're just Ryes with an honorary title—bucksheesh for loyalty to the Crown.'

Mr Doughty snorted contemptuously. 'These days it takes no more than an acre or two for a Baboo to style himself a More-Roger. And the way this one jaws on, you'd think he's the Padshaw of Persia. Wait till you hear the barnshoot bucking in English—like a bandar reading aloud from *The Times*.' He chuckled gleefully, twirling the knob of his cane. 'Now that'll be something else to look forward to this evening, apart from the chitchky—a spot of bandarbaiting.'

He paused to give Zachary a broad wink. 'From what I hear, the Rascal's going to be in for a samjaoing soon enough. The kubber is that his cuzzanah is running out.'

Zachary could no longer sustain the pretence of omniscience.

Knitting his eyebrows, he said: 'Cu—cuzzanah? Now there you go again, Mr Doughty: that's another word I don't know the meaning of.'

This naïve, if well-meant, remark earned Zachary a firm dressing-down: it was about time, the pilot said, that he, Zachary, stopped behaving like a right gudda—'that's a donkey in case you were wondering.' This was India, where it didn't serve for a sahib to be taken for a clodpoll of a griffin: if he wasn't fly to what was going on, it'd be all dickey with him, mighty jildee. This was no Baltimore—this was a jungle here, with biscobras in the grass and wanderoos in the trees. If he, Zachary, wasn't to be diddled and taken for a flat, he would have to learn to gubbrow the natives with a word or two of the zubben.

Since this admonishment was delivered in the strict but indulgent tone of a mentor, Zachary plucked up the courage to ask what 'the zubben' was, at which the pilot breathed a patient sigh: 'The zubben, dear boy, is the flash lingo of the East. It's easy enough to jin if you put your head to it. Just a little peppering of nigger-talk mixed with a few girleys. But mind your Oordoo and Hindee doesn't sound too good: don't want the world to think you've gone native. And don't mince your words either. Mustn't be taken for a chee-chee.'

Zachary shook his head again, helplessly. 'Chee-Chee? And what d'you mean by that, Mr Doughty?'

Mr Doughty raised an admonitory eyebrow. 'Chee-chee? Lip-lap? Mustee? Sinjo? Touch o'tar . . . you take my meaning? Wouldn't challo at all, dear fellow: no sahib would have one at his table. We're very particular about that kind of thing out East. We've got our BeeBees to protect, you know. It's one thing for a man to dip his nib in an inkpot once in a while. But we can't be having luckerbaugs running loose in the henhouse. Just won't ho-ga: that kind of thing could get a man chawbuck'd with a horsewhip!'

There was something in this, a hint or suggestion, that made Zachary suddenly uncomfortable. Over the last two days he had come to like Mr Doughty, recognizing, in the lee of his hectoring voice and meaty face, a kindly, even generous spirit. Now it was almost as if the pilot were trying to give him a word of warning, cautioning him in some roundabout way.

Zachary tapped the deck rail and turned away. 'By your leave, Mr Doughty, I'd best make sure I've got a change of clothes.'

The pilot nodded in agreement. 'Oh yes: we'll have to get ourselves all kitted out. Glad I thought to bring along a fresh pair of sirdrars.'

Zachary sent word to the deckhouse and shortly afterwards, Serang Ali came to his cabin and picked out a set of clothes, laying them on the bunk for Zachary to inspect. The pleasure of high-priming in someone else's finery had begun to wane now, and Zachary was dismayed by the array of clothes on his bunk: a blue dresscoat of fine serge, black nainsook trowsers, a shirt made of Dosootie cotton and a white silk cravat. 'Enough's enough, Serang Ali,' he said wearily. 'I'm done playin biggity.'

Serang Ali's demeanour became suddenly insistent. Picking up the trowsers, he held them up to Zachary. 'Mus wear,' he said in a voice that was soft but steely. 'Malum Zikri one big piece pukka sahib now. Mus wear propa cloths.'

Zachary was puzzled by the depth of feeling with which this was said. 'Why?' he asked. 'Why in the livin hell is it so important to you?'

'Malum must be propa pukka sahib,' said the serang. 'All lascar wanchi Malum be captin-bugger by'm'by.'

'Eh?'

Now, in a sudden, bright flash of illumination, Zachary understood why his transformation meant so much to the serang: he was to become what no lascar could be—a 'Free Mariner', the kind of sahib officer they called a malum. For Serang Ali and his men Zachary was almost one of themselves, while yet being endowed with the power to undertake an impersonation that was unthinkable for any of them; it was as much for their own sakes as for his that they wanted to see him succeed.

As the weight of this responsibility sank in, Zachary sat on the bunk and covered his face. 'You don know the livin deal of what you askin,' he said. 'Six months back I was nothin but the ship's carpenter. Lucked out getting to second mate. Forget Captain: that's way above my bend. Ain gon happen; not bimeby, not ever.'

'Can do,' said Serang Ali, handing him the Dosootie shirt. 'By'm'by can do. Malum Zikri plenty smart bugger inside. Can do 'come genl'man.'

'What makes you think I can do it anyways?'

'Zikri Malum sabbi tok pukka-talk no?' said Serang Ali. 'Hab heard Zikri Malum tok Mistoh Doughty sahib-fashion.'

'What?' Zachary shot him a startled glance: that Serang Ali should have noticed his talent for changing voices struck a chord of alarm. It was true that when called upon, his tongue could be as clipped as that of any college-taught lawyer: not for nothing had his mother made him wait at table when the master of the house, his natural father, was entertaining guests. But nor had she spared him her hand when he'd shown signs of getting all seddity and airish; to watch her son playing the spook would set her turning in her grave.

'Michman wanchi, he can 'come pukka genl'man by'm'by.'

'No.' Having long been compliant, Zachary was now all defiance. 'No,' he said, thrusting the serang out of his cuddy. 'This flumadiddle's got'a stop: ain havin it no more.' Throwing himself on his bunk, Zachary closed his eyes, and for the first time in many months, his vision turned inwards, travelling back across the oceans to his last day at Gardiner's shipyard in Baltimore. He saw again a face with a burst eyeball, the scalp torn open where a handspike had landed, the dark skin slick with blood. He remembered, as if it were happening again, the encirclement of Freddy Douglass, set upon by four white carpenters; he remembered the howls, 'Kill him, kill the damned nigger, knock his brains out'; he remembered how he and the other men of colour, all free, unlike Freddy, had held back, their hands stayed by fear. And he remembered, too, Freddy's voice afterwards, not reproaching them for their failure to come to his defence, but urging them to leave, scatter: 'It's about jobs; the whites won't work with you, freeman or slave: keeping you out is their way of saving their bread.' That was when Zachary had decided to quit the shipyard and seek a berth on a ship's crew.

Zachary got out of his bunk and opened the door, to find the serang still waiting outside. 'Okay,' he said wearily. 'I'll let you get back in here. But you bes do what you gon do blame quick, fore I change my mind.'

Just as Zachary had finished dressing, a series of shouts went echoing back and forth between ship and shore. A couple of minutes later Mr Doughty knocked on the door of his cabin. 'Oh I say, my boy!' he boomed. 'You'll never credit it, but the Burra Sahib has arrived in person: none other than Mr Burnham himself! Ridden chawbuckswar from Calcutta: couldn't wait to see his ship. Sent the gig for him: he's in it now, coming over.'

The pilot's eyes narrowed as he took in Zachary's new clothes. There was a moment of silence as he looked him up and down, subjecting his attire to careful examination. Then with a resounding thump of his cane, he announced: 'Tip-top, my young chuckeroo! You'd put a kizzilbash to shame in those togs of yours.'

'Glad to pass muster, sir,' said Zachary gravely.

Somewhere close by, Zachary heard Serang Ali hissing: 'What I tell you? Malum Zikri no pukka rai-sahib now?'

# three

~

Kalua lived in the Chamar-basti, a cluster of huts inhabited only by people of his caste. To enter the hamlet would have been difficult for Deeti and Kabutri, but fortunately for them, Kalua's dwelling lay on the periphery, not far from the main road to Ghazipur. Deeti had passed that way many times before and had often seen Kalua lumbering about, in his cart. To her eyes, his dwelling did not look like a hut at all, but had more the look of a cattle-pen; when she was within hailing distance of it, she came to a halt and called out: *Ey Kalua? Ka horahelba?* Oh Kalua? What're you up to?

After three or four shouts there was still no answer, so she picked up a stone and aimed it at the doorless entrance of his dwelling. The pebble vanished into the unlit darkness of the hut and a tinkle of pottery followed to tell her that it had struck a pitcher or some earthenware object. *Ey Kalua-ré!* she called out again. Now something stirred inside the hut and there was a deepening of the darkness around the doorway until at last Kalua showed himself, stooping low to make his way out. Following close behind, as if to confirm Deeti's notion that he lived in a cattle-pen, were the two small white oxen that pulled his cart.

Kalua was a man of unusual height and powerful build: in any fair, festival or mela, he could always be spotted towering above the crowd—even the jugglers on stilts were usually not so tall as he. But it was his colour rather than his size that had earned him the nickname Kalua—'Blackie'—for his skin had the shining, polished tint of an oiled whetstone. It was said of Kalua that as a child he had shown an insatiable craving for meat, which his family had satisfied by feeding him carrion; being leather-makers, it was their trade to collect the remains of dead cows and oxen—it was on the meat of these salvaged carcasses that Kalua's gigantic frame was said to have been nourished. But it was said also that Kalua's body had gained at the expense of his mind, which had remained slow, simple and trusting, so that even small children were able to take advantage of him. So easily was he duped, that on his parents' passing, his brothers and other relatives had not had the least difficulty in cheating him of the little that was his rightful due: he had raised no objection even when he was evicted from the family dwelling and sent to fend for himself in a cattle-pen.

At that time, help had come to Kalua from an unexpected quarter: one of Ghazipur's most prominent landowning families had three young scions, thakur-sahibs, who were much addicted to gambling. Their favourite pastime was to bet on wrestling matches and trials of strength, so on hearing of Kalua's physical prowess, they had sent an ox-cart to fetch him to the kothi where they lived, on the outskirts of town. *Abé Kalua*, they said to him, if you were to be given a reward, what would you want?

After much head-scratching and careful thought, Kalua had pointed to the ox-cart and said: Malik, I would be glad to have a bayl-gari like that one. I could make a living from it.

The three thakurs had nodded their heads and said that he would get an ox-cart if only he could win a fight and give a few demonstrations of his strength. Several wrestling matches followed and Kalua had won them all, defeating the local pehlwans and strongmen with ease. The young landlords earned a good profit and Kalua was soon in possession of his reward. But once having gained his ox-cart, Kalua showed no further inclination to fight—which was scarcely a surprise, for he was, as everyone knew, of a shy, timid and peaceable disposition and had no greater ambition than to make a living by transporting goods and people in his cart. But Kalua could not escape his fame: word of his deeds soon filtered through to the august ears of His Highness, the Maharaja of Benares, who expressed a desire to see the strongman of Ghazipur pitted against the champion of his own court.

Kalua demurred at first, but the landlords wheedled, cajoled and finally threatened to confiscate his cart and oxen, so to Benares they went and there, on the great square in front of the Ramgarh Palace, Kalua suffered his first defeat, being knocked unconscious within a few minutes of the bout's start. The Maharaja, watching in satisfaction, remarked that the outcome was proof that wrestling was a trial not just of strength, but also of intelligence—and in the latter field Ghazipur could scarcely hope to challenge Benares. All Ghazipur was humbled and Kalua came home in disgrace.

But not long afterwards, stories began to blow back that gave a different accounting of Kalua's defeat. It was said that on taking Kalua to Benares, the three young landlords, being seized by the licentious atmosphere of the city, had decided that it would be excellent sport to couple Kalua with a woman. They had invited some friends and taken bets: could a woman be found who would bed this giant of a man, this two-legged beast? A well-known baiji, Hirabai, was hired and brought to the kotha where the landlords were staying. There, with a select audience watching from the shelter of a marbled screen, Kalua had been led into her presence wearing nothing but a langot of white cotton around his waist. What had Hirabai expected? No one knew—but when she saw Kalua, she was rumoured to have screamed: This animal should be mated with a horse, not a woman. . .

It was this humiliation, people said, that cost Kalua the fight at Ramgarh Palace. Thus went the story that was told in the galis and ghats of Ghazipur.

It so happened that of all the people who could vouch for the truth of this tale, Deeti herself was one. This is how it came about: one night, after serving her husband his meal, Deeti had discovered that she had run short of water; to leave the dishes unwashed overnight was to invite an invasion of ghosts, ghouls and hungry pishaches. No matter: it was a bright, full-moon night and the Ganga was but a short walk away. Balancing a pot on her hip, she made her way through the waist-high poppies towards the silver gleam of the river. Just as she was about to step out of the poppy field, on to the treeless bank of sand that flanked the water, she heard the sound of hoofs, some distance away: looking to her left, in the direction of Ghazipur, she saw, in the light of the moon, four men on horses, trotting towards her.

A man on a horse never meant anything but trouble for a lone woman, and where there were four, riding together, the signs of danger were all too clear: Deeti lost no time in hiding herself among the poppies. When the horsemen had approached a little, she saw that she had been mistaken in thinking that they were four in number: there were only three mounted men; the fourth was following on foot. She took this last man to be a groom but when the men had come closer still, she saw that the fourth man had a halter around his neck and was being led like a horse. It was his size that had caused her to mistake him for a horseman: she saw that he was none other than Kalua. Now she recognized the horsemen too, for their faces were well known to everyone in Ghazipur: they were the three sport-loving landowners. She heard one of them call out to the others—*Iddhar*, here, this is a good spot; there's no one around—and she knew from his voice that he was drunk. When they were almost abreast of her, the men dismounted; of their three horses, they tied two together, turning them out to graze in the poppy fields. The third horse was a large black mare, and this animal they led towards Kalua, who was himself being held as if by a tether. Now she heard a whimpering, sobbing sound as Kalua fell suddenly to his knees, clutching at the thakurs' feet: *Mái-báp, hamke máf karelu* . . . forgive me, master . . . the fault wasn't mine . . .

This earned him volleys of kicks and curses:

. . . You lost on purpose, didn't you, *dogla* bastard?

. . . Do you know how much it cost us . . .?

. . . Now let's see you do what Hirabai said . . .

By pulling on his halter, the men forced Kalua to his feet and pushed him stumbling towards the mare's swishing tail. One of them stuck his whip into the fold of Kalua's cotton langot and whisked it off with a flick of his wrist. Then, while one of them held the horse steady, the others whipped Kalua's naked back until his groin was pressed hard against the animal's rear. Kalua uttered a cry that was almost indistinguishable in tone from the whinnying of the horse. This amused the landlords:

. . . See, the *b'henchod* even sounds like a horse . . .

. . . *Tatva dabá dé* . . . wring his balls . . .

Suddenly, with a swish of its tail, the mare defecated, unloosing a surge of dung over Kalua's belly and thighs. This excited yet more laughter from the three men. One of them dug his whip into Kalua's buttocks: Arre Kalua! Why don't you do the same?

Ever since the night of her wedding, Deeti had been haunted by images of her own violation: now, watching from the shelter of the poppy field, she bit the edge of her palm, to keep from crying out aloud. So it could happen to a man too? Even a powerful giant of a man could be humiliated and destroyed, in a way that far exceeded his body's capacity for pain?

In averting her eyes, her attention was drawn to the two grazing horses, which had strayed into the poppy field and were now quite close to her: another step and she would be within reach of their flanks. It was the work of a moment to find a poppy pod that had already shed its leaves; in falling, they had left behind a crown of sharp, dry prickles. Creeping towards one of the horses, she made a hissing sound as she dug the spiky pod into its withers. The animal reared, as if in response to a snakebite, and galloped off, pulling its tethered companion along in its fight. The horse's panic was instantly communicated to the black mare; in breaking free it lashed out with its hind legs, hitting Kalua in the chest. The three landlords, after standing a moment nonplussed, went racing off in pursuit of their mounts, leaving Kalua unconscious in the sand, naked and smeared in dung.

It took Deeti a while to summon the courage to take a closer look. When it became clear that the landlords were really gone, she crept out of her hiding-place and lowered herself to a squatting position beside Kalua's unconscious body. He was lying in shadow so she couldn't tell whether he was breathing or not. She put out a hand to touch his chest, but only to snatch it back: to think of touching a naked man was bad enough—and when that man was of Kalua's station, wasn't it almost a plea for retribution? She cast a furtive glance around her, and then, in defiance of the world's unseen presence, she put out a finger and allowed it to fall on Kalua's chest. The drumbeat of his heart reassured her and she quickly withdrew her hand, preparing to dart back into the poppies if his eyes showed any sign of coming open. But they remained shut and his body lay so peacefully inert that she felt no fear in examining him more closely. She saw now that his size was deceptive, that he was quite young, with no more than a faint feathering of hair on his upper lip; lying crumpled in the sand, he was no longer the dark giant who called at her home twice a day, without speaking, or allowing himself to be seen: he was just a fallen boy. Her tongue clicked involuntarily at the sight of the dung around his middle; she went to the riverside, pulled up a handful of rushes and used them to wipe away the smears. His langot was lying nearby, glowing white in the moonlight, and this too she fetched and fastidiously opened out.

It was when she was dropping the langot over him that her eyes were drawn, despite herself, to focus on his nakedness—somehow, even as she was cleaning him, she had managed not to take it in. She had never before, in a state of consciousness, been so close to this part of a man's body and now she found herself staring, both in fear and curiosity, seeing again that image of herself on her wedding night. As if of its own accord, her hand snaked out and laid itself down, and she felt, to her amazement, the softness of mere flesh: but then, as she grew accustomed to his breathing, she became aware of a faint stirring and swelling, and suddenly it was as if she were waking to a reality in which her family and her village were looking over her shoulder, watching as she sat with her hand resting intimately upon the most untouchable part of this man. Recoiling, she went quickly back into the field, where she hid herself among the poppies and waited as she had before.

After what seemed like a long time, Kalua rose slowly to his feet and looked around himself, as if in surprise. Then, knotting his langot around his loins, he staggered away, with a look of such confusion that Deeti was certain—or almost— that he had been totally unconscious of her presence.

Two years had passed since then, but far from fading, the events of that night had attained a guilty vividness in her memory. Often, as she lay beside her opium-dazed husband, her mind would revisit the scene, sharpening the details and refreshing certain particulars—all of this without her permission and despite her every effort to steer her thoughts in other directions. Her discomfort would have been greater still if she had believed that Kalua had access to the same images and recollections—but she had, as yet, seen no sign that he remembered anything from that night. Still, a nagging doubt remained, and since then she had always taken good care to avoid his eyes, shrouding her face in her sari whenever he was near.

So it was with some apprehension that Deeti observed Kalua now, from the shelter of her faded sari: the folds of fabric betrayed nothing of the concentration with which she watched for his response to her presence. She knew that if his eyes or his face were to betray any knowledge, any recollection, of her part in the events of that night, then she would have no option but to turn on her heel and walk away: the awkwardness would be too great to ignore, for not only was there the question of what the landlords had tried to do to him—the shame of which might well destroy a man if he knew that it had been witnessed—but there was also the shamelessness of her own curiosity, if that was indeed all it was.

To Deeti's relief, the sight of her seemed to kindle no spark in Kalua's dull eyes. His massive chest was clothed in a discoloured, sleeveless vest, and around his waist he was wearing his usual dirty cotton langot—out of the folds of which his oxen were now picking bits of straw, grass and fodder while he stood in front of his shack, shifting his weight between his pillar-like legs.

*Ka bhailé*? What's happening? he said at last in his hoarse, unmindful way, and she felt sure now that if he'd ever had any memory of that night, his slow, simple mind had long since lost track of it.

*Ey-ré Kalua*, she said, that man of mine is unwell at the factory; he has to be brought home.

He gave this some thought, cocking his head, and then nodded: All right; I'll bring him back.

Gaining confidence, she took out the package she had prepared and held it up in her hand: But this is all I can give you in payment, Kalua—don't expect anything more.

He stared at it: What is it?

Afeem, Kalua, she said briskly. At this time of year, what else do people have in their houses?

He began lumbering towards her, so she placed the package on the ground and stepped quickly back, clutching her daughter to her side: in the full light of day, it was unthinkable that any kind of contact should occur between herself and Kalua, even that which might result from the passing of an inert object. But she kept careful watch, as he picked up the leaf-wrapped package and sniffed its contents; it occurred to her to wonder, fleetingly, whether he too was an opium-eater—but she dismissed the thought instantly. What did it matter what his habits were? He was a stranger, not a husband. Yet, she felt oddly glad when, instead of putting the opium away for his own use, he broke the lump in two and fed the halves to his oxen. The animals chewed contentedly as he tied them to his yoke, and when the cart had drawn abreast of her, she climbed in with her daughter and sat facing backwards, with her legs dangling over the edge. And so they made their way towards Ghazipur, sitting at either end of the cart's bamboo platform, so far apart that not even the loosest of tongues could find a word to say, by way of scandal or reproach.

~

On that very afternoon, five hundred miles to the east of Ghazipur, Azad Naskar—known universally by his nickname, Jodu—was also preparing to embark on the journey that would bring him athwart the bows of the *Ibis* and into Deeti's shrine. Earlier that day, Jodu had buried his mother in the village of Naskarpara, using one of his last coins to pay a molla-shaheb to read the Qur'an over her freshly-dug grave. The village was some fifteen miles from Calcutta, in a featureless stretch of mud and mangrove, on the edge of the Sundarbans. It was little more than a huddle of huts, clustered around the tomb of the Sufi fakir who had converted the inhabitants to Islam a generation or two before. If not for the fakir's dargah the village might well have melted back into the mud, its inhabitants not being the kind of people to tarry long in one place: most of them earned their living by wandering on the water, working as boatmen, ferry-wallahs and fishermen. But they were humble folk, and few among them possessed the ambition or impetuosity to aspire to jobs on ocean-going ships—and of that small number, none had ever aspired more ardently to a lascar's livelihood than Jodu. He would have been long gone from the village if not for his mother's health, their family circumstances being such that in his absence, she was sure to have suffered complete neglect. Through the duration of her illness, he had tended to his mother in a fashion that was both impatient and affectionate, doing what little he could to provide some comfort in her last days: now, he had one final errand to perform on her behalf, after which he would be free to seek out the ghat-serangs who recruited lascars for deep-water ships.

Jodu too was a boatman's son, and he was, by his own reckoning, no longer a boy, his chin having become suddenly so fecund in its crop of hair as to require a weekly visit to the barber. But the changes in his physique were so recent and so volcanic that he had yet to grow accustomed to them: it was as if his body were a smoking crater that had just risen from the ocean and was still waiting to be explored. Across his left eyebrow, the legacy of a childhood mishap, there was a deep gash where the skin showed through, with the result that when seen from a distance, he seemed to have three eyebrows instead of two. This disfigurement, if it could be called that, provided an odd highlight to his appearance, and years later, when it came time for him to enter Deeti's shrine, it was this feature that was to determine her sketch of him: three gently angled slashes in an oval.

Jodu's boat, inherited years before from his father, was a clumsy affair, a dinghy made from hollowed-out logs and bound together with hemp ropes: within hours of his mother's burial, Jodu had loaded it with his few remaining possessions and was ready to leave for Calcutta. With the current behind him, it did not take long to cover the distance to the mouth of the canal that led to the city's docks: this narrow waterway, recently excavated by an enterprising English engineer, was known as Mr Tolly's Nullah, and for the privilege of entering it, Jodu had to hand the last of his coins to the keeper of its tollhouse. The narrow canal was busy, as always, and Jodu took a couple of hours to make his way through the city, past the Kalighat temple and the grim walls of Alipore Jail. Emerging into the busy waterway of the Hooghly, he found himself suddenly in the midst of a great multitude of vessels—crowded sampans and agile almadias, towering brigantines and tiny baulias, swift carracks and wobbly woolocks; Adeni buggalows with rakish lateen sails and Andhra bulkats with many-tiered decks. In steering through this press of traffic, there was no avoiding an occasional scrape or bump and for each of these he was roundly shouted out by serangs and tindals, coksens and bosmans; an irritable bhandari threw a bucket of slop at him and a lewd seacunny taunted him with suggestive gestures of his fist. Jodu responded by imitating the familiar shouts of sea officers—'What cheer ho? Avast!'—and left the lascars gaping at the fluency of his mimicry.

After a year spent in rural seclusion, it made his spirits soar to hear these harbour-front voices again, with their outpourings of obscenity and abuse, taunts and invitations—and to watch the lascars swinging through the ringeen made his own hands

*Amitav Ghosh*

grow restless for the feel of rope. As for the nearby shore, his gaze kept straying from the godowns and bankshalls of Kidderpore, to the twisting lanes of Watgunge where the women sat on the steps of their kothis, painting their faces in preparation for the night. What would they say to him now, those women who'd laughed and turned him away because of his youth?

Beyond Mr Kyd's shipyard, the traffic on the water thinned a little, and Jodu had no difficulty in pulling up to the embankment at Bhutghat. This part of the city lay directly opposite the Royal Botanical Gardens, on the far side of the Hooghly, and the ghat was much used by the Gardens' staff. Jodu knew that one of their boats would pull up here sooner or later, and sure enough, one such appeared within the hour, carrying a young English assistant curator. The lungi-clad coksen at the helm was well-known to Jodu, and once the sahib had stepped off, he pushed his own boat closer.

The coksen recognized him at once: *Arré Jodu na*? Isn't that you—Jodu Naskar?

Jodu made his salams: Salam, khalaji. Yes, it's me.

But where have you been? the coksen asked. Where's your mother? It's more than a year since you left the Gardens. Everyone's been wondering . . .

We went back to the village, khalaji, said Jodu. My mother didn't want to stay on after our sahib died.

I heard, said the coksen. And there was some talk that she was ill?

Jodu nodded, lowering his head: She died last night, khalaji.

*Allah'r rahem*! The coksen shut his eyes and muttered: God's mercy on her.

*Bismillah* . . . Jodu murmured the prayer after him and then added: Listen, khalaji—it's for my mother that I'm here: before she died she told me to be sure to find Lambert-sahib's daughter—Miss Paulette.

Of course, said the coksen. That girl was like a daughter to your mother: no ayah ever gave a child as much love as she did.

. . . But do you know where Paulette-missy is? It's more than a year since I last saw her.

The coksen nodded and raised a hand to point downriver: She lives not far from here. After her father died she was taken in by a rich English family. To find her, you'll have to go to Garden Reach. Ask for the mansion of Burnham-sahib: in the garden there's a chabutra with a green roof. You'll know it the moment you see it.

Jodu was delighted to have achieved his end with such little effort. *Khoda-hafej khálaji!* Waving his thanks, he pulled his oar from the mud and gave it a vigorous heave. As he was pulling away, he heard the coksen talking excitedly to the men around him: Do you see that boy's dinghy? Miss Paulette—the daughter of Lambert-sahib, the Frenchman—she was born in it: in that very boat . . .

Jodu had heard the story so many times, told by so many people, that it was almost as if he had witnessed the events himself. It was his kismat, his mother had always said, that accounted for the strange turn in their family's fate—if she hadn't gone home to her own village for Jodu's birth, it was certain that their lives would never have embraced Paulette.

It had happened soon after Jodu was born: his boatman father had come in his dinghy to fetch his wife and child from her parents' home, where she had gone for the delivery. They were on the Hooghly River when a brisk, squally wind had started to blow. With the day nearing its end, Jodu's father had decided that he would not risk crossing the river at that time: it would be safer to spend the night by the shore and make another attempt the next morning. Keeping to the bank, the boat had arrived eventually at the brick-bound embankment of the Royal Botanical Gardens: what better resting-place could there be than this fine ghat? Here, with the boat safely moored, they had eaten their evening meal and settled in to wait out the night.

They had not been long asleep when they were woken by a clamour of voices. A lantern had appeared, bringing with it the face of a white man: the sahib had thrust his face under their boat's thatched hood and uttered many words of frantic gibberish. It was clear he was very worried about something, so they were not surprised when one of his servants intervened to explain that there was a dire emergency; the sahib's pregnant wife was in great pain and in desperate need of a white doctor; there were none to be had on this side of the river, so she had to be taken to Calcutta, on the other bank.

Jodu's father had protested that his boat was too small to attempt a crossing, with no moon above, and the water churning beneath shifting winds. Far better that the sahib take a big bora or a budgerow—some boat with a large crew and many oars; surely there were some such at the Botanical Gardens?

So there were, came the answer; the Garden did indeed have a small fleet of its own. But as luck would have it, none of those boats were available that night: the head curator had commandeered them all, in order to take a party of his friends to the annual Ball of the Calcutta Exchange. The dinghy was the only boat presently moored at the ghat: if they refused to go, two lives would be lost—the mother's as well as the child's.

Having herself recently suffered the pains of childbirth, Jodu's mother was touched by the evident distress of the sahib and his mem: she added her voice to theirs, pleading with her husband to accept the commission. But he continued to shake his head, relenting only after the handing over of a coin, a silver tical worth more than the value of the dinghy itself. With this unrefusable inducement the bargain was sealed and the Frenchwoman was carried on board, in her litter.

One look at the pregnant woman's face was enough to know that she was in great pain: they cast off at once, steering towards Calcutta's Babughat. Even though it was windy and dark, there was no difficulty in setting a course because the lights of the Calcutta Exchange had been especially illuminated for the annual Ball and were clearly visible across the river. But the winds grew stronger and the water rougher as they pulled away from the shore; soon the boat was being buffeted with such violence that it became difficult to hold the litter still. As the rolling and tossing increased, the memsahib's condition grew steadily worse until suddenly, right in midstream, her waters broke and she went into the throes of a premature labour.

They turned back at once, but the shore was a long way off. The sahib's attention was now focused on comforting his wife and he could be of no help in the delivery: it was Jodu's mother who bit through the cord and wiped the blood from the girl's tiny body. Leaving her own child, Jodu, to lie naked in the boat's bilges, she took his blanket, wrapped the girl in it, and held her close to her dying mother. The child's face was the last sight the memsahib's eyes beheld: she bled to death before they could return to the Botanical Gardens.

The sahib, distraught and grieving, was in no position to deal with a screaming infant: he was greatly relieved when Jodu's mother quietened the baby by putting her to her breast. On their return, he made another request—could the boatman and his family stay on until an ayah or wet-nurse could be engaged?

What could they say but yes? The truth was that Jodu's mother would have found it hard to part from the girl after that first night: she had opened her heart to the baby the moment she held her to her breast. From that day on, it was as if she had not one child but two: Jodu, her son, and her daughter Putli—'doll'—which was her way of domesticating the girl's name. As for Paulette, in the confusion of tongues that was to characterize her upbringing, her nurse became 'Tantima'—'aunt-mother'.

This was how Jodu's mother entered the employment of Pierre Lambert, who had but recently come to India to serve as the assistant curator of Calcutta's Botanical Gardens. The understanding was that she would stay only until a replacement could be found—but somehow no one else ever was. Without anything ever being formally arranged, Jodu's mother became Paulette's wet-nurse, and the two children spent their infancy lying head-to-head in her arms. Such objections as Jodu's father might have had disappeared when the assistant curator bought him a new and much better boat, a bauliya: he soon went off to live in Naskarpara, leaving behind his wife and child, but taking his new vessel with him. From that time on, Jodu and his mother saw him but rarely, usually at the beginning of the month, around the time when she was paid; with the money he took from her, he married again and sired a great number of children. Jodu saw these half-siblings twice a year, during the 'Id festivals, when he was made to pay reluctant visits to Naskarpara. But the village was never home to him in the way of the Lambert bungalow, where he reigned as Miss Paulette's favoured playmate and mock-consort.

As for Paulette, the first language she learnt was Bengali, and the first solid food she ate was a rice-and-dal khichri cooked by Jodu's mother. In the matter of clothing she far preferred saris to pinafores—for shoes she had no patience at all, choosing, rather, to roam the Gardens in bare feet, like Jodu. Through the early years of their childhood they were all but inseparable, for she would neither sleep nor eat unless Jodu was present in her room. There were several other children in the bungalow's quarters, but only Jodu was allowed free access to the main house and its bedrooms. At an early age, Jodu came to understand that this was because his mother's relationship with her employer was special, in a way that required her to remain with him until late at night. But neither he nor Putli ever referred to this matter, accepting it as one of the many unusual circumstances of their peculiar household—for Jodu and his mother were not the only ones to be cut off from their own kind; Paulette and her father were perhaps even more so. Rarely, if ever, did white men or women visit their bungalow, and the Lamberts took no part in the busy whirl of Calcutta's English society. When the Frenchman ventured across the river, it was only for what he liked to call 'busy-ness': other than that he was wholly preoccupied with his plants and his books.

Jodu was more worldly than his playmate, and it did not escape him that Paulette and her father were at odds with the other white sahibs: he had heard it said that the Lamberts were from a country that was often at war with England, and at first it was to this that he attributed their apartness. But later, when his shared secrets with Putli deepened in import, he came to understand that this was not the only difference between the Lamberts and the English. He learnt that the reason why Pierre Lambert had left his country was that he had been involved, in his youth, in a revolt against his king; that he was shunned by respectable English society because he had publicly denied the existence of God and the sanctity of marriage. None of this mattered in the least to the boy—if such opinions served to insulate their household against other sahibs then he could only be glad of them.

But it was neither age nor sahibdom, but a much subtler intrusion that loosened the bonds between the children: at a certain moment Putli began to read, and then there was not enough time in the day for anything else. Jodu, on the other hand, lost interest in letters as soon as he learnt to decipher them; his own inclinations had always drawn him towards the water. He laid claim to his father's old boat—Putli's birthplace—and by the age of ten had become adept enough in its use, not just to serve as a boatman for the Lamberts but also to accompany them when they travelled in search of specimens.

Odd as their household was, its arrangements seemed so secure, permanent and satisfying that none of them were prepared for the disasters that followed on Pierre Lambert's unexpected death. He perished of a fever before he could set his affairs in order; shortly after his passing, it was discovered that he had accumulated substantial debts in furthering his researches—his mysterious 'busy-ness' trips to Calcutta were revealed to have consisted of surreptitious visits to moneylenders in Kidderpore. It was then too that Jodu and his mother paid the price of their privileged association with the assistant curator. The resentments and jealousies of the other servants and employees were quickly made manifest in angry accusations of deathbed theft. The hostility became so acute that Jodu and his mother were forced to slip away, in their boat. Left with no other option, they returned to Naskarpara, where they were given grudging refuge by their step-family. But years of comfortable bungalow-living had left Jodu's mother unfit for the privations of village life. The irreversible decline of her health started within a few weeks of their arrival and did not end until her death.

Altogether, Jodu had spent fourteen months in Naskarpara: in that time he had neither seen Paulette nor received any word from her. On her deathbed his mother had thought often of her old charge and had begged Jodu to meet with Putli one last time, so that she would know, at least, how much her old ayah had missed her in the last days of her life. Jodu, for his part, had long been aware that he and his erstwhile playmate would one day be reclaimed by their separate worlds and he would have been content to leave it at that: if not for his mother, he would not have set out to look for Paulette. But now that he knew he was nearing the place where she lived, he found himself growing both eager and apprehensive: Would Putli agree to meet him, or would she have him turned out by the servants? If he could but see her face to face, there'd be so much to talk about, so much to tell. Looking ahead, downriver, he spotted a little pavilion with a green roof and quickened his pace.

# four

~

Heading into Ghazipur, in Kalua's ox-cart, Deeti felt strangely light in spirit, despite the grim nature of her errand: it was as if she knew, in her heart, that this was the last time she would be travelling that road with her daughter, and was determined to make the best of it.

The cart was slow in making its way through the warren of lanes and bazars that lay at the heart of the town, but once the road curved towards the riverfront, the congestion eased a little and the surroundings became more gracious. Deeti and Kabutri rarely had occasion to come into town, and they stared in fascination at the walls of the Chehel Satoon, a forty-pillared palace built by a nobleman of Persian ancestry, in imitation of a monument in Isfahan. A short while later they passed a still-greater wonder, a structure of Grecian inspiration, with fluted columns and a soaring dome; this was the mausoleum of Lord Cornwallis, of Yorktown fame, who had died in Ghazipur thirty-three years before: as the ox-cart rumbled past, Deeti showed Kabutri the statue of the English Laat-Sahib. Then, suddenly, as the cart was trundling around a curve in the road, Kalua clicked his tongue, to rein in the oxen. Jolted by the abrupt change of pace, Deeti and Kabutri swivelled around to look ahead—and their smiles died on their lips.

The road was filled with people, a hundred strong or more; hemmed in by a ring of stick-bearing guards, this crowd was trudging wearily in the direction of the river. Bundles of belongings sat balanced on their heads and shoulders, and brass pots hung suspended from their elbows. It was clear that they had already marched a great distance, for their dhotis, langots and vests were stained with the dust of the road. The sight of the marchers evoked both pity and fear in the local people; some of the spectators clucked their tongues in sympathy but a few urchins and old women threw pebbles into the crowd, as if to ward off an unsavoury influence. Through all this, despite their exhaustion, the marchers seemed strangely unbowed, even defiant, and some threw the pebbles right back at the spectators: their bravado was no less disturbing to the spectators than their evident destitution.

Who are they, Ma? Kabutri asked, in a low whisper.

I don't know—prisoners maybe?

No, said Kalua immediately, pointing to the presence of a few women and children among the marchers. They were still speculating when one of the guards stopped the cart and told Kalua that their leader and duffadar, Ramsaran-ji, had hurt his foot, and would need to be driven to the nearby river-ghat. The duffadar appeared as the guard was speaking, and Deeti and Kabutri were quick to make room for him: he was an imposing man, tall and full-bellied, dressed in immaculate white, with leather shoes. He carried a heavy stick in one hand and wore a huge dome of a turban on his head.

At first they were too frightened to speak and it was Ramsaran-ji who broke the silence: Where've you come from? he said to Kalua. *Kahwãa se áwela?*

From a nearby village, malik; *parosé ka gaõ se áwat bani.*

Deeti and Kabutri had been straining their ears, and when they heard the duffadar speaking their own Bhojpuri tongue, they edged towards him, so as to be able to overhear all that was said.

At length, Kalua plucked up the courage to ask: Malik, who are these people who are marching?

They are girmitiyas, said Ramsaran-ji, and at the sound of that word Deeti uttered an audible gasp—for suddenly she understood. It was a few years now since the rumours had begun to circulate in the villages around Ghazipur: although she had never seen a girmitiya before, she had heard them being spoken of. They were so called because, in exchange for money, their names were entered on 'girmits'—agreements written on pieces of paper. The silver that was paid for them went to their families, and they were taken away, never to be seen again: they vanished, as if into the netherworld.

Where are they going, malik? said Kalua, in a hushed voice, as if he were speaking of the living dead.

A boat will take them to Patna and then to Calcutta, said the guard. And from there they'll go to a place called Mareech.

Unable to restrain herself any longer, Deeti joined in the conversation, asking, from the shelter of her sari's ghungta: Where is this Mareech? Is it near Dilli?

Ramsaran-ji laughed. No, he said scornfully. It's an island in the sea—like Lanka, but farther away.

The mention of Lanka, with its evocation of Ravana and his demon-legions, made Deeti flinch. How was it possible that the marchers could stay on their feet, knowing what lay ahead? She tried to imagine what it would be like to be in their place, to know that you were forever an outcaste; to know that you would never again enter your father's house; that you would never throw your arms around your mother; never eat a meal with your sisters and brothers; never feel the cleansing touch of the Ganga. And to know also that for the rest of your days you would eke out a living on some wild, demon-plagued island?

Deeti shivered. And how will they get to that place? she asked Ramsaran-ji.

A ship will be waiting for them at Calcutta, said the duffadar, a *jaház*, much larger than any you've ever seen: with many masts and sails; a ship large enough to hold hundreds of people . . .

*Hái Rám*! So that was what it was? Deeti clapped a hand over her mouth as she recalled the ship she had seen while standing in the Ganga. But why had the apparition been visited upon her, Deeti, who had nothing to do with these people? What could it possibly mean?

*Amitav Ghosh*

Kabutri was quick to guess what was on her mother's mind. She said: Wasn't that the kind of ship you saw? The one like a bird? Strange that it showed itself to you.

Don't say that! Deeti cried, throwing her arms around the girl. A tremor of dread went through her and she hugged her daughter to her chest.

~

Moments after Mr Doughty had announced his arrival, Benjamin Burnham's boots landed on the deck of the *Ibis* with a weighty thud: the shipowner's fawn breeches and dark jacket were dusty after the journey from Calcutta, and his knee-length riding boots were flecked with mud—but the ride had clearly invigorated him, for there was no trace of fatigue on his glowing face.

Benjamin Burnham was a man of imposing height and stately girth, with a full curly beard that cloaked the upper half of his chest like a plate of glossy chainmail. A few years short of fifty, his step had not lost the bounce of youth and his eyes still had the brilliant, well-focused sparkle that comes from never looking in any direction other than ahead. The skin of his face was leathery and deeply tanned, a legacy of many years of energetic activity in the sun. Now, standing erect on deck, he hooked his thumb in the lapel of his jacket and ran a quizzical eye over the schooner's crew before stepping aside with Mr Doughty. The two men conferred for a while and then Mr Burnham went up to Zachary and extended a hand. 'Mr Reid?'

'Yes, sir.' Zachary stepped up to shake his hand.

The shipowner looked him up and down, in approval. 'Doughty says for a rank griffin, you're a pucka sort of chap.'

'I hope he's right, sir,' said Zachary, uncertainly.

The shipowner smiled, baring a set of large, sparkling teeth. 'Well, do you feel up to giving me a tour of my new vessel?'

In Benjamin Burnham's bearing there was that special kind

of authority that suggests an upbringing of wealth and privilege—but this was misleading, Zachary knew, for the shipowner was a tradesman's son and prided himself on being a self-made man. Over the last two days, courtesy of Mr Doughty, Zachary had learnt a great deal about the 'Burra Sahib': he knew, for example, that for all his familiarity with Asia, Benjamin Burnham was not 'countryborn'—'that's to say he's not like those of us sahibs who drew our first breath in the East.' He was the son of a Liverpool timber merchant, but had spent no more than a scant ten years 'at home'—'and that means Blatty, my boy, not just any damned place you happen to be living in.'

As a child, the pilot said, young Ben was a 'right shaytan': a brawler, trouble-maker and general hurremzad who was clearly destined for a lifetime's journey through penitentiaries and houses of correction: it was to save him from his kismet that his family had shipped him out as a 'guinea-pig'—'that's what you called a cabin-boy on an Indiaman in the old days— because they were everyone's to step on and do with as they willed.'

But even the discipline of an East India Company tea-wagon had proved insufficient to tame the lad: 'A quartermaster lured the boy into the ship's store with a mind to trying a bit of udlee-budlee. But chota as he was, young Benjamin didn't lack for bawhawdery—set upon the old launderbuzz with a belaying-pin and beat him with such a will that his life-line was all but unrove.'

For his own safety Benjamin Burnham was sent off the ship at its next port of call, which happened to be the British penal colony of Port Blair, on the Andaman Islands. 'Best thing that could happen to a wild young chuckeroo: nothing like a jail-connah to tame a junglee.' At Port Blair, Ben Burnham found employment with the prison's chaplain: here, under a regime that was both punitive and forgiving, he acquired faith as well as an education. 'Oh those preachers have hard hands, my boy; they'll put the Lord's Word in your mouth even if they have to knock out your teeth to do it.' When sufficiently reformed, the boy drifted Atlantic-wards and spent some time on a blackbirder, sailing between America, Africa and England. Then, at the age of nineteen he found himself sailing China-wards on a ship that was carrying a well-known Protestant missionary. The accidental acquaintance between Ben Burnham and the English Reverend was to strengthen and deepen into a lasting friendship. 'That's how it goes in those parts,' said the pilot. 'Canton is a place where you get to know your friends. The Chinamen keep the Fanqui-devils penned inside the foreign factories, outside the town walls. No Fanqui can leave their little strip of shore; can't pass the city gates. Nowhere to go; no place to walk, no course to ride. Even to take a little hongboat out on the river, you have to get an official chop. No mems allowed; nothing to do but listen to your shroffs counting their taels. Man can get as lonely as a butcher on banyan-day. There's some who just can't take it and have to be sent home. There's some who go down to Hog Lane, to puckrow a buy-em-dear or get must on shamshoo wine. But not Ben Burnham: when he wasn't selling opium, he was with the missionaries. More often than not you'd find him at the American factory—the Yankees were more to his taste than his Company colleagues, being more churchy-like.'

Through the Reverend's influence, Benjamin Burnham found a position as a clerk with the trading firm of Magniac & Co., the predecessors of Jardine & Matheson, and from then on, as with every other foreigner involved in the China trade, his time was divided between the two poles of the Pearl River Delta—Canton and Macao, eighty miles apart. Only the winter trading-season was spent in Canton: for the rest of the year the traders lived in Macao, where the Company maintained an extensive network of godowns, bankshalls and factories.

'Ben Burnham did his time, offloading opium from receiving-ships, but he wasn't the kind of man who could be happy on another man's payroll, drawing a monthly tuncaw: he wanted to be a nabob in his own right, with his own seat at the Calcutta opium auction.' As with many another Fanqui merchant in Canton, Burnham's church connections were a great help, since several missionaries had close connections with opium traders. In 1817, the year the East India Company gave him his articles of indenture as a free merchant, an opportunity presented itself in the form of a team of Chinese converts who had to be escorted to the Baptist Mission College in Serampore, in Bengal. 'And what better man to bring them in than Ben Burnham? Before you know it, he's in Calcutta, looking for a dufter—and what's more he finds one too. The good old Roger of Rascally gives him a set of chabees to a house on the Strand!'

Burnham's intention in moving to Calcutta was to position himself to bid in the opium auctions of the East India Company: yet it was not the China trade that provided him with his first financial coup; this came, rather, from his boyhood training in another branch of the British Empire's commerce. 'In the good old days people used to say there were only two things to be exported from Calcutta: thugs and drugs—or opium and coolies as some would have it.'

Benjamin Burnham's first successful bid was for the transportation of convicts. Calcutta was then the principal conduit through which Indian prisoners were shipped to the British Empire's network of island prisons—Penang, Bencoolen, Port Blair and Mauritius. Like a great stream of silt, thousands of Pindaris, Thugs, dacoits, rebels, head-hunters and hooligans were carried away by the muddy waters of the Hooghly to be dispersed around the Indian Ocean, in the various island jails where the British incarcerated their enemies.

To find a kippage for a convict ship was no easy matter, for many a seaman would heave sharp about at the prospect of signing on to a vessel with a cargo of cutthroats. 'In his hour of need, Burnham broached his business by calling upon a friend from his chocolateering days, one Charles Chillingworth, a ship's master of whom it would come to be said that there was no better manganizer at large on the ocean—not a single slave, convict or coolie had ever escaped his custody and lived to gup about it.' With Chillingworth's help, Benjamin Burnham sieved a fortune from the tide of transportees that was flowing out of Calcutta, and this inflow of capital allowed him to enter the China trade on an even bigger scale than he had envisaged: soon he was running a sizeable fleet of his own ships. By his early thirties, he had formed a partnership with two of his brothers, and the firm had become a leading trading house, with agents and dufters in such cities as Bombay, Singapore, Aden, Canton, Macao, London and Boston.

'So there you are: that's the jadoo of the colonies. A boy who's crawled up through the hawse-holes can become as grand a sahib as any twice-born Company man. Every door in Calcutta thrown open. Burra-khanas at Government House. Choti hazri at Fort William. No BeeBee so great as to be durwauza-bund when he comes calling. His personal shoke might be for Low-Church evangelism, but you can be sure the Bishop always has a pew waiting for him. And to seal it all, Miss Catherine Bradshaw for a wife—about as pucka a memsahib as ever there was, a brigadier's daughter.'

~

The qualities that had made Ben Burnham into a merchant-nabob were amply in evidence during his tour of the *Ibis*: he examined the vessel from stem to stern, even descending to the keelson and mounting the jib-boom, noting everything that merited attention, either by way of praise or blame.

'And how does she sail, Mr Reid?'

'Oh she's a fine old barkey, sir,' said Zachary. 'Swims like a swan and steers like a shark.'

Mr Burnham smiled in appreciation of Zachary's enthusiasm. 'Good.'

Only when his inspection was over did the shipowner listen to Zachary's narrative of the disastrous voyage from Baltimore, questioning him carefully on the details while thumbing through the ship's log. At the end of the cross-examination, he pronounced himself satisfied and clapped Zachary on the back: 'Shahbash! You bore up very well, under the circumstances.'

Such reservations as Mr Burnham had concerned chiefly the lascar crew and its leader: 'That old Mug of a serang: what makes you think he can be trusted?'

'Mug, sir?' said Zachary, knitting his brows.

'That's what they call the Arakanese in these parts,' said Burnham. 'The very word strikes terror into the natives of the coast. Fearsome bunch, the Mugs—pirates to a man, they say.'

'Serang Ali? A pirate?' Zachary smiled to think of his own initial response to the serang and how absurd it seemed in retrospect. 'He may look a bit of a Tartar, sir, but he's no more a pirate than I am: if he was, he'd have made off with the *Ibis* long before we dropped anchor. Certainly I couldn't have stopped him.'

Burnham directed his piercing gaze directly into Zachary's eyes. 'You'll vouch for him, will you?'

'Yes, sir.'

'All right then. But I'd still keep a weather eye on him, if I were you.' Closing the ship's log, Mr Burnham turned his attention to the correspondence that had accumulated over the course of the voayge. M. d'Epinay's letter from Mauritius seemed particularly to catch his interest, especially after Zachary reported the planter's parting words about his sugar-cane rotting in the fields and his desperate need for coolies.

Scratching his chin, Mr Burnham said. 'What do you say, Reid? Would you be inclined to head back to the Mauritius Islands soon?'

'Me, sir?' Zachary had thought that he would be spending several months ashore, refitting the *Ibis*, and was hard put to respond to this sudden change of plan. Seeing him hesitate, the shipowner added an explanation: 'The *Ibis* won't be carrying opium on her first voyage, Reid. The Chinese have been making trouble on that score and until such time as they can be made to understand the benefits of Free Trade, I'm not going to send any more shipments to Canton. Till then, this vessel is going to do just the kind of work she was intended for.'

The suggestion startled Zachary: 'D'you mean to use her

as a slaver, sir? But have not your English laws outlawed that trade?'

'Yes indeed they have, Reid. It's sad but true that there are many who'll stop at nothing to halt the march of human freedom.'

'Freedom, sir?' said Zachary, wondering if he had misheard.

His doubts were quickly put at rest. 'Freedom, yes, exactly,' said Mr Burnham. 'Isn't that what the mastery of the white man means for the lesser races? As I see it, Reid, the Africa trade was the greatest exercise in freedom since God led the children of Israel out of Egypt. Consider, Reid, the situation of a so-called slave in the Carolinas—is he not more free than his brethren in Africa, groaning under the rule of some dark tyrant?'

Zachary tugged his ear-lobe. 'Well sir, if slavery is freedom then I'm glad I don't have to make a meal of it. Whips and chains are not much to my taste.'

'Oh come now, Reid!' said Mr Burnham. 'The march to the shining city is never without pain, is it? Didn't the Israelites suffer in the desert?'

Reluctant to enter into an argument with his new employer, Zachary mumbled: 'Well sir, I guess . . .'

This was not good enough for Mr Burnham, who quizzed him with a smile. 'I thought you were a pucka kind of fellow, Reid,' he said. 'And here you are carrying on like one of those Reformer fellows.'

'Am I, sir?' said Zachary quickly. 'I didn't mean to.'

'Thought not,' said Mr Burnham. 'Lucky thing that particular disease hasn't taken hold in your parts yet. Last bastion of liberty, I always say—slavery'll be safe in America for a while yet. Where else could I have found a vessel like this, so perfectly suited for its cargo?'

'Do you mean slaves, sir?'

Mr Burnham winced. 'Why no, Reid. Not slaves—coolies. Have you not heard it said that when God closes one door he opens another? When the doors of freedom were closed to the African, the Lord opened them to a tribe that was yet more needful of it—the Asiatick.'

Zachary chewed his lip: it was not his place, he decided, to interrogate his employer about his business; better to concentrate on practical matters. 'Will you be wishing to refurbish the 'tween-deck then, sir?'

'Exactly,' said Mr Burnham. 'A hold that was designed to carry slaves will serve just as well to carry coolies and convicts. Do you not think? We'll put in a couple of heads and piss-dales, so the darkies needn't always be fouling themselves. That should keep the inspectors happy.'

'Yes, sir.'

Mr Burnham ran a finger through his beard. 'Yes, I think Mr Chillingworth will thoroughly approve.'

'Mr Chillingworth, sir?' said Zachary. 'Is he to be the ship's master?'

'I see you've heard of him.' Mr Burnham's face turned sombre. 'Yes—this is to be his last voyage, Reid, and I would like it to be a pleasant one. He has suffered some reverses lately and is not in the best of health. He will have Mr Crowle as his first mate—an excellent sailor but a man of somewhat uncertain temper it must be said. I would be glad to have a sound kind of fellow on board, as second mate. What do you say, Reid? Are you of a mind to sign up again?'

This corresponded so closely to Zachary's hopes that his heart leapt: 'Did you say second mate, sir?'

'Yes of course,' said Mr Burnham, and then, as if to settle the matter, he added: 'Should be an easy sail: get under weigh after the monsoons and be back in six weeks. My subedar will be on board with a platoon of guards and overseers. He's had a lot of experience in this line of work: you won't hear a murmur from the thugs—he knows how to keep them shipshape. And if all goes well, you should be back just in time to join us on our Chinese junket.'

'I beg your pardon, sir?'

Mr Burnham slung an arm around Zachary's shoulders. 'I'm telling you this in confidence, Reid, so hold it close to your chest. The word is that London is putting together an expedition to take on the Celestials. I'd like the *Ibis* to be a part of it—and you too for that matter. What'd you say, Reid? Are you up for it?'

'You can count on me, sir,' said Zachary fervently. 'Won't find me wanting, not where it's a matter of effort.'

'Good man!' said Mr Burnham, clapping him on the back. 'And the *Ibis*? Do you think she'd be useful in a scrap? How many guns does she have?'

'Six nine-pounders, sir,' said Zachary. 'But we could add a bigger gun on a swivel mount.'

'Excellent!' said Mr Burnham. 'I like your spirit, Reid. Don't mind telling you: I could use a pucka young chap like you in my firm. If you give a good account of yourself, you'll have your own command by and by.'

~

Neel lay on his back, watching the light as it rippled across the polished wood of the cabin's ceiling: the blinds on the window filtered the sun's reflection in such a way that he could almost imagine himself to be under the river's surface, with Elokeshi by his side. When he turned to look at her, the illusion seemed even more real, for her half-unclothed body was bathed in a glow that swirled and shimmered exactly like flowing water.

Neel loved these intervals of quiet in their love-making, when she lay dozing beside him. Even when motionless, she seemed to be frozen in dance: her mastery of movement seemed not to be bounded by any limits, being equally evident in stillness and in motion, onstage and in bed. As a performer she was famed for her ability to outwit the quickest tabla-players: in bed, her improvisations created similar pleasures and surprises. The suppleness of her body was such that when he lay on her, mouth to mouth, she could curl her legs around him so as to hold his head steady between the soles of her feet; or when the mood took her, she could arch her back so as to lever him upwards, holding him suspended on the muscular curve of her belly. And it was with a dancer's practised sense of rhythm that she would pace their love-making, so that he was only dimly aware of the cycles of beats that governed their changes of tempo: and the moment of release, too, was always utterly unpredictable yet totally predetermined, as if a mounting, quickening *tál* were reaching the climactic stillness of its final beat.

But even more than the love-making, he liked these moments afterwards, when she lay spent on the bed, like a dancer after a dizzying tihai, with her sari and her dupattas scattered around her, their loops and knots passing over and around her torso and her limbs. There was never time, in the urgent preliminaries to the first love-making, to properly undress: his own six-yard-long dhoti would wind itself through her nine-yard sari, forming patterns that were even more intricate than the interleaving of their limbs; only afterwards was there the leisure to savour the pleasures of a slowly-conjured nakedness. Like many dancers, Elokeshi had a fine voice and could sing exquisite thumris: as she hummed, Neel would unwrap the garments from her limbs, lingering over each part of her body as his fingers bared them to his eyes and his lips: her powerful, arched ankles, with their tinkling silver anklets, her sinuous thighs, with their corded muscles, the downy softness of her mound, the gentle curve of her belly and the upswell of her breasts. And then, when every shred of clothing had been peeled away from both their bodies, they would start again, on their second bout of love-making, long, languid and lasting.

Today Neel had barely started to disentangle Elokeshi's limbs from the knotted cocoon of her clothing, when there was an untimely interruption in the form of a second altercation in the gangway outside the door: once again, the three girls were holding Parimal back from bringing news to his master.

Let him come in, Neel snapped in annoyance. He pulled a dupatta over Elokeshi, as the door was opening, but made no move to reattach his own disarranged clothing. Parimal had been his personal bearer and dresser since he was of an age to walk; he had bathed him and clothed him through the years of his childhood; on the day of Neel's wedding, it was he who had prepared the twelve-year-old boy for his first night with his bride, instructing him in what had to be done: there was no aspect of Neel's person that was unfamiliar to Parimal.

Forgive me, huzoor, Parimal said as he stepped inside. But I thought you should know: Burra-Burnham-sahib has arrived here. He is on the ship right now. If the other sahibs are coming to dinner, then what about him?

The news took Neel by surprise, but after a moment's thought, he nodded: You're right—yes, he must be invited too. Neel pointed to a gown-like garment hanging on a peg: Bring me my choga.

Parimal fetched the choga and held it open while Neel stepped out of bed and slipped his arms into its sleeves. Wait outside, Neel said: I'm going to write another note for you to deliver to the ship.

When Parimal had left the room, Elokeshi threw off her covers. What's happened? she said, sleepily blinking her eyes.

Nothing, said Neel. I just have to write a note. Stay where you are. It won't take long.

Neel dipped his quill in an inkpot and scrawled a few words, but only to change his mind and start again. His hands became a little unsteady as he wrote out a line expressing his pleasure at the prospect of welcoming Mr Benjamin Burnham on the Raskhali budgerow. He stopped, took a deep breath and added: 'Your arrival is indeed a happy coincidence, and it would have pleased my father, the late Raja, who was, as you know, a great believer in signs and omens . . .'

~

Some twenty-five years before, when his trading house was still in its infancy, Mr Benjamin Burnham had come to see the old Raja with an eye to leasing one of his properties as an office: he needed a Dufter but was short on capital, he said, and would have to defer the payment of the rent. Unbeknownst to Mr Burnham, while he was presenting his case, a white mouse had appeared under his chair—hidden from the trader, but perfectly visible to the zemindar, it sat still until the Englishman had had his say. A mouse being the familiar of Ganesh-thakur, god of opportunities and remover of obstacles, the old zemindar had taken the visitation to be an indication of divine will: not only had he allowed Mr Burnham to defer his rent for a year, he had also imposed the condition that the Raskhali estate be allowed to invest in the fledgling agency—the Raja was a shrewd judge of people, and in Benjamin Burnham he had recognized a coming man. Of what the Englishman's business would consist, the Raja made no inquiry: he was a zemindar after all, not a bania in a bazar, sitting cross-legged on a countertop.

It was on decisions like these that the Halders had built their fortunes over the last century and a half. In the era of the Mughals, they had ingratiated themselves with the dynasty's representatives; at the time of the East India Company's arrival, they had extended a wary welcome to the newcomers; when the British went to war against the Muslim rulers of Bengal, they had lent money to one side and sepoys to the other, waiting to see which would prevail. After the British proved victorious, they had proved as adept at the learning of English as they had previously been in the acquisition of Persian and Urdu. When it was to their advantage, they were glad to shape their lives to the world of the English; yet they were vigilant always to prevent too deep an intersection between the two circles. The inner determinations of the white mercantile community, and its private accountings of profit and opportunity, they continued to regard with aristocratic contempt—and never more so than where it concerned men like Benjamin Burnham, whom they knew to have been born into the commercial classes. The transactions of investing money with him and accepting the returns represented no challenge to their standing; but to display an interest in where the profits came from and how they had been accumulated would have been well below their place. The old Raja knew nothing more about Mr Burnham than that he was a shipowner, and there he was content to let the matter rest. Each year, from the time of their first meeting onwards, the zemindar gave a

*Amitav Ghosh*

sum of money to Mr Burnham to augment the consignments of his agency: every year he got back a much larger sum. He would laughingly refer to these payments as his tribute from the 'Faghfoor of Maha-chin'—the Emperor of Greater China.

That his money was accepted by the Englishman was the Raja's singular fortune—for in eastern India, opium was the exclusive monopoly of the British, produced and packaged entirely under the supervision of the East India Company; except for a small group of Parsis, few native-born Indians had access to the trade or its profits. As a result, when it came to be known that the Halders of Raskhali had entered into a partnership with an English trader, a great number of friends, relatives and creditors had begged to be allowed to share in the family's good fortune. By dint of much pleading and cajolery they persuaded the old zemindar to add their money to the sums that he annually deposited with Mr Burnham: for this privilege they were content to pay the Halder estate a ten-per-cent dasturi on the profits; so great were the returns that this commission seemed perfectly reasonable. Little did they know of the perils of the consignment trade and how the risks were borne by those who provided the capital. Year after year, with British and American traders growing ever more skilled in evading Chinese laws, the market for opium expanded, and the Raja and his associates made handsome profits on their investments.

But money, if not mastered, can bring ruin as well as riches, and for the Halders the new stream of wealth was to prove more a curse than a blessing. As a family, their experience lay in the managing of kings and courts, peasants and dependants: although rich in land and property, they had never possessed much by way of coinage; what there was of it, they disdained to handle themselves, preferring to entrust it to a legion of agents, gomustas and poor relatives. When the old zemindar's coffers began to swell, he tried to convert his silver into immovable wealth of the kind he best understood—land, houses, elephants, horses, carriages and, of course, a budgerow more splendid than any other craft then sailing on the river. But with the new properties there came a great number of

dependants who had all to be fed and maintained; much of the
new land proved to be uncultivable, and the new houses
quickly became an additional drain since the Raja would not
suffer them to be rented. Learning of the zemindar's new
source of wealth, his mistresses—of whom he had exactly as
many as there were days in the week, so as to be able to spend
each night in a different bed—grew more exigent, vying with
each other in asking for gifts, baubles, houses, and jobs for
their relatives. Always a doting lover, the old zemindar gave in
to most of their demands, with the result that his debts
increased until all the silver Mr Burnham earned for him was
being channelled directly to his creditors. Having no more
capital of his own to give to Mr Burnham, the Raja came
increasingly to depend on the commissions paid by those who
entrusted him to be their go-between: this being the case, he
had also to expand the circle of investors, signing a great many
promissory notes—or hundees as they were known in the
bazar.

As was the custom in the family, the heir to the title was
excluded from the estate's financial dealings; being studious by
inclination and dutiful by nature, Neel had not sought to
question his father about the running of the zemindary. It was
only in the final days of his life that the old zemindar informed
his son that the family's financial survival depended on their
dealings with Mr Benjamin Burnham; the more they invested
with him the better, for their silver would come back doubled
in value. He explained that in order to make the best of this
arrangement, he had told Mr Burnham that this year he would
like to venture the equivalent of one lakh sicca rupees. Knowing
that it would take time to raise such a large amount, Mr
Burnham had kindly offered to forward a part of the sum from
his own funds: the understanding was that the money would
be made good by the Halders if it wasn't covered by the profits
from that summer's opium sales. But there was nothing to
worry about, the old zemindar had said: in the past two
decades there had never been a single year when their money
had not come back with a large increase. This was not a debt,
he had said, it was a gift.

A few days later the old zemindar had died, and with his passing everything seemed to change. That year, 1837, was the first in which Burnham Bros. failed to generate profits for its clients. In the past, when the opium ships returned from China, at the end of the trading season, Mr Burnham had always come in person to the Raskhali Rajbari—the Halders' principal seat in Calcutta. It was the custom for the Englishman to bring auspicious gifts, like areca-nuts and saffron, as well as bills and bullion. But in the first year of Neel's incumbency there was neither a visit nor any promise of money: instead the new Raja received a letter informing him that the China trade had been severely affected by the sudden decline in the value of American bills of exchange; its losses aside, Burnham Bros. was now facing severe difficulties in remitting funds from England to India. At the end of the letter there was a polite note requesting the Raskhali estate to make good on its debts.

In the meanwhile, Neel had signed a great many hundees for merchants in the bazar: his father's clerks had prepared the papers and shown him where to make his mark. When Mr Burnham's note arrived, the Halder mansion was already under siege by an army of lesser creditors: some of these were wealthy merchants, who could, without compunction, be staved off for a while; but there were also many relatives and underlings who had entrusted what little they had to the zemindar—these impoverished and trusting dependants could not be refused. It was in trying to return their money that Neel discovered that his estate had no more cash available than was required to cover its expenses for a week or two. The situation was such that he demeaned himself to the point of sending a pleading letter to Mr Burnham, asking not just for time, but also a loan to tide the estate through until the next season.

In return he had received a note that was shocking in the peremptoriness of its tone. In reading it, Neel had wondered whether Mr Burnham would have struck a similar pitch with his father. He doubted it: the old Raja had always got on well with Englishmen, even though he spoke their language imperfectly and had no interest at all in their books. As if to compensate for his own limitations, the Raja had hired a British tutor for his son, to make sure that he had a thorough schooling in English. This tutor, Mr Beasley, had much in common with Neel, and had encouraged his interests in literature and philosophy. But far from putting him at ease in the society of Calcutta's Englishmen, Neel's education had served exactly the opposite end. For Mr Beasley's sensibility was unusual amongst the British colonials of the city, who tended to regard refinements of taste with suspicion, and even derision—and never more so than when they were evinced by native gentlemen. In short, by both temperament and education, Neel was little fitted for the company of such men as Mr Burnham, and they in turn tended to regard him with a dislike that bordered on contempt.

Of all this Neel was well aware, but he still found Mr Burnham's note startling. The Burnham firm was not in a position to extend a loan, it said, having itself suffered greatly because of the current uncertainty in the trade with China. The note went on to remind Neel that his debts to Burnham Bros. already far exceeded the value of the entire zemindary: these arrears had to be made good at once, it said, and asked him to consider transferring his landholdings to the Burnham firm in exchange for the liquidation of some part of his dues.

To give himself time, Neel had decided to visit his estate with his son: it was his duty, surely, to give the boy a glimpse of his threatened inheritance? His wife, Rani Malati, had wanted to come too, but he had refused to bring her, on the grounds of her ever-fragile health: he had settled on Elokeshi instead, thinking that she would provide a welcome diversion. It was true that she had helped to take his mind off his troubles from time to time—but now, at the prospect of meeting Benjamin Burnham face-to-face, his worries came flooding back.

Sealing his rewritten letter of invitation, Neel went to the door and handed it to Parimal. Take it over to the ship right now, he said. Make sure that Burnham-sahib gets it.

On the bed, Elokeshi stirred and sat up, holding the covers to her chin. Won't you lie down again? she said. It's still early.

*Ashchhi* . . . I'm coming.

But instead of taking him back to the bed, Neel's feet carried him away, dressed just as he was, in his flowing red choga. Holding the robe around his chest, he went running down the gangway and up the ladder, to the topmost deck of the budgerow, where his son was still flying kites.

Baba? cried the boy. Where were you? I've been waiting and waiting.

Neel went up to his son and swept him off the deck, folding him in his arms and hugging him to his chest. Unused to public displays of affection, the boy squirmed: What's the matter with you, Baba? What are you doing? Pulling away, he squinted at his father's face. Then he turned to the servants he had been playing with and gave a delighted shout: Look! Look at Baba! The Raja of Raskhali is crying!

# five

~

It was late in the afternoon when at last Kalua's cart came within view of its destination: the Sudder Opium Factory— fondly spoken of by old Company hands as the 'Ghazeepore Carcanna'. The factory was immense: its premises covered forty-five acres and sprawled over two adjoining compounds, each with numerous courtyards, water tanks and iron-roofed sheds. Like the great medieval forts that overlooked the Ganga, the factory was so situated as to have easy access to the river while being high enough to escape seasonal floods. But unlike such forts as Chunar and Buxar, which were overgrown and largely abandoned, the Carcanna was anything but a picturesque ruin: its turrets housed squads of sentries, and its parapets were manned by a great number of peons and armed burkundazes.

The day-to-day management of the factory was in the hands of a superintendent, a senior official of the East India Company who oversaw a staff of several hundred Indian workers: the rest of the British contingent consisted of overseers, accountants, storekeepers, chemists and two grades of assistant. The superintendent lived on the premises, and his sprawling bungalow was surrounded by a colourful garden, planted with many varieties of ornamental poppy. The English church was nearby and the passage of the day was marked by the ringing of its bell. On Sundays, worshippers were called to service by the firing of a cannon. The gun-crew was paid not by the Carcanna, but by the subscription of the congregation: the opium factory being an institution steeped in Anglican piety, none of the residents begrudged the expense.

Although the Sudder Opium Factory was indisputably large and well-guarded, there was nothing about its exterior to suggest to an onlooker that it was among the most precious jewels in Queen Victoria's crown. On the contrary, a miasma of lethargy seemed always to hang over the factory's surroundings. The monkeys that lived around it, for instance: Deeti pointed a few of these out to Kabutri as the ox-cart trundled towards the walls. Unlike others of their kind they never chattered or fought or stole from passers-by; when they came down from the trees it was to lap at the open sewers that drained the factory's effluents; after having sated their cravings, they would climb back into the branches to resume their stupefied scrutiny of the Ganga and its currents.

Kalua's cart rumbled slowly past the factory's outer compound: this was a complex of some sixteen enormous godowns that were used for the storage of processed opium. The fortifications here were formidable, and the guards particularly sharp-eyed—and well they might be, for the contents of those few sheds, or so it was said, were worth several million pounds sterling and could buy a good part of the City of London.

As Kalua's cart rolled on, towards the factory's main compound, Deeti and Kabutri began to sneeze; soon, Kalua and the oxen were sniffling too, for they had now drawn abreast of the godowns where farmers came to dispose of their 'poppy trash'—leaves, stalks and roots, all of which were used in the packaging of the drug. Ground up for storage, these remains produced a fine dust that hung in the air like a fog of snuff. Rare was the passer-by who could brave this mist without exploding into a paroxysm of sneezes and sniffles— and yet it was a miracle, plain to behold, that the coolies pounding the trash were no more affected by the dust than were their young English overseers.

Noses streaming, the oxen plodded on, past the massive brass-studded doors of the factory's Sudder Gateway, towards a humbler but more-frequented entrance at the south-western corner of the walls, a few steps from the Ganga. This stretch of riverbank was unlike any other, for the ghats around the Carcanna were shored up with thousands of broken earthenware gharas—the round-bottomed vessels in which raw opium was brought to the factory. The belief was widespread that fish were more easily caught after they had nibbled at the shards, and as a result the bank was always crowded with fishermen.

Leaving Kabutri in Kalua's cart, Deeti headed alone towards the factory's entrance, nearby. Here stood the weighing shed to which the farmers of the district brought their poppy-leaf wrappers every spring, to be weighed and sorted into grades of fine and coarse, 'chandee' and 'ganta'. This was where Deeti would have sent her own rotis, had she accumulated enough to make the trouble worthwhile. Around harvest time there was always a great press of people here, but the crop being late this year, the crowd was relatively small.

A small troop of uniformed burkundazes was on duty at the gate, and Deeti was relieved to see that their sirdar, a stately white-moustachioed elder, was a distant relative of her husband's. When she went up to him and murmured Hukam Singh's name, he knew exactly why she had come. Your husband's condition isn't good, he said, ushering her into the factory. Get him home quickly.

Deeti was about to step in when she glanced over the sirdar's shoulder, into the weighing shed: the sight made her pull back, with a sudden start of apprehension. Such was the length of the shed that the door at the far end looked like a distant pinprick of light; in between, arrayed along the floor, stood many gigantic pairs of scales, dwarfing the men around them; beside each set of scales sat a tall-hatted Englishman, overseeing teams of weighmen and accountants. Buzzing busily around the sahibs were turbaned muharirs bearing armloads of paper and dhoti-clad serishtas with thick registers; swarming everywhere were gangs of bare-bodied boys carrying improbably tall stacks of poppy-flower wrappers.

But where to go? Deeti said to the sirdar, in alarm. How will I find my way?

Go straight through this shed, came the answer: and keep on going, through the weighing hall, to the mixing room. When you get through, you'll find one of our relatives waiting. He works here too: he'll show you where to find your husband.

With her sari draped over her face, Deeti stepped in and made her way past columns of stacked poppy-flower rotis, ignoring the stares of serishtas, muharirs and other lesser carcoons: not another woman to be seen, but no matter—everyone was too busy to ask where she was going. Yet, it still took an age to reach the far door and here she stood blinded for a moment, in the bright sunlight.

Facing her was a doorway, leading into another immense iron-roofed structure, except that this one was even bigger and higher than the weighing shed—it was the largest building she had ever seen. She walked in, murmuring a prayer, and was brought again to a halt by the sight ahead: the space in front of her was so vast that her head began to spin and she had to steady herself by leaning against a wall. Bars of light were shining through slit-like windows that stretched from the floor to the roof; enormous square columns ran down the length of the hall and the ceiling soared so high above the beaten floor that the air inside was cool, almost wintry. The earthy, sickly odour of raw opium-sap hung close to the ground, like wood-smoke on a chilly day. In this hall too, gigantic pairs of scales stood against the walls, here used for the weighing of raw opium. Clustered around each set of scales were dozens of earthenware gharas, of exactly the kind she herself used in packing her harvest. How well she knew them, those vessels: they each held one maund of raw opium gum, of a consistency such that a ball of it would stick briefly to your palm if you upended it. Who would guess, in looking at them, how much time and trouble went into the filling of these vessels? So this was where they came, these offspring of her fields? Deeti could not help looking around in curiosity, marvelling at the speed and dexterity with which the vessels were whisked on and off the scales. Then, with paper battas attached, they were carried to a seated sahib, who proceeded to poke, prod and sniff their contents before marking them with a seal, allowing some through for processing, and condemning others to some lesser use. Nearby, held back by a line of lathi-carrying peons, stood the farmers whose vessels were being weighed; alternatively tense and angry, cringing and resigned, they were waiting to find out if their harvests for the year had fulfilled their contracts—if not, they would have to start the next year with a still greater load of debt. Deeti watched as a peon carried a slip of paper to a farmer and was rebuffed with a howl of protest: all over the hall, she noticed, there were quarrels and altercations breaking out, with farmers shouting at serishtas, and landlords berating their tenants.

Deeti saw now that she was beginning to attract attention, so she hunched her shoulders and stepped forward, hurrying through that endless cavern of a hall, not daring to pause till she found herself outside again, in the sun. Here, she would have liked to linger a little, to catch her breath, but from the cover of her sari she spotted an armed burkundaz striding in her direction. There was only one way to go—into a shed to her right. She did not hesitate; hitching up her sari she stepped quickly through the door.

Now once again Deeti was taken aback by the space ahead, but this time not because of the vastness of its dimensions, but rather the opposite—it was like a dim tunnel, lit only by a few small holes in the wall. The air inside was hot and fetid, like that of a closed kitchen, except that the smell was not of spices and oil, but of liquid opium, mixed with the dull stench of sweat—a reek so powerful that she had to pinch her nose to keep herself from gagging. No sooner had she steadied herself, than her eyes were met by a startling sight— a host of dark, legless torsos was circling around and around, like some enslaved tribe of demons. This vision—along with the overpowering fumes—made her groggy, and to keep herself from fainting she began to move slowly ahead. When her eyes had grown more accustomed to the gloom, she discovered the secret of those circling torsos: they were bare-bodied men, sunk waist-deep in tanks of opium, tramping round and round to soften the sludge. Their eyes were vacant, glazed, and yet somehow they managed to keep moving, as slow as ants in honey, tramping, treading. When they could move no more, they sat on the edges of the tanks, stirring the dark ooze only with their feet. These seated men had more the look of ghouls than any living thing she had ever seen: their eyes glowed red in the dark and they appeared completely naked, their loincloths—if indeed they had any—being so steeped in the drug as to be indistinguishable from their skin. Almost as frightening were the white overseers who were patrolling the walkways—for not only were they coatless and hatless, with their sleeves rolled, but they were also armed with fearsome instruments: metal scoops, glass ladles and long-handled rakes. When one of these overseers approached her she all but screamed; she heard him say something—what it was she did not wish to know, but the very shock of being spoken to by such a man sent her scurrying down the tunnel and out at the far end.

Not till she was through the door did she allow herself to breathe freely again: now, as she was trying to cleanse her lungs of the odour of raw, churned opium, she heard someone say: Bhauji? Are you all right? The voice proved to be that of their relative and it was all she could do not to collapse on him. Fortunately, he seemed to understand, without explanation, the effect the tunnel had had on her: leading her across a courtyard, he stopped at a well and poured water from a bucket, so she could drink and wash her face.

Everyone needs water after they come through the mixing room, he said. Better you rest here a bit, Bhauji.

Gratefully, Deeti squatted in the shade of a mango tree while he pointed to the buildings around them: there was the wetting shed, where the poppy-leaf wrappers were dampened before being sent into the assembly room; and there, set a little way back from the other buildings, was the house where medicines were made—all kinds of dark syrups and strange white powders that were much valued by the sahibs.

Deeti allowed the words to roll around and away from her, until she was once again impatient to deal with the errand at hand. Come, she said, let's go. They rose to their feet and he led her diagonally across the courtyard, into yet another gigantic shed, every bit as large as the weighing room—with the difference that where the latter had been filled with the clamour of altercation, this one was sepulchrally quiet, as if it were some cavernous shrine in the high Himalayas, chilly, damp and dimly lit. Stretching away, on either side, reaching all the way to the lofty ceiling, were immense shelves, neatly arranged with tens of thousands of identical balls of opium, each about the shape and size of an unhusked coconut, but black in colour, with a glossy surface. Deeti's escort whispered in her ear: This is where the afeem is brought in to dry, after it's been assembled. She noticed now that the shelves were joined by struts and ladders; glancing around, she saw troops of boys clinging to the timber scafolding, climbing as nimbly as acrobats at a fair, hopping from shelf to shelf to examine the balls of opium. Every now and again, an English overseer would call out an order and the boys would begin to toss spheres of opium to each other, relaying them from hand to hand until they had come to rest safely on the floor.

How could they throw so accurately with one hand, while holding on with the other—and that too at a height where the slightest slip would mean certain death? The sureness of their grip seemed amazing to Deeti, until suddenly one of them did indeed drop a ball, sending it crashing to the floor, where it burst open, splattering its gummy contents everywhere. Instantly the offender was set upon by cane-wielding overseers and his howls and shrieks went echoing through the vast, chilly chamber. The screams sent her hurrying after her relative and she caught up with him on the threshold of yet another of the factory's chambers. Here he lowered his voice reverentially, in the manner of a pilgrim who is about to step into the innermost sanctum of a temple. This is the assembly room, he whispered. It is not for everyone to work here—but your husband Hukam Singh, is one such.

It could indeed have been a temple that Deeti had entered now, for the long, well-aired passage ahead was lined with two rows of dhoti-clad men, sitting cross-legged on the floor, like Brahmins at a feast, each on his own woven seat, with an array of brass cups and other equipment arranged around him. Deeti knew, from her husband's tales, that there were no less than two hundred and fifty men working in that room, and twice that number of running-boys—yet such was the assemblers' concentration that there was very little noise, apart from the pattering of the runners' feet, and periodic shouts announcing the completion of yet another ball of opium. The assemblers' hands moved with dizzying speed as they lined hemispherical moulds with poppy-leaf rotis, moistening the wrappers with lewah, a light solution of liquid opium. Hukam Singh had told Deeti that the measure for every ingredient was precisely laid down by the Company's directors in faraway London: each package of opium was to consist of exactly one seer and seven-and-a-half chittacks of the drug, the ball being wrapped in five chittacks of poppy-leaf rotis, half of fine grade and half coarse, the whole being moistened with no more and no less than five chittacks of lewah. So finely honed was the system, with relays of runners carrying precise measures of each ingredient to each seat, that the assemblers' hands never had cause to falter: they lined the moulds in such a way as to leave half the moistened rotis hanging over the edge. Then, dropping in the balls of opium, they covered them with the overhanging wrappers, and coated them with poppy-trash before tapping them out again. It remained only for runners to arrive with the outer casing for each ball—two halves of an earthenware sphere. The ball being dropped inside, the halves were fitted into a neat little cannonshot, to hold safe this most lucrative of the British Empire's products: thus would the drug travel the seas, until the casing was split open by a blow from a cleaver, in distant Maha-Chin.

Dozens of the black containers passed through the assemblers' hands every hour and were duly noted on a blackboard: Hukam Singh, who was not the most skilled among them, had once boasted to Deeti of having put together a hundred in a single day. But today Hukam Singh's hands were no longer working and nor was he at his usual seat: Deeti spotted him as she entered the assembly room—he was lying on the floor with his eyes closed and he looked as if he had had some kind of seizure, for a thin line of bubbling spit was dribbling out of the corner of his mouth.

Suddenly, Deeti was assailed by the sirdars who supervised the packaging room. What took you so long? . . . Don't you know your husband is an afeemkhor? . . . Why do you send him here to work? . . . Do you want him to die?

Despite the shocks of the day, Deeti was not of a mind to ignore these attacks. From the shelter of her sari, she snapped back: And who are you to speak to me like that? How would you earn your living if not for afeemkhors?

The altercation drew the attention of an English agent, who waved the sirdars aside. Glancing from Hukam Singh's prone body to Deeti, he said, quietly: *Tumhara mard hai*? Is he your husband?

Although the Englishman's Hindi was stilted, there was a kindly sound to his voice. Deeti nodded, lowering her head, and her eyes filled with tears as she listened to the sahib berating the sirdars: Hukam Singh was a sepoy in our army; he was a balamteer in Burma and was wounded fighting for the Company Bahadur. Do you think any of you are better than him? Shut your mouths and get back to work or I'll whip you with my own chabuk.

The cowed sirdars fell silent, stepping aside as four bearers stooped to lift Hukam Singh's inert body off the floor. Deeti was following them out when the Englishman turned to say: Tell him he can have his job back whenever he wants.

Deeti joined her hands together, to express her gratitude— but in her heart she knew that her husband's days in the Carcanna had come to an end.

On the way home, in Kalua's cart, with her husband's head in her lap and her daughter's fingers in her hand, she had eyes neither for Ghazipur's forty-pillared palace nor for its memorial to the departed Laat-Sahib. Her thoughts were now all for the future and how they would manage without her husband's monthly pay. In thinking of this, the light dimmed in her eyes; even though nightfall was still a couple of hours away, she felt as if she were already enveloped in darkness. As if by habit she began to chant the prayer-song for the end of the day:

*Sājh bhailé*
*Sājha ghar ghar ghumé*
*Ke mora sājh*
*manayo ji*

Twilight whispers
at every door:
it's time
to mark my coming.

~

Just beyond the boundaries of Calcutta, to the south of the dock-side neighbourhoods of Kidderpore and Metia Bruz, lay a length of gently sloping bank that overlooked a wide sweep of the Hooghly River: this was the verdant suburb of Garden Reach, where the leading white merchants of Calcutta had their country estates. Here, as if to keep watch over the ships that bore their names and their goods, stood the adjacent properties of the Ballards, Fergusons, McKenzies, MacKays, Smoults and Swinhoes. The mansions that graced these estates were as varied as the owners' tastes would allow, some being modelled on the great manors of England and France, while others evoked the temples of classical Greece and Rome. The grounds of the estates were extensive enough to provide each mansion with a surrounding park, and these were, if anything, even more varied in design than the houses they enclosed—for the malis who tended the gardens, no less than the owners themselves, vied to outdo each other in the fancifulness of their plantings, creating here a little patch of topiary and there an avenue of trees, trimmed in the French fashion; and between the stretches of greenery, there were artfully placed bodies of water, some long and straight, like Persian qanats, and some irregular, like English ponds; a few of the gardens could even boast of geometrical Mughal terraces, complete with streams, fountains, and delicately-tiled bowries. But it was not by these extravagant extensions that the values of the properties were judged; it was rather by the view that each manse commanded—for a patch of garden, no matter how pretty, could not be held to materially affect the owner's prospects, while to be able to keep an eye on the comings-and-goings on the river had an obvious and direct bearing on the fortunes of all who were dependent on that traffic. By this criterion it was generally acknowledged that the estate of Benjamin Brightwell Burnham was second to none, no matter that it was an acquisition of relatively recent date. In some respects the estate's lack of a pedigree could even be counted as an advantage, for it had allowed Mr Burnham to give it a name of his choice, Bethel. What was more, having himself been responsible for the founding of his estate, Mr Burnham had felt no constraint in shaping the grounds to his needs and desires, ordering, without hesitation, the clearing of every unseemly weed and growth that obscured his view of the river—among them several ancient mango trees and a heathenish thicket of fifty-foot bamboo. Around Bethel, nothing interrupted the lines of sight between house and water, other than the chabutra that stood perched on the lip of the river, looking down on the estate's landing ghat and jetty. This shapely little gazebo differed from those on the neighbouring estates in that it was topped by a roof of Chinese design, with upturned eaves and curved green-glazed tiles.

Recognizing the pavilion from the coksen's description, Jodu plunged his oar into the mud and leant on the handle, to hold the dinghy stationary against the river's current. In passing the other estates of Garden Reach, he had come to realize that the problem of finding Putli would not be resolved by locating the house in which she lived: each of these mansions was a small fortress, guarded by servants who were certain to perceive all interlopers as possible competitors against whom their jobs would have to be defended. To Jodu's eye, it seemed that the garden with the green-roofed pavilion was the largest, and most impregnable, of all the neighbouring estates: deployed across its lawn was an army of malis and ghaskatas, some of whom were engaged in digging new beds, while others were weeding or mowing the grass with scythes. Dressed as he was, in a torn lungi and banyan, with a faded gamchha tied around his head, Jodu knew that his chances of penetrating these defences were very small; in all likelihood within moments of setting foot on the grounds, he would be captured and handed over to the chowkidars, to be thrashed as a thief.

Already, the stationary dinghy had attracted the attention of one of the estate's boatmen—evidently a calputtee, for he was busy caulking the bottom of a sleek-looking caique, applying liquid tar with a palm-leaf brush. Now, leaving his brush in the bucket, the caulker turned to frown at Jodu. What's the matter? he shouted. What's your business here?

Jodu gave him a disarming smile. Salam mistry-ji, he said, flattering the calputtee by raising him a rank or two in the grades of artisanship: I was just admiring the house. It must be the biggest around here?

The calputtee nodded: What else? Zaroor. Of course it is.

Jodu decided to chance his luck: It must be a large family that lives in it then?

The calputtee's lips curled into a sneer: Do you think a house like this would belong to the kind of people who'd live in a crowd? No; it's just the Burra Sahib, the Burra BeeBee and the Burra Baby.

That's all? No one else?

There's a young missy-mem, said the caulker, with a dismissive shrug. But she's not a part of the family. Just a charity-case they've taken in, from the goodness of their hearts.

Jodu would have liked to know more, but he saw that it would be imprudent to press the man any further—it might well get Putli into trouble if word got out that a boatman had come looking for her in a dinghy. But how then was he to get a message to her? He was puzzling over this when he noticed a sapling, growing in the shade of the green-tiled pavilion: he recognized it as a chalta tree, which produced fragrant white flowers and a fruit that had an unusual, sour favour, vaguely reminiscent of unripe apples.

He assumed a voice like that of his rustic half-siblings, who seemed never to be able to walk past a field without asking questions about the crops; in a tone of innocent inquiry, he said to the calputtee: Has that chalta tree been recently planted?

The caulker looked up and frowned. That one? He made a face and shrugged, as if to distance himself from the misbegotten growth. Yes, that's the new missy-mem's handiwork. She's always interfering with the malis in the garden, moving things around.

Jodu made his salams and turned the boat around, to head back the way he had come. He had guessed at once that the sapling had been planted by Putli: she had always craved the mouth-puckering taste of its fruit. At home, in the Botanical Gardens, a chalta tree had stood beside the window of her bedroom and every year, during its brief season, she had gathered handfuls of the fruit, to make into chutneys and pickles. She loved them so much that she even ate them raw, to the disbelief of others. Being thoroughly familiar with Putli's gardening habits, Jodu knew that she would be down to water the sapling early in the morning: if he spent the night somewhere nearby, then he might well be able to catch her before the servants were up and about.

Now, Jodu began to row upstream, watching the shore for a spot that would be at once hidden from view and near enough to habitation to be a discouragement to leopards and jackals. When one such appeared, he hitched up his lungi and waded through a bank of mud to tether the boat to the roots of a gigantic banyan tree. Then, climbing back inside, he washed the mud off his feet and set hungrily upon a pot of stale rice.

*Amitav Ghosh*

At the rear of the dinghy there was a small thatched shelter and this was where he spread his mat after finishing his meagre meal. It was twilight now; the sun was setting on the far bank of the Hooghly, and the shadowed outlines of the trees in the Botanical Gardens were still visible across the water. Although Jodu was very tired, he could not bring himself to close his eyes while the skies were still bright enough to shed light upon the bustling life of the river.

The tide was beginning to sweep in, and the Hooghly had filled with sails, as ships and boats hurried to take their berths or to stand out to mid-channel. From where he lay, on the slats of his gently rocking dinghy, Jodu could imagine that the world had turned itself upside down, so that the river had become the sky, crowded with banks of cloud; if you narrowed your eyes, you might almost think that the ships' masts and spars were bolts of lightning, forking through the billowing sails. And as for thunder, there was that too, booming out of the sheets of canvas, as they flapped, slackened and filled again. The noise never failed to amaze him: the whiplash crack of the sails, the high-pitched shriek of the wind in the rigging, the groan of the timbers and surf-like pounding of the bow-waves: it was as if each ship were a moving tempest and he an eagle, circling close behind to hunt in the ruins of its wake.

Looking across the river Jodu could count the flags of a dozen kingdoms and countries: Genoa, the Two Sicilies, France, Prussia, Holland, America, Venice. He had learnt to recognize them from Putli, who had pointed them out to him as they sailed past the Gardens; even though she herself had never left Bengal, she knew stories about the places from which they came. These tales had played no small part in nurturing his desire to see the roses of Basra and the port of Chin-kalan, where the great Faghfoor of Maha-chin held sway.

On the deck of a nearby three-master, a mate's voice could be heard, calling out in English: 'All hands to quarters, ahoy!' A moment later, the command became a hookum, relayed by a serang: *Sab admi apni jagah*!

'Fill the main topsails'—*Bhar bara gávi*! With a resounding crack the canvas billowed in the wind, and the mate called out: 'Ease the helm!'

*Gos daman ja*! came the serang's echo, and slowly the vessel's bows began to turn. 'Shiver the foretopsail!'—and almost before the serang had finished issuing the hookum— *Bajao tirkat gavi*!—the lofty square of canvas had sent its whiplash crack shooting through the wind.

From the silmagoors who sat on the ghats, sewing sails, Jodu had learnt the names of each piece of canvas, in English and in Laskari—that motley tongue, spoken nowhere but on the water, whose words were as varied as the port's traffic, an anarchic medley of Portuguese calaluzes and Kerala pattimars, Arab booms and Bengal paunch-ways, Malay proas and Tamil catamarans, Hindusthani pulwars and English snows—yet beneath the surface of this farrago of sound, meaning flowed as freely as the currents beneath the crowded press of boats.

By listening to the voices that echoed off the decks of oceangoing ships, Jodu had taught himself to recognize the officers' hookums to the point where he could say them aloud, even if only to himself—'Starboard watch ahoy!' *Jamna pori upar ao*!—understanding perfectly well the whole, while yet being unable to account for the meaning of the several parts. To shout the commands in earnest, on a ship that had been pushed on her beam-ends by a gale . . . that day would come, he was sure of it.

Suddenly, another call floated across the water—*Hayyá ilá assaláh . . .*—and was taken up in relay, by the ships in the channel, passing from one vessel to another as the Muslims amongst the crewmen began to chant the evening azan. Jodu roused himself from the torpor of his full stomach and made his preparations for prayer: covering his head with a folded cloth, he manoeuvred his boat to point in a westerly direction before kneeling for the first raka'a. He had never been particularly devout and it was only because his mother's interment was still so fresh in his mind that he felt compelled to pray now. But afterwards, when he had murmured the final syllables, he was glad that he had remembered: his mother would have wished it, he knew, and the knowledge of having done his duty would allow him to yield, without guilt, to the fatigue his body had accumulated over the last few weeks.

~

Ten miles downriver, on the Raskhali budgerow, the preparations for dinner had run afoul of some unexpected snags. The boat's lavish sheeshmahal for one: it had seen little use since the old Raja's time and was found to be in a state of some disrepair when opened up. The chandeliers had lost many of their candle-holders, and these had to be replaced by makeshift devices constructed out of bits of string, wood and even a few strips of coconut fibre. While the results were not unsatisfactory, they took some of the sparkle out of the fixtures and gave them a strangely wind-blown appearance.

The sheeshmahal was partitioned into two halves by a velvet curtain: the rear section was used as a dining room, and was graced by a table of fine calamander wood. Now, when the curtains were parted, it was found that the polished surface of the table had gone grey with neglect, and a family of scorpions had taken up residence under it. A platoon of stick-wielding paiks had to be summoned, to drive the creatures away, and then a duck had to be caught and killed, so that the table could be polished with its fat.

At the far end of the sheeshmahal, behind the dining table, there was a screened alcove, meant to accommodate women in purdah: from this sequestered vantage point, the old Raja's mistresses had been accustomed to observe his guests. But neglect had taken a toll on the delicately-carved observation screen, which was found to have rotted away. A curtain, with hastily-pierced peepholes, was installed in its place, at Elokeshi's insistence, for she felt it to be her right to appraise the guests. This in turn inspired a desire for a fuller participation in the evening so she decided that her three companions would provide some after-dinner entertainment by staging a few dances. But upon inspection it was found that the floor had warped: to dance barefoot on the crooked boards was to risk a rich crop of splinters. A carpenter had to be summoned to flatten the boards.

No sooner was this problem resolved than another arose: the sheeshmahal was equipped with a full set of ivory-handled silverware, as well as a complete dinner service, imported at great expense from the Swinton pottery in England. Being reserved for the use of unclean, beef-eating foreigners, these utensils were kept locked in cabinets, to prevent the contamination of the household's other crockery. Now, on opening the cabinet, Parimal discovered, to his shock, that many of the plates were missing, as was much of the silverware. There remained just about enough to provide for a dinner for four—but the discovery of the theft created an unpleasant climate of suspicion which resulted ultimately in an outbreak of internecine fighting on the kitchen-boat. After two paiks ended up with broken noses, Neel was forced to intervene: although peace was restored, the preparations for the evening were much delayed and Neel could not be provided with a proper meal, in advance of the dinner that would be served to his guests. This was a sore blow, for it meant that Neel would have to fast while his guests feasted: the rules of the Raskhali household were strict in regard to whom the Raja could eat with, and unclean beef-eaters were not a part of that small circle—even Elokeshi was not included in it, and had always to feed herself in secret when Neel came to spend the night in her house. So strict was the Halder family's usage in this regard, that when entertaining, it was their custom to sit politely at table with their guests but without ever touching any of the food that was heaped before them: so as not to be tempted, they always ate their dinner earlier, and this was what Neel would have liked to do—but with the kitchen-boat in disarray, he had to be content with a few handfuls of parched rice, soaked in milk.

Just as the sound of the sunset azan was floating across the water, Neel discovered that he had no more of the fine shanbaff dhotis and abrawan-muslin kurtas that he usually wore on public occasions: they had all been sent off to be laundered. He had to content himself with a relatively coarse dosooti dhoti and an alliballie kurta. Somewhere in his baggage, Elokeshi found gold-embroidered Lahori jooties for his feet: it was she who led him to his seat in the sheeshmahal and draped his shoulders in a shawl of fine Warangal nayansukh, with a border of zerbaft brocade. Then, with the *Ibis*'s jollyboat approaching, she whisked herself out of sight and went off to preside over her companions' rehearsals.

When the guests were shown in, Neel rose ceremonially to his feet: Mr Burnham, he noticed, had come in his riding clothes, but the other two men had evidently been at some pains to dress for the occasion. Both men were wearing double-breasted coats, and a ruby pin could be seen in the folds of Mr Doughty's cravat. Mr Reid's lapels were ornamented with the chain of an elegant watch. His guests' finery made Neel self-conscious, and he swirled his brocaded shawl protectively over his chest as he folded his hands together in welcome: 'Mr Burnham, Mr Doughty—I am most greatly honoured to be afforded this privilege.'

The two Englishmen merely bowed their heads in response, but Zachary startled Neel by moving forward as if to shake hands. He was rescued by Mr Doughty, who managed to intercept the American. 'Keep your hands to yourself, you gudda of a griffin,' whispered the pilot. 'Touch him and he'll be off to bathe, and we won't be fed till midnight.'

None of the visitors had been on the Raskhali budgerow before, so they accepted readily when Neel offered them a tour of the public parts of the barge. On the upper deck they came upon Raj Rattan, who was flying kites by moonlight. Mr Doughty made a harrumphing sound when the boy was introduced: 'Is this little Rascal your Upper-Roger, Raja Nil-Rotten?'

'The upa-raja, yes,' Neel nodded. 'My sole issue and heir. The tender fruit of my loin, as your poets might say.'

'Ah! Your little green mango!' Mr Doughty shot a wink in Zachary's direction. 'And if I may be so bold as to ask—would you describe your loin as the stem or the branch?'

Neel gave him a frosty glare. 'Why, sir,' he said coldly, 'it is the tree itself.'

Mr Burnham took a turn with a kite and proved to be adept at the sport, sending his kite soaring and dipping, its glass-coated string flashing in the moonlight. When Neel commented on the dabness of his hand, his response was: 'Oh I learnt in Canton: no better place to learn about kites!'

Back in the sheeshmahal, a bottle of champagne was waiting in a balty of muddy river water. Mr Doughty fell upon the wine with an expression of delight: 'Simkin! Shahbash—just the thing.' Pouring himself a glass, he gave Neel a broad wink: 'My father used to say, "Hold a bottle by the neck and a woman by the waist. Never the other way around". I'll wager that would have rung a ganta or two with your own father, eh Roger Nil-Rotten—now he was quite the rascal, wasn't he, your father?'

Neel gave him a chilly smile: repelled as he was by the pilot's manner, he could not help reflecting on what a mercy it was that his ancestors had excluded wine and liquor from the list of things that could not be shared with unclean foreigners—it would be all but impossible, surely, to deal with them, if not for their drink? He would have liked another glass of simkin but he noticed, from the corner of his eye, that Parimal was making signals to indicate that dinner was ready. He took the folds of his dhoti into his hands. 'Gentlemen, I am being given to believe that our repast has been readied.' As he rose to his feet, the sheeshmahal's velvet curtain was swept back to reveal a large, polished table, set in the English fashion, with knives, forks, plates and wineglasses. Two immense candelabra stood at either end, illuminating the settings; in the centre was an arrangement of wilted water lilies, piled together in such profusion that almost nothing could be seen of the vase that held them.There was no food on the table, for meals in the Raskhali household were served in the Bengali fashion, in successive courses.

Neel had arranged the seating so that he would have Mr Burnham across the table from him, with Zachary and Mr

Doughty to his left and right, respectively. There was a bearer behind each chair, as was the custom, and although they were all dressed in the Raskhali livery, Neel noticed that their uniforms—pyjamas, turbans and belted chapkan coats that came down to the knees—were strangely ill-fitting. It was then that he remembered that they were not bearers at all, but young boatmen, who had been hastily pressed into service by Parimal: their discomfort with the role was evident in their nervous twitches and shifty glances.

Now, on arriving at the table, there was a long pause during which Neel and his guests stayed on their feet, waiting for their chairs to be pushed forward. Catching Parimal's eye, Neel realized that the boatmen had not been told about this part of the ceremony: they, in turn, were waiting for the guests to come to them; clearly they were under the impression that the diners were to be seated at a distance of several feet from the table—and how indeed were they to know, it occurred to Neel to wonder, that chairs and tables belonged in much closer proximity?

In the interim, one of the young boatmen took the initiative and gave Mr Doughty's elbow a helpful tap, to indicate that his chair was empty and waiting to be occupied, some three feet to the rear. Neel saw the pilot reddening and intervened hastily in Bengali, ordering the boatmen to bring the chairs closer. The command was so sharply uttered that the youngest of the boatmen, a boy who happened to be attending upon Zachary, brought his chair forward in a startled rush, as though he were pushing a dinghy down a mudbank. The lip of the chair caught Zachary from behind, scooping him up and delivering him to the table—breathless, but otherwise unharmed.

Although he apologized profusely, Neel was pleased to see that Zachary was more amused than offended by the incident: in the short time they had spent together, the young American had made a considerable impression on him, as much for the innate elegance of his person as for the reserve of his bearing. The provenance and origins of strangers often provoked Neel's curiosity: in Bengal it was so easy to know who was who;

more often than not, just to hear someone's name would reveal their religion, their caste, their village. Foreigners were, by comparison, so opaque: it was impossible not to speculate about them. Mr Reid's demeanour, for example, suggested to Neel that he might be descended from an old, aristocratic family—he remembered having read somewhere that it was not unusual for the European nobility to send their younger sons to America. This thought led him to remark: 'Your city, Mr Reid, am I not right to think it was named for a certain Lord Baltimore?'

The answer was oddly unsure—'May . . . maybe—I'm not sure . . .'—but Neel persisted: 'Lord Baltimore was an ancestor of yours perhaps?' This elicited a startled shaking of the head and an abashed denial—which served only to persuade Neel all the more firmly of the noble origins of his reticent guest. 'Will you be sailing back to Baltimore soon . . .?' Neel asked. He was about to add 'my lord' but caught himself just in time.

'Why no, sir,' Zachary responded. 'The *Ibis* is bound first for the Mauritius. If we make good time, we may sail to China later in the year.'

'I see.' This recalled to Neel's mind his original purpose in hosting this meal, which was to discover whether there was any immediate prospect of a change in his chief creditor's fortunes. He turned to Mr Burnham: 'There is an improvement, then, in the situation in China?'

Mr Burnham answered with a shake of his head: 'No, Raja Neel Rattan. No. Truth to tell, the situation has worsened considerably—to the point where there is serious talk of war. Indeed that may well be the reason for the *Ibis*'s voyage to China.'

'A war?' said Neel in astonishment. 'But I have heard nothing about a war with China.'

'I am sure you haven't,' said Mr Burnham, with a thin smile. 'Why indeed should a man like you concern yourself with such matters? You have more than enough to occupy you, I'm sure, with all your palaces and zenanas and budgerows.'

Neel knew that he was being sneered at and his hackles rose, but he was saved from an intemperate response by the timely appearance of the first course—a steaming soup. The silver tureen having been stolen, the soup was presented in the one remaining utensil that was made of the same metal: a punch-bowl shaped like a seashell.

Mr Doughty permitted himself an indulgent smile. 'Do I smell duck?' he said, sniffing the air.

Neel had no idea of what was to be served, for the cooks on the kitchen-boat had been foraging for provisions almost till the last. Having reached the final leg of its journey, the budgerow's stocks of food had begun to run low: the news that there was to be a grand dinner had caused panic among the cooks; an army of piyadas, paiks and boatmen had been dispatched to fish and forage—with what results, Neel did not know. So it was Parimal who confirmed, in a whisper, that the soup had been made from the flesh of the very animal whose fat had been used to polish the table—but the latter part of the tale Neel kept to himself, conveying only that the soup was indeed concocted from the remains of a duck.

'Excellent!' said Mr Doughty, tipping back his glass. 'And a fine sherry-shrub too.'

Although glad of the interruption, Neel had not forgotten Mr Burnham's dismissive jibes about his preoccupations. He was convinced now that the shipowner was exaggerating in order to persuade him of the extent of his firm's losses. Taking care to keep his voice even, he said: 'You will no doubt be surprised to know, Mr Burnham, that I have been at some pains to be keeping myself informed—yet I know nothing about this war you speak of.'

'Well then, it falls to me to inform you, sir,' said Mr Burnham, 'that of late the officials in Canton have been moving forcefully to end the inflow of opium into China. It is the unanimous opinion of all of us who do business there that the mandarins cannot be allowed to have their way. To end the trade would be ruinous—for firms like mine, but also for you, and indeed for all of India.'

'Ruinous?' said Neel mildly. 'But surely we can offer China something more useful than opium?'

'Would that it were so,' said Mr Burnham. 'But it is not. To put the matter simply: there is nothing they want from us—they've got it into their heads that they have no use for our products and manufactures. But we, on the other hand, can't do without their tea and their silks. If not for opium, the drain of silver from Britain and her colonies would be too great to sustain.'

Here, Mr Doughty suddenly joined in: 'The trouble, you know, is that Johnny Chinaman thinks he can return to the good old days, before he got his taste for opium. But there's no going back—just won't hoga.'

'Going back?' said Neel, in surprise. 'But China's hunger for opium dates back to antiquity, does it not?'

'Antiquity?' scoffed Mr Doughty. 'Why, even when I first went out to Canton, as a lad, there was just a trickle of opium going in. Damned hard-headed gudda is Johnny Long-tail. I can tell you, it wasn't easy to get him to take to opium. No sir—to give credit where it's due, you would have to say that the yen for opium would still be limited to their twice-born if not for the perseverance of English and American merchants. It's happened almost within living memory—for which we owe a sincere vote of thanks to the likes of Mr Burnham.' He raised his glass to the shipowner. 'To you, sir.'

Neel was about to join in the toast when the next course appeared: it consisted of fledgling chickens that had been cooked whole. 'I'll be damned if it isn't a roast of Sudden-Death!' cried Mr Doughty, in delight. Spearing a bird's tiny head with his fork, he began to chew on it in dreamy contentment.

Neel stared at the bird on his plate in glum resignation: he was suddenly very hungry and had he not been in plain view of his retainers he would certainly have set upon the chicken—but he distracted himself instead by belatedly raising his glass to Mr Burnham. 'To you, sir,' he said, 'and your successes in China.'

*Amitav Ghosh*

Mr Burnham smiled. 'It wasn't easy, I can tell you,' he said. 'Especially in the early days, when the mandarins were somewhat less than amenable.'

'Really?' Not having given much thought to commerce, Neel had imagined that the traffic in opium enjoyed official approval in China—this seemed only natural since in Bengal the trade was not merely sanctioned but monopolized by the British authorities, under the seal of the East India Company. 'You amaze me, Mr Burnham,' he said. 'Is the sale of opium frowned on by the Chinese authorities then?'

'I'm afraid so,' said Mr Burnham. 'Trafficking in opium has been illegal there for some time. But they've never made a tumasher about it in the past: their mandarins and chuntocks always got their ten-per-cent destures and were glad to shut their eyes to it. The only reason they're making a fuss now is that they want a bigger share of the profits.'

'It's simple,' Mr Doughty announced, chewing on a wing. 'The Long-tails have got to be given a taste of the lattee.'

'I'm afraid I have to agree, Doughty,' said Mr Burnham, nodding. 'A timely dose of chastisement is always to the good.'

'So you are convinced then,' said Neel, 'that your government will go to war?'

'It may well come to that, alas,' said Mr Burnham. 'Britain has been nothing if not patient but there's a limit to everything. Look at what the Celestials did to Lord Amherst. There he was, on the very threshold of Pekin, with a shipload of presents—and the Emperor wouldn't so much as receive him.'

'Oh don't speak of it, sir, it is not to be borne!' said Mr Doughty indignantly. 'Wanted his lordship to kowtow in public! Why, they'll be asking us to grow long-tails next!'

'And Lord Napier fared no better either,' Mr Burnham reminded him. 'The mandarins paid him no more attention than they would this chicken.'

The mention of the bird drew Mr Doughty's attention back to his food. 'Speaking of chicken, sir,' he murmured. 'This certainly is a most excellent roast.'

Neel's eyes wandered back to the untouched bird on his

own plate: even without tasting it, he could tell that it was a toothsome little morsel, but of course it was not his place to say so. 'You are too generous in your praise, Mr Doughty,' he said, in a flourish of hospitable self-deprecation, 'it is no more than a verminous little creature, unworthy of such guests as yourselves.'

'Verminous?' said Zachary in sudden alarm. It was only now that he noticed that Neel had not touched any of the food that had been placed in front of him. Laying down his fork, he said: 'But you haven't touched your chicken, sir. Is it . . . is it not advisable, in this climate?'

'No,' said Neel, and quickly corrected himself. 'I mean yes—it is perfectly advisable for yourself . . .' He broke off, trying to think of a polite way to explain to the American why the chicken was forbidden to the Raja of Raskhali, but perfectly edible for an unclean foreigner. No words came to him, and in a mute plea for help, he glanced at the two Englishmen, both of whom were well aware of the dietary rules of the Halders. Neither of them would meet his gaze, but at length Mr Doughty made a bubbling sound, like a kettle coming to the boil. 'Just eat the bish, you gudda,' he hissed at Zachary. 'He was only foozlowing.'

The matter was resolved by the entry of a platter of fish: a crumbed fillet of bhetki, with an accompaniment of crisp vegetable pakoras. Mr Doughty subjected the dish to careful scrutiny. 'Cockup, if I'm not mistaken—and with fuleeta-pups too! Why, sir, your bobachees have done us proud.'

Neel was about to mouth a polite demurral when he made a discovery that shocked him to his core. His eyes having strayed to the wilted water lilies at the centre of the table, he realized to his utter horror that the flowers were sitting not in a vase, as he had thought, but in an old porcelain chamber-pot. Evidently the budgerow's present generation of boatmen had forgotten the function and history of this vessel, but Neel remembered very well that it had been purchased expressly for the use of an elderly district magistrate whose intestines had been sorely beset by worms.

Stifling an exclamation of disgust, Neel tore his eyes away and cast about for a subject that would keep his guests distracted. When one such suggested itself, he uttered a cry in which a lingering trace of revulsion could still be heard. 'But Mr Burnham! Are you saying the British Empire will go to war to force opium on China?'

This elicited an instantaneous response from Mr Burnham, who placed his wineglass forcefully on the table. 'Evidently you have mistaken my meaning, Raja Neel Rattan,' he said. 'The war, when it comes, will not be for opium. It will be for a principle: for freedom—for the freedom of trade and for the freedom of the Chinese people. Free Trade is a right conferred on Man by God, and its principles apply as much to opium as to any other article of trade. More so perhaps, since in its absence many millions of natives would be denied the lasting advantages of British influence.'

Here Zachary broke in. 'How so, Mr Burnham?'

'For the simple reason, Reid,' said Mr Burnham patiently, 'that British rule in India could not be sustained without opium—that is all there is to it, and let us not pretend otherwise. You are no doubt aware that in some years, the Company's annual gains from opium are almost equal to the entire revenue of your own country, the United States? Do you imagine that British rule would be possible in this impoverished land if it were not for this source of wealth? And if we reflect on the benefits that British rule has conferred upon India, does it not follow that opium is this land's greatest blessing? Does it not follow that it is our God-given duty to confer these benefits upon others?'

Neel had been listening to Mr Burnham with less than half a mind, his attention having been thoroughly distracted: he had just realized that the business of the chamber-pot might well have turned out a great deal worse than it had. What, for instance, would he have done if it had been presented at the table as a tureen, filled to the brim with steaming soup? Considering all that could have happened, he had every reason to be grateful for his deliverance from social ruin: indeed, the matter smacked so much of divine intervention that he could not help saying, in a tone of pious rebuke: 'Does it not trouble you, Mr Burnham, to invoke God in the service of opium?'

'Not in the slightest,' said Mr Burnham, stroking his beard. 'One of my countrymen has put the matter very simply: "Jesus Christ is Free Trade and Free Trade is Jesus Christ." Truer words, I believe, were never spoken. If it is God's will that opium be used as an instrument to open China to his teachings, then so be it. For myself, I confess I can see no reason why any Englishman should abet the Manchu tyrant in depriving the people of China of this miraculous substance.'

'Do you mean opium?'

'I certainly do,' said Mr Burnham tartly. 'Why, let me ask you, sir: would you like to return to such a time when men had to have their teeth pulled and their limbs sawn off without benefit of any palliative to ease the pain?'

'Why no,' said Neel, with a shudder. 'I certainly wouldn't.'

'I thought not,' said Mr Burnham. 'So you would do well to bear in mind that it would be well nigh impossible to practise modern medicine or surgery without such chemicals as morphine, codeine and narcotine—and these are but a few of the blessings derived from opium. In the absence of gripe water our children would not sleep. And what would our ladies— why, our beloved Queen herself?—do without laudanum? Why, one might even say that it is opium that has made this age of progress and industry possible: without it, the streets of London would be thronged with coughing, sleepless, incontinent multitudes. And if we consider all this, is it not apposite to ask if the Manchu tyrant has any right to deprive his helpless subjects of the advantages of progress? Do you think it pleases God to see us conspiring with that tyrant in depriving such a great number of people of this amazing gift?'

'But Mr Burnham,' Neel persisted, 'is it not true that there is a great deal of addiction and intoxication in China? Surely such ⟨...⟩ions are not pleasing to our Creator?'

⟨...⟩ttled Mr Burnham. 'These ills you mention, sir,' he ⟨...⟩ merely aspects of the fallen nature of Man. Should you ever happen to walk through the rookeries of London, Raja Neel Rattan, you will see for yourself that there is as much addiction and intoxication in the gin shops of the Empire's capital as there is in the dens of Canton. Are we then to raze every tavern in the city? Ban wine from our tables and whisky from our parlours? Deprive our sailors and soldiers of their daily dose of grog? And these measures being enacted, would addiction disappear and intoxication vanish? And would every member of Parliament bear the blame for every fatality should their efforts fail? The answer is no. No. Because the antidote for addiction lies not in bans enacted by Parliaments and emperors, but in the individual conscience—in every man's awareness of his personal responsibility and his fear of God. As a Christian nation this is the single most important lesson we can offer to China—and I have no doubt that the message would be welcomed by the people of that unfortunate country, were they not prevented from hearing it by the cruel despot who holds sway over them. It is tyranny alone that is to blame for China's degeneracy, sir. Merchants like myself are but the servants of Free Trade, which is as immutable as God's commandments.' Mr Burnham paused to pop a crisp fuleeta-pup in his mouth. 'And I might add, in this regard, that I do not think it sits well on a Raja of Raskhali to moralize on the subject of opium.'

'And why not?' said Neel, steeling himself for the affront that was sure to follow. 'Pray explain, Mr Burnham.'

'Why not?' Mr Burnham's eyebrows rose. 'Well, for the very good reason that everything you possess is paid for by opium—this budgerow, your houses, this food. Do you think you could afford any of this on the revenues of your estate and your half-starved coolie farmers? No, sir: it's opium that's given you all of this.'

'But I would not go to war for it, sir,' Neel said, in a tone that matched Mr Burnham's in its sharpness. 'And I do not believe the Empire will either. You must not imagine that I am unaware of the part that Parliament plays in your country.'

'Parliament?' Mr Burnham laughed. 'Parliament will not

know of the war until it is over. Be assured, sir, that if such matters were left to Parliament there would *be* no Empire.'

'Hear, hear!' said Mr Doughty, raising his glass. 'Truer words were never spoken . . .'

He was interrupted by the arrival of the next course, the presentation of which had required the mobilization of much of the budgerow's crew. They arrived one by one, bearing brass bowls of rice, mutton, prawns, and an assortment of pickles and chutneys.

'Ah, at last—the karibat,' said Mr Doughty. 'Just in time too!' As the covers were removed from the dishes, he cast an anxious glance over the table. When he found what he was looking for, he pointed a jubilant finger in the direction of a brass bowl that was filled with spinach and tiny slivers of fish. 'Isn't that the famous Rascally chitchky of pollock-saug? Why, I do believe it is!'

The smells had no effect on Neel, who had been so deeply stung by Mr Burnham's remarks that all thought of food, as well as worms and chamber-pots, had been purged from his mind. 'You must not imagine, sir,' he said to Mr Burnham, 'that I am an ignorant native, to be spoken to like a child. If I may say so, your youthful Queen has no more loyal subject than myself, and none who is more keenly aware of the rights that are enjoyed by the people of Britain. Indeed I am thoroughly familiar, I might add, with the writings of Mr Hume, Mr Locke and Mr Hobbes.'

'Please do not speak to me, sir,' said Mr Burnham, in the chilly tone of a man who wishes to snub a name-dropper, 'of Mr Hume and Mr Locke. For I would have you know that I have been acquainted with them since they served on the Bengal Board of Revenue. I too have read every word they've written—even their report on sanitation. And as for Mr Hobbes, why I do believe I dined with him at my club just the other day.'

'Fine fellow, Hobbes,' Mr Doughty broke in suddenly. 'Got a seat on the Municipal Council now, if I'm not mistaken. Went pig-sticking with him once. The shikarees scared up an old sow and a brood of piglets. Came charging at us! Scared the Nick's knackers out of the horses. Old Hobbes was tossed—right on a little suckling. Dead on the spot. The piglet I mean. Hobbes was unscathed. Damnedest thing I ever saw. Made a fine roast too. Piglet I mean.'

Mr Doughty had not quite finished his tale when another distraction presented itself: a tinkling sound, like that of anklets, now made itself heard in the purdah-screened alcove behind Neel. Evidently Elokeshi and the girls had come to take a look at the dinner guests: there followed some whispering and shifting of feet as they took turns at the peep-holes, and then Neel heard Elokeshi's voice, rising in excitement. *Eki-ré—* look, look!

Shh! said Neel over his shoulder, but his warning went unheard.

Do you see the fat, old one? Elokeshi continued, whispering in loud and urgent Bengali. He came to me twenty years ago; I couldn't have been more than fifteen; oh the things he did, *báp-ré*! If I told you, you would die laughing . . .

Neel noticed now that a silence had fallen over the table: the experienced older men were staring studiedly at the ceiling or at the table—but Zachary was looking around in astonished inquiry. Even less than before, could Neel think of a way to explain the situation to the newcomer: how was he to be told that he was being observed, through chinks in a curtain, by four dancers? At a loss for something to say, Neel muttered an apology: 'Just the ladies-in-waiting. Passing some wind.'

Now Elokeshi lowered her voice, and despite himself, Neel strained to follow: No really . . . made me sit on his face . . . *chhi, chhi*! . . . and then licked there with his tongue . . . no silly, right there, yes . . . *sheje ki chatachati*! . . . Oh what a licking! You'd think he was tasting a chutney . . .

'Hot cock and shittleteedee!' There was a crash as Mr Doughty sprang suddenly to his feet, knocking his chair over. 'Damned badzat pootlies. You think I don't samjo your bloody bucking? There's not a word of your black babble I don't understand. Call me a cunnylapper, would you? 'D rather bang the bishop than charter your chute. Licking, did you say? Here's my lattee to give you a licking . . .'

He began to advance on the alcove, with his cane upraised, but Mr Burnham jumped nimbly from his chair and headed him off. Zachary came quickly to his aid, and between the two of them they were able to get the pilot out of the sheeshmahal and on to the foredeck, where they handed him over to Serang Ali and his team of lascars.

'Catchi too muchi shamshoo,' said Serang Ali matter-of-factly, as he took hold of the pilot's ankles. 'More better go sleep chop-chop.'

This did nothing to soothe Mr Doughty. As he was being wrestled into the jollyboat, his voice could be heard, railing: 'Hands off my gander! . . . Avast with your launderbuzzing! . . . or I'll stuff your laurels between your teeth . . . tear out your jaunties . . . chowder your chutes . . . damned luckerbaugs and wanderoos! . . . where's my dumbpoke and pollock-saug . . .?'

'How-fashion to chow-chow this-time?' scolded Serang Ali. 'Too muchi shamshoo hab got inside. Allo come topside, no?'

Leaving Zachary behind to restrain the pilot, Mr Burnham came back to the sheeshmahal, where Neel was still sitting at the head of the table, contemplating the ruins of the dinner: would the evening have taken such a turn if his father had been presiding over the table? He could not imagine that it would.

'Very sorry about that,' Mr Burnham said. 'Just had a nipperkin too much of shrob our good Mr Doughty: a bit out of his altitude.'

'But it is I who should apologize,' said Neel. 'And surely you are not leaving already? The ladies have planned a *nách*.'

'Indeed?' said Mr Burnham. 'Well you must give them our apologies. I'm afraid I'm not up for that kind of thing.'

'I'm sorry to hear that,' said Neel. 'Are you not feeling well? Did the food not agree with you?'

'The food was splendid,' said Burnham gravely. 'But as for

*Amitav Ghosh*

a nautch—you may be aware that I have certain responsibilities to my church. It is not my practice to participate in spectacles that are injurious to the dignity of the fairer sex.'

Neel bowed his head in apology. 'I understand, Mr Burnham.'

Mr Burnham took a cheroot from his waistcoat and tapped it on his thumb. 'But if you don't mind, Raja Neel Rattan, I would like to have a few words with you in private.'

Neel could think of no way to refuse this request. 'Certainly, Mr Burnham. Shall we proceed to the upper deck? There some privacy should certainly be available.'

~

Once they were on the top deck, Mr Burnham lit his cheroot and blew a plume of smoke into the night air. 'I am very glad to have this opportunity to speak with you,' he began. 'It is an unexpected pleasure.'

'Thank you,' said Neel warily, every defensive instinct on the alert.

'You will recall that I wrote to you recently,' Mr Burnham said. 'May I ask if you have been able to give some thought to my proposal?'

'Mr Burnham,' Neel said flatly, 'I regret that at the present time, I cannot restore to you the funds that are owed. You must understand that it is impossible for me to entertain your proposal.'

'And why so?'

Neel thought of his last visit to Raskhali and the public meetings where his tenants and managers had pleaded with him not to sell the zemindary and deprive them of the lands they had farmed for generations. He thought of his last visit to his family's temple, where the priest had fallen at his feet, begging him not to give away the temple where his forefathers had prayed.

'Mr Burnham,' Neel said, 'the zemindary of Raskhali has been in my family for two hundred years; nine generations of

Halders have sat in its guddee. How can I give it away to settle my debts?'

'Times change, Raja Neel Rattan,' Mr Burnham said. 'And those who don't change with them, are swept away.'

'But I have a certain obligation to the people,' said Neel. 'You must try to understand—my family's temples are on that land. None of it is mine to sell or give away: it belongs also to my son and his yet unborn children. It is not possible for me to make it over to you.'

Mr Burnham blew out a mouthful of smoke. 'Let me be honest with you,' he said quietly. 'The truth is you have no option. Your debts to my company would not be covered even by the sale of the estate. I am afraid I cannot wait much longer.'

'Mr Burnham,' said Neel firmly, 'you must forget about your proposal. I will sell my houses, I will sell the budgerow, I will sell everything I can—but I cannot part with the Raskhali lands. I would rather declare bankruptcy than hand over my zemindary to you.'

'I see,' said Mr Burnham, not unpleasantly. 'Am I to take that as your final word?'

Neel nodded. 'Yes.'

'Well then,' said Mr Burnham, staring at the glowing tip of his cheroot. 'Let it be understood then, that whatever happens, you have only yourself to blame.'

The candle in Paulette's window was the first to pierce the pre-dawn darkness that surrounded Bethel: of all the residents of the house, master and servant alike, she was always up the earliest and her day usually began with the hiding of the sari she had slept in at night. It was only in the seclusion of her bedroom, sheltered from the prying gaze of the staff, that she dared wear a sari at all: Paulette had discovered that at Bethel, the servants, no less than the masters, held strong views on what was appropriate for Europeans, especially memsahibs. The bearers and khidmutgars sneered when her clothing was not quite pucka, and they would often ignore her if she spoke to them in Bengali—or anything other than the kitchen-Hindusthani that was the language of command in the house. Now, on rising from her bed, she was quick to lock her sari in her trunk: this was the one place where it would be safe from discovery by the procession of servants who would file through to clean the bedroom later in the day—the bed-making bichawnadars, the floor-sweeping farrashes and the commode-cleaning matranees and harry-maids.

The apartment that Paulette had been assigned was on the uppermost floor of the mansion, and it consisted of a sizeable bedroom and a dressing room; more remarkably, it also had an adjoining water-closet. Mrs Burnham had made sure that her residence was among the first in the city to do away with outhouses. 'So tiresome to have to run outside,' she liked to say, 'every time you have to drop a chitty in the dawk.'

As with the rest of the mansion, Paulette's water-closet boasted of many of the latest English devices, among them a comfortable, wood-lidded commode, a painted porcelain basin and a small footbath made of tin. But from Paulette's point of view the water-closet lacked the most important amenity of all—it had no arrangements for bathing. Through years of habit, Paulette had grown accustomed to daily baths and frequent dips in the Hooghly: it was hard for her to get through a day without being refreshed at least once by the touch of cool, fresh water. At Bethel a daily bath was permitted only to the Burra Sahib, when he returned, hot and dusty, from a day at the Dufter. Paulette had heard rumours that Mr Burnham had created a special contraption for the purpose of this daily wash: holes had been bored into the bottom of a common tin balty, and the bucket had been strung up in such a way as to permit it to be constantly filled by a bearer, while the sahib stood underneath, revelling in the flow. Dearly would Paulette have loved to make use of this device, but her one attempt to broach this subject had scandalized Mrs Burnham, who, with her usual indirection, had made puzzling reference to the many reasons why frequent cold baths were necessary for a man but unseemly, even perverse, in the gentler, less excitable sex; she had made it clear that, so far as she was concerned, a bathtub was the pucka amenity for a memsahib, to be used at decent intervals of every two or three days.

At Bethel there were two enormous goozle-connahs—bathrooms outfitted with cast-iron tubs, imported directly from Sheffield. But to have the tubs filled required at least half a day's advance notice to the ab-dars, and Paulette knew that if she were to issue this command more than twice a week, word would quickly get back to Mrs Burnham. In any event, to bathe in those tubs was not much to Paulette's taste: it gave her no pleasure to soak in a tepid pool of her own scum; nor did she relish the ministrations of the three female attendants—the 'cushy-girls' as Mrs Burnham liked to call them—who would fuss over her as she lay in the tub, soaping her back and scrubbing her thighs, tweezing wherever they saw fit, and all the while murmuring 'khushi-khushi?' as if there were some great joy in being pinched, prodded and rubbed all over one's body. When they reached for her most intimate recesses, she would fight them off, which always left them looking surprised and wounded, as if they had been prevented from properly performing their duties: this was a trial to Paulette, for she could not imagine what it was that they intended to do and wasn't inclined to find out.

Desperation had led Paulette to devise her own method of washing, inside her water-closet: standing in her tin footbath, she would reach carefully into a balty, with a mug, and then allow the water to trickle gently down her body. In the past she had always bathed in a sari, and to be wholly unclothed had made her uncomfortable at first, but after a week or two she had grown used to it. Inevitably, there was a certain amount of spillage and she always had to spend a good deal of time afterwards, in towelling the floor, to remove all trace of the ritual: the servants were ever-curious about the doings of Bethel's inmates and Mrs Burnham, for all her vagueness, seemed to have an efficient way of extracting gossip from them. Despite her precautions, Paulette had reason to think that word of her surreptitious bathing had somehow trickled through to the mistress of the house: of late, Mrs Burnham had made several derisive remarks about the incessant bathing of the Gentoos and how they were always dipping their heads in the Ganges and muttering bobberies and baba-res.

Recalling these strictures, Paulette went to considerable trouble to make sure that no water remained on the floor of her water-closet. But immediately after this struggle, there followed several more: first she had to grapple with the stays of a pair of knee-length drawers; next, she had to twist herself into knots to find the fastenings of her bodice, her chemise, and her petticoat; only then could she wriggle into one of the many dresses her benefactress had bequeathed to her upon her arrival at Bethel.

Although Mrs Burnham's clothes were severe in cut, they

were made of much finer stuffs than any that Paulette had ever worn before: not for her common Chinsurah calicoes, nor even the fine shabnam muslins and zaituni satins that many memsahibs made do with; the Burra BeeBee of Bethel would have nothing less than the finest kerseymere, the best silks from China, crisp linens from Ireland and soft Surat nainsooks. The trouble with these fine fabrics, as Paulette had discovered, was that once having been cut and stitched, they could not easily be adapted for the use of another wearer, especially one as maladroit as herself.

At seventeen, Paulette was unusually tall, of a height where she could look over the heads of most of those around her, men and women alike. Her limbs, too, were of such a length that they tended to wave like branches in a wind (years later, this would be her chief complaint about the way she was represented in Deeti's shrine—that her arms looked like the fronds of a coconut palm). In the past, Paulette's awareness of her unusual stature had led to a shy indifference to her appearance: but in a way this awkwardness had also amounted to a charter of freedom, in that it had rid her of the burden of having to care about her looks. But since her arrival at Bethel, her diffidence about her appearance had been transformed into an acute self-consciousness: in repose, her nails and fingertips would seek out small blemishes and tease them until they became ugly blotches on her pale complexion; while walking she would lean forward as if she were striding into a powerful wind; while standing, she would stoop, with her hands clasped behind her back, swaying back and forth, as though she were about to deliver an oration. In the past, she had worn her long, dark hair in pigtails, but of late she had taken to tying it back, in a severe little knot, as if it were a corset for her skull.

On her arrival at Bethel, Paulette had found four dresses laid out on her bed, with all the necessary chemises, blouses and petticoats: Mrs Burnham had assured her that they had all been properly altered to fit and were ready to be worn to dinner. Paulette had taken Mrs Burnham at her word: she had dressed hurriedly, ignoring the cluckings of the maid who'd been sent to help her. Eager to please her benefactress, she had run enthusiastically down the stairs and into the dining room. 'But only regard, Mrs Burnham!' she'd cried. 'Look! Your robe is perfectly of my cut.'

There was no answer: only a sound like that of a large crowd collectively drawing its breath. Coming through the doors, Paulette had noticed that the dining room seemed strangely full, especially considering that this was meant to be a family supper, with only the Burnhams and their eight-year-old daughter, Annabel, at table. Being unaccustomed to the ways of the house, she had not allowed for the others who were present at every meal: the turbaned bearers who stood behind each chair; the masalchie with the sauceboat; the chobdar whose job it was to ladle soup from the sideboard tureen; the three or four young chuckeroos who always followed at the feet of the more senior retainers. And nor were these the only servants present that night: curiosity about the newly arrived missy-mem had spread to the bobachee-connah and many of the kitchen staff were lurking in the anterior vestibule, where the punkah-wallahs sat, pulling the overhead fans by means of ropes attached to their toes: among them were the curry consumah, the caleefa who roasted the kabobs and the bobachees who were responsible for the stews and the joints of beef. The indoors servants had even contrived to smuggle in a few whose place was strictly out-of-doors—malis from the garden, syces and julibdars from the stables, durwauns from the gatehouse, and even some beasties from the gang that kept the house supplied with water. The servants held their breath as they waited for their master's response: the sauceboat wobbled on the masalchi's tray, the chobdar lost his ladle, and the ropes on the punkah-wallahs' toes went slack as they watched the eyes of the Burra Sahib and the Burra BeeBee descending from Paulette's ill-fitting bodice—the stays of which had come undone—to the hem of her dress, which was so short as to expose Paulette's ankles, in all their nakedness. The only voice to be heard was little Annabel's who gave a gleeful shout of laughter: 'Mama! she forgot to bundo her jumma!

And oh dekko mama, do: there's her ankle! Do you see it? Look what the puggly's done!'

The name stuck, and from then on Paulette was Puggly to Mrs Burnham and Annabel.

The next day a contingent of tailors, consisting of some half-dozen darzees and rafoogars, had been summoned to adapt Mrs Burnham's clothing to the measure of the newly-arrived missy-mem. Yet, for all their diligence, their efforts had met with limited success: such was Paulette's build that even with the hems let out to the fullest, Mrs Burnham's gowns did not come quite as far down as they should—around the waist and arm, on the other hand, they seemed always to be much wider than was necessary. As a result, when draped upon Paulette, those finely tailored gowns had a tendency to slip and flap; memsahib costume of this kind being, in any case, unfamiliar to her, the lack of fit greatly compounded her discomfort: often, when the loose fabric chafed against her skin, she would pinch, pull and scratch—sometimes causing Mrs Burnham to ask if little chinties had got into her clothes.

Since that awful night, Paulette had laboured hard to behave and speak exactly as she should, but not always with success. Just the other day, in referring to the crew of a boat, she had proudly used a newly-learnt English word: 'cock-swain'. But instead of earning accolades, the word had provoked a disapproving frown. When they were out of Annabel's hearing, Mrs Burnham explained that the word Paulette had used smacked a little too much of the 'increase and multiply' and could not be used in company: 'If you must buck about that kind of thing, Puggly dear, do remember the word to use nowadays is "roosterswain".'

But then, unaccountably, the BeeBee had burst into giggles and slapped Paulette's knuckles with her fan. 'As for that other thing, dear,' she said, 'no mem would ever let it past her lips.'

~

One reason why Paulette had risen early was to give herself time to work on the unfinished manuscript of her father's

*Materia Medica* of the plants of Bengal. Dawn was the only time of day that she felt to be entirely her own; in the spending of that hour, there was no need to feel any guilt, even if she chose to do something that she knew to be displeasing to her benefactors. But rare were the days when she was actually able to devote any time to the manuscript: more often than not, her gaze would stray across the river, to the Botanical Gardens, and she would find herself slipping into a spell of melancholy remembrance. Was it cruel or kind of the Burnhams to have given her a room with a window that commanded so fine a view of the river and the shore beyond? She could not decide: the fact was that even when seated at her desk, she had only to crane her head a little to catch a glimpse of the bungalow she had left some fourteen months before—its presence, beyond the water, seemed a mocking reminder of all that she had lost with her father's death. Yet, even to revisit those memories, was to be assailed by a wave of guilt—to hanker after that earlier life seemed not just ungrateful, but disloyal to her benefactors. Whenever her thoughts strayed across the river, she would conscientiously remind herself of her good fortune in being where she was, and in receiving all that the Burnhams had given her—her clothes, her bedroom, pin-money to spend, and most of all, instruction in things of which she had been sadly ignorant, such as piety, penitence and Scripture. Nor was gratitude hard to summon, for to be mindful of her luck she had only to think of the fate that would otherwise have been hers: instead of sitting in this spacious room, she would have found herself in a barracks in Alipore, an inmate of the newly-instituted poorhouse for destitute Eurasians and white minors. Such indeed was the lot to which she'd resigned herself when she was summoned before Mr Kendalbushe, a stern-faced judge of the Sudder Court. Instructing her to offer thanks to a merciful heaven, Mr Kendalbushe had let her know that her case had come to the notice of none other than Benjamin Brightwell Burnham, a leading merchant and philanthropist with a distinguished record of receiving destitute white girls into his house. He had written to the presiding officer of the court, offering to provide the orphaned Paulette Lambert with a home.

The judge had shown Paulette the letter: it was prefaced with the line: 'Above all things have fervent charity among yourselves: for charity shall cover the multitude of sins.' To her shame, Paulette had not been able to identify the provenance of the verse: it was the judge who told her that it was from 'The Book of the Lord: I Peter, chapter 4, verse 8'. Mr Kendalbushe had then proceeded to ask her a few simple scriptural questions; her answers, or rather, the lack of them, had shocked him into delivering a caustic judgement: 'Miss Lambert, your godlessness is a disgrace to the ruling race: there is many a Gentoo and Mom'den in this city, who is better informed than yourself. You are but a step away from chanting like a Sammy or shrieking like a Sheer. In the opinion of this court you will be better served by Mr Burnham's tutelage than ever you were by your father's. It falls to you now to show yourself worthy of this good fortune.'

In the months she had spent at Bethel, Paulette's knowledge of Scripture had grown apace, for Mr Burnham had undertaken to personally instruct her. As with her predecessors, it had been made clear to her that nothing would be asked of her other than regular churchgoing, good behaviour and a willingness to open herself to religious instruction. Before her arrival, Paulette had imagined that the Burnhams would expect her to make herself useful in the manner of a poor relative: the discovery that she had little to offer them, by way of compensatory services, had come as something of a shock. Her offers of help in tutoring Annabel had been politely declined, for reasons that had soon become apparent to Paulette: not only was her command of English far from perfect, her education had followed a path exactly contrary to that which Mrs Burnham deemed appropriate for a girl.

For the most part, Paulette's schooling had consisted of assisting her father as he went about his work. This provided a wider range of instruction than might be supposed, for it was Pierre Lambert's practice to label his plants, when possible, in

Bengali and Sanskrit, as well as in accordance with the system recently invented by Linnaeus. This meant that Paulette had learnt a good deal of Latin from her father, while also absorbing Indian languages from the learned munshis who had been enlisted to assist the curator with his collections. French she had studied of her own volition, reading and re-reading her father's books until she knew them almost by heart. Thus, through effort and observation, Paulette had become, while still quite young, an accomplished botanist and a devout reader of Voltaire, Rousseau, and most particularly M. Bernardin de Saint-Pierre, who had once been her father's teacher and mentor. But Paulette had not thought to mention any of this at Bethel, knowing that the Burnhams would not wish to have Annabel instructed in botany or philosophy or Latin, their dislike of Romish popery being almost equal to their detestation of Hindus and Muslims—or 'Gentoos and Musselmen' as they liked to put it.

By default, since it was not in her nature to be idle, Paulette had assigned herself the task of overseeing the Burnhams' gardens. But this too had proved no easy matter, for the Head Malley had quickly made it clear that he would not willingly take instructions from a girl of her age. It was over his objections that she had planted a chalta tree by the chabutra, and only with the greatest difficulty had she prevailed on him to put a pair of latanias in a bed on the main driveway: these palms, a great favourite of her father's, were another slender link with her past.

Not the least of the reasons why Paulette so often found herself slipping into a state of melancholy was that she had not yet been able to find a way of being properly useful to her benefactors. Now, just as a wave of despair was beginning to build, Paulette was startled out of her despondency by the sound of hoofs and wheels, crackling urgently on the conkers of the gravelled driveway that led to the main entrance of Bethel. She glanced up at the sky and saw that the darkness of night had begun to yield to the first rosy streaks of dawn: but even so, it was very early for a visitor. Opening her door, she crossed the vestibule that ran past her room and unlatched a window on the far side of the house. She was just in time to see a carriage pulling up to the portico of the Burnham mansion: the vehicle was a caranchie, a ramshackle coach constructed from the remains of an old hackney carriage. These humble carriages were common in the Bengali quarters of the city, but Paulette could not remember ever having seen one at Bethel; certainly none had ever pulled up to the main entrance of the house. As she was looking down from above, a man dressed in a kurta and dhoti climbed out and leant over to spit a mouthful of paan into a bed of cobra-lilies: Paulette caught a glimpse of a braided tail of hair hanging down from an enormous head and she knew that the visitor was Baboo Nobokrishna Panda, Mr Burnham's gomusta—the agent responsible for the shipping of indentured migrants. Paulette had seen him about the house a few times, usually carrying armloads of paper for Mr Burnham's perusal—but never before had he presented himself so early in the morning and nor had he ever summoned the courage to bring his caranchie up the main driveway, to the front door.

Paulette guessed that there would be no one about to let the Baboo in at this hour: this was the one time of day when the outdoors durwauns could be counted on to fall asleep, while the indoors khidmutgars would not yet have risen from their charpoys. Always eager to make herself useful, she went flying down the stairs, and after a brief struggle with the brass latches, pushed the durwauza open to find the gomusta standing outside.

The gomusta was a man of middle age, with cheeks that hung down as if weighted with melancholy; he was stout in girth, with dark shapeless ears that stuck out from his huge head like outgrowths of fungus on a mossy rock. Although he still had a full head of hair, his brow was shaven clean, while the locks at the back of his head were braided into a long, priestly tikki. The Baboo was clearly surprised to see her and even though he smiled and dipped his head, in a gesture that was at once a greeting and a signal of submission, she sensed

*Amitav Ghosh*

a hesitation in his manner and guessed that it had something to do with an uncertainty about her situation: was she to be treated as an extension of the Burnham family or was she an employee or dependant, not unlike himself? To set him at ease, she joined her hands in the Indian way, and was about to say, in Bengali:—Nomoshkar Nobokrishno-babu—when she recalled, just in time, that the gomusta preferred to be spoken to in English, and liked to be addressed by the *anglice* of his name, which was Nob Kissin Pander.

'Please but enter, Baboo Nob Kissin,' she said, stepping well away from the door to let him in. Noticing the three lines of sandalwood paste on his forehead, she quickly dropped the hand she had almost offered in greeting: the gomusta was a fervent devotee of Sri Krishna, she recalled, and as a celibate Seeker, he might well look askance upon a woman's touch.

'Miss Lambert, you are well today?' he said, as he came in, nodding and bobbing his head, while also stepping backwards to maintain a safe distance from the possible pollutions of Paulette's person. 'Motions were not loose, I hope?'

'Why no, Baboo Nob Kissin. I am very well. And you?'

'I have come running like anything,' he said. 'Master only has told to reach message—his caique-boat is urgently required.'

Paulette nodded. 'I will send word to the boatmen.'

'That will be most appreciable.'

Looking over her shoulder, Paulette noticed that a khidmutgar had entered the hallway. She sent him off to alert the boatmen and led Baboo Nob Kissin towards the small withdrawing room where visitors and petitioners were usually seated before being admitted to Mr Burnham's presence.

'Perhaps you would like to attend here until the boat is ready?' she said. She was about to close the door when she noticed, somewhat to her alarm, that the gomusta's expression had changed: baring his teeth in a smile, he shook his head in such a way as to set his tikki wagging. 'Oh Miss Lambert,' he said, in a strangely ardent voice, 'so many times I'm coming to Bethel and always I am wanting to meet and raise up one matter. But never you are lonely with me one minute also—how to commence discussions?'

She drew back, startled. 'But Baboo Nob Kissin,' she said. 'If there is anything you wish to say to me, surely it can be said all in the open?'

'That you only can be judging, Miss Lambert,' he said, and his tikki danced in such a comical way that Paulette could not but bite back a laugh.

~

Paulette was not alone in seeing something absurd in the gomusta: many years and thousands of miles later, when Baboo Nob Kissin Pander found his way into Deeti's shrine, his was the only likeness to figure as a caricature, a great potato of a head sprouting two fernlike ears. Yet Nob Kissin Pander was always full of surprises, as Paulette was imminently to discover. Now, from the pocket of his black jacket, he pulled out a small object that was wrapped in cloth. 'Only one minute, Miss: then you dekho.'

Laying the bundle on his palm, he began to undo the folds, very fastidiously, using just the tips of his fingers, without once touching the thing itself. When the wrappings had been undone and the object lay nested in a bed of cloth, he extended his palm towards Paulette, moving his arm slowly, as if to remind her not to approach too close: 'Kindly do not catch.' Despite the distance, Paulette recognized instantly the tiny face that smiled up at her from the gold-framed locket in the gomusta's palm; it was an enamelled miniature of a woman with dark hair and grey eyes—her mother, whom she had lost at the very moment of her birth and of whom she possessed no other token or likeness.

Paulette glanced at the gomusta in confusion: 'But Baboo Nob Kissin!' After her father's death, she had looked for the miniature everywhere, without success, and had been forced to conclude that it had been stolen, in the confusion that befell the house after his sudden passing. 'But how you have found this? Where?'

'Lambert-sahib only gave,' said the gomusta. 'Just one

week before shifting to heavenly-abode. His conditions were extremely parlous; hands were trembling like anything and tongue was also coated. Rigorous constipation must have been there, but still he is reaching to my daftar, in Kidderpore. Just imagine!'

She recalled the day, in a clarity of detail that brought tears to her eyes: her father had told her to summon Jodu and his boat and when she asked why, his answer was that he had business in the city and needed to cross the river. She had demanded to know what business he might have that she couldn't see to, but he gave her no answer, insisting that Jodu be called. She'd watched as Jodu's boat made its way slowly across the river: when they were almost at the far side, she was surprised to see that they were heading not towards the centre of the city but to the docks at Kidderpore. What business could he have there? She could not imagine, and he never answered her questions about it; not even Jodu could do anything to enlighten her, upon their return. All he could tell her was that her father had left him to wait in his boat, while he disappeared into the bazar.

'That time was not his first to my chamber,' the gomusta said. 'As such, many sahibs and mems are coming when some funds are required. They give some jewelleries and trinkets for disposal. Lambert-sahib graced with his presence only two-three times, but he is not like others—not loocher, not gambler, not shrubber. For him, difficulty is that he is too-much good-hearted, all the time doing charities and giving up funds. Naturally many villains are taking advantage . . .'

This description was neither unjust nor inaccurate, Paulette knew, but that was not how she chose to remember her father: for of course the great majority of those who benefited from his kindness were people desperately in need—waifs and urchins, porters crippled by their loads and boatmen who had lost their boats. And even now, after being thrown into the care of people who were, after all, strangers, no matter how kind, she could not bring herself to reproach her father for the greatest of his virtues, the one thing she had loved in him most. But yes, it was also true, and there was no denying it, that her lot would have been different if he had been—like most other Europeans in the city—bent upon his own enrichment.

'Lambert-sahib always discussing with me in Bangla,' the gomusta continued. 'But I am always replying in chaste English.'

But now as if to belie his own pronouncement, he surprised Paulette by switching to Bengali. With the change of language, she noticed, a weight of care seemed to lift from his huge, sagging face: *Shunun.* Listen: when your father came to me for money, I knew, even without his saying so, that he would be giving it away to some beggar or cripple. I'd say to him: 'Arre Lambert-shaheb, I've seen many a Christian trying to buy his way into heaven, but I've never come across one who worked as hard at it as you do.' He'd laugh like a child—he liked to laugh, your father—but not this time. This time there was no laughter, and hardly a word was said before he stretched out his hand and asked: How much will you give me for this, Nob Kissin Baboo? I knew at once that it was of great value to him; I could tell from the way he held it—but of course, such is the evil of this age that things that are of value to us are not necessarily so to the world at large. Not wishing to disappoint him, I said: 'Lambert-sahib, tell me, what is the money for? How much do you need?' 'Not much,' was his answer, 'just enough for a passage back to France.' I said, in surprise: 'For yourself, Lambert-sahib?' He shook his head. 'No,' he said,'for my daughter, Putli. Just in case something happens to me. I want to be sure she has the means to return. Without me this city would be no place for her.'

The gomusta's fist closed on the locket as he broke off to glance again at his watch. Your father, Miss Lambert—how well he knew our language. I used to marvel as I listened to him speak . . .

But now, even as the gomusta continued, in the same sonorous tones, Paulette heard his words as though they were being spoken by her father, in French: . . . a child of Nature, that is what she is, my daughter Paulette. As you know I have educated her myself, in the innocent tranquillity of the Botanical

Gardens. She has had no teacher other than myself, and has never worshipped at any altar except that of Nature; the trees have been her Scripture and the Earth her Revelation. She has not known anything but Love, Equality and Freedom: I have raised her to revel in that state of liberty that is Nature itself. If she remains here, in the colonies, most particularly in a city like this, where Europe hides its shame and its greed, all that awaits her is degradation: the whites of this town will tear her apart, like vultures and foxes, fighting over a corpse. She will be an innocent thrown before the money-changers who pass themselves off as men of God . . .

'Stop!' Paulette raised her hands to her ears, as if to shut out her father's voice. How wrong he was! How mistaken he had always been in his understanding of her, making her into that which he himself wished to be, rather than seeing her for the ordinary creature that she was. Yet, even as she chafed against his judgement, Paulette's eyes misted over at the thought of those childhood years, when she and her father had lived with Jodu and Tantima, as though their bungalow were an island of innocence in a sea of corruption.

She shook her head, as if to rid herself of a dream: So what did you tell him then, Nob Kissin Baboo—about the worth of the locket?

The gomusta smiled, tugging at his tikki. 'After careful considerations I clarified that passage to France, even in steerage, would definitely be costing more than this locket. Maybe two-three similar items would be required. For the cost of this one he could send only up to *Mareech-díp*.'

*Mareech-díp*? she wrinkled her eyebrows, wondering what place he could be thinking of: the expression meant 'pepper-island' but she had never heard it used before. Where is that?

'The Mauritius Islands, they call in English.'

O les îles Maurice? cried Paulette. 'But that is where my mother was born.'

'That is what he told,' the gomusta said, with a thin smile. 'He said: Let Paulette go to Mauritius—it is like her native-place. There she can cope up with the joys and agonies of life.'

And then? Did you get him the money?

'I told him to come back after some days and funds would be there. But how he is to come? Expired, no, after one week?' The gomusta sighed. 'Even before, I could tell that his conditions were already parlous. Eyes were red and tongue was wheatish colour, indicating stoppages of bowels-movement. I advised to him: Lambert-sahib, just for some days, kindly refrain from meat-eating—vegetarian stool is easier to pass. But no doubt he ignored, leading to untimely demise. After that I had too much difficulties in obtaining back the item. The moneylender had already delivered at pawnshop; and so on and so forth. But as you see, now it is again in my possession.'

Only then did it occur to Paulette that he need not have told her any of this: he could have kept the money for himself and she would never have known any better. 'I am truly grateful to you for bringing back the locket, Nob Kissin Baboo,' she said. Unthinkingly she extended a hand towards his arm, only to see him back away as if from a hissing snake. 'I do not know how you to remercy.'

The gomusta's head reared in indignation and he switched back to Bengali: What do you think, Miss Lambert? Do you think I would keep something that is not my own? I may be man of commerce in your eyes, Miss—and in this age of evil, who is not?—but are you aware that eleven generations of my ancestors have been pandas at one of Nabadwip's most famous temples? One of my forefathers was initiated into the love of Krishna by Shri Chaitanya himself. I alone was not able to fulfil my destiny: it is my misfortune . . .

'Even now I am searching Lord Krishna left and right,' continued the gomusta. 'But what to do? He is not heeding . . .'

But even as he was extending his hand towards Paulette's open palm, the gomusta hesitated and drew back his arm. 'And the interest? My means are deficient, Miss Lambert, and I am saving for higher purpose—to build temple.'

'You shall have the money, never fear,' said Paulette. She saw a look of doubt enter the gomusta's eyes, as though he were already beginning to rethink his generosity. 'But you must let me have the locket: it is my mother's only picture.'

Now, in the distance, she heard a footfall that she knew to be the sound of the khidmutgar returning from the boathouse. This made her suddenly desperate, for it mattered very much to her that no one at Bethel should know of this dealing between herself and Mr Burnham's gomusta—not because she took any pleasure in deceiving her benefactor, but only because she did not wish to provide them with any further material for their recurrent indictments of her father and his godless, improvident ways. She lowered her voice and whispered urgently in English: 'Please Baboo Nob Kissin; please, I beg you . . .'

At this, as if to remind himself of his better instincts, the gomusta reached up and gave his tikki a tug. Then, opening his fingers, he allowed the cloth-wrapped locket to fall into Paulette's waiting hands. He stepped back just as the door opened to admit the khidmutgar, who had returned to let them know that the boat was ready.

'Come, Baboo Nob Kissin,' said Paulette, making an effort to be cheerful. 'I will walk you to the boathouse. Come: to there one goes!'

As they were walking through the house, towards the garden, Baboo Nob Kissin came suddenly to a halt beside a window that looked towards the river: he raised his hand to point and Paulette saw that a ship had entered the rectangular frame—the chequered flag of the Burnham firm was clearly visible on the vessel's mainmast.

'*Ibis* is there!' cried Baboo Nob Kissin. 'At last, by Jove! Master waiting, waiting, all the time breaking my head and collaring me—why my ship is not coming? Now he will rejoice.'

Paulette flung open a door and went hurrying across the garden towards the riverfront. Mr Burnham was standing on the schooner's quarter-deck, waving a hat triumphantly in the direction of Bethel. He was answered by the crew of the caique, who waved back from the boathouse.

While the men were waving, on ship and shore, Paulette's

gaze strayed towards the river and she caught sight of a dinghy that seemed to have come loose from its moorings: it was floating adrift, with no one at the helm. Caught by the river's current, it had been pulled out to midstream and was on its way to a collision with the oncoming schooner.

Paulette choked on her breath as she looked more closely: even from that distance, the boat looked very much like Jodu's. Of course there were hundreds of similar dinghies on the Hooghly—yet, there was only one that she herself had known intimately: that was the boat on which she was born and on which her mother had died; it was the boat she had played in as a child and in which she had travelled with her father, to collect specimens in the mangrove forests. She recognized the thatch, the crooked turn of the prow, and the stubby jut of the stern: no, there could be no doubt that it was Jodu's boat, and it was just a few yards from the *Ibis*, in imminent danger of being rammed by its knife-edged cutwater.

In a desperate attempt to avoid a collision, she began to mill her arms through the air, shouting as loud as she could. 'Look out! Dekho! Dekho! *Attention*!'

~

After weeks of anxious wakefulness at his mother's side, Jodu had slept so deeply as to be unaware that his boat had slipped its moorings and was drifting out into mid-river, right into the path of the ocean-going ships that were using the incoming tide to make their way to Calcutta. The *Ibis* was almost upon him when the flapping of her foretopsail roused him; the sight that met his eyes was so unexpected that he could not immediately respond: he lay motionless in the boat, his gaze locked on the protruding bill of the vessel's carved figurehead, which seemed now to be bearing directly down on him, as if to snatch him from the water like prey.

Lying as he was, flat on his back, on the bamboo slats of his dinghy, Jodu could have been an offering to the river, set afloat on a raft of leaves by some pious pilgrim—yet he did not fail to recognize that this was no ordinary ship bearing down on him, but an iskuner of the new kind, a 'gosi ka jahaz', with agil-peechil ringeen rather than square sails. Only the trikat-gavi was open to the wind and it was this distant patch of canvas that had woken him as it filled and emptied with the early-morning breeze. Some half-dozen lascars sat perched like birds on the crosswise purwan of the trikatdol, while on the tootuk beneath the serang and the tindals were waving as if to catch Jodu's attention. He could tell, because their mouths were open, that they were shouting too, although nothing was audible of their voices because of the sound of the wave created by the ship's knife-like taliyamar as it cut through the water.

The iskuner was so close now that he could see the green glint of the copper that sheathed the taliyamar; he could even see the shells of the siyala-insects that were clinging to the wet, slime-covered surface of the wood. If his boat were to take the impact of the taliyamar squarely in its flank, it would split, he knew, like a bundle of twigs hit by a falling axe; he himself would be pulled under by the suction of the wake. All this while, the long oar that served as the dinghy's rudder was only a step and a stretch away—but by the time he leapt to put his shoulder to the handle, it was too late to significantly alter the boat's course; he was able to turn it just enough so that instead of being hit smack in the middle, the boat bounced off the hull of the *Ibis*. The impact rolled the dinghy steeply to one side, at exactly the moment when the ship's bow wave was crashing down on it, like a breaker on a beach; the hemp ropes snapped under the weight of the water, and the logs flew apart. As the boat was disintegrating under him, Jodu managed to catch hold of one of the logs; he clung on as it bobbed under and back again to the top. When his head was clear of the water, he saw that he had floated almost to the stern of the ship, along with the rest of the wreckage; now he could feel the powerful suction of the awari beginning to tug at the log he was holding on to.

'Here! Here!' he heard a voice shouting in English, and

looked up to see a curly-haired man, whirling a weighted rope above his head. The line snaked out and Jodu succeeded in getting a grip on it just as the ship's stern was sweeping past, sucking the remains of his boat under its keel. The turbulence spun him around and around, but in such a way as to wrap the rope securely around him, so that when the sailor began to pull, at the other end of the line, his body broke quickly free of the water and he was able to use his feet to scramble up the iskuner's side and over the bulwark, to collapse in a heap on the after-tootuk.

While lying on the scrubbed planks, coughing and spluttering, Jodu became aware of a voice, speaking to him in English, and he looked up to see the bright-eyed face of the man who had thrown him the rope. He was kneeling beside him, saying something incomprehensible; arrayed behind him were the looming figures of two sahibs, one tall and bearded, the other big-bellied and bewhiskered: the latter was armed with a cane, which he was tapping excitedly on the tootuk. Fixed as he was, under the scrutiny of the sahibs' eyes, Jodu became suddenly aware that he was naked except for the thin, cotton gamchha that was wrapped around his waist. Lowering his chest to his knees, he hunched his body into a defensive huddle and tried to shut their voices out of his head. But soon enough he heard them calling out the name of one Serang Ali; then a hand fell on his neck, forcing him to look up into a sternly venerable face, with a thin moustache.

*Tera nám kyá?* What's your name? said the serang.

Jodu, he said, and added quickly, in case this sounded too childish: That's what people call me, but my good-name is Azad—Azad Naskar.

Zikri Malum's gone to get some clothes for you, continued the serang, in broken Hindusthani. You go below deck and wait. Don't need you under our feet while we're berthing.

Keeping his head lowered, Jodu followed Serang Ali off the quarter-deck and through the staring phalanx of the crew, to the hatch that led down to the 'tween-deck. There's the dabusa, said the serang. Stay down there till you're sent for.

Standing on the tip of the dabusa, with his feet on the ladder, Jodu became aware of a sickly, fetid odour, welling upwards from the darkness below: it was a smell that was at once offensive and disturbing, familiar and unrecognizable, and it became stronger as he descended. When he reached the bottom of the ladder, he looked around and saw that he had entered a shallow, empty space, unlit but for the shaft of light that was pouring through the open hatch. Although as wide as the vessel, the dabusa had a close, cramped feel—partly because its ceiling was not much taller than a man, but also because it was divided, by timber ribs, into open compartments, like cattle-pens. As his eyes became accustomed to the dim light, Jodu stepped warily into one of these pens and immediately stubbed his toe upon a heavy iron chain. Falling to his knees, he discovered that there were several such chains in the pen, nailed into the far beam: they ended in bracelet-like clasps, each fitted with eyeholes, for locks. The weight and heft of the chains made Jodu wonder what sort of cargo they were intended to restrain: it occurred to him that they might be meant for livestock—and yet the stench that permeated the hold was not that of cows, horses or goats; it was more a human odour, compounded of sweat, urine, excrement and vomit; the smell had leached so deep into the timbers as to have become ineradicable. He picked up one of the chains, and on looking more closely at the bracelet-like clasps, he became convinced that it was indeed meant for a human wrist or ankle. Now, running his hands along the floor, he saw that there were smooth depressions in the wood, of a shape and size that could only have been made by human beings, over prolonged periods of time. The depressions were so close to each other as to suggest a great press of people, packed close together, like merchandise on a vendor's counter. What kind of vessel would be equipped and outfitted to carry human beings in this way? And why had the serang sent him, Jodu, down here to wait, out of sight of other people? Suddenly he remembered stories, told on the river, of devil-ships that would descend on the coast to kidnap entire villages—the victims were eaten alive, or so the rumour went. Like an invasion of ghosts, unnamed apprehensions rushed into his mind; he pushed himself into a corner and sat shivering, falling gradually into a trance-like state of shock.

The spell was broken by the sound of someone coming down the hatch: Jodu focused his eyes on the ladder, expecting to see Serang Ali—or perhaps the curly-haired man who'd thrown him the rope. But he saw, instead, the figure of a woman, dressed in a long, dark gown and a close-fitting bonnet that kept her face hidden. The thought of being discovered, almost naked, by this unknown memsahib prompted him to slip quickly into another pen. He tried to hide himself, by flattening his body against the bulwark, but his foot struck a chain, sending a rattle of iron through the cavern of the hold. Jodu froze as the memsahib's shoes came tapping towards him. Suddenly he heard his own name spoken: Jodu? The whisper echoed through the hold as the bonneted face stepped around a beam and came closer: Jodu? The woman paused to remove the bonnet and he found himself looking into a familiar face.

It's just me, Putli. Paulette smiled into his wide-eyed, disbelieving face: Aren't you going to say anything?

∼

In his cabin, up on the quarter-deck, Zachary was upending a ditty-bag on his bunk, looking for some clothes to give to Jodu, when along with a heap of banyans, shirts and trowsers, something he had long given up for lost came tumbling out— his old penny-whistle. Zachary grinned as he reached for it: this was beyond praise, it seemed like a sign, a portent of good things to come. Forgetting all about the errand that had brought him to his cabin, he put the whistle to his lips and began to play 'Heave Away Cheerily', one of his favourite sea-shanties.

It was this tune, as much as the sound of the instrument, that arrested Baboo Nob Kissin's hand just as it was about to knock on the cabin door. He froze, listening intently, and soon every inch of his upraised arm was prickling with gooseflesh.

For more than a year now, ever since the untimely death of the woman who had been his spiritual preceptor and Guruma, Baboo Nob Kissin's heart had been filled with premonitory foreboding: Ma Taramony, as she was known to her disciples, had promised him that his awakening was at hand and had told him to watch carefully for its signs, which were sure to be manifested in the unlikeliest places and in the most improbable forms. He had promised her that he would do his best to keep his mind open, and his senses watchful, so that the signs would not elude him when they were revealed—yet, now, despite his best efforts, he could not believe the evidence of his own ears. Was it really a flute, Lord Krishna's own instrument, that had started to play, just as he, Nob Kissin Pander, stepped up to the door of this cabin and raised his hand? It seemed impossible, but there could be no denying it—just as there was no denying that the tune, although unfamiliar in itself, was set to Gurjari, one of the most favoured ragas for the singing of the Dark Lord's songs. So long, and so anxiously, had Baboo Nob Kissin awaited the sign that now, as the tune breathed itself to an end and a hand made itself heard on the doorknob inside, he fell to his knees and covered his eyes, trembling in fear of what was imminently to be revealed.

This was why Zachary all but tripped over the gomusta's kneeling body as he made to leave his cabin with a banyan and a pair of trowsers tucked under his arm. 'Hey!' he said, gaping in surprise at the stout, dhoti-clad man who was crouching in the gangway with his hands over his eyes. 'What the hell you doin down there?'

Like the leaves of some shrinking, touch-averse plant, the gomusta's fingers prised themselves apart, to allow a full view of the figure that had appeared in front of him. His first response was one of intense disappointment: he had heeded well his preceptor's warning, that the message of awakening might be delivered by the unlikeliest of messengers, but he still could not bring himself to believe that Krishna—whose very name meant 'black' and whose darkness had been celebrated in thousands of songs, poems and names—would choose as his emissary someone of so pale a cast of countenance, one who showed no trace of the monsoonal tint of Ghanshyam, the Cloud-Dark Lord. And yet, even as he was yielding to his disappointment, Baboo Nob Kissin could not help but notice that the face was comely, not unbecoming of an emissary of the Slayer of Milkmaids' Hearts, and the eyes were dark and quick, so that it was not too great a stretch to imagine them as night-birds drinking from the moonlit pool of a maiden's love-thirsty lips. And surely it was, if not quite a sign, then at least a minor indication that his shirt was yellowish, of the same colour as the clothes in which the Joyful Lord was known to disport himself with the lovelorn girls of Brindavan? And it was true too that the shirt was stained with sweat, as Careless Krishna's was said to be after the fatigue of a tumultuous love-making. Could it be, then, that this ivory-tinted Rupa was exactly what Ma Taramony had warned him of: a Guise, wrapped in veils of illusion by the Divine Prankster, so as to test the quality of his devotee's faith? But even then, surely there would be some additional sign, some other mark . . .?

The gomusta's protuberant eyes started further forward in his head as a pale hand came winding down to help him to his feet. Could this be a limb blessed by the Butter-Thieving Lord himself? Snatching at the proffered limb, Baboo Nob Kissin turned it over, examining the palm, the lines, the knuckles—but nowhere was a trace of darkness to be seen except beneath the nails.

The intensity of this scrutiny, and the eye-rolling that accompanied it, caused Zachary no little alarm. 'Hey, quit that!' he said. 'What're you lookin at?'

Choking back his disappointment, the gomusta released the hand. No matter: if the Guise was who he thought him to be, then a sign was sure to be concealed somewhere else on his person—it was just a question of guessing where it was. A thought occurred to him: could it be that to compound the deception, the Master of Mischief had chosen to give his emissary an attribute that belonged properly to the Blue-Throated Lord—Shiva Neel-Kunth?

In the urgency of the moment, this seemed self-evident to Nob Kissin Baboo: heaving himself tremulously to his feet, the gomusta made a grab at the fastened collar of Zachary's shirt.

Startled as he was by the gomusta's lunge, Zachary was quick enough to slap his hand away. 'What you gettin up to?' he cried in disgust. 'You crazy or somethin?'

Chastened, the gomusta dropped his hands. 'Nothing, sir,' he said, 'just only searching to see if kunth is blue.'

'If what is *what*?' Raising his fists, Zachary squared his shoulders. 'You cussin me now?'

The gomusta shrank back in dread, amazed at the dexterity with which the Guise had assumed the Warrior's stance. 'Please sir—no offence. Myself only Burnham-sahib's accountant. Good-name is Baboo Nob Kissin Pander.'

'And what're you doin here, on the quarter-deck?'

'Burra sahib has sent to get ship's papers from your kind self. Logs, crew manifests, all-type papers are required for insurance purposes.'

'Wait here,' said Zachary gruffly, slipping back into his cuddy. He had prepared the papers already, so it took no more than a moment to fetch them. 'Here they are.'

'Thank you, sir.'

Zachary was disconcerted to note that the gomusta was still examining his throat with all the intensity of a professional strangler. 'You'd best be on your way, Pander,' he said curtly. 'I've got other business to take care of now.'

~

In the gloom of the dabusa, Jodu and Paulette were holding each other tight, as they so often had in their childhood, except that they had never then had to reach around the stiff, crackling barrier of a dress like the one she was now wearing.

He scratched the rim of her bonnet with a fingernail: You look so different . . .

He had half-expected that she wouldn't understand, that she had lost her Bengali since he'd seen her last. But when she answered it was in the same language: You think I look different? she said. But it's you who's changed. Where were you all this while?

I was in the village, he said. With Ma. She was very sick.

She gave a start of surprise: Oh? And how is Tantima now?

He buried his face in her shoulder and she felt a tremor running up the sinews of his back. Suddenly alarmed, she pulled his nearly-naked body still closer, trying to warm him with her arms. His loincloth was still wet and she could feel the dampness seeping through the folds of her dress. Jodu! she said. What's happened? Is Tantima all right? Tell me.

She died, said Jodu through his clenched teeth. Two nights ago . . .

She died! Now Paulette lowered her head too, so that they each had their noses buried in the other's neck. I can't believe it, she whispered, wiping her eyes on his skin.

She was thinking of you to the last, said Jodu, sniffing. You were always . . .

He was cut short by a cough and the clearing of a throat.

Paulette felt Jodu stiffen even before the sound of the intrusion reached her ears. Pulling free of his arms, she spun around and found herself face to face with a sharp-eyed, curly-haired young man in a faded yellow shirt.

Zachary too was taken utterly by surprise, but he was the first to recover. 'Hullo there, Miss,' he said, sticking out a hand. 'I'm Zachary Reid, the second mate.'

'I'm Paulette Lambert,' she managed to say, as she was shaking his hand. Then in a rush of confusion, she added: 'I witnessed the mishap from the rivage, and I came to see what had happened to the unfortunate victim. I was much concerned about his fate . . .'

'So I see,' said Zachary drily.

Now, looking into Zachary's eyes, Paulette's mind brimmed over with wild imaginings of what he must think of her, and of what Mr Burnham would do when he learnt that his memsahib-in-the-making had been discovered in an embrace with a native boatman. A stream of exonerating lies tumbled through her head: that she had fainted because of the stench of the 'tween-deck, that she had stumbled in the darkness: but none of these would be as convincing, she knew, as to say that Jodu had assaulted her and taken her unawares—and that she could never do.

But oddly, Zachary did not seem to be disposed to make much of what he had seen: far from giving vent to an explosion of sahib-ish outrage, he was going quietly about the errand that had brought him to the 'tween-deck, which was to hand Jodu a set of clothes—a shirt and a pair of canvas trowsers.

After Jodu had stepped away to change, it was Zachary who broke the awkward silence: 'I take it you're acquainted with this gawpus of a boatman?'

Faced with this, Paulette could not bring herself to mouth any of the fictions that were bubbling in her head. 'Mr Reid,' she said, 'you were no doubt shocked to find me in an embracement of such intimacy with a native. But I assure you there is nothing compromising. I am able to explicate all.'

'Not necessary,' said Zachary.

'But yes indeed, I must explain,' she said. 'If for no other reason, then only to show you the depth of my gratitude for your saving of him. You see, Jodu, who you rescued, is the son of the woman who brought me up. Our growing was together; he is like my brother. It was as a sister that I was holding him, for he has suffered a great loss. He is the only family I have in this world. All this will seem strange to you no doubt . . .'

'Not at all,' he said, shaking his head. 'Miss Lambert, I know very well how such a connection might arise.'

She noticed that there was a tremor in his voice, as if to indicate that her story had touched a chord in him. She laid a hand on his arm. 'But please,' she said guiltily, 'you must not speak of it to others. There are some, you know, who might look askance upon the chouteries of a memsahib and a boatman.'

'I'm good with secrets, Miss Lambert,' he said. 'I won't blow the gaff on you. You can be sure of that.'

Paulette heard a footfall behind her and turned away to find Jodu standing there, dressed in a blue sailor's banyan and a pair of old canvas trowsers. This was the first time Paulette had ever seen him in anything but lungis and gamchhas, vests and chadars—and because she was looking at him anew she saw also how much he had changed since she had seen him last: he had grown leaner, taller, stronger, and she could see in his face the shadow of what he had almost become, a man, and thus necessarily a stranger: this was deeply unsettling, for she could not imagine that she would ever know anyone as well as she had known Jodu. In other circumstances, she would have started at once to tease him, with the peculiar savagery they had always reserved for each other, when either of them had shown signs of taking too long a step outside the boundaries of their intimate universe: what a setting-to they would have had, a fierce bout of baiting and mockery that would have ended in slaps and scratches—but here, constrained by Zachary's presence, all she could do was give him a smile and a nod.

As for Jodu, his eyes went from Paulette's face to Zachary's and he knew at once, from the stiffness of their attitudes, that something of significance had passed between them. Having lost everything he owned, he had no qualms in using their new-found friendship to his advantage. *O ké bol to ré*, he said in Bengali to Paulette: Tell him to find me a place on this ship's lashkar. Tell him I have nowhere to go, nowhere to live—and it's their fault, for running down my boat . . .

Here Zachary broke in. 'What's he saying?'

'He says that he would like to gain a place on this ship,' said Paulette. 'Now that his boat is destroyed, he has nowhere to go . . .'

As she was speaking, her hands had risen to toy with the ribbons of her bonnet: in her awkwardness she presented a picture that was so arresting to Zachary's starved eyes that there was nothing he would not have done for her at that moment. She was, he knew, the boon promised by the rediscovery of his penny-whistle, and if she had asked him to throw himself at her feet or take a running jump into the river, he would have paused only to say: 'Watch me do it.' An eager flush rose to his face as he said: 'Consider it done, Miss: you can count on me. I will speak to our serang. A place on the crew won't be hard to arrange.'

Just then, as if summoned by the mention of his office, Serang Ali came stepping down the ladder. Zachary lost no time in drawing him aside: 'This fellow here is out of a job. Since we've sunk his boat and given him a laundering, I think we have to take him on, as a ship's-boy.' Here, Zachary's eyes strayed back to Paulette, who flashed him a smile of gratitude. Neither this, nor the shy grin with which it was reciprocated, eluded Serang Ali's notice; his eyes narrowed in suspicion.

'Malum hab cuttee he head?' he said. 'What for wanchee this-piece boy? He blongi boat-bugger—no can learn ship-pijjin. Better he wailo chop-chop.'

Zachary's voice hardened. 'Serang Ali,' he said sharply; 'I don need no explateratin here: I'd like you to do this, please.'

Serang Ali's eyes darted resentfully from Paulette to Jodu before he gave his reluctant assent. 'Sabbi. Fixee alla propa.'

'Thank you,' said Zachary with a nod, and his chin rose in pride as Paulette stepped up to whisper in his ear: 'You are too kind, Mr Reid. I feel I should give you an explanation more complete—for what you have seen, of me and Jodu.'

He gave her a smile that made her sway on her feet. 'You don't owe me no explanation,' he said softly.

'But maybe we can speak—as friends, perhaps?'

'I would be . . .'

Then suddenly Mr Doughty's voice went booming through the hold: 'Is that the gooby you fished out of the water today, Reid?' His eyes bulged as they took in Jodu's newly-clothed form. 'Well I'll be damned if the blackguard hasn't squeezed his wedding-tackle into a pair of trowsers? There he was, a naked little cockup half a puhur ago, and now he's tricked out like a wordy-wallah!'

~

'Ah! I see you've met,' said Mr Burnham as Zachary and Paulette emerged from the booby-hatch into the heat of the sunlit deck.

'Yes, sir,' said Zachary, taking good care to keep his eyes away from Paulette, who was holding her bonnet over the spot where her dress had been dampened by Jodu's wet loincloth.

'Good,' said Mr Burnham, reaching for the ladder that led to his caique. 'And now we must be off. Come along now—Doughty, Paulette. You too, Baboo Nob Kissin.'

At the mention of this name Zachary glanced over his shoulder and was perturbed to see that the gomusta had cornered Serang Ali and was conferring with him in a manner so furtive, and with so many glances in his own direction, that there could be no doubt of who was being talked about. But the annoyance of this was not enough to eclipse his pleasure in shaking Paulette's hand again. 'Hope we'll meet again soon, Miss Lambert,' he said softly as he released his hold on her fingers.

'Me also, Mr Reid,' she said, lowering her eyes. 'It would give me much pleasure.'

Zachary lingered on deck until the caique had faded completely from view, trying to fix in his mind the lineaments of Paulette's face, the sound of her voice, the leaf-scented smell of her hair. It was not till much later that he remembered to ask Serang Ali about his conversation with the gomusta: 'What was that man talkin to you about—what's his name? Pander?'

Serang Ali directed a contemptuous jet of spit over the deck rail. 'That bugger blongi too muchi foolo,' he said. 'Wanchi sabbi allo foolo thing.'

'Like what?'

'He ask: Malum Zikri likee milk? Likee ghee? Ever hab stole butter?'

'Butter?' Zachary began to wonder whether the gomusta was not some kind of investigator, looking into a report of misplaced or manarveled provisions. Yet, why would he concern himself with butter of all things? 'Why the hell'd he ask bout that?'

Serang Ali tapped his knuckles on his head. 'He blongi too muchi sassy bugger.'

'What'd you tell him?'

'Told: how-fashion Malum Zikri drinki milk in ship? How can catch cow on sea?'

'Was that all?'

Serang Ali shook his head. 'Also he ask—hab Malum ever changi colour?'

'Change colour?' Suddenly Zachary's knuckles tightened on the deck rail. 'What the devil did he mean?'

'He say: Sometimes Malum Zikri turn blue, no?'

'And what'd you say?'

'I say: maski, how-fashion Malum blue can be? He is sahib no? Pink, red, all can do—but blue no can.'

'Why's he asking all these questions?' said Zachary. 'What's he up to?'

'No need worry,' said Serang Ali. 'He too muchi foolo.'

Zachary shook his head. 'I don't know,' he said. 'He may not be as much of a fool as you think.'

~

Deeti's intuition that her husband would not be able to go back to work was soon confirmed. Hukam Singh's condition, after his seizure at the factory, was so enfeebled that he had not the strength to protest even when she took away his pipe and his brass box. But instead of initiating an improvement, deprivation provoked a dramatic turn for the worse: he could neither eat nor sleep and he soiled himself so often that his bed had to be moved out of doors. Drifting in and out of consciousness, he would scowl and mutter in incoherent rage: Deeti knew that if he had possessed the strength, he would not have stopped at killing her.

A week later, Holi arrived, bringing neither colour nor laughter to Deeti's home: with Hukam Singh muttering deliriously on his bed, she did not have the heart to step outside. In Chandan Singh's house, across the fields, people were drinking bhang and shouting '*Holi hai*!' The joyful cheers prompted Deeti to send her daughter over, to join in the fun— but even Kabutri had no appetite for merrymaking and was back within the hour.

As much to keep up her own spirits as to ease her husband's suffering, Deeti exerted herself to find a cure. First she brought in an ojha to exorcise the house, and when this produced no effect, she consulted a hakim, who purveyed Yunani medicines, and a vaid who practised Ayurveda. The doctors spent long hours sitting at Hukam Singh's bedside and consumed great quantities of satua and dalpuris; they dug their fingertips into the patient's stick-like wrists and exclaimed over his pallid skin; they prescribed expensive medicines, made with gold foil and shavings of ivory, to obtain which Deeti had to sell several of her bangles and nose-rings. When the treatments failed, they confided secretly that Hukam Singh was not long for this world, one way or another—why not ease his passage by allowing him a taste of the drug his body craved? Deeti had decided never to return her husband's pipe and she was true to her resolve; but she relented to the point where she allowed him a few mouthfuls of akbari opium to chew on every day. These doses were not enough to bring him to his feet, but they did ease his suffering and for Deeti, it was a relief to look into his eyes and know that he had slipped away from the mundane pains of the world and escaped into that other, more vivid reality where Holi never ceased and spring arrived afresh every day. If that was what was necessary to postpone the prospect of widowhood, then she was not the woman to flinch from it.

In the meanwhile there was the harvest to attend to: within a short frame of time each poppy would have to be individually incised and bled of its sap; the coagulated gum would then have to be scraped off and collected in earthenware gharas, to be taken to the factory. It was slow, painstaking work, impossible for a woman and child to undertake on their own. Being unwilling to ask for her brother-in-law's help, Deeti was forced to hire a half-dozen hands, agreeing to pay them in kind when the harvest was done. While they were at work she had often to be away, to attend to her husband, and thus could not keep as close a watch as she would have liked: the result, predictably, was that her tally of sap-filled jars was a third less than she had expected. After paying the workers, she decided it wouldn't be wise to entrust the delivery of her jars to anyone else: she sent word to Kalua to come around with his ox-cart.

By this time Deeti had abandoned the thought of paying for a new roof with the proceeds of her poppies: she would have been content to earn enough to provide provisions for the season, with perhaps a handful or two of cowries for other expenses. The best she could hope for, she knew, was to come away from the factory with a couple of silver rupees; with luck, depending on the prices in the bazar, she might then have two or three copper dumrees left—maybe even as much as an adhela, to spend on a new sari for Kabutri.

But a rude surprise was waiting at the Carcanna: after her gharas of opium had been weighed, counted and tested, Deeti was shown the account book for Hukam Singh's plot of land. It turned out that at the start of the season, her husband had taken a much larger advance than she had thought: now, the meagre proceeds were barely enough to cover his debt. She looked disbelievingly at the discoloured coins that were laid before her: *Aho se ka karwat?* she cried. Just six dams for the whole harvest? It's not enough to feed a child, let alone a family.

The muharir behind the counter was a Bengali, with heavy jowls and a cataract of a frown. He answered her not in her native Bhojpuri, but in a mincing, citified Hindi: Do what others are doing, he snapped. Go to the moneylender. Sell your sons. Send them off to Mareech. It's not as if you don't have any choices.

I have no sons to sell, said Deeti.

Then sell your land, said the clerk, growing peevish. You people always come here and talk about being hungry, but tell me, who's ever seen a peasant starve? You just like to complain, all the time khichir-michir . . .

On the way home, Deeti decided to stop at the bazar

anyway: having hired Kalua's cart, it made no sense now to return without any provisions. As it turned out, she was able to afford no more than a two-maund sack of broken rice, thirty seers of the cheapest arhar dal, a couple of tolas of mustard oil and a few chittacks of salt. Her frugality was not lost on the shopkeeper who happened to be also a prominent seth and moneylender. What's happened-ji, O my sister-in-law? he said, with a show of concern. Do you need a few nice bright Benarsi rupees to see you through till the shravan harvest?

Deeti resisted the offer till she thought of Kabutri: after all, the girl had just a few years left at home—why make her live through them in hunger? She gave in and agreed to place the impression of her thumb on the seth's account book in exchange for six months' worth of wheat, oil and gurh. Only as she was leaving did it occur to her to ask how much she owed and what the interest was. The seth's answers took her breath away: his rates were such that her debt would double every six months; in a few years, all the land would be forfeit. Better to eat weeds than to take such a loan: she tried to return the goods but it was too late. I have your thumbprint now, said the seth, gloating. There's nothing to be done.

On the way home Deeti sat bowed with worry and forgot about Kalua's fare. By the time she remembered he was long gone. But why hadn't he reminded her? Had things come to the point where she had become an object of pity for a carrion-eating keeper of oxen?

Inevitably, word of Deeti's plight filtered across the fields to Chandan Singh, who appeared at her door with a sackful of nourishing satua. For her daughter's sake, if not her own, Deeti could not refuse, but once having accepted, nor could she shut the door on her brother-in-law with the same finality as before. After this, on the pretext of visiting his brother, Chandan Singh took to invading her home with increasing frequency. Although he had never before shown any interest in Hukam Singh's condition, he now began to insist on his right to enter the house in order to sit beside his brother's bed. But once past the door, he paid no attention to his brother and had eyes only for Deeti: even as he was entering he would brush his hand against her thigh. Sitting on his brother's bed, he would look at her and fondle himself through the folds of his dhoti; when Deeti knelt to feed Hukam Singh, he would lean so close as to brush her breasts with his knees and elbows. His advances became so aggressive that Deeti took to hiding a small knife in the folds of her sari, fearing that he might attack her, right on her husband's bed.

The assault, when it came, was not physical, but rather an admission and an argument. He cornered her inside the very room where her husband was lying supine on his bed. Listen to me, Kabutri-ki-ma, he said. You know very well how your daughter was conceived—why pretend? You know that you would be childless today if not for me.

Be quiet, she cried. I won't listen to another word.

It's only the truth. He nodded dismissively at his brother's bed. He couldn't have done it then any more than he can now. It was me; no one else. And that is why I say to you: wouldn't it be best for you to do willingly now what you did before without your knowledge? Your husband and I are brothers after all, of the same flesh and blood. Where is the shame? Why should you waste your looks and your youth on a man who cannot enjoy them? Besides, the time is short while your husband is still alive—if you conceive a son while he is still living, he will be his father's rightful heir. Hukam Singh's land will pass to him and no one will have the right to dispute it. But you know yourself that as things stand now, my brother's land and his house will become mine on his death. *Jekar khet, tekar dhán*—he who owns the land, owns the rice. When I become master of this house, how will you get by except at my pleasure?

With the back of his hand, he wiped the corners of his mouth: This is what I say to you, Kabutri-ki-ma: why not do willingly now what you will be compelled to do a short while hence? Don't you see that I'm offering you your best hope for the future? If you keep me happy, you will be well looked after.

There was a part of Deeti's mind that acknowledged the reasonableness of this proposal—but by this time her loathing of her brother-in-law had reached such a pitch that she knew she would not be able to make her own body obey the terms of the bargain, even if she were to accede to it. Following her instincts, she dug her elbow into his bony chest and pushed him aside; baring just enough of her face to expose her eyes, she bit the hem of her sari, drawing it aslant across her face. What kind of devil, she said, can speak like this in front of his own dying brother? Listen to my words: I will burn on my husband's pyre rather than give myself to you.

He drew back a step and his slack mouth curled into a mocking smile. Words are cheap, he said. Do you think it's easy for a worthless woman like you to die as a sati? Have you forgotten that your body ceased to be pure on the day of your wedding?

All the more reason then, she said, to burn it in the fire. And it will be easier than to live as you say.

Big-big words, he said. But don't depend on me to stop you, if you try to make yourself a sati. Why should I? To have a sati in the family will make us famous. We'll build a temple for you and grow rich on the offerings. But women like you are all words: when the time comes, you'll escape to your family.

*Dikhatwa*! We'll see, she said, slamming the door in his face.

Once the idea had been planted in her mind, Deeti could think of little else: better by far to die a celebrated death than to be dependent on Chandan Singh, or even to return to her own village, to live out her days as a shameful burden on her brother and her kin. The more she thought about it, the more persuasive the case—even where it concerned Kabutri. It was not as if she could promise her daughter a better life by staying alive as the mistress and 'keep' of a man of no account, like Chandan Singh. Precisely because he was her daughter's natural father, he would never allow the girl to be the equal of his other children—and his wife would do everything in her power to punish the child for her parentage. If she remained here, Kabutri would be little more than a servant and working-woman for her cousins; far better to send her back to her brother's village, to be brought up with his children—a lone child would not be a burden. Deeti had always got on well with her brother's wife, and knew that she would treat her daughter well. When looked at in this way, it seemed to Deeti that to go on living would be nothing more than selfishness—she could only be an impediment to her daughter's happiness.

A few days later, with Hukam Singh's condition growing steadily worse, she learnt that some distant relatives were travelling to the village where she was born: they agreed readily when she asked them to deliver her daughter to the house of her brother, Havildar Kesri Singh, the sepoy. The boat was to leave in a few hours and the pressure of time made it possible for Deeti to remain dry-eyed and composed as she tied Kabutri's scant few pieces of clothing in a bundle. Among her few remaining pieces of jewellery were an anklet and a bangle: these she fastened on her daughter, with instructions to hand them over to her aunt: She'll look after them for you.

Kabutri was overjoyed at the prospect of visiting her cousins and living in a household filled with children. How long will I stay there? she asked.

Until your father gets better. I'll come to get you.

When the boat sailed away, with Kabutri in it, it was as if Deeti's last connection with life had been severed. From that moment she knew no further hesitation: with her habitual care, she set about making plans for her own end. Of all her concerns, perhaps the least pressing was that of being consumed by the cremation fire: a few mouthfuls of opium, she knew, would render her insensible to the pain.

seven

~

Well before he looked at the papers that Zachary had given him, Baboo Nob Kissin knew that they would provide the sign he needed to confirm what was already clear in his heart. So confident was he of this, that on the way back from Bethel, in his caranchie, he was already dreaming of the temple he had promised to build for Ma Taramony: it would sit upon the edge of a waterway and it would have a soaring, saffron-coloured spire. There would be a wide, paved threshold in front, where great numbers of devotees could assemble, to dance, sing and worship.

It was in just such a temple that Nob Kissin Baboo had spent much of his own childhood, some sixty miles north of Calcutta. His family's temple was in the town of Nabadwip, a centre of piety and learning consecrated to the memory of Chaitanya Mahaprabhu—saint, mystic, and devotee of Sri Krishna. One of the gomusta's ancestors, eleven generations removed, was said to have been among the saint's earliest disciples: he had founded the temple, which had been tended ever since by his descendants. Nob Kissin himself had once been in line to succeed his uncle as the temple's custodian, and in his boyhood he had been carefully groomed for his inheritance, being given a thorough education in Sanskrit and logic, as well as in the performance of rites and rituals.

When Nob Kissin was fourteen his uncle fell ill. Summoning the boy to his bedside, the old man had entrusted him with one last duty—his days were drawing to a close, he said, and it was his wish that his young wife, Taramony, be sent to an ashram in the holy city of Brindavan, to live out her widowhood: the journey being difficult and dangerous, he wanted Nob Kissin to escort her there personally before assuming his duties in the family temple.

It will be done, said Nob Kissin, touching his uncle's feet, you need say no more.

A few days later, the old man died, and shortly afterwards Nob Kissin set off for Brindavan, with his widowed aunt and a small retinue of servants. Although Nob Kissin was well past the usual age of marriage, he was still a brahmachari—a virginal celibate—as befitted a student who was undergoing the rigours of an old-fashioned education. The widow, as it happened, was not much older than Nob Kissin, for her late husband had married her only six years before, in a final effort to beget an heir. Through those years, Nob Kissin had rarely had occasion to meet or speak with his aunt, for he was often away, living with his gurus, in their tols, pathshalas and ashrams. But now, as the party travelled slowly westwards, towards Brindavan, the boy and his aunt were inevitably often in each other's company. That his aunt was a woman of uncommon charm and comeliness, Nob Kissin had always known—but he discovered now, to his astonishment, that she was also a person of extraordinary spiritual accomplishment, a devotee of a kind that he had never encountered before: one who spoke of the Lotus-Eyed Lord as if she had personally experienced the grace of his presence.

As a student and a brahmachari, Nob Kissin had been trained to turn his mind from sensual thoughts; in his education, so much stress was laid on the retention of semen that it was rarely, if ever, that the image of a woman succeeded in penetrating his mental defences. But now, rattling and rolling towards Brindavan, in a succession of boats and carriages, the boy's defences crumbled. Never once did Taramony permit him to touch her in an unchaste way—yet he would find himself trembling in her presence; at times his body would go into a kind of seizure, leaving him drenched in shame. At first he was merely confused and could think of no words to describe what was happening to him. Then he understood that his feeling for his aunt was but a profane version of what she herself felt for the divine lover of her visions; he understood also that only her tutelage could cure him of his bondage to his earthly desires.

I can never leave your side, he told her. I cannot abandon you in Brindavan. I would rather die.

She laughed and told him he was a foolish, vain fellow; Krishna was her only man, she said, the only lover she would ever have.

No matter, he said. *You* will be my Krishna and I will be your Radha.

She said incredulously: And you will live with me without touching me, without knowing my body, without knowing any other woman?

Yes, he said. Isn't that how you are with Krishna? Isn't that how the Mahaprabhu was?

And what of children?

Did Radha have children? Did any of the Vaishnav saints?

And your duties to your family? To the temple? What of all that?

I care nothing for such things, he said. *You* will be my temple and I will be your priest, your worshipper, your devotee.

When they reached the town of Gaya, she gave her assent: slipping away from their retainers, they turned around and made their way to Calcutta.

Although neither of them had been to the city before, they were not without resources. Nob Kissin still had their travel funds in his possession, as well as the silver that was to have provided the endowment for Taramony's incarceration in Brindavan. Put together, the sum was quite substantial, and it allowed them to rent a small house in Ahiritola, an inexpensive waterfront neighbourhood of Calcutta: there they took up residence, making no pretence of being anything other than they were, a widowed woman living with her nephew.

No scandal ever attached to them, for Taramony's saintliness was so patently evident that she soon attracted a small circle of devotees and followers. Nob Kissin would have loved nothing better than to join this circle: to call her 'Ma', to be accepted as a disciple, to spend his days receiving spiritual instruction from her—this was all he wanted, but she would not allow it. You are different from the others, she told him, yours is a different mission; you must go into the world and make money—not just for our upkeep but as an endowment for the temple that you and I will build one day.

At her bidding, Nob Kissin went out into the city where his shrewdness and intelligence did not go long unnoticed. While working at the counter of a moneylender, in Rajabazar, he discovered that keeping accounts was no great challenge for someone of his education; having mastered it, he decided that his best hope for advancement lay in finding a place with one of the city's many English firms. To this end, he began to attend tutorial meetings in the house of a Tamil dubash—a translator who worked for Gillanders & Company, a big trading agency. He quickly established himself as one of the best students in the group, stringing together sentences with a fluency that astounded his master as well as his fellow pupils.

One recommendation led to another and one job to the next: starting as a serishta at Gillanders', Nob Kissin rose to become, successively, a carcoon at the Swinhoe factory, a cranny at Jardine & Matheson, a munshi at Ferguson Bros., and a mootsuddy at Smoult & Sons. It was from there that he found his way into the offices of Burnham Bros. where he rose quickly to the rank of gomusta and was entrusted with the shipping of migrant labour.

It was not just for his acumen and his fluency in English that Baboo Nob Kissin's employers valued his services: they appreciated also his eagerness to please and his apparently limitless tolerance of abuse. Unlike many others, he never took offence if a sahib called him a dung-brained gubberhead, or compared his face to a bandar's bunghole; if shoes or paperweights were hurled his way, then he would merely step aside, displaying a surprising agility for a man of his girth and weight. Insults he would endure with a detached, almost pitying smile: the one thing that put him out of countenance was to be struck by his employer's shoes or feet—which was scarcely to be wondered at, since such blows necessitated the inconvenience of a bath and a change of clothes. Indeed, he twice switched jobs to rid himself of employers who were too much in the habit of kicking their local staff. This too was one of the reasons why he found his present position particularly congenial: Mr Burnham might be a hard-driving man and a difficult taskmaster, but he never kicked or beat his employees and rarely swore. It was true that he often mocked his gomusta by addressing him as 'my Nut-Kissing Baboon' and the like, but he was generally careful to avoid these familiarities in public—and 'baboon', in any case, was not a term to which Baboo Nob Kissin could really object, since that creature was but an avatar of Lord Hanuman.

While furthering his employer's interests, Baboo Nob Kissin had not neglected to pursue a few opportunities of his own. Since much of his work consisted in acting as an intermediary and facilitator, he had acquired, over time, a wide circle of friends and acquaintances, many of whom relied on him for advice in matters pecuniary and personal. In time, his role as adviser turned into a thriving moneylending operation, often resorted to by gentlefolk who were in need of a discreet and reliable source of funding. There were some who came to him also for help in matters still more intimate: abstinent in all things but food, Baboo Nob Kissin regarded the carnal appetites of others with the detached curiosity with which an astrologer might observe the movements of the stars. He was unfailingly attentive to the women who appealed to him for assistance—and they in turn found him easy to trust, knowing that his devotion to Taramony would prevent him from exacting favours for himself. It was thus that Elokeshi had come to regard him as an indulgent and kindly uncle.

Yet, for all his success, there was one great sorrow in the gomusta's life: the experience of divine love that he had hoped to achieve with Taramony had been denied him by the pressing exigencies of his career. The house he shared with her was large and comfortable, but when he returned to it, at the end of the day, it was usually to find her surrounded by a circle of disciples and devotees. These hangers-on would linger late into the night, and in the morning, when the gomusta left for the daftar, his aunt was almost always asleep.

I've worked so hard, he would say to her; I've made plenty of money. When will you set me free from this wordly life? When will it be time to build our temple?

Soon enough, she would answer. But not yet. When the moment comes you will know.

Such were her promises and Baboo Nob Kissin accepted without question that they would be redeemed at a time of her choosing. But suddenly one day, with the temple still unbuilt, she was seized by a wasting fever. For the first time in two decades, Baboo Nob Kissin stopped going to work; he banished Ma Taramony's disciples and hangers-on from his house and nursed her himself. When he saw that his devotion was powerless against her disease, he begged her: Take me with you; don't abandon me to live alone in this world. Other than you there is nothing of value in my life; it is a void, an emptiness, an eternity of wasted time. What will I do on this earth without you?

You won't be on your own, she promised him. And your work in this world is not done yet. You must prepare yourself— for your body will be the vessel for my return. There will come a day when my spirit will manifest itself in you, and then the two of us, united by Krishna's love, will achieve the most perfect union—you will become Taramony.

Her words caused a wild surging of hope in his heart. When will that day come? he cried. How will I know?

There will be signs, she said. You must keep careful watch, for the indications may be obscure and unexpected. But when they show themselves, you must not hesitate or hold back: you must follow them wherever they lead, even if they take you across the sea.

You give me your word? he said, falling to his knees. You promise it will not be too long?

You have my word, she replied. A day will come when I will pour myself into you: but till then you must be patient.

How long ago that was! Nine years and fifty weeks had passed since the day of her death and he had continued to live his accustomed life, clothed in the garb of a busy gomusta, working harder and harder, even as he grew ever more weary of the world and his work. As the tenth anniversary of her death approached he had begun to fear for his reason and had come to the decision that if the day passed without any sign yet being manifested, then he would renounce the world and go to Brindavan to live the life of a mendicant. And in making this pledge, he came to be convinced that the moment was at hand, the manifestation was on its way. He had grown so certain of this that now he felt no further anxiety or disquiet: it was at a calm, unhurried pace that he stepped off his caranchie and carried the ship's books into his silent, empty house. Spreading the papers on his bed, he leafed through them one by one until he came to the schooner's original crew manifest. When at last he saw the notation beside Zachary's name—'Black'—he uttered no wild cry of joy—it was rather with a sigh of quiet jubilation that he rested his eyes on the scribbled word that revealed the hand of the Dark Lord. This was the confirmation he needed, he was certain of it—just as he was certain, also, that the messenger himself knew nothing of his mission. Does an envelope know what is contained in the letter that is folded inside it? Is a sheet of paper aware of what is written upon it? No, the signs were contained in the transformation that had been wrought during the voyage: it was the very fact of the world's changeability that proved the presence of divine illusion, of Sri Krishna's leela.

Separating the manifest from the other papers, Baboo Nob Kissin carried it to an almirah and placed it inside. Tomorrow he would roll it up tightly and take it to a coppersmith, to have it encased inside an amulet, so that it could be worn like a necklace. Should Mr Burnham ask for the manifest, he would tell him it was lost—such things happened often enough on long voyages.

As he was closing the almirah, Baboo Nob Kissin's eyes fell on a saffron-coloured alkhalla—one of the long, loose gowns that Taramony had liked to wear. On an impulse, he slipped it on, over his dhoti and kurta, and went over to a looking-glass. He was amazed by how well the robe fitted him. Reaching up to his head he undid the bindings of his tikki, shaking out his hair so that it fell to his shoulders. From now on, he decided, he would never again tie it or cut it; he would leave it open, to grow, so that it hung down to his waist, like Taramony's long, black locks. As he gazed at his own image, he became aware of a glow, spreading slowly through his body, as if it were being suffused by another presence. Suddenly his ears were filled by Taramony's voice: he heard her saying, once again, the words she had spoken in this very room—she was telling him that he must be prepared to follow the signs wherever they led, even across the sea. All at once, everything was clear and he knew why things had happened as they had: it was because the *Ibis* was to take him to the place where his temple would be built.

~

Neel and Raj Rattan were flying kites, on the roof of the Raskhali mansion in Calcutta, when the Commissioner of Police arrived with a detachment of silahdars and darogas. It was early evening, on a hot April day, with the last light of the setting sun shimmering on the Hooghly River. The nearby ghats were crowded with bathers, scrubbing away the dust of the day, and the moss-darkened roofs and terraces around the Raskhali Rajbari were filled with people, out to enjoy the sunset breeze. Everywhere in the neighbourhood conch-shells were sounding, to mark the lighting of the first lamps, and the muezzin's call could be heard at a distance, floating over the city.

When Parimal burst in, Neel's attention was centred on his

kite, which was soaring high on the swirling green breeze of the month of Phalgun: he had no ears for what was said. Huzoor, Parimal repeated himself. You have to go down. He wants you.

Who? said Neel.

The English afsar from the jel-khana—he's come with a police paltan.

The news made little impression on Neel: it often happened that officials from the constabulary came to see him on some matter related to the zemindary. Still intent on his kite, Neel said: What's happened? Has there been a burglary or dacoity nearby? If they want help, tell them to talk with the gomusta-babus.

No, huzoor: it's you they want.

Then they should come back in the morning, Neel said sharply. This is not the time of day to come to a gentleman's house.

Huzoor: they won't listen to us. They insist . . .

Now, with the drum-like spindle of the kite-string still spinning in his hands, Neel shot a glance at Parimal and was surprised to see that he was on his knees, and that his eyes were overflowing. Parimal? he said, in astonishment. *Yeh kya bát hai*? Why are you making such a tamasha? What is going on?

Huzoor, Parimal said again, choking. They want you. They're in the daftar. They were on their way up here. I had to beg them to wait downstairs.

They were coming up here? Neel was speechless for a moment: this part of the roof lay in the most secluded part of the house, above the zenana; it defied credence that an outsider should think of setting foot in it.

Have they gone mad? he said to Parimal. How could they even think of such a thing?

Huzoor, Parimal implored him, they said not to waste time. They're waiting.

All right. Neel was more intrigued than alarmed by the sudden summons, but as he was leaving the roof, he stopped to ruffle Raj Rattan's hair.

Where are you going, Baba? said the boy, impatient of the interruption. Didn't you say we would fly kites till sunset?

And so we will, said Neel. I'll be back in ten minutes. The boy nodded and his attention veered back to his kite as Neel went down the staircase.

At the bottom of the stairs lay the interior courtyard of the zenana, and in crossing this space Neel noticed that a hush had fallen over the house—unaccountably, for this was the time of day when all his elderly aunts, widowed cousins, and other female relatives and dependants were always at their busiest. There were at least a hundred of them in the house, and at this hour they were usually bustling from room to room, with freshly lit lamps and incense, watering the tulsi plants, ringing the bells of the temple, blowing conch-shells and making preparations for the night-time meal. But today the rooms around the courtyard were in darkness, with not a lamp to be seen, and the balustraded verandas were filled with the white-robed figures of his widowed relatives.

Leaving behind the silence of the interior courtyard, Neel stepped into the street-facing part of the compound, where lay the office wing of the house, and the barracks that accommodated the hundred or so guards employed by the Raskhali zemindary. Here too, the spectacle that met Neel's eyes was astonishing in its novelty: on stepping into the open space, he saw that the piyadas, paiks and lathiyals who made up his guard force had been penned into a corner of the grounds by a detachment of armed police. The guards were milling about in confusion, disarmed of their sticks, staves and swords, but on catching sight of the zemindar, they began to shout their cry: *Joi Má Kali! Joi Raskhali!* Neel raised a hand to silence them but their voices grew steadily louder, rising to a roar that rang through the neighbouring streets and alleys. Looking up, Neel saw that the terraces and balconies of the buildings that overlooked the courtyard were jammed with people, all staring down in curiosity. He quickened his pace and went quickly up the stairs that led to his office, on the second floor.

The zemindar's daftar was a large, disorderly room, strewn with furniture and files. As Neel entered, a red-uniformed English officer rose to his feet, with his high-crowned hat tucked under his arm. Neel recognized him at once: his name was Hall and he was a former infantry major who was now in charge of the city's constabulary; he had visited the Raskhali Rajbari several times—sometimes to discuss matters of public security, but also often as a guest.

Neel joined his hands together in greeting, and tried to summon a smile. 'Ah, Major Hall! What can I do for you? Pray allow me to oblige . . .'

The sombre expression on the Major's face remained unchanged as he said, in a stifly official voice: 'Raja Neel Rattan, I regret that it is an unfortunate duty that brings me here today.'

'Oh?' said Neel: he noticed, abstractedly, that the Commissioner of Police was wearing his sword; although he had seen Major Hall in the Rajbari many times, he could not recall that he had ever come armed before. 'And what is the nature of your errand, Major Hall?'

'It is my painful duty to inform you,' the Major said formally, 'that I come bearing a warrant for your arrest.'

'Arrest?' The word was too outlandish to make immediate sense. 'You are here to arrest me?'

'Yes.'

'May I know what for?'

'For the crime of forgery, sir.'

Neel stared at him in incomprehension. 'Forgery? By Jove, sir, I must confess I do not find this the most amusing of jests. What am I said to have forged?'

Reaching into his pocket, the Major laid a piece of paper on an inlaid marble table. Neel did not have to look very closely to know what it was: it was one of the many dozen hundees he had signed over the last year. He smiled: 'This is no forgery, Major. I myself can vouch that it is not a counterfeit.'

The Major's finger descended to indicate a line where the name 'Benjamin Burnham' had been inscribed with a flourish.

'Do you deny, sir,' the Major said, 'that it was you who made this mark?'

'Not for a moment, Major,' Neel said evenly. 'But the matter is easily explained: there exists an agreement between Mr Burnham's firm and the Raskhali zemindary. This is a fact universally known . . .'

So far as Neel knew, the Raskhali hundees had always carried Mr Burnham's name: his gomustas had assured him that this was the time-honoured practice of the old Raja, who had agreed with his partner long ago that there was no need to send every note across town for endorsement—it was quicker and more efficient to have the needful done at the Halder residence. As it happened, the old Raja had never had a good hand in English, and the task had been performed for him by an underling; Neel, being something of a perfectionist in matters of calligraphy, had disliked the secretaries' crude script and had insisted on doing the job himself. All this was well known to Benjamin Burnham.

'I am afraid,' Neel said, 'that you have gone to much trouble for no reason. Mr Burnham will resolve this misunderstanding in a matter of minutes.'

The Major coughed into his fist in embarrassment. 'I am afraid I must still do my duty, sir.'

'But surely,' Neel protested, 'there will be no need, if Mr Burnham explains what happened?'

After a brief pause, the Commissioner said: 'It was Mr Burnham, sir, who alerted us to the crime.'

'What?' Neel gave a start of disbelief. 'But there is no crime . . .'

'This is a forged signature, sir. And there is a great deal of money at stake.'

'To write a man's name is not the same, surely, as forging his signature?'

'That depends on the intent, sir, which is for the court to decide,' said the Major. 'You may be sure that you will be given ample opportunity to make your case.'

'And in the meanwhile?'

'You must permit me to accompany you to Lalbazar.'

'To the jail?' said Neel. 'Like a common criminal?'

'Hardly that,' the Major said. 'We will make sure of your comfort; in consideration of your place in native society, we will even allow you to receive food from home.'

Now, at last, it began to sink in that the inconceivable was about to happen: the Raja of Raskhali was to be taken away by the police and locked in prison. Certain as he was that he would be acquitted, Neel knew that his family's reputation would never again be what it was, not after a crowd of neighbours had witnessed his arrest and forcible removal—all his relatives, his dependants, his son, even Elokeshi, would be mired in the shame.

'Do we have to go now?' Neel demurred. 'Today? In front of all my people?'

'Yes,' said Major Hall, 'I am afraid I can give you no more than a few minutes—to gather some clothes and personal effects.'

'Very well.'

Neel was turning to go when the Major said, sharply: 'I see that your men are in a state of some excitement. You should be aware that in the event of a disturbance, you will be held responsible and your case will suffer in court.'

'I understand,' Neel said. 'You need have no fear.'

The veranda adjoining the zemindar's office looked down upon a courtyard, and as he was stepping out, to make his way downstairs, Neel saw that this enclosure had suddenly turned white: his female relatives and dependants had come pouring out, in their widow's garb; catching sight of him now, they began a soft keening that turned quickly louder and more agitated; some flung themselves on the ground, while others began to beat their breasts. There was no question now of going back to the main house: Neel knew he would not be able to bring himself to force a passage through that throng. He waited just long enough to make sure that his wife, Malati, was not present among the women: even in the confusion of that moment, it was a great relief to know that she had not stepped out of the zenana—he was spared, at least, the humiliation of having the veil of her seclusion torn away.

Huzoor: Parimal appeared beside him, with a bag in hand. I have packed a few things—all that you will need.

Neel reached out in gratitude and squeezed his retainer's hands: all his life, Parimal had known exactly what he needed; often before he himself had known the want, but he had never felt as deeply indebted to him as he did now. He put out a hand to take the bag, but Parimal would not give it to him.

How can you carry your own luggage, huzoor? In front of the world's eyes?

The absurdity of this brought a smile to Neel's lips; he said: Do you know where they're taking me, Parimal?

Huzoor . . . Parimal lowered his voice to a whisper: If you but give the word, our men will fight back. You could escape . . . you could be concealed . . .

For a wild instant, the idea of escape lodged in Neel's mind—but only to vanish, as he recalled the map that hung in his daftar, and the red stain of Empire that had spread so quickly across it. Where would I hide? he said. The piyadas of Raskhali can't fight the battalions of the East India Company. No, there's nothing to be done.

Neel turned away from Parimal to step back into his daftar, where the Major was waiting for him, with a hand on the hilt of his sword. 'I am ready,' said Neel. 'Let us be done with this.'

Ringed by a half-dozen uniformed constables, Neel made his way down the stairs. When he stepped into the courtyard the voices of the white-clad women rose once again to a shriek and they threw themselves at the constables, trying to reach across their batons, to the prisoner. Neel held his head high, but he could not bring himself to meet their gaze; it was only when he was at the gates that he allowed himself to glance back. No sooner did he turn than his eyes met those of his wife, Malati, and it was as if he had never seen her before. The covers had dropped from her ever-veiled face, and she had torn open the bindings of her braids so that her hair lay on her shoulders like a dark shroud of grief. Neel stumbled and lowered his eyes; he could not bear for her to look at him; it was as if the uncovering of her face had stripped the veil from his own manhood, leaving him naked and exposed to the gloating pity of the world, to a shame that could never be overcome.

A covered hackney carriage was waiting in the lane outside and when Neel sat down in it, the Major took the seat opposite his. He was clearly relieved to have accomplished his end without violence, and as the horses began to move, he said, in a kinder tone than he had earlier used: 'I am sure it will all be sorted out quite soon.'

The carriage arrived at the end of the lane, and as it was turning the corner, Neel swivelled in his seat to take a last look at his house. He could see only the roof of the Raskhali Rajbari, and on it, outlined against the dimming sky, his son's head, leaning on a parapet, as if in wait: he recalled that he had said he would be back in ten minutes, and this seemed to him now the most unpardonable of all the lies in his life.

~

Ever since that night by the river, when Deeti had come to his help, Kalua had kept count of the days on which he was granted a glimpse of her, and the empty days in between. The tally was kept neither with any specific intention, nor as an expression of hope—for Kalua knew full well that between her and himself, none but the most tenuous connection could exist—yet the patient enumeration happened in his head whether he liked it or not: he was powerless to make it cease, for his mind, slow and plodding in some respects, had a way of seeking the safety of numbers. Thus it was that when Kalua heard of Deeti's husband's death, he knew that exactly twenty days had elapsed since that afternoon when she asked for his help in bringing Hukam Singh back from the opium factory.

The news came to him by chance: it was evening, and he was on his way back to his dwelling, in his cart, at the end of the day, when he was stopped by two men who were travelling

*Amitav Ghosh*

on foot. Kalua knew they had come a long way because their dhotis were dark with dust and they were leaning heavily on their sticks. They held up their hands as he was passing by, and when his cart rumbled to a stop, they asked if he knew the dwelling of Hukam Singh, the former sepoy. I know it, said Kalua, and he pointed down the road and told them that to get there they would have to walk straight for two kos, and turn left after reaching a large tamarind tree. Then, after following a path through the fields for one hundred and twenty paces, they would have to turn left again, to walk another two hundred and sixty. The men were dismayed: It's almost dark, how will we find these paths? Just keep looking, said Kalua. And how long will it take? An hour, said Kalua, but maybe less.

The men began to plead with him to take them there in his cart: or they would be late, they said, and would miss everything. Late for what? Kalua asked, and the older of the two men said: For Hukam Singh's cremation and . . .

He was about to say something else, when his companion nudged him sharply with his stick.

Has Hukam Singh passed away? Kalua asked.

Yes, late last night. We set out as soon as we heard the news.

All right then, said Kalua. Come. I'll take you there.

The two men climbed on to the rear of the cart and Kalua shook his reins to set his oxen moving. After a good while had passed, Kalua inquired cautiously: And what of Hukam Singh's wife?

Let's see what happens, said the older man. Maybe we'll know tonight . . .

But here again he was interrupted by his companion and the sentence was never finished.

The oddly surreptitious behaviour of the two men set Kalua to wondering whether something untoward was under way. He made it his practice to think hard about everything he saw around him: as the cart rolled down the road, he asked himself why these men, who didn't know Hukam Singh well enough to be aware of the location of his dwelling, would come such a great distance to be present at his cremation. And why was the cremation to be near the dead man's home rather than in the cremation ghat? No: there was something in this that was out of the ordinary. Kalua became more and more convinced of this as they approached their destination—for he saw now that there were a great many others heading towards the same place, more than seemed likely to attend the funeral of a man like Hukam Singh, known by the world to be an incorrigible afeemkhor. When they reached the dwelling, his suspicions deepened, for he saw that the pyre was a great mound of wood, on the banks of the Ganga. Not only was it far larger than was necessary for the cremation of a single man, it was surrounded by a profusion of offerings and objects, as if it were being readied for some larger purpose.

It was dark now, and after the two travellers had alighted, Kalua tethered his ox-cart in a field, some distance away, and returned on foot to the pyre. There were some hundred or so people there, and by listening to their conversations, he soon picked up the whispered sibilance of a word—'sati'. It was all clear now: he understood. He made his way back, in the dark, to his tethered cart, and lay in it a while, to think through his next move. He thought slowly and carefully, examining the merits and drawbacks of several possible courses of action. Only one plan survived the winnowing, and when he rose to his feet again, he knew exactly what he had to do. First, he took the yoke of his oxen and freed them, to wander off along the riverbank: this was the most difficult part of all, for he loved those two animals as if they were his kin. Then, one nail at a time, he ripped the bamboo platform from the axle of his cart, and tied a rope tightly and securely around its middle. The platform was a large unwieldy object, but for Kalua the weight was negligible, and he had no trouble slinging it over his back. Keeping to the shadows, he crept along the river till he came to a sandbank that overlooked the pyre. He laid the bamboo platform on the sand and flattened himself on it, taking care to stay out of sight.

*Amitav Ghosh*

The clearing around the pyre was illuminated by many small fires, so when Hukam Singh's body was carried out of his dwelling, in procession, and laid upon the mound, Kalua had a clear view. Following close behind was a second procession, and upon its entry into the clearing, Kalua saw that it was headed by Deeti, in a resplendent white sari— except that she was slumped over, barely upright: she would not have been able to stand on her own feet, much less walk, had she not been supported by her brother-in-law, Chandan Singh, and several others. Half dragged and half carried, she was brought to the pyre and made to sit cross-legged on it, beside her husband's corpse. Now there was an outbreak of chanting as heaps of kindling were piled around her, and doused with ghee and oil to ready them for the fire.

On the sandbank, Kalua bided his time, counting, counting, to calm himself: his main asset, he knew, was neither his power nor his agility, but rather the element of surprise—for even he, with all his strength, could not hope to fight off fifty men or more. So he waited and waited, until the pyre was lit and everyone was intent upon the progress of the flames. Now, still keeping to the shadows, he crept down to the edge of the crowd and rose to his feet. Unloosing a roar, he began to whirl the bamboo platform above his head, holding it by the end of its rope. The heavy, sharp-edged object became a blur, cracking heads and breaking bones, clearing a path through the crowd— people fled from the hurtling projectile, like cattle scattering before some whirling demon. Racing to the mound, Kalua placed the platform against the fire, scrambled to the top, and snatched Deeti from the flames. With her inert body slung over his shoulder, he jumped back to the ground and ran towards the river, dragging the now-smouldering bamboo rectangle behind him, on its rope. On reaching the water, he thrust the platform into the river and placed Deeti upon it. Then, pushing free of the shore, he threw himself flat on the improvised raft and began to kick his heels in the water, steering out towards midstream. All of this was the work of a minute or two and by the time Chandan Singh and his cohorts gave chase, the river had carried Kalua and Deeti away from the flaming pyre, into the dark of the night.

~

The raft wobbled and spun as the currents swept it downstream, and every once in a while, a slick of water would run streaming over its surface. Under the impact of these dousings, the fog that clouded Deeti's mind began slowly to dispel and she became aware that she was on a river and there was a man beside her, holding her in place with his arm. None of this was surprising, for it was in exactly this way that she had expected to awaken from the flames—afloat in the netherworld, on the Baitarini River, in the custody of Charak, the boatman of the dead. Such was her fear of what she would see that she did not open her eyes: every wave, she imagined, was carrying her closer to the far bank, where the god of death, Jamaraj, held sway.

At length, when the journey showed no signs of ending, she plucked up the courage to ask how long the river was and how far the destination. There was no answer, so she called out the name of the boatman of the dead. Then, through the whisper of a deep, hoarse voice it was made known to her, that she was alive, in the company of Kalua, on the Ganga— and there was no destination or aim to their journey except to escape. Even then she did not feel herself to be living in the same sense as before: a curious feeling, of joy mixed with resignation, crept into her heart, for it was as if she really had died and been delivered betimes in rebirth, to her next life: she had shed the body of the old Deeti, with the burden of its karma; she had paid the price her stars had demanded of her, and was free now to create a new destiny as she willed, with whom she chose—and she knew that it was with Kalua that this life would be lived, until another death claimed the body that he had torn from the flames.

Now there was a soft lapping and grinding, as Kalua nudged the raft to shore, and when it was lodged in the sand, he picked her up in his arms and placed her on the bank. Then, lifting up the raft, he disappeared into a stand of tall rushes, and when he came back to fetch her, she saw that he had laid the platform down in such a way as to turn it into a palette, a small, level island, hidden within the riverbank's greenery. After he had laid her on this bamboo floor, he drew back, as if to retreat and go elsewhere, and she understood that he was afraid, unsure of how she would respond to his presence, now that she was safe on land. She called to him, Kalua, come, don't leave me alone in this unknown place, come here. But when he lay down, she too was afraid: all of a sudden she was aware of how cold her body was, after its long immersion, and of the sopping wetness of her white sari. She began to shiver, and her hand, shaking, came upon his and she knew that he too was trembling, and slowly their bodies inched closer: as each sought the other's warmth, their damp, sodden clothing came unspooled, his langot and her sari. Now it was as though she was on the water again: she remembered his touch and how he had held her to his chest with his arm. On the side of her face that was pressed to his, she could feel the gentle abrasion of his unshaved cheek—on the other side, which was flattened against the deck, she could hear the whispering of the earth and the river, and they were saying to her that she was alive, alive, and suddenly it was as if her body was awake to the world as it had never been before, flowing like the river's waves, and as open and fecund as the reed-covered bank.

Afterwards, when she lay enveloped in his arms, he said, in his rough, hoarse voice: *Ká sochawá?* What're you thinking?

. . . Thinking how you saved me today; *sochat ki tu bacháwelá* . . .

It was myself I saved today, he said in a whisper. Because if you had died, I couldn't have lived; *jinda na rah sakelá* . . .

Shh! Don't say any more. Always superstitious, she shuddered at the mention of death.

But where will we go now? he said. What will we do? They'll hunt for us everywhere, in the cities and the villages.

Although she had no more of a plan than he did, she said: We'll go away, far away, we'll find a place where no one will know anything about us except that we are married.

Married? he said.

Yes.

Squirming out of his arms, she wrapped herself loosely in her sari and went off towards the river. Where are you going? he shouted after her. You'll see, she called over her shoulder. And when she came back, with her sari draped over her body like a veil of gossamer, it was with an armload of wild-flowers, blooming on the bank. Plucking a few long hairs from her head, she strung the flowers together to make two garlands: one she gave to him, and the other she took herself, lifting it up above his head and slipping it around his neck. Now he too knew what to do and when the exchange of garlands had bound them together, they sat for a while, awed by the enormity of what they had done. Then she crept into his arms again and was swept into the embracing warmth of his body, as wide and sheltering as the dark earth.

part two

~

River

# eight

~

Once the *Ibis* had been berthed, Zachary and Serang Ali opened the account books and paid the crew their accumulated addlings. Many of the lascars disappeared immediately into the gullies of Kidderpore, with their copper and silver coins carefully hidden in the folds of their clothing. Some would never see the *Ibis* again, but some were back in a matter of days, having been robbed or cheated, or having squandered their earnings in toddyshacks and knockingdens— or having discovered, simply, that life ashore was far more attractive when you were at sea than when your feet were a-trip on the slick turf of lubber-land.

It would be some time yet before the *Ibis* could be accommodated at the Lustignac dry docks in Kidderpore, where she was to be repaired and refurbished. During the time she was moored in the river, only a skeleton crew remained on board, along with Zachary and Serang Ali. Although shrunken in size, the crew continued to function much as at sea, being divided into two pors, or watches, each of which was headed by a tindal; as at sea, each por was on deck for four hours at a stretch, except during the chhota-pors, which were the two-hour dogwatches of dawn and dusk. The safety of port came at the price of an increased risk of pilferage and theft, so there was no slackening in the vigilance required of the por; nor was there any easing in the pace of work on board, for there were inventories to be made, inspections to be completed and most of all, a great deal of cleaning to be done. Serang Ali made no secret of his view that a sailor who would send his ship untended to the dry dock was worse than the worst shorebound scum, worse than a ma-chowdering pimp.

Gali was one domain of the Laskari tongue in which no one could outdo the serang: in no small measure was it because of the fluency of his swearing that Jodu held him in unbounded respect. It was a matter of great disappointment to him that his regard was entirely unreciprocated.

Jodu knew well enough that freshwater-jacks like himself were held in contempt by ocean-going lascars: often, while rowing past some towering three-master, he had looked up to see a grinning seacunny or kussab shouting taunts, calling him a stick-man—a *dandiwálá*—and spinning out insults about the uses to which sticks could be put. For taunts and jibes, Jodu was well-prepared and would even have been glad of, but the serang would allow no familiarities between him and the other lascars: indeed he lost no opportunity to make it clear that he had taken Jodu into the crew against his will and would prefer to see him gone. If he had to be put up with, at Zachary's insistence, then it would only be as a topas, the lowliest of lascars—a sweeper, to scrub piss-dales, clean heads, wash utensils, scour the decks and the like. To make things as unpleasant as possible, he even made Jodu saw his jharu in half: the shorter the broom, he said, the cleaner the work—this way you'll be so close to the droppings you'll know what the tatti was made of when it went in the mouth. On the serang's right foot, there was a single, carefully-tended toenail, a half-inch in length and filed to a sharp point. When Jodu was on all fours, scouring the deck, the serang would sometimes steal up to kick him: *Chal sálá!* You think it hurts to be spiked in the stern? Be glad it's not a cannon up your gundeck.

During his first weeks on the *Ibis*, the serang would not allow Jodu to go below for any reason other than to clean the heads: even at night, he had to sleep on deck. This was a problem only when it rained, which didn't happen often—at other times, Jodu was by no means the only hand to be looking for the 'softest plank on deck'. It was thus that he was befriended by Roger Cecil David, known as Rajoo-launder to his shipmates. Tall and thin, Rajoo had the upright mien of a tent-pole, and a complexion that almost matched the tarry tint of the schooner's masts. Having been raised in a succession of Christian missions, he liked to wear shirts and trowsers, and was often to be seen in a cloth cap—not for him the lungis and bandhnas of the other lascars. These were ambitious tastes for a ship-launder, and they earned him much derision—not least because his garments were patched together from scraps of sailcloth. The joke about him, in short, was that he was the schooner's third dol—a human mizzenmast—and his forays into the ringeen were often accompanied by much hilarity, with the foretopmen vying with each other to make cracks at his expense. The possibilities of suggestion here were very rich, for unlike sailors elsewhere, lascars often spoke of their ships in the masculine, referring to the vessels' masts as their manhood—the word for which was much the same as the commonly used term for 'ship's-boy', with but a syllable removed.

> . . . *lund to yahā, par launda kahā . . .?*
> . . . here's the prick, but where's the pricker . . .?
> . . . lowering his canvas . . .
> . . . waiting for a blow . . .

Rajoo, for his part, would have been overjoyed to give up his place among the foretopmen—not only because of their jokes, but also because he had no head for heights and was always queasy while aloft. It was his fond ambition to move off the yards, into some position such as as mess-boy, steward, or cook, where his feet would be firmly planted on deck. Since Jodu, on the other hand, wanted nothing more than to be up on the foremast with the trikat-wale, they quickly decided to put their heads together, to make the exchange come about.

It was Rajoo who took Jodu through the cramped companionway that led to the fo'c'sle, where the lascars' hammocks were hung. The lascars' word for this space was *faná*, or hood, as in the outspread crown of a cobra—for if a ship were to be thought of as a sinuous, living creature, then the head was the exact part to which the fana would correspond, being tucked between the bows, below the main deck and above the cutwater, just aft of the fang of the bowsprit. Although he had never before set foot on the exalted precincts of an ocean-going vessel, Jodu was familiar with the word fana, and had often wondered what it would be like to live and sleep inside the skull of the great living creature that was a ship. To be a fana-wala—a fo'c'sleman of the hood—and to live above the taliyamar, forging through the oceans, was the stuff of his dreams: but in the sight that met his eyes now, as he entered the fana, there was nothing of wonder, and certainly no trace of the fabled jewels of a cobra's crown. The fana was airless, hot and dark, with no source of lighting except a single oil-lamp hanging on a hook; in the glow of the sputtering flame, it seemed to Jodu that he had tumbled into some musty cave that was densely festooned with cobwebs—for everywhere he looked there was a webbing of hammocks, hanging in double rows, suspended between wooden beams. The cramped, shallow space had the form of an elliptical triangle, with sides that curved inwards to meet at the bows. In height, it was not quite as tall as a full-grown man, yet the hammocks were hung one above another, no more than sixteen regulation inches apart, so that every man's nose was inches away from a solid barrier: either the ceiling or an arse. Strange to think that these hanging beds were called 'jhulis', as if they were swings, like those given to brides or infants; to hear the word said was to imagine yourself being rocked gently to sleep by a ship's motion—but to see them strung up in front of you, like nets in a pond, was to know that your dreaming hours would be spent squirming like a trapped fish, fighting for space to breathe.

Jodu could not resist climbing into one of the jhulis—but only to leap out again when he caught a noseful of its odour, which consisted not just of the stench of bodies, but of the accumulated smell of sleep itself, compounded of the reek of unwashed bedding, hair-oil, soot, and several months'-worth of dribbles, trickles, leaks, spurts and farts. As luck would have it, the next job to which he was set was that of scrubbing and washing the hammocks: so thoroughly were the jhulis steeped in soot and grime that it seemed to Jodu that not all the water of the Ganga would clean them of the sweat and sin of their former occupants. And when at last the job seemed done, the serang clipped him on the ear, and made him start all over again: Call that clean, do you, you tatter-arsed plugtail of a launder? Many a backslit is cleaner than this.

With his nose in the grime, Jodu yearned to leap up into the ringeen, to be with the trikat-wale, chatting in the crosstrees—not for nothing did lascars call that lofty chair a 'kursi', for that was where they went when they chose to lounge at ease, cooled by the breeze. How wasted was this privilege on Rajoo-launder, who never made use of it—and yet for him, Jodu, to so much as glance aloft was to risk a stinging blow from the serang's foot. To think of all the years he'd spent learning to tell one mast from another, one sail from the next—the *kalmí* from the *dráwal*, the *dastúr* from the *sawái*—all that effort and knowledge wasted while he squatted by the scuppers, washing a fana-ful of jhulis.

Unpleasant though it was, the task had one fortunate consequence: with the fana emptied of its jhulis, all its occupants now had to sleep on the main deck. This was no great trial, for the weather was growing ever hotter, in anticipation of the coming monsoons, and it was better to be out in the open, even if it meant sleeping on wood. What was more, the fresh air seemed to have the effect of loosening everyone's tongue, and the lascars often gossiped late into the night as they lay under the stars.

Serang Ali never joined in these sessions: along with the steward, the silmagoor, the seacunnies, and a few others, he had his quarters not in the fana but the deckhouse. But the serang kept himself aloof, even from the other inhabitants of the deckhouse. This was only partly because he was, by nature, a crusty and unforgiving disciplinarian (no shortcoming in the eyes of the lascars, none of whom liked to serve with serangs who were excessively familiar or played at favourites): the serang stood apart also because of his origins, which were obscure even to those who had served with him longest. But this again was not unusual, for many of the lascars were itinerants and vagrants, who did not care to speak too much about their past; some didn't even know where their origins lay, having been sold off as children to the ghat-serangs who supplied lascars to ocean-going vessels. These riverside crimps cared nothing about who their recruits were and where they came from; all hands were the same to them, and their gangs would kidnap naked urchins from the streets and bearded sadhus from ashrams; they would pay brothel-keepers to drug their clients and thugs to lie in wait for unwary pilgrims.

Yet, varied as they were, most of the lascars on the *Ibis* knew themselves to be from one part or another of the subcontinent. The serang was one of the few exceptions: if asked, he would always say that he was a Muslim from the Arakan, a Rohingya, but there were those who claimed that he had served his launder-hood with a Chinese crew. That he was fluent in Chinese was soon common knowledge, and was regarded as a blessing, for it meant that often, of an evening, the serang would take himself off to the Chinese quarters of Calcutta's docklands, leaving the lascars free to make merry on board.

At times when both Serang Ali and Zachary were gone the *Ibis* was a vessel transformed: someone would be sent aloft to watch for their return, and someone else would be dispatched to fetch a pitcher or two of arrack or doasta; then the whole lashkar would gather, on deck or in the fana, to sing, drink and pass around a few chillums. If there was no ganja at hand, they would burn a few shavings of sailcloth, which was, after all, made from the same plant that had given canvas its name and provided something of a cannabis savour.

The two tindals—Babloo-tindal and Mamdoo-tindal—had served together since their launder-hood: they were as devoted as a pair of nesting cranes although they were from places far apart, one being a Cooringhee Hindu and the other a Shia

Muslim from Lucknow. Babloo-tindal, whose face was pitted with the scars of a childhood duel with smallpox, had a quick pair of hands and a knack for beating out rhythms on the backs of metal pots and khwanchas; Mamdoo-tindal was tall and lissom and when the mood was on him he would doff his lungi and banyan and change into a sari, choli and dupatta; with kohl in his eyes and brass rings dangling from his ears, he would assume his other identity, which was that of a silver-heeled dancer who went by the name of Ghaseeti-begum. This character had a complicated life of her own, strewn with heart-breaking flirtations, sparkling exchanges of wit and many besetting sorrows—but it was for her dancing that Ghaseeti-begum was best known, and her performances in the fana were such that few among the crew ever felt the need to visit a shoreside nautchery: why pay on land for what was free on board?

Sometimes, the lascars would gather between the bows to listen to the stories of the greybeards. There was the steward, Cornelius Pinto: a grey-haired Catholic from Goa, he claimed to have been around the world twice, sailing in every kind of ship, with every kind of sailor—including Finns, who were known to be the warlocks and wizards of the sea, capable of conjuring up winds with a whistle. There was Cassem-meah, who, as a young man, had gone to London as a shipowner's dress-boy, and had spent six months living in the Cheapside boarding house where lascars were lodged: his tales of the taverns set everyone afire for those shores. There was Sunker, a wizened man-boy of indeterminate age, with bandy legs and the sad face of a chained monkey: he had been born into a family of high-caste landlords, he claimed, but a vengeful servant had kidnapped him and sold him to a ghat-serang. Then there was Simba Cader, of Zanzibar, who was deaf in one ear: he was the oldest of all of them, and claimed to have lost his eardrum while serving on an English man-o'-war; when primed with a few swallows of doasta, he would tell of the terrible battle in which his eardrums had been punctured by a cannon-blast. He would speak of it as if it had really happened, with hundreds of ships unloosing cannonades at each other—but the lascars were too wise to give any credence to these entertaining tales: for who could be so foolish as to believe that some great battle had really been fought at a place called 'Three-fruit-house'—Tri-phal-ghar?

Dearly would Jodu have liked to be fully of this contingent, to be assigned to a watch and to find a place on the yardarms aloft—but Serang Ali would have none of it, and on the only occasion when Jodu mentioned his ambition, he was answered with a kick in the buttocks: This is the only part of you that's going to be up on that mast, with the laddu in your scuppers.

It was Steward Pinto, who had seen everything there was to be seen on a ship, who gave Jodu an inkling of why the serang had taken against him. It's because of the young memsahib, said the steward. The Serang-ji has plans for the malum and he's afraid that she's going to lead him off course.

What plans?

Who knows? But this much is for sure, he doesn't want anything to get in the malum's way, least of all a girl.

A few days later, almost as if to confirm the steward's suggestion, Jodu was summoned to the capstan for a talk with Zikri Malum. The malum seemed somewhat ill at ease, and it was in a rather gruff voice that he asked: 'You know Miss Lambert well, boy?'

Drawing on his limited supply of hookums, Jodu answered: 'Fore and aft, sir!'

This appeared to offend the malum, who responded sharply: 'Hey there! Is that any way to talk about a lady?'

'Sorry, sir. Hard-a-weather!'

Since this was going nowhere, the malum decided, to Jodu's horror, to call upon Serang Ali to translate. Squirming under the serang's narrow-eyed gaze, Jodu veered sharp about, providing laconic answers to the malum's questions, doing all he could to suggest that he knew Miss Lambert hardly at all, having merely been a servant in her father's house.

He breathed a sigh of relief when Serang Ali turned away from him to report to the mate: 'Launder say father-blongi-she go hebbin. That bugger do too muchi tree-pijjin. Allo time pickin plant. Inside pocket hab no cash. After he go hebbin cow-chilo catchi number-two-father, Mr Burnham. Now she too muchi happy inside. Eat big-big rice. Better Malum Zikri forgetting she. How can learn sailor-pijjin, allo time thinking ladies-ladies? More better keep busy with laund'ry till marriage time.'

The malum took unexpected umbrage at this. 'Hell and scissors, Serang Ali!' he cried, springing to his feet. 'Don you never think of nothin but knob-knockin and gamahoochie!'

The malum went stalking off, in exasperation, and as soon as he was out of sight, the serang dealt Jodu's ear a vicious little clip: Trying to hitch him to a bride, are you? I'll see you dead first, you little holemonger . . .

When told of this encounter, the steward shook his head in puzzlement. The way the serang carries on, he said, you'd think he was trying to save the malum for a daughter of his own.

~

Both Deeti and Kalua knew that their best chance of escape lay in travelling downriver, on the Ganga, in the hope of reaching a town or city where they would be able to disappear into a crowd: some place such as Patna perhaps, or even Calcutta. Although Patna was by far the nearer of the two cities, it was still a good ten days' journey away, and to cover the distance by road would be to risk being recognized: news of their flight was sure to have spread by this time, and in the event of capture, they knew they could expect no mercy, even from their own kin. Caution demanded that they keep to the water, continuing their journey on Kalua's makeshift raft for as long as it was able to bear their weight. Fortunately, there was enough driftwood on the riverbank to buttress the bamboos, and plenty of rushes from which to fashion lengths of rope; after spending a day on repairing and reinforcing the flimsy craft, they set off again, floating eastwards on the river.

Two days later they were within sight of the dwelling where Kabutri was now living with the family of Deeti's absent brother. Once having spotted the house, it was impossible for Deeti to proceed any further without making an attempt to meet her daughter. She knew that a meeting with Kabutri would be, at best, a brief, stolen encounter, requiring much stealth and patience, but being familiar with the terrain, she was confident of being able to stay hidden until she found her alone.

Deeti's childhood home—now inhabited by her brother's family—was a straw-thatched dwelling that overlooked a confluence where the Ganga was joined by a lesser river, the Karamnasa. As witnessed by its name—'destroyer of karma'—this tributary of the holy river had an unfortunate reputation: it was said that the touch of its water could erase a lifetime of hard-earned merit. The two rivers—the holy Ganga and its karma-negating tributary—were equidistant from Deeti's old home, and she knew that the women of the household preferred to go to the more auspicious of the two when they needed to bathe or fetch water. It was on the shores of the Ganga that she chose to wait, leaving Kalua a mile upriver with the raft.

There were many outcrops of rock along the shore and Deeti had no trouble in finding a place of concealment. Her vantage point commanded a good view of both rivers, and her long vigil afforded her plenty of time to reflect on the stories that were told of the Karamnasa and of the taint it could cast upon the souls of the dead. The landscape on the rivers' shores had changed a great deal since Deeti's childhood and looking around now, it seemed to her that the Karamnasa's influence had spilled over its banks, spreading its blight far beyond the lands that drew upon its waters: the opium harvest having been recently completed, the plants had been left to wither in the fields, so that the countryside was blanketed with the parched remnants. Except for the foliage of a few mango and jackfruit trees, nowhere was there anything green to relieve the eye. This, she knew, was what her own fields looked like, and were she at home today, she would have been asking herself what she would eat in the months ahead: where were the vegetables, the grains? She had only to look around to know that here, as in the village she had left, everyone's land was in hock to the agents of the opium factory: every farmer had been served with a contract, the fulfilling of which left them with no option but to strew their land with poppies. And now, with the harvest over and little grain at home, they would have to plunge still deeper into debt to feed their families. It was as if the poppy had become the carrier of the Karamnasa's malign taint.

The first day afforded two sightings of Kabutri, but on both occasions Deeti was forced to keep to her concealment because the girl was accompanied by her cousins. But to have seen her at all was ample reward: it seemed a miracle to Deeti that her daughter had changed so little, in a period of time in which she herself had stepped between life and death and back again.

With nightfall, Deeti retraced her steps to the raft, where she found Kalua kindling a fire, for their evening meal. At the time of her escape, Deeti had been wearing only one ornament, a silver nose-ring: the rest of her jewellery Chandan Singh had been careful to remove before leading her to the pyre. But this remaining trinket had proved invaluable, for Deeti had been able to barter it, at a riverside hamlet, for some satua—a flour made from roasted gram, a reliable and nutritious staple of all travellers and pilgrims. Every evening Kalua would light a fire and Deeti would knead and cook a sufficient number of rotis to see them through the day. With the Ganga close at hand, they had so far lacked for neither food nor water.

At dawn Deeti retraced her steps to her hiding-place, and the day passed without offering another glimpse of Kabutri. It was not till sunset, the day after, that Deeti spotted her daughter, walking alone to the Ganga, with an earthen pitcher balanced on her waist. Deeti kept to the shadows as the girl waded into the water and only after she'd made sure that her daughter was unaccompanied, did she follow her in. So as not to startle her, she whispered a familiar prayer: *Jai Ganga Mayya ki . . .*

This was unwise, for Kabutri recognized her voice at once: she turned around and on seeing her mother behind her, let go of her pitcher and gave a terrified shriek. Then she lost consciousness and fell sidewise into the water. The pitcher was swept away by the current, and so too would Kabutri have been, if Deeti had not thrown herself into the water and taken hold of the end of her sari. The water was only waist-deep, so Deeti was able to get her hands under the girl's arms to drag her to the shore. Once on the sand, she picked her up, slung her over her shoulder and carried her to a sheltered hollow between two shoals of sand.

*Ei Kabutri . . . ei beti . . . meri ján*! Cradling her daughter in her lap, Deeti kissed her face until her eyelids began to flicker. But when the girl's eyes opened, Deeti saw that they were dilated with fear.

Who are you? Kabutri cried. Are you a ghost? What do you want with me?

Kabutri! Deeti said sharply. *Dekh mori suratiya*—look at my face. It's me—your mother: don't you see me?

But how can it be? They said you were gone, dead. Kabutri reached up to touch her mother's face, running her fingertips over her eyes and lips: Can it really be you? Is it possible?

Deeti hugged her daughter still closer. Yes, it's me, it's me, Kabutri; I'm not dead; I'm here: look. What else did they tell you about me?

That you died before the cremation pyre could be lit; they said a woman like you could not become a sati; that the heavens would not allow it—they said your corpse was taken by the water.

Deeti began to nod, as if in assent: it was best that this be the version that was believed; so long as she was thought to be dead, no one would set out in search of her; she, Kabutri, must never say anything that might suggest otherwise, never let slip a word about this meeting . . .

But what really happened? said the girl. How did you get away?

Deeti had prepared a carefully considered explanation for

her daughter: she would say nothing, she had decided, about Chandan Singh's behaviour and Kabutri's true paternity; nor would she speak about the man the girl had known as her father: all she would tell her was that she, Deeti, had been drugged, in an attempt at immolation, and had been rescued while still unconscious.

But how? By whom?

The evasions that Deeti had invented for Kabutri's benefit slipped her mind; with her daughter's head in her lap, she could not bring herself to practise a wilful deception. Abruptly she said: My escape was Kalua's doing. *Woh hi bacháwela*— It was he who saved me.

*Kalua bacháwela*? Kalua saved you?

Was it outrage or disbelief that she heard in Kabutri's voice? Already prey to many kinds of guilt, Deeti began to tremble, in anticipation of her daughter's verdict on her flight with Kalua. But when the girl continued, it was in a tone, not of anger, but of eager curiosity: Is he with you now? Where will you go?

Far away from here; to a city.

A city! Kabutri flung a beseeching arm around Deeti's waist. I want to go too; take me with you; to a city.

Deeti had never wanted to yield to her daughter as much as she did now. But her parental instincts dictated otherwise: How can I take you, beti? *Saré jindagi aisé bhatkátela*? To wander all your life? Like me?

Yes; like you.

No, Deeti shook her head; no matter how fiercely her heart longed to take her daughter along, she knew she must resist: she had no idea of where her next meal would come from, far less where she might be next week or next month. At least with her aunt and her cousins the girl would be looked after; it was best that she stay there until . . .

. . . Until the time is right, Kabutri—and when it is I will be back for you. Do you think I don't want you with me? Do you think so? Do you know what it will mean for me to leave you here? Do you know, Kabutri? Do you know?

Kabutri fell silent and when she spoke again it was to say something that Deeti would never forget.

And when you come back, will you bring me bangles? *Hamré khátir churi lelaiya?*

~

Weary though he was of the world, Baboo Nob Kissin realized that he would have to endure it for a while yet. His best hope of finding a place on the *Ibis* was to be sent out as the ship's supercargo, and the job was unlikely to come his way, he knew, if he gave the appearance of having lost interest in his work. And this too he knew, that if Mr Burnham were to have the least suspicion that there was some heathenish intent behind his seeking of the post of supercargo, then that would put an abrupt end to the matter. So for the time being, Baboo Nob Kissin decided, it was imperative that he apply himself to his duties and display as few signs as possible of the momentous transformations that were taking place within him. This was no easy task, for no matter how closely he tried to keep to his accustomed routines, he was ever more conscious that everything had changed and that he was seeing the world in new, unexpected ways.

There were times when insights passed before his eyes with blinding suddenness. One day while travelling in a boat, up Tolly's Nullah, his eye fell upon a wooden shack, on a stretch of mangrove-covered wasteland; it was just a primitive thatch-covered bamboo platform, but it stood in the shade of a luxuriant kewra tree, and its very simplicity put the gomusta in mind of those sylvan retreats where the great sages and rishis of the past were said to have sat in meditation.

It so happened that just that morning Baboo Nob Kissin Pander had received a chit from Ramsaran-ji, the recruiter: he was still deep in the hinterland, the duffadar wrote, but he expected to arrive in Calcutta in a month's time with a large party of indentured workers, men and women. The news had added a note of urgency to the gomusta's many worries: where were these migrants to be accommodated when they arrived?

One month was so little time to provide for so many people.

In the past, duffadars like Ramsaran-ji had usually kept their recruits in their own homes until they were shipped out. But this practice had proved unsatisfactory for several reasons: for one, it plunged the would-be migrants into city life, exposing them to all kinds of rumours and temptations. In a place like Calcutta there was never any lack of people to prey upon simple-minded rustics, and in years past, many recruits had run away because of stories told by troublemakers; some had found other employment in the city and some had gone straight back to their villages. A few duffadars had tried to keep their recruits indoors by locking them in—but only to be faced with riots, fires and break-outs. The city's unhealthy climate was yet another problem, for every year a good number of migrants perished of communicable diseases. From an investor's point of view, each dead, escaped and incapacitated recruit represented a serious loss, and it was increasingly clear that if something wasn't done about the problem, the business would cease to be profitable.

It was the answer to this question that appeared before his eyes that day: a camp had to be built, right here, on the shore of Tolly's Nullah. As if in a dream, Baboo Nob Kissin saw a cluster of huts, standing there, like the dormitories of an ashram; the premises would have a well, for drinking water, a ghat for bathing, a few trees for shelter, and a paved space where the inmates' food would be cooked and eaten. At the heart of the complex there would be a temple, a small one, to mark the beginning of the journey to Mareech: he could already envision its spire, thrusting through the wreathed smoke of the cremation ghat; he could imagine the migrants, standing clustered at its threshold, gathering together to say their last prayers on their native soil; it would be their parting memory of sacred Jambudwipa, before they were cast out upon the Black Water. They would speak of it to their children and their children's children, who would return to it over generations, to remember and recall their ancestors.

~

Lalbazar Jail lay upon Calcutta's crowded centre like a gargantuan fist, holding the city's heart clenched in its grasp. The severity of the jail's exterior was deceptive, however, for behind its massive red-brick façade lay a haphazard warren of courtyards, corridors, offices, barracks and tope-khanas for the storage of weaponry. Prison cells were only a small part of this enormous complex, for despite its name, Lalbazar was not really a centre of incarceration but rather a lock-up where prisoners were held while under trial. Being also the administrative headquarters of the city's constabulary, it was a busy, bustling place, constantly enlivened by the comings and goings of officers and peons, prisoners and darogas, vendors and hurkarus.

Neel's quarters were in the administrative wing of the jail, well removed from the areas where other, less fortunate, prisoners were detained. Two sets of ground-floor offices had been cleared out for him, creating a comfortable apartment with a bedroom, a receiving room, and a small pantry. Neel was also allowed the privilege of having a servant with him during the day, to clean his rooms and serve his meals; as for food and water, everything he ate and drank came from his own kitchens—for his jailers could scarcely permit it to be said that they had obliged the Raja of Raskhali to lose caste even before his case was brought to court. At night the doors of Neel's apartment were lightly guarded, by constables who treated him with the greatest deference; if sleep eluded him, these sentries would keep him entertained with games of dice, cards and pachcheesi. During the day Neel was allowed as many visitors as he wished and the zemindary's gomustas and mootsuddies came so often that he had little difficulty in prosecuting the estate's business from the confines of the jail.

Although grateful for all these concessions, the privilege that mattered most to Neel was one that could not be publicly mentioned: it was the right to use the clean and well-lit outhouse that was reserved for officers. Neel had been brought up to regard his body and its functions with a fastidiousness that bordered almost on the occult: this was largely the doing

*Amitav Ghosh*

of his mother, for whom bodily defilement was a preoccupation that permitted neither peace nor rest. Although a quiet, gentle and loving woman in some ways, the usages of her caste and class were, for her, not just a set of rules and observances, but the very core of her being. Neglected by her husband, and living sequestered within a gloomy wing of the palace, she had devoted her considerable intelligence to the creation of fantastically elaborate rituals of cleanliness and purification: it was not enough that she wash her hands for a full half-hour, before and after every meal—she had also to make sure that the vessel from which the water was poured was properly cleaned, as also the bucket in which it had been fetched from the well; and so on. Her most potent fears centred upon the men and women who emptied the palace's outhouses and disposed of its sewage: these sweepers and cleaners of night-soil she regarded with such loathing that staying out of their way became one of her besetting preoccupations. As for the sweepers' tools—jharus made from palm-leaf bristles—neither sword nor serpent inspired a deeper unease in her than these objects, the sight of which could haunt her for days. These fears and anxieties created a way of life that was too unnatural to be long sustained and she died when Neel was only twelve years old, leaving him a legacy of extreme fastidiousness in regard to his own person. So it was that for Neel, no aspect of his captivity held greater terror than the thought of sharing a shit-hole with dozens of common prisoners.

To get to the officers' outhouse, Neel had to pass through several corridors and courtyards, some of which afforded glimpses of the jail's other inmates—often they seemed to be fighting for light and air, with their noses pressed against the bars, like trapped rats. These sightings of the hardships suffered by other prisoners gave Neel a keen sense of the consideration that he himself had been afforded: it was clear that the British authorities were intent on reassuring the public that the Raja of Raskhali was being treated with the utmost fairness. So slight indeed were the inconveniences of Neel's imprisonment at Lalbazar that he could almost have imagined himself to be on holiday, were it not for the ban on visits from women and children. Yet even this was no great loss, since Neel would not, in any case, have permitted his wife or son to defile themselves by entering the jail. Elokeshi, on the other hand, he would have been glad to receive, but there had been no news of her since the time of Neel's arrest: it was thought that she had slipped out of the city, to avoid being questioned by the police. Neel could not rightfully complain about so well-judged an absence.

The ease of his incarceration was such that Neel was hard put to take his legal difficulties very seriously. His relatives among Calcutta's gentry had told him that his was to be a show-trial, intended to persuade the public of the even-handedness of British justice: he was sure to be acquitted, or let off lightly, with some token punishment. They were insistent in assuring him that he had no cause for anxiety: great efforts were being mounted on his behalf by many prominent citizens, they said; everyone in his circle of acquaintance was extending their reach as far as they possibly could: between all of them they would almost certainly be able to move some important levers, maybe even in the Governor-General's Council. In any event, it was unthinkable that a member of their class would be treated as a common criminal.

Neel's lawyer, too, was cautiously optimistic: a small fidgety man, Mr Rowbotham had the bristling pugnacity of one of those hirsute terriers that could sometimes be seen in the Maidan, straining upon a memsahib's leash. Generously eyebrowed and lavishly whiskered, almost nothing was visible of his face except for a pair of bright, black eyes and a nose that was of the shape and colour of a ripe litchi.

Having reviewed Neel's brief, Mr Rowbotham offered his first opinion. 'Let me tell you, dear Raja,' he said bluntly. 'There's not a jury on earth that would acquit you—far less one that consists mainly of English traders and colonists.'

This came as a shock to Neel. 'But Mr Rowbotham,' he said. 'Are you suggesting that I may be found guilty?'

'I will not deceive you, my dear Raja,' said Mr Rowbotham.

'I think it very possible that such a verdict will be returned. But there's no reason to despair. As I see it, it's the sentence that concerns us, not the verdict. For all you know, you could get away with a fine and a few forfeitures. If I remember right there was a similar case recently when the penalty consisted of nothing more than a fine and a sentence of public ridicule: the culprit was led around Kidderpore sitting backwards on a donkey!'

Neel's mouth fell open and he uttered an appalled whisper: 'Mr Rowbotham, could such a fate befall the Raja of Raskhali?'

The lawyer's eyes twinkled: 'And what if it did, dear Raja? It isn't the worst that could happen, is it? Would it not be worse if all your properties were to be seized?'

'Not at all,' said Neel promptly. 'Nothing could be worse than such a loss of face. By comparison, it would be better even to be rid of my encumbrances. At least I would then be free to live in a garret and write poetry—like your admirable Mr Chatterton.'

At this, the attorney's ample eyebrows knitted themselves into a puzzled tangle. 'Mr Chatterjee, did you say?' he asked in surprise. 'Do you mean my head clerk? But I assure you, dear Raja, he does not live in a garret—and as for his poetry, why this is the first I've heard of it . . .'

## nine

~

It was at the riverside township of Chhapra, a day's journey short of Patna, that Deeti and Kalua again encountered the duffadar they had met at Ghazipur.

Many weeks had passed since the start of Deeti and Kalua's journey, and their hopes of reaching a city had foundered, along with their raft, in the treacherous labyrinth of sand-shoals that mark the confluence of the Ganga with her turbulent tributary, the Ghagara. The last of their satua was gone and they had been reduced to begging, at the doors of the temples of Chhapra, where they had arrived after walking away from the wreckage of their raft.

Both Deeti and Kalua had tried to find work, but employment was hard to come by in Chhapra. The town was thronged with hundreds of other impoverished transients, many of whom were willing to sweat themselves half to death for a few handfuls of rice. Many of these people had been driven from their villages by the flood of flowers that had washed over the countryside: lands that had once provided sustenance were now swamped by the rising tide of poppies; food was so hard to come by that people were glad to lick the leaves in which offerings were made at temples or sip the starchy water from a pot in which rice had been boiled. Often, it was on gleanings like these that Deeti and Kalua got by: sometimes, when they were lucky, Kalua managed to earn a little something by working as a porter on the riverfront.

As a market town and river port, Chhapra was visited by

many vessels, and the town's ghats were the one place where a few coppers could sometimes be earned by loading or unloading boats and barges. When they were not begging at the temple, it was there that Deeti and Kalua spent most of their time. At night, the riverfront was much cooler than the town's congested interior, and that was where they usually slept: once the rains came they would have to find some other spot, but until then this was as good a place as any. Every night, as they made their way there, Deeti would say: *Suraj dikhat áwé to rásta mil jáwé*—when the sun rises the path will show itself—and so strongly did she believe this that not even at the worst of times did she allow her hopes to slacken.

It happened one day that as the eastern sky was beginning to glow with the first light of the sun, Deeti and Kalua woke to find a tall babu of a man, well-dressed and white-moustached, pacing the ghat and complaining angrily about the tardiness of his boatman. Deeti recognized the man almost at once. It's that duffadar, Ramsaran-ji, she whispered to Kalua. He rode with us that day, at Ghazipur. Why don't you go and see if you can be of help?

Kalua dusted himself off, folded his hands respectfully together, and stepped over to the duffadar. A few minutes later he returned to report that the duffadar wanted to be rowed to the far side of the river, to pick up a group of men. He needed to leave at once because he'd received word that the opium fleet was arriving and the river was to be closed to other traffic later in the day.

He offered me two dams and an adhela to take him across, said Kalua.

Two dams and an adhela! And you're still standing here like a tree? said Deeti. *Kai sochawa?* Why are you stopping to think? Go, na, jaldi.

Several hours later, Deeti was sitting at the entrance to Chhapra's famous Ambaji temple when she saw Kalua coming up the lane. Before she could ask any questions, he said: I'll tell you everything, but first, come, let's eat: *chal, jaldi-jaldi khanwa khá lei.*

*Khanwa*? Food? They gave you food?

Chal! He elbowed away the hungry throng that had gathered around them and only when they were safely out of sight did he show her what he had brought: a leaf-wrapped package of succulent satua-stuffed parathas, mango pickle, potatoes mashed with masalas to make aloo-ka-bharta, and even a few sugared vegetables and other sweets—parwal-ka-mithai and succulent khubi-ka-lai from Barh.

After the food had been devoured, they sat a while under the shade of a tree, and Kalua gave her a detailed account of all that had happened. They had arrived on the far side of the river to find eight men waiting, along with one of the duffadar's sub-agents. Right there, on the shore, the men had entered their names on paper girmits; after these agreements were sealed, they had each been given a blanket, several articles of clothing, and a round-bottomed brass lota. Then, to celebrate their new-found status as girmitiyas, they had been served a meal—it was the remains of this feast that had been handed to Kalua by the duffadar. The gift was not given without protest: none of the recruits were strangers to hunger, and replete though they might be, they had been shocked to see so much food being given away. But the duffadar had told them they needn't worry; they would have their fill at every meal; from now on, until they arrived in Mareech, that was all they needed to do—to eat and grow strong.

This assertion had evoked much disbelief. One of the men had said, Why? Are we being fattened for the slaughter, like goats before 'Id?

The duffadar had laughed and told him that it was he who would be feasting on fattened goats.

On the way back, all of a sudden, the duffadar had told Kalua that if he had a mind to join up, he would be happy to have him: he could always use big, strong men.

This had set Kalua's head a-spinning. Me? he said. But malik, I'm married.

No matter, said the duffadar. Many girmitiyas go with their wives. We've had letters from Mareech asking for more women. I will take you and your wife as well, if she wants to go.

After thinking about this for a bit, Kalua asked: And *ját*— what about caste?

Caste doesn't matter, said the duffadar. All kinds of men are eager to sign up—Brahmins, Ahirs, Chamars, Telis. What matters is that they be young and able-bodied and willing to work.

At a loss for words, Kalua had put all his strength behind his oars. As the boat was pulling up to shore, the duffadar had repeated his offer. But this time he had added a warning: Remember—you have only one night to decide. We leave tomorrow—if you come, it must be at dawn . . . *sawéré hí áwat áni.*

Having told his story, Kalua turned to look at Deeti and she saw that his huge, dark eyes were illuminated by questions that he could not bring himself to ask. The sensation of a full stomach had made Deeti groggy enough to hear Kalua out in silence, but now, her head boiled over with the heat of many inadmissible fears and she jumped to her feet in agitation. How could he imagine that she would agree to abandon her daughter forever? How could he conceive that she would go to a place which was, for all she knew, inhabited by demons and pishaches, not to speak of all kinds of unnameable beasts? How could he, Kalua, or anyone else, know that it wasn't true that the recruits were being fattened for the slaughter? Why else would those men be fed with such munificence? Was it normal, in these times, to be so profligate without some unspoken motive?

Tell me, Kalua, she said, as tears welled into her eyes. Is this what you saved me for? To feed me to the demons? Why, it would have been better if you'd left me to die in that fire . . .

~

One of the small ways in which Paulette attempted to make herself useful to her benefactors was by writing the place-cards for their dinners, suppers, church tiffins and other entertainments. Being of a comfortable, placid disposition, Mrs Burnham rarely exercised much effort over these meals, preferring to make the arrangements while lying in bed. The head-bobachee and chief consumah were generally shown in first, to discuss the fare: for reasons of propriety, Mrs Burnham would keep her nightcap on her head and her mosquito-net down while this consultation was in progress. But when it was Paulette's turn to enter, the drapes would be pulled back and more often than not Paulette would be invited to sit on the Burra BeeBee's bed, to look over her shoulder as she puzzled over the seating for the meal, writing names and drawing diagrams on a slate tablet. Thus it was that Paulette was summoned to Mrs Burnham's bedroom one afternoon to help with the arrangements for a burra-khana.

For Paulette, the examination of Mrs Burnham's seating charts was usually an exercise in misery: coming as low as she did in the order of social precedence, it almost always fell to her to be seated amidships—or beech-o-beech, as the BeeBee liked to say—which meant that she was usually placed between the least desirable guests: colonels who'd been deafened by gunpowder; collectors who could speak of nothing but the projected revenues of their district; lay preachers who ranted about the obduracy of the heathens; planters with indigo-stained hands, and other such nincumnoodles. Such being her experience of the Burnham burra-khanas, it was with some trepidation that Paulette asked: 'Is this a special occasion, Madame?'

'Why yes, Puggly,' said Mrs Burnham, stretching languidly. 'Mr Burnham wants us to put on a tumasher. It's for Captain Chillingworth, who's just arrived from Canton.'

Paulette glanced at the slate and saw that the Captain had already been placed at the BeeBee's end of the table. Glad of an opportunity to show off her knowledge of memsahib etiquette, she said: 'Since the Captain is next to you, Madame, must not his wife be placed beside Mr Burnham?'

'His wife?' the tip of the chalk withdrew from the slate in

surprise. 'Why, dear, Mrs Chillingworth has been gone many a long year.'

'Oh?' said Paulette. 'So he is—how do you say—a veuf?'

'A widower do you mean, Puggly? No, dear, he's not that either. It's rather a sad story . . .'

'Yes, Madame?'

This was all the prompting Mrs Burnham needed to settle back comfortably against her pillows. 'He's from Devonshire, Captain Chillingworth, and bred to the sea, as they say. These old salts like to go back to their home ports to marry, you know, and that's what he did: found himself a rosy-cheeked West Country lass, fresh from the nursery, and brought her out East. Our country-born larkins weren't mem enough for him. As you might expect—no good came of it.'

'Why, Madame? What was it that came to pass?'

'The Captain went off to Canton one year,' said the BeeBee. 'As usual, months went by and there she was, all alone, in a strange new place. Then at last there was news of her husband's ship—but instead of the Captain, who should turn up at her door, but his first mate. The Captain had been struck down by the hectic-fever, he told her, and they'd had to leave him in Penang to convalesce. The Captain had decided to arrange a passage for Mrs Chillingworth and had deputed the mate to see to it. Well, dear, that was that: hogya for the poor old Captain.'

'How do you mean, Madame?'

'This mate—his name was Texeira as I recall—was from Macao, a Portuguese, and as chuckmuck a rascal as ever you'll see: eyes as bright as muggerbees, smile like a xeraphim. He put it about that he was escorting Mrs Chillingworth to Penang. They got on a boat and that was the last that was seen of them. They're in Brazil now I'm told.'

'Oh Madame!' cried Paulette. 'What a pity for the Captain! So he never remarried?'

'No, Puggly dear. He never really recovered. Whether it was because of the loss of his mate or his wife, no one knows, but his seafaring went all to pieces—couldn't get along with his officers; scared the cabobs out of his crews; even turned a ship oolter-pooter in the Spratlys, which is considered a great piece of silliness amongst sailing men. Anyway, it's all over now. The *Ibis* is to be his last command.'

'The *Ibis*, Madame?' Paulette sat up with a jolt. 'He will be Captain of the *Ibis*?'

'Why yes—didn't I tell you, Puggly?' Here the BeeBee cut herself short with a guilty start. 'Look at me, rattling on like a gudda when I should be getting on with the tumasher.' She picked up the slate, and scratched her lip pensively with the tip of the chalk. 'Now tell me, Puggly dear, what on earth am I to do with Mr Kendalbushe? He's a puisne judge now you know, and has to be treated with the greatest distinction.'

The BeeBee's eyes rose slowly from the slate and came to rest appraisingly on Paulette. 'The judge does so enjoy your company, Puggly!' she said. 'Just last week I heard him say that you deserve a shahbash for your progress with your Bible studies.'

Paulette took fright at this: an evening spent at the side of Mr Justice Kendalbushe was not a pleasant prospect, for he invariably subjected her to lengthy and disapproving catechisms on scriptural matters. 'The judge is too kind,' said Paulette, recalling vividly the frown with which Mr Kendalbushe had afixed her on seeing her take a second sip from her wineglass: '"Remember the days of darkness,"' he had muttered, '"for they shall be many . . ."' And of course she had not been able to identify either the chapter or the verse.

Some quick thinking was called for and Paulette's wits did not fail her. 'But Madame,' she said, 'will not the other Burra Mems take offence if someone like me is placed beside a man so puisne as Judge Kendalbushe?'

'You're right, dear,' said Mrs Burnham after a moment's consideration. 'It would probably give Mrs Doughty an attack of the Doolally-tap.'

'She is to be present?'

'Can't be avoided I'm afraid,' said the BeeBee. 'Mr Burnham is set on having Doughty. But what on earth am I to do with her? She's completely dottissima.'

Suddenly Mrs Burnham's eyes lit up and the tip of her chalk flew down to the slate again. 'There!' she said triumphantly, inscribing Mrs Doughty's name on the empty seat to Captain Chillingworth's left. 'That should keep her quiet. And as for that husband of hers, he'd better be sent off beech-o-beech where I don't have to listen to him. I'll let you have the windy old poggle . . .' The chalk came down on the blank centre of the table and seated Mr Doughty and Paulette side by side.

Paulette had barely had time to reconcile herself to the prospect of making conversation to the pilot—of whose English she understood mainly the Hindusthani—when the tip of the BeeBee's chalk began to hover worriedly once again.

'But that still leaves a problem, Puggly,' the BeeBee complained. 'Who on earth am I to lagow on your left?'

A bolt of inspiration prompted Paulette to ask: 'Are the ship's mates to be invited, Madame?'

Mrs Burnham shifted her weight uncomfortably on her bed. 'Mr Crowle? Oh my dear Puggly! I couldn't have him in my house.'

'Mr Crowle? Is he the first mate?' said Paulette.

'So he is,' said the BeeBee. 'He's a fine sailor they say—Mr Burnham swears that Captain Chillingworth would have been all adrift without him these last few years. But he's the worst kind of sea-dog: piped out of the Navy because of some ghastly goll-maul with a foretopman. Lucky for him the Captain is none too particular—but my dear, no mem could have him at her table. Why, it would be like dining with the moochy.' The BeeBee paused to lick her chalk. 'It's a pity, though, because I've heard the second mate is quite personable. What's his name? Zachary Reid?'

A tremor passed through Paulette, and when it ceased it was as if the very motes of dust had ceased their dance and were waiting in suspense. She dared not speak, or even look up, and could only offer a nod in answer to the BeeBee's question.

'You've already met him, haven't you—this Mr Reid?' the

BeeBee demanded. 'Wasn't he on the schooner when you went over to take a dekko last week?'

Having made no mention of her visit to the *Ibis*, Paulette was more than a little put out to find that Mrs Burnham knew of it already. 'Why yes, Madame,' she said cautiously. 'I did have a brief rencounter with Mr Reid. He seemed aimable enough.'

'Aimable, was he?' Mrs Burnham gave her a shrewd glance. 'The kubber is that there's more than one young missy-mem who's got a mind to bundo the fellow. The Doughties have been dragging him all over town.'

'Oh?' said Paulette, brightening. 'Then maybe they could bring Mr Reid with them, as their guest? Surely Mr Crowle need not know?'

'Why, you sly little shaytan!' The BeeBee gave a delighted laugh. 'What a clever contrivance! And since you thought of it, I'll put you beside him. There. Chull.'

And with that her chalk came swooping down on the slate, like the finger of fate, and wrote Zachary's name on the seat to Paulette's left: 'There you are.'

Paulette snatched the tablet from the BeeBee and went racing upstairs, only to find her rooms under invasion by a troop of cleaners. For once, she summarily bundled them all out, the farrashes, bichawnadars and harry-maids—'Not today, not now . . .'—and seated herself at her desk, with a stack of place-cards.

Mrs Burnham liked the cards to be inscribed in an elaborately ornamental script, with as many curlicues and flourishes as could possibly be squeezed in: even on ordinary days it often took Paulette an hour or two to fill them to the BeeBee's satisfaction. Today, the task seemed to stretch on endlessly, with her quill spluttering and faltering: of all the letters, it was the 'Z' that gave her the most trouble, not only because she had never before had cause to inscribe it in capitals, but also because she had never known that it offered so many curves and curls and possibilities: in exploring its shape and size, her pen turned it around and around, shaping it into loops and whorls that seemed, somehow, to want to knot itself with the humble P of her own initials. And when she grew tired of this, she felt impelled, inexplicably, to stare at herself in the mirror, taking alarm at the straggling mess of her hair, and at the blotches of red where her nails had dug into her skin. Then her feet took her to the wardrobe and held her imprisoned in front of it, rifling through the dresses that Mrs Burnham had given her: now, as never before, she wished that they were not all so severe in their colour, nor so voluminous in shape. On an impulse, she opened her locked trunk and took out her one good sari, a scarlet Benarasi silk, and ran her hands over it, remembering how even Jodu, who always laughed at her clothes, had gasped when he first saw her wearing it—and what would Zachary say if he saw her in it? That notion took her eyes straying out of the window, in the direction of the bungalow in the Gardens, and she fell on her bed, defeated by the impossibility of everything.

# ten

As he stepped past the tall mahogany doors of Mr Burnham's Dufter, it seemed to Baboo Nob Kissin that he had left the heat of Calcutta behind and arrived in another country. The dimensions of the room, with its apparently endless stretch of floor and soaring walls, were such as to create a climate peculiar to itself, temperate and free of dust. From the massive beams of the ceiling, an enormous cloth-fringed punkah hung down, sweeping gently back and forth, creating a breeze that was strong enough to paste the gomusta's light cotton kurta against his limbs. The veranda that adjoined the Dufter was very broad, so as to keep the sun at bay by creating a wide threshold of shade; now, at midday, the balcony's khus screens were hanging low, and the tatties were being wetted constantly by a team of punkah-wallahs, to create a cooling effect.

Mr Burnham was sitting at a massive desk, bathed in the muted glow of a skylight, far above. His eyes widened as he watched Baboo Nob Kissin walking across the room. 'My good Baboon!' he cried, as he took in the sight of the gomusta's oiled, shoulder-length hair and the necklace that was hanging around his neck. 'What on earth has become of you? You look so . . .'

'Yes, sir?'

'So strangely womanish.'

The gomusta smiled wanly. 'Oh no, sir,' he said. 'It is outward appearance only—just illusions. Underneath all is same-same.'

'Illusion?' said Mr Burnham scornfully. 'Man and woman? God made them both as they were, Baboon, and there's nothing illusory about either, nor is there anything in between.'

'Exactly, sir,' said Baboo Nob Kissin, nodding enthusiastically. 'That is what I am also saying: on this point no concession can be made. Unreasonable demands must be strenuously opposed.'

'Then may I ask, Baboon,' said Mr Burnham, frowning, 'why you have chosen to adorn yourself with that'—he raised a finger to point at the gomusta's bosom, which seemed somehow to have attained an increased salience within the contours of his body—'may I ask why you are wearing that large piece of jewellery? Is it something you got from your sammy-house?'

Baboo Nob Kissin's hand flew to his amulet and slipped it back inside his kurta. 'Yes, sir; from temple only I got.' Improvising freely, he rushed to add: 'As such it is mainly for medicinal purposes. Made from copper, which enhances digestion. You can also try, sir. Bowel movements will become smooth and copious. Colour will also be nice, like turmeric.'

'Heaven forbid!' said Mr Burnham with a gesture of distaste. 'Enough of that. Now tell me, Baboon, what's this urgent business you wanted to see me about?'

'Just I wanted to raise up some issues, sir.'

'Yes, go on. I haven't got all day.'

'One thing is about camp for coolies, sir.'

'Camp?' said Mr Burnham. 'What do you mean, camp? I know of no camp for coolies.'

'Yes, sir, that is the discussion I want to raise up. What I am proposing is, why not to build a camp? Here, just see and you will be convinced.' Taking a sheet of paper from a file, Baboo Nob Kissin laid it in front of his employer.

The gomusta was well aware that Mr Burnham considered the transportation of migrants an unimportant and somewhat annoying part of his shipping enterprise, since the margins of profit were negligible in comparison to the enormous gains offered by opium. It was true that this year was an exception, because of the interruption in the flow of opium to China—but he knew that he would still have to present a strong case if he was to persuade the Burra Sahib to make a significant outlay in this branch of his business.

'Look here, sir, and I will show . . .' With the numbers written down, Baboo Nob Kissin was able to demonstrate, quickly and graphically, that the cost of buying the campsite, erecting huts and so on, would be earned back in a couple of seasons. 'One big advantage, sir, you can sell camp to gov'ment in one, two years. Profit could be healthy.'

This caught Mr Burnham's attention. 'How so?'

'Simple, sir. You can tell to Municipal Council that proper immigrant depot is needed. Otherwise cleanliness will suffer and progress will be delayed. Then to them only we can sell, no? Mr Hobbes is there—he will ensure payment.'

'Splendid idea,' Mr Burnham sat back in his seat and stroked his beard. 'There's no denying it, Baboon, from time to time you do serve up some excellent notions. You have my permission to do whatever's necessary. Go on. Don't waste any time.'

'But, sir, one other issue is also raising its head.'

'Yes? What is it?'

'Sir, supercargo for *Ibis* has not been appointed yet, no sir?'

'No,' said Mr Burnham. 'Not yet. Do you have someone in mind?'

'Yes, sir. The proposal I would like to moot out, sir, is that I myself should go.'

'You?' Mr Burnham looked up at his gomusta in surprise. 'But Baboo Nob Kissin! Whatever for?'

The gomusta had his answer ready: 'Just, sir, the reason is to observe the field situation. It will facilitate my work with coolies, sir, so I can provide fulsome services. It will be like plucking a new leaf for my career.'

Mr Burnham cast a dubious glance at the gomusta's matronly form. 'I am impressed by your enthusiasm, Baboo Nob Kissin. But are you sure you'll be able to cope with the conditions on a ship?'

'Definitely, sir. Already I have been on one ship—to Jagannath temple, in Puri. No problem was there.'

'But Baboon,' said Mr Burnham, with a satirical curl of his lip. 'Are you not afraid of losing caste? Won't your Gentoo brethren ban you from their midst for crossing the Black Water?'

'Oh no, sir,' said the gomusta. 'Nowadays all are going for pilgrimage by ship. Pilgrims cannot lose caste—this can also be like that. Why not?'

'Well I don't know,' said Mr Burnham, with a sigh. 'Frankly, I don't have time to think about it right now, with this Raskhali case coming up.'

This was the time, Baboo Nob Kissin knew, to play his best card. 'Regarding case, sir, can I kindly be permitted to forward one suggestion?'

'Why, certainly,' said Mr Burnham. 'As I recall, it was all your idea in the first place, wasn't it?'

'Yes, sir,' said the gomusta with a nod, 'it was myself only who suggested you this scheme.'

Baboo Nob Kissin took no little pride in having been the first to alert his employer to the advantages of acquiring the Raskhali estate: for some years, it had been rumoured that the East India Company was to relinquish its control on opium production in eastern India. Were that to happen, poppies might well become a plantation crop, like indigo or sugar-cane: with the demand rising annually in China, merchants who controlled their own production, rather than depending on small farmers, would stand to multiply their already astronomical profits. Although there was, as yet, no clear sign that the Company was ready to make the necessary concessions, a few far-sighted merchants had already started looking for sizeable chunks of land. When Mr Burnham began to make inquiries, it was Baboo Nob Kissin who reminded him that he need look no further than the hugely-indebted Raskhali estate, which was already within his grasp. He was well acquainted with several crannies and mootsuddies in the Raskhali daftar, and they had kept him closely informed of all the young zemindar's missteps: like them, he regarded the new Raja as a dilettante, who had his nose in the air and his head in the clouds, and he fully shared their opinion that anyone so foolish as to sign everything that was put before him, deserved to lose his fortune. Besides, the Rajas of Raskhali were well known to be bigoted, ritual-bound Hindus, who were dismissive of heterodox Vaishnavites like himself: people like that needed to be taught a lesson from time to time.

The gomusta lowered his voice: 'Rumours are reaching, sir, that Raja-sahib's "keep-lady" is hiding in Calcutta. She is one dancer, sir, and her name is Elokeshi. Maybe she can provide affidavits to seal his fate.'

The shrewd glint in Baboo Nob Kissin's eye was not lost on his employer. Mr Burnham leant forward in his chair. 'Do you think she might testify?'

'Cannot say for sure, sir,' said the gomusta. 'But there is no harm in launching efforts.'

'I'd be glad if you would.'

'But then, sir,' the gomusta allowed his voice to trail away softly so that it ended on a note of interrogation: 'what to do about appointment of supercargo?'

Mr Burnham pursed his lips, as if to indicate that he understood precisely the bargain that was being proposed. 'If you can provide the affidavit, Baboon,' he said, 'the job is yours.'

'Thank you, sir,' said Baboo Nob Kissin, reflecting, once again, on what a pleasure it was to work for a reasonable man. 'You can repose all trust, sir. I will do maximum best.'

~

On the eve of Neel's first appearance in court the monsoons came crashing down, which was regarded as a good sign by all his well-wishers. To add to the general optimism, the Raskhali estate's court astrologer determined that the date of the hearing was extremely auspicious, with all the stars aligned in the Raja's favour. It was also learnt that a clemency petition had been signed by Bengal's wealthiest zemindars: even the Tagores of Jorasanko and the Debs of Rajabazar, who could agree on nothing else, had put aside their differences in this matter since it concerned a member of their own class. These bits of news provided so much cheer to the Halder family that Neel's wife, Rani Malati, paid a special visit to the Bhukailash temple where she provided a feast for a hundred Brahmins, serving each of them with her own hands.

The news was not enough, however, to dispose entirely of Neel's apprehensions, and he could not sleep at all the night before his first court appearance. It had been arranged that he would be transported to the courthouse before daybreak, under light guard, and his family had been given permission to send a team of retainers to help with his preparations. Dawn was still a couple of hours away when a rattle of wheels announced the approach of the estate's phaetongari; shortly afterwards, the Raskhali retinue arrived at Neel's door and from that point on, mercifully, he had no time to worry.

Parimal had brought two of the family priests with him, along with a cook and a barber. The Brahmin purohits had come bearing the most 'awake' of the images in the Raskhali temple, a gold-encrusted statue of Ma Durga. While the outer room of the apartment was being prepared for the puja, Neel was taken off to the bedchamber inside, where he was shaved, bathed and anointed with fragrant oils and flower-scented attars. By way of clothing, Parimal had brought along the finest Raskhali regalia, including a chapkan jacket ornamented with Aljofar seed-pearls, and a turban fitted with the famous Raskhali sarpech—a gold spray, inlaid with rubies from the Shan highlands. It was Neel himself who had asked for these accoutrements, but once they had been laid out on his bed he began to reconsider. Might it make the wrong impression if he presented himself in court in such a rich array of finery? But on the other hand, wasn't it also possible that a simpler outfit might be seen as an acknowledgement of guilt? It was hard to know what the proper attire was for a forgery trial. In the end, deciding that it would be best not to call attention to his clothes, Neel asked Parimal for a kurta of plain mushru' mulmul and an unbordered dhoti of Chinsura cotton. Parimal was kneeling to tuck in his dhoti when Neel asked: And how is my son?

He was busy with his kites till late last night, huzoor. He thinks you are away in Raskhali. We've made sure that he knows nothing of all this.

And the Rani?

Huzoor, said Parimal, since the moment you were taken away, she is without sleep or rest. She spends the days in prayer and there is not a temple or holy man she has omitted to visit. Today again she will spend the day in our temple.

And Elokeshi? said Neel. Has there been any word of her yet?

No, huzoor, none.

Neel nodded—it was best that she stay in hiding till the trial was over.

With his clothing completed, Neel was impatient to be on his way, but there was much else still to be done: the puja took the better part of an hour and then, after the priests had smeared his brow with sandalwood paste and sprinkled him with holy water and sacred durba grass, he was made to eat a meal composed of various kinds of auspicious foods— vegetables and puris, fried in the purest ghee, and sweets made with patali syrup, from his household's own sugar palms. When at last it was time to leave, the Brahmins led the way, clearing Neel's path of such impure objects as jharus and toilet buckets, and ushering away all carriers of ill-omen—sweepers, porters of night-soil and such. Parimal had already gone ahead to make sure that the constables who were accompanying Neel to the court were Hindus of respectable caste and could be entrusted with his food and water. Now, as Neel was climbing into the shuttered carriage, his retainers joined together to remind him, yet again, to make sure of keeping the windows closed, so that his gaze would encounter no ill-augured sights— on this of all days, it was best to take every possible precaution.

The carriage was slow and took the better part of an hour

to cover the distance from Lalbazar to the New Courthouse, on the Esplanade, where Neel's case was to be tried. On arriving there, Neel was whisked quickly through the damp, gloomy building, past the vaulted room where most prisoners were held while awaiting their turn in court. The corridors filled with hisses and whispers as the other defendants began to speculate about who Neel was and what he'd done.

The ways of zemindars were not unfamiliar to these men:

. . . If this was the one who crippled my son, even these bars couldn't hold me . . .

. . . Let me get a hand on him—he'll get a touching he won't forget . . .

. . . Give his chute the ploughing my land's longing for . . .

To get to the courtroom they had to climb several staircases and pass through many corridors. It was clear, from the noise that was reverberating through the New Courthouse, that the trial had drawn a large crowd. Yet, even though Neel was well aware of the public interest in his case, he was in no way prepared for the sight that was waiting for him when he stepped into the venue of his trial.

The courtroom was shaped like a halved bowl, with the witness stand at the bottom, and the spectators ranged in rows along the steep, curved sides. On Neel's entry the hubbub ceased abruptly, leaving a few last threads of sound to float gently to the floor, like the torn ends of a ribbon; among these was a clearly audible whisper: 'Ah, the Rascally-Roger! Here at last.'

The first few rows were occupied by whites, and this was where Mr Doughty was seated. Behind, stretching all the way to the skylights at the top of the room, were the faces of Neel's friends, acquaintances and kin: at one glance, he could see, arrayed before him, all his fellow members of the Bengal Landowners' Association as well as the innumerable relatives who had accompanied him on his wedding procession. It was as if every male of his class, all of Bengal's acreocracy, had assembled to watch the progress of his trial.

Looking away, Neel caught sight of Mr Rowbotham, his advocate. He had risen to his feet when Neel entered, and he now proceeded to make a confident show of welcoming Neel to the courtroom, ushering him to his seat with much ceremony. Neel had just seated himself when the bailiffs began to bang their maces on the floor, to announce the entry of the judge. Neel stood a moment with his head lowered, like everyone else, and on raising his eyes he saw that the man who was to preside over his trial was none other than Mr Justice Kendalbushe. Being well aware of the judge's friendship with Mr Burnham, Neel turned to Mr Rowbotham in alarm: 'Is that indeed Justice Kendalbushe? Is he not closely linked with Mr Burnham?'

Mr Rowbotham pursed his lips and nodded. 'That may be so, but I am confident he is a man of unimpeachable fairness.'

Neel's eyes strayed to the jury-box, and he found himself exchanging nods with several of the jurymen. Of the twelve Englishmen in the box, at least eight had known his father, the old Raja, and several had been present at the celebration of his son's First Rice ceremony. They had brought gifts of silver and gold, ornamented spoons and filigreed cups; one of them had gifted little Raj Rattan an abacus from China, made of ebony and jade.

Mr Rowbotham had been watching Neel closely in the meantime and he leant over now to whisper in his ear. 'I'm afraid there is some other, somewhat unwelcome news . . .'

'Oh?' said Neel. 'What is it?'

'I have only this morning received an official chitty from the government's solicitor. They are to introduce a new piece of evidence: a sworn affidavit.'

'From whom?' said Neel.

'A lady—a woman I should say—who claims to have had a liaison with you. I gather she is a dancer . . .' Mr Rowbotham peered closely at a sheet of paper. 'The name I think is Elokeshi.'

Neel's disbelieving eyes moved away, to glance once again at the assembled crowd. He saw that his wife's oldest brother had appeared in the courtroom and taken a seat at the rear. For a brief but nightmarish instant he wondered whether Malati had come too and great was his relief when he noted that his brother-in-law was alone. In the past he had sometimes regretted Malati's strictness in the observation of the rules of caste and purdah—but today he felt nothing but gratitude for her orthodoxy, for if there was any one thing that could possibly make the situation even worse than it already was, it was the thought of her being present to witness his betrayal by his mistress.

It was this consideration that sustained him through the ordeal of Elokeshi's affidavit, which proved to be a fanciful account, not just of the incriminating conversation in which Neel had spoken of the Raskhali estate's dealings with Mr Burnham, but also of the circumstances in which it had taken place. The Raskhali budgerow, the stateroom, even the coverings on the bed, were described in such painstaking, even salacious, detail that each fresh revelation was greeted by gasps of surprise, exclamations of shock and outbursts of laughter.

When at last the reading was over, Neel turned in exhaustion to Mr Rowbotham: 'How long will this trial last? When will we know the outcome?'

Mr Rowbotham gave him a wan smile: 'Not long, dear Raja. Perhaps no more than a fortnight.'

~

When Deeti and Kalua went down to the ghat they saw why the duffadar had been in such a hurry that morning: now, the river ahead was clogged by a huge fleet that was bearing slowly down on the ghats of Chhapra, from upstream. In the lead was a flotilla of pulwars—single-masted boats, equipped with oars as well as sails. These quick-moving craft were ranging ahead of the main body of the fleet, clearing the waterways of other traffic, scouting the navigable channels, and marking the many shoals and sandbars that lurked just beneath the water's surface. Behind them, advancing under full sail, were some twenty patelis. Double-masted and square-rigged, these were the largest vessels on the river, not much smaller than ocean-going ships, and they carried a full complement of canvas on each mast, both dols being hung with three sails—bara, gavi and sabar.

Deeti and Kalua knew at a glance where the ships were coming from and where they were going: this was the fleet of the Ghazipur Opium Factory, carrying the season's produce to Calcutta, for auction. The fleet was accompanied by a sizeable contingent of armed guards, burkundazes and peons, most of whom were distributed among the smaller pulwar boats. The large vessels were still a good hour away when some half-dozen pulwars pulled in. Squads of guards jumped ashore, wielding lathis and spears, and set about clearing the ghats of people, securing them for the docking of the stately patelis.

The opium fleet was commanded by two Englishmen, both junior assistants from the Ghazipur Carcanna. By tradition, the senior of the two occupied the pateli that headed the fleet while the other sailed in the ship that brought up the rear. These two vessels were the largest in the fleet and they took the places of honour at the shore. The ghats at Chhapra were not of a size to accommodate many large vessels at one time and the other patelis had to drop anchor at midstream.

Despite the line of guards around the ghat, a crowd soon assembled to gape at the fleet, their attention being drawn particularly to the two largest patelis. Even by daylight, these vessels presented a handsome sight—and after nightfall, when their lamps were lit, they looked so spectacular that few of the townsfolk could resist taking a dekho. From time to time, prodded by lathis and spears, the crowd would be forced to part, clearing a path for those of the local zemindars and notabilities who wished to offer their salams to the two young assistants. Some were sent away without being granted an audience, but a few were accorded a brief reception, on board: one or the other of the Englishmen would come on deck for a few minutes, to acknowledge the proffered obeisances. At each such appearance, the crowd pressed forward to get a closer look at the white men, in their jackets and trowsers, their tall black hats and white cravats.

As the night wore on, the crowd thinned and those of the spectators who remained were able to press a little closer to the stately patelis—Deeti and Kalua among them. The night was hot and the windows in the patelis' staterooms were left open to invite in the breeze. These openings provided occasional glimpses of the two young assistants, as they sat down to their meal—not on the floor, it was observed, but at a table that was brilliantly illuminated with candles. Transfixed with curiosity, the transients of the waterfront kept watch as the two men were served their food by a team of more than a dozen khidmutgars and khalasis.

While jostling for a better view, many spectators speculated about the food that was being put before the white men.

. . . That's a jackfruit they're eating now, look, he's cutting up the *katthal* . . .

. . . It's your brain that's a jackfruit, you fool—what they're eating is the leg of a goat . . .

Then, all of a sudden, the crowd was put to flight by a detachment of guards and chowkidars, from the kotwali that was responsible for policing this part of the town. Deeti and Kalua scattered into the shadows as the kotwal himself came waddling down the steps that led to the ghats. A large, officious-looking man, he seemed none too pleased to be summoned to the riverfront at this time of night. He raised his voice in annoyance as he made his way down to the water: Yes? Who is it? Who asked for me at this hour?

He was answered in Bhojpuri, by one of the men who had accompanied the fleet: Kotwal-ji, it was I, sirdar of the burkundazes, who wanted to meet with you: might I trouble you to come down to my pulwar?

The voice was familiar, and Deeti's instincts were instantly alert. Kalua, she whispered, get away from here, run to the sandbanks. I think I know that man. There'll be trouble if you're recognized. Go, hide.

And you?

Don't worry, said Deeti, I've got my sari to hide me. I'll be all right. I'll come as soon as I find out what's happening. Go now, chal.

The kotwal was flanked by two peons who were carrying burning branches, to show him the way. When he had reached the water's edge, the light from the torches fell on the man in the boat, and Deeti saw that he was none other than the sirdar who had let her into the opium factory on the day of her husband's collapse. The sight of him inflamed her ever-combustible curiosity: what business could the sirdar have with the kotwal of Chhapra's river-ghat? Determined to know more, Deeti crept closer, through the shadows, until the two men were just within earshot. The sirdar's voice came wafting through the darkness, in snatches:

. . . Stole her from the cremation fire . . . they were seen here together recently, near the Ambaji temple . . . you're of our caste, you understand . . .

*Kya áfat*—what a calamity! It was the kotwal speaking now: What do you want me to do? I'll do anything I can . . . *tauba, tauba* . . .

. . . Bhyro Singh will pay generously for any help you can offer him . . . as you can understand, the family's honour won't be restored till they're dead . . .

I'll put the word out, the kotwal promised. If they're here, you can be sure we'll catch them.

There was no need to wait any longer: Deeti hurried into the sandbanks, where Kalua was waiting. When they were a safe distance away, they found a place to sit and she told him what she had learnt—that her dead husband's family was determined to hunt them down, and had somehow come to know of their presence in Chhapra. It would not be safe to remain there one more day.

Kalua listened thoughtfully but said little. They lay beside each other on the sand, under a crescent moon, and neither of them spoke. They lay awake until the hooting of the owls ceased and the call of a hoopoe signalled the approach of day. Then Kalua said, quietly: The girmitiyas will leave at daybreak . . .

Do you know where their boat is moored?

It's just outside the town, to the east.

Come. Let's go.

Keeping away from the waterfront, they circled through the centre of the town, drawing howls from the packs of dogs that roamed the lanes at night. On reaching the town's eastern boundary, they were intercepted by a chowkidar, who took Deeti for a prostitute and was seized by a desire to take her into his chokey. Instead of arguing, she told him that she had been working all night and was too soiled to go with him without first taking a bath in the river. He let them go after making her promise to return, but by the time they got away from him, the sun had already risen. They reached the river just in time to see the migrants' boat pushing off from its moorings: the duffadar was on deck, supervising the boatmen as they hoisted the sails.

Ramsaran-ji! They ran down a sandy slope shouting his name. Ramsaran-ji! Wait . . .

The duffadar looked over his shoulder and recognized Kalua. It was too late to bring the pulwar back to the shore, so he made a beckoning motion with his hands: Come! Come through the water; it's not too deep . . .

Just as they were about to step into the river, Kalua said to Deeti: There's no turning back after this. Are you sure about going on?

Is it even something to ask? she snapped impatiently. Is this the time to stand there like a tree? Come! Let's go—chal, na . . .

Kalua had no other questions, for his own doubts had been resolved a while before, in his heart. It was without any hesitation now that he swept Deeti into his arms and strode through the water, towards the pulwar.

~

Jodu was on deck when Captain Chillingworth and Mr Crowle came to inspect the *Ibis*, so he was one of the few to see the whole tamasha from the start. The timing could not have been worse: they came the day before the *Ibis* was due to be towed to the dry docks, when things were a little out of sneer anyway. Worse still, they arrived shortly after the midday meal, when every crewman's head was slowed by the heat and their bodies were sluggish and replete. For once, Serang Ali had allowed the watch to go below for a siesta. He had stayed on deck himself to keep an eye on Jodu, whose turn it was to wash the utensils—but the heat was such as to wilt anyone's vigilance, and soon enough he too was stretched out under a strip of shade beneath the binnacle.

With the passage of the sun, the shadows of the masts had dwindled into small circles of shade, and Jodu was sitting in one of these, clothed in nothing but a chequered langot, scouring metal khwanchas and earthen chatties. The only other man on deck was Steward Pinto, who was on his way back to the galley, tray in hand, after having taken Zachary's midday meal to the cuddy. It was the steward who first spotted Mr Crowle and it was his expression of alarm—*Burra Malum áyá*!—that alerted Jodu: pushing the pots and pans aside, he took refuge in the shadows of the bulwark and thought himself lucky when the Burra Malum's gaze passed over him without pause.

The Burra Malum had the look of a man who expected nothing but trouble from the world; although tall and broad-chested, he walked with his shoulders hunched and his neck braced, as if in readiness to run head-on into all impediments and obstructions. He was neatly, even carefully, dressed in a dark, broadcloth jacket, narrow pantaloons and wide-brimmed hat, but on the sides of his narrow face there was a coarse, reddish stubble that gave him a look of indefinable slovenliness. Jodu observed him carefully as he went by, and noticed that his mouth had an odd twitch, which laid bare the tips of a few cracked and wolfish teeth. Elsewhere, he might well have been a nondescript, unremarkable kind of man, but here, as a sahib amongst a shipload of lascars, he knew himself to be a figure of command, and it was clear, from the start, that he was

*Amitav Ghosh*

looking to establish his authority: his blue eyes were darting here and there, as if in search for things to take issue with. And it wasn't long before they chanced upon one such: for there, stretched out beneath the binnacle, was Serang Ali in a tattered banyan and lungi, stupefied by the heat, his chequered bandhna covering his face as he snored.

The sight of the sleeping lascar seemed to light some kind of wick in the malum's head and he began to swear: '. . . drunk as a fiddler's bitch . . . at midday too.' The Burra Malum pulled back a foot and was about to unloose a kick, when Steward Pinto bethought himself of a ruse and dropped his tray: the clatter of the metal did what it was meant to, and the serang jumped to his feet.

Cheated of his kick, the Burra Malum swore even louder, telling the serang he was an over-shrubbed sniplouse, and what did he think he was doing lying incog on deck at this time of day? Serang Ali was slow to answer, for he had stuffed, as was his custom, a large wad of paan into his cheek after his midday meal: his mouth was now so full that his tongue could not move. He turned his head, to spit over the rails, but for once his aim failed him and he spewed the macerated red remains over the bulwarks and the deck.

At this, the Burra Malum snatched a bitt-stopper off the bulwark and ordered the serang to get down on his knees and clean up the mess. He had been swearing all the while, of course, but now he used an oath that everyone understood: Soor-ka-batcha.

Son of a pig? Serang Ali? By this time, several other members of the crew had emerged from the fana to see what was happening, and Muslim or not, there was not one among them who did not bridle at this curse. Despite his oddities, Serang Ali was a figure of unquestioned respect and authority, occasionally harsh but usually fair, and always supremely competent in his seamanship: to insult him in this way was to piss on the whole fana. Some of the men bunched their fists and took a step or two in the Burra Malum's direction, but it was the serang himself who signalled to them to stay back. To defuse the situation he got down on his knees and began to swab the deck with his bandhna.

All this had happened so quickly that Zikri Malum had yet to emerge from the cuddy. Now, running up on deck, he found the serang on his hands and knees: 'Hey, what's going on here? What's all this bellerin?' Then he caught sight of the first mate and cut himself short.

For a minute the two officers eyed each other from a distance, and then a heated argument began. To look at the Burra Malum, you'd think a flying gob-line had hit him on the nose: that a sahib should speak up for a lascar, and that too, in front of so many others, was more than he could stand. Brandishing the bitt-stopper, he stepped towards Zikri Malum in a distinctly threatening way: he was by far the bigger man, and much older too, but Zikri Malum didn't give any ground, standing toe to toe with him, and keeping himself under control in a way that won him a lot of respect among the fanawale. Many of the lascars thought he might even get the better of it in a fight, and they would have been none too sorry to see the malums come to blows—whatever happened, it would have made a rare spectacle to see two officers beating each other up, and they'd have had a tale to tell for years to come.

Jodu was not among those who was hoping for an all-out fight, and he was unreservedly glad when another voice rang across the deck to put an end to the altercation: 'Avast there . . . Bas!'

With the two malums going at it hank for hank, no one had noticed the Kaptan coming on deck: spinning around now, Jodu saw a large, bald sahib holding on to the labran ropes, trying to catch his breath. He was much older than Jodu would have expected, and clearly not in the best of health, for the effort of climbing up the side-ladder had robbed him of his wind, sending streams of perspiration down his face.

But well or not, it was in a voice of authoritative assertion that the Kaptan put a stop to the malums' dispute: 'Stash it there, you two! Enough with your mallemarking.'

The Kaptan's hookum sobered the two mates and they made an effort to put a good face on the incident, even bowing and shaking hands. When the Kaptan headed off to the quarter-deck, they followed in step.

But after the officers had disappeared, there was yet another surprise in wait: Steward Pinto, whose dark face had turned a strange, ashy colour, said: I know this Burra Malum— Mr Crowle. I served on a ship with him once . . .

Word flew from lip to lip, and by common consent, the lascars retreated into the gloom of the fana, where they gathered in a circle around the steward.

It was some years ago, said Steward Pinto, maybe seven or eight. He won't remember me—I wasn't a steward then; I was a cook, in the galley. My cousin Miguel, from Aldona, was on that ship too: he was a little younger than me, still a mess-boy. One day, while serving dinner in bad weather, Miguel spilled some soup on this Crowle. He flew into a rage and said Miguel wasn't fit to be a mess-boy: took hold of him by the ear, led him out on deck, and told him he would be working up on the foremast from then on. Now Miguel was a hard worker, but he couldn't climb well. The thought of going all the way up to the tabar scared him half to death. He begged and begged— but Crowle paid him no mind. Even the serang went and explained the problem: whip the boy, he said, or make him scrub the heads, but don't send him up there; he can't climb and he'll fall and die. But the serang's efforts only made things worse—for do you know what this Crowle bastard did? When he heard of Miguel's fears, he deliberately made the climb even harder, by taking down the iskat: without the ladders, the trikat-wale could only go aloft by climbing the labran, which were made of coir rope and could slice up your hands and toes. It was hard even for experienced men because you were often climbing with your body hanging down, like a weighted jhula. For someone like Miguel it was close to impossible, and Crowle must have known what would come of it . . .

What happened? said Cassem-meah. Did he fall on deck?

The steward stopped to brush a hand across his eyes. No;

the wind took him—carried him away like a kite.

The lascars exchanged glances, and Simba Cader shook his head despondently: Nothing good will come from staying on this boat: I can feel it, in my elbow.

We could vanish, said Rajoo hopefully. The ship's going into dry dock tomorrow. By the time it comes back, we could all be gone.

Now, suddenly, Serang Ali took command, in a voice that was low but authoritative. No, he said. If we desert, they'll blame Zikri Malum. He's come a long way with us—look at him: anyone can see he's on his way to making good. No other malum's ever shared our bread and salt. We can only gain by keeping faith with him: it may be hard for a while, but in the end it'll be to our good.

Here, sensing himself to be at odds with the others, the serang glanced around the circle, as if in search of someone who would join him in affirming allegiance to the malum.

Jodu was the first to respond. Zikri Malum helped me, he said, and I'm in his debt; I'll stay even if no one else does.

Once Jodu had committed himself, many others said they'd steer the same course—but Jodu knew that it was he who'd steadied the tiller, and Serang Ali acknowledged as much by giving him a nod.

That was when Jodu knew that he was no longer a dandiwala; he was a real lascar now, assured of his place in the crew.

# eleven

~

The migrants had been on the Ganga only a few days when the monsoons came sweeping up the river and deluged them with a thunderous downpour. They greeted the rains with cries of gratitude, for the preceding few days had been searingly hot, especially in the crowded hold. Now, with powerful winds filling its single, tattered sail, the ungainly pulwar began to make good time, despite having to tack continually between the banks. When the winds died and the showers stopped, the vessel would make use of its complement of twenty long-handled oars, the manpower being supplied by the migrants themselves. The oarsmen were rotated every hour or so and the overseers were careful to ensure that every man served his proper turn. While under weigh, only the oarsmen, the crew and the overseers were allowed on deck—everyone else was expected to remain in the hold below, where the migrants were quartered.

The hold ran the length of the vessel, and had no compartments or internal divisions: it was like a floating storage shed, with a ceiling so low that a grown man could not stand upright in it for fear of hurting his head. The hold's windows, of which there were several, were usually kept shut for fear of thieves, thugs and river-dacoits; after the rains came down they were almost permanently sealed, so that very little light penetrated inside, even when the clouds cleared.

The first time Deeti looked into the hold, she had felt as though she were about to tumble into a well: all she could see, through the veil of her ghungta, were the whites of a great many eyes, shining in the darkness as they looked up and blinked into the light. She went down the ladder with great deliberation, being careful to keep her face veiled. When her eyes had grown accustomed to the gloom, she saw that she had descended into the middle of a packed assembly: several dozen men were gathered around her, some squatting on their haunches, some lying curled on mats, and some sitting with their backs against the hull. A ghungta seemed but a paltry shield against the assault of so many curious eyes, and she was quick to seek shelter behind Kalua.

The women's section of the hold lay well forward, in a curtained alcove between the bows: Kalua led the way there, clearing a path through the press of bodies. When they reached the alcove, Deeti came to an abrupt halt and her hand shook as she reached for the curtain. Don't go far, she whispered nervously in Kalua's ear. Stay close by—who knows what these women are like?

*Theekba*—don't worry, I'll be nearby, he said, ushering her through.

Deeti had expected the women's part of the hold to be just as crowded as the men's, but on stepping past the curtain, she found only a half-dozen figures inside, veiled by their ghungtas. Some of the women were lying sprawled on the floor planks, but on Deeti's entry they moved up to make room for her; she lowered herself slowly to her haunches, taking care to keep her face covered. With everyone squatting and every face covered, there followed a sizing-up that was as awkward and inconclusive as the examination of a new bride by her husband's neighbours. At first no one spoke, but then a sudden gust of wind caused the pulwar to lurch, and the women found themselves tumbling and spilling over each other. Amidst the groans and giggles, Deeti's ghungta slipped from her face, and when she had righted herself, she found that she was looking at a woman with a wide mouth from which a lone tooth protruded like a tilted gravestone. Her name, Deeti would discover later, was Heeru, and she was given to fits of forgetfulness during which she would sit gazing vacantly at her fingernails. It would not take Deeti long to learn that Heeru was the most harmless of women, but at that first meeting, she was more than a little disconcerted by the directness of her curiosity.

Who are you? Heeru demanded. *Tohar nám patá batáv tani*—if you don't identify yourself, how will we know who you are?

As the newcomer, Deeti knew that she would have to account for herself before she could expect the same of the others. It was on her lips to identify herself as Kabutri-ki-ma— the name by which she had been known ever since her daughter's birth—when it occurred to her that if she was to prevent her husband's kinsmen from learning of her whereabouts, both she and Kalua would have to use names other than those by which they were generally known. What then was to be her name? Her proper, given name was the first to come to mind, and since it had never been used by anyone, it was as good as any. Aditi, she said softly, I am Aditi.

No sooner had she said it than it became real: this was who she was—Aditi, a woman who had been granted, by a whim of the gods, the boon of living her life again. Yes, she said, raising her voice a little, so that Kalua could hear her. I am Aditi, wife of Madhu.

The significance of a married woman using her own name was not lost on the others. Heeru's eyes grew clouded with pity: she too had been a mother once and her name was, properly speaking, Heeru-ki-ma. Although her child had died a while ago, through a cruel irony of abbreviation, his name had lived on in his mother. Heeru clicked her tongue sadly as she mulled over Deeti's plight: So your lap is empty then? No children?

No, said Deeti.

Miscarriages? The question was asked by a thin, shrewd-looking woman, with streaks of grey in her hair: this was Sarju, Deeti would discover later, the oldest among the women. Back in her village, near Ara, she had been a *dái*, a midwife, but a mistake in the delivery of a thakur's son had caused her to be driven from her home. On her lap lay a large cloth bundle, over which her hands were protectively clasped, as if to safeguard a treasure.

That day on the pulwar, Deeti did not have the presence of mind to think of a proper answer when the midwife repeated her question: Miscarriages? stillborn? how did you lose the little ones?

Deeti said nothing, but her silence was suggestive enough to elicit an outburst of sympathy: Never mind . . . you are young and strong . . . your lap will soon be filled . . .

In the midst of this, one of the others edged closer, a teenaged girl with long-lashed, trusting eyes: the mound of her chin, Deeti noticed, bore an embellishment that perfectly complemented the oval shape of her face—a tattoo of three tiny dots, arrayed in an arrowhead pattern.

*É tohran ját kaun ha?* the girl asked eagerly. And your caste?

I am . . .

Once again, just as she was about to provide an accustomed answer, Deeti's tongue tripped on the word that came first to her lips: the name of her caste was as intimate a part of herself as the memory of her daughter's face—but now it seemed as if that too were a part of a past life, when she had been someone else. She began again, hesitantly: We, my *jora* and I . . .

Confronted with the prospect of cutting herself loose from her moorings in the world, Deeti's breath ran out. She stopped to suck in a deep draught of air before starting again: . . . We, my husband and I, we are Chamars . . .

At this, the girl gave a squeal and threw her arm delightedly around Deeti's waist.

You too? said Deeti.

No, said the girl. I'm from the Mussahars, but that makes us like sisters, doesn't it?

Yes, said Deeti smiling, we could be sisters—except that you're so young you should be my niece.

This delighted the girl: That's right, she cried, you can be *bhauji hamár*—my sister-in-law.

This exchange annoyed some of the other women, who began to scold the girl: What's wrong with you, Munia? How does all that matter any more? We're all sisters now, aren't we?

Yes, that's right, said Munia, with a nod—but under the cover of her sari, she gave Deeti's hand a little squeeze as if to affirm a special and secret bond.

~

'Neel Rattan Halder, the time has come . . .'

No sooner had Mr Justice Kendalbushe begun his concluding address than he had to start pounding his gavel, for a disturbance broke out in the courtroom when it came to be noted that the judge had omitted the defendant's title. After order had been restored, the judge began again, fixing his eyes directly upon Neel, who was stationed below the podium, in a dock.

'Neel Rattan Halder,' said the judge, 'the time has come to bring these proceedings to a close. Having given due consideration to all the evidence brought before this court, the jury has found you guilty, so it now becomes my painful duty to pass upon you the sentence of the law for forgery. Lest you be unaware of the seriousness of your offence, let me explain that under English law your offence is a crime of the utmost gravity and was until recently considered a capital crime.'

Here the judge broke off and spoke directly to Neel: 'Do you understand what that means? It means that forgery was a hanging offence—a measure which played no small part in ensuring Britain's present prosperity and in conferring upon her the stewardship of the world's commerce. And if this crime proved difficult to deter in a country such as England, then it is only to be expected that it will be very much more so in a land such as this, which has only recently been opened to the benefits of civilization.'

Right then, through the muted patter of a monsoon shower,

Neel's ears caught the faint echo of a vendor's voice, hawking sweetmeats somewhere in the distance: *Joynagorer moa* . . . At the sound of that faraway call, his mouth filled with the remembered taste of a crisp, smoky sweetness as the judge went on to observe that since it was said, and rightly, that a parent who failed to chasten a child was thereby guilty of shirking the responsibilities of guardianship, then might it not also be said, in the same spirit, that in the affairs of men, there was a similar obligation, imposed by the Almighty himself, on those whom he had chosen to burden with the welfare of such races as were still in the infancy of civilization? Could it not equally be said that the nations that had been appointed to this divine mission would be guilty of neglecting their sacred trust, were they to be insufficiently rigorous in the chastisement of such peoples as were incapable of the proper conduct of their own affairs?

'The temptation that afflicts those who bear the burden of governance,' said the judge, 'is ever that of indulgence, the power of paternal feeling being such as to make every parent partake of the suffering of his wards and offspring. Yet, painful as it is, duty requires us sometimes to set aside our natural affections in the proper dispensation of justice . . .'

From his place in the dock, all that Neel could see of Mr Justice Kendalbushe was the top half of his face, which was, of course, framed by a heavy white wig. He noticed that every time the judge shook his head, for emphasis, a little cloud of dust seemed to rise from the powdered curls, to hang suspended above like a halo. Neel knew something of the significance of haloes, having seen a few reproductions of Italian paintings, and it occurred to him to wonder, momentarily, whether the effect was intentional or not. But these speculations were cut short by the sound of his own name.

'Neel Rattan Halder,' rasped the judge's voice. 'It has been established beyond a doubt that you repeatedly forged the signature of one of this city's most respectable merchants, Mr Benjamin Brightwell Burnham, with the intention of wilfully defrauding a great number of your own dependants, friends

*Amitav Ghosh*

and associates, people who had honoured you with their trust because of their regard for your family and because of the blameless reputation of your father, the late Raja Ram Rattan Halder of Raskhali, of whom it could well be said that the only reproach ever to attach to his name is that of having fathered as infamous a criminal as yourself. I ask you, Neel Rattan Halder, to reflect that if an offence such as yours merits punishment in an ordinary man, then how much more loudly does it call for reproof when the person who commits it is one in affluent circumstances, a man in the first rank of native society, whose sole intention is to increase his wealth at the expense of his fellows? How is society to judge a forger who is also a man of education, enjoying all the comforts that affluence can bestow, whose property is so extensive as to exalt him greatly above his compatriots, who is considered a superior being, almost a deity, among his own kind? How dark an aspect does the conduct of such a man assume when for the sake of some petty increase to his coffers, he commits a crime that may bring ruin to his own kinsmen, dependants and inferiors? Would it not be the duty of this court to deal with such a man in exemplary fashion, not just in strict observance of the law, but also to discharge that sacred trust that charges us to instruct the natives of this land in the laws and usages that govern the conduct of civilized nations?'

As the voice droned on, it seemed to Neel that the judge's words too were turning into dust so that they could join the white cloud that was circling above the wig. Neel's schooling in English had been at once so thorough and so heavily weighted towards the study of texts that he found it easier, even now, to follow the spoken language by converting it into script, in his head. One of the effects of this operation was that it also robbed the language of its immediacy, rendering its words comfortingly abstract, as distant from his own circumstances as were the waves of Windermere and the cobblestones of Canterbury. So it seemed to him now, as the words came pouring from the judge's mouth, that he was listening to the sound of pebbles tinkling in some faraway well.

'Neel Rattan Halder,' said the judge, brandishing a sheaf of papers, 'it appears that despite the waywardness and depravity of your nature, you do not lack for adherents and supporters, for this court has received several petitions in your favour, some of them signed by the most respectable natives and even by a few English men. This court is also in receipt of an opinion, offered by pandits and munshis who are learned in the laws of your religion: they hold that it is not lawful to punish a man of your caste and station as others are punished. In addition, the jury has taken the extraordinary and unusual step of commending you to the merciful consideration of the court.'

With a gesture of dismissal the judge allowed the papers to slip from his hand. 'Let it be noted that there is nothing this court values more than a recommendation from a jury, for they understand the habits of the people and may be aware of mitigating circumstances that have escaped the attention of the judge. You may be assured that I have subjected every submission placed before me to the most serious scrutiny, in the hope of discovering therein some reasonable grounds for diverting from the straight path of justice. I confess to you that my efforts have been in vain: in none of these petitions, commendations and opinions, have I been able to discover any grounds whatsoever for mitigation. Consider, Neel Rattan Halder, the view, offered by the learned pandits of your religion, that a man of your station ought to be exempted from certain forms of punishment because these penalties might also be visited on your innocent wife and child by causing them to lose caste. I freely acknowledge the necessity of accommodating the law to the religious uses of the natives, so far as it can be done in a manner consistent with justice. But we see no merit whatsoever in the contention that men of high caste should suffer a less severe punishment than any other person; such a principle has never been recognized nor ever will be recognized in English law, the very foundation of which lies in the belief that all are equal who appear before it . . .'

There was something about this that seemed so absurd to

Neel that he had to drop his head for fear of betraying a smile: for if his presence in the dock proved anything at all, it was surely the opposite of the principle of equality so forcefully enunciated by the judge? In the course of his trial it had become almost laughably obvious to Neel that in this system of justice it was the English themselves—Mr Burnham and his ilk—who were exempt from the law as it applied to others: it was they who had become the world's new Brahmins.

But now there was a sudden deepening in the hush of the court, and Neel raised his eyes to find the judge glaring directly at him again: 'Neel Rattan Halder, the petition submitted in your favour implores us to mitigate your sentence on the grounds that you have been a person of wealth, that your young and innocent family will lose caste and be shunned and ostracized by their kinsmen. As to the latter, I have too great a regard for the native character to believe that your kin would be guided by so erroneous a principle, but in any event, this consideration cannot be permitted to have a bearing on our reading of the law. As to your wealth and your position in society, in our view these serve only to aggravate your offence in our eyes. In pronouncing your sentence I have a stark choice: I can choose either to let the law take its course without partiality, or I can choose to establish, as a legal principle, that there exists in India a set of persons who are entitled to commit crimes without punishment.'

And so there does, thought Neel, and you are one of them and I am not.

'Being unwilling to add further to your distress,' said the judge, 'it is sufficient to say that none of the applications made on your behalf have suggested a single proper ground for altering the course of the law. Recent precedent, in England as well as in this country, has established forgery to be a felony for which the forfeiture of property is an inadequate penalty: it carries the additional sanction of transportation beyond the seas for a term to be determined by the court. It is in keeping with these precedents that this court pronounces its sentence, which is that all your properties are to be seized and sold, to make good your debts, and that you yourself are to be transported to the penal settlement on the Mauritius Islands for a period of no less than seven years. So let it be recorded on this, the twentieth day of July, in the year of Our Lord, 1838 . . .'

~

Soon, by virtue of his prodigious strength, Kalua became the most valued oarsman on the pulwar and he alone, among all the migrants, was allowed to take turns whenever the weather permitted. The privilege pleased him greatly, the strain of rowing being more than amply compensated by the rewards of being on deck, where he could watch the rain-freshened countryside going by.The names of the settlements on the banks made a great impression on him—Patna, Bakhtiyarpur, Teghra—and it became a game with him to compute the number of strokes that separated the next from the last. Occasionally, when some storied town or city came into view, Kalua would go down to let Deeti know: Barauni! Munger! The women's enclosure boasted more than its fair share of windows, being endowed with two, one on either bow. With each of Kalua's reports, Deeti and the others would prise the shutters briefly open to gaze upon the settlements as they approached.

Every day at sunset, the pulwar would stop for the night. Where the banks were dangerously unpeopled, it would drop anchor at midstream, but if they happened to be in the vicinity of some populous town, like Patna, Munger or Bhagalpur, then the boatmen would attach their moorings directly to the shore. The greatest treat of all was when the pulwar pulled up to the ghats of some busy town or river port: in the intervals between showers of rain the women would sit on deck, watching the townsfolk and laughing at the evermore-outlandish accents in which they spoke.

When the pulwar was under weigh, the women were permitted on deck only for the serving of the midday meal: at all other times, they were kept in seclusion, in their curtained enclosure between the bows. To spend three weeks in that small, dark and airless space should have been, by rights, an experience of near-unbearable tedium. Yet, strangely, it was anything but that: no two hours were the same and no two days alike. The close proximity, the dimness of the light, and the pounding drumbeat of the rain outside, created an atmosphere of urgent intimacy among the women; because they were all strangers to each other, everything that was said sounded new and surprising; even the most mundane of discussions could take unexpected twists and turns. It was astonishing, for example, to discover that in making mango-achar, some were accustomed to using fallen fruit while others would use none that were not freshly picked; no less was it surprising to learn that Heeru included heeng among the pickling spices and that Sarju omitted so essential an ingredient as kalonji. Each woman had always practised her own method in the belief that none other could possibly exist: it was bewildering at first, then funny, then exciting, to discover that the recipes varied with every household, family and village, and that each was considered unquestionable by its adherents. So absorbing was this subject that it kept them occupied from Ghoga to Pirpainti: and if so trivial a thing could generate so much talk, then what of such pressing matters as money and the marital bed?

As for stories, there was no end to them: two of the women, Ratna and Champa, were sisters, married to a pair of brothers whose lands were contracted to the opium factory and could no longer support them; rather than starve, they had decided to indenture themselves together—whatever happened in the future, they would at least have the consolation of a shared fate. Dookhanee was another married woman, travelling with her husband: having long endured the oppressions of a violently abusive mother-in-law, she considered it fortunate that her husband had joined in her escape.

Deeti, too, felt no constraint in speaking of the past, for she had already imagined, in fulsome detail, a history in which she had been Kalua's wife since the age of twelve, living with him and his cattle in his roadside bier. And if called upon to account for the decision to cross the Black Water, she would blame it all on the jealousies of the pehlwans and strongmen of Benares, who, unable to beat her husband in combat, had contrived to have him driven from the district.

To some of the stories, they returned again and again: the tale of Heeru's separation from her husband, for example, was told so many times that they all felt as though they had lived through it themselves. It had happened the previous year, at the start of the cold season, during the great cattle mela of Sonepur. Heeru had lost her firstborn and only child the month before and her husband had persuaded her that if she was ever to bear another son, she would need to do a puja at the temple of Hariharnath, during the fair.

Heeru knew, of course, that a great many people went to the mela, but she was not prepared for the multitudes that were assembled on the sand-flats of Sonepur: the dust raised by their feet was so thick as to make a moon of the midday sun, and as for cattle and other animals, there were so many that it seemed as if the river's banks would collapse under their weight. It took them a whole day to make their way to the gates of the temple and while they were waiting to enter, an elephant, brought there by a zemindar, ran suddenly amuck, scattering the crowd. Heeru and her husband ran in opposite directions, and afterwards, when she knew herself to be lost, she fell prey to one of her bouts of distracted forgetfulness. For hours she sat on the sand, staring at her fingernails, and when at last she bethought herself to go looking for her man, he was nowhere to be found: it was like searching for a grain of rice in an avalanche of sand. After two days of fruitless wandering, Heeru decided to make her way back to her village—but this was no easy matter for there was a distance of sixty kos to be covered, and that, too, through a stretch of country that was preyed-upon by ruthless dacoits and murderous Thugs: for a woman to embark on that journey alone was to invite murder, or worse. She got as far as Revelganj and decided to wait until she encountered relatives or acquaintances who might agree to take her with them. Several months passed during which she sustained herself by begging, washing clothes and carting dust at a saltpetre mine. Then one day she saw someone she knew, a neighbour from the village; she rushed towards him, in delight, but when he recognized her, he fled, as if from a ghost. At length, when she managed to catch up with him, he told her that her husband had given her up for dead and married again; his new wife was already pregnant.

At first Heeru was determined to go back and reclaim her place in her home—but then she began to wonder. Why had her husband taken her to Sonepur in the first place? Had he perhaps intended to abandon her all along, seizing any opportunity that arose? Certainly he had berated and beaten her often enough in the past: what would he do if she returned to him now?

And as luck would have it, just as she was mulling over these questions, a pulwar, filled with migrants, drew up to the ghat . . .

Munia's story was apparently the simplest of all: when questioned about her presence on the pulwar, she would say that she was on her way to join her two brothers, who had both left for Mareech some years before. If asked why she wasn't married she would say that there was no one at home to find a husband for her, both her parents having recently died. Deeti guessed that this was not all there was to this tale, but she was careful not to pry: she knew that when the time was right, Munia would tell of her own accord—wasn't she, Deeti, the girl's surrogate bhauji, the sister-in-law that everyone dreamed of, friend, protector and confidant? Wasn't it to her that Munia always came when some overly forward man flirted or teased or tried to entice her into assignations? She knew that Deeti would put those men in their places by reporting her tales to Kalua: Look at that filthy luchha over there, making eyes at Munia. He thinks he can tease and provoke and do all kinds of *chherkáni* just because she's young and pretty. Go and set him right; tell him *aisan mat kará*—

don't you dare do it again, or you'll find your liver on the wrong side of your belly.

Kalua would go lumbering over and ask, in his polite way: *Khul ke batáibo*—tell me truthfully, were you bothering that girl? Could you tell me why?

This was usually enough to put an end to the trouble for to be asked such a question by someone of Kalua's size was not to the taste of most.

It was after one such episode that Munia poured her story into Deeti's ear: it was about a man from Ghazipur, a pykari agent from the opium factory. While visiting their village, he had seen her working at the harvest and had made it his business to pass that way again and again. He had brought her trinkets and baubles and told her that he was besotted with her—and she, trusting and openhearted as she was, had believed everything he said. They had started meeting secretly, in the poppy fields, during festivals and weddings, when the whole village was distracted. She had enjoyed the secrecy and the romance and even the fondling, until the night when he forced himself on her: after that, for fear of public exposure, she had continued to do his bidding. When she became pregnant, she assumed her family would cast her out or have her killed, but miraculously, her parents had stood by her, despite the ostracism of their community. But they were people of desparately straitened circumstances—so much so that they had had to sell two of their sons into indenture, just to make ends meet. When Munia's child was eighteen months old, they had decided to take the baby to the agent's house—not to threaten or blackmail, but just to show him that he had given them another mouth to feed. He heard them out patiently and then sent them back, saying he would provide all the help that was needed. A few days later some men had stolen up to their dwelling, in the dead of night, and set it on fire. It so happened that it was Munia's time of the month, so she was sleeping away from the others, out in the fields: she had watched the hut burn down, killing her mother, her father and her child. After that, to remain in the district would have been to court death: she had set off to look for the duffadar's pulwar, just as her brothers had done, before her.

Oh you foolish, dung-brained girl! said Deeti. How could you let him touch you . . .?

You won't understand, Munia sighed. I was mad for him; when you feel like that, there's nothing you won't do. Even if it happens again, I'll be helpless, I know.

What are you saying, you silly girl? Deeti cried. How can you talk like that? After all you've been through, you must make sure it never happens again.

Never again? Munia's mood changed suddenly, in a way that made Deeti despair of her. She giggled, covering her mouth with her hand. Would you stop eating rice, she said, because you broke a tooth once, on a kanker? But how would you live . . .?

Shh! Thoroughly scandalized, Deeti began to scold: Be quiet, Munia! Have a thought for yourself. How can you prattle so loosely? Don't you know what would happen if the others found out?

Why would I tell them? said Munia, making a face. I only told you because you're my bhauji. To the others I won't say a thing: they talk too much anyway . . .

It was true that conversation rarely flagged amongst the women—and when it did they had only to prick up their ears to listen to the tales that were being told on the other side of the curtain, among the men. Thus they learnt the story of the quarrelsome Jhugroo, whose enemies had contrived to ship him away by bundling him into the pulwar while drunk; of Cullookhan, the sepoy, who had returned to his village after completing his military service, but only to find that he could no longer bear to be at home; of Rugoo, the dhobi who had sickened of washing clothes, and Gobin, the potter, who had lost the use of his thumb.

Sometimes, when the pulwar stopped for the night, new recruits would come on board, usually in ones and twos, but occasionally in small bands of a dozen or more. At Sahibganj, where the river turned southwards, there were forty men waiting—hills-men from the plateaus of Jharkhand. They had names like Ecka and Turkuk and Nukhoo Nack, and they brought with them stories of a land in revolt against its new rulers, of villages put to flames by the white man's troops.

Soon after this, the pulwar crossed an invisible boundary, taking them into a watery, rain-drowned land where the people spoke an incomprehensible tongue: now, when the barge stopped for the night, they could no longer understand what the spectators were saying, for their jeers and taunts were in Bengali. To add to the migrants' growing unease, the landscape changed: the flat, fertile, populous plains yielded to swamps and marshes; the river turned brackish, so that its water could no longer be drunk; every day the water rose and fell, covering and uncovering vast banks of mud; the shores were blanketed in dense, tangled greenery, of a kind that was neither shrub nor tree, but seemed to grow out of the river's bed, on roots that were like stilts: of a night, they would hear tigers roaring in the forest, and feel the pulwar shudder, as crocodiles lashed it with their tails.

Up to this point, the migrants had avoided the subject of the Black Water—there was no point, after all, in dwelling on the dangers that lay ahead. But now, as they sweated in the steamy heat of the jungle, their fears and apprehensions bubbled over. The pulwar became a cauldron of rumours: it began to be whispered that their rations on the Black Water ship would consist of beef and pork; those who refused to eat would be whipped senseless and the meats would be thrust down their throats. On reaching Mareech, they would be forced to convert to Christianity; they would be made to consume all kinds of forbidden foods, from the sea and the jungle; should they happen to die, their bodies would be ploughed into the soil, like manure, for there was no provision for cremation on that island. The most frightening of the rumours was centred upon the question of why the white men were so insistent on procuring the young and the juvenile, rather than those who were wise, knowing, and rich in experience: it was because they were after an oil that was to be found only in the human brain—the coveted *mimiái-ka-tel*, which was known to be most plentiful among people who had recently reached maturity. The method employed in extracting this substance was to hang the victims upside down, by their ankles, with small holes bored into their skulls: this allowed the oil to drip slowly into a pan.

So much credence did this rumour accumulate that when at last Calcutta was sighted, there was a great outburst of sorrow, in the hold: looking back now, it seemed as if the journey down the Ganga had given the migrants their last taste of life before the onset of a slow and painful death.

~

On the morning of the tumasher, Paulette rose to find that her anxious fingernails had raised an alarming crop of weals on her face during the night. The sight brought tears of vexation to her eyes, and she was tempted to send a chit to Mrs Burnham, claiming that she was ill and could not leave her bed—but instead, presently, she instructed the ab-dars to fill the tub in the goozle-connah. For once she was glad to avail herself of Mrs Burnham's cushy-girls, allowing them to pluck her arms and champo her hair. But the question of what she was to wear had still to be faced, and in addressing it, Paulette found herself yet again on the brink of tears: this was a matter that she had never worried about before and she was at a loss to understand why it should concern her now. What did it matter that Mr Reid was coming? For all she knew, he would scarcely notice her presence. And yet, when she tried on one of Mrs Burnham's hand-me-downs, she found herself examining the rich but stern-looking gown with unaccustomedly critical eyes: she could not face the thought of going down to the tumasher dressed like a marmot in mourning. But what else could she do? To buy a new dress was beyond her capabilites, not just because she had no money, but also because she could not trust her own taste in memsahib fashion.

With no other recourse, Paulette sought help from Annabel,

who was wise beyond her years in some things. Sure enough, the girl was a great source of support, and hit upon the expedient of using bits of one of her own chikan-worked dooputties, to brighten the pelerine collar of Paulette's black silk gown. But Annabel's aid did not come without a price. 'Why, look at you, Puggly—you're flapping about like a titler!' she said. 'I've never seen you worry about your jumma before. It's not because of a chuckeroo, is it?'

'Why no,' said Paulette quickly. 'Of course not! It is only that I feel I should not let down your family at such an important evenment.'

Annabel was not taken in. 'You're trying to bundo someone, aren't you?' she said with her wicked smile. 'Who is it? Do I know him?'

'Oh Annabel! It is nothing like that,' cried Paulette.

But Annabel was not easily silenced, and later that day, when she saw Paulette coming down the stairs, fully outfitted, she uttered a squeal of admiration: 'Tip-top, Paulette—shahbash! They'll be showering choomers on you before the night's out.'

'Really Annabel—how you do exagere!' Hitching up her skirts, Paulette bolted away, glad to see that there was no one within earshot except a passing chobdar, two hurrying farrashes, three mussack-laden beasties, two chisel-wielding mysteries, and a team of flower-bearing malis. She would have been mortified if Mrs Burnham had overheard her, but fortunately the BeeBee was still at her toilette.

At the front of the Burnham house, adjoining the portico, lay a reception room that Mrs Burnham laughingly referred to as her shishmull, because of the great quantity of gilt-framed Venetian mirrors that hung on its walls: it was here that guests were usually received and seated before the serving of dinner. Although grand enough, this room was by no means the largest in the house, and when all its chandeliers and sconces were ablaze the shishmull offered very few dark or quiet corners—which was something of a nuisance for Paulette, whose principal expedient, in dealing with the Burnham burra-khanas, was to make herself as inconspicuous as possible. In

*Amitav Ghosh*

the shishmull, by dint of experimentation, she had found that her purpose was best served by retiring to a corner where a single, straight-backed chair stood in isolation against an unmirrored patch of wall: here she had succeeded in sitting out the preliminary phases of many an evening without attracting the attention of anyone other than the khidmutgars who were serving iced simkin and sherbert. It was to this corner therefore that she made her way, but tonight her customary refuge did not shelter her for long: she had just accepted a cold tumlet of tart-sweet tamarind sherbert when she heard Mrs Burnham calling out her name. 'Oh Paulette! Where have you been chupowing yourself? I've been looking everywhere for you: Captain Chillingworth has a question.'

'For me, Madame?' said Paulette in alarm, rising to her feet.

'Yes indeed—and here he is.' Mrs Burnham took a half-step aside, bringing Paulette face-to-face with the Captain.

'Captain Chillingworth, may I present Mademoiselle Paulette Lambert?'

Mrs Burnham was gone almost as soon as she had said the words, and Paulette was now alone with the Captain who was breathing rather heavily as he bowed.

'. . . Honoured, Miss Lambert.'

His voice was low, she noticed, and it had the crunching sound of conkers rattling beneath the wheel of a carriage. Even if he had not been so visibly short of wind, it would have been clear at a glance that he was not in the best of health: the colour of his face was a mottled red, and his figure seemed oddly bloated. Like his body, his face seemed to sag upon a frame that had once been large, square and confident of its power; its lines drooped in apparent exhaustion—the fleshy jowls, the watery eyes and the deep dark pouches beneath them. When he raised his hat, his head was revealed to be almost completely bald, except for a tattered ring of hair that hung down from its edges, like a fringe of peeling bark.

Mopping the sweat from his face, the Captain said: 'I

noticed a row of lataniers on the drive. I'm told they were your doing, Miss Lambert.'

'That is true, sir,' Paulette replied, 'it was indeed I who planted them. But they are still so small! I am surprised you noticed them.'

'Pretty plants, latanias,' he said. 'Don't see them much in these parts.'

'I have a great fondness for them,' said Paulette, 'especially the *Latania commersonii.*'

'Oh?' said the Captain. 'May I ask why?'

Paulette was embarrassed now, and she looked down at her shoes. 'The plant was identified, you see, by Philippe and Jeanne Commerson.'

'And who, pray, were they?'

'My grand-uncle and grand-aunt. They were botanists, both of them, and lived many years in the Mauritius.'

'Ah!' His frown deepened, and he began to ask another question—but the query was lost on Paulette who had just caught sight of Zachary, coming through the door. Like the other men, he was in his shirtsleeves, having handed his coat to a khidmutgar before stepping into the shishmull. His hair was neatly tied, with a black ribbon, and his Dosootie shirt and nainsook trowsers were the plainest in the room—yet he looked improbably elegant, mainly because he was the only man present who was not dripping with sweat.

After Zachary's arrival, Paulette was unable to summon much more than a monosyllable or two in response to the Captain's inquiries, and she scarcely noticed when Mr Justice Kendalbushe frowned disapprovingly at her finery and murmured: '"Hell is naked and destruction hath no covering."'

To add to her trials, when it came time to go in to dinner, Mr Doughty began to compliment her effusively on her appearance. ''Pon my sivvy, Miss Lambert! Aren't you quite the dandyzette today? Fit to knock a feller oolter-poolter on his beam-ends!' Then, fortunately, he caught sight of the dinner-table and forgot about Paulette.

*Amitav Ghosh*

The table for the evening was of modest size, having been fitted with only two of its six leaves, but what it lacked in length, it more than made up for in the height and weight of its fare, which was laid out in a single spectacular service, with platters and dishes arranged in a spiralling ziggurat of comestibles. There was green turtle soup, served artfully in the animals' shells, a Bobotie pie, a dumbpoke of muttongosht, a tureen of Burdwaun stew, concocted from boiled hens and pickled oysters, a foogath of venison, a dish of pomfrets, soused in vinegar and sprinkled with petersilly, a Vinthaleaux of beef, with all the accompaniments, and platters of tiny roasted ortolans and pigeons, with the birds set out in the arrowhead shapes of flocks in fight. The table's centrepiece was a favourite of the Bethel bobachee-connah: a stuffed roast peacock, mounted upon a silver stand, with its tail outspread as if for an imminent mating.

The spectacle briefly deprived Mr Doughty of his breath: 'I say,' he muttered at last, wiping his forehead, which was already streaming in anticipation of the feast, 'now here's a sight for Chinnery's paintbrush!'

'Exactly, sir,' said Paulette, although she had not quite heard what he had said—for her attention, if not her gaze, was focused upon the place to her left, where Zachary had now appeared. Yet she dared not turn away from the pilot, for she had more than once been reprimanded by Mrs Burnham for the solecism of speaking with a left-hand neighbour out of turn.

Mr Doughty was still exclaiming over the fare when Mr Burnham cleared his throat in preparation for the saying of grace: 'We thank you Lord . . .' In emulation of the others, Paulette held her clasped hands to her chin and shut her eyes— but she couldn't resist stealing a surreptitious glance at her neighbour, and was greatly discomposed when her eyes encountered Zachary's, who was also peering sideways, over his fingertips. They both flushed and looked hurriedly away, and were just in time to echo Mr Burnham's sonorous 'Amen'.

Mr Doughty wasted no time in spearing an ortalan.

'Tantivy, Miss Lambert!' he whispered to Paulette, as he dropped the bird on her plate. 'Take it from an old hand: have to be jildee with the ortolans. They're always the first to go.'

'Why thank you.' Paulette's words were lost on the pilot, whose attention was now focused on the dumbpoke. With her senior dinner-partner thus distracted, Paulette was free at last to turn to Zachary.

'I am glad, Mr Reid,' she said formally, 'that you could spare an evening for us.'

'Not as glad as I am, Miss Lambert,' said Zachary. 'It's not often that I'm invited to such a feast.'

'But Mr Reid,' said Paulette, 'my little finger has told me that you have been sortieing a great deal of late!'

'Sort . . . sortieing?' said Zachary in surprise. 'And what might you mean by that, Miss Lambert?'

'Forgive me,' she said. 'I mean dining out—you have been doing so a great deal, no, of late?'

'Mr Doughty and his wife have been very kind,' said Zachary. 'They've taken me with them to a few places.'

'You are lucky,' said Paulette, with a conspiratorial smile. 'I believe your colleague, Mr Crowle, is not so fortunate?'

'Wouldn't know about that, Miss.'

Paulette lowered her voice: 'You know, you must be careful with Mr Crowle. Mrs Burnham says he is an awful thug.'

Zachary stiffened. 'I'm not a'feared of Mr Crowle.'

'But have a care Mr Reid: Mrs Burnham says she will not have him in the house. You must not tell him you were here tonight.'

'Don't worry Miss,' said Zachary smiling. 'Mr Crowle's not a man I'm likely to be sharing confidences with.'

'Is he not on the ship then?'

'No,' said Zachary. 'None of us are. The *Ibis* is in dry dock and we're all liberty-men in the meantime. I've moved into a boarding house.'

'Really? Where?'

'In Kidderpore—Watsongunge Lane. Jodu found it for me.'

'Oh?' Paulette glanced over her shoulder to make sure that no one else had heard Jodu's name, and turned back to Zachary reassured.

Recently, Mr Burnham had installed a new fixture to cool the dining room. Known as a Thermantidote, the device was a winnowing machine that had been fitted with a propeller and a thick mat of fragrant khus-khus.The men who had once pulled the ropes of the overhead punkahs were now employed in operating the Thermantidote: while one wetted the machine's rush screen the other turned the propeller by means of a handle, forcing a constant stream of air through the dampened mat. Thus, by means of evaporation, the machine was supposed to create a wonderfully cooling breeze. Such at least was the theory—but in rainy weather the Thermantidote added greatly to the humidity, making everyone sweat even more than usual, and it also produced a loud, grinding noise that often drowned the conversation. Mr Burnham and Mr Doughty were among the few who could make themselves heard effortlessly, above the machine—but those with feebler voices often had to shout, which only added to the prevailing sweatiness. In the past, when seated beside deaf colonels and infirm accountants, Paulette had often had cause to regret the introduction of the new machine—but today she was unreservedly glad of its presence, since it allowed her to speak with Zachary without fear of being overheard.

'If I may ask, Mr Reid,' she said, 'where is Jodu now? What has become of him?'

'He's trying to earn a little money while the *Ibis* is being refitted,' said Zachary. 'He asked me for a small loan so he could rent a little ferry-boat. He'll be back on board when we're ready to sail.'

Paulette thought back to the lazy days when she and Jodu had sat in the trees of the Botanical Gardens, watching the ships on the Hooghly. 'So he is to have his wish then? He will be on your crew?'

'That's right: just as you wanted. He will be going to Port Louis with us when we sail in September.'

'Oh? He will go to the Mauritius?'

'Yes,' said Zachary. 'Do you know the islands?'

'No,' said Paulette, 'I have never been there, although it was once my family's home. My father was a botanist, you see, and in the Mauritius there is a very famous botanical garden. It was there that my father and mother were married. That is why I have a great envy to go there . . .' She broke off: suddenly it seemed intolerably unjust that Jodu should be able to go to this island while she, Paulette, with all her prior claims, could not.

'Is something the matter?' Zachary said, alarmed by her pallor. 'Are you all right, Miss Lambert?'

'An idee came to my mind,' said Paulette, trying to make light of her sudden turn of thought. 'It struck me that I too would love to go to the Mauritius on the *Ibis*. Just like Jodu, working on a ship.'

Zachary laughed. 'Believe me, Miss Lambert, a schooner's no place for a woman—lady, I mean, begging your pardon. Especially not someone who is accustomed to living like this . . .' He made a gesture in the direction of the loaded table.

'Is that indeed so, Mr Reid?' said Paulette, raising her eyebrows. 'So it is not possible, according to you, for a woman to be a marin?'

Often, when at a loss for a word, Paulette would borrow a term from the French, trusting that it would pass for English if pronounced exactly as it was spelled. This strategy worked well enough to provide reason to persist, but every once in a while it produced unexpected results: from the look on Zachary's face, Paulette knew that this was one such occasion.

'Marine?' he said in surprise. 'No, Miss Lambert, there sure aren't any woman marines that I ever heard of.'

'"Sailor",' said Paulette triumphantly. 'That is what I meant. You think it is not possible for a woman to sail under a mast?'

'As a captain's wife, perhaps,' said Zachary, shaking his

head. 'But never as a member of the crew: not a sailor worth his salt would put up with that. Why, there's many a sailor won't so much as utter the word "woman" at sea, for fear of bad luck.'

'Ah!' said Paulette. 'But then it is clear, Mr Reid, that you have never heard of the famous Madame Commerson!'

'Can't say as I have, Miss Lambert,' said Zachary with a frown. 'What flag does she fly?'

'Madame Commerson was not a ship, Mr Reid,' said Paulette. 'She was a scientist: to be precise, she was my own grand-aunt. And I beg to inform you that she was but a young woman when she joined a ship and sailed all around the world.'

'Is that a fact?' said Zachary sceptically.

'Yes, indeed it is,' said Paulette. 'You see, before she was married, my grand-aunt's name was Jeanne Baret. Even as a girl, she had a passion most heated for science. She read about Linnaeus, and the many new species of plants and animals that were being named and discovered. These diverse facts made her burn with the volontee to see for herself the riches of the earth. What should happen then, Mr Reid, but that she should learn of a great expedition, being organized by Monsieur de Bougainville, with the intention of doing exactly that which she wished? This idee set her afire and she decided that she too, by all hasard, would be an expeditionnaire. But of course it was not to be expected that the men would permit a woman to join the ship . . . so can you imagine Mr Reid, what my grand-aunt did?'

'No.'

'She did the simplest thing, Mr Reid. She tied up her hair like a man and applied to join under the name of Jean Bart. And what is more, she was accepted—by none other than the great Bougainville himself! And it was none too hard, Mr Reid—this I would have you know: it was no more than a matter of wearing a tight band over her chest and lengthening her stride when she walked. Thus she set sail, wearing trowsers, just like you, and not one of the sailors or scientists guessed her secret. Can you but imagine, Mr Reid, all those savants, so knowledgeable about the anatomy of animals and plants?—not one of them knew that there was a fillie among them, so completely was she male? It was only after two years that she was undone, and do you know how, Mr Reid?'

'Wouldn't like to guess, Miss,' said Zachary.

'In Tahiti, when the expeditionnaires went ashore, the people took but one look and they knew! The secret that no Frenchman had guessed through two years of living on the same ship, day in, day out, the Tahitians knew tootsweet. But now it did not matter, for of course, Monsieur de Bougainville could not abandonne her so he agreed to let her come along. They say it was she who, out of gratitude, named the flower that is called after the admiral: bougainvillea. This was how it happened that Jeanne Baret, my grand-aunt, became the first woman to sail around the earth. And this too was how she found her husband, my grand-uncle, Philippe Commerson, who was among the expeditionnaires and a great savant himself.'

Pleased to have trumped Zachary, Paulette treated him to a beaming smile. 'So you see, Mr Reid, sometimes it happens after all that a woman does indeed join a crew.'

Zachary took a long sip from his wineglass, but the claret was not of much help in digesting Paulette's tale: he tried to think of a woman attempting a similar impersonation on the *Ibis* and was certain that she would be detected within days if not hours. He remembered the hammocks, hung so close that one man's tossing would set the whole fo'c'sle astir and a-shake; he thought of the boredom of the small hours, and those contests where the men of the watch would open their trowsers to leeward to see how much of the sea's phosphorescence they could light up; he thought of the ritual of the weekly bath, on deck, by the lee scuppers, with every tar's body bared to the waist and many having to strip naked to wash their one pair of underclothes. How could a woman join in any of this? Perhaps on a shipful of frog-eating crappos—who knew what devilment they got up to?—

but a Baltimore clipper was a man's world and no true salt would want it otherwise, no matter how great his love of women.

Noting his silence, Paulette asked: 'Do you not believe me, Mr Reid?'

'Well, Miss Lambert, I'll believe it could happen on a French ship,' he said grudgingly. He couldn't resist adding: ''Tisn't the easiest thing anyway to tell a Mamzelle from a Monsoo.'

'Mr Reid . . .!'

'No offence meant . . .'

As Zachary was making his apologies, a tiny pellet of bread came flying over the table and struck Paulette on the chin. She glanced across to find Mrs Doughty smiling and rolling her eyes as if to indicate that some matter of great significance had just transpired. Paulette looked around, nonplussed, and could see nothing of note, except Mrs Doughty herself: the pilot's wife was extremely stout, with a round face that hung, like a setting moon, under a great cloud of henna-red hair; now, with her gestures and grimaces, she appeared to be undergoing some kind of planetary convulsion.

Paulette looked quickly away, for she harboured a great dread of attracting the attention of Mrs Doughty, who tended to speak, at length and with exceptional rapidity, about matters she could not quite comprehend.

Fortunately, Mr Doughty saved her the trouble of having to respond to his wife. 'Shahbash dear!' he exclaimed. 'Perfect shot!' Then, turning to Paulette, he said: 'Tell me, Miss Lambert, have I ever told you how Mrs Doughty once pelleted me with an ortolan?'

'Why no, sir,' said Paulette.

'Happened at Government House,' the pilot continued. 'Right under the Lat-Sahib's eye. Bird caught me smack on my nose. Must have been a good twenty paces. Knew right then she was the woman for me—eyes like a shoe-goose.' Here, having speared the last ortolan with his fork, he waved it in the direction of his wife.

Paulette seized the opportunity to turn her attention back to Zachary: 'But tell me, Mr Reid, how is it that you communicate with your lascars? Do they speak English?'

'They know the commands,' said Zachary. 'And sometimes, when it's needed, Serang Ali translates.'

'And how do you hold converse with Serang Ali?' Paulette asked.

'He speaks a little English,' said Zachary. 'We manage to make ourselves understood. Odd thing is, he can't even say my name.'

'What does he call you then?'

'Malum Zikri.'

'Zikri?' she cried. 'What a beautiful name! Do you know what it means?'

'I didn't even know it meant anything,' he said in surprise.

'It does,' she said. 'It means the "one who remembers". How nice that is. Would you mind if I called you by this name?'

Now, seeing a flush rise to his face, she quickly regretted her forwardness: it seemed a godsend when the khidmutgars distracted everyone by bringing in an enormous jelly-tree—a three-layered stand with many branching arms, each of these loaded with miniature custards, jellies, puddings, trifles, fools, blancmanges, syllabubs and sugared fruits.

Paulette was about to recommend a mango fool to Zachary when Mr Doughty reclaimed her attention with a melancholy story about how a goose hurled at a Government House dinner had led to a duel and brought official disapproval upon the custom of pelleting. Before he had quite finished, Mrs Burnham caught Paulette's eye in the special way that indicated that it was time for the ladies to withdraw to the gol-cumra. The khidmutgars came forward to pull back their chairs, and the women stepped away to follow their hostess out of the dining room.

Mrs Burnham led the way out at a serenely regal pace, but the moment they were out of the dining room, she abandoned

Paulette with Mrs Doughty. 'I'm off to the dubber,' she whispered slyly in Paulette's ear. 'Good luck with old fustilugs.'

~

In the dining room, where the men had gathered around the host's end of the table, Mr Burnham's offer of a cigar was politely declined by Captain Chillingworth. 'Thank you, Mr Burnham,' said the Captain, reaching for a candlestick, 'but I prefer my buncuses, if it's all the same to you.'

'As you please,' said Mr Burnham, pouring a glass of port. 'But come now, Captain: give us the news from Canton. Does it appear that the celestials will see reason before it is too late?'

The Captain sighed: 'Our friends in the English and American factories do not think so. Almost to a man they believe that a war with China is inevitable. Frankly, most of them welcome the prospect.'

'So the Chuntocks are still set, are they,' said Mr Burnham, 'on putting a stop to the trade in opium?'

'I am afraid so,' said the Captain. 'The mandarins do indeed seem quite set in their course. The other day, they beheaded some half-dozen opium-sellers, right at the gates of Macao. Strung up the bodies in full public view, for everyone to see, Europeans included. It's had an effect, no doubt about it. In February the price of the best Patna opium had sunk to four hundred and fifty dollars a chest.'

'Good God!' said Mr Doughty. 'Was it not twice that last year?'

'So it was.' Mr Burnham nodded. 'You see, it's clear now—the Long-tails will stop at nothing to drive us out of business. And they'll succeed too, no doubt about it, unless we can prevail upon London to fight back.'

Mr Justice Kendalbushe broke in, leaning across the table: 'But tell me, Captain Chillingworth: is it not true that our representative in Canton, Mr Elliott, has had some success in persuading the mandarins to legalize opium? I've heard it said that the mandarins have begun to consider the benefits of free trade.'

Mr Doughty laughed. 'You are too optimistic, sir. Damned hardheaded gudda is Johnny Chinaman. Not a chance of changing his mind.'

'But what the judge says is not unfounded,' said the Captain quickly. 'There's a party in Pekin that is rumoured to be in favour of legalization. But the word is that the Emperor's shrugged them off and decided to destroy the trade root and branch. I'm told he's appointed a new governor to do the job.'

'We should not be surprised,' said Mr Burnham, looking around the table in satisfaction, with his thumbs hooked in his lapels. 'Certainly I am not. I knew from the start it would come to this. Jardine and Matheson have said so all along, and I'm of the same mind. No one dislikes war more than I do—indeed I abhor it. But it cannot be denied that there are times when war is not merely just and necessary, but also humane. In China that time has come: nothing else will do.'

'Quite right, sir!' said Mr Doughty emphatically. 'There is no other recourse. Indeed, humanity demands it. We need only think of the poor Indian peasant—what will become of him if his opium can't be sold in China? Bloody hurremzads can hardly eat now: they'll perish by the crore.'

'I fear you are right,' said Justice Kendalbushe gravely. 'My friends in the Missions are agreed that a war is necessary if China is to be opened up to God's word. It's a pity, of course, but it's best to get it over and done with.'

Eyes twinkling, Mr Burnham looked around the candlelit table: 'Since we are all agreed, gentlemen, perhaps I can share a bit of news that has just come my way? In the strictest confidence, of course.'

'Of course.'

'Mr Jardine has written to say that he has prevailed on the Prime Minister at last.'

'Oh, is it true then?' cried Mr Justice Kendalbushe. 'Lord Palmerston has agreed to send a fleet?'

'Yes,' Mr Burnham nodded in confirmation. 'But fleet is perhaps too grand a word. Mr Jardine reckons that no great show of force will be needed to overwhelm China's antique defences. A few frigates, perhaps, and a couple of dozen merchantmen.'

'Shahbash!' cried Mr Doughty, with a handclap. 'So war it is then?'

'I think we can take it as a certainty now,' said Mr Burnham. 'I'm sure there'll be some pretence of a palaver with the Celestials. But it will all come to naught—we can depend on the Long-tails for that. And then the fleet will go in and wrap it all up in short order. It'll be the best kind of war— quick and inexpensive with the outcome never in doubt. Won't need more than a handful of English troops: a couple of sepoy battalions will get it done.'

Mr Doughty gave a stomach-shaking laugh. 'Oh that's for sure! Our darkies will rout the yellowbellies in short order. It'll be over in a couple of weeks.'

'And I shouldn't be surprised,' said Mr Burnham, stabbing the air with his cigar, 'if there's cheering in the streets of Canton, when the troops go marching in.'

'That's a pucka certainty,' said Mr Doughty. 'The Celestials will be out in force, lighting up their joss-sticks. Ooloo though he might be in some ways, Johnny Chinaman knows a good thing when he sees it. He'll be delighted to be rid of his Manchu tyrant.'

Zachary could no longer hold himself aloof from the excitement that was simmering around the table. He broke in to ask Mr Burnham: 'When do you think the fleet will be ready, sir?'

'I believe two frigates are already on their way,' said Mr Burnham. 'As for the merchantmen, Jardine and Matheson's ships will begin assembling soon, as will ours. You'll be back in plenty of time to join in.'

'Hear, hear!' said Mr Doughty, raising his glass.

Captain Chillingworth alone seemed to be unaffected by the high spirits and general good cheer: his silence having grown too pronounced to be ignored, Mr Justice Kendalbushe bestowed a kindly smile on him: 'A great pity, Captain Chillingworth, that your health will not permit you to join the expedition. No wonder you are gloomy. In your place I would be sorry too.'

Suddenly Captain Chillingworth bristled. 'Sorry?' His voice was emphatic enough to startle everyone. 'Why, no: I am not sorry in the least. I have seen enough of such things in my time; I can well do without another round of butchery.'

'Butchery?' The judge blinked in surprise. 'But Captain Chillingworth, I am sure there will be no more killing than is strictly necessary. There is always a price, is there not, for doing good?'

'"Good", sir?' said Captain Chillingworth, struggling to pull himself upright in his chair. 'I am not sure whose good you mean, theirs or ours? Though why I should include myself in your number I cannot think—heaven knows that very little good has come to me from my doings.'

Two bright spots of colour rose to the judge's cheeks as he absorbed this. 'Why Captain,' he said sharply. 'You do credit neither to yourself nor to us. Is it your implication that no good will come of this expedition?'

'Oh it will, sir; there's no denying that.' Captain Chillingworth's words emerged very slowly, as if they had been pulled up from a deep well of bitterness. 'I am sure it will do a great deal of good for some of us. But I doubt I'll be of that number, or that many Chinamen will. The truth is, sir, that men do what their power permits them to do. We are no different from the Pharaohs or the Mongols: the difference is only that when we kill people we feel compelled to pretend that it is for some higher cause. It is this pretence of virtue, I promise you, that will never be forgiven by history.'

Here Mr Burnham intervened by placing his glass forcefully on the table. 'Well, gentlemen! We can't keep the ladies waiting till we've solved every problem in the world; it's time we joined them.'

An outburst of relieved laughter broke the awkwardness, and the men rose to their feet and began to file out. Zachary was the last through the door, and he stepped out to find the host waiting for him. 'You see, Reid,' Mr Burnham whispered,

*Amitav Ghosh*

placing an arm around his shoulder; 'you see why I'm worried about the Captain's judgement? Much will depend on you, Reid.'

Zachary could not help being flattered. 'Thank you, sir,' he said. 'You can trust me to do my best.'

~

Mrs Doughty's eyes twinkled as she looked at Paulette, over the rim of her cup. 'Well, my dear!' she said. 'You've certainly worked a bit of jadoo tonight.'

'I pray your pardonne, Madame?'

'Oh, don't think you can play the gull with me!' cried Mrs Doughty, wagging a finger. 'I'm sure you noticed, didn't you?'

'Noticed what, Madame? I do not follow.'

'Didn't you dekko? How he wouldn't touch his ortolans and hardly tasted the foogath? Such a waste! Asked ever so many questions too.'

'Who, Madame?' said Paulette. 'Of whom do you speak?'

'Why, Justice Kendalbushe of course: you've certainly scored quite a hit there! Couldn't take his eyes off you.'

'Justice Kendalbushe!' cried Paulette in alarm. 'Did I do something wrong Madame?'

'No, you silly bandar,' said Mrs Doughty, tweaking her ear. 'Not at all. But I'm sure you noticed, didn't you, how he jawaub'd the dumbpoke and sniffed at the peacock? It's always a sign, I say, when a man won't eat. I can tell you, dear, he was all a-chafe every time you turned to talk to Mr Reid!' She went prattling on, leaving Paulette ever more convinced that the judge had spotted her using the wrong fork or an inappropriate knife, and was sure to report the solecism to Mrs Burnham.

To make things worse, when the door opened to admit the men, the judge headed straight over to Paulette and Mrs Doughty and proceeded to deliver a homily on the subject of gluttony. Paulette pretended to listen although all her senses were focused on Zachary's unseen presence, somewhere behind her. But between Mrs Doughty and the Captain, there was no getting away until the evening was all but over. It was only when the guests were taking their leave that Paulette was able to speak with Zachary again. Despite her efforts to remain collected, she found herself saying, with much greater vehemence than she had intended: 'You will look after him, won't you— my Jodu?'

To her surprise, he answered with an intensity that seemed to match her own. 'You can be sure I will,' he said. 'And should there be anything else I can do, Miss Lambert, you need only ask.'

'You must be careful, Mr Reid,' said Paulette, playfully. 'With a name like Zikri you may be held to your word.'

'And gladly too, Miss,' said Zachary. 'You can call on me for sure.'

Paulette was touched by the sincerity of his tone. 'Oh Mr Reid!' she cried. 'You have already done too much.'

'What have I done?' he said. 'I've done nothing, Miss Lambert.'

'You have kept my secret,' she whispered. 'Perhaps you cannot conceive what that means in this world I live in? Look around you, Mr Reid: do you see anyone here who would for a moment believe that a memsahib could think of a native— a servant—as a brother? No: the worst possible imputations would be ascribed.'

'Not by me, Miss Lambert,' said Zachary. 'You can be sure of that.'

'Really?' she said, looking him full in the eyes. 'It does not seem uncroyable to you that a bond so intimate and yet so innocent should exist between a white girl and a boy of another race?'

'Not at all, Miss Lambert—why, I myself . . .' Zachary suddenly began to cough into his fist, cutting himself short. 'I assure you, Miss Lambert, I know of many, much stranger things.'

Paulette sensed that he had something to add, but now there was a sudden interruption, caused by a thunderous detonation. In the awkward silence that followed, nobody glanced in the direction of Mr Doughty, who was examining the knob of his cane with an air of pretended nonchalance. It fell to Mrs Doughty to make an attempt to retrieve the situation. 'Ah!' she cried, clapping her hands cheerily together. 'The wind is rising and we must make sail. Anchors aweigh! We must be off!'

# twelve

~

Many days passed with no word being received about when exactly Neel was to be moved to the jail at Alipore, where convicts were usually sent to await transportation. In the meanwhile, although he was allowed to remain in his former apartment at Lalbazar, the change in his circumstances was made evident to him in dozens of different ways. No longer was he allowed visitors at all times, and days went by when he met with no one at all; the constables who stood guard at his door no longer exerted themselves to provide him with diversions; their manner, once obsequious, now became gruff and surly; at night they took to chaining his doors and he was not allowed to leave his rooms without shackles on his wrists. No longer was he waited on by his own servants, and when he complained of an accumulation of dust in his rooms, the constable on guard answered by asking if he would like to be brought a jharu, so he could do the job for himself. If it were not for the mockery in the man's voice, Neel might have said yes, but instead he shook his head: It's just a few days more, isn't it?

Yes, said the guard, with a guffaw of laughter. And after that you'll be off to your in-laws' palace, in Alipore. You'll be nicely looked after over there—nothing to worry about.

For a short while more, Neel's food continued to come from the Raskhali palace, but then, abruptly, it stopped. Instead, he was handed a wooden basin, a tapori of the kind that was used to serve all the lock-up's inmates: looking under the lid he saw that it contained a gruel-like mixture of dal and coarse rice. 'What's this?' he asked the constable, and was answered by nothing more than a negligent shrug.

He took the basin inside, placed it on the floor and walked away, resolving to ignore it. But in a while hunger drove him back and he seated himself cross-legged beside the basin and removed the lid. The contents had congealed into a grey slop and the smell made him gag, but he forced himself to scoop up a few grains with his fingertips. As he was raising his hand to his lips, it occurred to him that this was the first time in all his years that he had ever eaten something that was prepared by hands of unknown caste. Perhaps it was this thought, or perhaps it was just the smell of the food—it happened, at any rate, that he was assailed by a nausea so powerful that he could not bring his fingers to his mouth. The intensity of his body's resistance amazed him: for the fact was that he did not believe in caste, or so at least he had said, many, many times, to his friends and anyone else who would listen. If, in answer, they accused him of having become too *tāsh*, overly Westernized, his retort was always to say, no, his allegiance was to the Buddha, the Mahavira, Shri Chaitanya, Kabir and many others such—all of whom had battled against the boundaries of caste with as much determination as any European revolutionary. Neel had always taken pride in laying claim to this lineage of egalitarianism, all the more so since it was his prerogative to sit on a Raja's guddee: but why, then, had he never before eaten anything prepared by an unknown hand? He could think of no answer other than ease of habit: because he had always done what was expected of him; because the legion of people who controlled his daily existence had seen to it that it happened in that way and no other. He had thought of his everyday routines as a performance, a duty and nothing more; one of the many little enactments that were required by the demands of a social existence, by samsara—none of it was meant to be real; it was just an illusion, no more than a matter of playing a part in the great charade of conducting a householder's life. And yet there was nothing unreal about the nausea that had seized him now; it was not an illusion that his body was convulsed by a sensation of *ghrina*, a stomach-clenching revulsion that made him recoil from the wooden container in front of him.

Neel stood up and walked away, trying to steady himself: it was clear now that this was not just a matter of a single meal; it was a question of life and death, whether he'd be able to survive or not.

Returning to the tapori, he seated himself beside it, lifted a few morsels to his lips and forced himself to swallow them. It was as if he had ingested a handful of burning embers, for he could feel each grain blazing a trail of fire through his entrails—but he would not stop; he ate a little more, and a little more, until his very skin seemed to be peeling from his body. That night his dreams were plagued by a vision of himself, transformed into a moulting cobra, a snake that was struggling to free itself of its outworn skin.

Next morning he woke to find a sheet of paper under his door. It was a notice, printed in English: 'Burnham Bros. announce the sale of a property awarded by a decision of the Supreme Court of Judicature, a handsome residence known as the Raskhali Rajbari . . .'

He stared at the sheet in a daze, running his eyes over it again and again. This was a possibility he had not allowed himself to contemplate: the deluge of his misfortunes was such that to protect himself from drowning under them, he had chosen not to inquire too closely into the precise implications of the Supreme Court's judgement. Now, his hands began to shake as he thought of what the sale of the Rajbari would mean for his dependants: what would become of the family's servants and retainers, the widowed female relatives?

And what indeed would become of Malati and Raj? Where would they go? His wife's family home, where her brothers now lived, was not a grand residence, like the Raskhali Rajbari, but it was certainly large enough to accommodate her. But now that she had irretrievably lost caste, along with her husband, there could be no question of her seeking shelter

*Amitav Ghosh*

there; if her brothers took her in, their own sons and daughters would never be able to find spouses of their own station. Malati was too proud, he knew, to put her brothers in the situation of having to turn her away.

Neel began to pound upon his chained door. He kept at it until it was opened by a guard. He needed to send a message to his family, he told the constable; some arrangement had to be made to take a letter; he would insist until it was done.

Insist? sneered the constable, waggling his head in derision, and who did he think he was, some kind of raja?

But word must have percolated through, because later in the day, he heard a key turning in the lock. At that hour of the afternoon the sound could only herald a visitor, so he went eagerly to the door, expecting to find Parimal on the threshold—or perhaps one of his gomustas or daftardars. But when the doors swung open, it was to reveal his wife and son, standing outside.

You? he could scarcely bring himself to speak.

Yes. Malati was wearing a red-bordered cotton sari, and although her head was covered, the garment was not draped in such a way as to veil her face.

You've come like this? Neel moved quickly to one side, so she could step out of public view. To a place where everyone can see you?

Malati tossed her head, so that her sari dropped to her shoulders baring her hair. How does it matter any more? she said quietly. We are no different now from anyone on the street.

He began to chew his lip, in concern. But the shame, he said. Are you sure you will be able to bear it?

Me? she said matter-of-factly. What's it to me? It wasn't for my own sake that I kept purdah—it was because you and your family wanted it. And it means nothing now: we have nothing to preserve and nothing to lose.

Now Raj's arm came snaking around Neel's waist, as the boy buried his face in his father's midriff. Looking down at his head, it seemed to Neel that his son had shrunk somehow—or was it just that he could not remember ever seeing him in a coarse cotton vest and knee-length dhoti?

Our kites . . . are they . . .? He had been trying to keep his tone light and his voice punished him by dying in his throat.

I threw them all in the river, said the boy.

We've given away most of our things, Malati added quickly. Tucking in her sari, she took the jharu from the corner where the guard had left it and set to sweeping the floor. We've kept only what we can take with us.

Take where? said Neel. Where are you thinking to go?

It's all been arranged, she said, sweeping busily. You shouldn't worry.

But I must know, he insisted. Where are you going? You have to tell me.

To Parimal's place.

Parimal's place? Neel repeated the words after her, in bewilderment: he had never thought of Parimal as having a home of his own, other than his quarters in the Rajbari.

But where is Parimal's place?

Not far from the city, she said. I didn't know of it either, till he told me. He bought some land, years ago, with money saved from his earnings. He's going to give us a corner of it.

Neel sank helplessly on to his string bed, holding his son by the shoulders. He could feel the dampness of Raj's tears on his skin now, soaking through his tunic, and he pulled the boy closer, sinking his chin into his thick black hair. Then his own face began to smart and he realized that his eyes had welled up with a substance that was as corrosive as acid, tinged with the bitter gall of his betrayals of his wife and child, and with the bile that came from knowing that he had spent all his years as a somnambulist, walking through his days as if his life mattered no more than a bit-part in a play written by someone else.

Malati put away the jharu and came to sit beside him. We'll be all right, she said insistently. Don't worry about us; we'll manage. It's you who must be strong. For our sakes, if not your own, you have to stay alive: I could not bear to be a widow, not after all this.

As her words sank in, his tears dried on his cheeks and he spread out his arms to pull his wife and son to his chest. Listen to me, he said: I *will* stay alive. I make you this promise: I will. And when these seven years are over, I will return and I will take you both away from this accursed land and we will start new lives in some other place. That is all I ask of you: do not doubt that I will come back, for I will.

~

The tumasher for Captain Chillingworth, with all its fuss and goll-maul, was not long in the past when Paulette received yet another summons to the Burra BeeBee's bedchamber. The call came shortly after Mr Burnham's departure for his Dufter, and the wheels of his carriage were still crackling on the conkers of Bethel's drive when a khidmutgar knocked on Paulette's door to deliver the summons. This was not an hour of day which often found Mrs Burnham fully awakened from her nightly dose of laudanum, so it seemed only natural to assume that the call was of especial urgency, prompted by an unannounced church tiffin or some other unexpected entertainment. But on being admitted to the BeeBee's bedchamber it became apparent to Paulette that this was an occasion truly without precedent— for not only was Mrs Burnham fully awake, she was actually on her feet, skipping prettily around the room, throwing open the shutters.

'Oh Puggly!' she cried, as Paulette stepped in. 'Pray, where *have* you been, dear?'

'But Madame,' said Paulette. 'I came all-a-sweet, as soon as I was told.'

'Really, dear?' said the BeeBee. 'It seems like I've been waiting an age. I thought for sure you were off to bake a brinjaul.'

'Oh, but Madame!' protested Paulette. 'It is not the bonne hour.'

'No, dear,' Mrs Burnham agreed. 'It would never do to be warming the coorsy when there's kubber like this to be heard.'

'News?' said Paulette. 'There is some news?'

'Why yes, so there is; but we must sit on the cot, Puggly dear,' said Mrs Burnham. 'It's not the kind of thing you want to be gupping about on your feet.' Taking Paulette by the hand, the BeeBee led her across the room and cleared a place for the two of them at the edge of her bed.

'But what is it that has arrived, Madame?' said Paulette, in rising alarm. 'Nothing bad, I hope?'

'Good heavens, no!' said Mrs Burnham. 'It's the best possible news, dear.'

Mrs Burnham's voice was so warm and her blue eyes so filled with fellow-feeling, that Paulette became a little apprehensive. Something was amiss, she knew: could it be that the BeeBee, with her uncanny powers of divination, had somehow uncovered the most pressing of her secrets? 'Oh Madame,' she blurted out, 'it is not about . . . ?'

'Mr Kendalbushe?' Mrs Burnham prompted her delightedly. 'Why, how did you know?'

Robbed of her breath, Paulette could only repeat, stupefied: 'Mr Kendalbushe?'

'You sly little shaytan!' said the BeeBee, slapping her wrist. 'Did you guess or did someone tell you?'

'Neither, Madame. I you assure, I do not know . . .'

'Or was it just a case,' continued the BeeBee archly, 'of two hearts chiming together, like gantas in a clock-tower?'

'Oh Madame,' cried Paulette, in distress. 'It is nothing like that.'

'Well then I can't imagine how you knew,' declared the BeeBee, fanning herself with her nightcap. 'As for myself, a talipot in a gale could not be knocked over as easily as I was when Mr Burnham told me this morning.'

'Told you what, Madame?'

'About his meeting with the judge,' said Mrs Burnham. 'You see, Puggly, they had dinner at the Bengal Club yesterday, and after they'd bucked about this and that, Mr Kendalbushe asked if he might broach a rather delicate matter. Now, as you know, dear, Mr Burnham holds Mr Kendalbushe in the highest esteem so of course he said yes. And would you like to hazard a guess, Puggly dear, about what this matter was?'

'A point of law?'

'No, dear,' said Mrs Burnham, 'far more delicate than that: what he wanted to ask was whether you, dear Puggly, might look favourably upon his suit.'

'Suit?' said Paulette, in confusion. 'But Madame, I cannot say. I have no memory of his costume.'

'Not that kind of suit, you gudda,' said Mrs Burnham, with a good-natured laugh. 'Suit of marriage is what he meant. Don't you samjo, Puggly? He's planning to propose to you.'

'To me?' cried Paulette in horror. 'But Madame! Why?'

'Because, my dear,' said Mrs Burnham with a good-natured laugh, 'he is most greatly impressed by your simple manners and your modesty. You have quite won his heart. Can you imagine, dear, what a prodigious stroke of kismet it will be for you to bag Mr Kendalbushe? He's a nabob in his own right—made a mountain of mohurs out of the China trade. Ever since he lost his wife every larkin in town's been trying to bundo him. I can tell you, dear, there's a paltan of mems who'd give their last anna to be in your jooties.'

'But with so many splendid memsahibs vying for him, Madame,' said Paulette, 'why would he choose so poor a creature as myself?'

'He is evidently very impressed by your willingness to improve yourself, dear,' said the BeeBee. 'Mr Burnham has told him that you are the most willing pupil he has ever had. And as you know, dear, Mr Burnham and the judge are completely of a mind in these things.'

'But Madame,' said Paulette, who could no longer control her trembling lip, 'surely there are many who know the Scriptures far better than I? I am but the merest novice.'

'But my dear!' laughed Mrs Burnham. 'That's exactly why you have won his regard—because you're a clean slate and willing to learn.'

'Oh Madame,' moaned Paulette, wringing her hands, 'surely you are pleasanting. It is not kind.'

The BeeBee was surprised by Paulette's distress. 'Oh Puggly!' she said. 'Are you not glad of the judge's interest? It is a great triumph, I assure you. Mr Burnham approves most heartily and has assured Mr Kendalbushe that he will do everything in his power to sway you. The two of them have even agreed to share the burden of your instruction for a while.'

'Mr Kendalbushe is too kind,' said Paulette, wiping her eyes on her sleeve. 'And so is Mr Burnham. I am greatly honoured, Madame—yet I must confess that my sentiments are not the same as those of Mr Kendalbushe.'

At this, Mrs Burnham frowned and sat upright. 'Sentiments, my dear Puggly,' she said sternly, 'are for dhobis and dashies. We mems can't let that kind of thing get in the way! No, dear, let me tell you—you're lucky to have a judge in your sights and you mustn't let your bunduk waver. This is about as fine a shikar as a girl in your situation could possibly hope for.'

'Oh Madame,' said Paulette, weeping freely now, 'but are not the things of this world mere dross when weighed against love?'

'Love?' said Mrs Burnham, in mounting astonishment. 'What on earth are you bucking about? My dear Puggly, with your prospects, you can't be letting your shokes run away with you. I know the judge is not as young as he might be, but he's certainly not past giving you a butcha or two before he slips into his dotage. And after that, dear, why, there's nothing a mem needs that can't be cured by a long bath and a couple of cushy-girls. Believe me, Puggly, there's a lot to be said for men of that age. No badmashee at all hours of the night, for one thing. I can tell you, dear, there's nothing more annoying than to be puckrowed just when you're looking forward to a sip of laudanum and a nice long sleep.'

'But Madame,' said Paulette, miserably, 'do you not feel it would be penible to spend one's life thus?'

'That's the best part of it, dear,' said Mrs Burnham cheerfully. 'You won't have to. He's no chuckeroo after all, and I doubt he is long for this world. And just imagine—after the dear, sainted man is gone you'll be able to swan off to Paris with his cuzzanah and before you know it, some impoverished duke or marquis will come begging for your hand.'

'But Madame,' said Paulette, sobbing, 'what will be my profit from this, if my youth is forfeit and I have wasted the love that is in my heart?'

'But Puggly dear,' protested the BeeBee. 'You could learn to love the judge, could you not?'

'But one cannot learn to love, Madame,' Paulette protested. 'Surely it is more like a coup de foudre—how do you say in English—like being shot by his bolt?'

'Shot by his bolt!' Mrs Burnham clapped her hands over her scandalized ears. 'Puggly! You really must watch what you say.'

'But is it not true, Madame?'

'I'm sure I wouldn't know.' Her suspicions awakened, Mrs Burnham turned to rest her chin on her hand and directed a long, searching glance at Paulette. 'Pray tell me, dear Puggly—there isn't someone else, is there?'

Paulette was in a panic now, knowing that she had given away more than she should have. But denial was futile too, she knew, for to tell a direct lie to someone as shrewd as Mrs Burnham, was merely to double the risks of detection. So instead she hung her head, in silence, and lowered her streaming eyes.

'I knew it!' said the BeeBee triumphantly. 'It's that American, isn't it—Hezekiah or Zebediah or whatever? But you're out of your mind, Puggly! It would never serve. You're too poor to throw yourself away on a sailor, no matter how handsome or well-spoken. A young seaman—why, that's the worst kismet any woman could wish for, even worse than a wordy-wallah! They're gone when you need them, they never have a dam's worth of silver to call their own, and they're dead before the children are out of their langoots. With a classy for a husband, you'd have to find a job as a harry-maid just to get by! I don't think it would suit you at all, dear, cleaning up other people's cabobs and emptying their dawk-dubbers. No, dear, it can't be allowed, I won't hear of it . . .'

Suddenly, as her suspicions deepened, the BeeBee cut herself short and clamped her hands on her mouth. 'Oh! dear, dear Puggly—tell me—you haven't . . . ? . . . you haven't . . . No! Tell me it isn't so!'

'What, Madame?' said Paulette, in puzzlement.

The BeeBee's voice sank to a whisper. 'You haven't compromised yourself, Puggly dear, have you? No. I will not credit it.'

'Compromise, Madame?' Paulette proudly raised her chin and squared her shoulders. 'In matters of the heart, Madame, I do not believe that half-measures and compromises are possible. Does not love demand that we give our all?'

'Puggly . . .!' Mrs Burnham gasped, fanning herself with a pillow.'Oh my dear! Oh heavens! Tell me, dear Puggly: I must know the worst.' She swallowed faintly and clutched her fluttering bosom: '. . . is there? . . . no surely there isn't! . . . no . . . Lud! . . .'

'Yes, Madame?' said Paulette.

'Puggly, tell me the truth, I conjure you: there isn't a rootie in the choola, is there?'

'Why, Madame . . .'

Paulette was a little surprised to see Mrs Burnham making such a to-do about a matter she usually touched upon so lightly—but she was glad, too, to have the conversation turned in this new direction, since it presented a good opportunity for escape. Hugging her stomach, she made a moaning sound: 'Madame, you are prefectly right: I am indeed a little foireuse today.'

'Oh dear, dear Puggly!' The BeeBee dabbed her streaming eyes and gave Paulette a pitying hug. 'Of course you're furious! Those budzat sailors! With all their udlee-budlee, you'd think they'd leave the larkins alone! My lips are sealed, of course—no one will learn of it from me. But Puggly dear, don't you see? For your own sake, you must marry Mr Kendalbushe at once! There is no time to waste!'

'No indeed, Madame, there is not!' Just as Mrs Burnham was reaching for her laudanum, Paulette leapt to her feet and ran to the door. 'Forgive me, Madame, I must away. The coorsy will not wait.'

~

The word 'Calcutta' had no sooner been uttered than every window in the girmitiyas' pulwar flew open. In the men's section, with its greater press of numbers, there was a good deal of jostling and pushing and not everyone was able to find a desirable vantage point; the women were luckier—with two windows to share between them, they were all able to look at the shorefront as the city approached.

On the journey downriver, the pulwar had stopped at so many large and populous towns—Patna, Bhagalpur, Munger— that urban vistas were no longer a novelty. Yet, even the most worldly of the girmitiyas was caught unawares by the spectacle that unfolded around them now: the ghats, buildings and shipyards that lined the Hooghly were so numerous, so crowded and of such a size that the migrants fell into a silence that was in equal measure awestruck and appalled. How was it possible that people could live in the midst of such congestion and so much filth, with no fields or greenery anywhere in sight; such folk were surely another species of being?

As they drew closer to the docks, the river traffic thickened and the pulwar was soon surrounded by a forest of masts, spars and sails. In this company, the pulwar seemed a paltry vessel, but Deeti was suddenly filled with affection for it: in the midst of so much that was unfamiliar and intimidating, it seemed like a great ark of comfort. Like everyone else, she too had often been impatient for this stage of the journey to end— but now it was with deepening dread that she listened to the duffadar and the sirdars as they made preparations for the migrants' disembarkation.

Silently, the women collected their belongings and crept out of their enclosure; Ratna, Champa and Dookhanee hurried off to join their husbands, but Deeti, having appointed herself the guardian of the single women, gathered Munia, Sarju and Heeru around her and took them along to wait with Kalua. Soon the sirdars came down to let the migrants know that from here they would be taken to their camp in hired rowboats, ten or twelve at a time. The women were the first to be called on to make the switch; along with their spouses, they emerged on deck to find a rowboat waiting beside the pulwar.

But how are we going to get down there? said Sarju, in alarm—for the boat sat low in the water, well beneath the deck of the pulwar.

Yes, how? cried Munia. I can't jump that far!

That far! A shout of mocking laughter came echoing back to them from the boat. Why, a baby could do it. Come, come—there's nothing to be afraid of . . .

It was the boatman speaking, in a quicksilver, citified Hindusthani that Deeti could just about follow. He was a stripling of a fellow, dressed not in the usual lungi and vest, but in *patloon* pants and a blue banyan that billowed around his wiry chest. His dark, thick hair had a coppery tint because of prolonged exposure to the sun, and it was held in place by a rakishly-tied bandhna. He was laughing, with his head thrown back, and his bright, impudent eyes seemed sharp enough to pierce the cover of their veils.

What a dandy of a fellow! Munia whispered to Deeti, from under her ghungta.

Don't so much as look at him, warned Deeti. He's one of those townie flirts, a real bāka-bihari.

But the boatman was still laughing, beckoning them on: What're you waiting for? Jump, na! Do I have to spread my net, to catch you like so many fishes?

Munia giggled and Deeti couldn't help laughing too; it had to be admitted that there was something quite fetching about the fellow: perhaps it was the brightness of his eyes, or the carefree mischievousness of his expression—or was it the quirky little scar on his forehead that gave him the appearance of possessing three eyebrows rather than two?

Ey! said Munia giggling. And what if we jump and you drop us? What'll happen then?

Why should I drop a thin little thing like you? said the boatman, winking. I've caught many fish that are bigger: just take a jump and see . . .

This had gone far enough now, Deeti decided; as the senior married woman of the group, it was her duty to enforce the proprieties. She turned upon Kalua and began to scold: What's the matter with you? Why don't you step into the boat and help us climb down? Do you want this lecher of a lucchha to be putting his hands on us?

Chastened, Kalua and the other men stepped into the boat and reached up to help the women down, one by one. Munia hung back and waited until there was only one pair of hands that was unoccupied—the boatman's. When she made her jump, he caught her neatly, by the waist, and deposited her gently in the boat: but in the process, somehow, Munia's ghungta slipped—whether by accident or design Deeti could not tell—and there followed a long instant when there was no barrier at all between her coquettish smile and his hungry eyes.

How long the girl would have allowed herself this liberty, Deeti did not know and was not willing to find out. Munia! she said in a tone of sharp admonition. *Tu kahé aisan kaíl karala*? Why do you act like this? Don't you have any shame? Cover up at once!

Obediently, Munia draped her sari over her head and went to sit beside Deeti. But despite the demureness of her attitude, Deeti knew, from the angle of her head, that the girl's eyes were still entangled with the boatman's.

*Aisan mat kará*! she said sharply, elbowing the girl's flanks. Don't carry on like this . . . what will people think?

I'm just listening to what he's saying, Munia protested. Is that a crime?

Deeti had to admit that it was hard to ignore the boatman, for he was talking almost without interruption, keeping up a continuous patter as he pointed out the sights: . . . there to your left are the opium godowns . . . fine place to lose yourself, eh? . . . no end to the happiness to be found there . . .

But even as he was speaking, he kept turning around so that Deeti knew full well that he and Munia were fencing with their eyes. In indignation, she appealed to the men: Look at how this launda talks! Are you going to let him get away with all his loochergiri? Isn't there something you can do? Show him you have some spirit too—*josh dikháwat chalatbá*!

But it was to no avail, for the men too were listening open-mouthed: although they had heard stories about the fast-talking haramzadas of the city, they had never seen one in person before; they were mesmerized, and as for remonstrating with him, they knew all too well that the rascal would only make a mockery of their rustic tongues.

The boat made a turn from the river into a nullah, and in a while the boatman pointed to a grim set of walls, looming in the distance. Alipore Jail, he announced gravely; the most fearsome dungeon in the land . . . oh if you but knew of the horrors and tortures of that place! . . . of course, it won't be long before you find out . . .

Mindful of the many rumours they had heard, the migrants exchanged nervous glances. One of them inquired: Why are we going towards the jail?

Didn't they tell you? said the boatman, off-handedly. That's where I've been ordered to take you. They're going to make candles out of the wax in your brains . . .

There were several audible gasps of alarm, to which the boatman responded with a cackle of knowing laughter: . . . No, just joking . . . no, that's not where you're going . . . no, I'm taking you to the cremation ghat over there . . . do you see the flames, and smoke? . . they're going to cook the lot of you—alive at that . . .

This too was met with gasps, which amused the boatman all the more. Goaded beyond endurance, Champa's husband shouted: *Hasé ka ká bátbá ré*? What're you laughing at? *Hum kuchho na ho*? You think we're nothing? Want a beating, do you?

From an idiot rustic like you? said the boatman, laughing

all the louder. You *deháti*—one flick of my oar and you'll be in the water . . .

Suddenly, just as a fight was about to break out, the boat pulled up to a jetty and was tied fast: beyond lay a newly-cleared stretch of shore, still littered with the stumps of recently felled trees. Three large, straw-thatched sheds stood in a circle at the centre of the clearing; a short distance away, next to a well, was a modest little shrine, with a red pennant flying aloft on a pole.

. . . This is it, said the boatman, this is where you get off: the new depot for girmitiyas, just built and readied, in time for the arrival of the sheep . . .

This? What're you saying? Are you sure?

. . .Yes, this is it . . .

It was a while before anyone stirred: the encampment seemed so peaceful that they could not believe that it really was meant for them.

. . . Be off with you now . . . think I've got nothing else to do?

While stepping off the boat, Deeti was careful to herd Munia in front of her—but her protective presence did nothing to inhibit the boatman, who flashed them a smile and said: . . . Ladies, please to forgive any offence . . . no harm meant . . . name's Azad . . . Azad the Lascar . . .

Deeti could tell that Munia was longing to linger near the jetty, so she ushered her smartly along, trying to draw her attention to the camp ahead: Look, Munia—this is it! Our last place of rest, before we're cast out on the Black Water . . .

Instead of going indoors, to join the others, Deeti decided to pay a visit to the campground's shrine. Come, she said to Kalua, let's go to the mandir first; a safe arrival calls for a prayer.

The temple was built of plaited bamboo, and there was something reassuringly domestic about its simplicity. Walking towards it, Deeti's steps quickened in eagerness, but then she saw, somewhat to her surprise, that there was a stout, long-haired man dancing in front of it, whirling around and around, with his eyes closed in ecstasy and his arms clasped around his bosom as if he were embracing an invisible lover. Sensing their presence, he came to a stop and his eyes opened wide in surprise. *Kyá*? What? he said, in heavily-accented Hindi. Coolies? Here already?

He was a strangely shaped man, Deeti noticed, with an enormous head, flapping ears and a pair of bulging eyes that gave him the appearance of goggling at the world around him. She could not tell whether he was angry or merely surprised, and took the precaution of seeking shelter behind Kalua.

The man took a minute or two to take account of Kalua's imposing size and once he had looked him up and down, his tone softened a little.

Are you girmitiyas? he asked.

*Ji*, nodded Kalua.

When did you get here?

Just now, said Kalua. We're the first.

So soon? We weren't expecting you till later . . .

Devotions forgotten, the man was suddenly thrown into a frenzy of excitable activity. Come, come! he cried, with hectic gestures. You have to go to the daftar first, to be registered. Come with me—I'm the gomusta and I'm in charge of this camp.

Not without some misgivings, Deeti and Kalua followed him across the camp to one of the sheds. With barely a pause to open the door, the gomusta called out aloud: 'Doughty-sahib—coolies are coming; registration proceedings must at once be commenced.' There was no answer, so he hurried in, gesturing to Deeti and Kalua to follow.

Inside, there were several desks, and one capacious planter's chair, in which a large, heavy-jowled Englishman was presently revealed to be reclining. He was snoring gently, his breath bubbling slowly through his lips. The gomusta had to call out his name a couple of times before he stirred: 'Doughty-sahib! Sir, kindly to arouse and uprise.'

Mr Doughty had just half an hour before left the table of a district magistrate, where he had been served a large lunch, copiously lubricated with many brimming beakers of porter and ale. Now, between the heat and the beer, his eyes were gummed together with sleep, so that a good few minutes followed between the opening of his right eye and then the left. When at last he became conscious of the gomusta's presence, he was in no mood for pleasantries: it was much against his will that he had been prevailed upon to help with the registration of the coolies, and he was not about to let himself be taken advantage of. 'God damn your eyes, Baboon! Can't you see I'm having a little rest?'

'What to do, sir?' said the gomusta. 'I do not wish to intrude into your privates, but alas it cannot be helped. Coolies are arriving like anything. As such, registration proceedings must be commenced without delay.'

Turning his head a little, the pilot caught a glimpse of Kalua and the sight prompted him to struggle to his feet. 'Now there's a burrasize budzat if ever I saw one.'

'Yes sir. Thumping big fellow.'

Muttering under his breath, the pilot lurched unsteadily to one of the desks and threw open a massive, leather-bound register.

Dipping a quill, he said to the gomusta: 'Right then, Pander, go ahead. You know the bandobast.'

'Yes, sir. I will supply all necessary informations.' The gomusta inclined his head in Deeti's direction. The woman? he said to Kalua. What's her name?

Her name is Aditi, malik; she is my wife.

'What did he say?' Mr Doughty bellowed, cupping his ear. 'Speak up there.'

'The lady's good-name is reported as Aditi, sir.'

'"Aditty?"' The tip of Mr Doughty's nib touched down on the register and began to write. 'Aditty it is then. Bloody ooloo name, if you ask me, but if that's what she wants to be called so be it.'

Caste? said the gomusta to Kalua.

We are Chamars, malik.

District?

Ghazipur, malik.

'You bloody bandar of a Baboon,' Mr Doughty broke in. 'You forgot to ask him his name.'

'Sorry, sir. Immediately I will rectify.' Baboo Nob Kissin turned to Kalua: And you: who are you?

Madhu.

'What was that, Pander? What did the brute say?'

As he was about to say the name, Baboo Nob Kissin's tongue tripped on the final dipthong: 'He is Madho, sir.'

'Maddow?'

The gomusta seized upon this. 'Yes, sir, why not? That is extremely apt.'

'And his father's name?'

The question flummoxed Kalua: having stolen his father's name for his own, the only expedient he could think of was to make a switch: His name was Kalua, malik.

This satisfied the gomusta, but not the pilot. 'But how on earth am I to spell it?'

The gomusta scratched his head: 'If I can moot out one proposal, sir, why not do like this? First write C-o-l—just like "coal" no?—then v-e-r. Colver. Like-this like-this we can do.'

The pink tip of the pilot's tongue appeared at the corner of his mouth, as he wrote the letters in the register. 'Theek you are,' said the pilot. 'That's how I'll put him down then—as Maddow Colver.'

'Maddow Colver.'

Deeti, standing beside her husband, heard him whisper the name, not as if it were his own but as if it belonged to someone else, a person other than himself. Then he repeated it, in a tone of greater confidence, and when it came to his lips again, a third time, the sound of it was no longer new or unfamiliar: it was as much his own now as his skin, or his eyes, or his hair—Maddow Colver.

Later, within the dynasty that claimed its descent from him, many stories would be invented about the surname of the founding ancestor and the reasons why 'Maddow' occurred so frequently among his descendants. While many would choose to recast their origins, inventing grand and fanciful lineages for themselves, there would always remain a few who clung steadfastly to the truth: which was that those hallowed names were the result of the stumbling tongue of a harried gomusta, and the faulty hearing of an English pilot who was a little more than half-seas over.

~

Although the prisons at Lalbazar and Alipore were both known as jails, they no more resembled each other than a bazar does a graveyard: Lalbazar was surrounded by the noise and bustle of Calcutta's busiest streets, while Alipore lay at the edge of a deserted stretch of land on the city's outskirts and silence weighed down on it like the lid of a coffin. It was the largest prison in India and its fortress-like battlements loomed over the narrow waterway of Tolly's Nullah, well within view of those who travelled by boat to the migrants' depot. But few indeed were the passersby who would willingly rest their gaze upon those walls: such was the dread inspired by the grim edifice that most chose to avert their eyes, even paying their boatmen extra to warn of its approach.

It was late at night when the carriage came to take Neel from Lalbazar to Alipore Jail. To cover the distance took about an hour as a rule, but tonight the carriage took a much longer route than usual, circling around Fort William and keeping to the quiet roadways that flanked the riverfront. This was done to forestall trouble, for there had been some talk of demonstrations of public sympathy for the convicted Raja: but Neel was unaware of this and to him the journey seemed like a prolongation of a special kind of torment, in which the desire to be done with the uncertainties of the recent past was at war with a longing to linger forever on this final passage through the city.

Accompanying Neel was a group of some half-dozen guards who whiled away their time with ribald banter, their jokes being premised on the pretence that they were a marriage party, escorting a bridegroom to his in-laws' house—his *sasurál*—on the night of his wedding. From the practised nature of their exchanges, Neel understood that they had enacted this charade many times before, while transporting prisoners. Ignoring their sallies, he tried to make the most of the journey—but there was little to be seen, in the darkness of the small hours, and it was largely through memory that he had to chart the progress of the carriage, envisioning in his mind the lapping water of the river and the tree-shaded expanse of the city's Maidan.

The carriage picked up speed when the jail came into view, and Neel willed himself to concentrate on other things: the howls of nearby jackals and the faint smell of night-time flowers. When the sound of the wheels changed, he knew the carriage was crossing the jail's moat, and his fingers dug into the cracked leather of his seat. The wheels creaked to a halt and the door opened, allowing Neel to sense the presence of a multitude of people, waiting in the darkness. In much the way that the legs of a reluctant dog lock themselves against the tug of a leash, his fingers dug into the horsehair stuffing of his seat: even when the guards began to prod and push—Chalo! We're here! Your in-laws are waiting!—they would not yield. Neel tried to say he wasn't ready yet and needed a minute or two more, but the men who had accompanied him were not of a mind to be indulgent. One of them gave Neel a shove that broke his hold; in stumbling off the carriage, Neel happened to step on the edge of his own dhoti, pulling it undone. Flushed with embarrassment, he tore his arms free, in order to rearrange his garments: Wait, wait—my dhoti, don't you see . . .?

In descending from the carriage, Neel had passed into the custody of a new set of jailers, men of a wholly different cast from the constables of Lalbazar: hard-bitten veterans of the East India Company's campaigns, they wore the red coattees of the sepoy army; recruited from the deep hinterlands, they held all city folk in equal contempt. It was in surprise rather than anger that one of them kneed Neel in the small of his back: Get moving b'henchod, it's late already . . .

The novelty of this treatment confused Neel into thinking that some sort of mistake had been made. Still grappling with his dhoti, he protested: Stop! You can't treat me like this; don't you know who I am?

There was a momentary check in the motion of the hands that had been laid upon him; then someone caught hold of the end of his dhoti and gave it a sharp tug. The garment spun him around as it unravelled, and somewhere nearby a voice said:

. . . Now here's a real Draupadi . . . clinging to her sari . . .

Now another hand took hold of his kurta and tore it apart so as to lay bare his underclothing.

. . . More of a Shikandi if you ask me . . .

The butt of a spear caught him in the small of his back, sending him stumbling along a dark vestibule, with the ends of his dhoti trailing behind him like the bleached tail of a dead peacock. At the end of the vestibule lay a torch-lit room where a white man was seated behind a desk. He was wearing the uniform of a serjeant of the jail, and it was clear that he had been sitting in the room for a considerable length of time and had grown impatient of waiting.

It came as a relief to Neel to enter the presence of someone in authority. 'Sir!' he said. 'I must protest against this treatment. Your men have no right to hit me or tear away my clothes.'

The serjeant looked up and his blue eyes hardened with an incredulity that could not have been greater than if the words had been spoken by one of the chains on the wall—but from what happened next, it was clear that his initial response was prompted not by the burden of what Neel had said, but rather by the mere fact of being spoken to in his own language, by a native convict: without addressing a word to Neel, he turned to the sepoys who had led him in, and said, in rough Hindusthani: *Mooh khol . . .* open his mouth.

At this, the guards on either side of Neel took hold of his face and expertly prised his mouth open, sticking a wooden wedge between his teeth to hold his jaws apart. Then an orderly in a white chapkan stepped forward and began to count Neel's teeth, tapping them with a fingertip; his hand, the smell of which filled Neel's head, reeked of dal and mustard oil—it was as if he were carrying the remnants of his last meal under his nails. On coming to a gap, the finger dug down into the jaw, as if to make sure the missing molar wasn't hidden somewhere within. The unexpectedness of the pain transported Neel suddenly to the moment when he'd lost that tooth: how old he was he could not remember, but in his mind's eye, he saw a sunlit veranda, with his mother at the far end, swinging on a jhula; he glimpsed his own feet, carrying him towards the sharp edge on the corner of the swing . . . and it was almost as if he could hear her voice again, and feel the touch of her hand as it reached into his mouth to take the broken tooth from his lips.

'Why is this necessary, sir?' Neel began to protest as soon as the wedge was removed from his mouth. 'What is the purpose?'

The serjeant did not look up from the log-book in which he was entering the results of the examination, but the orderly leant over to whisper something about marks of identification and signs of communicable disease. This was not enough for Neel, who was now seized by a determination not to be ignored: 'Please, sir, is there a reason why I cannot have an answer to my question?'

Without a glance in his direction, the serjeant issued another order, in Hindusthani: *Kapra utaro* . . . take off his clothes.

The sepoys responded by pinning Neel's arms to his side: long practice had made them expert in stripping the clothes from convicts, many of whom would gladly have died—or killed—rather than be subjected to the shame of having their nakedness exposed. Neel's struggles presented no challenge to them and they quickly tore off the remnants of his clothing; then they held him upright, pinioning his limbs so as to fully expose his naked body to his jailers' scrutiny. Unexpectedly, Neel felt the touch of a hand, grazing against his toes, and he looked down to see the orderly brushing his feet with his fingertips, as if to ask forgiveness for what he was about to do. The gesture, in all its unforeseen humanity, had scarcely had time to register when the orderly's fingers dug into Neel's groin.

Lice? Crabs? Vermin?

None, sahib.

Birthmarks? Lesions?

No.

The touch of the orderly's fingers had a feel that Neel could never have imagined between two human beings— neither intimate nor angry, neither tender nor prurient—it was the disinterested touch of mastery, of purchase or conquest; it was as if his body had passed into the possession of a new owner, who was taking stock of it as a man might inspect a house he had recently acquired, searching for signs of disrepair or neglect, while mentally assigning each room to a new use.

'Syphilis? Gonorrhoea?'

These were the first English words the serjeant had used, and in speaking them he looked at the prisoner with the faintest hint of a smile.

Neel was now standing with his legs apart and his arms extended over his head while the orderly searched his flanks for birthmarks and other ineradicable signs of identification. But he did not miss the mockery in his jailer's glance, and was quick to respond. 'Sir,' he said, 'can you not afford me the dignity of a reply? Or is it that you do not trust yourself to speak English?'

The man's eyes flared and Neel saw that he had nettled him, simply by virtue of addressing him in his own tongue— a thing that was evidently counted as an act of intolerable insolence in an Indian convict, a defilement of the language. The knowledge of this—that even in his present state, stripped to his skin, powerless to defend himself from the hands that were taking an inventory of his body—he still possessed the ability to affront a man whose authority over his person was absolute: the awareness made Neel giddy, exultant, eager to explore this new realm of power; in this jail, he decided, as in the rest of his life as a convict, he would speak English whenever possible, everywhere possible, starting with this moment, here. But such was the urgency of this desire that words failed him and he could think of nothing to say; no words of his own would come to mind—only stray lines from passages that he had been made to commit to memory:

'. . . this is the excellent foppery of the world . . . to make guilty of our disasters, the sun, the moon and the stars . . .'

The serjeant interrupted him with an angry command: *Gánd dekho . . .* bend him over, check his arse . . .

With his head bowed between his legs, Neel still would not stop: 'Proud man, drest in a little brief authority, his glassy essence like an angry ape . . .' His voice rose till the words were echoing off the stone walls. The serjeant rose from his seat as Neel was straightening up. An arm's-length away, he came to a halt, drew his hand back and struck Neel across the face: 'Shut yer gob, quoddie.'

In some reflexive part of his mind, Neel noted that the serjeant had hit him with his left hand, and that had he been at home, he would have had to bathe and change. But that was in some other life: here what mattered was that he had succeeded at last in making the man speak to him in English. 'A very good day to you, sir,' he muttered, bowing his head.

'Get his bleedin arse out o' me sight.'

In a small adjoining room, Neel was handed a bundle of folded clothing. A sepoy enumerated the articles as he handed them over: one gamchha, two vests, two dhotis of *dungri* weave, one blanket; better take care of them, they're all you'll have for the next six months.

The unwashed dungaree cloth was thick and rough, its texture more like jute sacking than woven cotton. When shaken loose, the dhoti proved to be half the size, in length as well as breadth, of the six-yard stretch of fabric to which Neel was accustomed. Tied at the waist, it would fall no lower than the knees and was clearly meant to be worn as a langot—but Neel had never had occasion to tie a loincloth before and his hands fumbled so much that one of the sepoys snapped: What are you waiting for? Cover yourself!—as if it were by his own choice that he had been stripped of his clothes. The blood rushed to Neel's head and he thrust his pelvis forward, pointing at himself with a lunatic's abandonment: Why? What have you not seen? What's left?

A look of pity came into the eyes of the sepoy: Have you lost all shame? And Neel nodded, as if to say yes, that's right: for it was true that at this moment he felt no shame at all, nor any other form of responsibility for his body; it was as if he had vacated his own flesh in the process of yielding it to the tenancy of the prison.

Move, come on! Losing patience, the sepoys took the dhoti out of Neel's hands and showed him how to knot it so that the ends could be pulled between his legs and tucked in at the back. Then, using their spear-butts as prods, they hurried him down a dim corridor into a cell that was small but brilliantly lit, with candles and oil-lamps. In the centre of the room, a bare-bodied, white-bearded man sat waiting on an ink-stained mat: his torso was covered with an intricate network of tattoos and on a folded square of cloth in front of him lay an array of glistening needles. The man could only be a *godna-wala*, a tattooist: when this dawned on Neel he spun around, as if to make a lunge for the exit—but the gambit was familiar to the sepoys who wrestled him quickly to the ground; holding him immobile, they carried him over to the mat and positioned him so that his head was resting on the tattooist's knee and he was looking up at his venerable face.

There was a gentleness in the old man's eyes that allowed Neel to find his voice. Why? he said, as the needle came towards his forehead. Why are you doing this?

It's the law, said the tattooist peaceably. All transportees have to be marked so they'll be recognized if they try to escape.

Then the needle hissed against his skin, and there was no space in Neel's mind for anything but the spasms of sensation that were radiating outwards from his forehead: it was as if the body that he had thought to have vacated, were taking revenge on him for having harboured that illusion, reminding him that he was its sole tenant, the only being to whom it could announce its existence through its capacity for pain.

The tattooist paused, as if in pity, and whispered: Here, eat this. His hand circled over Neel's face and pushed a little ball of gum between his lips. It will help; eat it . . .

As the opium began to dissolve in his mouth, Neel realized that it was not the intensity of the pain that was dulled by the drug, but rather its duration: it so blunted his consciousness of time that the operation, which must have taken hours of painstaking work, seemed to last only for a few concentrated moments. Then, as if through a dense winter fog, he heard the tattooist's voice whispering in his ear: Rajasah'b . . . Raja-sah'b . . .

Neel opened his eyes to see that his head was still in the old man's lap; the sepoys, in the meanwhile, had drowsed off in the corners of the cell.

What is it? he said, stirring.

Don't worry, Raja-sahib, the tattooist whispered. I've watered the ink; the mark will not last beyond a few months.

Neel was too befuddled to make sense of this: Why? why would you do that for me?

Raja-sahib, don't you know me?

No.

The tattooist brought his lips still closer: My family is from Raskhali; your grandfather gave us land to settle there; for three generations we've eaten your salt.

Placing a mirror in Neel's hands, he bowed his head: Forgive me, Raja-sahib, for what I had to do . . .

Raising the mirror to his face, Neel saw that his hair had been cut short and two rows of tiny Roman letters had been inscribed unevenly upon the right side of his forehead:

forgerer
alipore 1838

# thirteen

~

Zachary's room, in the Watsongunge boarding house, was just about wide enough to turn around in, and the bed was a string pallet, on which he had spread a layer of his own clothes, to protect his skin from the barbed roughness of its coconut-fibre ropes. At the foot of the bed, so close that he could almost rest his toes on its edge, was a window—or rather a square hole that had long since lost its shutters. The opening looked out on Watsongunge Lane—a winding string of grag-ghars, poxparlours and boarding houses that unspooled into the shipyard where the *Ibis* was being careened, caulked and re-fitted in preparation for her next voyage. Mr Burnham had been none too pleased to know of Zachary's choice of lodging: 'Watsongunge? There's no more godless place on earth, save it be the North End in Boston. Why would a man step into a galavant like that when he could enjoy the simple comforts of the Reverend Johnson's Mission House for Sailors?'

Zachary had dutifully gone to take a look at the Mission House, but only to come away after catching sight of Mr Crowle, who had already taken a room there. On Jodu's advice he had decided to go instead to the boarding house on Watsongunge Lane: the fact that it was a few minutes' walk from the shipyard had served as his excuse. Whether or not his employer was satisfied by this reasoning was not quite clear to Zachary, for of late he had begun to suspect that Mr Burnham had set a spy on him. Once, answering a knock at a suspiciously late hour of the night, Zachary had opened his door to find Mr

Burnham's gomusta standing outside. The man had leant this way and that, as if he were trying to see if Zachary had smuggled anyone into his room. When asked what he was doing there, he claimed to be the bearer of a present, which turned out to be a pot of half-melted butter: sensing that it was a snare of some kind, Zachary had refused to accept it. Later, the proprietor of the boarding house, an Armenian, had informed him that the gomusta had asked if Zachary was ever to be seen in the company of prostitutes—except that the word he'd used apparently was 'cowgirls'. Cowgirls! As it happened, after his meeting with Paulette, the thought of buying a woman had become repugnant to Zachary so the gomusta's snooping had gone unrewarded. But he'd carried on undeterred: just a few nights ago, Zachary had caught sight of him, skulking in the lane, wearing a bizarre disguise—an orange robe that made him look like some kind of duppy madwoman.

This was why, when woken one night by a quiet but persistent knocking, Zachary's first response was to bark: 'Is that you, Pander?'

There was no answer, so he struggled drowsily to his feet, tightening the lungi that he had taken to wearing at night. He had bought several of them from a vendor: one he had strung across the unshuttered window, to keep out the crows and the dust that rose in clouds from the unpaved lane. But the cloth barrier did nothing to lessen the noise that welled upwards from the street at night as sailors, lascars and stevedores sought their pleasures in the nearby nautcheries. Zachary had discovered that he could almost tell the time by the volume of sound, which tended to peak at about midnight, tapering off into silence at dawn. He noticed now that the street was neither at its loudest nor quietest—which suggested that dawn was still two or three hours away.

'I swear, Pander,' he snarled, as the knocking continued, 'you'd better have a good reason for this, or it's my knob you gon be kissin.' Undoing the latch, he opened the door but there was no light in the corridor and he could not tell immediately who was outside. 'Who're you?'

*Amitav Ghosh*

He was answered by a whisper: 'Jodu-launder, sir.'

'Grease-us twice!' Taken aback, Zachary allowed his visitor to step inside his room. 'What the hell you pesticatin me for this time o'night?' A gleam of suspicion came into his eyes. 'Wait a minute—wasn't Serang Ali sent you, was it?' he said. 'You go tell that ponce-shicer my mast don need no fiddin.'

'Avast sir!' said Jodu. 'Muffle oars! Serang Ali not sent.'

'Then what're you doin here?'

'Bring to messenger, sir!' Jodu made a beckoning gesture as if he were asking to be followed. ''Bout ship.'

'Where'd you want me to go?' said Zachary, irritably. In response, Jodu merely handed him his banyan, which was hanging on the wall. When Zachary reached for his trowsers, Jodu shook his head, as if to indicate that a lungi was all that was necessary.

'Anchor a-weigh, sir! Haul forward.'

Sticking his feet into his shoes, Zachary followed Jodu out of the boarding house. They walked quickly down the lane, towards the river, past the arrackshacks and knockingdens, most of which were still open. In a few minutes they had left the lane behind, to arrive at an unfrequented part of the shore where several dinghies lay moored. Pointing to one of these, Jodu waited for Zachary to step in before casting off the ropes and pushing the boat away from shore.

'Wait a minute!' said Zachary as Jodu began to row. 'Where you takin me now?'

'Look out afore!'

As if in answer, there came the sound of someone striking a flint. Spinning around, Zachary saw that the sparks were coming from the other end of the boat, which was covered by a roof of curved thatch. The spark flared again, to reveal for an instant the hooded figure of a woman in a sari.

Zachary turned angrily on Jodu, his suspicions confirmed. 'Just like I thought—lookin to do some snatchpeddlin huh? So let me tell you this: if I needed to pudden anchor, I'd know to find my own way to the jook. Wouldn't need no hairdick to show me the way . . .'

He was interrupted by the sound of his own name, spoken in a woman's voice: 'Mr Reid.'

He was turning to look more closely when the woman in the sari spoke again. 'It is I, Mr Reid.' The flint sparked again and the light lasted just long enough to allow him to recognize Paulette.

'Miss Lambert!' Zachary clapped a hand on his mouth. 'You must forgive me,' he said. 'I didn't know . . . didn't recognize . . .'

'It is you who must forgive me, Mr Reid,' said Paulette, 'for so greatly imposing.'

Zachary took the flint from her and lit a candle. When the fumbling was over, and their faces were lit by a small glow of light, he said: 'If you don't mind my asking, Miss Lambert—how come you're dressed like this, in a . . . in a . . .'

'Sari?' prompted Paulette. 'Perhaps you could say I am in disguise—although it seems less of a travesti to me than what I was wearing when you saw me last.'

'And what brings you here, Miss Lambert, if I may be so bold?'

She paused, as if she were trying to think of the best way to explain. 'Do you remember, Mr Reid, that you said you would be glad to help me, if I needed it?'

'Sure . . . but'—the doubt in his voice was audible even to him.

'So did you not mean it?' she said.

'I certainly did,' he said. 'But if I'm to be of help I need to know what's happening.'

'I was hoping you would help me find a passage, Mr Reid.'

'To where?' he said in alarm.

'To the Maurice Islands,' she said. 'Where you are going.'

'To the Mauritius?' he said. 'Why not ask Mr Burnham? He's the one can help you.'

She cleared her throat. 'Alas, Mr Reid,' she said. 'That is not possible. As you can see, I am no longer under Mr Burnham's protection.'

'And why so, if you don't mind me asking?'

*Amitav Ghosh*

In a small voice, she mumbled: 'Is it really necessary for you to know?'

'If I'm going to be of help—sure.'

'It is not a pleasant subject, Mr Reid,' she said.

'Don't worry about me, Miss Lambert,' Zachary said. 'My pate's not easily rattled.'

'I will tell—if you insist.' She paused to collect herself. 'Do you remember, Mr Reid, the other night? We spoke of penitence and chastisement? Very briefly.'

'Yes,' he said, 'I remember.'

'Mr Reid,' Paulette continued, drawing her sari tightly over her shoulders, 'when I came to live at Bethel I had no idee of such things. I was ignorant of Scripture and religious matters. My father, you see, had a great detestation of clergymen and held them in abhorrence—but this was not uncommon in men of his epoch . . .'

Zachary smiled. 'Oh it's still around, Miss Lambert, that aversion for parsons and devil-dodgers—in fact, I'd say it has a while yet to live.'

'You laugh, Mr Reid,' said Paulette. 'My father too would have pleasanted—his dislike of bondieuserie was very great. But for Mr Burnham, as you know, these are not subjects for amusement. When he discovered the depths of my ignorance, he was quite bouleversed and said to me that it was most imperative that he take personal charge of my instruction, notwithstanding other more pressing calls on his time. Is it possible to imagine, Mr Reid, to what point my face was put out of countenance? How could I refuse the offer so generous of my benefactor and patron? But also I did not wish to be a hypocrite and pretend to believe what I did not. Are you aware, Mr Reid, that there are religions in which a person may be put to death for hypocrisy?'

'That so?' said Zachary.

Paulette nodded. 'Yes, indeed. So you may imagine, Mr Reid, how I discuted with myself, before deciding that there could be no cause for reproach in proceeding with these lessons—in Penitence and Prayer, as Mr Burnham was pleased to describe them. Our lessons were held in the study where his Bible is kept, and almost always they were in the evenings, after dinner, when the house was quiet and Mrs Burnham had retired to her bedchamber with her beloved tincture of laudanum. At this time, the servants too, of whom, as you have seen, there are a great many in that house, could be counted on to retire to their own quarters, so there would be no paddings-about of their feet. This was the best possible time for contemplation and penitence, Mr Burnham said, and juste indeed was his description, for the atmosphere in his study was of the most profonde solemnity. The curtain would be drawn already when I entered, and he would then proceed to fasten the door—to prevent, as he said, interruptions in the work of righteousness. The study would be cast into darkness for there was never a light except for the branch of candles that glowed over the high lectern where the Bible lay open. I would walk in to find the passage for the day already chosen, the page marked with a silken placeholder, and I would take my own seat, which was a small footstool, beneath the lectern. When I had myself seated, he would take his place and start. What a tableau did he present, Mr Reid! The flames of the candles shining in his eyes! His beard glowing as if it were about to burst into light, like a burning bush! Ah, but if you had been there, Mr Reid: you too would have marvelled and admired.'

'I wouldn't wager long chalks on it, Miss,' said Zachary drily. 'But please go on.'

Paulette turned away, to look over her shoulder, at the far bank of the river, now visible in the moonlight. 'But how to describe, Mr Reid? The scene would bring before your eyes a tableau of the ancient patriarchs of the Holy Land. When he read, his voice was like a mighty waterfall, breaking upon the silence of a great valley. And the passages he chose! It was as if heaven had transfixed me in its gaze, like a Pharisee upon the plain. If I closed my eyes, the words would scorch my eyelids: "As the weeds are pulled up and burned in the fire so it will be at the end of the age. The Son of Man will send out his angels and they will weed out of his kingdom everything that causes sin and all who do evil." Are you familiar with those words, Mr Reid?'

'I believe I've heard them,' said Zachary, 'but don't be asking me for chapter and verse now.'

'The passage impressioned me very much,' Paulette said. 'How I trembled, Mr Reid! My whole body shook as if with the ague. So it went, Mr Reid, and I did not wonder that my father had neglected my scriptural education. He was a timid man and I dreaded to think of the anguish these passages would have caused him.' She drew her ghungta over her head. 'So did we proceed, lesson after lesson, until we came to a chapter of Hebrews: "If ye endure chastening, God dealeth with you as sons; for what son is he whom the father chasteneth not? But if ye be without chastisement, whereof all are partakers, then are ye bastards, and not sons." Do you know these lines, Mr Reid?'

"'Fraid not, Miss Lambert,' said Zachary, 'not being much of a churchgoer an all.'

'Nor did I know that passage,' Paulette continued. 'But for Mr Burnham it contained much meaning—so he had told me before he started his lecture. When he stopped I could see that he was greatly emotioned, for his voice was shaking and there was a tremor in his hands. He came to kneel beside me and asked, in a manner most severe, whether I was without chastisement. Now was I thrown into the profondest confusion, for I knew, from the passage, that to admit being unchastened was to acknowledge bastardy. Yet what was I to say, Mr Reid, for the verity is that not once in my life had my father ever beaten me? Shamefully I confessed my lack of chastening, at which he asked whether I should not like to learn of it, since it was a lesson very necessary for true penitence. Can you think, Mr Reid, how legion were my fears at the thought of being chastised by so large and powerful a man? But I hardened the bone of my courage and said, yes, I am ready. But here lay a surprise, Mr Reid, for it was not I who had been chosen for chastening . . .'

'But then who?' Zachary broke in.

'He,' said Paulette. 'He-the-same.'

'B'jilliber!' said Zachary. 'You're not tellin me it was Mr Burnham who wanted to be beat?'

'Yes,' Paulette continued. 'I had understood wrong. It was he who wished to endure the chastening, while I was but to be the instrument of his punishment. Imagine my nervosity, Mr Reid. If your benefactor asks you to be the instrument of his chastisement, with what face can you refuse? So I agreed, and he then proceeded to assume a most singular posture. He begged me to remain seated and then lowered his face to my feet, cupping my slippers in his hands and crouching, as a horse kneels to drink from a puddle. Then he urged me to draw my arm back and strike him upon his—his fesse.'

'On his face? Come now, Miss Lambert! You're ironing, for sure.'

'No—not his face. How do you say, the posterior aspect of the torso . . . the de-rear?'

'Stern? Taffrail? Poop-deck?'

'Yes,' said Paulette, 'his poop-deck as you call it was now raised high in the air, and it was there he wished me to aim my chastisements. You may imagine, Mr Reid, my distress at the thought of attacking my benefactor thus—but he would not be denied. He said my spiritual education would not progress otherwise. "Strike!" he cried, "smite me with thine hand!" So what could I do, Mr Reid? I made pretence there was a mosquito there, and brought my hand down on it. But this did not suffice. I heard a groan issuing from my feet—somewhat muffled, for the toe of my slipper was now inside his mouth— and he cried, "Harder, harder, smite with all thine strength." And so we went on for a while, and no matter how hard I struck, he bade me strike still harder—even though I knew him to be in pain, for I could feel him biting and sucking on my slippers, which were now quite wet. When at last he rose to his feet, I was sure that I would meet with reproofs and protests. But no! He was as pleased as ever I have seen him. He tickled me under the chin and said: "Good girl, you have learnt your lesson well. But mind! All will be undone if you should speak

of this. Not one word—to anyone!" Which was unnecessary—
for of course I would not have dreamt of making mention of
such things.'

'Jee-whoop!' Zachary let out a low whistle. 'And did it
happen again?'

'But yes,' said Paulette. 'Many times. Always these lessons
would begin with lectures and end thus. Believe me, Mr Reid,
I tried always to administer my correctionments to the best of
my ability, yet even though he appeared often to be in pain,
my arm seemed never to be of sufficient strength. I could see
that he was growing deceived. One day he said: "My dear, I
regret to say as a weapon of punishment your arm is not all
that could be wished for. Perhaps you need another tool? I
know just the thing . . ."'

'What did he have in mind?'

'Have you ever seen . . .?' Paulette paused here, rethinking
the word she was about to use. 'Here in India there is a kind
of broom that is used by sweepers to clean commodes and
lavatories. It is made of hundreds of thin sticks, tied together—
the spines of palm fronds. These brooms are called "jhatas" or
"jharus" and they make a swishing noise . . .'

'He wanted to be beat with a broom?' gasped Zachary.

'No ordinary broom, Mr Reid,' cried Paulette. 'A sweeper's
broom. I told him: But are you aware, sir, that such brooms
are used in the cleaning of lavatories and are regarded as most
unclean? He was not at all deterred. He said: Why then, it is
the perfect instrument for my abasement; it will be a reminder
of Man's fallen nature and of the sinfulness and corruption of
our bodies.'

'Now that's got to be a new way of getting your ashes
hauled.'

'You cannot image, Mr Reid, what a labour it was to find
that instrument. Such things are not to be found in a bazar.
Not till I tried to acquire one did I find out that they are made
at home, by those who use them, and are no more available to
others than a doctor's instruments are to his patients. I had to
summon a sweeper and it was no easy matter, believe me, to

interview him, for half the household staff gathered around to listen, and I could hear them discuting with each other as to why I might wish to procure this object. Was it my purpose to become a sweeper? To rob them of their employment? But to be brief, at length I did succeed in procuring such a jharu, last week. And a few nights ago I took it to his study for the first time.'

'Pay away, Miss Lambert.'

'Oh Mr Reid, had you but been there you would have remarked the mixture of joy and anticipation with which he regarded the instrument of his impending oppression. This was as I said, just a few days ago, so I remember well the passage he chose for his lecture. "And they utterly destroyed all that was in the city, both man and woman, young and old, and ox, and sheep, and ass, with the edge of the sword." Then he put the jharu in my hands and said: "I am the city and this your sword. Strike me, smite me, burn me with your fire." He knelt, as always, with his face at my feet and his poop-deck in the air. How he squirmed and squealed when I flailed the broom upon his rear. Mr Reid, you would have thought him to be in agony: I myself was sure that I was doing him some dreadful injury, but when I paused to inquire whether he would not wish me to stop, he positively shrieked: "No, no, go on! Harder!" So I swung back my arm and lashed him with the jhata, using all my strength—which, you may be sure, is not inconsiderable—until finalmently he moaned and his body went slack on the floor. What horror! I thought, the worst has come to pass! I have killed him for sure. So I leant down and whispered: "Oh poor Mr Burnham—are you all right?" Vaste was my relief, you can be sure, when he stirred and moved his head. But yet he would not rise to his feet, no, he lay flat on the floor and squirmed over the parquet like some creature of the soil, all the way to the door. "Are you hurt, Mr Burnham?" I inquired, following him. "Have you broken your back? Why do you lie thus on the floor? Why do you not rise?" He answered me with a moan: "All is well, do not worry, go to the lectern and read again the lesson." I went to obey him, but no sooner was my back turned than he leapt nimbly to his feet, undid the latch and hurried away up the stairs. I was retracing my steps to the lectern when I saw on the floor a curious mark, a long, wet stain, as if some thin, damp creature had crawled over the parquet. Now was I certain that in a moment's inattention a millipede or a serpent had intruded into the room—for such a thing is often known to happen, Mr Reid, in India. To my shame, I must admit, I shrieked . . .'

She broke off in agitation and wrung the hem of her sari between her hands. 'I know this may cause me to sink in your esteem, Mr Reid—for I am well aware that a serpent is as much our brother in Nature as is a flower or a cat, so why should we fear it? My father essayed often to reason with me on this subject, but I regret to say that I have not been able to make myself fond of those creatures. I trust you will not judge me too harshly?'

'Oh I'm with you, Miss Lambert,' said Zachary. 'Snakes are not to be messed with, blind or not.'

'You will not be surprised then,' Paulette said, 'to know that I screamed and screamed until at last one of the old khidmutgars appeared. I said to him: 'Sāp! Sāp! A serpent of the jungle has entered the room. Hunt it out!' He stooped to examine the stain and presently when he rose he said the strangest thing, Mr Reid, you will not credit it . . .'

'Go on, Miss: tip me the grampus.'

'He said: "This was not made by a serpent of the jungle; this is a mark of the snake that lives in Man." I took this to be a Biblical allusion, Mr Reid, so I said, "Amen." Indeed I was wondering whether I should not add an "Hallelujah!"— but then the old khidmutgar burst into laughter and hurried away. And still, Mr Reid, I did not see the meaning of any of this. All night, I lay awake, thinking of it, but at dawn, suddenly I knew. And after that, of course, I could not remain any more in that house, so I sent a message to Jodu, through another boatman, and here I am. But to hide from Mr Burnham in Calcutta is very hard—it would only be a matter of time before I am discovered, and who knows what the consequences might be? So I must flee the country, Mr Reid, and I have decided where I must go.'

'And where is that?'

'The Mauritius Islands, Mr Reid. That is where I must go.'

~

All this while, even as he was working the oars, Jodu had been listening intently to Paulette, so that Zachary was led to conclude that this was the first he'd heard of what had happened between her and Mr Burnham. Now, as if in confirmation, a heated argument broke out and the boat began to drift, with Jodu resting on his oars as he poured out a stream of plaintive Bengali.

Glancing shorewards, Zachary's eye was caught by a glimmer of moonlight, on the roof of a green-tiled pavilion, and he realized that they had drifted far enough downriver to draw level with the Burnham estate. Bethel loomed in the distance, like the hull of a darkened ship, and the sight of it transported Zachary suddenly to the evening when Paulette had sat beside him at dinner, looking rosily virginal in her severe black gown; he remembered the musical breeze of her voice and how, through the evening, his head had been all a-sway at the thought that this girl, with her strange mixture of worldliness and innocence, was the same Paulette he'd stumbled upon in the 'tween-deck, locked in an embrace with the laundered lascar that she called her brother. Even then he had glimpsed a kind of melancholy behind her smile: now, in thinking of what might have caused it, a memory came to him, of listening to his mother as she told the story of the first time she was summoned by the master—his father—to the cabin in the woods that he kept for bedding his slaves: she was fourteen then, she'd said, and had stood trembling by the door, her feet unwilling to move, even when old Mr Reid told her to quit her snivelling and git over to the bed.

The question of whether Mr Burnham was a better or worse human being than the man who had fathered him, seemed, to Zachary, without meaning or purpose, for he took for granted that power made its bearers act in inexplicable ways—no matter whether a captain or bossman or just a master, like his father. And once this was accepted, it followed also that the whims of masters could be, at times, kind as well as cruel, for wasn't it just such an impulse that had caused old Mr Reid to grant his mother her freedom so that he, Zachary, would not be born a slave? And wasn't it true equally that Zachary himself had benefited enough from Mr Burnham to make it impossible for him to leap easily to judgement? Yet, it had still twisted him in a knot to hear his mother speak of that first time, in Mr Reid's cabin in the woods, and although Paulette's experience with Mr Burnham was in no wise similar, her story too had caused a nippering in the stays of his heart— a stirring, not just of sympathy, but also an awakening of an instinct of protectiveness. 'Miss Lambert,' he blurted out suddenly, breaking in on her altercation with Jodu, 'Miss Lambert, believe me, if I had the means to be a settled man, I would this minute offer to make you . . .'

Paulette cut him off before he could finish. 'Mr Reid,' she said proudly, 'you are yourself trumping very much if you imagine me to be in search of a husband. I am not a lost kitten, Mr Reid, to be sheltered in a menage. Indeed I can conceive of no union more contemptible than one in which a man adopts a wife out of pity!'

Zachary bit his lip. 'Didn't mean no offence, Miss Lambert. Believe me: wasn't pity made me say what I did.'

Squaring her shoulders, Paulette tossed the ghungta of her sari off her head. 'You are mistaken, Mr Reid, if you imagine that I asked you here to seek your protection—for if there is anything that Bethel has taught me it is that the kindness of men comes always attached to some prix . . .'

The word stunned Zachary. 'Avast, Miss Lambert! I didn say nothin like that. I know to watch my mouth around a lady.'

'Lady?' said Paulette scornfully. 'Is it to a lady that an offer like yours is made? Or rather to a woman . . . who sits in the window?'

'You're on the wrong tack, Miss Lambert,' said Zachary. 'Never meant nothin like that.' He could feel his face colouring in mortification now, and to calm himself, he took the oars out of Jodu's hands and began to row. 'So why did you want to see me then, Miss Lambert?'

'I asked you here, Mr Reid, because I wish to discover whether you are fit to bear the name you have been given: Zikri.'

'I don't take your meaning, Miss.'

'May I then rappel for you, Mr Reid,' said Paulette, 'that a few nights ago you told me that if I ever needed anything, I had only to ask? I asked you here tonight because I wish to know whether your promise was a mere bagatelle, lightly uttered, or whether you are indeed a man who honours his parole.'

Zachary could not help smiling. 'You're wrong there again, Miss: many a bar I've seen, but never those of a jail.'

'Word,' said Paulette, correcting herself. 'That is what I mean. I want to know whether you are a man of your word. Come: tell the truth. Are you a man of your word or not?'

'That depends, Miss Lambert,' said Zachary cautiously, 'on whether it's in my power to give you what you want.'

'It is,' said Paulette firmly. 'It most certainly is—or else I would not ask.'

'What is it then?' said Zachary, his suspicions deepening.

Paulette looked him in the eye and smiled. 'I would like to join the crew of the *Ibis*, Mr Reid.'

'What?' Zachary could not believe that he had heard aright: in that moment of inattention his grip slackened and the current tore the oars from his hands and would have swept them away but for the vigilance of Jodu, who snatched one from the water and used it to pole the other one in. Leaning over the gunwale to retrieve the oar, Zachary found himself exchanging glances with Jodu, who shook his head as if to indicate that he knew perfectly well what Paulette had in mind and had already decided that it could not be allowed. United by this secret understanding, each man took an oar for himself and they started to row together, sitting shoulder to shoulder, with their faces turned towards Paulette: no longer were they lascar and malum, but rather a confederacy of maleness, banding together to confront a determined and guileful adversary.

'Yes Mr Reid,' Paulette repeated, 'that is my request to you: to be allowed to join your crew. I will be one of them: my hair will be confined, my clothing will be as theirs . . . I am strong . . . I can work . . .'

Zachary leant hard against the oar and the boat surged forward against the current, leaving the Burnham estate in its wake: he was glad to be rowing now, for there was a certain comfort in the hardness of the wooden handle that was grating against the calluses of his palms; there was something reassuring, even, about the dampness on his shoulder, where his arms were grinding against Jodu's: the proximity, the feel and smell of sweat—these were all reminders of the relentless closeness of shipboard life, the coarseness and familiarity which made sailors as heedless as animals, thinking nothing of saying aloud, or even being seen to do, that which elsewhere would have caused agonies of shame. In the fo'c'sle lay all the filth and vileness and venery of being a man, and it was necessary that it be kept contained to spare the world the stench of the bilges.

But Paulette, in the meanwhile, had not ceased to make her case: '. . . Nobody will know who I am, Mr Reid, except for yourself and Jodu. It is now only a matter of whether you will honour your word or not.'

An answer could no longer be delayed, so Zachary replied by shaking his head. 'You've got to put this out of your mind, Miss Lambert. It just won't do.'

'Why?' she said defiantly. 'Give me a reason.'

'Can't happen,' said Zachary. 'See: it's not only that you're a woman—it's also that you're white. The *Ibis* will be sailing with an all-lascar crew which means that only her officers will be "European", as they say here. There are only three such: first mate, second mate and Captain. You've already met the

Captain; and the first mate, let me tell you, is as mean a hard-horse as I've ever seen. This isn't a kippage you'd want to be in, even if you were a man—and all the white berths are taken anyway. No room for another buckra on board.'

Paulette laughed. 'Oh but you don't understand, Mr Reid,' she said. 'Of course I don't expect to be an officer, like yourself. What I want is to join as a lascar, like Jodu.'

'Shitten hell . . .!' Once again Zachary's grip went slack and this time the oar caught a wallop of a crab, dealing him a blow to the stomach that left him gasping and spluttering.

Jodu tried to keep them on a steady course, but by the time Zachary recovered, the current had dragged them backwards and they were again within view of the Burnham estate—but Paulette was as oblivious to the sight of her former home as she was to the groans of pain issuing from the centre of the boat. 'Yes, Mr Reid,' she continued, 'if only you agreed to help me, it could be quite easily done. Anything Jodu can do, I can do also—that has been true since we were children, he himself will tell you so. I can climb as well as he, I can swim and run better, and I can row almost as well. As for languages, I can speak Bengali and Hindusthani as well as he. It is true that he is darker, but I am not so pale that I could not be taken for an Indian. I assure you there has never been a time in our lives when we could not persuade an outsider that we were brothers—it was always just a question of changing my pinafore for a lungi, and tying a gamchha around my head. In this way we have been everywhere together, on the rivers and in the streets of the city: ask him—he cannot deny it. If he can be a lascar then, you may be sure, so can I. With kajal in my eyes, a turban on my head and a lungi around my waist, no one will know me. I will work below deck and never be seen.'

An image of Paulette, dressed in a lungi and turban, flashed before Zachary's eyes—it was so distasteful, so unnatural, that he shook his head to rid himself of it. It was hard enough to reconcile the girl in the sari with the Paulette who had invaded his dreams: the delicate rose he'd first met on the deck of the *Ibis*, with her face framed in a bonnet, and a

*Amitav Ghosh*

spoondrift of lace bubbling at her throat. The sight of her had caught more than his eyes: that he might speak with her, walk out with her—he had wanted nothing more. But to think of that girl dressed in a sarong and headcloth, clinging barefoot to the ratlines, wolfing rice from a tapori and strutting the decks with the smell of garlic on her breath—that would be like imagining himself to be in love with a lascar; he would be like a man who'd gone sweet on an ape.

'Miss Lambert,' said Zachary firmly, 'this notion of yours is just a smoke-sail: it's never going to catch the least breath of wind. To start with, it's our serang who does the 'gagement of the lascars, not us. He procures them through a ghaut-serang . . . and for all I know, there's not a man among them who's not his cousin or uncle or worse. I have no say in who he signs on: that's for him to decide.'

'But the serang took Jodu, didn't he?'

'Yes, but it wasn't on my say-so—it was because of the accident.'

'But if Jodu spoke for me,' said Paulette, 'he would take me, would he not?'

'Maybe.' Glancing to his side, Zachary saw that Jodu's face was screwed into an angry scowl: there could be no doubt that they were of one mind on this, so there was no reason not to let him speak for himself. 'Have you asked Jodu what he thinks?'

At this, a hissing sound issued from Jodu's mouth and was followed by a succession of words and exclamations that left no doubt about where he stood—'Avast! . . . how she live beech-o-beech many mans? Don know hook from hinch . . . bumkin or wank . . .' In a final rhetorical flourish, he posed the question: 'Lady lascar? . . .'—and answered by spitting over the deck rail, with a contemptuous: 'Heave the lead!'

'You must pay the dear little choute no attention,' said Paulette quickly. 'He is blablating because he is jealous and does not wish to admit that I can be just as good a sailor as he can. He likes to believe that I am his helpless little sister. Anyway it does not matter what he thinks, Mr Reid, because he will do as you tell him. It is all up to you, Mr Reid, not Jodu.'

'Miss Lambert,' said Zachary gently, 'it was you as told me that he's like a brother to you. Don't you see you'd be putting him in danger if you went through with this? What'd you think the other lascars would do to him if they knew he'd fooled them into taking a woman into the fo'c'sle? Many a sailor has been killed for less. And think, Miss Lambert, about what would be done to *you* if you were found out—and you surely would be, no mojo nor conjuration can stop it. When that happens, believe me, Miss, it would not be something that any of us would wish to think about.'

All this while Paulette had been sitting proudly upright, but now her shoulders began to sag. 'So you will not help me then?' she said in a slow, halting voice. 'Even though you gave your word?'

'If I could help in some other way, I would be only too glad,' said Zachary. 'Why, I have some little money saved, Miss Lambert—it might be enough to buy a passage on another ship.'

'It's not your charity I want, Mr Reid,' Paulette said. 'Don't you see that I must give proof of myself? Do you think a few little obstacles would have stopped my grand-aunt from making her voyage?' Paulette's lip trembled and swelled and she had to brush a tear of vexation from her eye. 'I had thought you were a better man, Mr Reid, a man of your word, but I see that you are nothing but a paltry hommelette.'

'An omelette?'

'Yes; your word is not worth a dam.'

'I'm sorry to disappoint you, Miss Lambert,' said Zachary, 'but I do believe it's for the best. A clipper is no place for a girl like yourself.'

'Oh, so that is it—a girl cannot do it?' Paulette's head snapped up and her eyes flashed. 'To listen to you one would think you had invented hot water, Mr Reid. But you are wrong: I can do it and I will.'

'I wish you good luck with that, Miss,' said Zachary.

*Amitav Ghosh*

'Don't you dare sneer at me, Mr Reid,' Paulette cried. 'I may be in difficulties now but I will get to the Mauritius and when I do I will laugh in your face. I will call you names such as you have never heard.'

'Really?' With the end of the battle in sight, Zachary permitted himself a smile. 'And what might they be, Miss?'

'I will call you . . .' Paulette broke off, searching her memory for an oath that would be insulting enough to express the anger in her heart. Suddenly a word exploded from her lips: 'Cock-swain! That is what you are, Mr Reid—a horrid cock-swain!'

'Cockswain?' said Zachary, in puzzlement, and Jodu, glad to hear a familiar word, translated, as if by habit, Coksen?

'Yes,' said Paulette, in a voice that was tremulous with indignation. 'Mrs Burnham says that it is a most unspeakable thing and should never be in a lady's mouth. You may think the King is your cousin, Mr Reid, but let me tell you what you really are: an unutterable cock-swain.'

Zachary was so taken by the absurdity of this that he burst out laughing and whispered, in an aside to Jodu: 'Is it "dick-swain" she means?'

'Dix?' This exchange had not eluded Paulette. 'A fine pair the two of you, cockson and dixon, neither one man enough to keep his word. But you wait and see—you're not going to leave me behind.'

# fourteen

~

It was only to the outside world that Alipore Jail presented the semblance of an unitary realm: to its inmates, it appeared rather as an archipelago of fiefdoms, each with its own rules, rulers and ruled. Neel's transition from the outer sphere of the prison, where the British authorities held sway, into the jail's inner domain, took more than a day to complete: he spent his first night in a holding cell and it was not till the evening of the second day that he was assigned to a ward. By this time, he had been seized by a strange sense of dissociation, and even though he knew very little about the internal arrangements of the jail, he betrayed no surprise when his guards delivered him into the custody of another convict, a man who was also dressed in white dungaree cloth, except that his dhoti was of ankle length and his tunic was clean and well-washed. The man had the heavy build of an ageing wrestler and Neel was quick to notice the marks of eminence that he bore on his person: the well-fed surge of his belly, the trimmed grey beard and the massive ring of keys at his waist; when they walked past cells, the prisoners invariably saluted him with deferential greetings, addressing him as Bishu-ji. It was clear that Bishu-ji was one of the prison's jemadars—a convict who, by reason either of seniority, or force of character, or brute strength, had been appointed to a position of authority by the jail's governors.

The ward in which Neel now found himself was laid out around a square courtyard that had a well at one side and a tall neem tree at the other. This courtyard was where the ward's inmates cooked, ate and bathed: at night they slept in shared cells and their mornings were spent working in labour gangs—but the courtyard was otherwise the centre of their lives, the hearth where their days ended and began. Now, the evening meal having been served and consumed, the cooking fires were dying out and the barred gates that ringed the courtyard were clanging loudly as each group of convicts was returned to its cell for the night. Of the men who remained, one lot were clustered around the well, where they were scrubbing cooking pots and other utensils; the others were the ward's jemadars, and they were sitting at leisure under the neem tree, where four charpoys had been arranged in a circle. The jemadars were all attended by a few of their loyalists, for they each headed a band that was part gang and part family. Within these groupings, the jemadars functioned as both bosses and heads of household, and in much the way that zemindars were served by members of their zenanas, they too were waited on by their favourite chokras and followers. Now, at the end of the day, the overseers were taking their ease with their equals, while their attendants busied themselves in lighting their hookahs, preparing chillums of ganja and massaging their masters' feet.

What followed was not unlike a hearing at a meeting of village elders, with the particulars of Neel's case being presented to the others by Bishu-ji. Speaking with the cogency of a lawyer, he told them about the Raskhali zemindary, the charge of forgery and the proceedings of the Supreme Court. How he had come by this information, Neel could not imagine, but he sensed that Bishu-ji wished him no harm and was grateful for his painstaking elaboration of the facts of his case.

From the exclamations of shock that greeted the end of Bishu-ji's recital, Neel understood that even among these long-term tenants of the jail, the penalty of transportation was regarded with an inexpressible horror. He was summoned to the centre of the gathering and made to display his tattooed forehead, which was examined with fascination and revulsion, sympathy and awe. Neel participated in the display without reluctance, hoping that the marks on his skin would entitle him to certain privileges, setting his lot apart from that of lesser convicts.

Presently, a silence fell, to indicate that the deliberations of the panchayat had ended, and Bishu-ji signalled to Neel to follow him across the courtyard.

Listen, he said, as they walked away, let me explain our rules to you: it is the custom here, when a new prisoner arrives, for him to be allotted to one or other of the jemadars, according to his origins and his character. But with someone such as yourself, this does not apply because the sentence you have been given will tear you forever from the ties that bind others. When you step on that ship, to go across the Black Water, you and your fellow transportees will become a brotherhood of your own: you will be your own village, your own family, your own caste. That is why it is the custom here for such men as you to live apart, in their own cells, separate from the rest.

Neel nodded: I understand.

At this time, continued Bishu-ji, there is only one other man here who bears the same sentence as you: he too is to be transported to Mareech, and the two of you will no doubt travel together. Therefore it is only right that you should share his cell.

There was an undertone in his voice that sounded a warning. Neel said: Who is this man?

Bishu-ji's face creased into a smile: His name is Aafat.

Aafat? said Neel, in surprise: the word meant 'calamity' and he could not imagine that anyone would choose it for a name. Who is this man? Where is he from?

He is from across the sea: the land of Maha-Chin.

He is Chinese?

So we think, from the look of him, said Bishu-ji. But it's hard to be sure, for we know almost nothing about him, except that he is an afeemkhor.

An addict? said Neel. But from where does he get his opium?

*Amitav Ghosh*

That's the thing, said the jemadar. He is an afeemkhor who has no opium.

They had reached the cell now and Bishu-ji was sorting through his keys to find the right one. This corner of the courtyard was dimly lit, and the cell was so silent that at first glance, Neel had the impression that it was empty. He asked where the addict was and Bishu-ji answered by opening the gate to push him inside.

He's there; you'll find him.

Inside there were two charpoys, both covered with a webbing of rope, and in the far corner there was a toilet bucket with a wooden lid. By the wall there stood an earthen pitcher of drinking water: apart from these few things, the cell seemed to contain nothing else.

But he's not here, said Neel.

He's there, said the jemadar. Just listen.

Gradually, Neel became aware of a whimpering sound, accompanied by a soft clicking, like the chattering of teeth. The sound was so close that its source had to be somewhere inside the cell: he dropped to his knees and looked under the charpoys, to discover an unmoving heap lying beneath one of them. He recoiled, more in fear than revulsion, as he might from an animal that was badly wounded or grievously sick— the creature was making a sound that was more like a whine than a moan, and all he could see of its face was a single glinting eye. Then Bishu-ji poked a stick through the bars and thrust it under the charpoy: Aafat! Come on out! Look, we've found you another transportee.

Prodded by the stick, a limb came snaking out from under the bed and Neel saw that it was a man's arm, encrusted with filth. Then the head showed itself, barely visible because of a thick coating of matted hair, and a straggling black beard that was twisted into ropes. As the rest of the body slowly emerged, it showed itself to be so thickly mired in dirt and mud that it was impossible to tell whether the man was naked or clothed. Then suddenly the cell was filled with the smell of ordure and Neel realized that it was not just mud the man was covered in, but also faeces and vomit.

Spinning around in disgust, Neel clutched the bars of the cell, calling out after Bishu-ji: You can't leave me here, have some pity, let me out . . .

Bishu-ji turned around and walked back.

Listen, he said, wagging a finger at Neel: Listen—if you think you can hide from this man you are wrong. From now on, you will never be able to escape this Aafat. He will be on your ship and you will have to travel with him to your jail across the Black Water. He is all you have, your caste, your family, your friend; neither brother nor wife nor son will ever be as close to you as he will. You will have to make of him what you can; he is your fate, your destiny. Look in a mirror and you will know: you cannot escape what is written on your forehead.

~

Jodu was not surprised to find Paulette growing increasingly morose and resentful after her late-night meeting with Zachary: it was clear that she blamed him, Jodu, for the failure of her plan, and often now, there was an unaccustomedly ugly edge to their usually harmless bickering. For two people to live in rancour, in a small boat, was far from pleasant, but Jodu understood that Paulette was in a cruel, even desperate, situation, with no money and few friends, and he could not bring himself to refuse her the refuge of his pansari. But the boat was just a rental, from a ghat-side boat-owner, due to be returned when the *Ibis* was ready to set sail. What would Paulette do after that? She refused to discuss the subject, and he could not blame her for this, since he could scarcely bear to think of it himself.

In the meanwhile, it was still raining hard, and one day Paulette got caught in a ferocious monsoonal downpour. Either because of the drenching or by reason of her state of mind, she fell ill. It was beyond Jodu's power to nurse her back in the boat, so he decided instead to take her to a family who had known her father well: they had long been malis at the

Botanical Gardens, and had benefited greatly from Mr Lambert's generosity. With them she would be safe and well looked after.

The family lived in a village a little to the north of Calcutta, in Dakshineshwar, and on arriving at their door, Paulette received a welcome that was warm enough to allay any remaining qualms that Jodu may have had. Rest and get better, he said to her as he was leaving. I'll be back in two-three months and we can decide then what to do next. She answered with a wan nod, and that was where they left the matter.

Jodu rowed back to Calcutta, hoping to make some quick money with his boat. This was not to be, for the last few rainstorms of the monsoons proved to be the most furious of the season, and he had to spend almost all his time moored at the ghats. But when at last the rains ended, the air was cleaner and crisper than ever before, and the winds brisk and redolent of renewal: after the rain-slowed months of the monsoons, the rivers and roadways quickly filled up with traffic, as farmers hurried to bring their freshly-harvested crops to the markets, and shoppers swarmed to the bazars, to buy new clothes for Durga Puja, Dussehra and 'Id.

It was on one such busy evening, while ferrying passengers in his boat, that Jodu looked downriver and caught sight of the *Ibis*, freshly released from dry dock: she was at a berth, moored between two buoys, but even with her masts bare, she looked like a token of the season itself, scrubbed and refreshed, with a new sheathing of copper along her watermark, her masts taunt and a-gleam. Wisps of smoke were curling out of the chuldan chimney, so Jodu knew that many of the lascars were already on board, and for once he wasted no time in haggling over fares and taunting the miserly: he got rid of his passengers as soon as he could, and rowed over to the schooner at full speed.

And there they were, lounging around the deckhouse, all the old familiar faces, Cassem-meah, Simba Cader, Rajoo, Steward Pinto, and the two tindals, Babloo and Mamdoo. Even Serang Ali unbent far enough to give him a smile and a nod. After the slapping and the gut-punching, his boat became the focus of much laughter—Is its roof made from old jharus? Is that an oar or a punkha? No one, he was told, had expected him to return: they thought he'd been lost to the stick-men—wasn't it common knowledge that no dandi-wala could ever be happy without a stick in his stern?

And the malums? The Kaptan? Where are they?

Not aboard yet, said Rajoo.

This delighted Jodu, for it meant that the lascars had the run of the vessel. Come on, he said to Rajoo, let's look the ship over while we can.

They headed first for the officers' section of the vessel, the peechil-kamre—the after-cabins—which lay directly beneath the quarter-deck: they knew they would never again set foot there, except as topas or mess-boy, and were determined to make the most of it. To get to the peechil-kamre they had to go through one of two companionways that were tucked under the overhang of the quarter-deck: the entrance on the dawa side led to the officers' cabins and the other to the adjoining compartment, which was known as the 'beech-kamra' or midships-cabin. The dawa companionway opened into the cuddy, which was where the officers ate their meals. Looking around it, Jodu was astonished by how carefully everything was made, how every eventuality had been thought of and provided for: the table at the centre even had rims around its sides, with little fenced enclosures in the middle, so that nothing could slip or slide when the schooner was rolling. The mates' cabins were on either side of the cuddy, and they were, in comparison, somewhat plain, just about large enough to turn around in, with bunks that were not quite long enough for a man to stretch out his legs in comfort.

The Kaptan's stateroom was furthest aft, and there was nothing about this kamra that was in the least bit disappointing: it extended along the width of the stern and its wood and brass shone brightly with polish; it seemed grand enough to belong in a Raja's palace. At one end of it there was a small, beautifully carved desk, with tiny shelves and an inkwell that was built into the wood; at the other end was a spacious bunk with a polished candle-holder affixed to one side. Jodu threw himself on the mattress and bounced up and down: Oh, if only you were a girl—a Ranee instead of a Rajoo! Can you think what it would be like, on this . . .?

For a moment they were both lost in their dreams.

One day, sighed Jodu, one day, I'll have a bed like this for myself.

. . . And I'll be the Faghfoor of Maha-chin . . .

Forward of the after-cabins lay the midships-cabin—the beech-kamra, where the overseers and guards were to be accommodated. This part of the schooner was also relatively comfortable: it was equipped with bunks rather than hammocks, and was fairly well lit, with portholes to let in the daylight and several lamps hanging from the ceiling. Like the after-cabins, this kamra was connected to the main deck by its own companionway and ladder. But the ladder to the midships-cabin had an extension that led even further into the bowels of the vessel, reaching down to the holds, storerooms and istur-khanas where the ships' provisions and spare equipment were stored.

Next to the beech-kamra lay the migrants' part of the ship: the 'tween-deck, known to the lascars as the 'box', or dabusa. It was little changed since the day Jodu first stepped into it: it was still as grim, dark and foul-smelling as he remembered— merely an enclosed floor, with arched beams along the sides— but its chains and ring-bolts were gone and a couple of heads and piss-dales had been added. The dabusa inspired a near-superstitious horror in the crew, and neither Jodu nor Rajoo remained there for long. Shinning up the ladder, they went eagerly to their own kamra, the fana. This was where the most startling change was found to have occurred: the rear part of the compartment had been boxed off to make a cell, with a stout door.

If there's a chokey, said Rajoo, it can only mean there'll be convicts on board.

How many?

Who knows?

The chokey's door lay open so they climbed into it. The cell was as cramped as a chicken coop and as airless as a snake-pit: apart from a lidded porthole in its door, it had only one other opening, which was a tiny air duct in the bulwark that separated it from the coolies' dabusa. Jodu found that if he stood on tiptoe, he could put his eye to the air duct. Two months in this hole! he said to Rajoo. With nothing to do but spy on the coolies . . .

Nothing to do! scoffed Rajoo. They'll be picking istup till their fingers fall off: they'll have so much work they'll forget their names.

And speaking of work, said Jodu. What about our exchange? Do you think they're going to let me take your place on the mast?

Rajoo pulled a doubtful face: I spoke to Mamdoo-tindal today, but he said he'd have to try you out first.

When?

They did not have to wait long for an answer. On returning to the main deck, Jodu heard a voice shouting down from aloft: You there! Stick-man! Jodu looked up to see Mamdoo-tindal looking down from the kursi of the foremast, beckoning with a finger. Come on up!

This was a test, Jodu knew, so he spat on his palms and muttered a bismillah before reaching for the iskat. Less than halfway up, he knew his hands were scraped and bleeding—it was as if the hempen rope had sprouted thorns—but his luck held. Not only did he get to the kursi, he even managed to wipe his bloody hands on his hair before the tindal could see his cuts.

*Chalega*! said Mamdoo-tindal, with a grudging nod. It'll do—not bad for a dandi-wala . . .

For fear of saying too much, Jodu responded only with a modest grin—but if he had been a king at a coronation, he could not have felt more triumphant than he did as he eased himself into the kursi: what throne, after all, could offer as grand a view as the crosstrees, with the sun sinking in the west, and a river of traffic flowing by below?

Oh you'll like it up here, said Mamdoo-tindal. And if you ask nicely, Ghaseeti might even teach you her way of reading the wind.

Reading the wind? How?

Like this. Stepping on the purwan, the tindal laid himself down and turned his legs to point at the horizon, where the sun was setting. Then, lifting his feet, he shook out his lungi, so that it opened out like a funnel. When the tube of cloth filled with wind, he gave a triumphant moan. Yes! Ghaseeti predicts that the wind will rise. She feels it! It's on her ankles, on her legs, its hand is inching its way up, she feels it *there* . . .

On her legs?

In her wind-maker, you faltu-chute, where else?

Jodu laughed so hard he almost fell out of the kursi. There was only one thing, he realized, with a twinge of regret, that could have made the joke still more enjoyable, and that was if Paulette had been there to share it with him: this was the kind of silliness that had always delighted them both.

～

It did not take long for Neel to discover that his cell-mate's torments were ordered by certain predictable rhythms. His paroxysms of shivering, for instance, would begin with a mild, almost imperceptible trembling, like that of a man in a room that is just a little too cold for comfort. But these gentle shivers would mount in intensity till they became so violent as to tip him off his charpoy, depositing his convulsing body on the ground. The outlines of his muscles would show through the grime on his skin, alternately contracting into knots and then briefly relaxing, but only to seize up again: it was like looking at a pack of rats squirming in a sack. After the convulsions subsided, he would lie unconscious for a while and then something inside him would stir again; his breathing would grow laboured and his lungs would rattle, yet his eyes would remain closed; his lips would begin to move and form words, and he would pass into the grip of a delirium that somehow permitted him to remain asleep, even as he tossed from side to side, in a frenzy of movement, while shouting aloud in his own language. Then a fire would seem to come alight under his skin and he would begin to slap himself all over, as if to snuff out the spreading flames. When this failed, his hands would become claws, gouging into his flesh as if to rip off a coating of charred skin. Only then would his eyes come open: it was as if his exhausted body would not allow him to wake up until he had tried to flay himself.

Horrible as these symptoms were, none of them affected Neel as much as his cell-mate's chronic incontinence. To watch, hear and smell a grown man dribbling helplessly on the floor, on his bed, and on himself, would have been a trial for anyone—but for a man of Neel's fastidiousness, it was to cohabit with the incarnate embodiment of his loathings. Later, Neel would come to learn that not the least of opium's properties is its powerful influence on the digestive system: in proper doses it was a remedy for diarrhoea and dysentery; taken in quantity it could cause the bowels to freeze—a common symptom in addicts. Conversely, when withdrawn abruptly, from a body that had grown accustomed to consuming it in excess, it had the effect of sending the bladder and sphincter into uncontrollable spasms, so that neither food nor water could be retained. It was unusual for this condition to last for more than a few days—but to know this would have provided little comfort to Neel, for whom every minute spent in the proximity of his dribbling, leaking, spewing cell-mate had a duration beyond measure. Soon, he too began to shiver and hallucinate: behind the lids of his closed eyes, the lashings of shit on the floor would come alive and send out tentacles that dug into his nose, plunged into his mouth and took hold of his throat. How long his own seizures lasted Neel did not know, but from time to time he would open his eyes to catch sight of the faces of other convicts, gaping at him in amazement; in one of these moments of wakefulness, he noticed that someone had opened the gratings of the cell and placed two objects inside: a jharu and a scoop, like those used by sweepers for the removal of night-soil.

If he was to keep his sanity, Neel knew he would have to take hold of the jharu and scoop; there was no other way. To rise to his feet and take the three or four steps that separated him from the jharu took as intense an effort as he had ever made, and when he was finally within touching distance of it, he could not prevail upon his hand to make contact: the risk involved seemed unimaginably great, for he knew that he would cease to be the man he had been a short while before. Closing his eyes, he thrust his hand blindly forward, and only when the handle was in his grasp did he allow himself to look again: it seemed miraculous then that his surroundings were unchanged, for within himself he could feel the intimations of an irreversible alteration. In a way, he was none other than the man he had ever been, Neel Rattan Halder, but he was different too, for his hands were affixed upon an object that was ringed with a bright penumbra of loathing; yet now that it was in his grip it seemed no more nor less than what it was, a tool to be used according to his wishes. Lowering himself to his heels, he squatted as he had often seen sweepers do, and began to scoop up his cell-mate's shit.

Once having started, Neel found himself to be possessed by a fury for the task. Only one part of the cell did he leave untouched—a small island near the waste-bucket, where he had pushed his cell-mate's charpoy in the hope of keeping him confined in a single corner. As for the rest, he scrubbed the walls as well as the floor, washing the refuse into the gutter that drained the cell. Soon many another convict was stopping by to watch him at work; some even began to help, unasked, by fetching water from the well and by throwing in handfuls of sand, of a kind that was useful in scouring floors. When he went into the courtyard, to bathe and wash his clothes, he was offered a welcome at several of the cooking-fires where meals were being prepared.

. . . Come, here . . . eat with us . . .

While he was eating, someone asked: Is it true that you know how to read and write?

Yes.

In Bengali?

In English too. And also Persian and Urdu.

A man approached, on his haunches: Can you write a letter for me then?

To whom?

The zemindar of my village; he wants to take some land away from my family and I want to send him a petition . . .

At one time, the daftars of the Raskhali zemindary had received dozens of such requests: though Neel had rarely taken the trouble to read them himself, he was not unfamiliar with their phrasing. I'll do it, he said, but you will have to bring me paper, ink and a quill.

Back in his cell, he was dismayed to find much of his work undone, for his cell-mate, gripped by one of his paroxysms, had rolled across the floor, leaving a trail of filth behind him. Neel was able to prod him back into his corner, but was too exhausted to do any more.

The night passed more peaceably than those before and Neel sensed a change in the rhythm of his cell-mate's seizures: they seemed to be waning in their intensity, allowing him longer intervals of rest; his incontinence, too, seemed somewhat moderated, possibly because there was nothing left in him to eject. In the morning, while unlocking the gratings, Bishu-ji said: It's Aafat you'll have to clean next. No way around it: once he feels the touch of water, he'll start to improve. I've seen it happen before.

Neel looked at the starved, emaciated body of his cell-mate, with its caking of ordure and its matted hair: even if he bathed him, overcoming his revulsion, what would be achieved? He would only soil himself again, and as for clothing, the only garment he seemed to possess was a drawstringed pyjama that was soaked in his own waste.

Shall I send someone to help you? Bishu-ji asked.

No, said Neel. I'll do it myself.

Having spent a few days in the same space, Neel had already begun to feel that he was somehow implicated in his

*Amitav Ghosh*

cell-mate's plight: it was as if their common destination had made their shame and honour a shared burden. For better or for worse it was he who would have to do whatever had to be done.

It took a while to make the necessary preparations: bartering his services as a letter-writer, Neel acquired a few slivers of soap, a pumice stone, an extra dhoti and a banyan. To persuade Bishu-ji to leave the gratings of the cell unlocked proved unexpectedly easy: as prospective transportees, neither Neel nor his cell-mate were expected to participate in work-gangs, so they had the courtyard mostly to themselves in the first part of the day. Once the other inmates were gone, Neel drew several buckets of water from the well and then half lifted and half dragged his cell-mate across the courtyard. The addict offered little resistance and his opium-wasted body was unexpectedly light. At the first dousing, he stirred his limbs feebly as if to fight off Neel's hands, but he was so weakened that his struggles were like the squirming of an exhausted bird. Neel was able to hold him down without difficulty, and within a few minutes his twitching subsided and he lapsed into a kind of torpor. After scouring his chest with a pumice stone, Neel wrapped his slivers of soap in a rag and began to wash the man's limbs: the addict's frame was skeletal and his skin was covered with scabs and sores, caused by vermin, yet it was soon apparent, from the elasticity of his sinews, that he was not in late middle-age, as Neel had thought: he was much younger than he appeared, and had evidently been in the full vigour of youth when the drug took control of his body. On reaching the knot of his drawstring, Neel saw that it was too tangled to be undone, so he cut through it and ripped away what little was left of his pyjamas. Gagging at the stench, Neel began to sluice water between the man's legs, breaking off occasionally to draw breath.

To take care of another human being—this was something Neel had never before thought of doing, not even with his own son, let alone a man of his own age, a foreigner. All he knew of nurture was the tenderness that had been lavished on him by his own caregivers: that they would come to love him was something he had taken for granted—yet knowing his own feelings for them to be in no way equivalent, he had often wondered how that attachment was born. It occurred to him now to ask himself if this was how it happened: was it possible that the mere fact of using one's hands and investing one's attention in someone other than oneself, created a pride and tenderness that had nothing whatever to do with the response of the object of one's care—just as a craftsman's love for his handiwork is in no way diminished by the fact of it being unreciprocated?

After swaddling his cell-mate in a dhoti, Neel propped him against the neem tree and forced a little rice down his throat. To put him back on his verminous charpoy would be to undo all the cleaning he had done, so he made a nest of blankets for him in a corner. Then he dragged the filthy bedstead to the well, gave it a thorough scrubbing and placed it, top down, in the open, as he had seen the other men do, so that the sunlight would burn away its pale, wriggling cargo of blood-sucking insects. Only after the job was done did it occur to Neel that he had lofted the stout bedstead on his own, without any assistance—he, who by family legend had been sickly since birth, subject to all manner of illness. In the same vein, it had been said of him, too, that he would choke on anything other than the most delicate food—but already many days had passed since he'd eaten anything but the cheapest dal and coarsest rice, small in grain, veined with red and weighted with a great quantity of tooth-shattering conkers and grit—yet his appetite had never been more robust.

Next day, through a complicated series of exchanges, involving the writing of letters to chokras and jemadars in other wards, Neel struck a bargain with a barber for the shaving of his cell-mate's head and face.

In all my years of hair-cutting, said the barber, I've never seen anything like this.

Neel looked over the barber's shoulder at his cell-mate's scalp: even as the razor was shaving it clean, the bared skin was sprouting a new growth—a film that moved and shimmered like mercury. It was a swarming horde of lice, and as the matted hair tumbled off, the insects could be seen falling to the ground in showers. Neel was kept busy, drawing and pouring bucketfuls of water, so as to drown the insects before they found others to infest.

The face that emerged from the vanished matting of hair and beard was little more than a skull, with shrunken eyes, a thin beak of a nose, and a forehead in which the bones had all but broken through the skin. That some part of this man was Chinese was suggested by the shape of his eyes and the colour of his skin—but in his high-bridged nose and his wide, full mouth, there was something that hinted also at some other provenance. Looking into that wasted face, Neel thought he could see the ghost of someone else, lively and questing: although temporarily exorcized by the opium, this other being had not entirely surrendered its claim upon the site of its occupancy. Who could say what capacities and talents that other self had possessed? As a test, Neel said, in English: 'What is your name?'

There was a flicker in the afeemkhor's dulled eyes, as if to indicate that he knew what the words meant, and when his head dropped, Neel chose to interpret the gesture not as a refusal but as a postponement of a reply. From then on, with his cell-mate's condition improving steadily, Neel made a ritual of asking the question once a day and even though his attempts to communicate met with no success, he never doubted that he would soon have a response.

~

The afternoon that Zachary came on board the *Ibis*, Mr Crowle was on the quarter-deck, pacing its width with a slow, contemplative tread, almost as if he were rehearsing for his day as Captain. He came to a halt when he caught sight of Zachary, with his ditty-bags slung over his shoulder. 'Why, lookee here!' he said in mock surprise. 'Blow me if it isn't little

Lord Mannikin hisself, primed to loose for the vasty deep.'

Zachary had resolved that he would not allow himself to be provoked by the first mate. He grinned cheerfully and dropped his ditty-bags. 'Good afternoon, Mr Crowle,' he said, sticking out a hand. 'Trust you've been well?'

'Oh do you now?' said Mr Crowle, shaking his hand brusquely. 'Truth to tell, I wasn't sure we'd have the pleasure o'yer company after all. Thought ye'd claw off and cut the painter, to be honest. Tofficky young tulip like y'self—reckon'd y'might prefer to find gainful employment onshore.'

'Never entered my mind, Mr Crowle,' said Zachary promptly. 'Nothing'd make me give up my berth on the *Ibis*.'

'Too soon to tell, Mannikin,' said the first mate with a smile. 'Much too early yet.'

Zachary shrugged this off, and over the next few days, what with stowing provisions and tallying the spare equipment, there was no time for any but the most perfunctory exchanges with the first mate. Then, one afternoon, Steward Pinto came aft to let Zachary know that the schooner's contingent of guards and overseers was in the process of embarking. Curious about the newcomers, Zachary stepped out to the quarter-deck to watch, and within a few minutes he was joined at the fife-rail by Mr Crowle.

The guards were for the most part turbaned silahdars—former sepoys with bandoliers crossed over their chests. The overseers were known as maistries, prosperous-looking men in dark chapkans and white dhotis. What was striking about them, maistries and silahdars alike, was the swagger with which they came aboard: it was as if they were a conquering force, that had been deputed to take possession of a captured vessel. They would not demean themselves by shouldering their own baggage; they deigned only to carry weapons and armaments—lathis, whips, spears and swords. Their firearms, which consisted of an impressive cache of muskets, gunpowder and tamancha handguns, were carried aboard by uniformed porters and deposited in the schooner's armoury. But as for the rest of their luggage, it fell to the lascars to fetch, carry and

*Amitav Ghosh*

stow their belongings and provisions, to the accompaniment of many a kick, cuff and gali.

The leader of the paltan, Subedar Bhyro Singh, was the last to step on board, and his entry was the most ceremonious of all: the maistries and silahdars received him as though he were a minor potentate, forming ranks and bowing low to offer their salams. A large, barrel-chested, bull-necked man, the subedar stepped on deck wearing a spotless white dhoti and a long kurta with a shimmering silk cummerbund: his head was wrapped in a majestic turban and he had a stout lathi tucked under his arm. He curled his white moustaches as he surveyed the schooner, looking none too pleased until his eyes fell on Mr Crowle. He greeted the first mate by beaming broadly and joining his hands together and Mr Crowle, too, seemed glad to see him, for Zachary heard him muttering, under his breath, 'Well, if it isn't old Muffin-mug!' Then he called out aloud, in the most cordial tone that Zachary had yet heard him employ: 'A very good day to you, Subby-dar.'

This unusual display of affability prompted Zachary to ask: 'Friend of yours, Mr Crowle?'

'We've shipped together in the past, and it's always the same, inn'it, for us Rough-knots? "Shipmates afore strangers, strangers afore dogs".' The first mate's lip curled as he looked Zachary up and down. 'Not that ye'd know about that, Mannikin, not in the company y'keep.'

This caught Zachary unawares: 'I don't know what you mean, Mr Crowle.'

'Oh don't y'now?' The first mate gave him a grimace of a smile. 'Well, maybe it's best that way.'

Here, before he could be pressed any further, the first mate was taken away by Serang Ali to oversee the fidding of the foremast, and Zachary was left to puzzle over the meaning of what he had said. As luck would have it, the Captain went ashore that night so the two mates dined alone, with Steward Pinto waiting on them. Scarcely a word was said until Steward Pinto carried in some chafing-dishes and laid them on the table. From the smell, Zachary could tell that they were about to be served a dish for which he had once expressed a liking, prawn curry with rice, and he gave the steward a smile and a nod. But Mr Crowle, in the meanwhile, had begun to sniff the air suspiciously and when the steward removed the covers from the dishes, a snarl of revulsion broke from his lips: 'What's this?' He took one look inside and slammed the lid back on the curry. 'Take this away, boy, and tell cookie to fry up some lamb chops. Don't y'ever set this mess o' quim-slime in front o'me again.'

The steward rushed forward, mumbling apologies, and was about to remove the containers when Zachary stopped him. 'Wait a minute, steward,' he said. 'You can leave that where it is. Please bring Mr Crowle what he wants, but this'll do just fine for me.'

Mr Crowle said nothing until the steward had disappeared up the companionway. Then, squinting at Zachary with narrowed eyes, he said: 'Ye're awful familiar with these here lascars, in'ye?'

'We sailed together from Cape Town,' said Zachary, with a shrug. 'I guess they know me and I know them. That's all there is to it.' Reaching for the rice, Zachary raised an eyebrow: 'With your permission.'

The first mate nodded, but his lips began to twitch in disgust as he watched Zachary helping himself. 'Was't them lascars as taught y'ter t'stomach that nigger-stink?'

'It's just karibat, Mr Crowle. Everyone eats it in these parts.'

'Do they so?' There was a pause and then Mr Crowle said: 'So is that what y'feeds on, when ye're up there with the Nabbs and Nobs and Nabobs?'

Suddenly Zachary understood the allusion of that afternoon; he glanced up from his plate, to find Mr Crowle watching him with a smile that bared the points of his teeth.

'I'll bet ye'thought I wouldn't find out, didn'yer, Mannikin?'

'About what?'

'Yer hobnobbin with the Burnhams and such.'

Zachary took a deep breath and answered quietly, 'They

invited me, Mr Crowle, so I went. I thought they'd asked you too.'

'Right! And black's the white o'me eye!'

'It's true. I did think they'd asked you,' said Zachary.

'Jack Crowle? Up at Bethel?' The words emerged very slowly, as if they had been dragged up from the bottom of a deep well of bitterness. 'Not good enough to get through that front door, is Jack Crowle—not his face, nor his tongue, nor his hands neither. Missus'd worry about stains on her linen. If ye're born with a wooden ladle, Mannikin, it don't matter if y'can eat the wind out o'a topsail. There's always the little Lord Mannikins and Hobdehoys and Loblolly-boys to gammon the skippers, and pitch slum to the shipowners. Ne'er mind they don't know a pintle from a gudgeon, nor a pawl from a whelp, but there they are—at the weather end of the quarter-deck with Jack Crowle eating their wind.'

'Listen, Mr Crowle,' said Zachary slowly, 'if you think I was born with a silver spoon in my mouth, let me tell you, you're half a clock off course.'

'Oh, I know y'for what y'are, Mannikin,' the first mate growled. 'Ye're a snob's cat, full o'piss and tantrums. I'se seen the likes o'yer before with yer pretty face and yer purser's grins. I know y'mean nothing but trouble, for y'self and fer me. Best y'get off this barkey, while y'can: save me as much pain as yer goin'ter save y'self.'

'I'm just here to do a job, Mr Crowle,' said Zachary stonily. 'And nothing's going to stop me doing it.'

The first mate shook his head: 'Too soon to tell, Mannikin. It's a couple of days yet afore we weigh. Time enough that something could happen to help yer change yer mind.'

For the sake of preserving the peace, Zachary bit back the rejoinder that sprang to his tongue and ate the rest of his dinner in silence. But the effort of keeping himself under control left his hands shaking, his mouth dry, and afterwards, to calm himself, he took a couple of turns around the main deck. Bursts of animated conversation were welling out of the fo'c'sle and the galley, where the lascars were eating their evening meal. He stepped up to the fo'c'sle deck, leant his elbows on the saddle of the jib-boom, and looked down at the water: there were many lights flickering on the river, some hanging from the sterns and binnacles of moored ships, and some lighting the way for the flotilla of boats and dinghies that were weaving between the cables of the ocean-going fleet. One of these rowboats was pulling towards the *Ibis* with a number of drunken voices echoing out of it. Zachary recognized the boat as Jodu's, and a twinge shot up his spine as he remembered the night when he'd sat in it, arguing with Paulette.

Turning away, Zachary peered into the looming darkness upriver: he knew that Paulette was in a village somewhere north of Calcutta—he had been alarmed to hear from Jodu that she had been ill and was being looked after by friends. When the boat pulled up beside the schooner, he was powerfully tempted to jump into it and row off, to go looking for her. The impulse was so strong that he might have obeyed it, if not for one thing: it stuck in his craw that Mr Crowle would imagine that he had succeeded in running him off the *Ibis*.

# fifteen

~

With the rains over, the sunlight turned crisp and golden. The dry weather speeded Paulette's recovery and she decided to leave for Calcutta, to put in motion the plan that had been gestating in her mind through her illness.

The first step required a private meeting with Nob Kissin Baboo and she gave the matter much thought before setting off. Burnham Bros.'s main offices were on Calcutta's fashionable Strand Road, but the firm's dockside premises were in a dingy corner of Kidderpore, a half-hour's boat ride away: this distance Baboo Nob Kissin Pander was required to traverse almost daily, in the discharge of his duties, and being of a thrifty turn of mind, he chose usually to travel on the crowded kheya-boats that transported people up and down the waterfront.

The Burnham compound in Kidderpore was a large one, consisting of several godowns and bankshalls. The shed that served as the gomusta's private daftar lay in one corner of the compound, adjoining a lane. When prospective clients wished to avail themselves privately of Baboo Nob Kissin's services as a bespoke moneylender, it was there, Paulette knew, that they went to meet with him. This, for instance, was what her father had done—but for herself, in her current situation, the risks attendant upon venturing into a property owned by her former benefactor were too great to make this a comfortable option; she decided instead to waylay the gomusta as he stepped off his ferry, at the nearby ghat.

The ghat in question—known as Bhutghat—proved to be ideal for her purposes: it was narrow enough to be kept easily under watch, and sufficiently busy for a lone woman to loiter without attracting attention. Better still, it was overlooked by an ancient tree, growing on a knoll: the tree was a banyan and its hanging roots formed a beard so dense as to offer easy concealment. Slipping inside this tangled thicket Paulette came upon a root that had looped down in such a way as to form a swinging bench. Here she seated herself, rocking gently, and watched the ghat through a gap in the carefully draped folds of cloth that covered her face.

Her vigil almost came to naught, for the gomusta was so changed, with his long, shoulder-length hair, that he was nearly gone before she recognized him: even the way he walked seemed different, with smaller steps and swaying hips, so she took the precaution of following for a minute or two before she accosted him with a sibilant whisper: Gomusta-babu . . . *shunun* . . . listen . . .

He spun around in alarm, looking from the river's edge to the nearby lane. Although Paulette was well within the ambit of his gaze, his eyes, which were lined with a thin touch of kajal, passed without check over her sari-shrouded face.

Paulette hissed again, but in English this time: 'Baboo Nob Kissin . . . it's me . . .'

This surprised him even more but brought him no closer to recognizing her; on the contrary he began to mutter prayers, as if to ward off a ghost: *Hé Radhé, hé Shyam* . . .

'Nob Kissin Baboo! It is me, Paulette Lambert,' she whispered. 'I am here, look!' When his bulging eyes had turned in her direction, she whisked her sari momentarily off her face. 'You see? It is me!'

The sight of her made him leap backwards in shock, so that he landed heavily on the toes of several passers-by—but the drizzle of abuse that rained down on him went unheeded for his attention was transfixed on Paulette's sari-shrouded face. 'Miss Lambert? Why, I cannot believe! You have turned up in my backside? And wearing native garbs also. So nicely you have hidden your face I could not tell . . .'

'Shh!' Paulette pleaded. 'I pray you, Baboo Nob Kissin, please abase your voice.'

The gomusta switched to a piercing whisper. 'But Miss, what you are doing in this nook-and-cranny, kindly can you inform? We all are searching you left and right, to no avail. But never mind—Master will rejoice like anything. Let us return back right now-itself.'

'No, Baboo Nob Kissin,' said Paulette. 'It is not my intention to go to Bethel. I searched you out for it is with you I must most pressingly speak. May I pray you to spare a little time to sit with me? If it will not too much derange you?'

'Sit?' The gomusta directed a disapproving frown at the mud-splattered, refuse-strewn steps of the ghat. 'But this locality is sorely lacking in furnitures. How to sit? Our saris—I mean, our clothings may become soiled.'

'Do not fear, Baboo Nob Kissin,' said Paulette, pointing to the knoll. 'Up on that monticule we can put ourselves in the shelter of the tree. Personne will see us, I assure you.'

The gomusta eyed the tree with some concern: of late he had developed a housewifely aversion to all creatures that crept and crawled and was at pains to stay away from anything that might harbour these forms of life. But today his curiosity prevailed over his distrust of greenery: 'Very well,' he said reluctantly. 'I shall comply your demands. Let us put our foot in it.'

With Paulette in the lead, they climbed up the slope and made their way into the thicket of tangled roots; although Baboo Nob Kissin's pace was slow, he made no complaint until Paulette ushered him towards the swinging root that had served as her seat. Having inspected this gnarled offshoot, he made a dismissive gesture. 'This place is not apt for sitting,' he announced. 'Insects are indulging in all type of activities. Ferocious caterpillars may also be there.'

'But caterpillars do not habitate on the roots of such trees,' said Paulette. 'It is safe to sit, I assure you.'

'Kindly do not persist,' said Baboo Nob Kissin. 'I prefer to opt out for foot-standing.' Thus having spoken, he crossed his arms over his bosom and positioned himself so that no part of his clothing or person was in contact with any kind of foliage.

'As you please, Baboo Nob Kissin,' said Paulette. 'I do not wish to impose . . .' She was interrupted by the gomusta, who could no longer restrain his curiosity. 'But so tell, no? Where you have been putting up all this time? Which side you went?'

'It is not important, Baboo Nob Kissin.'

'I see,' said the gomusta, narrowing his eyes. 'So then must be true what everyone is telling.'

'And what is that?'

'I do not like to wash dirty linens, Miss Lambert,' said the gomusta, 'but actually, all are saying that you have indulged in unproper behaviours and are now expecting. That is why you have absconded.'

'Expecting?' said Paulette. 'Expecting what?'

'Infructuous issue. You only told to Mrs Burnham, no, that native-bread is cooking in the coal-oven?'

Paulette went bright red and clapped her hands to her cheeks. 'Baboo Nob Kissin!' she said. 'I have indulged in nothing and am expecting nothing. You must believe me: I left Bethel of my own will; it was my decision to escape.'

The gomusta leant closer. 'You can freely admit—with me, formalities need not be there. Chastity is highly depleted, no? Maiden's-head has also been punctured, isn't it?'

'Not at all, Nob Kissin Baboo,' said Paulette indignantly. 'I do not know how you can imagine such things.'

The gomusta mulled this over for a moment and then leant furtively forward, as if to give voice to a thought that he could scarcely bring himself to articulate: 'So tell then: is it because of Master you are absconding?'

Paulette slipped her ghungta down so as to bare her eyes, and looked him full in the face. 'Maybe.'

'Oh my, my!' said the gomusta, passing his tongue over his lips. 'Must be then hanky-pankies were taking place?'

It was clear to Paulette that a desire to learn of his employer's private compulsions was smouldering brightly in the gomusta's head: what use he would make of this knowledge she could not tell, but she understood that his curiosity might well be turned to her advantage. 'I cannot say any more, Nob Kissin Baboo. Not unless . . .'

'Yes. Kindly proceed.'

'Not unless you are able to provide me with a little morceau of help.'

Ever alert to the hint of a bargain, the Baboo was suddenly watchful. 'And what morsel of assistance is required? Please to spell it out.'

Paulette gave him a long, steady look. 'Baboo Nob Kissin,' she said. 'Do you recall why my father came to see you? And when?'

'Just before departure for heavenly abode, no?' said the gomusta. 'How I could forget, Miss Lambert? You think I am a ninnyhammer? What is said with dying breaths cannot be lightly disposed of.'

'You recall that he wanted to procure me a passage to the Mauritius?'

'Naturally,' said Baboo Nob Kissin. 'This item I only conveyed, no?'

Paulette's right fist crept slowly out of her sari. 'And you told him, did you not, that you could do it in exchange for this?' Opening her palm she thrust towards him the locket he had handed to her a few weeks before.

Baboo Nob Kissin glanced briefly at her palm. 'What you are intimating is correct. But what is the relevance I do not see.'

Paulette took a deep breath. 'Baboo Nob Kissin—I propose to hold you to your words. In exchange for this locket I wish to obtain a passage on the *Ibis*.'

'*Ibis*!' Baboo Nob Kissin's mouth dropped open. 'You are mad or what? How you shall go on *Ibis*? Only coolies and quoddies may be accommodated on said vessel. Passenger traffic is not existing.'

'That matters nothing to me,' said Paulette. 'If I could join the labourers I would be content. It is you who is in charge of them, are you not? No one will be advised of it if you add another name.'

'Miss Lambert,' said the gomusta frostily. 'I daresays you are trying to pull out my legs. How you could forward such a proposal I cannot realize. At once you must scrap it off.'

'But Baboo Nob Kissin,' Paulette beseeched him, 'tell me: what difference will arrive to you if you add one more name to the list? You are the gomusta and there are so many labourers. One more will not be remarked. And as you can see, you yourself would not have recognized me in this sari. No one will learn of my identity: you need have no fear, I assure you, and in return you will have the locket.'

'No, by Jupiter!' Baboo Nob Kissin shook his head so violently that his huge ears flapped like wind-blown ferns. 'Do you know what Master shall do if this scheme is exposed and I am spotted out as the culprit? He shall break my head. And Captain Chillingworth is too much colour-conscious. If he finds I have consigned one memsahib as coolie, he will strangulate and make into tiffin for sharks. Baba-re . . . no, no, no . . .'

Spinning around, the gomusta went crashing through the curtain of hanging roots. His voice carried back to Paulette as his steps receded: '. . . No, no, this scheme will lead only to a big-big mischief. Must immediately be scotched . . .'

'Oh please, Baboo Nob Kissin . . .'

Paulette had invested all her hopes in this meeting and her lips began to tremble now as she contemplated the failure of her plan. Just as the tears were beginning to trickle from her eyes, she heard Baboo Nob Kissin's heavy tread coming back through the thicket. There he was again, standing before her, sheepishly twisting the fringe of his dhoti.

'But listen, one thing,' he said. 'You have overlooked to inform about the escapade with Master . . .'

Under the cover of her ghungta, Paulette quickly dabbed her eyes and hardened her voice. 'You will learn nothing from me, Baboo Nob Kissin,' she said. 'Since you have offered me no assistance nor any recourse.'

She heard him swallow and looked up to see his Adam's apple bobbing pensively in his throat. 'Might be, one recourse is there,' he muttered at last. 'But it is endowed with many pitfalls and loopholes. Implementation will be extremely difficult.'

'Never mind, Nob Kissin Baboo,' said Paulette eagerly. 'Tell me, what is your idee? How can it be done?'

~

Through the season of festivities, the city resounded with celebrations, which made the silence within the camp all the more difficult to bear. When Diwali came, the migrants marked it by lighting a few lamps, but there was little cheer in the depot. There was still no word of when they would leave and every new day sent a fresh storm of rumours blowing through the camp. There were times when it seemed that Deeti and Kalua were the only people there who believed that a ship really would come to take them away; there were many who began to say, no, it was all a lie, that the depot was just a kind of jail where they had been sent to die; that their corpses would be turned into skulls and skeletons, so that they could be cut up and fed to the sahibs' dogs, or used as bait for fish. Often these rumours were started by the spectators and camp-followers who lurked perpetually outside the fence—vendors, vagrants, urchins, and others in whom the sight of the girmitiyas inflamed an inexhaustible curiosity: they would stand around for hours, watching, pointing, staring, as if at animals in a cage. Sometimes they would bait the migrants: Why don't you try to escape? Come, we'll help you run away; don't you see they're waiting for you to die so they can sell your bodies?

But when a migrant did run off, it was those very spectators who brought him back. The first to try was a grizzled, middle-aged man from Ara, a little weak in the head, and he had no sooner broken through the fence than they caught hold of him, tied his hands and dragged him back to the duffadar: they received a nice little reward for their pains. The would-be escapee was beaten and made to go without food for two days.

The climate of the city—hot, humid and damp—made

things worse, for many people fell ill. Some recovered, but others seemed to want to sicken and fade away, so disheartened were they by the waiting, the rumours, and the disquieting feeling of being held captive. One night a boy became delirious: although very young, he had long, ash-smeared locks, like a mendicant's; people said he had been kidnapped and sold off by a sadhu. When the fever took hold of him, his body became scalding hot, and horrible sounds and imprecations began to pour from his mouth. Kalua and some of the other menfolk tried to fetch help, but the sirdars and maistries were drinking toddy and would pay no attention. Before daybreak there was a final outbreak of shouts and curses, and then the boy's body went cold. His death seemed to arouse much more interest among the overseers than his illness had done: they were unaccustomedly prompt in arranging to have the corpse carried away—for cremation, they said, at the nearby burning ghats—but who could know for sure? None of the girmitiyas was allowed to leave the depot to see what happened, so no one could say anything to the contrary when a vendor whispered through the fence that the boy had not been cremated at all: a hole had been bored in his skull and his corpse had been hung up by the heels, to extract the oil—the *mimiái-ka-tel*—from his brain.

To counter the rumours and ill auguries, the migrants spoke often of the devotions they would perform the day before their departure: they talked of pujas and namazes, of recitations of the Qur'an and the Ramcharitmanas and the Alha-Khand. When they spoke of these rituals, it was in eager tones, as though the occasion was much to be looked forward to—but this was only because the dread inspired by the prospect of departure was so profound as to be inexpressible, the kind of feeling that made you want to squat in a corner, hugging your knees and muttering aloud, so that your ears would not be able to hear the voices in your head. It was easier to speak of the details of rituals, and to plan them minutely, comparing them all the while with the pujas and namazes and recitations of the past.

When the day finally came, it was not as they had envisioned: the only augury of their departure consisted of the sudden arrival at the camp of the gomusta, Nob Kissin Baboo. He hurried into the overseers' hut and was closeted with them for a while; afterwards, the sirdars and maistries gathered everyone together and then Ramsaran-ji, the duffadar, announced that the time had come for him to take his leave of them: from here on, until they reached Mareech and were each allotted to a plantation, they would be in the custody of a different set of guards, overseers and supervisors. This team had boarded their ship already and had made sure that the vessel was ready to receive them: they themselves would be boarded tomorrow. He ended by wishing them *sukh-shánti*, peace and happiness, in their new home and said he would pray to the Lord of Crossings to keep them safe: *Jai Hanumán gyán gun ságar . . .*

~

In Alipore Jail the season of festivals had been celebrated with no little fanfare: Diwali, in particular, was an occasion for the jemadars and their gangs to compete in a fiery display and many of the jail's inner courtyards had been lit up with lamps and improvised sparklers. The noise, food and festivity had had a perverse effect on Neel, causing a sudden collapse in the resolve that had sustained him thus far. On the night of Diwali, when the courtyard was ablaze with light, he had trouble rising from his charpoy and could not bring himself to step beyond the bars: his thoughts were only of his son, of the fireworks of years past, and the dimness, silence and denial that would be the boy's lot this season.

Over the next few days Neel's spirits sank lower and lower, so that when Bishu-ji came to announce that the date of their departure had been fixed, he responded with bewilderment: Where are they taking us?

To Mareech. Have you forgotten?

Neel rubbed his eyes with the heel of his palm. And when is that to be?

Tomorrow. The ship is ready.

Tomorrow?

Yes. They'll come for you early. Be ready. And tell Aafat too.

That was all: having said what he had to, Bishu-ji turned on his heel and walked away. Neel was about to slump back into his charpoy when he noticed his cell-mate's eyes resting on him, as if to ask a question. Many days had passed since Neel had last performed the ritual of asking for his cell-mate's name, but now he stirred himself to say, in gruff English: 'We're leaving tomorrow. The ship is ready. They'll come for us in the morning.' Apart from a slight widening of the eyes, there was no response, so Neel shrugged and turned over on his charpoy.

With departure looming, the images and memories Neel had tried to bar from his mind came flooding back: of Elokeshi, of his home, of his husband-less wife and fatherless child. When he dozed off, it was only to be visited by a nightmare, in which he saw himself as a castaway on the dark void of the ocean, utterly alone, severed from every human mooring. Feeling himself to be drowning, he began to toss his arms, trying to reach towards the light.

He woke to find himself sitting up, in the darkness. Gradually he became aware that there was an arm around his shoulder, holding him steady, as if in consolation: in this embrace there was more intimacy than he had ever known before, even with Elokeshi, and when a voice sounded in his ear, it was as if it were coming from within himself: 'My name Lei Leong Fatt,' it said. 'People call Ah Fatt. Ah Fatt your friend.' Those faltering, childlike words offered more comfort than was in all the poetry Neel had ever read, and more novelty too, because he had never before heard them said— and if he had, they would only have been wasted before, because he would not have been able to value them for their worth.

~

It was no human agency but rather a quirk of the tides that was responsible for fixing the date of the *Ibis*'s departure. That year, as in many others, Diwali fell close to the autumn equinox. This would have had little bearing on the sailing of the *Ibis* if not for one of the more dangerous oddities of the waterways of Bengal: namely the *bán*, or bore—a tidal phenomenon that sends walls of water hurtling upriver from the coast. Bores are never more hazardous than in the periods around Holi and Diwali, when the seasons turn upon an equinoctial hinge: at those times, rising to formidable heights and travelling at great speed, the waves can pose a serious threat to the river's traffic. It was one such wave that determined when the *Ibis* would weigh anchor: the announcement of the hazard having been made well in time, it was decided that the schooner would ride the bore out at her moorings. Her passengers would come on board the day after.

On the river, the day began with a warning from the harbour-master that the bore was expected around sunset. From then on, the riverfront was a-buzz with preparations: fishermen worked together to carry dinghies, pansaris and even the lighter paunchways out of the water and up the embankments, taking them beyond the river's reach. Patelis, budgerows, batelos and other river craft that were too heavy to be lifted from the water, were spaced out at safe intervals, while brigs, brigantines, schooners and other ocean-going vessels struck their royal and t'gallant yards, and unbent their sails.

During his stay in Calcutta, Zachary had twice joined the crowds that gathered on the river's banks to watch the passing of the bore: he had learnt to listen for the distant murmur that heralded the wave's approach; he had watched the water rising suddenly into a great, roaring head that was topped by a foaming white mane; he had turned to see the bore go by, on its coiled and tawny haunches, racing upstream as if in pursuit of some elusive prey. He too, like the urchins along the shore, had cheered and shouted, without quite knowing why, and afterwards, like everyone else, he had felt a little twinge of embarrassment at all the excitement—because it took no more than a few minutes for the water to resume its normal flow and for the day to return to the even tenor of its ordinariness.

Although no stranger to these waves, Zachary had no shipboard experience of them, having only watched them from shore. Mr Crowle, on the other hand, was well-practised in dealing with bores and macareos, having ridden out many such, on the Irrawaddy as well as the Hooghly. The Captain put him in charge of the preparations and stayed below, letting it be known that he would not come on deck until later in the day. But as it happened, about an hour before the bore was expected, a message was received from Mr Burnham, summoning the Captain to the city on some urgent last-minute business.

As a rule, when the Captain had to be ferried ashore, it was a tindal or seacunny who rowed him over in the ship's gig—a small but handy little rowboat that was kept permanently tethered to the stern while the schooner was in port. But today the *Ibis* was shorthanded because many of the lashkar were still ashore, either recovering from their pre-departure excesses or making preparations for the long absence ahead. With every available hand occupied in snugging the ship down, Zachary went to Mr Crowle and offered to row the Captain's gig himself.

The offer was made on an impulse, without any forethought, and Zachary regretted it the moment it was out of his lips—for Mr Crowle took a while to chew over it, and his face darkened as he tried the taste of his conclusions.

'So what'd you think, Mr Crowle?'

'What do I think? I'll tell y'Mannikin: I don't think the skipper needs to be jibbering the kibber with yer. If he has to be rowed, then it's best I be the one to do it.'

Zachary shifted his weight uncomfortably. 'Sure. Suit yourself, Mr Crowle. Was just tryin to help.'

'Help? It's no help to anyone to have yer pitching the gammon to the skipper. Ye'll stay where ye're needed and look sharp about it too.'

This exchange was beginning to attract attention from the lascars, so Zachary brought it to an end: 'Yes, Mr Crowle. As you please.'

The first mate went off in the gig, with the Captain, while Zachary stayed on board, to oversee the lascars who were unbending the topgallants and royals. By the time the mate returned, the sky was beginning to turn colour and spectators were gathering along the embankments, to wait for the bore.

'Take y'self aft, Reid,' the first mate growled as he came aboard. 'Don't need yer swilkering about for'ard.'

Zachary shrugged this off and went aft, to the wheelhouse. The sun had set now and the fishermen onshore were hurrying to secure their upturned boats. Zachary was looking downstream, watching for the first signs of the wave, when Steward Pinto came running to the stern. 'Burra Malum calling Chhota Malum.'

'What for?'

'Problem with langar-boya.'

Zachary hurried forward to find the first mate standing between the bows, squinting at the water ahead. 'Something amiss, Mr Crowle?'

'You tell me, Reid,' said the first mate. 'What do y'see over there?'

Shading his eyes, Zachary saw that Mr Crowle was pointing to a cable that linked the schooner's bow to the underside of a buoy, some fifty feet ahead. Having been on board during the initial berthing of the *Ibis*, Zachary knew that the Hooghly's bore entailed special procedures for the mooring of ocean-going sailing ships: they were usually berthed far out in the river's stream, where, instead of dropping their anchors, they were tethered between buoys anchored deep in the river's muddy bed. The holdfasts to which the ship's cables were attached lay on the underside of the buoys, beneath the water's surface, and could only be accessed by divers who were accustomed to the near-blind conditions of the muddy river. It was one such mooring-cable that had attracted Mr Crowle's attention—but Zachary was at a loss to see why, for there was not much to be seen of the rope, which disappeared underwater halfway to the buoy.

'Don't see nothing wrong, Mr Crowle.'

'Don't you now?'

There was just enough light to get another look: 'Sure don't.'

Mr Crowle's index finger rose to pick a morsel from his teeth. 'Don't say much for yer know, Mannikin. What if I told you the cable's a-foul of the buoy's anchor-chain?' He raised an eyebrow as he examined his fingernail. 'Didn't think o'that, did'ye now?'

Zachary had to acknowledge the truth of this. 'No, Mr Crowle. I didn't.'

'Care to go out in the gig and take a look?'

Zachary paused, trying to reckon whether he would have time enough to get to the buoy and back before the wave came bearing down. It was hard to judge because of the current, which was flowing so swiftly as to carve deep fissures on the river's surface.

As if to preclude his doubts, the first mate said: 'Not a nidget are'ye, Reid?'

'No, Mr Crowle,' Zachary said promptly. 'I'll go if you think it's necessary.'

'Stubble yer whids then, and heave on.'

If he was to do it, Zachary knew he would have to be quick. He went aft at a run, heading for the stern where the gig was still tethered—pulling it out of the water was to have been the last item in the preparations for the bore. Looking at it now, Zachary decided that it would take too long to draw the boat around to the side-ladder: better, if trickier, to vault over the stern-rail. He was tugging on the boat's painter when Serang Ali stepped out of the wheelhouse to whisper: 'Malum 'ware: gig-bot broken.'

'What . . .?'

Zachary's question was cut short by the first mate, who had followed him aft: 'What's this now? 'Fraid o'wettin yer feet Mannikin?'

Without another word, Zachary handed the gig's painter to Serang Ali who looped it around a stanchion and pulled it taut. Climbing over the stern-rail, Zachary took hold of the rope and lowered himself into the gig, signalling to Serang Ali to set the boat loose. Almost at once the current took hold of the little craft and pulled it along the length of the schooner, propelling it towards midstream.

The gig's oars were on the floorboards and on reaching for them, Zachary was surprised to find that there was a good inch or so of water sloshing around the bottom. He thought nothing of it, for the boat's sides were so low that waves often lapped over them, even when the craft was stationary. When he began to row, the gig responded well enough until he was some twenty feet past the schooner's bow. He noticed then that the water in the boat's bottom had risen past his ankles and was creeping up his calves. He had, so far, concentrated his attention on the buoy, so he was taken aback when he looked over the gig's side—for only an inch or two remained between the gunwale and the fast-flowing river. It was as if holes had been drilled into the gig's hull, with great care, so as not to open up fully until the boat was under oar.

He pushed his shoulders hard against the oars now, trying to turn the gig about, but the stern was wallowing so deep in the water that the bows would not respond. The buoy was only some twenty feet ahead, clearly visible even in the rapidly-dimming light, but the current was sweeping the boat wide of its mark, towards the middle of the river. The schooner's cable was tantalizingly close and Zachary knew that if he could but reach it, he would be able to pull himself to safety. But the gap was widening quickly, and although he was a strong swimmer, Zachary guessed that it would not be easy to get to the cable before the wave swept in, not with the current flowing against him. Clearly, his best hope lay in being picked up by another boat—but the Hooghly, usually so tightly packed with river craft, was ominously empty. He looked towards the *Ibis* and saw that Serang Ali knew he was in trouble. The lascars were labouring to lower the starboard longboat—but there was nothing to be hoped for here, for the process could take as much as fifteen minutes. Glancing shorewards, he saw that he was being observed by a great number of spectators—fishermen, boatmen and others—all of whom were watching with helpless concern. The sound of the approaching bore was clearly audible now, loud enough to leave no doubt that anyone who ventured into the water would do so at the risk of his life.

This much was clear: it wouldn't do to remain in the foundering gig. Using his toes and heels, Zachary worked his sodden shoes off his feet and tore off his canvas shirt. Just as he was about to jump, he saw a boat sliding down the mudbank: the slim, long craft hit the water with such force that its momentum carried it halfway to Zachary.

The sight of the boat lent Zachary's arms a burst of strength, and he did not pause for breath until he heard a voice, shouting: 'Zikri Malum!' He raised his head from the water and looked up to see a hand reaching towards him; looming behind it was Jodu's face; he was stabbing a finger to point downriver, where the sound of the wave had risen to a rumble. Zachary didn't stop to listen; snatching at Jodu's hand, he tumbled into the boat. Pulling him upright, Jodu thrust an oar into his hands and pointed to the buoy ahead: the wave was too close now to think of rowing back to shore.

As he dug his oar into the water, Zachary threw a glance over his shoulder: the wave was streaking towards them and its foaming crest was a blur of white. He turned away, rowing furiously, and did not look back again till they had drawn level with the buoy. Behind them, the bore was rearing out of the water at an impossible angle, as if springing into a leap.

'Zikri Malum!' Jodu had already leapt on the buoy and was knotting the boat's rope to the hooped holdfast on its crown. He gestured to Zachary to leap too, extending a hand to steady him as he stepped on the slippery, algae-covered surface.

Now, with the wave almost upon them, Zachary threw himself flat, beside Jodu. There was just enough time to pass a rope around their bodies and loop it through the holdfast.

Linking one arm with Jodu's, Zachary hooked the other through the iron hoop and sucked a huge draught of air into his lungs.

Suddenly everything went quiet and the wave's deafening sound was transformed into an immense, crushing weight, flattening them against the buoy, holding them down so hard that Zachary could feel the barnacles on its surface slicing into his chest. The heavy float strained against its cable, spinning around and around as the water swept past. Then suddenly, like a windswept kite, it changed direction and shot upwards, with a momentum that lifted it out of the water with a skip and a bounce. Zachary shut his eyes and let his head fall against the metal.

When his breath returned, he extended his hand to Jodu. 'Thank you, my friend.'

Jodu flashed him a grin and grasped his hand with a slap: eyebrows dancing wildly in his face, he said. 'Cheerily there! Alzbel!'

'Sure,' said Zachary with a laugh. 'Alzbel that's end's well.'

Miraculously Jodu's boat had survived unscathed and he was able to row Zachary back to the *Ibis* before going off to return the hired craft to its owner.

Zachary hauled himself aboard the schooner to find the first mate waiting, with his arms crossed over his chest. 'Had enough Reid? Changed yer mind yet? Still time to turn around and get y'self ashore.'

Zachary glanced down at his dripping clothes. 'Look at me Mr Crowle,' he said. 'I'm here. And I'm not going anywhere the *Ibis* isn't going.'

part three

Sea

## sixteen

~

It happened that Deeti went early to the nullah next morning, so she was among the first to come upon the rowboats that were moored around the camp's jetty: the scream that broke from her lips—*nayyá á gail bá*!—was such as to freeze your liver, and by the time its echoes had faded, there was not a soul in the campsite who was still at rest. In twos and threes they came creeping out of their huts to ascertain that the boats were real and that this was indeed the day when they would take leave of the camp. Now that disbelief was no longer possible, a great uproar broke out and people began to mill around, gathering together their belongings, taking down their washing, and hunting for their pitchers, lotas and other necessary utensils. The long-planned-for rituals of departure were forgotten in the confusion, but strangely, this great outburst of activity became itself a kind of worship, not so much intended to achieve an end—their bundles and bojhas were so small and so many times packed and unpacked that there was not much to be done to them—but rather as an expression of awe, of the kind that might greet a divine revelation: for when a moment arrives that is so much feared and so long awaited, it perforates the veil of everyday expectation in such a way as to reveal the prodigious darkness of the unknown.

Within minutes the maistries were going from hut to hut, swinging their lathis, rooting out those who had shrunk fearfully into corners, and kicking loose the knots of whispering men who were blocking the campsite's paths and doorways. In the women's hut, the prospect of departure caused such a rout that Deeti had to put aside her own fears in order to organize the evacuation: Ratna and Champa could do little but cling to each other; Heeru had prostrated herself on the floor and was rolling from side to side; Sarju, the midwife, had buried her face in her precious bundles and bojhas; Munia could think of nothing but braiding tassels into her hair. Fortunately, Deeti's own bundle of possessions was packed and ready, so she could apply herself fully to the task of organizing the others, prodding, slapping and shouting as was necessary. To such good effect did she apply herself that by the time Kalua appeared in the doorway, every last belonging, the smallest pot and the thinnest shred of cloth, had been accounted for and packed away.

A pile of baggage was clustered around the doorway: picking up her own, Deeti led the women out of the hut with their saris draped carefully over their heads and faces. The women kept close to Kalua's giant frame, as they made their way through the milling migrants. Nearing the jetty, Deeti caught sight of Baboo Nob Kissin: he was in one of the boats, wearing his hair loose so that it fell to his shoulders in shining ringlets. He greeted the women almost as if he were an elder sister, ordering the maistries to let them through first.

When Deeti had crossed the quaking gangplank, the gomusta pointed her to a thatched section at the rear that had been screened off for the women: there was someone already seated inside, but Deeti did not notice her—she had no eyes now but for the pennant-topped temple at the edge of the camp, the sight of which filled her with remorse for her unperformed devotions. No good could come, surely, of a journey embarked upon without a puja? She joined her hands together, closed her eyes, and was soon lost in prayer.

The boat's moving! squealed Munia, and her cry was quickly echoed by another voice, an unfamiliar one: *Hã, chal rahe hãi*! Yes, we're on our way!

It was only now that Deeti realized that there was a

stranger in their midst. Opening her eyes, she saw, sitting opposite her, a woman in a green sari. Deeti's skin began to prickle, as if to tell her that this was someone she had seen before, perhaps in a dream. Seized by curiosity, she pulled her own ghungta back from her head, laying bare her face. We're all women here, she said; *ham sabhan merharu*. We don't need to be covered up.

Now the stranger too pulled back her sari, revealing a face that was long and finely-shaped, with an expression in which innocence was combined with intelligence, sweetness with resolution. Her complexion had a soft, golden glow, like that of the cosseted daughter of a village pandit, a child who had never worked a day in the fields and had never had to endure the heat of the sun.

Where are you travelling to? said Deeti, and such was her sense of familiarity with the stranger, that she had no hesitation in addressing her in her native Bhojpuri.

The girl answered in the bastardized Hindusthani of the city: I'm going where you are going—*jahā áp játa . . .*

But you aren't one of us, said Deeti.

I am now, said the girl smiling.

Deeti was not so bold as to ask the girl directly about her identity, so she chose instead the more circuitous course of revealing her own name and those of the others: Munia, Heeru, Sarju, Champa, Ratna and Dookhanee.

I'm called Putleshwari, said the girl in response, and just as everyone was beginning to wonder how they were ever going to pronounce this tongue-tripping Bengali farrago, she rescued them by adding: But my nickname is Pugli, and that's what people call me.

'Pugli?' Why, said Deeti, with a smile. You don't look at all mad.

That's just because you don't know me yet, said the girl, with a sweet smile.

And how is it that you are here with us? Deeti asked.

Baboo Nob Kissin, the gomusta, is my uncle.

Ah! I knew it, said Deeti. You are a *bamni*, a Brahmin's

daughter. But where are you travelling to?

To the island of Mareech, said the girl, just like you.

But you're not a girmitiya, said Deeti. Why would you go to such a place?

My uncle has arranged a marriage for me, said the girl. With a maistry who is working on a plantation.

A marriage? Deeti was amazed to hear her speaking of crossing the sea for a wedding, as if it were no different from going to another village downriver. But aren't you afraid, she said, of losing caste? Of crossing the Black Water, and being on a ship with so many sorts of people?

Not at all, the girl replied, in a tone of unalloyed certainty. On a boat of pilgrims, no one can lose caste and everyone is the same: it's like taking a boat to the temple of Jagannath, in Puri. From now on, and forever afterwards, we will all be ship-siblings—*jaház-bhais* and *jaház-bahens*—to each other. There'll be no differences between us.

This answer was so daring, so ingenious, as fairly to rob the women of their breath. Not in a lifetime of thinking, Deeti knew, would she have stumbled upon an answer so complete, so satisfactory and so thrilling in its possibilities. In the glow of the moment, she did something she would never have done otherwise: she reached out to take the stranger's hand in her own. Instantly, in emulation of her gesture, every other woman reached out too, to share in this communion of touch. Yes, said Deeti, from now on, there are no differences between us; we are jahaz-bhai and jahaz-bahen to each other; all of us children of the ship.

Somewhere outside, a man's voice was shouting: There she is! The ship—our jahaz . . .

And there she was, in the distance, with her two masts, and her great beak of a bowsprit. It was now that Deeti understood why the image of the vessel had been revealed to her that day, when she stood immersed in the Ganga: it was because her new self, her new life, had been gestating all this while in the belly of this creature, this vessel that was the Mother-Father of her new family, a great wooden *mái-báp*, an adoptive ancestor and parent of dynasties yet to come: here she was, the *Ibis*.

~

From his perch on the foremast, high up in the kursi of the crosstrees, Jodu had as fine a view as ever he could have wished: the wharves, the river and the schooner were spread out beneath him like treasure on a moneylender's counter, waiting to be weighed and valued. On deck, the subedar and his men were busy making preparations for the embarkation of the convicts and the migrants. All around them, lascars were swarming about, coiling hansils, rolling bimbas, penning livestock and stowing crates, trying to clear the deck of its last-minute clutter.

The convicts arrived first, preceding the migrants by some fifteen minutes: they came in a jel-bot, a large vessel of the budgerow type, except that all its windows were heavily barred. It looked as if it could hold a small army of cutthroats, so it came as a surprise when it disgorged only two men, neither of whom looked very threatening despite the chains on their ankles and wrists. They were wearing dungaree pyjamas and short-sleeved vests, and each had a lota under one arm and a small cloth bundle in the other. They were handed over to Bhyro Singh without much ceremony, and the jail-boat left almost immediately afterwards. Then, as if to show the convicts what they were in for, the subedar took hold of their chains and herded them along like oxen, prodding them in the arse and occasionally flicking the tips of their ears with his lathi.

On the way to the chokey, before stepping into the fana, one of the convicts turned his head, as if to catch a last glimpse of the city. This brought Bhyro Singh's lathi crashing down on his shoulder with a thwacking sound that made the trikat-wale wince, all the way up in their perch.

Haramzadas, these guards and maistries, said Mamdoo-tindal. Squeeze your balls at any chance.

One of them slapped Cassem-meah yesterday, said Sunker. Just for touching his food.

I'd have hit him back, said Jodu.

You wouldn't be here now if you had, said the tindal. Don't you see? They're armed.

In the meantime, Sunker had pulled himself upright, so that he was standing on the footropes. Suddenly he called out: They're here!

Who?

The coolies. Look. That must be them in those boats.

They all rose to their feet now, and leant over the purwan to look down below. A small flotilla of some half-dozen dinghies was coming towards the schooner, from the direction of Tolly's Nullah; the boats were filled with groups of men, uniformly clad in white vests and knee-length dhotis. The dinghy in the lead was a little different from the rest in that it had a small shelter at the back: when it pulled up alongside the side-ladder, a sunburst of colour seemed to explode inside it, with eight sari-clad figures stepping out of the shelter.

Women! said Jodu, in a hushed voice.

Mamdoo-tindal was not impressed: so far as he was concerned, few indeed were the women who could match the allure of his alter-ego. Hags the lot of them, he said darkly. Not one a match for Ghaseeti.

How do you know, said Jodu, with their faces hidden?

I can see enough to know they're bringing trouble.

Why?

Just count the number, said the tindal. Eight women on board—not counting Ghaseeti—and over two hundred men, if you include the coolies, silahdars, maistries, lascars and malums. What good do you think will come of it?

Jodu counted and saw that the tindal was right: there were eight sari-clad figures advancing towards the *Ibis*. It was the number that led him to suspect that they might be the same people he had rowed to the camp: had there been seven women in the group that day, or eight? He could not remember, for his attention had been focused mainly on the girl in the pink sari.

Suddenly, he leapt up. Stripping the bandhna from his

*Amitav Ghosh*

head, he began to wave, with a foot in the tanni and an elbow hooked through the labran.

What're you doing, you crazed launder? snapped Mamdoo-tindal.

I think I know one of the girls, said Jodu.

How can you tell? said Mamdoo-tindal. Their faces are all covered up.

Because of the sari, said Jodu. See the pink one? I'm sure I know her.

Shut your chute and sit down! said the tindal, tugging on his pants. You're going to be lundbunded if you don't take care. The Burra Malum's already got it in for you after your stunt with Zikri Malum yesterday. If he sees you honeying up to those coolie girls you're going to be a launder without a mast.

~

Down by the boat, the sight of Jodu, rising to his feet to wave, gave Paulette such a scare that she nearly fell into the water. Although her ghungta was certainly her most important means of concealment, it was by no means the only one; she had also disguised her appearance in a number of other ways: her feet were lacquered with bright vermilion *alta*; her hands and arms were covered with intricate, hennaed designs that left very little of her skin visible; and under the cover of her veil, the line of her jaw was obscured by large, tasselled earrings. In addition, she was balancing her cloth-wrapped belongings on her waist, in such a fashion as to give her the gait of an elderly woman, shuffling along under the weight of a crushing burden. With these many layers of masking, she had felt reasonably confident that not even Jodu, who knew her as well as anyone in the world, would harbour any suspicions about who she was. Yet, evidently, all her efforts had been in vain, for no sooner had he set eyes on her than he had begun to wave, and from a long way off, at that. What was she to do now?

Paulette was convinced that Jodu, whether out of a

misplaced brotherly protectiveness, or by reason of the competitiveness that had always marked their quasi-siblingship, would stop at nothing to prevent her from sailing on the *Ibis*: if he had recognized her already, then she might as well turn back right now. She was contemplating exactly that when Munia took hold of her hand. Being close in age, the girls had gravitated towards each other on the boat; now, as they were going up the stepladder, Munia whispered in Paulette's ear: Do you see him, Pugli? Waving at me from all the way up there?

Who? Who do you mean?

That lascar up there—he's crazy for me. Do you see him? He's recognized my sari.

You know him then? said Paulette.

Yes, said Munia. He rowed us to the camp when we came to Calcutta. His name's Azad Lascar.

Oh, is that so? Azad Lascar, is he?

Paulette smiled: she was halfway up the stepladder now, and as a further test of her disguise, she tilted her face upwards so that she was looking directly at Jodu, through the cover of her ghungta. He was hanging from the shrouds in an attitude she knew all too well: exactly so had they played together in the tall trees of the Botanical Gardens across the river. She was aware of a twinge of envy: how she would have loved to be up there, hanging on the ropes with him; but instead, here she was, on the stepladder, swathed from head to toe, while he was free and at large in the open air—the worst of it was that it was she who had always been the better climber. Ushered along by the maistries, she stepped on deck and paused to look up again, defiantly, daring him to expose her—but he had no eyes except for her companion, who was giggling as she clung to Paulette's arm: See? Didn't I tell you? He's mad for me. I could make him dance on his head if I liked.

Why don't you? said Paulette tartly. He looks like he needs a lesson or two.

Munia giggled and glanced up again: Maybe I will.

Be careful, Munia, Paulette hissed. Everyone's watching.

And so they were: not just the lascars and mates and

maistries, but also Captain Chillingworth, who was standing at the weather end of the quarter-deck, with his arms folded over his chest. As Paulette and Munia approached, the Captain's lips curled into an expression of disgust.

'I tell you, Doughty,' he declared, in the confident voice of a man who knows that his words will be understood only by the person for whom they are intended: 'The sight of these miserable creatures makes me long for the good old days, on the Guinea Coast. Look at these hags, treading five over five to Rotten Row.'

'Theek you are,' boomed the pilot, who was standing beside the wheelhouse. 'About as sorry a lot of pootlies as I ever did see.'

'This old crone here, for instance,' said the Captain, looking directly at Paulette's hooded face. 'A virgin-pullet if ever I saw one—often trod and never laid! What conceivable purpose is served by transporting her across the sea? What will she do there—a bag of bones that can neither bear a burden nor warm a bed?'

'Damned shame,' agreed Mr Doughty. 'Probably ridden with disease too. Shouldn't be surprised if she spreads it through the herd.'

'If you ask me, Doughty, it'd be a mercy to have her put down; at least she'd be spared the pains of the journey—why tow a frigate on fire?'

'Save on provisions too: I'll wager she eats like a luckerbaug. The scrawny ones always do.'

~

And, at this very moment, who should appear before Paulette but Zachary? And he too was looking directly into her ghungta, so that she could see his eyes fill with pity as they took in the bent shape of the ageless hag in front of him. 'A ship's no place for a woman,' she remembered him saying: how smug he had looked then, just as he did now, doling out his sympathy from on high; it was as if he'd forgotten that he owed his mate's berth to nothing more than the colour of his skin and a few misbegotten muscles. Paulette's fingers quivered in indignation, loosening her hold on her load. Suddenly the bundle slipped from her grasp and landed heavily on the deck, so close to Zachary's feet that he leant over instinctively to help her pick it up.

The gesture drew a shout from the quarter-deck. 'Leave her be, Reid!' Mr Doughty called out. 'You'll get no thanks for your bawhawdery.'

But the warning came too late: Zachary's hand was almost on the bundle when Paulette slapped it smartly away: her father's manuscript was concealed inside, along with two of her most beloved novels—and she could not take the risk of letting him feel the bindings through the cloth.

A look of injured surprise appeared on Zachary's face as he dropped his reprimanded hand. As for Paulette, her only thought was of escaping to the 'tween-deck. Picking up her bundle, she hurried over to the booby-hatch and took hold of the ladder.

Halfway down, she remembered her last visit to the dabusa: how quickly she had skipped down that ladder then—but now, with her sari wrapped around her calves, and her bundle on her head, it was another matter altogether. Nor was the 'tween-deck immediately recognizable as the same dabusa she'd been in before: its dark, unlit interior was now illuminated by several lamps and candles, and she saw, by their light, that dozens of mats had been laid out in concentric circles, covering most of the floor space. Strangely, the dabusa seemed to have shrunk in the meanwhile, and she discovered why when she glanced ahead: its forward end had been cut short by a new wooden bulwark.

There was a maistry inside, directing operations, and he pointed Munia and Paulette towards the newly-made partition. The women's section's over there, he said, right next to the chokey.

You mean there's a chokey behind that wall? cried Munia, in fright. Then why have you put us right next to it?

Nothing to worry about, said the maistry. The entrance is on the other side. There's no way the qaidis can get at you. You'll be safe over there, and you won't have the men stepping all over you to get to the heads.

There was no arguing with this: as she was making her way to the women's enclosure, Paulette noticed a small air duct, in the chokey's bulwark; if she stood on tiptoe it was on a level with her eye. She could not resist peeking in as she went past, and having stolen one glimpse, she returned quickly for another: she saw that there were two men inside the chokey, as curious a pair as ever she had laid eyes on. One had a shaven head, a skeletal face, and looked as if he might be Nepali; the other had a sinister tattoo on his forehead and appeared to have been dragged in from the Calcutta waterfront. Stranger still, the darker one was weeping while the other one had an arm around his shoulder, as if in consolation: despite their chains and bindings, there was a tenderness in their attitudes that seemed scarcely conceivable in a couple of criminal transportees. After yet another stolen glance, she saw that the two men were now speaking to each other, and this further excited her curiosity: what could they be saying—and with such absorption as not to notice the commotion in the adjoining compartment? What language might they share, this skeletal Easterner and this tattooed criminal? Paulette moved her mat around, so that it was placed right beside the bulwark: when she put her ear to a seam in the wood, she found, to her astonishment, that she could not only hear what was being said, but understand it too—for, amazingly, the two convicts were conversing in English.

~

Moments after Zachary's hand had been slapped, Baboo Nob Kissin Pander appeared at his side. Although the gomusta was wearing his accustomed dhoti and kurta, his shape, Zachary noticed, had acquired a curious, matronly fullness, and when he swept his shoulder-length hair off his face, it was with the practised gesture of a stout dowager. The expression on his face was at once indulgent and admonitory as he wagged a finger in Zachary's face: 'Tch! Tch! Despite beehive activities you still cannot suspend your mischiefs?'

'There you go again, Pander,' said Zachary. 'What the hell you talkin bout now?'

The gomusta lowered his voice: 'It is all right. No formalities. Everything is known to me.'

'What's that mean?'

'Here,' said Baboo Nob Kissin, helpfully. 'I will show what is hidden in the bosom.'

The gomusta thrust a hand through the neckline of his kurta, reaching so deep inside that Zachary would not have been surprised to see a plump breast laid bare. But instead, the hand emerged holding a cylindrical copper locket. 'See how nicely I have hidden? This way maximum securities can be maintained. However, one warning I must give.'

'What?'

'I regret to inform that this place is not apt.'

'Apt for what?'

Leaning towards Zachary's ear, the gomusta hissed: 'For mischiefs with cowgirls.'

'What the hell you talkin bout, Pander?' cried Zachary in exasperation. 'I was just tryin to help the woman pick up her stuff.'

'Better to leave ladies alone,' said the gomusta. 'Flute also better not show. They may get too much excited.'

'Show my flute?' Not for the first time, Zachary wondered whether the gomusta was not merely eccentric but actually mad. 'Oh hie off, Pander; leave me alone!'

~

Zachary turned on his heel and took himself off to the deck rail. The back of his hand was still red from the woman's slap; Zachary frowned as he looked at it—it disturbed him in a way that he could not quite understand. He had noticed the woman

in the red sari well before she dropped her baggage: she had
been the first to come up the gangplank, and something about
the tilt of her head had given him the impression that she was
watching him, from the shelter of her headcloth. Her tread had
seemed to grow slower and heavier as she came on deck. Even
when her sorry little bundle was giving her such a hard time,
she would not allow herself to use more than one of her
gnarled, henna-veined hands in wrestling with her burden; the
other claw, similarly disfigured, was employed solely in holding
her shroud in place. There was a fervour in her concealment
which seemed to suggest that a man's glance was as much to
be feared as a tongue of fire—the thought made him smile, and
a twinge of memory reminded him suddenly of the burning
scowl that Paulette had directed at him, at the end of their last
meeting. This notion, in turn, made him look towards the
shore, wondering if she might be somewhere nearby, keeping
watch on the *Ibis*. He had heard, from Jodu, that she had
recovered from her illness: surely she wouldn't allow the ship
to leave without saying goodbye—if not to him, then at least
to Jodu? Surely she would see that both he and Jodu had acted
in her own best interest?

Suddenly, as if conjured up by some rite of divination,
Serang Ali appeared at his elbow. 'No hab heard?' he whispered.
'Lambertmissy hab run way to marry nother-piece man. More
better Malum Zikri forgetting she. Anyway she too muchi
thin. China-side can catch one nice piece wife-o. Topside,
backside same-same. Make Malum Zikri too muchi happy
inside.'

Zachary banged a despairing fist on the deck rail: 'Oh, by
all the hoaky, Serang Ali! Will you stop it? You with your
damned wife-o and Pander with his cowgirls! To listen to you
two anyone'd think I was some crazy crannyhunter on the
prowl . . .'

He was cut short by Serang Ali, who pushed him suddenly
to one side, with a shout: 'Mich'man! 'Ware! 'Ware.' Zachary
looked over his shoulder just in time to see Crabbie, the ship's
cat, racing along the deck rail as though she were fleeing from

some unseen predator. Launching into a flying leap, the cat touched down once upon the side-ladder, and then bounced off to land on a boat that was moored alongside the schooner. Then, without so much as a glance at the vessel that had carried her halfway around the world, the tabby disappeared.

On deck the lascars and migrants stared aghast after the vanished animal, and even Zachary experienced a touch of apprehension: he had heard superstitious old sailors speaking of misgivings that 'made buttons in the belly', but had never before known what it meant to have his own stomach serve up such a tremor.

Up above, Mamdoo-tindal's knuckles had turned white on the yard.

Did you see that? he said to Jodu. Did you see?

What?

That cat jumped ship: now there's a sign if ever I saw one.

~

The last woman to come on board was Deeti, and she was climbing up the side-ladder when the cat leapt across her path. She would gladly have fallen in the water rather than be the first to cross the line of its flight, but Kalua was right behind her, holding her steady. At his back there were so many others, crowding on to the ladder, that there was no resisting their collective weight. Driven on by the maistries, the migrants surged forward and Deeti was carried across the invisible mark, to be deposited on the schooner's deck.

Through the veil of her sari, Deeti looked up at the masts, towering above. The sight made her a little giddy, so she kept her head bent and her eyes lowered. A number of maistries and silahdars were positioned along the deck, ushering the migrants along with their lathis, shoving them in the direction of the booby-hatch. *Chal! Chal!* Despite their shouts, progress was slow because of all the clutter on deck; everywhere you looked there were ropes, casks, pipas, bimbas, and even the occasional runaway chicken and bleating goat.

Deeti was almost abreast of the foremast when she became aware of a voice that sounded strangely familiar: it was shouting obscenities in Bhojpuri: *Toré mái ké bur chodo*!

Looking ahead, through a tangle of ropes and spars, she caught sight of a bull-necked, heavy-bellied man with luxuriant white moustaches; her feet froze and a cold hand took hold of her heart. Even though she knew who it was, there was a voice in her ear telling her that it was not a mortal man at all, but Saturn himself: It's him, Shani, he's been hunting you all your life and now he has you in his grasp. Her knees buckled under her, sending her crashing to the planks, at her husband's feet.

By this time a great press of people had poured on to the deck, and they were being herded steadily aft by the guards and overseers, with their swishing lathis. Had the person behind Deeti been someone of lesser size and strength than Kalua, she might well have been trampled where she lay. But on seeing her fall, Kalua braced himself against the deck and was able to bring the flow of people to a sudden halt.

What's happening there?

The disturbance had caught Bhyro Singh's attention and he began to advance upon Kalua, lathi in hand. Deeti lay where she was and pulled her sari tight over her face: but what was the point of hiding when Kalua was standing right above her, in full view and sure to be recognized? She shut her eyes and began to mutter prayers: *Hé Rám, hé Rám* . . .

But the next thing she heard was Bhyro Singh's voice, saying to Kalua: What's your name?

Was it possible that the subedar would not recognize Kalua? Yes, of course: he had been away from the village these many years and had probably never seen him, except as a child—and what interest would he have had in a leather-tanner's child anyway? But the name, Kalua—that he was sure to know because of the scandal of Deeti's escape from her husband's funeral pyre. Oh, fortunate the kismat that had prompted her to be careful with their real names; if only Kalua did not mention it now. To give him warning, she dug a fingernail into his toe: Beware! Beware!

What's your name? the subedar asked again.

Her prayer was answered. After a moment's hesitation, Kalua said: Malik, my name is Madhu.

And is that your wife, lying there?

Yes, malik.

Pick her up, said Bhyro Singh, and carry her to the dabusa. Don't let me see either of you making trouble again.

Yes, malik.

Kalua slung Deeti across his shoulder and carried her down the ladder, leaving their bundles on deck. After he had laid her on a mat, he would have gone back to fetch the bundles, but Deeti would not let him: No, listen to me first: do you know who that man was? He's Bhyro Singh, my husband's uncle; it's he who arranged my marriage, and it's he who sent people out to look for us. If he knows we're here . . .

~

'Are you ready, ho?' The pilot's call was answered promptly by Serang Ali: *Sab taiyár, sáhib.*

The sun was at its zenith now, and the booby-hatch that led to the dabusa had long since been battened down. Along with every other lascar, Jodu had been set to work on clearing the main deck—stowing pipas of drinking water, tirkaoing hamars, and hauling zanjirs through the hansil-holes. Now, with the chickens and goats safely stowed in the ship's boats, nothing else remained to be cleared and Jodu was impatient to be up on the trikat-yard again, for it was from aloft that he envisioned himself taking a last look at his native city: his were the first hands on the iskat when at last the command came— 'Foretopmen aloft!'—*Trikatwalé úpar chal!*

From Calcutta to Diamond Harbour, some twenty miles to the south, the *Ibis* was to be towed by the *Forbes*, one of several steam-tugs that had recently been put into commission on the Hooghly River. Jodu had seen these diminutive boats from afar, puffing consequentially along the river, towing mighty barques and brigantines as if they weighed no more than his own frail dinghy: not the least part of his eagerness to be under way lay in the prospect of a tow from one of these amazing vessels. Looking upriver, he saw that the round-nosed tug was already approaching, tolling its bell to clear a path through the traffic on the river.

On the far bank lay the Botanical Gardens and Jodu's perch was high enough that he could see the familiar trees and pathways. The sight made him think, for one fleeting and wistful instant, of what it would have been like to have Putli balancing on the trikat-yard beside him: that it would be sport, there was no denying, and she could have done it too, had it been possible. Of course, such a thing could not be permitted under any circumstances—but still, he couldn't help wishing that he had parted from her on some better, less contentious note: there was no telling when, if ever, he would see her again.

His attention had strayed so far that he was taken by surprise when Sunker said: Look, over there . . .

The heads of a pair of divers could be seen bobbing around the anchor buoys as they loosed the schooner's cables. It was almost time now: in a matter of moments they would be pulling away. Mamdoo-tindal tossed back his hair, and closed his long-lashed eyes. Then his lips began to move in prayer, murmuring the first words of the Fatiha. Jodu and Sunker were quick to join in: *B'ism'illáh ar-rahmán ar-rahím, hamdu'l'illáh al-rabb al-'alamín* . . . In the name of God, the Compassionate, the Merciful, Praise to the Lord of all Creation . . .

~

'All hands to quarters, ahoy!' The pilot's shout was followed by a cry from the serang: *Sab ádmi apna jagah!*

As the tug drew closer, the hammering of its engine grew louder and louder, and in the enclosed, airless gloom of the dabusa, it sounded as if some enraged demon were trying to rip apart the wooden planks of the hull in order to devour the people who sat huddled within. It was very dark inside, for the maistries had extinguished the candles and lamps on their way out: there was no need for them, they'd said, now that the migrants were all nicely packed in—to keep them burning would only increase the risk of fire. No one had disputed this but everyone understood that the overseers were merely saving themselves an extra expense. With no flame lit and the hatch secured, such light as there was came from cracks in the timber and the openings of the piss-dales. The leaden gloom, combined with the midday heat and the fetid stench of hundreds of enclosed bodies, gave the unstirred air a weight like that of sewage: it took an effort even to draw breath.

Already now, the girmitiyas had moved their mats about to their liking: everyone knew, from the first, that the maistries cared very little about what actually happened below: their chief concern was to escape the heat and stench of the dabusa so that they could settle into their own bunks, in the midships-cabin. No sooner had the overseers departed, shutting the hatch behind them, than the migrants began to disrupt the careful circle of their mats, scuffling and shouting as they fought for space.

As the noise of the tugboat mounted, Munia began to tremble, and Paulette, guessing that she was on the verge of hysteria, drew her closer. Despite her pretence of self-possession, even Paulette was beginning to feel the onset of panic when she heard a voice she knew to be Zachary's: he was right above her, on the main deck, so close that she could almost hear the shuffle of his feet.

'Pay out the cable!'—*Hamár tirkao*!

'Haul together!'—*Lag sab barábar*!

The hawsers that connected the *Ibis* to the steam-tug drew tight and a tremor ran through the schooner as if she were waking suddenly to life, like a bird startled out of a long night's sleep. From below the waterline, the spasms ran upwards, through the dabusa and into the deckhouse, where Steward Pinto crossed himself and dropped to his knees. As his lips began to move, the mess-boys, in all their many faiths, knelt beside him and bowed their heads: *Ave Maria, gratia plena, Dominus tecum* . . . Hail Mary, full of grace, the Lord is with thee . . .

~

On the main deck, Mr Doughty's hands were on the wheel as he shouted: 'Heave, you dogs, heave!'

*Habés—habés kutté, habés! habés!*

The schooner lurched to its jamna side and down in the darkness of the dabusa, people slipped and slid and tumbled upon each other like crumbs on a tilted tray. Neel put his eye to the air duct, and saw that a riot had broken out in the adjacent dabusa, with dozens of terriffied migrants hurling themselves at the ladder, pounding on the fastened hatch, in a belated attempt at escape: *Chhoro, chhoro*—let us out, let us off . . .

There was no response from above, except for a series of hookums, ringing across the deck: 'Haul you bastards! Haul!'— *Sab barábar! Habés salé, habés!*

Exasperated by the futile thrashings of the girmitiyas, Neel shouted through the air duct: Be quiet you fools! There's no escape; no turning back . . .

Slowly, as the vessel's motion made itself felt in the pit of every stomach, the noise yielded to a pregnant, fearful stillness. Now the migrants began to absorb the finality of what was under way: yes, they were moving, they were afloat, heading towards the void of the Black Water; neither death nor birth was as fearsome a passage as this, neither being experienced in full consciousness. Slowly, the rioters backed away from the ladder and returned to their mats. Somewhere in the darkness, a voice, trembling in awe, uttered the first syllables of the Gayatri Mantra—and Neel, who had been made to learn the words almost as soon as he could speak, now found himself saying them, as if for the first time: *Om, bhur bhuvah swah, tat savitur varenyam* . . . O giver of life, remover of pain and sorrow . . .

~

'Ready about!'—*Taiyár jagáh jagáh*!

Up on the foremast, as the shudder of the *Ibis*'s awakening ran from a-low to aloft, Jodu felt a tremor in the trikat-yard and knew that he had arrived at the moment his life had been building towards through many a long year; now, at last, he was leaving behind these muddy shores to meet the waters that led to Basra and Chin-kalan, Martaban and Zinjibar. As the mast began to sway, his chest swelled with pride to see how fine a figure the *Ibis* cut amongst the craft that clogged the river—the caramoussals and perikoes and budgerows. At this lofty elevation, it seemed as if the schooner had given him a pair of wings to soar above his past. Giddy with exhilaration, he hooked an arm around the shrouds and tore off his headcloth.

My salams to all of you, he shouted, waving to the unheeding shore: Jodu is on his way . . . oh you whores of Watgunge . . . you crimps of Bhutghat . . . Jodu's turned a lascar and he is gone . . . Gone!

## seventeen

~

Twilight brought the *Ibis* back to the Narrows, at Hooghly Point, and there, in the river's broad curve, she dropped anchor to wait out the night. Not till darkness had swallowed the surrounding banks were the girmitiyas allowed on deck; until then the gratings of the hatchway were kept firmly closed. The subedar and the overseers were agreed that the migrants' first taste of shipboard conditions had probably increased the likelihood of attempted break-outs: seen in daylight, the shore might present an irresistible temptation. Even after nightfall, when the attractions of land had been diminished by the howls of foraging jackal-packs, the maistries did not relax their vigilance: past experience had taught them that in every group of indentured migrants there were always a few who were desperate—or suicidal—enough to throw themselves into the water. When it came time to prepare the evening meal, they kept every migrant under watch. Even those who had been designated to serve as bhandaris were kept under guard while they stirred the chattas in the deckhouse chuldan. As for the rest, they were allowed up only in small groups, and were herded back into the dabusa as soon as they had finished their rice, dal and lime-pickle.

While the bhandaris and maistries were seeing to the feeding of the migrants, Steward Pinto and his mess-boys were serving roast lamb, mint sauce and boiled potatoes in the officers' cuddy. The portions were generous, for the steward had laid in two whole sides of fresh mutton before leaving

Calcutta, and the meat was not likely to last long in the unseasonable heat. But in spite of the plenitude of food and drink, there was less conviviality in the cuddy than there was around the chuldan, where, from time to time, the migrants could even be heard singing a few snatches of song.

*Májha dhára mé hai bera merá*
*Kripá kará ásrai hai tera*

My raft's adrift in the current
Your mercy is my only refuge . . .

'Damned coolies,' muttered the Captain, through a mouthful of lamb. 'Bloody Doomsday couldn't put a stop to their caterwauling.'

~

A ship could take as long as three days, depending on the weather and the winds, to sail downriver from Calcutta to the Bay of Bengal. Between the river's estuary and the open sea lay the island of Ganga-Sagar, the last of the holy waterway's many pilgrimages. One of Neel's ancestors had endowed a temple on the island, and he had visited it several times himself. The erstwhile Halder zemindary lay about halfway between Calcutta and Ganga-Sagar, and Neel knew that the *Ibis* would pass his estate towards the end of the second day. This was a journey that he had made so often that he could feel the zemindary's approach in the river's bends and turns. As it drew near, his head filled with shards of recollection, some of them as bright and sharp as bits of broken glass. When the time came, almost as if to mock him, he heard the lookout cry out, above: Raskhali, we're passing Raskhali!

He could see it now: it couldn't have been clearer if the schooner's hull had turned into glass. There it was: the palace and its colonnaded verandas; the terrace where he had taught Raj Rattan to fly kites; the avenue of palash trees his father had planted; the window of the bedroom to which he had taken Elokeshi.

'What is it, eh?' said Ah Fatt. 'Why you hitting your head, eh?' When Neel made no answer, Ah Fatt shook him by the shoulders till his teeth rattled.

'The place we pass now—you know it, not know it?'

'I know it.'

'Your village, eh?'

'Yes.'

'Home? Family? Tell everything.'

Neel shook his head: 'No. Maybe some other time.'

'Achha. Other time.'

Raskhali was so close that Neel could almost hear the bells of its temple. What he needed now, was to be elsewhere, in a place where he could be free of his memories. 'Where's *your* home, Ah Fatt? Tell me about it. Is it in a village?'

'Not village.' Ah Fatt scratched his chin.'My home very big place: Guangzhou. English call Canton.'

'Tell me. Tell me everything.'

Hou-hou . . .

Thus it happened that while the *Ibis* was still on the Hooghly, Neel was being transported across the continent, to Canton—and it was this other journey, more vivid than his own, that kept his sanity intact through the first part of the voyage: no one but Ah Fatt, no one he had ever known, could have provided him with the escape he needed, into a realm that was wholly unfamiliar, utterly unlike his own.

It was not because of Ah Fatt's fluency that Neel's vision of Canton became so vivid as to make it real: in fact, the opposite was true, for the genius of Ah Fatt's descriptions lay in their elisions, so that to listen to him was a venture of collaboration, in which the things that were spoken of came gradually to be transformed into artefacts of a shared imagining. So did Neel come to accept that Canton was to his own city as Calcutta was to the villages around it—a place of fearful splendour and unbearable squalor, as generous with its pleasures as it was unforgiving in the imposition of hardship. In listening and prompting, Neel began to feel that he could almost see with Ah Fatt's eyes: there it was, the city that had conceived and nurtured this new half of himself—a seaport that lay far inland, in the recesses of a nook-shotten coast, separated from the ocean by an intricate tangle of swamps, sands, creeks, marshes and inlets. It was shaped like a ship, this river port, its hull outlined by a continuous bulwark of towering, grey walls. Between the water and the city's walls lay a shoulder of land that was as turbulent as a ship's wake: although it fell outside the city limits, this stretch of shore was so thickly settled that nobody could tell where the land stopped and the water began. Sampans, junks, lorchas and smug-boats were moored here in such numbers as to form a wide, floating shelf that reached almost halfway across the river's width: everything was jumbled, water and mud, boats and godowns—but the confusion was deceptive, for even in this teeming, bustling length of silt and water, there were distinct little communities and neighbourhoods. And of these, the strangest, without a doubt, was the small enclave allotted to the foreigners who came to trade with China: the extra-Celestials who were known to the Cantonese as Fanquis—Aliens.

It was on this spit of land, just beyond the south-western gates of the walled city, that the Aliens had been permitted to build a row of so-called factories, which were nothing but narrow, red-tiled buildings, part warehouse, part residence and part accounts office for the shrofing of cash. For the few months of the year during which they were allowed to reside at Canton, the Aliens had perforce to confine their devilry to this one narrow enclave. The precincts of the walled city were forbidden to them, as to all foreigners—or so at least the authorities declared, claiming that such had been the case for almost a hundred years. Yet anyone who had been inside could tell you that of certain kinds of Alien there was no lack within the city walls: why, you had only to walk past the Hao-Lin temple, on the Chang-shou Road, to see monks from dark, westerly places; and if you stepped inside the precincts, you could even see a statue of the Buddhist preacher who had founded the temple: nobody could dispute that this proselyte was as foreign as the Sakyamuni himself. Or else, if you ventured still further into the city, walking up the Guang-li Road to the Huai-shang temple, you would know at once, from the shape of the minaret, that this was not, despite the outward resemblance, a temple at all, but a mosque; you would see too that the people who lived in and around this edifice were not all Uighurs, from the western reaches of the Empire, but included, besides, a rich display of devilry— Javanese, Malays, Malayalis, and Black-Hat Arabs.

Why, then, were some Aliens allowed in and some kept out? Was it the case that only a certain kind of Alien was truly an extra-Celestial being, to be kept under careful confinement, in the enclave of the factories? So it had to be, for the Fanquis of the factories were undeniably of a certain cast of face and character: there were 'Redfaced' Aliens from England, 'Flowery-flag' Aliens from America, and a good sprinkling of others, from France, Holland, Denmark and so on.

But of these many kinds of creature, the most easily recognizable, without a doubt, was the small but flourishing tribe of White-hatted Aliens—Parsis from Bombay. How was it that the White-hatted ones came to be counted as Fanquis, of the same breed as the Red-faces and Flowery-flags? No one knew, since a matter of appearance it surely could not be—for while it was true that some of the white-hatted faces were no less florid than those of the Flowery-flags, it was true also that there were many among them who were as dark as any of the lascars who sat imp-like upon the mastheads of the Pearl River. As for their clothes, the White-hats' garments were in no whit the same as those of the Fanquis: they wore robes and turbans, not unlike those of Black-hatted Arabs, presenting an aspect utterly unlike that of the other factory-dwellers—whose wont it was to strut about in absurdly tight leggings and jerkins, their pockets stuffed with the kerchiefs in which they liked to store their snot. No less was it plain for all to see that the other Fanquis looked somewhat askance upon the White-hats, for they were often excluded from the councils and revelries of the rest, just as their factory was the smallest and narrowest. But they too were merchants, after all, and profits were their business, for the sake of which they seemed perfectly willing to live the Fanqui life, migrating like birds between their homes in Bombay, their summer chummeries in Macao, and their cold-weather quarters in Canton, where the vistas of the walled city were not the least of the pleasures forbidden them—for while in China, they had to live, as did the other Fanquis, not just without women, but in the strictest celibacy. On no measure did the city's authorities so firmly insist as on the chop, issued annually, that forbade the people of Guangzhou to provide the Aliens with 'women or boys'. But could such an edict really be enforced? As in so many things, what was said and what transpired were by no means the same. It was impossible, surely, for those self-same authorities to be unaware of the women on the flower-boats that trolled the Pearl River, importuning lascars, merchants, linkisters, shroffs and whoever else was of a mind for some diversion; impossible, equally, that they should not know that in the very centre of the Fanqui enclave there lay a filth-clogged mews called Hog Lane, which boasted of any number of shebeens serving not just shamshoo, hocksaw and other liberty-liquors, but all manner of intoxicants of which the embrace of women was not the least. The authorities were certainly aware that the Dan boat-people who manned many of the sampans and lanteas and chop-boats of the Pearl River, also performed many small but essential services for the Fanquis, including taking in their washing—of which there was always a great deal, not just by way of clothing, but also of bed- and table-linen (the latter particularly, since food and drink did not fall within the purview of the luxuries denied to the poor devils). Such being the case, the business of laundering could not be transacted without frequent visits and outcalls—which was how it happened that a young White-hat of devilish charm, Bahramji Naurozji Moddie, came to cross paths with a fresh-faced Dan girl, Lei Chi Mei.

It began as a prosaic matter of handing over tablecloths soaked in Sunday dhansak, and napkins wetted with kid-nu-gosht, all of which young Barry—as he was known among the Fanquis—had to enter and account for in a laundry-book, this

*Amitav Ghosh*

duty being assigned to him by right of his status as the junior-most of the White-hatted tribe. And it was nothing other than a white hat that led to the pair's first coupling—or rather, it was one of those long spools of cloth which held the headgear in place: for it so happened that one of the great seths of the factory, Jamshedji Sohrabji Nusserwanji Batliwala, discovered a rent in his turban cloth one day and subjected young Barry to such a dumbcowing that when it came time to display the sundered object to Chi Mei, the young man burst into tears, weeping so artfully that the turban wound itself around and around the couple till they were sealed inside a snug cocoon.

A few years of loving and laundering were still to pass before a child was born to Chi Mei, but when at last the infant made his appearance, the event inspired a great fever of optimism in his father, who bestowed upon him the impressive name of Framjee Pestonjee Moddie, in the hope that it would ease his acceptance into the world of the White-hats. But Chi Mei, who knew far better the probable fate of children who were neither Dan nor Fanqui, took the precaution of naming the boy Leong Fatt.

~

The maistries quickly let it be known that the female migrants would be expected to perform certain menial duties for the officers, guards and overseers. Washing their clothes was one such; sewing buttons, repairing torn seams and so on, was another. Eager for exercise of any sort, Paulette elected to share the washing with Heeru and Ratna, while Deeti, Champa and Sarju opted to do the sewing. Munia, on the other hand, managed to snag the only job on board that could be considered remotely glamorous: this was the task of looking after the livestock, which was housed in the ship's boats and consumed almost exclusively by the officers, guards and overseers.

The *Ibis* was equipped with six boats: two small, clinker-built jollyboats, two mid-size cutters, and two carvel-built longboats, each a full twenty feet in length. The jollyboats and cutters were stowed on the roof of the deckhouse, one of each kind being nested in the other, with the whole ensemble held in place by chocks. The longboats, on the other hand, were amidships, swung up on davits. The longboats' crane-like davits were known to the lascars as 'devis', and not without reason, for their ropes and guys intersected with the mainshrouds in such a way as to create small niches of semi-concealment, as might be found in the sheltering lap of a goddess: in these recesses it was not impossible for one or two people to elude the unceasing bustle of the main deck for several minutes at a time. The scuppers, where the washing was done, lay under the devis, and Paulette quickly learnt to take her time over the task, so she could linger in the open air. The Ibis was now deep in the watery labyrinth of the Sundarbans, and she was glad to seize every opportunity to gaze at the river's mangrove-cloaked shores. The waterways here were strewn with mudbanks and other hazards, so the navigable channel followed a twisting, looping course, occasionally drawing close enough to the banks to provide clear views of the jungle. Some of Paulette's happiest memories were of helping her father catalogue the flora of this forest, during weeks-long collecting trips in Jodu's boat: now, as she watched the banks through the screen of her ghungta, her eyes sifted through the greenery as if by habit: there, beneath the upthrust elbow-roots of a mangrove, was a little shrub of wild basil, *Ocimum adscendens*; it was Mr Voight, the Danish curator of the Gardens at Serampore—and her father's best friend—who had confirmed that this plant was indeed to be found in these forests. And here, growing thick along the banks, was *Ceriops roxburgiana*, identified by the horrible Mr Roxburgh, who'd been so unkind to her father that the very sound of his name would make him blanch; and there, on the grassy verge, just visible above the mangroves, was a spiky-leafed shrub she knew all too well: *Acanthus lambertii*. It was at her own insistence that her father had given it this name—

because she had literally stumbled upon it, having been poked in the leg by one of its spiny leaves. Now, watching the familiar foliage slip by, Paulette's eyes filled with tears: these were more than plants to her, they were the companions of her earliest childhood and their shoots seemed almost to be her own, plunged deep into this soil; no matter where she went or for how long, she knew that nothing would ever tie her to a place as did these childhood roots.

For Munia, on the other hand, the forest was a place of dread. One afternoon, as Paulette was gazing at the mangroves, under the pretence of scrubbing clothes, Munia appeared beside her and uttered a horrified gasp. Clutching at Paulette's arm, she pointed to a sinuous form, hanging from the branch of a mangrove. Is that a snake? she whispered.

Paulette laughed. No, you ullu; it's just a creeping plant that grows on the bark. Its flowers are very beautiful . . .

It was, in fact, an epiphytic orchid; she'd first encountered this species three years ago when Jodu brought one back home. Her father had taken it for *Dendrobium pierardii* at first, but on examination had decided that it wasn't. What would you like to call it? he had asked Jodu with a smile, and Jodu had glanced at Paulette before replying, with a sly grin: Call it Putli-phool. She knew he was teasing, that it was his way of making fun of her for being so thin, flat-chested and weedy. But her father was much taken by the idea, and sure enough the epiphyte became *Dendrobium pauletii*.

Munia shuddered: I'm glad I'm not down here. It's much nicer where I work, on the roof of the deckhouse. The lascars pass right by when they're climbing up to fix the sails.

Do they ever say anything? Paulette asked.

Only him. Munia glanced over her shoulder at the trikat-yard, where Jodu could be seen standing on the footropes, at full stretch, reeling the foretopsail. Look at him! Always showing off. But he's a sweet boy, no denying that, and nice-looking too.

The terms of their siblingship being what they were, Paulette had given little thought to Jodu's appearance: now, as she looked up at his boyishly mobile face, his upturned lips, and the coppery glint in his raven's-wing hair, she could see why Munia might be attracted to him. Vaguely embarrassed by this, she said: What did you talk about?

Munia giggled: He's like a fox, that one: made up a story about how a hakim in Basra had taught him to tell people's fortunes. How? I said, and do you know what his answer was?

What?

He said: let me put my ear on your heart, and I'll tell you what the future holds. Better still, if I can use my lips.

That Jodu might have a strong amatory streak had never occurred to Paulette: she was shocked to hear of his boldness. But Munia! weren't there people around?

No, it was dark; no one could see us.

And did you let him? said Paulette. Listen to your heart? What do you think?

Paulette slipped her head under Munia's ghungta, so she could look into her eyes. No! Munia, you didn't!

Oh Pugli! Munia gave a teasing laugh and pulled her ghungta away. You may be a devi, but I'm a shaitan.

Suddenly, over Munia's shoulder, Paulette saw Zachary stepping down from the quarter-deck. He seemed to be heading forward, on a course that would take him right past the devis. As he approached, Paulette's limbs tensed involuntarily and she pulled away from Munia to flatten herself against the bulwark. As it happened, she had one of his shirts in her hands, and she tucked it quickly out of sight.

Surprised by Paulette's fidgeting, Munia said: What's the matter?

Although Paulette's face was buried in her knees, and her ghungta was drawn almost to her ankles, Munia had no difficulty in following the direction of her gaze. Just as Zachary was walking past, she gave a hiccup of laughter.

Munia, be quiet, Paulette hissed. That's no way to behave.

For who? said Munia, tittering in delight. Look at you, acting the devi. But you're no different from me. I saw who

*Amitav Ghosh*

you had your eye on. He's got two arms and a flute just like any other man.

~

Right from the start, it was made clear to the convicts that their days would be spent largely in picking and rolling istup— or oakum, as Neel insisted on calling it, giving the fibre its English name. At the start of each day, a large basket of the stuff was brought to them, and they were expected to turn it into usable pickings by nightfall. They were told also that, unlike the migrants, they would not be allowed on deck at mealtimes: their food would be sent to them below, in taporis. But once each day, they would be released from the chokey and given time to empty their shared toilet bucket and to wash their bodies with a few mugfuls of water. Afterwards, they would be taken above and given a few minutes' exercise, consisting, usually, of a turn or two around the main deck.

This last part of the convicts' routine, Bhyro Singh was quick to appropriate: the pretence that they were a pair of plough-oxen and he a farmer, tilling a field, seemed to give him endless delight; he would loop their chains around their necks, in such a way that they were forced to stoop as they walked; then, shaking their fetters like reins, he would make a clicking, tongue-rolling noise as he drove them along, occasionally slicing at their legs with his lathi. It wasn't just that the infliction of pain gave him pleasure (though this was no small part of it): the blows and insults were also intended to show everyone that he, Bhyro Singh, was uncontaminated by the degraded creatures who had been placed in his power. Neel had only to look into his eyes to know that the disgust that he and Ah Fatt inspired in the subedar far surpassed anything he might have felt for more commonplace criminals. Thugs and dacoits, he would probably have regarded as kindred spirits and treated with some respect, but Neel and Ah Fatt did not fit that mould of man: for him they were misbegotten, befouled creatures—one because he was a filthy foreigner and the other because he was a fallen outcaste. And even worse, if possible, was the fact that the two convicts appeared to be friends and that neither seemed to want to overmaster the other: to Bhyro Singh this was a sign that they were not men at all, but castrated, impotent creatures—oxen, in other words. While driving them around the deck, he would shout, for the amusement of the maistries and silahdars: . . . *Ahó*, keep going . . . don't weep for your balls now . . . tears won't bring them back.

Or else he would rap them on the genitals and laugh when they doubled up: What's the matter? Aren't you hijras, you two? There's no pleasure or pain between your legs.

In order to turn the convicts against each other, the subedar would sometimes give one an extra helping of food, or make the other take a double turn at cleaning the toilet buckets: Come, let's see if you have a taste for your sweetheart's dung.

In the failure of these stratagems, he evidently perceived a subtle undermining of his own position, for if ever he saw Neel and Ah Fatt coming to each other's assistance on deck, he would vent his anger with furious lashings of his lathi. What with the swaying of the schooner, the unsteadiness of their legs, and the weight of their fetters, it was difficult for Ah Fatt and Neel to take more than a few steps at a time without falling or faltering. Any attempt by either to help the other would result in kicks and swipes of the lathi.

It was in the midst of one such flurry of blows that Neel heard the subedar say: Sala, get up. The Chhota Malum's heading this way: on your feet now—don't dirty his shoes.

Neel was struggling to his feet when he found himself looking into a face that he remembered well. Before he could stop himself, he said aloud: 'Good afternoon, Mr Reid.'

That a convict should have the spleen to address an officer was so incredible to Bhyro Singh that he slammed his lathi on Neel's shoulder, knocking him to his knees: B'henchod! You dare look the sahib in the eye?

'Wait!' Zachary stepped forward to stop the subedar's hand. 'Wait a minute there.'

The mate's intervention so inflamed the subedar that for a moment he glowered as if he were about to hit Zachary next. But then, thinking the better of it, he stepped back.

In the meanwhile, Neel had risen to his feet and was dusting his hands.'Thank you, Mr Reid,' he said. Then, unable to think of anything else, he added: 'I trust you are well?'

Zachary peered into his face, frowning. 'Who are you?' he said. 'I know the voice, but I confess I can't place . . .'

'My name is Neel Rattan Halder. You may remember, Mr Reid, that you dined with me some six months ago, on—on what was then—my budgerow.' This was the first time in many months that Neel had spoken to anyone on the outside, and the experience was so strangely exhilarating that he could almost have imagined himself back in his own sheeshmahal. 'You were served, if my memory does not fail me, some duck soup and a roast of Sudden-Death. Forgive me for mentioning these details. Food has been much on my mind of late.'

'Gollation!' cried Zachary suddenly, in astonished recognition. 'You're the Roger, aren't you? The Raja of . . .?'

'Your memory does not mislead you, sir,' said Neel, bowing his head. 'Yes, I was indeed once the Raja of Raskhali. My circumstances are very different now, as you can see.'

'I had no idea you were aboard this vessel.'

'No more was I aware of your presence on board,' said Neel, with an ironic smile. 'Or I would certainly have tried to send up my card. I had imagined somehow that you had already returned to your estates.'

'My estates?'

'Yes. Did you not say you were related to Lord Baltimore? Or am I imagining it?' Neel was amazed by how easy it was, and how strangely pleasurable, to fall back into the snobberies and small talk of his past life. Those gratifications had seemed insignificant when they were freely available, but now it was as if they were life's very essence.

Zachary smiled. 'I think you may be misremembering. I'm no lordling and possess no estates.'

'In that at least,' said Neel, 'our lot is shared. My present zemindary consists of no more than a toilet bucket and a set of rusty chains.'

Zachary made a wondering gesture as he looked Neel over, from his tattooed head to his unshod feet: 'But what happened to you?'

'It is a tale that cannot be briefly told, Mr Reid,' said Neel. 'Suffice it to say that my estate has passed into the possession of your master, Mr Burnham: it was awarded to him by a decision of the Supreme Court of Judicature.'

Zachary whistled in surprise: 'I'm sorry . . .'

'I am but another of Fortune's fools, Mr Reid.' Now, with a guilty start, Neel remembered Ah Fatt, standing mutely beside him. 'Forgive me, Mr Reid. I have not introduced my friend and colleague, Mr Framjee Pestonjee Moddie.'

'How do you do?' Zachary was about to stick out his hand when the subedar, provoked beyond endurance, shoved his lathi into the small of Ah Fatt's back: *Chal! Hatt!* Move on, you two.

'It was a pleasure to see you again, Mr Reid,' said Neel, wincing under the subedar's blows.

'For me too . . .'

As it turned out, the encounter produced nothing to be glad of, either for Zachary or the convicts. For Neel it earned a slap across the face from the subedar: You think you can impress me with two words of angrezi? I'll show you how this ingi-lis is spoken . . .

For Zachary, it earned a summons from Mr Crowle: 'What's this I hear about you jawin with the quoddies?'

'I'd met one of them before,' said Zachary. 'What was I to do? Pretend he doesn't exist?'

'Exactly,' said Mr Crowle. 'Pretend he don't exist. 'S not yer place to be talkin with the quoddies and coolies. Subby-dar don like it. He don't like you too much neither, to be honest. There'll be trouble if 'n you try it agin. Warnin you I am, Mannikin.'

~

*Amitav Ghosh*

The encounter between Zachary and the convicts had another witness—one on whom it produced a more momentous effect than on anyone else. This was Baboo Nob Kissin Pander, who had woken that morning to a powerful and prophetic rumbling in his bowels. As was his wont, he had paid close attention to these symptoms and had been led to conclude that the spasms were too forceful to be ascribed entirely to the motion of the schooner: they seemed more akin to the tremors that betoken the coming of a great earthquake or upheaval.

With the progress of the day, this sense of foreboding and expectation had grown steadily stronger, driving the gomusta finally to make his way agil, to the fo'c'sle-deck, where he positioned himself between the bows, allowing the wind to fill out his loose-flowing robes. As he peered ahead, at the silvery waters of the ever-broadening river, the mounting suspense made his stomach go pit-a-pat and he was forced to cross his legs, to hold back the threatened eruption. It was in the process of squirming and twisting that he caught sight of the two convicts being marched around the deck by Subedar Bhyro Singh.

The countenance of the former Raja was not unknown to Baboo Nob Kissin: he had glimpsed it several times, in Calcutta, through the window of the Raskhali phaeton. Once, when the carriage was thundering past, the gomusta had lost his footing and toppled backwards in fright: he remembered well the smile of disdainful amusement with which Neel had regarded him, as he wallowed haplessly in a pool of mud. But the pale, refined countenance of his memory, with its rosebud mouth and world-weary eyes, bore no resemblance to the gaunt, swarthy face that he saw before him now. Had Baboo Nob Kissin not known that the disgraced Raja was one of the two convicts on the *Ibis*, he would not have imagined this to be the same man, so striking was the change, not just in his appearance but also in his demeanour, which was just as alert and watchful now as it had been bored and languid then. It was somehow thrilling to imagine that he, Baboo Nob Kissin Pander, had played a part in humbling this proud and arrogant aristocrat, in subjecting this effete, self-indulgent sensualist to privations that he could not have envisioned in his worst nightmares. In a way it was like midwiving the birth of a new existence—and no sooner had this thought crossed his mind than the gomusta experienced the upwelling of a sensation that was so intense and so unfamiliar that he knew that Taramony had to be its source. What other provenance could there be for the tumult of pity and protectiveness that seized him at the sight of Neel's begrimed face and chained extremities? Who else could be responsible for the upsurge of maternal tenderness in his bosom, as he watched the convict being driven around the deck like a draught animal? He had always harboured the suspicion that the great regret of Taramony's life was that she had no child of her own. This was confirmed now by the welter of emotions emanating from the presence inside him, the instinct that made him yearn to wrap his arms around the convict to shield him from pain: it was as if Taramony had recognized, in Neel, the son, now grown, whom she had been unable to bear for her husband, Baboo Nob Kissin's uncle.

So powerful indeed were the gomusta's maternal stirrings that had not the fear of an embarrassing accident compelled him to keep his legs knotted, he might well have gone racing down the deck to interpose himself between Neel and the subedar's failing lathi. And could it be a coincidence that it was exactly then that Zachary stepped forward to stop the subedar's hand and anoint the convict with his recognition? It was as if two aspects of Taramony's capacity for womanly love had been brought into conjunction: that of the mother, longing to nurture a wayward son, and that of the seeker, yearning to transcend the things of this world.

The sight of the encounter between these two beings, both of whom concealed inner truths known only to him, was so moving as to actually set in motion the long-threatened earthquake: the gurgling in the gomusta's interior was now like that of molten lava, and even the fear of embarrassment could not prevent him from racing aft, in search of the heads.

~

*Amitav Ghosh*

During the day, when the schooner's movement could be felt in the pit of every stomach, the heat and stench of the dabusa were made bearable only by the knowledge that every moment of it brought the end of the voyage a little closer. But there was no such consolation when the schooner anchored at night in the bends of the jungle: with tigers roaring and leopards coughing nearby, even the least excitable of the migrants were seized by wild imaginings. Nor was there any lack of people to stoke rumours and set people against each other. The worst of these was Jhugroo, who had been bundled out of his own village because of his propensity for making trouble: his face was as ugly as his disposition, with a jutting, twisted lower jaw, and tiny bloodshot eyes, yet his tongue and his wits were quick enough to earn him a certain kind of authority among the younger and more credulous girmitiyas.

On the first night, when no one could sleep, Jhugroo began to tell a story about the jungles of Mareech and how the younger and weaker migrants were destined to be used as bait for the wild animals that lived in those forests. His voice could be heard through the whole dabusa, and it terrorized the women, especially Munia, who broke down in tears.

In the suffocating heat, her fear had the virulence of a fever and soon infected those around her: as the women collapsed, one after another, Paulette realized that she would have to act quickly if she was to stem their panic. *Khamosh*! Quiet! she cried out. Listen to me, listen: what this man is telling you is all *bakwás* and nonsense. Don't believe these stories—they aren't true. There are no wild animals in Mareech, except for birds and frogs and a few goats, pigs and deer—most of them brought there by human beings. As for snakes, there's not one on the whole island.

No snakes!

This pronouncement was so remarkable that the crying stopped and many heads, including Jhugroo's, turned to stare at Paulette. It fell to Deeti to ask the question that was foremost in every mind: No snakes? Can there really be such a jungle?

Yes, there are such jungles, said Paulette. Mainly on islands.

Jhugroo would not let this pass unchallenged. How would you know? he demanded. You're just a woman: who can take your word for it?

Paulette answered calmly: I know because I've read it in a book. It was written by a man who knew about such things and had lived a long time in Mareech.

A book? Jhugroo gave a satirical laugh. The bitch is lying. How would a woman know what's written in a book?

This stung Deeti, who retorted: Why shouldn't she be able to read a book? She's the daughter of a pandit—she's been taught her letters by her father.

Lying rundees, Jhugroo cried. You should clean your mouths with dung.

What? Kalua rose slowly to his feet, stooping low to keep his head clear of the ceiling. What was that you said to my wife?

Confronted with Kalua's massive frame, Jhugroo retreated into a sulky, vengeful silence, while his followers edged away to join those who had gathered around Paulette: Is it true? There are no snakes there? What trees do they have? Is there rice? Really?

~

On the other side of the bulwark, Neel too was listening intently to Paulette. Although he had spent a fair amount of time peering at the migrants, through the air duct, he had not paid her much attention till then: like the other women, she was always ghungta'd, and he had not set eyes on her face, nor indeed on any other part of her, apart from her henna-darkened hands and alta-reddened feet. From the intonations of her voice, he had surmised that she differed from the other migrants in that her language was Bengali rather than Bhojpuri, and it had struck him once that her head was sometimes inclined in such a way as to listen in on his conversations with

*Amitav Ghosh*

Ah Fatt—but this seemed absurd. It was impossible surely, that a coolie-woman would understand English?

It was Deeti who brought Neel's attention to bear on Paulette anew: if what she'd said was true—that this female was educated—then it seemed to Neel that he would almost certainly know her parents or relatives: small indeed was the number of Bengali families who encouraged their daughters to read, and few among them were unrelated to his own. The names of the handful of Calcutta women who could claim any kind of punditry were well known in his circle, and there was not, to his knowledge, one among them who would publicly admit to knowing English—that was a threshold that even the most liberal families had yet to cross. And here was another puzzle: the educated women of the city were almost all from well-to-do families; it was inconceivable that any of them would allow a daughter of theirs to sail off with a boatload of indentured labourers and convicts. Yet here, apparently, was one such: or was she?

Only when the general interest in the girl had waned did Neel put his lips to the air duct. Then, addressing her ghungta-draped head, he said, in Bengali: One who has been so courteous in dealing with her interlocutors will have no objection, surely, to answering yet another query?

The silky phrasing and refined accent put Paulette instantly on her guard: although her back was turned towards the chokey, she knew exactly who had spoken and she understood immediately that she was being put to some kind of test. Paulette was well aware that her Bengali tended to have a rafish, riverfront edge to it, much of it having been acquired from Jodu; she was careful now in choosing her words. Matching her tone to the convict's, she said: There is no harm in a question; should the answer be known it will certainly be provided.

The accent was neutral enough to deny Neel any further clues to the speaker's origins.

Would it be possible then, he continued, to inquire after the title of the book that was referred to earlier: this volume that is said to have contained such a rich trove of information about the island of Mareech?

Paulette, playing for time, said: The name eludes me—it is of no consequence.

But indeed it is, said Neel. I have searched my memory for a book in our language that might contain these facts and I can think of none.

There are many books in the world, parried Paulette, and surely no one can know all their names?

Not of all the books in the world, Neel conceded, that is certainly true. But in Bengali the number of books in print is yet to exceed a few hundred, and I once prided myself on possessing every single one of them. Thus my concern—is it possible that I had missed a volume?

Thinking quickly, Paulette said: But the book of which I speak has yet to see print. It is a translation from the French.

From the French! Indeed? And would it be too much to ask the name of the translator?

Paulette, thoroughly rattled, uttered the first name to come to mind, which was that of the munshi who had taught her Sanskrit and helped her father with the cataloguing of his collection: His name was Collynaut-baboo.

Neel recognized the name at once: Really? Do you mean Munshi Collynaut Burrell?

Yes, that is he.

But I know him well, said Neel. He was my uncle's munshi for many years. I can assure you he speaks not a syllable of French.

Of course not, said Paulette, parrying quickly. He was collaborating with a Frenchman—Lambert-sahib of the Botanical Gardens. Since I was Collynaut-baboo's pupil, he sometimes gave me pages to transcribe. That is how I read them.

Not a word of this was convincing to Neel, but he could think of no way to shake the story. May I presume to ask, he said at last, what the good-name of the lady's family might be?

Paulette was ready with her riposte. Would it not be intolerably forward, she answered politely, to speak of so intimate a matter upon such a brief acquaintance?

As you please, said Neel. I will say no more except that you are wasting your time in trying to educate these oafs and bumpkins. They might as well be left to rot in ignorance, since rot they surely will.

All this while, Paulette had been sitting so that she would not have to look at the convict. But now, nettled by the arrogance of his tone, she turned her ghungta-covered face in his direction and allowed her eyes to travel slowly up to the air duct. All she could see, in the dimness of the dabusa, was a pair of eyes, glowing crazily in the depths of a stubbled face. Her anger turned to a kind of pity and she said, softly: If you are so clever, then what are you doing here with us? If there was to be a panic or a riot in here, do you think your learning would save you? Haven't you ever heard of the saying: we're all in the same boat?—*amra shob-i ek naukoye bháshchhi?*

Neel burst into laughter. Yes, he said, triumphantly: I have heard it said—but never in Bengali. It's an English saying that you've just translated—very prettily, if I may say so—but it begs the question of where and how you learnt the English language.

Paulette turned away without answering, but he persisted: Who are you, my good lady? You may as well tell me. You can be sure I'll find out.

I'm not of your kind, said Paulette. That is all you need to know.

Yes, indeed it is, he said, in a tone of mockery—for in uttering her final retort, Paulette's tongue had betrayed just enough of the waterfront's sibilance for the mystery to be solved. Neel had heard Elokeshi speak of a new class of prostitute who had learnt English from their white clients—no doubt this was one such, on her way to join some island brothel.

~

The space which Deeti and Kalua had chosen for themselves lay under one of the massive beams that arched over the 'tween deck. Deeti's mat was pushed right up to the side, so that the hull provided a backrest when she sat up. But when she lay down, the wooden ridge was no more than an arm's length from her head, so that a moment's inattention could mean a nasty blow to the head. After cracking her brow against the edge a few times, she learnt to slip out safely, and after that, she quickly came to be grateful for the shelter of the beam: it was like a parental arm, holding her in place when everything else was becoming more and more unsteady.

Never was Deeti more grateful for the beam's proximity than during the first days of the voyage, when she was still unaccustomed to the vessel's motion: it gave her something to hold on to, and she found that she could lessen the whirling sensation in her head by focusing her eyes on the wood. In this way, despite the half-light of the dabusa, she became intimately familiar with that length of timber, learning to recognize its grain, its whorls and even the little scratches that had been carved into its surface by the nails of others who had lain where she lay. When Kalua told her that the best remedy for queasiness was to look up at the open sky, she told him tartly to look where he pleased, but for herself, she had all the sky she could deal with in the wood above her head.

For Deeti, the stars and constellations of the night sky had always recalled the faces and likenesses of the people she remembered, in love or in dread. Was it this, or was it the shelter afforded by the arched limb that reminded her of the shrine she had left behind? It happened anyway that on the morning of the third day she dipped the tip of her index finger into the vermilion-filled parting of her hair and raised it to the wood to draw a tiny face with two pigtails.

Kalua understood at once: It's Kabutri, isn't it? he whispered—and Deeti had to jab him in the ribs, to remind him that her daughter's existence was a secret.

Later that day, at noon, when the migrants were making their way out of the dabusa, a strange affliction took hold of

*Amitav Ghosh*

everyone who climbed up the ladder: when they set foot on the last rung, they became immobile and had to be shoved up bodily by those who were following at their heels. No matter how loud or impatient the voices below, everyone was stricken in turn as they stepped on the main deck, even those who had but a moment before been cursing the clumsy clodhoppers who were weighing down the line. When it was her turn to emerge from the hatch, Deeti too was seized by the malady: for there it was, dead ahead of the schooner's bows, the Black Water.

The wind had fallen off, so there was not a fleck of white visible on the surface, and with the afternoon sun glaring down, the water was as dark and still as the cloak of shadows that covers the opening of an abyss. Like the others around her, Deeti stared in stupefaction: it was impossible to think of this as water at all—for water surely needed a boundary, a rim, a shore, to give it shape and hold it in place? This was a firmament, like the night sky, holding the vessel aloft as if it were a planet or a star. When she was back on her mat, Deeti's hand rose of itself and drew the figure she had drawn for Kabutri, many months ago—of a winged vessel flying over the water. Thus it happened that the *Ibis* became the second figure to enter Deeti's seaborne shrine.

eighteen

~

At sundown, the *Ibis* cast anchor at the last place from which the migrants would be able to view their native shore: this was Saugor Roads, a much-trafficked anchorage in the lee of Ganga-Sagar, the island that stands between the sea and the holy river. Except for some mudbanks and the pennants of a few temples, there was little to be seen of the island from the *Ibis*, and none of it was visible in the unlit gloom of the dabusa: yet the very name Ganga-Sagar, joining as it did, river and sea, clear and dark, known and hidden, served to remind the migrants of the yawning chasm ahead; it was as if they were sitting balanced on the edge of a precipice, and the island were an outstretched limb of sacred Jambudvipa, their homeland, reaching out to keep them from tumbling into the void.

The maistries too were jitterily aware of the proximity of this last spit of land, and that evening they were even more vigilant than usual when the migrants came on deck for their meal; lathis in hand, they positioned themselves warily around the bulwarks and any migrant who looked too closely at the distant lights was hustled quickly below: What're you staring at, sala? Get back down there, where you belong . . .

But even when removed from view, the island could not be put out of mind: although none of them had set eyes on it before, it was still intimately familiar to most—was it not, after all, the spot where the Ganga rested her feet? Like many other parts of Jambudvipa, it was a place they had visited and revisited time and again, through the epics and Puranas, through myth, song and legend. The knowledge that this was the last they would see of their homeland, created an atmosphere of truculence and uncertainty in which no provocation seemed too slight for a quarrel. Once fights broke out, they escalated at a pace that was bewildering to everyone, including the participants: in their villages they would have had relatives, friends, and neighbours to step between them, but here there were no elders to settle disputes, and no tribes of kinsfolk to hold a man back from going for another's throat. Instead, there were troublemakers like Jhugroo, always eager to set one man against another, friend against friend, caste against caste.

Among the women, the talk was of the past, and the little things that they would never see, nor hear, nor smell again: the colour of poppies, spilling across the fields like *ábír* on a rain-drenched Holi; the haunting smell of cooking-fires drifting across the river, bearing news of a wedding in a distant village; the sunset sounds of temple bells and the evening azan; late nights in the courtyard, listening to the tales of the elderly. No matter how hard the times at home may have been, in the ashes of every past there were a few cinders of memory that glowed with warmth—and now, those embers of recollection took on a new life, in the light of which their presence here, in the belly of a ship that was about to be cast into an abyss, seemed incomprehensible, a thing that could not be explained except as a lapse from sanity.

Deeti fell silent as the other women spoke, for the recollections of the others served only to remind her of Kabutri and the memories from which she would be forever excluded: the years of growing she would not see; the secrets she would never share; the bridegroom she would not receive. How was it possible that she would not be present at her child's wedding to sing the laments that mothers sang when the palanquins came to carry their daughters away?

> *Talwa jharáilé*
> > *Kāwal kumhláile*
> *Hansé royé*
> > *Birahá biyog*

The pond is dry
> The lotus withered
The swan weeps
> For its absent love

In the escalating din, Deeti's song was almost inaudible at first, but when the other women grew aware of it they joined their voices to hers, one by one, all except Paulette, who held back shyly, until Deeti whispered: It doesn't matter whether you know the words. Sing anyway—or the night will be unbearable.

Slowly, as the women's voices grew in strength and confidence, the men forgot their quarrels: at home too, during village weddings, it was always the women who sang when the bride was torn from her parents' embrace—it was as if they were acknowledging, through their silence, that they, as men, had no words to describe the pain of the child who is exiled from home.

*Kaisé katé ab*
> *Birahá ki ratiyá?*

How will it pass
> This night of parting?

~

Through the opening of the air duct, Neel too was listening to the women's songs, and neither then nor afterwards was he able to explain why it happened that the language he had been surrounded by for the last two days, now poured suddenly into his head, like flood water cascading over a breached bund. It was either Deeti's voice, or some fragment of her songs, that made him remember that hers was the language, Bhojpuri, in which Parimal had been accustomed to speak to him, in his infancy and childhood—until the day when his father put a stop to it. The fortunes of the Halders were built, the old Raja had said, on their ability to communicate with those who held the reins of power; Parimal's rustic tongue was the speech of those who bore the yoke, and Neel ought never to use it again for it would ruin his accent when it came time for him to learn Hindusthani and Persian, as was necessary for the heir to a zemindary.

Neel, ever the obedient son, had allowed the language to wither in his head, yet, unbeknownst to him, it had been kept alive—and it was only now, in listening to Deeti's songs, that he recognized that the secret source of its nourishment was music: he had always had a great love of dadras, chaitis, barahmasas, horis, kajris—songs such as Deeti was singing. Listening to her now, he knew why Bhojpuri was the language of this music: because of all the tongues spoken between the Ganges and the Indus, there was none that was its equal in the expression of the nuances of love, longing, and separation—of the plight of those who leave and those who stay at home.

How had it happened that when choosing the men and women who were to be torn from this subjugated plain, the hand of destiny had strayed so far inland, away from the busy coastlines, to alight on the people who were, of all, the most stubbornly rooted in the silt of the Ganga, in a soil that had to be sown with suffering to yield its crop of story and song? It was as if fate had thrust its fist through the living flesh of the land in order to tear away a piece of its stricken heart.

∼

The urge to use his remembered words was strong upon Neel that night and he could not sleep. Much later, after the women had sung themselves hoarse, and a fitful quiet had descended upon the dabusa, he heard a few of the migrants trying to recall the story of Ganga-Sagar Island. He could not keep himself from telling the tale: speaking through the air duct, he reminded his listeners that if not for this island neither the Ganga nor the sea would exist; for according to the myths, it was here that Lord Vishnu, in his avatar as the sage Kapila, was sitting in meditation, when he was disturbed by the sixty thousand sons of King Sagar who were marching through the land to claim it for the Ikshvaku dynasty. It was here too, exactly where they were now, that those sixty thousand princes were punished for their impudence, being incinerated by a single glance from one of the sage's burning eyes; it was here that their unhallowed ashes had lain until another scion of their dynasty, the good king Bhagiratha, was able to persuade the Ganga to pour down from the heavens and fill the seas: this was how the ashes of the sixty thousand Ikshvaku princes were redeemed from the underworld.

The listeners were dumbfounded—not by the tale so much as by Neel himself. Who would have thought that this filthy qaidi would show himself to be possessed of so much telling and so many tongues? To think that he could even speak an approximation of their own Bhojpuri! Why, if a crow had begun to sing a kajri they could not have been more amazed.

Deeti too was awake and listening, but she found little assurance in the story. I'll be glad when we're gone from this place, she whispered to Kalua. There's nothing worse than to sit here and feel the land pulling us back.

~

At dawn, with much greater regret than he had anticipated, Zachary said goodbye to Mr Doughty, who was now headed back to shore with his team. Once the pilot was gone it remained only to refresh a few supplies before weighing anchor and standing out to sea. The re-provisioning was quickly done, for the schooner was soon beseiged by a flotilla of bumboats: cabbage-carrying coracles, fruit-laden dhonies, and machhwas that were filled with goats, chickens and ducks. In this floating bazar there was everything a ship or a lascar might need: canvas by the gudge, spare jugboolaks and zambooras, coils of istingis and rup-yan, stacks of seetulpatty mats, tobacco by the batti, rolls of neem-twigs for the teeth, martabans of isabgol for constipation, and jars of columbo-root for dysentery: one ungainly gordower even had a choola going with a halwai frying up fresh jalebis. With so many vendors to set against each other, it took Steward Pinto and the mess-boys very little time to acquire everything that was needed by way of provisions.

By noon the schooner's anchors were a-trip and the trikat-wale were ready to haul on her hanjes—but the wind, which had been faltering all morning, chose just this time, or so the tindals said, to trap the vessel in a kalmariya. With her rigging taut, and her crew set to make sail, the *Ibis* lay becalmed in a looking-glass sea. At every change of watch, a man was sent aloft with instructions to sound the alert if any breath of wind should be felt to stir. But hour after hour went by, and the serang's shouted queries—*Hawá?*—met with nothing but denial: *Kuchho nahi.*

Sitting in the full glare of the sun, without a breeze to cool her, the schooner's hull trapped the heat so that down below, in the dabusa, it was as if the migrants' flesh were melting on their bones. To let in some air, the maistries removed the wooden hatch, leaving only the grating in place. But it was so still outside that scarcely a breath of air trickled through: instead, the perforations of the iron screen allowed the stench of the hold to rise slowly into the sky, summoning kites, vultures and sea-mews. Some circled lazily above, as if waiting for carrion, while others settled on the yards and shrouds, screeching like witches and peppering the decks with their droppings.

The rules for the rationing of drinking water were still new and unfamiliar to the girmitiyas: the system had not been put to any kind of test before, and now, as it began to break down, the patterns of order that had ruled the dabusa thus far broke down with it. By early afternoon, the day's allowance of drinking water had dwindled to a point where men were fighting for possession of those gharas that still contained a few sips. Egged on by Jhugroo, some half-dozen migrants climbed the ladder and began to beat on the gratings of the hatch: Water! Listen, up there! Our gharas need to be filled.

When the maistries came to remove the gratings there was

a near riot: dozens of men scrambled up the ladder in a desperate effort to force their way out on deck. But the hatch was only wide enough for a single man to pass through at a time and every head that was thrust out of it presented an easy target to the maistries. Their lathis came crashing down on the girmitiyas' skulls and shoulders, knocking them back inside, one after another. Within minutes both the grating and the hatch were slammed shut again.

Haramzadas!—the voice belonged to Bhyro Singh—I swear I'm going to straighten you out; you're the unruliest mob of coolies I've ever seen . . .

The disturbance, however, was not entirely unexpected, for it was rare for a contingent of girmitiyas to adapt themselves to the shipboard regimen without some resistance. The overseers had dealt with this kind of trouble before and knew exactly what to do: they shouted through the gratings to let the girmitiyas know that the Kaptan had ordered them to muster on the main deck; they were to come up the ladder in orderly fashion, one by one.

The maistries directed the women to come out of the hold first, but some of them were in such a bad way that they couldn't climb the ladder and had to be carried up. Paulette was the last woman to leave the hold and she did not realize how unsteady she was till she stepped on deck. Her knees shook, as if about to buckle, and she had to hold on to the deck rail to keep her balance.

A pipa of fresh water had been placed in the shade of the deck-house and a mess-boy was dipping into it to pour a couple of ladlefuls into each woman's lota. The jamna longboat was hanging a few steps aft of it and Paulette saw that several women had taken shelter beneath it, some squatting on their haunches and some lying prostrate: she pulled herself along the rails and squatted beside them, in the last remaining patch of shade. Like the others, Paulette drank deeply from her vessel before pouring the last trickle of moisture on her head, allowing it to seep slowly down the sweat-drenched ghungta that was draped over her face. With the water percolating through her parched innards, she began to feel the first tremors of life returning, not just to her body but also to her mind, which seemed to wake to consciousness after having lain long-dormant beneath her thirst.

Till this moment, defiance and determination had made Paulette wilfully blind to the possible privations of the voyage: she had told herself that she was younger and stronger than many of the others and had nothing to fear. But it was clear now that the weeks ahead would be hard beyond anything she had imagined; it was even possible that she would not live to see the journey's end. As the awareness of this took hold of her, she turned to look over her shoulder, at Ganga-Sagar Island, and found herself almost unconsciously trying to gauge the distance.

Then Bhyro Singh's voice rang out, signalling the completion of the muster: *Sab házir hai*! All present!

Turning aft, Paulette saw that Captain Chillingworth had appeared on the quarter-deck and was standing like a statue behind its balustrade of fife-rails. On the main deck, a ring of lascars, maistries and silahdars had been posted around the schooner's bulwarks to keep watch over the assembled girmitiyas.

Facing the assembly, lathi in hand, Bhyro Singh shouted: *Khamosh*! Silence! The Kaptan is going to speak and you will listen; the first to make a sound will feel my lathi on his head.

Up on the quarter-deck, the Captain was still motionless, with his hands clasped behind his back, calmly surveying the crowd on the deck. Although a light breeze had begun to blow now, it had little or no cooling effect, for the air seemed only to grow hotter under the Captain's gaze: when at last he spoke, his voice carried to the bows with the crackle of a leaping flame: 'Listen carefully to what I say, for none of it will be said again.'

The Captain paused to allow Baboo Nob Kissin to translate, and then, for the first time since he had appeared on the quarter-deck, his right hand came into view and was seen to be holding a tightly-coiled whip. Without turning his head, he gestured towards Ganga-Sagar Island, pointing with the weapon's tip.

. . . In that direction lies the coast from which you came. In the other lies the sea, known to you as the Black Water. You may think that the difference between the one and the other can be seen clearly with the naked eye. But that is not so. The greatest and most important difference between land and sea is not visible to the eye. It is this—and note it well . . .

Now, as Baboo Nob Kissin was translating, the Captain leant forward and put his whip and his white-knuckled hands on the fife-rails.

. . . The difference is that the laws of the land have no hold on the water. At sea there is another law, and you should know that on this vessel I am its sole maker. While you are on the *Ibis* and while she is at sea, I am your fate, your providence, your lawgiver. This chabuk you see in my hands is just one of the keepers of my law. But it is not the only one—there is another . . .

Here, the Captain held up his whip and curled the lash around the handle to form a noose.

. . . This is the other keeper of the law, and do not doubt for a moment that I will use it without hesitation if it should prove necessary. But remember, always, there is no better keeper of the law than submission and obedience. In that respect, this ship is no different from your own homes and villages. While you are on it, you must obey Subedar Bhyro Singh as you would your own zemindars, and as he obeys me. It is he who knows your ways and traditions, and while we are at sea he will be your *mái-báp*, just as I am his. You should know that it is because of his intercession that no one is being punished today; he has pleaded for mercy on your behalf, since you are new to this ship and its rules. But you should know also that the next time there is any disorder on board, the consequences will be severe, and they will be visited upon everyone who plays a part in it; anyone who thinks to make trouble should know that this is what awaits them . . .

*Amitav Ghosh*

Now the lash of the whip coiled out to make a crack that split the overheated air like a bolt of lightning.

Despite the heat of the sun the Captain's words had chilled Paulette to the marrow. As she looked around her now, she could see that many of the girmitiyas were in a trance of fear: it was as if they had just woken to the realization that they were not only leaving home and braving the Black Water— they were entering a state of existence in which their waking hours would be ruled by the noose and the whip. She could see their eyes straying to the island nearby; it was so close that its attraction was almost irresistible. When a grizzled, middle-aged man began to babble, she knew by instinct that he was losing his struggle against the pull of land. Although forewarned, she was still among the first to scream when this man made a sudden turn, shoved a lascar aside, and vaulted over the deck rail.

The silahdars raised the alarm by shouting—*Admi girah*! Man overboard!—and the girmitiyas—most of whom had no idea what was happening—began to mill about in panic. Under cover of the commotion, two more migrants broke through and made the leap, hurling themselves over the bulwark.

This sent the guards into a frenzy and they started to flail their lathis in an effort to herd the men back into the dabusa. To add to the confusion, the lascars were busy ripping the covers off the jamna longboat; when they tilted it sideways a flock of squawking hens and roosters descended upon the deck. The malums too had converged upon the boat, shouting hookums and pulling at the devis, raising clouds of chicken-muck that plastered them in feathers, shit and feed.

Temporarily forgotten, the women were left to huddle around the jamna devis. Craning over the deck rail, Paulette saw that one of the three swimmers had already disappeared below water; the other two were thrashing against a current that was sweeping them towards the open sea. Then a great flock of birds appeared above the swimmers, swooping down from time to time, as if to check whether they were still alive. Within a few minutes the swimmers' heads vanished, but still the birds remained, wheeling patiently above, as they waited for the corpses to float back to the surface. Although the bodies were not seen again, it was clear, from the way the birds were circling in the sky, that the corpses had been seized by the outgoing tide and were being swept towards the horizon.

This was why, when at last the long-awaited wind began to blow, the crew was exceptionally slow in making sail: because, after everything that had happened already, the prospect of crossing wakes with the three mutilated corpses had filled the lascars with an unspeakable dread.

*Amitav Ghosh*

# nineteen

~

Next morning, under a lamb's-wool sky, the *Ibis* ran into swells and gusts that set her to a frolicsome pitching. Many of the girmitiyas had begun to experience stirrings of discomfort while the *Ibis* was still on the Hooghly, for even at her most placid the schooner was a great deal livelier than the slow river-boats to which they were accustomed. Now, with the *Ibis* tipping all nines in a jabble-sea, many were reduced to a state of infantile helplessness.

Some half-dozen pails and wooden buckets had been distributed through the 'tween-deck, in preparation for the onset of seasickness. For a while, these were put to good use, with the steadier of the migrants helping the others to reach the balties before they spewed. But soon the containers were filled to overflowing, and their contents began to slop over the sides. As the vessel plunged and climbed, more and more of the migrants lost the use of their legs, emptying their stomachs where they lay. The smell of vomit added to the already noxious odours of the enclosed space, multiplying the effects of the vessel's motion. Soon it seemed as if the hold would be swamped by a rising tide of nausea. One night a man drowned in a pool of his own vomit, and such were the conditions that his death went unremarked for the better part of a day. By the time it was noticed, so few migrants could stand upright that the consigning of the corpse to the water was not witnessed by any of them.

Deeti, like many of the others, was oblivious to the fatality that had occurred nearby: even if she had known, she would not have had the strength to look in the dead man's direction. For several days she could not rise to her feet, far less leave the dabusa; it was a near-intolerable effort even to roll off her mat when Kalua wanted to wipe it clean. As for food and water, the very thought of them were enough to bring her gorge rushing to her lips: *Ham nahin tál sakelan*—I can't bear it, I can't . . .

Yes you can; you will.

As Deeti began to recover, Sarju grew steadily worse. One night her moaning became so piteous that Deeti, who was feeling none too spry herself, took her head into her own lap, and covered her forehead with a piece of moistened cloth. Suddenly she felt Sarju's body growing tense under her fingers. Sarju? she cried: Are you all right?

Yes, whispered Sarju. Hold still for a moment . . .

Alerted by Deeti's cry, some of the others turned to ask: What's happened to her? What's the matter?

Sarju raised a wavering finger to silence them, and then lowered her ear to Deeti's belly. The women held their breath until Sarju opened her eyes.

What? said Deeti. What's happened?

God has filled your lap, Sarju whispered. You are with child!

~

The one time when Captain Chillingworth was unfailingly present on deck was at noon, when he was joined by the two mates in shooting the sun. This was the part of the day that Zachary most looked forward to, and not even Mr Crowle's presence could diminish his pleasure in the ritual. It wasn't just that he enjoyed using his sextant, though that was no small part of it; for him this moment was a reward for the unceasing tedium of watch-on-watch and the constant aggravation of having to be at close quarters with the first mate: to see the schooner changing position on the charts was a reminder that this was not a journey without end. Every day, when Captain Chillingworth produced the schooner's chronometer, Zachary would go to great pains to synchronise his watch with it: the moving of the minute hand was evidence, too, that despite the unchanging horizon ahead, the schooner was steadily altering her place in the universe of time and space.

Mr Crowle did not possess a watch, and it irked him that Zachary had one. Every noon there was some new jibe: 'There he goes again, like a monkey with a nut . . .' Captain Chillingworth, on the other hand, was impressed by Zachary's exactitude: 'Always good to know where you stand in the world: never does a man any harm to know his place.'

One day, as Zachary was tweaking his watch, the Captain said: 'That's a pretty little gewgaw you've got there, Reid: would you mind if I took a look?'

'No, sir—not in the least.' Zachary snapped the cover shut and handed over his watch.

The Captain's eyebrows rose as he examined the filigreed designs. 'Fine little piece Reid; Chinese craftsmanship I should think: probably made in Macao.'

'Do they make watches there?'

'Oh yes,' said the Captain. 'Some very good ones too.' He flipped the lid open, and his eye went immediately to the lettering on the inside cover. 'What's this now?' He read the name out loud—Adam T. Danby—and repeated it, as if in disbelief: 'Adam Danby?' He turned to Zachary with a frown. 'May I ask how this came into your possession, Reid?'

'Why, sir . . .'

Had they been alone, Zachary would have had no hesitation in telling the Captain that Serang Ali had given him the watch: but with Mr Crowle within earshot, Zachary could not bring himself to hand over a fresh load of ammunition to be added to the first mate's armoury of jibes. 'Why, sir,' he said, with a shrug, 'I got it at a pawnshop, in Cape Town.'

'Did you now?' said the Captain. 'Well that's very interesting. Very interesting indeed.'

'Really, sir? How so?'

The Captain looked up at the sun and mopped his face. 'The tale's a bit of a breezo and will take some telling,' he said. 'Let's go below where we can sit down.'

Leaving the deck to the first mate, Zachary and the Captain went down to the cuddy and seated themselves at the table.

'Did you know this Adam Danby, sir?' said Zachary.

'No,' said the Captain. 'Never met him in person. But there was a time when he was well-known in these parts. Long before your day, of course.'

'Who was he, sir, if I might ask?'

'Danby?' the Captain gave Zachary a half-smile. 'Why he was none other than "the White Ladrone".'

'"Ladrone", sir . . .?'

'Ladrones are the pirates of the South China Sea, Reid; named after a group of islands off the Bocca Tigris. Not much left of them now, but there was a time when they were the most fearsome band of cutthroats on the high seas. When I was a younker they were skippered by a man called Cheng-I— savage brute he was too. Up and down the coast he'd go, as far as Cochin-China, pillaging villages, taking captives, putting people to the sword. Had a wife too—a bit of bobtail from a Canton fancy-house. Madame Cheng we used to call her. But the woman wasn't enough for Mr Cheng-I. Captured a young fisherman on one of his raids and made a mate of him too! Enough to put Madame Cheng's nose out of joint, you'd think? Not a bit of it. When old Cheng-I died, she actually married her rival! Two of them set themselves up as the King and Queen of the Ladrones!'

The Captain shook his head slowly, as if at the memory of an ancient and long-lingering bemusement. 'You might think this pair would be strung up by their own crew, wouldn't you? But no: in China nothing is ever as you expect; just when you think you've made sense of them, they'll send you up Tom Cox's traverse.'

'How do you mean, sir?'

'Well just think of it: not only were Madame Cheng and

her rival-turned-husband accepted as the cutthroats' leaders—they went on to build themselves a pirate empire. Ten thousand junks under their command at one time, with over a hundred thousand men! Caused so much trouble the Emperor had to send an army against her. Her fleet was broken up and she surrendered, with her husband.'

'And what became of them?' said Zachary.

The Captain gave a snort of laughter. 'You'd think they'd get the hempen habeas, wouldn't you? But no—that would be too straight a course for the Celestials. They put a mandarin's hat on the boy's head and as for Madame Cheng, she was let off with a earwigging and a fine. Still at large in Canton. Runs a snuggery, I'm told.'

'And Danby, sir?' said Zachary. 'Was he mixed up with Madame Cheng and her crew?'

'No,' said the Captain. 'She'd been beached by the time he came into these waters. Her followers, or what was left of them, had broken up into small bands. You wouldn't know their junks from any other country boat—little floating kampungs they were, with pigs and chickens, fruit trees and vegetable gardens. Had their women and children with them too. Some of their junks were really no better than the usual Canton flower-boat, part gambling-den and part knockingshop. They'd hide in the coves and inlets, raiding coastal vessels and preying on shipwrecks. That's how Danby fell into their hands.'

'Shipwrecked was he, sir?'

'That's right,' said the Captain, scratching his chin. 'Let me see: when did the *Lady Duncannon* run aground? Must have been '12 or '13—about twenty-five years ago I'd say. Foundered off Hainan Island. Most of her crew managed to get back to Macao. But one of the ship's boats was lost, with some ten or fifteen hands, Danby among them. What happened to the others I can't say, but this much is for sure, that Danby ended up with a band of Ladrones.'

'Did they capture him?'

'Either that, or found him washed ashore. Probably the latter, if you think about the course he took afterwards.'

'Which was . . .?'

'Turned into a catspaw for the Ladrones.'

'A catspaw, sir?'

'Yes,' said the Captain. 'Went native, did Danby. Married one of their women. Togged himself up in sheets and dishcloths. Learnt the lingo. Ate snakes with sticks. The lot. Can't blame him in a way. He was just a joskin of a cabin-boy, from Shoreditch or some other London rookery. Packed off to sea as soon as he could walk. No easy thing to be a drudge, you know. Pulley-hauley all day and fighting off the old cadgers all night. Not much to eat but lobscouse and old horse; Gunner's Daughter the only woman in sight. Between the bawdy-baskets and the food, a Ladrone junk must have been a taste of paradise. Shouldn't think it took too much for them to bring him sharp about—probably had him horizontalized under a staff-climber as soon as he was strong enough to stand. But he was no pawk, Danby, had a good head on him. Invented a devilish clever bit of flummery. He'd get togged out in his best go-ashores and hie off to some port like Manila or Anjer. The Ladrones would slip in after him and they'd pick a vessel that was short-handed. Danby'd sign on as a mate, and the Ladrones as lascars. No one'd suspect a thing, of course. White man playing catskin for a kippage of Long-tails? Last thought to enter any shipmaster's head. And Danby was a fine old glib-gabbet too. Bought himself the best clothes and gewgaws to be found in the East. Wouldn't show his hand till the vessel was safe out at sea—and then suddenly there they were, flying their colours, boarding her in the smoke. Danby would disarm the officers and the Ladrones would deal with the rest. They'd pack their captives into the ship's boats and cut them adrift. Then away they'd go, galing off with their prize. It was the most fiendishly clever ruse. Their luck ran out somewhere off Java Head as I remember. Intercepted by an English ship-o'-the-line while trying to sail off with a prize. Danby was killed, along with most of the gang. But a few of the Ladrones got away. I imagine it was one of them who pawned this watch of yours.'

'Do you really think so, sir?'

'Why yes, of course,' said the Captain. 'Do you think you might remember where you got it?'

Zachary began to stutter. 'I think . . . I think I might, sir.'

'Well,' said the Captain, 'when we get to Port Louis, you must be sure to take your tale to the authorities.'

'Really, sir? Why?'

'Oh I should think they'd be very interested in tracing your watch to its last owner.'

Chewing his lip, Zachary looked at the watch again, remembering the moment when the serang had handed it to him. 'And if they caught the last owner, sir?' he said. 'What do you think they'd do?'

'Oh they'd have a lot of questions for him I don't doubt,' said the Captain. 'And if there was any hint of a connection with Danby I'm sure they'd hang him. Not the least doubt about it: there's a nubbing-chit waiting for any member of the Danby gang who's still on the prowl.'

~

After a few days the majority of the migrants began to recover from their seasickness. Yet, even as the others were getting better, a few showed no signs of improvement at all, and some grew steadily weaker and more helpless so that their bodies could be seen to be wasting away. Although their number was not large, they had a disproportionate effect on the others: following upon all the other mishaps of the journey, their deteriorating condition created an atmosphere of despondency and demoralization in which many who had recovered began to ail afresh.

Every few days, the maistries would sprinkle vinegar or powdered lime around the edges of the hold, and a few of the patients would be given foul-smelling, gummy potions to drink. Many would spit out the liquid as soon as the guards' backs were turned, for it was rumoured that the so-called medicine had been concocted from the hoofs and horns of pigs, cows and horses. In any case, the medicines seemed to have no effect at all on the worst-affected migrants, of whom there were about a dozen.

The next to die was a thirty-year-old coppersmith from Ballia, a man whose once-robust body had dwindled almost to a skeleton. He had no relatives on board, and only one friend, who was himself too ill to go on deck when the dead man's body was cast into the water.

At that time Deeti was still too weak to sit up or take notice, but by the time the next death occurred, she was well on her way to recovery: in this instance, the deceased was a young Muslim julaha from Pirpainti, who was travelling with two cousins. The dead weaver's companions were even younger than he, and neither of them was in a state to protest when a squad of silahdars came down to the dabusa and ordered them to heave the body up so that it could be tipped overboard.

Deeti was not especially inclined to intervene, but when it became clear that no one else was going to say anything, what could she do but speak up? Wait! she told the two boys. This isn't right, what they're telling you to do.

The three silahdars rounded on her angrily: You stay out of this; it's none of your business.

But of course it is, she retorted. He may be dead but he's still one of us: you can't just throw him away like the skin of a peeled onion.

So what do you expect? said the silahdars. Do you want us to stop and make a big tamasha every time a coolie dies?

Just a little *izzat*; some respect . . . it's not right to treat us like this.

And who's going to stop us? came the sneering response. You?

Not me maybe, said Deeti. But there are others here . . .

By this time, many of the girmitiyas had risen to their feet, not with the intention of confronting the silahdars, but mostly out of curiosity. The guards, however, had noted the stir of movement with no little apprehension. The three silahdars began to edge nervously towards the ladder, where one of them paused to ask, in a voice that was suddenly conciliatory: What's to be done with him, then?

Give his relatives some time to talk things over, said Deeti. They can decide what is necessary.

We'll see what the subedar says.

With that, the guards went back on deck, and after a half-hour or so, one of them shouted through the hatch to let the migrants know that the subedar had agreed to let the dead man's kin sort the matter out for themselves. This concession was met with jubilation below, and more than a dozen men offered their help in carrying the body up to the deck.

Later, the dead man's kin sought Deeti out to let her know that the body had been cleaned as prescribed before being consigned to the sea. Everyone agreed that this was a signal victory, and not even the most quarrelsome or envious men could deny that it was largely Deeti's doing.

Kalua alone was less than completely happy about the outcome. Bhyro Singh may have given in this time, he whispered in Deeti's ear, but he's not glad about it. He's been asking who was behind the trouble and whether it was the same woman as before.

Deeti, elated by her success, shrugged this off. What can he do now? she said. We're at sea—he can't send us back, can he?

~

'Take in the flying jib!'—*Tán fulána-jíb*!

Through most of the morning the schooner had been close-hauled to the strengthening wind and the masts had been crowded thesam-thes, with a great press of sail. But now, with the sun overhead, the swells in the heaving sea had mounted to a height where the schooner was being continually pooped by surging waves. Zachary, glorying in the power of the vessel, would have kept all her canvas aloft, but was over-ruled by the Captain, who ordered him to reduce sail.

'Standy by!'—*Sab taiyár*!

Taking in the flying-jib required only one man to go aloft,

usually the quickest and lightest of the trikat-wale. Ascending almost to the truck of the foremast, the lascar would unloose the hinch that secured the sail's head, while the others waited below, between the bows, in order to wrestle the canvas down and stow it on its boom. By rights it should have fallen to Jodu to go up alone, but Mamdoo-tindal hated to work on the jib-boom, especially when the thirty-foot spar was ploughing in and out of the water, drenching all those who were clinging to it. Under the pretext of making sure the job was done right, the tindal followed Jodu up the mast and made himself comfortable on the baopar side of the sabar-purwan, seating himself on the yard while Jodu climbed still further up, to wrestle with the hinch.

'Haul aft the sheet!'—*Dáman tán chikár*!

Hold on! Mamdoo-tindal's warning came just as the knot sprung loose.

Suddenly, as if seized by panic, the canvas reared up and flung itself against Jodu: it was as if a hunted swan were trying to beat off a pursuer with a frenzied thrashing of its wings. Just in time, Jodu fastened both arms around the mast and clung on, while the men below began to haul on the hanjes, to sheet the sail home. But with the updraughts blowing strong, the sail did not go easily and the canvas kept rearing up, as if to snap at Jodu's heels.

You see, said Mamdoo-tindal, with no little satisfaction. It's not as easy as you launders think.

Easy? Who'd think that?

Slipping down from the masthead, Jodu seated himself astride the sabar yard so that he was sitting with his back to the tindal, with the mast in between. On either side of the schooner, the sea was striped with wide swathes of black shadow, marking the valleys between the swells. Up on the yard, where the ship's motions were exaggerated by the height of the mast, it was if they were sitting on a palm tree that was swaying from side to side. Jodu tightened his hold, weaving his arms through the sawais, knowing full well that with the water heaving as it was, a fall would mean certain death. With the wind gusting like this, it would take at least an hour to bring the schooner about, and the chances of survival were so slight that the afsars were unlikely even to change course: yet, there was no denying that the danger added a dash of mirch to the masala of the masts.

Mamdoo-tindal was of the same mind. He pointed to the outermost tip of the jib-boom, which was known to the lascars as the *Shaitán-jíb*—the Devil's-tongue—because so many sailors had lost their lives there. We're lucky to be here, he said. Just look at those poor buggers down there—the gandus are getting a bath like they've never had. *Chhi*! How it would make Ghaseeti's kajal run!

Glancing down at the schooner's bows, Jodu saw that the Devil's-tongue was plunging in and out of the swells, ducking the lascars who were sitting astride it, and tossing plumes of water over the deck, drenching the migrants who were emerging from the hatch for their midday meal. Under Jodu's feet, below the footropes, there was an elliptical opening between the billowing trikat and the bara: this gap afforded a view of the waist of the schooner, and looking through it now, Jodu saw two sari-clad figures sitting crouched under the jamna devis. He knew, from the colour of the sari, that one of them was Munia, and he knew, too, from the incline of her veiled head, that she was looking at him.

This exchange of glances did not elude Mamdoo-tindal, who curled his elbow around the mast to give Jodu a jab in the ribs. Are you staring at that girl again, you fuckwit of a launder?

Surprised by the severity of his tone, Jodu said: What's wrong with looking, Mamdoo-ji?

Listen to me, boy, said Mamdoo-tindal. Can't you see? You're a lascar and she's a coolie; you're a Muslim and she's not. There's nothing for you in this: nothing but a whipping. Do you understand?

Jodu burst into laughter. Arre Mamdoo-ji, he said, you take things too seriously sometimes. What's wrong with a couple of jokes and a laugh? Doesn't it help the time pass?

And wasn't it you said that when Ghaseeti was my age she always got whoever she wanted—no jhula or bunk was safe from her?

*Tchhi*! Turning away from the wind, the tindal ejected a gob of spittle that sailed away across the length of the yard, landing in the sea on the far side of the schooner. Listen, boy, he muttered darkly, under his breath. If you don't know why this is different, then a dismasting may be just what you need.

~

Even with fetters on his wrists, Ah Fatt possessed a sureness of hand that was astonishing to Neel. That he should be able to pluck flies out of the air—not swat, but pluck, trapping the insects between the tips of thumb and forefinger—was remarkable enough, but that he should be able to do this in the dark seemed scarcely credible. Often, at night, when Neel was ineffectually flailing his hands at a fly or mosquito, Ah Fatt would catch hold of his arm and tell him to lie still: 'Shh! Let me listen.'

To ask for silence in the chokey was to expect too much: what with the creaking of the ship's timbers, the lapping of the water beneath the hull, the tread of the sailors above, and the voices of the migrants on the far side of the bulwark, it was never quiet within its confines. But Ah Fatt seemed to be able to use his senses in such a way as to block out some noises while focusing on others: when the insect made itself heard again, his hand would come shooting out of the darkness to put an end to its drone. It didn't seem to matter even if the insect settled on Neel's body: Ah Fatt would pluck it out of the darkness in such a way that Neel would feel nothing but a slight pinch on his skin.

But tonight it was neither the hum of an insect nor Neel's flailing that made Ah Fatt say: 'Shh! Listen.'

'What is it?'

'Listen.'

Suddenly Ah Fatt's fetters moved, and their rattle was

followed by a frantic, high-pitched squeaking. Then there was a snapping sound, like that of a bone breaking.

'What was it?' said Neel.

'Rat.' An odour of excrement filled the chokey as Ah Fatt removed the cover of the toilet bucket to drop the dead creature inside.

Neel said: 'I don't understand how you can catch it with your bare hands.'

'Learnt.'

'To catch flies and mice?'

Ah Fatt laughed. 'No. Learnt to listen.'

'From whom?'

'Teacher.'

Neel, for all his connoisseurship of teachers and tutors, could think of none who would teach this particular skill. 'What kind of teacher would teach you that?'

'Teacher who teach to box.'

Neel was more than ever mystified. 'A boxing teacher?'

Ah Fatt laughed again. 'Strange no? Father made to learn.'

'But why?'

'He want me be like English Man,' said Ah Fatt. 'Want me learn things that Man must know—rowing, hunting, cricket. But in Guangzhou, there is no hunting and there is no garden for cricket. And rowing is done by servant. So he makes to learn boxing.'

'Your father? Did you live with your father then?'

'No. Live with Grandmother. In junk.'

The vessel was actually a Canton kitchen-boat, with a wide, flat prow, where dishes could be washed and pigs butchered. Aft of the prow was the galley, with a four-fire oven, sheltered by a bamboo roof; the middle section was sunken, and shaded by an awning, with a low table and benches for customers; the stern was square and high, with a double-decked house perched on it: this was where the family lived—Ah Fatt, his mother, his grandmother and whichever cousins or other relatives happened to be passing through.

The kitchen-boat was a gift from Ah Fatt's father, and it

was a step up in the world for the family: before the boy was born they had lived in a snail-boat that was half the size. Barry would have liked to do still better by his son, the guilt of whose illegitimacy lay heavy on him: he would gladly have bought Chi Mei and her family a house, in the city or in one of the nearby villages—Chuen-pi, for instance, or Whampoa. But this was a Dan family, bred to the river and unwelcome on land. Barry knew this, and raised no objection, although he did make it clear that he would have liked them to acquire a vessel that did him some credit: a big, colourful pleasure-barge, for instance, of the kind that he could have boasted of to his comprador, Chunqua. But Chi Mei and her mother were of thrifty stock, and a dwelling that provided no income was, to them, as useless a thing as a barren sow. Not only did they insist on buying a kitchen-boat, they moored it within sight of the Fanqui-town, so it happened that when Ah Fatt was put to work, helping with customers—which began almost as soon as he learnt to keep his footing on a tilted deck—he could be seen clearly from the windows of the White-hat factory.

*Kyá-ré*? the other Parsis would laugh; fine fellow you are, Barry—letting your bastard grow up like a boat-boy. For your daughters you're building mansions on Queensway—nothing for this bugger? True he's not one of us, but there's something there, no? Can't just turn your back on him . . .

This was unjust, for it was patent for all to see, Parsis and others alike, that Barry was an indulgent and ambitious father, who had every intention of providing his only son with the wherewithal to set himself up as a gentleman of good standing: the boy was to be erudite, active, and urbane, as handy with rod and gun as with book and pen; a Man who spouted Manliness like a whale exhales spray. If schools refused to accept the illegitimate son of a boatwoman, then he would hire special tutors, to teach him reading and penmanship, in Chinese and English—that way, he could always make a career for himself as a linkister, translating between the Fanquis and their hosts. There were many such in Canton, but most were utterly incompetent; the boy could easily learn to outdo them all and might even make a name for himself.

To find tutors who were willing to teach in a Dan kitchen-boat was no easy matter, but through Chunqua's good offices, some were found. Ah Fatt took readily to his lessons and every year when his father returned to Canton for the season, the records of his progress grew longer and longer, the calligraphy ever more stylish. Every year, Barry would bring extravagant gifts from Bombay, to thank his comprador for keeping an eye on the progress of the boy's education; every year Chunqua in turn would reciprocate with a present of his own, usually a book for the boy.

In Ah Fatt's thirteenth year, the present was a fine edition of that famous and beloved tale, *Journey to the West.*

Barry was much enthused when the name was translated for him: 'It'll do him good to read about Europe and America. Some day I will send him on a visit.'

Not without some embarrassment, Chunqua explained that the West in question was somewhat nearer at hand; in fact it was intended to be none other than Mr Moddie's very own homeland—Hindusthan, or Jambudvipa as it was called in the old books.

'Oh?' Although no longer so enthusiastic, Barry gave the boy his present anyway, little knowing that he would soon regret this offhand decision. Later, he came to be convinced that it was this book that was responsible for the fancies that entered Ah Fatt's head: 'Want to go West . . .'

Every time the boy saw him, he would plead to visit his father's homeland. But this was the one indulgence Barry could not grant: to think of letting the boy sail to Bombay on one of his father-in-law's ships; to imagine him walking down the gangplank, into a crowd of waiting relatives; to conceive of presenting his mother-in-law, his wife, his daughters, with fleshly evidence of his other life, in Canton, which they knew of only as a provenance for finely embroidered silks, pretty fans and torrents of silver—none of these notions could be entertained for more than a moment; why, it would be like unloosing an army of termites on the parqueted floors of his Churchgate mansion. The other Parsis in Canton might know about the boy, but he knew he could trust them to be discreet back home: after all, he, Barry, was not the only one to lapse from bachelordom during these long months of exile. And even if a whisper or two were to reach his hometown, he knew people would ignore them so long as the evidence was kept safely hidden from view. If, on the other hand, he were to bring the boy back, for people to see with their own eyes, then a great flame of scandal would erupt from the doors of the fire-temple, to light a conflagration that would ultimately consume his lucrative living.

No, Freddy, listen to me, he said to Ah Fatt. This 'West' you've got in your head is just something that was made up in a silly old book. Later, when you're grown up, I'll send you to the real West—to France or America or England, some place where people are civilized. When you get there you'll be able to set yourself up as a prince or a fox-hunting man. But don't think of Hindusthan; forget about it. It's the one place that's not good for you.

'And he was right,' said Ah Fatt. 'Was not good for me.'

'Why? What did you do?'

'Robbery. Did robbery.'

'When? Where?'

Ah Fatt rolled away, burying his face. ''Nother time,' he said, in a muffled voice. 'Not now.'

~

The turbulence of the open sea had a calamitous effect on Baboo Nob Kissin's processes of digestion and many days passed before he was able to make his way from the midships-cabin to the main deck. But when at last he stepped into the open air and felt the moisture of the sea on his face, he understood that all those days of dizziness, diarrhoea and vomiting were the necessary period of suffering that precedes a moment of illumination: for he had only to look at the spindrift that was flying off the schooner's bows to know that the *Ibis* was not a ship like any other; in her inward reality she

*Amitav Ghosh*

was a vehicle of transformation, travelling through the mists of illusion towards the elusive, ever-receding landfall that was Truth.

Nowhere was this transformation more evident than in himself, for the presence of Taramony was so palpable within him now that his outer body felt increasingly like the spent wrappings of a cocoon, destined soon to fall away from the new being that was gestating within. Every day offered some fresh sign of the growing fullness of the womanly presence inside him—for example, his mounting revulsion at the coarseness of the maistries and silahdars with whom he had perforce to live: when he heard them speaking of breasts and buttocks, it was as if his own body were being discussed and derided; at times, his need to veil himself was so intense that he would pull a sheet over his head. His maternal stirrings too had now grown so exigent that he could not walk across the main deck without lingering awhile over that part of it which lay above the convicts' cell.

This proclivity earned him many earfuls of galis from the lascars, and several angry tirades from Serang Ali: 'What for you standi here likee cock-a-roach? Bugger too muchi foolo—nevva hit any use.'

Mr Crowle was even more direct: 'Pander, y'spigot-sucking gobble-prick! With all the wide welkin around us, why d'ye always have to be beating the booby right here? I tell yer, Pander, I see yer here again and I'm going to splice a cuntline to yer arse.'

To these assaults on his dignity the gomusta tried always to respond with queenly self-possession. 'Sir, I must deplore to your fulsome remarks. There is no need to pass dirty-dirty comments. Why all the time you are giving dagger-looks and criticizing? Only I have come to take air and refresh. If you are busy you need not bestow undue attention.'

But the semi-proximity of his lingering presence on deck was galling not just to the sailors, but also to Taramony, whose voice was now often in Baboo Nob Kissin's head, urging him to enter the very precincts of the chokey, to bring her closer to her adopted son. These promptings precipitated a raging conflict between the emergent mother, seeking to comfort her child, and that part of Baboo Nob Kissin which continued to be a worldly gomusta, bound by all manner of everyday proprieties.

But I can't go down there! he would protest. What will people think?

How does it matter? she would respond. You can do what you like: aren't you the ship's supercargo?

There was no denying that Baboo Nob Kissin was one of the few people on the *Ibis* who had the right of access to every part of the ship. As the supercargo, he often had business with the Captain and was regularly to be seen making his way into the officers' part of the ship, where he would sometimes lurk at Zachary's door, in the hope of hearing his flute once again. In his official capacity, he had also been empowered, by Mr Burnham, to inspect the other parts of the vessel, and he even had in his possession a set of spare keys for the chokey.

None of this was a secret from Taramony, and as the days passed it became clear to Baboo Nob Kissin that if she was ever to manifest herself in him, then he would have to embrace every aspect of her being, including her capacity for maternal love. There was no getting out of it: he would have to find a way to the chokey.

~

Like an animal returning to its natural element, the *Ibis* seemed to grow ever more exuberant as she went lasking along on the open sea. The schooner had been on the Bay of Bengal for exactly a week when Paulette looked up from her washing one afternoon, and noticed that the sky above was a luminous, radiant blue, its colour deepened by flecks of cloud that mirrored the crests on the water below. The wind was blowing strong and hard, and the waves and clouds seemed to be racing each other across a single, vast firmament, with the schooner straining in pursuit, her timbers groaning with the effort of the chase. It was as if the alchemy of the open water had endowed her with her own will, her own life.

Leaning over the rail, Paulette gingerly lowered her balty to draw some water. As she was pulling the bucket up again a flying fish came rocketing out but only to leap back into the waves. The flutter of its wings drew a squeal of laughter from Paulette and startled her into tipping her balty over, spilling the water partly on herself and partly on the deck. Alarmed at the mess, she fell to her knees and was busily pushing the water down the scuppers when she heard a peremptory shout: 'You there—yes you!'

It was Mr Crowle, and much to Paulette's relief, he was shouting not at her, but at someone else: since his voice was pitched to the tone he commonly employed with the lowest of the lascars, Paulette assumed that he was shouting at some unfortunate launder or topas. But such was not the case; looking aft, she saw that it was Zachary who had been thus addressed. He was on the quarter-deck, heading back to his cabin after the end of his watch. His face went red as he came to the fife-rails. 'Were you speaking to me, Mr Crowle?'

'That's right.'

'What is it?'

'What's this hugger-mugger business over here? Were y'fuckin asleep on yer watch?'

'Where, Mr Crowle?'

'Come'n see for yer own bleedin self.'

This being a mealtime, the deck was about as noisy as it ever was, with dozens of girmitiyas, overseers, lascars and bhandaris, talking, jostling, and arguing over the food. The exchange between the mates brought the hubbub to an abrupt end: that there was bad blood between the malums was a secret to no one, and every eye turned to watch as Zachary made his way forward, towards the bows.

'What's wrong, Mr Crowle?' said Zachary, stepping up to the fo'c'sle-deck.

'You tell me.' The first mate pointed at something ahead and Zachary leant over the bows to take a look. 'D'ye have the eyes to see it, Mannikin—or do you need it explained?'

'I see the problem, Mr Crowle,' said Zachary straightening up. 'The traveller is unseized and the jib and martingale are afoul of the dolphin-striker. How it happened I cannot imagine, but I'll fix it.'

Zachary had begun to roll up his sleeves when Mr Crowle stopped him. 'Not yer job, Reid. Not yer place to tell me how it's to be fixed neither. Nor who's to do it.'

Turning aft, the first mate surveyed the deck with a hand over his eyes, squinting hard, as though he were looking for someone in particular. The search ended when he caught sight of Jodu, who was lounging in the kursi of the foremast: 'You there, Sammy!' He curled his finger to summon Jodu to the bows.

'Sir?' Taken by surprise, Jodu pointed to himself, as if to ask for confirmation.

'Yes, you! Get a move on, Sammy.'

'Sir!'

While Jodu was climbing down, Zachary was remonstrating with the first mate: 'He'll only do himself harm, Mr Crowle. He's a raw hand . . .'

'Not so raw he couldn't pick y'out o'the water,' said the first mate. 'Let's see him try his luck with the jib-boom.'

Alarmed now, Paulette elbowed her way to the forward bulwarks, where many migrants were standing clustered, and found herself a spot from which she could watch Jodu as he climbed out on the schooner's bowsprit, over the heaving sea. Till now, Paulette had paid little attention to the vessel's architecture, treating its masts, sails and rigging as a crazed cat's-cradle of canvas and hemp, pulleys and pins. She saw now that the bowsprit, for all that it looked like a mere extension of the schooner's ornamental figurehead, was actually a third mast, a lateral one, that stuck out over the water. Like the other two masts, the bowsprit was equipped with an extension, the jib-boom, so that the whole ensemble, when fitted together, jutted a good thirty feet beyond the schooner's cutwater. Strung out along the boom were three triangular lateen sails: it was the outermost of these that had somehow wrapped itself into a tangle and that was where Jodu was making his way, to the farthest tip of the jib-boom—the Devil's-tongue.

The *Ibis* was mounting a wave as Jodu began his advance, and the first part of his journey was an ascent, in which he was pulling himself along a pole that was pointing skywards. But when the crest of the wave passed, the climb became a descent, with the Devil's-tongue angled towards the depths. He reached the jib just as the *Ibis* went nose-first into the trough between two swells. The momentum of the schooner's slide sent it plunging into the water, with Jodu clinging on, like a barnacle to the snout of a sounding whale. Down and down he went, the white of his banyan becoming first a blur, and then disappearing wholly from view as the sea surged over the bowsprit and lapped over the bulwark. Paulette caught her breath as he went under, but he was gone so long that she was forced to breathe again—and yet again—before the *Ibis* began to raise her nose from the water, riding the next upswell. Now, as the bowsprit rose from the water, Jodu was seen to be lying flat, with his arms and legs wrapped tightly around the wooden tongue. When it reached the end of its trajectory, the jib seemed to flip upwards, as if to send its rider catapulting into the clouds of canvas above. A stream of water came sluicing back, along the bowsprit, drenching many of the spectators who were standing crowded around the bows. Paulette scarcely noticed the water: she wanted only to know that Jodu was alive, and still able to hold on—after a ducking like that, surely he would need whatever strength he had left for the climb back to the deck?

Zachary, in the meanwhile, was stripping off his shirt: 'The hell with you, Mr Crowle; I'm not going to stand by and see a man lost.'

The schooner was mounting a swell when Zachary leapt on the bowsprit, and the Devil's-tongue was still above water when he passed the dolphin-striker. During the next few seconds, with the schooner's head clear of the waves, Jodu and Zachary worked fast, cutting away ropes and cables, thrusting blocks and pulleys into their pockets. Then the schooner began its downwards plunge and both men flattened themselves on the boom—but their hands were now hampered with so many odds and ends of rope and canvas that it seemed impossible that they would be able to find a proper hold.

*Hé Rám*! A collective cry went up from the migrants as the Devil's-tongue plunged into the water, pushing the sailors below the surface. Suddenly, with the shock of an epiphany, it dawned on Paulette that the sea now had in its grasp the two people who mattered most to her in all the world. She could not bear to watch and her gaze strayed instead to Mr Crowle. He too, had his eyes fixed on the bowsprit, and she saw, to her astonishment, that his face, usually so hard and glowering, had turned as liquid as the sea, with currents of cross-cutting emotion whirling across it. Then a spirited cheer—*Jai Siyá-Rám*!—drew her eyes back to the bowsprit, which had emerged from the water with the two men still clinging on.

Tears of relief sprung to her eyes as Zachary and Jodu slid off the bowsprit, to drop safely back on deck. By some quirk of fate, Jodu's feet came to rest within inches of her own. Even if she had wanted to, she could not have stopped herself from saying something: her lips breathed his name as if of their own accord: Jodu!

His eyes widened as he turned to look at her ghungta'd head, and she made only the tiniest motion to caution him— as in childhood, it was enough; he was not one to betray a secret. Bowing her head, she slipped away and went back to her washing.

It was only when she was stepping away from the scuppers, to hang the washing on the after-shrouds, that she saw Jodu again. He was whistling nonchalantly, carrying a pintle in his hands. As he went past, the pintle dropped and he fell to his knees, scrambling about, as if he were chasing it across the tilted deck.

Putli? he hissed as he passed her. Is it really you?

What do you think? Didn't I say I'd be on board?

He gave a muffled laugh: I should have known.

Not to a word to anyone, Jodu.

Done. But only if you put in a word for me.

With who?

Munia, he whispered, as he rose to his feet.

Munia! Stay away from her, Jodu; you'll only get yourself in trouble . . .

But her warning was wasted, for he was already gone.

# twenty

~

Was it because of the glow of Deeti's pregnancy? Or was it because of her success in dealing with the maistries? Either way, it happened that more and more people took to calling her Bhauji: it was as if she had been appointed the matron of the dabusa by common consent. Deeti gave the matter no thought: there was nothing to be done, after all, if everybody wanted to treat her as if she were their older brother's wife. She might have been less sanguine if she had considered the responsibilities that went with being a Bhauji to the world at large—but not having done so, she was caught unawares when Kalua told her that he had been approached by someone who wanted her advice on a matter of grave importance.

Why me? she said in alarm.

Who else but Bhauji? said Kalua, with a smile.

All right, she said. Tell me: *Ká? Káwan? Kethié?* What? Who? Why?

The man in question, Kalua told her, was Ecka Nack, the leader of the group of hillsmen who had joined the migrants at Sahibganj. Deeti knew him by sight: a bandy-legged, muscular man, he had the grizzled look and thoughtful mien of a village elder, although he was probably no older than thirty-five.

What does he want? said Deeti.

He wants to know, said Kalua, whether Heeru would be willing to set up house with him when we reach Mareech.

Heeru? This so amazed Deeti that she could not speak for

several minutes. She had noticed of course—and who could not?—the hungry glances that came the way of every woman on the ship. Yet, she would never have thought that Heeru—poor, simple-minded Heeru, who had become a girmitiya almost by accident, after being abandoned by her husband at a mela—would be the first to elicit a serious offer.

And here was another puzzle: if this was indeed a serious proposal, then what was it for? Surely it could not be marriage? Heeru was, by her own account, a married woman, whose husband was still alive; and no doubt Ecka Nack himself had a wife or two, back in the hills of Chhota Nagpur. Deeti tried to think of what his village might be like, but such was her plainswoman's horror of the hills that she could only shudder. Had they been at home, the match would have been inconceivable—but over there, on the island, what would it matter whether you were from the plains or the hills? For Heeru to set up house with a hillsman would be no different from what she, Deeti, had done herself. Surely all the old ties were immaterial now that the sea had washed away their past?

If only it were so!

If the Black Water could really drown the past, then why should she, Deeti, still be hearing voices in the recesses of her head, condemning her for running away with Kalua? Why should she know that no matter how hard she tried, she would never be able to silence the whispers that told her she would suffer for what she had done—not just today or tomorrow, but for kalpas and yugas, through lifetime after lifetime, into eternity. She could hear those murmurs right now, asking: Do you want Heeru to share the same fate?

This thought made her groan in annoyance: what right did anyone have to thrust her into this tangle? Who was Heeru to her after all? Neither aunt nor cousin nor niece. Why should she, Deeti, be made to bear the burden of her fate?

Yet, despite her resentment of the imposition, Deeti could not help but recognize that Ecka Nack was, by his own lights, trying to do what was right and honourable. Now that they were all cut off from home, there was nothing to prevent men and women from pairing off in secret, as beasts, demons and pishaches were said to do: there was no pressing reason for them to seek the sanction of anything other than their own desires. With no parents or elders to decide on these matters, who knew what was the right way to make a marriage? And wasn't it she herself who had said, at the start, that they were all kin now; that their rebirth in the ship's womb had made them into a single family? But true as that might be, it was true also that they were not yet so much a family as to make decisions for one another: Heeru would have to decide for herself.

~

In the past few days Zachary's mind had returned often to Captain Chillingworth's account of the White Ladrone. In trying to fit the pieces of the story together, Zachary had extended to Serang Ali the benefit of every possible doubt— but no matter how charitably he looked at it, he could not rid himself of the suspicion that the serang had been priming him, Zachary, to step into Danby's shoes. The thought gave him no rest and he longed to discuss the matter with someone. But who? His relationship with the first mate being what it was, there was no question of broaching it with him. Zachary decided instead that he would take the Captain into his confidence.

It was the *Ibis*'s eleventh day on the open sea, and as the sun began to descend the heavens filled with sonder-clouds and mares' tails: soon enough the schooner was beating to windward under what was undeniably a mackerel sky. At sunset the wind changed too, with the schooner being assailed by gusts and squalls that kept turning her sails aback, with thunderous detonations of canvas.

Mr Crowle was on the first watch of the night, and Zachary knew that the cluttery weather would serve to keep him occupied on deck. But just to be sure of having him out of the way, he waited till the second bell of the watch before crossing the cuddy to the Captain's stateroom. He had to knock twice before the Captain answered: 'Jack?'

'No, sir. It's me, Reid. Wondered if I might have a word? In private?'

'Can't it wait?'

'Well . . .'

There was a pause followed by a snort of annoyance. 'Oh very well then. But you'll have to ship your oars for a minute or two.'

Two minutes went by, and then some more: though the door remained closed, Zachary could hear the Captain padding about and splashing water into a basin. He seated himself at the cuddy table and after a good ten minutes the door swung open and Captain Chillingworth appeared in the gap. A beam from the cuddy's lantern revealed him to be wearing an unexpectedly sumptuous garment, an old-fashioned gentleman's banyan—not a striped sailor's shirt of the kind the word had lately come to designate, but a capacious, ankle-length robe, intricately embroidered, of the sort that English nabobs had made popular a generation ago.

'Come in, Reid!' Although the Captain was careful to keep his face averted from the light, Zachary could tell that he had been at some pains to freshen up, for droplets of water were glistening in the folds of his jowls and on his bushy grey eyebrows. 'And shut the door behind you, if you please.'

Zachary had never been inside the Captain's stateroom before: stepping through the door now, he noticed the signs of a hurried straightening-up, with a spread thrown haphazardly over the bunk and a jug lying upended in the porcelain basin. The stateroom had two portholes, both of which were open, but despite a brisk cross-breeze a smoky odour lingered in the air.

The Captain was standing beside one of the open portholes, breathing deeply as if to clear his lungs. 'You've come to give me an ear-wigging about Crowle, have you Reid?'

'Well, actually, sir . . .'

The Captain seemed not to hear him, for he carried on

without a break: 'I heard about the business on the jib-boom, Reid. I wouldn't make too much of it if I were you. Crowle's a knaggy devil, no doubt about it, but don't be taken in by his ballyragging. Believe me, he fears you more than you do him. And not without reason either: we may sit at the same table while at sea, but Crowle knows full well that a man like you wouldn't have him for a groom if we were ashore. That kind of thing can eat a fellow up you know. To fear and be feared is all he's ever known—so how do you think it sits with him, to see that you can conjure loyalty so easily, even in the lascars? In his place would it not seem equally unjust to you? And would you not be tempted to visit your grievance on somebody?'

Here the schooner rolled to leeward, and the Captain had to reach for the bulwark to steady himself. Taking advantage of the pause, Zachary said quickly: 'Well, actually sir, I'm not here about Mr Crowle. It's about something else.'

'Oh!' This seemed to knock the wind out of Captain Chillingworth, for he began to scratch his balding head. 'Are you sure it can't wait?'

'Since I'm here, sir, maybe we should just get it done with?'

'Very well,' said the Captain. 'I suppose we may as well sit down then. It's too blashy to be on our feet.'

The only source of light in the stateroom was a lamp with a blackened chimney. Dim though it was, the flame seemed too bright for the Captain and he held up a hand to shield his eyes as he crossed the cabin to seat himself at his desk.

'Go on, Reid,' he said, nodding at the armchair on the other side of the desk. 'Sit yourself down.'

'Yes, sir.'

Zachary was about to sit when he glimpsed a long, lacquered object lying on the upholstery. He picked it up and found it warm to the touch: it was a pipe, with a bulb the size of a man's thumbnail, sitting on a stem that was as thin as a finger and as long as an arm. It was beautifully crafted, with carved knuckles that resembled the nodes of a stalk of bamboo.

The Captain too had caught sight of the pipe: half rising

to his feet, he thumped his fist on his thigh, as if to chide himself for his absent-mindedness. But when Zachary held the pipe out to him, he accepted with an unaccustomedly gracious gesture, extending both his hands and bowing, in a fashion that seemed more Chinese than European. Then, placing the pipe on the desk, he cradled his jowls in his palm and stared at it in silence, as though he were trying to think of some way of accounting for its presence in his stateroom.

At last, he stirred and cleared his throat. 'You're not a fool on the march, Reid,' he said. 'I'm sure you know what this is and what it's used for. I'll be bail'd if I make any apologies for it, so please don't be expecting any.'

'I wasn't, sir,' said Zachary.

'You were bound to find out sooner or later, so maybe it's for the best. It's scarcely a secret.'

'None of my business, sir.'

'On the contrary,' said the Captain, with a wry smile, 'in these waters it's everyone's business and it'll be yours, too, if you intend to continue as a seaman: you'll be stowing it, packing it, selling it . . . and I know of no salt who doesn't sample his cargo from time to time, especially when it's of a kind that might help him forget the blores and bottom-winds that are his masters of misrule.'

The Captain's chin had sunk into his jowls now, but his voice had grown steadier and stronger. 'A man's not a sailor, Reid, if he doesn't know what it's like to be becalmed in a dead-lown, and there's this to be said for opium that it works a strange magic with time. To go from one day to another, or even one week to the next, becomes as easy as stepping between decks. You may not credit it—I didn't myself until I had the misfortune of having my vessel detained for many months in a ghastly little port. It was somewhere on the Sula Sea—as ugly a town as I've ever seen; the kind of place where all the giglets are travesties, and you can't step ashore for fear of being becketed by the forelift. Never had I felt as flat aback as I did in those months, and when the steward, a Manila-man, offered me a pipe, I confess I took it with a will. No doubt you expect me to blame myself for my weakness—but no sir, I do not regret what I did. It was a gift like none I've ever known. And like all the gifts that Nature gives us—fire, water and the rest—it demands to be used with the greatest care and caution.'

The Captain looked up to fix his glowing eyes briefly on Zachary. 'There were many years, believe me, when I smoked no more than a single pipe each month—and if you should happen to think that such moderation is not possible, then I would have you know that not only is it possible, it is even the rule. They are fools, sir, who imagine that everyone who touches a pipe is condemned instantly to wither away in a smoke-filled den. The great majority of those who chase the dragon, I'll wager, do so only once or twice a month—not for nip-cheesing reasons at that, but because it is that very restraint that produces the most exquisite, the most refined pleasure. There are some, of course, who know with their first taste that they will never leave that smoky paradise—those are the true addicts and they are born, not made. But for the common run of men—and I include myself in that number—to come unballasted over the black mud takes something else, some turn of fate, some vulnerability of fortune . . . or perhaps, as was the case with me, reverses of a personal nature, that happened to coincide with a debilitating illness. Certainly, at the time when it happened, I could not have had a better remedy for my ills . . .'

The Captain broke off to glance at Zachary. 'Tell me, Reid: do you know what the most miraculous property of this substance is?'

'No, sir.'

'I will tell you then: it kills a man's desires. That is what makes it manna for a sailor, balm for the worst of his afflictions. It calms the unceasing torment of the flesh that pursues us across the seas, drives us to sin against Nature . . .'

The Captain looked down at his hands, which had begun to shake. 'Come, Reid,' he said suddenly. 'We've wasted enough breath. Since we are launched on this tack, let me ask: would you not like to try a whiff? You will not be able to avoid this experiment forever, I assure you—curiosity alone will drive you to it. You would be amazed . . .'—he broke off with a laugh—'oh you'd be amazed by the passengers I've known who've wanted to hoist the smoke-sail: Bible-thumping devil-scolders; earnest Empire-builders; corseted matrons, impregnable in their primness. If you're to sail the opium route, there will come a day when you too will bleed the monkey. So why not now? Is it not as good a time as any?'

Zachary stared, as if hypnotized, at the pipe and its delicate, polished stem. 'Why yes, sir,' he said. 'I should like that.'

'Good.'

Reaching into a drawer, the Captain brought out a box which was, in the lacquered sheen of its gloss, every bit a match for his pipe. When he opened the lid, several objects were revealed to be lying inside, on a lining of red silk, nested ingeniously together. One by one, like an apothecary at a counter, the Captain picked the objects apart and placed them on the table in front of him: a needle with a metal tip and a bamboo stem; a long-handled spoon of similar design; a tiny silver knife; a small round container, made of ivory and so ornately carved that Zachary would not have been surprised to see a ruby or diamond lying inside. But instead there was a lump of opium, dull in appearance, muddy in colour and texture. Arming himself with the knife, Captain Chillingworth cut off a minuscule piece and placed it in the bowl of the long-handled spoon. Then, removing the chimney from the lamp, he held the spoon directly over the flame, keeping it there until the gum changed consistency and turned liquid. Now, with the ceremonious air of a priest performing a ritual of communion, he handed Zachary the pipe: 'Be sure to work your bellows hard when I put the droplet in: a gulp or two is all you'll get before it's gone.' Now, moving with the greatest care, the Captain dipped the needle's tip into the opium and held it over the flame. As soon as the drop began to sizzle, he thrust it into the pipe's bulb. 'Yes! Now! let not a wisp escape!'

Zachary put the stem to his lips and drew in a breath of rich, oily smoke.

'Work the pump! Hold it in!'

After Zachary had drawn on the stem twice more, the pipe was exhausted of its smoke.

'Sit back in your chair,' said Captain Chillingworth. 'Do you feel it? Has the earth lost its hold on your body yet?'

Zachary nodded: it was true that somehow the pull of gravity seemed to have eased; his body had become as light as a cloud; every trace of tension had drained out of his muscles; they had become so relaxed, so yielding that he could not be sure that his limbs still existed. To sit in a chair now was the last thing he wanted to do; he wanted to be prone, to lie down. He put out a hand to steady himself, and watched his fingers travel, like slow-worms, to the edge of the table. Then he pushed himself up, half expecting his feet to be unusable—but they were perfectly steady and well capable of supporting his weight.

He heard the Captain speaking, as if from a great distance: 'Are you too be-dundered to walk? You are welcome to the use of my cot.'

'My cabin's just a step away, sir.'

'As you please, as you please. The effects will pass in an hour or two and you will wake refreshed.'

'Thank you, sir.' Zachary felt himself to be floating as he moved to the door. He was almost there when the Captain said: 'Wait a minute, Reid—what was it that you wanted to see me about?'

Zachary came to a stop with his hand on the door; to his surprise he found that the loosening of his muscles and the clouding of his senses had not led to any loss of memory. His mind was, if anything, unnaturally clear: not only did he recall that he had come to speak to the Captain about Serang Ali, he also understood that the opium had saved him from choosing a coward's course. For it was clear to him now that whatever had happened between himself and the serang had to be resolved between the two of them, and them alone. Was it because the fumes had given him a clearer vision of the world? Or was it because they had allowed him to look into parts of himself where he had never ventured before? Whatever the case, he saw now that it was a rare, diffcult and improbable thing for two people from worlds apart to find themselves linked by a tie of pure sympathy, a feeling that owed nothing to the rules and expectations of others. He understood also that when such a bond comes into being, its truths and falsehoods, its obligations and privileges, exist only for the people who are linked by it, and then in such a way that only they can judge the honour and dishonour of how they conduct themselves in relation to each other. It was for him, Zachary, to find an honourable resolution to his dealings with Serang Ali; in this would lie his manumission into adulthood, his knowledge of the steadiness of his helm.

'Yes, Reid? What did you want to talk about?'

'It was about our position, sir,' said Zachary. 'When I looked at the charts today, I had the feeling that we had strayed quite a long way eastwards.'

The Captain shook his head. 'No, Reid—we're exactly where we should be. In this season there's a southerly current off the Andamans and I thought to take advantage of it; we'll stay on this tack for a while yet.'

'I see, sir, I'm sorry. If you'll forgive me . . .'

'Yes go, go.'

Crossing the cuddy, Zachary felt none of the unsteadiness that accompanies inebriation; his movements were slow, but in no wise irregular. Once inside his cabin, he took off his banyan and trowsers and stretched out on his bunk in his underclothing. On closing his eyes he lapsed into a state of rest that was far deeper than sleep, and yet also more awake, for his mind was filled with shapes and colours: although these visions were extraordinarily vivid they were utterly tranquil, being untroubled by sensuality or desire. How long this state lasted he did not know, but his awareness of its waning started when faces and figures entered his visions again. He fell into a state of dreaming, in which a woman kept approaching and receding, keeping her face hidden, eluding him even though he knew her to be tantalizingly close. Just as he was becoming conscious of a distant ringing sound, the veil fell away from her face and he saw that she was Paulette; she was coming towards him, walking into his arms, offering him her lips. He woke to find himself drenched in sweat, dimly conscious that the last chime of the eighth bell had just sounded and that it was his watch next.

~

A marriage proposal being a sensitive affair, Deeti had to be careful in picking a time and place where she could discuss the matter with Heeru without being overheard. No opportunity arose until early the next morning, when the two women happened to find themselves alone on the main deck. Seizing the moment, Deeti took Heeru's elbow and led her to the jamna devis.

What is it, Bhauji?

It wasn't often that anyone paid Heeru much attention, and she began to stammer in apprehension, thinking she'd done something wrong and was in for a scolding: *Ká horahelba?* Is something wrong?

Under the cover of her ghungta, Deeti smiled: There's nothing wrong, Heeru—to tell the truth, I am happy today—*áj bara khusbáni*. I have some news for you.

News? What news? *Ká khabarbá?* Heeru dug her knuckles into her cheeks and whimpered: Is it good or bad?

That's for you to decide. Listen . . .

No sooner had Deeti started to explain than she began to wish she'd chosen some other venue for this talk, some place where they could have dropped their ghungtas: with their faces covered, it was impossible to know what Heeru was thinking. But it was too late now, she would have to go through with it.

When the news of the proposal had been conveyed in full, she said: *Ká ré*, Heeru? What do you think: tell me?

*Ká kahatbá Bhauji?* What can I say?

From the sound of her voice, Deeti knew she was crying, so she put an arm around her, pulling her into a huddle: Heeru, don't be afraid; you can say what you like.

Several minutes passed before Heeru could speak, and even then it was in a sobbing, disjointed rush: Bhauji . . . I hadn't thought, didn't expect . . . are you sure? Bhauji, they say in Mareech, a woman on her own will be torn apart . . . devoured . . . so many men and so few women . . . can you think what it would be like, Bhauji, to be alone there . . . Oh Bhauji . . . I never thought . . .

Deeti could not figure out where exactly this was heading. *Ágé ke bát kal hoilé*, she said sharply. You can talk about the future tomorrow. What's your answer for now?

What else, Bhauji? Yes, I'm ready . . .

Deeti laughed. Arre Heeru! You're a bold one!

Why do you say that, Bhauji? said Heeru anxiously. Do you think it's a mistake?

No, said Deeti firmly. Now that you've decided, I can tell you: I don't think it's a mistake. I think he's a good man. Besides, he has all those followers and relatives—they'll look after you. You'll be the envy of everyone, Heeru—a real queen!

~

It was not unusual for Paulette, when going through her washing, to come upon a shirt, banyan, or pair of trowsers that she recognized as Zachary's. Almost unconsciously, she would slip these garments to the bottom of her pile, saving them for the last. When she came to them, depending on her mood, she would sometimes subject them to an angry scrubbing, even beating them upon the deck-planks, with all the vigour of a washerwoman at a dhobi-ghat. But there were times also when she would linger over their collars and cuffs and seams, going to great lengths to scrub them clean. It was in this fashion that she was cleaning a shirt of his one day when

Baboo Nob Kissin Pander appeared at her side. Goggling at the garment in her hands, he said, in a furtive whisper: 'I do not wish to trespass into your preserves, Miss, but kindly may I inquire if that shirt belongs to Mr Reid?'

Paulette answered with a nod, whereupon he said, even more furtively: 'Just for one minute can I feel?'

'The shirt?' she asked in astonishment, and without another word, the gomusta snatched the damp twist of cloth from her and pulled it this way and that before handing it back. 'Seems he has been wearing from times-immemorial,' he said with a puzzled frown. 'Cloth feels extremely aged. Strange, no?'

Although Paulette was by now well-accustomed to the gomusta's oddities, she was puzzled by this cryptic statement. 'But why is it strange that Mr Reid should have old clothes?'

'Tch!' The gomusta clicked his tongue, as if mildly irritated by her ignorance. 'If avatar is new, how clothes can be old? Height, weight, privates, all must be changing, no, when there is alteration in externalities? Myself, I have had to buy many new clothings. Heavy financial outlay was required.'

'I don't understand, Nob Kissin Baboo,' said Paulette. 'Why was that necessary?'

'You cannot see?' The gomusta's eyes grew even rounder and more protuberant. 'You are blind or what? Bosoms are burgeoning, hair is lengthening. New modalities are definitely coming to the fore. How old clothes will accommodate?'

Paulette smiled to herself and lowered her head. 'But Baboo Nob Kissin,' she said, 'Mr Reid has not undergone such a change; his old clothes will surely suffice for a while yet?'

To Paulette's astonishment, the gomusta responded with startling vehemence: his face seemed to swell in outrage, and when he spoke again, it was as if he were defending some deeply cherished belief. 'How you can make such sweeping-statements? At once I will clear this point.' Thrusting a hand through the neckline of his flowing tunic, he pulled out an amulet and unrolled a yellowing piece of paper. 'Come here and see.'

Rising to her feet, Paulette took the list from him and

began to examine it under the glowing, sunlit penumbra of her ghungta.

'It is crew-list for *Ibis* from two years ago. Look at Mr Reid's good-name and you will see. Cent-per-cent change is there.'

As if mesmerized, Paulette's eyes ran back and forth along the line until they came to the word 'Black' scribbled beside Zachary's name. Suddenly so much that had seemed odd, or inexplicable, made perfect sense—his apparently intuitive sympathy for her circumstances, his unquestioning acceptance of her sisterly relationship with Jodu . . .

'It is a miracle no? Nobody can deny.'

'Indeed, Baboo Nob Kissin. You are right.'

She saw now how miraculously wrong she had been in some of her judgements of him: if there was anyone on the *Ibis* who could match her in the multiplicity of her selves, then it was none other than Zachary. It was as if some divine authority had sent a messenger to let her know that her soul was twinned with his.

There was nothing now to stop her from revealing herself to him—and yet the mere thought of it made her cringe in fear. What if he assumed that she had chased him on to the *Ibis*? What else indeed *could* he assume? What would she do if he laughed at her for humiliating herself? She could not bear to think of it.

She lifted her head to look at the sea, rushing by, and a glimmer of memory flashed through her head: she remembered a day, several years ago, when Jodu had found her crying over a novel. Taking the book out of her hands, he had flipped through it in puzzlement, even shaking it by the spine, almost as if he were expecting to dislodge a needle or a thorn—some sharp object that might account for her tears. Finding nothing, he said at last—it's the story, is it, that's turned on the flow?—and on this being confirmed, he had demanded a full recounting of the tale. So she'd told him the story of Paul and Virginie, growing up in exile on an island, where an innocent childhood attachment had grown into an abiding passion, but only to be sundered when Virginie was sent back to France. The last part of the book was Paulette's favourite, and she'd described at length the novel's tragic conclusion, in which Virginie is killed in a shipwreck, just as she is about to be reunited with her beloved. To her outrage, Jodu had greeted the melancholy tale with guffaws of laughter, telling her that only a fool would cry over this skein of weepy nonsense. She had shouted at him, telling him that it was he who was the fool, and a weakling too, because he would never have the courage to follow the dictates of his heart.

How was it that no one had ever told her that it was not love itself, but its treacherous gatekeepers which made the greatest demands on your courage: the panic of acknowledging it; the terror of declaring it; the fear of being rebuffed? Why had no one told her that love's twin was not hate but cowardice? If she had learnt this earlier she would have known the truth of why she had gone to such lengths to stay hidden from Zachary. And yet, even knowing this, she could not summon the courage to do what she knew she must—at least not yet.

~

It was late in the night, shortly after the fifth bell of the midnight watch, that Zachary spotted Serang Ali on the fo'c'sle-deck: he was alone and he seemed to be deep in thought, looking eastwards, at the moonlit horizon. All through the day, Zachary had had the feeling that the serang was avoiding him, so he lost no time now in stepping up to stand beside him at the rail.

Serang Ali was clearly startled to see him: 'Malum Zikri!'

'Can you spare a moment, Serang Ali?'

'Can, can. Malum, what-thing wanchi?'

Zachary took out the watch Serang Ali had given him and held it in his palm. 'Listen, Serang Ali, it's time you told me the truth about this timmyknocky here.'

Serang Ali gave the ends of his drooping moustache a puzzled tug. 'What Malum Zikri mean? No sabbi.'

Zachary opened the watch's cover. 'Time's come to cut playing the fool, Serang Ali. I know you been putting me on about Adam Danby. I know who he was.'

Serang Ali's eyes went from the watch to Zachary's face and he gave a shrug, as if to indicate that he was weary of pretence and dissimulation. 'How? Who tell?'

'That don matter none: what counts is I know. What I *don't* know is what you had in mind for me. Were you planning on teaching me Danby's tricks?'

Serang Ali shook his head and spat a mouthful of betel-juice over the deck rail. 'No true, Malum Zikri,' he said in a low, insistent voice. 'You cannot believe all what the buggers say. Malum Aadam, he blongi like son for Serang Ali—he my daughter husband. Now he hab makee die. Also daughter and all they chilo. Serang Ali 'lone now. When I look-see Malum Zikri, my eyes hab done see Malum Aadam. Both two same-same for me. Zikri Malum like son also.'

'Son?' said Zachary. 'Is that what you'd do for your son? Turn him to crime? Piracy?'

'Crime, Malum Zikri?' Serang Ali's eyes flashed. 'Smuggling opium not blongi crime? Running slave-ship blongi better'n piracy?'

'So you admit it then?' said Zachary. 'That's what you had in mind for me—to do a Danby for you?'

'No!' said Serang Ali, slapping the deck rail. 'Want only Zikri Malum do good for he-self. 'Come officer. Maybe Cap'ting. All thing Malum Aadam can not 'come.'

The Serang's body seemed to wilt as he was speaking, so that he looked suddenly older, and somehow strangely forlorn. Despite himself, Zachary's voice softened. 'Lookit, Serang Ali,' he said. 'You been plenty freehanded with me, can't deny it. Last thing I want is to turn you in. So let's just settle this between us. Let's agree that when we put into Port Louis, you'll light out. That way we can just forget any of this happened.'

Serang Ali's shoulders sagged as he answered. 'Can do—Serang Ali so can do.'

Zachary took a last look at the watch before handing it over. 'Here—this belongs in your poke, not mine. You better keep it.'

Serang Ali sketched a salam as he knotted the watch into the waist of his lungi.

Zachary stepped away but only to come back again. 'Look, Serang Ali,' he said. 'Believe me, I'm cut down bout it ending like this between us. Sometimes I just wish you'd'a left me alone and never come anigh. Maybe things would'a been different then. But it was you as showed me that what I do counts for more than where I was born. And if I'm to care bout my work, then I need to live by its rules. Else it wouldn't be worth doing. You see the sense of that?'

'See.' Serang Ali nodded. 'Can see.'

Zachary was about to step away again when Serang Ali stopped him. 'Malum Zikri—one thing.'

'What?' Zachary turned to find Serang Ali pointing ahead, in a south-easterly direction.

'Look-see. There.'

Zachary could see nothing in the dark. 'What'd you want me to look at?'

'Over there blongi Sumatra channel. From here maybe forty-fifty mile. From there Sing'pore very close. Six-seven day sail.'

'What're you getting at, Serang Ali?'

'Malum Zikri wanchi Serang Ali go, no? Can do. Can go very soon, that way.'

'How?' said Zachary in bemusement.

Serang Ali turned to point to one of the longboats. 'In that boat can go. Little food, little water. Can go Sing'pore seven days. Then China.'

Now Zachary understood. In disbelief he said: 'Are you talking of jumping ship?'

'Why not?' said Serang Ali. 'Malum Zikri wanchi me go, no? Better go now, much better. Only cause of Malum Zikri,

Serang Ali come on *Ibis*. Or else not come.' Serang Ali broke off to dump a mouthful of paan in the sea. 'Burra Malum, he no-good bugger. See what trouble he make with Shaitan-jib? Bugger make plenty bad joss.'

'But the *Ibis*?' Zachary slapped the schooner's deck rail. 'What about her? What about the passengers? Don't you owe them anything? Who's going to get them where they're going?'

'Plenty lascar hab got. Can reach *Ibis* to Por'Lwee. No problem.'

Zachary began to shake his head even before the serang had finished. 'No. I can't allow it.'

'Malum Zikri not hab do nothing. Only must sleep on watch one night. Just twenty minute.'

'I can't allow it, Serang Ali.' Zachary was absolutely sure of himself now, confident that this was where he had to stake out the lines of his own sovereignty. 'I can't let you make off with one of the longboats. What if something goes wrong later and we have to abandon ship? We can't afford to be a boat short, with so many people on board.'

'Other boats hab got. Will be enough.'

'I'm sorry, Serang Ali,' said Zachary. 'I just can't let it happen, not on my watch. I offered you a reasonable deal— that you wait till Port Louis before lighting out. That's as far as I'm going to go; no farther.'

The serang was about to say something but Zachary stopped him. 'And don't push me, cause if you do I'll have no choice but to go to the Captain. Do you understand?'

Serang Ali gave a deep sigh and a nod. 'Yes, Zikri Malum.'

'Good.'

Stepping off the fo'c'sle, Zachary turned around for one last word. 'And don't think of pulling anything smart, Serang Ali. Cause I'm goin to be watching you.'

Serang Ali smiled and stroked his moustache. 'Malum Zikri too muchi smart bugger, no? What Serang Ali can do?'

~

The news of Heeru's wedding broke upon the dabusa like a wave, creating eddies and whirlpools of excitement: after all the unfortunate things that had happened, here at last was something, as Deeti said, to make everyone laugh in their sorrow—*dukhwá me sabke hasáweli.*

As everybody's Bhauji, it fell, as if by right, to Deeti to think of all the organizing and bandobast that lay ahead. Should there be a tilak ceremony? Deeti allowed her voice to rise to the querulous pitch that was appropriate for someone who had been burdened, yet again, with the tiresome business of making all the arrangements for a family event: And what about a haldi, with a proper smearing of turmeric?

These were exactly the questions that arose when the other women heard the news: Was there to be a kohbar? Could a wedding be real without a marriage chamber? Surely it would be no great matter to set one up, with a few sheets and mats? And what about the fire, for the seven sacramental circlings? Would it be enough to have a candle, or a lamp instead?

We're all talking too much, scolded Deeti. We can't decide this on our own! We don't even know what the customs are like on the boy's side.

Boy? *Larika?*—this raised gales of laughter—he's no boy, that man!

At a wedding everyone's a boy: what's to stop him from being one again?

And what about a dowry? gifts?

Tell him, we'll give him a goat when we get to Mareech.

. . . Be serious . . . *hasé ka ká bátba ré . . .?* What's to laugh at?

The one thing everyone agreed about was that no purpose was to be served by dragging things out: best to get everything done with the greatest possible dispatch. Between the two sides, it was decided that the next day would be devoted entirely to the wedding.

Among the women, the only one who was less than enthused was Munia. Can you imagine living your life with any of these men? she said to Paulette. Wouldn't do it for anything.

So who're you aiming for then?

I need someone who'll show me a bit of the world.

Oh? said Paulette, teasing. A lascar, for example?

Munia giggled. Why not?

~

Among the women Sarju, the midwife, was the only one who still showed no signs of recovering from her seasickness: unable to keep down any food or water, she had dwindled away until it seemed that the last sparks of life in her body had retreated into her dark, fiery eyes. Since she was unable to go up to the main deck for her meals, the women took it in turns to bring a little food and water down to the dabusa, in the hope of coaxing a little nourishment between her lips.

That evening, it was Deeti's turn to fetch Sarju's food. She came down the ladder while most of the girmitiyas were still on deck, eating their meal: the dabusa was lit only by a couple of lamps, and in that dim, near-empty space, Sarju's worn, withered figure seemed even more forlorn than usual.

Deeti tried to sound cheerful as she seated herself beside her: How are you, Sarju-didi? Feeling better today?

Sarju made no answer; instead she raised her head and looked quickly around the dabusa. When she saw that there was no one within earshot, she caught hold of Deeti's wrist and pulled her close. Listen, she said, listen to me; there's something I have to tell you.

Yes, didi?

*Hamra sé chalal nā jálé,* Sarju whispered. I can't take this any more; I can't go on . . .

Why are you talking like that? Deeti protested. You'll be fine once you start eating properly.

Sarju dismissed this impatiently. Listen to me, she said, there's no time to waste. I'm telling you the truth; I will not live to see the end of this journey.

How do you know? said Deeti. You may get better.

It's too late for that. Sarju fixed her feverishly bright eyes on Deeti and whispered: I've dealt with these things all my life. I know, and before I go I want to show you something.

Moving her head off the cloth bundle that served as her pillow, Sarju pushed it towards Deeti: Here. Take this; open it.

Open it? Deeti was amazed, for Sarju had never before been known to open her bojha in anyone's sight: indeed her furtiveness about her baggage was so extreme that the others had often joked and speculated about the contents. Deeti had never joined in the teasing because Sarju's protectiveness seemed to her to be merely the fixation of a middle-aged woman who had precious few possessions to boast of. But she knew also that such manias were not easily overcome, so it was with some caution that she asked Sarju: Are you sure you want me to look inside?

Yes, said Sarju. Quickly. Before the others come.

Deeti had assumed that the bundle contained not much more than a few old clothes, maybe some masalas, and perhaps a couple of copper utensils: when she peeled away the first flaps of cloth she found more or less what she had expected—some old clothes and a few wooden spoons.

Here. Give it to me. Sarju thrust a twig-like hand into the bundle and pulled out a small pouch, not much bigger than her fist. She put it to her nose, took a deep breath and handed it to Deeti: Do you know what this is?

From the feel of the pouch, Deeti knew that it was filled with tiny seeds. When she raised it to her nose, she recognized the smell at once: Ganja, she said. These are seeds of ganja.

Sarju acknowledged this with a nod and handed over another pouch. And this?

This time it took Deeti several whiffs before she recognized what it was: Datura.

Do you know what datura can do? whispered Sarju.

Yes, said Deeti.

Sarju gave her a thin smile. I knew that you and you alone, would know the value of these things. This most of all . . .

Sarju pushed yet another pouch into Deeti's hands. In this, she whispered, there is wealth beyond imagining; guard it like your life—it contains seeds of the best Benares poppy.

Deeti thrust her fingers into the pouch and rubbed the tiny, speck-like seeds between her fingertips. The familiar grainy feel transported her back to the environs of Ghazipur; suddenly it was as if she were in her own courtyard, with Kabutri beside her, making posth out of a handful of poppy seeds. How was it possible that after spending so much of her life with these seeds she had not had the foresight or wisdom to bring some with her—as a keepsake if nothing else?

Deeti extended her hand to Sarju, as if to give back the pouch, but the midwife pushed it back towards her. It's yours; take it, keep it. This, the ganja, the datura: make of them the best use you can. Don't let the others know. Don't let them see these seeds. They'll keep for many years. Keep them hidden till you can use them; they are worth more than any treasure. Inside my bojha, there are some spices, ordinary ones. When I'm gone, you can distribute them to the rest. But these seeds— these are for you alone.

Why? Why me?

Sarju raised a trembling hand to point to the images on the beam above Deeti's head. Because I want to be there too, she said. I want to be remembered in your shrine.

You will be, Sarju-didi, said Deeti, squeezing her hand. You will be.

Now put the seeds away quickly, before the others come.

Yes, didi, yes . . .

Afterwards, when Deeti took Sarju's untouched food back to the main deck, she found Kalua squatting under the devis and sat down beside him. As she was listening to the sighing of the sails, she became aware that there was a grain lodged under her thumbnail. It was a single poppy seed: prising it out, she rolled it between her fingers and raised her eyes, past the straining sails, to the star-filled vault above. On any other night she would have scanned the sky for the planet she had always thought to be the arbiter of her fate—but tonight her eyes dropped instead to the tiny sphere she was holding between her thumb and forefinger. She looked at the seed as if she had never seen one before, and suddenly she knew that it was not the planet above that governed her life: it was this minuscule orb—at once bountiful and all-devouring, merciful and destructive, sustaining and vengeful. This was her Shani, her Saturn.

When Kalua asked what she was looking at she raised her fingers to his lips and slipped the seed into his mouth.

Here, she said, taste it. It is the star that took us from our homes and put us on this ship. It is the planet that rules our destiny.

~

The first mate was one of those men who like to boost their sense of their own worth by coining nicknames for others. As always with those who play this trick, he was careful to thrust his epithets only on those who could not refuse his coin. Thus Captain Chillingworth's cognomen—'Skipper Nabbs'—was used only behind his back, while Zachary's—'Mannikin'—was said to his face, but usually out of earshot of others (this being a concession to the collective prestige of sahibs, and thus malums). As for the rest, only a few were notable enough to merit names of their own. Serang Ali—'Sniplouse'—was one such, but the migrants were indifferently 'sukies' and 'slavies'; the silahdars and maistries were either 'Achhas' or 'Rum-Johnnies'; and the lascars were either 'Bub-dool' or 'Rammer-Sammy'—or just 'Sammy' for short.

Of all the people on the schooner, there was only one whose nickname denoted some measure of camaraderie on the part of the first mate: this was Subedar Bhyro Singh, whom he called 'Muffin-mug'. Unbeknownst to the mate, the subedar too had a name for him, which he used only in his absence: it was Malum na-Malum (Officer Don't-Know). This symmetry was not accidental, for between these two men there was a natural affinity that extended even to their appearance: although the subedar was much older and darker—heavier in the belly and whiter in the head—both were tall, barrel-chested men. Their mutuality of disposition, too, was such as to transcend the barriers of language and circumstance, allowing them to communicate almost without benefit of words, so that between them there could be said to exist, if not exactly a friendship, then certainly a joining of interests, and a mutual ease that made possible certain familiarities that would otherwise have been unthinkable in men of their respective stations—for example, the occasional sharing of grog.

One of the many matters in which the subedar and the first mate were perfectly in accord was their attitude towards Neel and Ah Fatt—or the 'Two Jacks' as Mr Crowle liked to call them (Neel being Jack-gagger and Ah Fatt, Jackin-ape). Often, of an afternoon, when Bhyro Singh led the two convicts around the deck on their daily Rogues' March, the first mate would join in the entertainment, urging Bhyro Singh on, as he prodded the convicts with his lathi: 'With a will there, Muffin-mug! Lay about cheerily now! Rattle their ruffles!'

Occasionally the mate would even step in to take the subedar's place. Flicking a length of rope like a whiplash, he would slash at the convicts' ankles, making them skip and jump, to the tune of:

Handy-spandy, Jack o'dandy
Loved plum cake and sugar candy
Bought some at a grocer's shop
And off he went with a hop-hop-hop.

These encounters invariably occurred during the day, when the convicts were up on deck: this being so, both Neel and Ah Fatt were taken unawares when a couple of guards came to the chokey, late one night, to tell them that the Burra Malum had ordered that they be brought above.

What for? said Neel.

Who knows? said one of the silàhdars, grumbling. The two of them are up there, drinking grag.

The bandobast for taking the convicts on deck required that their wrists and ankles be bound and chained, which took some doing, and it was soon clear that the silahdars were none too pleased to be called upon to go through the procedures at this late hour.

So what do they want with us? said Neel.

They're must with sharab, said the guard. Out for maza.

Fun? said Neel. What fun can we provide?

What do I know? Keep your hands steady, b'henchod.

It was a time of night when the fana was crowded with lascars, sleeping in their jhulis, and to walk through it was like trying to negotiate a thicket of low-hanging beehives. Because of their long confinement Neel and Ah Fatt were already unsteady on their feet and their clumsiness was now compounded by the motion of the ship and by their chains. Every roll sent them carroming into the hammocks, butting butts and ramming heads, provoking kicks, shoves and outbursts of angry galis.

. . . B'henchod slipgibbet qaidis . . .

. . . Your balls aren't meant for walking . . .

. . . Try using your feet . . .

Clanking and clattering, the two convicts were led out of the fana and taken up to the fo'c'sle deck, where they found Mr Crowle enthroned on the capstan. The subedar was waiting attendance on him, standing between the bows.

'Where's ye'been, quoddies? It's low hours for the likes of you.'

Neel saw now that both the first mate and the subedar had tin mugs in their hands, and it was clear from the slurred sound of Mr Crowle's voice that this was not his first drink of the night: even when sober, these two men were cause enough for trouble so it was hard to imagine what they might, or might not, do now. Yet, despite a tightening in his guts, Neel did not fail to take notice of the singular spectacle of the moonlit sea.

The schooner was on the starboard tack, and the deck was aslant, dipping and rising as the sails strained in the wind. From time to time, as the tilt lessened, waves would break on the port beam and wash across the deck, dripping out of the starboard scuppers when the schooner leant sidewise again before the wind. The phosphorescent glow of these whirling runnels of water seemed to add footlights to the masts, illuminating the soaring wings of canvas overhead.

'Where're ye'lookin, Jack-gagger?'

The sting of a rope-end, biting into his calves, brought Neel suddenly back to the moment. 'I'm sorry, Mr Crowle.'

'Sir to you, pillicock.'

'Yes, sir.' Neel pronounced the words slowly, cautioning himself to keep a hold on his tongue.

Draining his mug, the mate held it out to the subedar, who filled it from a bottle. The mate took another sip, watching the convicts over the rim of the mug. 'Jack-gagger—ye're a ready one with the red-rag. Let's hear it: do y'know why we called yer up on deck?'

'No, sir,' said Neel.

'Here's the gaff then,' said Mr Crowle. 'Me and my good friend Subby-dar Muffin-mug, we was coguing our noses with a nipperkin of the boosey and he says to me: Jackin-ape and Jack-gagger are as topping a pair of pals as I'se ever seen. So I says to him, I says, never saw a brace of jail-birds who wouldn't turn on each other. And he says to me: not these two. So I says: Muffin-mug, what'll you bet me that I can talk one o'em into pumping ship on t'other? And blow me if he doesn't show me a quartereen! So there's the nub of it, Jack: ye're here to settle our bet.'

'What's the wager, sir?' said Neel.

'That one o'yer is a-going to empty the Jordan on t'other.'

'The Jordan, sir?'

'Jordan's greek for piss-dale, Jack,' said the mate impatiently. 'I'm betting one o'yer is going to squeeze his taters on t'other's phizz. So there y'have it. No blows or beating, mind: nothing but suasion. Yer a-going to do it o'yer own will or not at all.'

'I see, sir.'

'So what do y'make of me chances, Jack-gagger?'

Neel tried to think of himself urinating on Ah Fatt, for the entertainment of these two men, and his stomach turned. But he knew he would have to pick his words carefully if he was not to provoke the mate. He produced an inoffensive mumble: 'I'd say the odds are not good, sir.'

'Cocky, in'e?' The mate turned to flash a smile at the subedar. 'Won't do it, Jack?'

'Don't want to, sir.'

'Sure o'y'self, are ye, quoddie?'

'Yes, sir,' said Neel.

'What if you go first?' said the mate. 'Spray his clock with yer pecnoster and ye're done and dry. How's tha' for a bargain? Give yer pal a wetting and that's that. What'd y'say, Jack-gagger? Roll the dibbs?'

Short of having a knife held to his throat, Neel knew that he would not be able to do it. 'Not me, sir, no.'

'Won't do it?'

'Not of my will, sir, no.'

'And yer pal here?' said the mate. 'What o'him?'

Suddenly the deck tilted, and Ah Fatt, always the steadier of the two, grabbed hold of Neel's elbow to keep him from falling. On other days, this might well have earned them swipes of Bhyro Singh's lathi, but today, as if in deference to some grander design, the subedar let it pass.

'Sure yer pal won't neither?' said the mate.

Neel glanced at Ah Fatt, who was looking stoically at his feet: strange to think, that having known each other for only a few weeks, the two of them—pitiful pair of convicts and transportees that they were—already possessed something that could excite the envy of men whose power over them was absolute. Could it be that there was something genuinely rare in such a bond as theirs, something that could provoke others to exert their ingenuity in order to test its limits? If that were so, then he, Neel, was no less curious on that score than they.

'If y'won't play along, Jack-gagger, I'll have to take my chances with yer pal.'

'Yes, sir. Go ahead.'

Mr Crowle laughed, and just then a foaming mop of

spindrift washed over the fo'c'sle-deck, so that for an instant his teeth sparkled in the phosphorescent glow. 'Let's hear it, Jack-gagger, do y'know why yer pal was quodded?'

'Robbery, sir, as far as I know.'

'That's all he's told yer?'

'Yes, sir.'

'Di'n't tell you he was a gull-choker, did'e now?'

'Don't follow, sir.'

'Robbed a nest of devil-scolders, he did.' The first mate shot a glance at Ah Fatt. 'In'it true, Jackin-apes? Cabbaged the Mission House that took you in and fed you?'

Now, as Neel turned to look at him, Ah Fatt mumbled: 'Sir. Is true I join Mission House in Canton. But was not for rice. Is because I want to travel West.'

'West?'

'To India, sir,' said Ah Fatt, shifting his feet. 'I want to travel and I hear Mission House send Chinese churchmen to college, in Bengal. So I join and they send to Mission College in Serampore. But I did not like. Could see nothing, could not leave. Only study and pray. Like prison.'

The mate guffawed: 'Is't true then? Y'stole the print off their machines? Beat a round dozen of them Amen-curlers half to death? While they were printing Bibles at that? And all for a penn'orth of elevation?'

Ah Fatt hung his head and made no answer, so Mr Crowle prompted him again: 'Go on then—let's hear it. Is it true or not that ye'did it 'cause of yer yinyan for the black mud?'

'For opium, sir,' said Ah Fatt hoarsely, 'man can do anything.'

'Anything?' The mate reached inside his shirt and produced a paper-wrapped ball of black gum, no larger than a thumbnail. 'So what'd ye' do for this then, Jackin-ape?'

Ah Fatt was standing so close that Neel could feel his friend's body going suddenly rigid. He turned to look and saw that his jaw muscles had seized up and his eyes had turned feverishly bright.

'Let's hear it then, Jackin-ape,' said the mate, twirling the ball between his fingertips. 'What would y'give for this?'

Ah Fatt's chains began to rattle softly, as if in response to the trembling of his body. 'What you want, sir? I have nothing.'

'Oh ye've got something right enough,' said the mate cheerfully. 'Ye've got a bellyful of the pale ale. Just a matter of where y'want to pu'it.'

Neel nudged Ah Fatt with his elbow: 'Don't listen—it's just a trick . . .'

'Stow yer jawin tackle, Jack-gagger.'

With a swipe of his boots, the mate kicked Neel's feet out from under, so that he fell heavily on the tilted deck, rolling headfirst against the bulwark. With his hands and feet bound, he could not do much more than flop around like an upturned beetle. With a great effort he managed to turn away from the bulwark, towards Ah Fatt, and was just in time to see his friend fumbling with the strings of his pyjamas.

'Ah Fatt, no!'

'Don't y'mind him, Jackin-ape,' said the mate. 'Y'do what ye're doin and don't be in no bleedin hurry. He's yer pal, in'e? He can wait for a taste o'yer brew.'

Ah Fatt was swallowing convulsively now and his fingers were trembling so much that he could not pick apart the knot in his drawstrings. In a fury of impatience, he sucked in his stomach and pushed his pyjamas down to his knees. Then, with shaking, unsteady hands he took hold of his penis and pointed it at Neel, who was lying curled at his feet.

'Go on then!' urged the mate. 'Do it, Jackin-ape. Never let yer prick or yer purse fail ye, as the cockqueans say.'

Closing his eyes, Ah Fatt turned his face to the sky and squeezed out a thin trickle of urine over Neel.

'That's the barber, Jackin-ape!' cried the mate, slapping his thigh triumphantly. 'Won me my wager, y'did.' He extended his hand towards the subedar, who duly placed a coin in it while muttering a word of congratulation: 'Mubarak malum-sahib!'

In the meanwhile, with his pyjamas still undone, Ah Fatt had fallen to his knees and was inching towards the mate, his hands cupped like a begging-bowl: 'Sir? For me?'

The mate gave him a nod. 'Ye've earned yer reward, Jackin-ape, no doubt about it, and ye're going to get it too. This here mud is good akbarry: has to be eaten whole. Open yer gobbler and I'll chise it to yer.'

Leaning forwards, Ah Fatt opened his mouth, trembling in anticipation, and the mate flicked the ball of gum out of the paper so that it dropped straight on to his tongue. Ah Fatt's mouth closed and he chewed once. Then suddenly he began to spit and cough, shaking his head as if to rid it of something unspeakably vile.

The sight raised howls of laughter from the mate and the subedar.

'Good day's work, Jackin-ape! There's a lesson in how to use a sprat to catch a mackerel. Gave yer mate a taste o'yer piss and earned y'self a gobful of goatshit to boot!'

# twenty-one

~

The wedding began in the morning, after the first meal of the day. The hold was divided in two, one part being designated the groom's and the other being allotted to the bride. Everybody chose a side and Kalua was picked to be the head of the bridal family: it was he who led the team that went over to the groom's half of the dabusa for the tilak ceremony, where the engagement was solemnly sealed with a reddening of foreheads.

The women had thought that they'd easily outdo the men in the matter of music, but a rude shock awaited them: it turned out that the groom's team included a group of Ahir singers, and when they began to perform, it became clear that the women would be hard put to compete.

> . . . *uthlé há chháti ke jobanwá*
> *piyá ké khélawna ré hoi . . .*

> . . . her budding breasts are ready
> to be her lover's toys . . .

Worse still, it turned out that one of the Ahirs was also a dancer, and knew how to do women's parts, having been trained as a dancing-launda back home. Despite the lack of proper costumes, make-up and accompaniment, he was persuaded to rise to his feet. A small space was cleared for him, in the centre of the deck, and even though he could scarcely stand without hitting his head, he performed so well that the women knew they would have to come up with something special if they were not to be put to shame.

Deeti, as the Bhauji who had organized the wedding, could not allow herself to be bested. When it was time for the midday meal, she gathered the women together and made them hang back in the dabusa. Come now, she said. What are we going to do? We have to think of something, or Heeru won't be able to hold up her head.

~

It was a withered piece of turmeric, from Sarju's bundle, that gave the bride's side a means of saving face: this root, so common on land, seemed as precious as ambergris now that they were at sea. Fortunately there was just about enough of it to produce a sufficient quantity of paste for the anointing of both bride and groom. But how was the turmeric to be ground, with neither stone nor mortar available? A way was found, eventually, involving the rear ends of two lotas. The effort and ingenuity that went into the grinding added an extra touch of brightness to the ceremony of yellowing, drawing chuckles even from the gloomiest of the girmitiyas.

What with the laughter and the singing, time went by so fast that everyone was amazed when the hatch was thrown open again, for the evening meal: it was hard to believe that it was already dark. The sight of the full moon, hanging upon the horizon with a great red halo around it, produced an awed hush among the migrants when they came on deck. No one had ever seen a moon so large or so strangely coloured: it was almost as if this were some other lunar body than that which lit the plains of Bihar. Even the wind, which had been blowing strongly through the day, seemed to be refreshed by the brightness of the light, for it picked up another knot or two, deepening the swells that were rolling towards the schooner from the eastern horizon. With the light and the waves coming from the same direction, the sea took on a furrowed appearance that reminded Deeti of the fields around Ghazipur at the time of year when the winter's crop was budding into bloom: then, too, if you looked out at night, you would see deep, dark channels in the fields, separating the endless rows of bright, moonlit blossoms—just like the red-flecked lines of foam that sat gleaming upon the dark troughs of the waves.

The schooner's masts were thesam-thes and the vessel was yawing steeply, with sharp saccades of her sails, leaning to leeward as she rode up the swells, and then easing off as she plunged into the troughs: it was as if she were dancing to the music of the wind, which rose in pitch as the vessel leant to leeward, and fell when she righted her keel.

Even though Deeti had grown accustomed to the motion of the ship, today she could not stay on her feet. For fear of tumbling overboard, she pulled Kalua down to squat on the deck-planks, and wedged herself between him and the solid bulwark beneath the deck rail. Whether it was because of the excitement of the wedding, or the moonlight, or the motion of the ship, she was never to know, but it was just then that she felt, for the first time, an unmistakable movement in her womb. Here! Under cover of the bulwark's shadow, she took Kalua's hand and placed it on her belly: Do you feel it?

She saw the flash of his teeth in the darkness and knew he was smiling: Yes, yes, it's the little one, kicking.

No, she said, not kicking—rolling, like the ship.

How strange it was to feel the presence of a body inside her, lurching in time to her own movements: it was as if her belly were the sea, and the child a vessel, sailing towards its own destiny.

Deeti turned to Kalua and whispered: Tonight it's like we too are being married again.

Why? said Kalua. Wasn't the first time good enough? When you found the flowers for the garlands and strung them together with your own hair?

But we didn't do the seven circles, she answered. There was no wood and no fire.

No fire? he said. But didn't we make our own?

Deeti blushed and pulled him to his feet: Chall, na. It's time to get back to Heeru's wedding.

～

The two convicts were sitting in the gloom of the chokey, silently picking oakum, when the door opened to admit the large, lamp-lit face of Baboo Nob Kissin.

The long-contemplated visit had not been easy to organize: only with the greatest reluctance had Subedar Bhyro Singh agreed to Baboo Nob Kissin's proposed 'tour of inspection', and on giving his assent, had imposed the condition that two of his silahdars would accompany the gomusta to the chokey and be present at the entrance all the while that he was inside. Having agreed to the arrangement, Baboo Nob Kissin had gone to great pains to prepare for the occasion. For his costume, he had chosen a saffron-coloured alkhalla, a robe voluminous enough to be suitable for male and female devotees alike. Hidden under the flowing folds of this garment, in a strip of cloth that was tied around his chest, was the small hoard of edible treats that he had gathered over the last few days—a couple of pomegranates, four hard-boiled eggs, a few crusty parathas and a lump of jaggery.

This contrivance served its purpose well enough at the start, and Baboo Nob Kissin was able to cross the main deck at a stately pace, walking in a manner that was not undignified, although perhaps a little top-heavy. But when he came to the entrance of the chokey, the matter took quite another turn: it was not easy for a man of his girth to pass through a low, narrow doorway, and in the process of bending and wriggling, some of the gifts seemed to acquire a life of their own, with the result that the gomusta had to use both his hands to hold his heaving bosom in place. Since the two silahdars were waiting at the door, he could not let go of his burden even after he had made his way in: sitting cross-legged in the tiny cell, he was forced into a posture like that of a wet-nurse cupping a pair of sore and milk-heavy breasts.

Neel and Ah Fatt stared at this weighty apparition in astonished silence. The convicts had yet to recover from their run-in with Mr Crowle: although the incident on the fo'c'sle deck had lasted no more than a few minutes, it had hit them with the force of a flash flood, sweeping away the fragile scaffolding of their friendship and leaving a residue that consisted not just of shame and humiliation, but also of a profound dejection. Once again, as through their time at Alipore Jail, they had fallen into an uncommunicative silence. The habit had taken hold so quickly that Neel could not now think of a word to say as he sat staring at Baboo Nob Kissin across a heap of unpicked oakum.

'To check up the premises, I have come.'

Baboo Nob Kissin made this announcement very loudly, and in English, so as to cast the visit in a properly official light. 'As such, all irregularities will be spotted out.'

The speechless convicts made no reply, so the gomusta seized the opportunity to subject their foul-smelling surroundings to a close scrutiny by the flickering light of his lamp. His attention was immediately arrested by the toilet balty and for a few moments his spiritual quest was interrupted by a more earthly interest.

'In this utensil you are passing urine and doing latrine?'

For the first time in a long while, Neel and Ah Fatt exchanged glances. 'Yes,' said Neel. 'That is correct.'

The gomusta's protuberant eyes grew still larger as he contemplated the implications of this. 'So both are present during purging?'

'Alas,' said Neel, 'we have no choice in the matter.'

The gomusta shuddered to think of what this would do to bowels as sensitive as his own. 'So stoppages must be extremely rigorous and frequent?'

Neel shrugged. 'We endure our lot as best we can.'

The gomusta frowned as he looked around the chokey. 'By Jove!' he said. 'Spaces are so scanty here, I do not know how you can refrain to make your ends meet.'

This met with no response and nor did the gomusta require any. He realized now, as he sniffed the air, that Ma Taramony's presence was struggling to reassert itself—for only the nose of a mother, surely, could transform the odour of her child's ordure to an almost-pleasing fragrance? As if to confirm the urgency of his inner being's claim for attention, a

*Amitav Ghosh*

pomegranate leapt from its hiding-place and came to rest atop the pile of oakum. The gomusta peered outside in alarm, and was relieved to see that the two silahdars were chatting with each other and had not noticed the fruit's sudden jump.

'Here, quickly, take,' said the gomusta, rapidly disbursing his trove of fruit, eggs, parathas and jaggery into Neel's hands. 'All is for you—extremely tasteful and beneficial to health. Motions may also be enhanced.'

Taken by surprise, Neel switched to Bengali: You are too generous . . .

The gomusta cut him abruptly short. Gesturing conspiratorially in the direction of the silahdars, he said: 'Kindly eschew native vernaculars. Guards are big trouble-shooters—always making mischiefs. Better they do not listen. Chaste English will suffice.'

'As you please.'

'It is advisable also that concealment of edibles is expedited.'

'Yes of course.'

Neel quickly slipped the food behind him—and just in time too, for the hoard was no sooner hidden than one of the silahdars poked his head through the door, urging the gomusta to be done with whatever he was doing.

Seeing that their time was short, Neel said quickly: 'I am most grateful to you for these gifts. But may I inquire as to the reason for your generosity?'

'You cannot connect it up?' cried the gomusta in evident disappointment.

'What?'

'That Ma Taramony has sent? Recognition is not there?'

'Ma Taramony!' Neel was perfectly familiar with the name, having often heard it on Elokeshi's lips—but the mention of it, now, took him by surprise. 'But has she not passed away?'

Here, after shaking his head vigorously in denial, Baboo Nob Kissin opened his mouth to issue an explanation. But then, faced with the task of finding words that were adequate to the enormous complexity of the matter, he changed his mind and chose instead to make a movement of the hands, a sweeping, fluttering gesture that ended with his forefinger pressed against his bosom, pointing to the presence that was blossoming within.

It was never clear whether it was because of the eloquence of this signal, or merely out of gratitude for the food the gomusta had brought—but it happened anyway that the gesture succeeded in disclosing something of more than trivial importance to Neel. He was left with the impression of having understood a little of what Baboo Nob Kissin was trying to convey; and he understood also that there was something at work within this strange man that was somehow out of the ordinary. What exactly it was he could not say, and nor was there time to think about the matter, for the silahdars had now begun to hammer on the door, to speed the gomusta's departure.

'Further discussions must wait for rainy day,' said Baboo Nob Kissin. 'I will try to prepone to earliest opportunity. Until then, please note that Ma Taramony has asked to bestow blessings-message.'

With that, the gomusta patted both convicts lightly on their foreheads and plunged headfirst out of the chokey's door.

After he was gone, the chokey seemed even dimmer than usual. Without quite knowing what he was doing, Neel divided the hoard of food into two parts and held one out to his cell-mate: 'Here.'

Ah Fatt's hand stole out of the darkness to receive his share. Then, for the first time since their encounter with the first mate, he spoke: 'Neel . . .'

'What?'

'Was bad, what happen . . .'

'Don't say that to me. You should say it to yourself.'

There was a brief silence before Ah Fatt spoke again. 'I going to kill that bastard.'

'Who?'

'Crowle.'

'With what?' Neel was tempted to laugh. 'Your hands?'

'You wait. See.'

~

*Amitav Ghosh*

The matter of a sacramental flame was much on Deeti's mind. A proper fire, even a small one, was not to be thought of, given all the hazards. Something safe would have to be provided instead. But what? The wedding being a special occasion, the migrants had pooled their resources and gathered a few lamps and candles to light the dabusa for the last part of the nuptials. But a shuttered lamp or lantern, like those that were commonly used on the ship, would rob the ceremony of all meaning: who could take seriously a wedding in which the bride and groom performed their 'seven circles' around a single, sooty flame? Candles would have to serve the purpose, Deeti decided, as many as could safely be stuck on a single thali. The candles were found and duly lit, but when they were carried to the centre of the dabusa, the fiery thali was found to have developed a mind of its own: with the ship rolling and pitching, it went shooting around the deck, threatening to set the whole dabusa alight. It was clear that someone would have to be stationed beside it, to hold it in place—but who? There were so many volunteers that a half-dozen men had to be assigned to the task, so as not to give anyone cause for offence. Then, when the bridal couple attempted to stand up, it was only to underscore, yet again, that this ritual had not been conceived with the Black Water in mind: for no sooner had they risen than their feet were knocked out from under them by the heaving of the ship. They both flopped belly-first on the deck-planks and went tobogganing towards the jamna side of the hull. Just when a head-cracking collision seemed inevitable the schooner tilted again, to send them shooting off in the other direction, feet first. The hilarity created by this spectacle ended only when the most agile young men came forward to surround the bride and groom with a webbing of shoulders and arms, holding them upright. But soon the young men began to slip and slide too, so that many others had to join in: in her eagerness to circle the flames, Deeti made sure that she and Kalua were among the first to leap into the scrum. Soon it was as if the whole dabusa were being united in a sacramental circle of matrimony: such was the enthusiasm that when it came time for the newlyweds to enter the improvised bridal chamber, it was with some difficulty that other revellers were prevented from accompanying them as they went in.

With the bride and groom closeted in the kohbar, the ribaldry and singing mounted to a crescendo. There was so much noise that no one in the dabusa had the faintest awareness that events of an entirely different order were transpiring elsewhere. Their first inkling of it came when something fell on the deck, above their heads, with a huge thud, shaking the vessel. The sound produced a moment of startled calm, and this was when they heard a scream, in a woman's voice, echoing down from somewhere high above: *Bacháo*! They're killing him! They've thrown him down . . .

Who's that? said Deeti.

Paulette was the first to think of Munia: Where's she gone? Is she here? Munia, where are you?

There was no answer and Deeti cried: Where could she be?

Bhauji, I think in all the confusion of the wedding, she must have sneaked out somehow, to meet . . .

A lascar?

Yes. I think she hid herself on deck and stayed on after we came down. They must have got caught.

~

From the roof of the deckhouse to the main deck was a drop of a little more than five feet. Jodu had made the jump many times of his own accord, never with any ill effect. But to be slung down by a silahdar was a different matter: he had fallen headfirst and had been lucky to hit the deck with his shoulder rather than his crown. Now, in trying to rise to his feet, he was conscious of a searing pain in his upper arm and when pushing himself up, he found that his shoulder would not bear his weight. As he was trying to find his footing on the slick, slippery deck, a hand took hold of his banyan and pulled him upright.

*Sala*! *Kutta*! You lascar dog . . .

Jodu tried to twist his head around to look the subedar in the face. I didn't do anything, he managed to say. We were only talking, just a few words—that's all.

You dare look me in the eye, you son of a pig?

Raising his arm, the subedar winched Jodu bodily off the deck, holding him suspended in the air, legs and arms flailing helplessly. Then he drew his other hand back and drove his clenched fist into the side of Jodu's face. Jodu felt a spurt of blood, leaking on to his tongue from a newly opened fissure between his teeth. His vision was suddenly blurry, so that Munia, who was now crouching under a longboat, looked like a heap of canvas pickings.

He began again—I didn't do anything—but the ringing in his head was so loud he could hardly hear his own voice. Then the back of the subedar's hand slammed into the other side of his face, knocking the air from his lungs, blowing his cheek out, like a stu'nsail caught by a thod of wind. The force of the blow wrenched him out of the subedar's grip, sending him sprawling on the deck.

You cut-prick lascar—where did you get the balls to go sniffing after our girls?

Jodu's eyes were half-closed now, and the ringing in his head made him insensible to the pain in his shoulder. He managed to struggle to his feet, swaying drunkenly as he tried to find his balance on the tilted deck. By the light of the binnacle-lamp he saw that the fana-wale had crowded around to watch: they were all there, Mamdoo-tindal, Sunker, Rajoo, looking over the shoulders of the silahdars, waiting to see what he, Jodu, would do next. His awareness of his shipmates' presence made him doubly conscious of his hard-earned standing among them, and in a rush of bravado, he spat the blood from his mouth and snarled at the subedar: B'henchod—who do you think you are? You think we're your slaves?

Kyá? Sheer astonishment at this piece of effrontery slowed the subedar's reactions by an instant. In that moment Mr Crowle stepped up to take his place, in front of Jodu.

'Why, in't it Reid's little scumsucker, again?'

The first mate had a length of rope in his hands, which he was holding by its bight. Now, drawing his arm back, he lashed the knotted end of the rope across Jodu's shoulders, forcing him to his hands and knees: 'Down, y'little claw-buttock.'

The rope came down again, hitting Jodu so hard that he was propelled forwards on all fours. 'That's right. Crawl, y'dog, crawl—I'll see yer crawling like an animal afore I'm done with yer.'

When next the rope came down, Jodu's arms were knocked out from under him and he fell flat on the deck-planks. The mate took hold of his Osnaburg banyan and pulled Jodu back on all fours, tearing the garment down the middle. 'Din't I say crawl? Don't lie there grindin yer gutstick on the deck—crawl like the dog that y'are.'

A kick sent Jodu tottering forward on his hands and knees, but his shoulder could not long take the weight and after a few more paces, he collapsed on his stomach again. His banyan was torn down the middle now, hanging in shreds under his armpits. There was no handhold to be found on those ragged strips of cloth, so instead the mate reached for his trowsers. Seizing the waistband, he gave it a jerk that ripped the frayed canvas apart at the seams. It was on the bare skin of Jodu's buttocks that the rope slammed down now, and the pain forced a cry from his lips.

*Allah*! *Bacháo*!

'Don't y'waste yer breath now,' said the mate grimly. 'Jack Crowle's the one to call on; no one else can save yer bacon here.'

Again the rope descended on the small of Jodu's back, and the pain was so intense, so numbing, that he no longer had the strength even to fall on his face. He went a couple more paces on all fours, and then, with his head hanging down, he saw, framed in the triangular gap between his naked thighs, the faces of the trikat-wale, watching him in pity and shame.

'Crawl, y'sonky dog!'

He lurched another couple of paces, and then two more,

while in his head a voice was saying—yes, you're an animal now, a dog, they've made a beast out of you: crawl, crawl . . .

He had crawled far enough to satisfy the first mate. Mr Crowle dropped his rope and gestured to the silahdars: 'Take the shit-heel down to the chokey and lock him in.'

They were done with him now—he was no better than a carcass to be carted away. As the guards were dragging him towards the fana, Jodu heard the subedar's voice, somewhere aft.

And now, you coolie whore—it's your turn; it's time you were taught a lesson too.

~

The dabusa was now in a state of utter confusion: everyone was milling about trying to make sense of what was happening above. It was as if they were ants, trapped inside a drum, trying to understand what was taking place on the other side of the skin: Was that heavy scraping sound, going agil, an indication that Jodu was being dragged to the fana? Was that tattoo of knocks over there, heading peechil, the sound of Munia kicking her heels as she was dragged away?

Then they heard Munia's voice: *Bacháo!* Save me, oh you people, they're taking me down to their kamra . . .

Munia's words were cut suddenly short, as if a hand had been clamped over her lips.

Paulette snatched at Deeti's elbow. Bhauji! We have to do something! Bhauji! There's no telling what they might do to her.

What can we do, Pugli?

It passed through Deeti's mind to say no, this wasn't her burden, she wasn't really everyone's Bhauji and couldn't be expected to fight every battle. But then she thought of Munia, all alone, amongst a roomful of silahdars and maistries, and her body rose as of itself. Come: let's go to the ladder.

With Kalua clearing a path, she went up the ladder and

began to bang on the hatch: Ahó! Who's there? Where are you—oh, you great paltans of maistries and silahdars?

Receiving no answer, she turned to face the dabusa: And you? she said to her fellow migrants. Why're you all so quiet now? You were making enough noise a few minutes ago. Come on! Let's see if we can't rattle the masts on this ship; let's see how long they can ignore us.

It began slowly, the noise-making, with the hills-men rising to their feet to stamp on the deck-planks. Then someone began to bang her bangles on a thali and others joined in, beating gharas and pots, or just shouting or singing, and within a few minutes it was as if some uncontainable force had been released inside the dabusa, an energy that was capable of shaking the oakum from the schooner's seams.

Suddenly, the hatch-cover flew open and the voice of an unseen silahdar came echoing through the opening. The gratings were still in place and Deeti could not see who was speaking nor follow his words. She set Kalua and Paulette to the task of silencing the others and raised her ghungta'd face to the hatch: Who are you up there?

What's going on with you coolies? came the answer. What's this noise?

You know very well what's going on, said Deeti. You've taken one of our girls away. We're worried about her.

Worried, are you?—the sneer was audible—why weren't you worried when she was whoring herself to a lascar? A Muslim at that?

Malik, said Deeti. Let her come back to us, and we'll settle the matter amongst us. It's best that we deal with our own.

It's too late for that; the Subedar-ji says she has to be kept in a safe place from now on.

Safe? said Deeti. Amongst all of you? Don't tell me that stuff: I've seen it all—*sab dekhchukalbáni*. Go: tell your subedar that we want to see our girl and won't rest till we do. Go. Right now.

There was a brief silence, during which they could hear the

maistries and silahdars consulting with each other. In a while, one of them said: Keep quiet for now, and we'll see what the subedar says.

All right.

An excited hubbub broke out in the 'tween-deck as the hatch-cover slammed back into place:

. . . You've done it again, Bhauji . . .

. . . They're scared of you . . .

. . . What you say, Bhauji, they cannot but do . . .

These premature comments filled Deeti with dread. Nothing's happened yet, she snapped; let's wait and see . . .

A good quarter of an hour passed before the hatch-cover opened again. Then a finger came through the gratings to point to Deeti. You there, said the same voice. The subedar says you can go and see the girl; no one else.

Alone? said Deeti. Why alone?

Because we don't want another riot. Remember what happened at Ganga-Sagar?

Deeti felt Kalua's hand slipping into hers, and she raised her voice: I won't go without my *jora*, my husband.

This led to another whispered consultation and another concession: All right then—let him come up too.

The gratings creaked open and Deeti climbed slowly out of the dabusa, with Kalua following behind her. There were three silahdars on deck, armed with long staves, their faces shadowed by their turbans. As soon as Deeti and Kalua stepped out, the gratings and hatch-cover were slammed shut, with such finality that Deeti began to wonder whether the guards had been waiting all along to separate the two of them from the other migrants: could it be that they had walked into a trap?

Her misgivings deepened when the sirdars produced a length of rope and ordered Kalua to put out his hands.

Why are you binding his wrists? cried Deeti.

Just to keep him quiet while you're gone.

I won't go without him, said Deeti.

Do you want to be dragged then? Like the other one?

Kalua jogged her elbow: Go, he whispered. If there's

trouble, just raise your voice. I'm here; I'll be listening and I'll find a way—*ham sahára khojat* . . .

~

Deeti lengthened her ghungta as she followed the silahdar down the ladder that led to the beech-kamra. In comparison with the dabusa, this part of the vessel was brightly lit, with several lamps suspended from the ceiling. The lights were swinging in wide arcs, with the rolling of the ship, and their pendulum-like movement multiplied the shadows of the men inside, so that the cabin seemed to be filled with a crowd of hurtling figures and shapes. Stepping off the last rung, Deeti averted her eyes and clung to the ladder to steady herself. She could tell from the mingled smell of smoke and sweat that there were many men inside the compartment; even with her head lowered she could feel their eyes boring into the shield of her ghungta.

. . . This is the one . . .

. . . *Jobhan sabhanké hamré khiláf bhatkáwat rahlé* . . .

. . . The one who's always inciting the others against us . . .

Deeti's courage almost failed her now, and her feet would have ceased to move if the silahdar had not muttered: What are you stopping for? Keep moving.

Where are you taking me? said Deeti.

To the girl, said the silahdar. Isn't that what you wanted?

Candle in hand, the silahdar led her down another turn of the ladder, stepping off when they came to a warren of storerooms. The smell of the bilges was so strong now that Deeti had to pinch her nostrils between finger and thumb.

The silahdar came to a halt at a latched door. This is where she is, he said. You'll find her inside.

Deeti glanced fearfully at the door. In there? she said. What is that place?

A bhandar, said the silahdar as he pushed the door open.

The smell of the storeroom was pungently reminiscent of

*Amitav Ghosh*

a bazar, with the gummy, oily reek of heeng overpowering even the stink of the schooner's bilges. It was very dark, and Deeti could see nothing, but she heard a sob and cried out: Munia?

Bhauji? Munia's voice rose in relief. Is it really you?

Yes, Munia, where are you? I can't see anything.

The girl rushed into her arms: Bhauji! Bhauji! I knew you would come.

Deeti held her off with extended arms. You fool, Munia, you fool! she cried. What were you doing up there?

Nothing, Bhauji, said Munia. Nothing, believe me—he was just helping me with the chickens. They stole up on us and started beating him. Then they threw him down.

And you? said Deeti. Have they done anything to you?

Just a few slaps and kicks, Bhauji, not much. But it's you they've been waiting for . . .

Suddenly Deeti became aware that someone else was standing behind her now, with a candle in hand. Then she heard a deep, heavy voice, saying to the silahdar: Take the girl away—it's the other one I want. I'll talk to her alone.

~

In the flickering light, Deeti could see sacks of grain and dal, piled high on the floor of the storeroom. The shelves along the sides were crammed with jars of spices, bundles of onion and garlic, and huge martabans of pickled limes, chillies and mangoes. The air was befogged with white dust, of the kind that is sweated by bags of grain; as the door of the storeroom slammed shut, a flake of red chilli entered Deeti's eye.

So?

Unhurriedly, Bhyro Singh latched the door of the storeroom and stuck his candle upright, in a sack of rice. Deeti had been facing away from him all this while, but she turned around now, holding her ghungta in place with one hand and rubbing her eye with the other.

What does this mean? she said, in a show of defiance. Why did you want to see me alone?

Bhyro Singh was wearing a langot and a banyan, and now, as Deeti turned towards him, the mound of his belly surged out of the confinement of the two flimsy garments. The subedar made no attempt to pull his vest down: instead, he cupped his hands under his belly and moved it tenderly up and down, as though he were weighing it. Then, he picked a bit of lint out of the gaping mouth of his belly-button and examined it closely.

So? he said again. How long did you think you could hide from me, Kabutri-ki-ma?

Deeti felt herself choke and stuffed a fistful of her ghungta into her mouth, to keep from crying out loud.

Why so quiet? Nothing to say to me? Bhyro Singh reached for her ghungta: No need to cover up any more. It's just you and me here. Just us.

Pulling her veil down, he tipped her head back with a finger and nodded in satisfaction: The grey eyes; I remember them, filled with witchery. The eyes of a chudail, some people thought—but I always said, no, those are the eyes of a whore.

Deeti tried to strike his hand away from her neck, but it stayed where it was. If you knew who I was, she said, still defiant, why didn't you say something earlier?

His lips curled in derision: And bring shame on myself? Acknowledge a tie with a woman like you? A whore who's run away with a filth-sweeper? An overheated bitch who's brought shame on her family, her village, her in-laws? You take me for a fool? Don't you know I have daughters of my own, to marry off?

Deeti narrowed her eyes and spat back: Be careful. My jora is waiting, above.

Your *jora*? said Bhyro Singh. You can forget about that scavenging piece of filth. He'll be dead before the year's out.

*I ká káhat ho*? she gasped. What's this you're saying?

He ran a finger up her neck and tweaked her ear-lobe: Don't you know, he said, that I'm the one who's in charge of your allotments? Don't you know it's me who decides who your master will be in Mareech? I've already set your *jora*'s name down for a plantation up north. He'll never come out from there alive. You can take my word for it: that shit-shoveller you call a husband is as good as dead.

And me? said Deeti.

You? He smiled and stroked her neck again. For you I have other plans.

What?

The tip of his tongue flicked over his lips and there was a rasp in his voice as he said: What does anyone want from a whore? His hand slipped through the neck of her choli and began to fumble for a handhold.

For shame, said Deeti, pushing his hand away. For shame . . .

There's nothing here that's new to me, he said, smiling. I've seen the grain-bag and I know it's full—*dekhlé tobra, janlé bharalba.*

*Áp pe thuki!* cried Deeti. I spit on you and your filth.

He leant forward so that his belly was against her breasts. He smiled again: Who do you think it was who held your legs open on your wedding night? Did you think that green twig of a launda, your brother-in-law, could have done it on his own?

Have you no shame? said Deeti, choking. Is there nothing you won't say? Do you know I'm with child?

Child? Bhyro Singh laughed. A child from that scavenger? By the time I'm done with you, his spawn will be dribbling out of you like an egg-yolk.

Tightening his hold on her neck, he reached up to a shelf with his other hand. His fist came back to brandish a foot-long roti-rolling *belan* under her nose.

So what do you say, Kabutri-ki-ma? he said. Are you whore enough for this?

~

It wasn't Deeti's cry for help but Munia's echo of it that was audible on the main deck, where Kalua was squatting between two silahdars with his hands bound by a length of rope. He had stayed quietly in place since Deeti was led away, giving careful thought to what he would have to do if it came to the worst. The silahdars were lightly armed, with knives and lathis, and it would be no great matter, Kalua knew, to break away from them. But after that, what? If he were to storm into the guard's kamra, he would run into many more men, and more armaments too: they would kill him before he could do Deeti any good. Far better to sound an alarm that would be heard in every quarter of the ship—and the perfect instrument for that was no more than a few paces away, the deckhouse ghanta. If he could but set the bell ringing, the migrants would be alerted and the officers and lascars would come on deck in force.

Back at home, in his ox-cart, it had been a habit with Kalua to count the squeaks of his wheel to keep an accurate measure of time and distance. Now, he found that the same purpose was served by counting the swells that were advancing towards the vessel, lifting her bows and setting them down, as they passed. After ten such had gone by, he knew something must be wrong, and it was exactly then that he caught the sound of Munia's voice, shouting: Bhauji? What're they doing . . .?

The schooner was in a steep roll, so that Kalua could feel the tilted bulwark lying aslant against the soles of his feet. Ahead of him, the deck was like a hillside, sloping upwards. Using the bulwark as a springboard, he jumped forwards, frog-like, covering half the distance to the bell in one leap. His move was so sudden the silahdars had yet to stir when he reached the lanyard that was attached to the bell's clapper. But the line had to be unwound from its eyebolt before it could be tugged, and this pause gave the guards the time they needed to fall upon him; one of them brought a lathi crashing down on his hands, while the other threw himself on his back, trying to wrestle him to the deck.

Kalua made a double fist out of his bound hands and swung out at the lathi-wielding silahdar, knocking him off his feet. Turning with the momentum of the swing, he took hold of the other man's arm and pulled him off his back, headfirst, slamming him down on the deck. Then he caught hold of the bell's lanyard, tore it free, and set the clapper swinging.

As the first, furious chimes were ringing out, another swell took hold of the vessel, tipping her sharply on her side. One of the guards was knocked down as he tried to rise to his feet, and the other, who had been working his way towards Kalua, slipped sideways so that the bulwark caught him in the belly. He lingered on the deck rail for a moment, with half his body hanging overboard, clutching wildly at the slippery stanchions. Then, almost as if to shake him off, the *Ibis* dipped her flank still further, and a lapping crest of turbulence reached up to claim him for the deep.

~

Once again, the ringing of the bell transformed the dabusa into a drum. The migrants gathered together in uncomprehending huddles, as the sound of the feet above them rose to a crescendo. Through the percussive tattoo an even more bewildering sound could be heard—a chorus of alarms and hookums: *Admi giráh! Man overboard! Look out aft! Peechil dekho! Dekho peechil!* Yet despite the shouts and the noise, there was no change in the schooner's movement: she went ploughing on as before.

Suddenly the dabusa's hatch cover flew open and Deeti and Munia came tumbling through. Paulette lost no time in elbowing through the milling crowd that collected around them: What happened? What happened? Are you all right?

Deeti was shaking so much she could hardly speak: Yes, we're all right, Munia and I. It was the ghanta that saved us.

Who rang it?

My husband . . . there was a fight and one of the silahdars fell . . . it was an accident, but they're calling it murder . . . they've tied him to the mast, my *jora* . . .

What're they going to do, Bhauji?

I don't know, sobbed Deeti, wringing her hands. I don't

know, Pugli: the subedar's gone to speak to the afsars. It's up to the Kaptan now. Maybe he'll have mercy . . . we can only hope . . .

In the darkness Munia slipped over to Paulette and took hold of her arm: Pugli, tell me: Azad? How is he?

Paulette glared at her: Munia, after all the trouble you've caused, how can you even dare to ask?

Munia began to sob: We weren't doing anything, Pugli, believe me—just talking. Is that so bad?

Bad or not, Munia, he's the one who's paying the price. He's so badly hurt he's barely conscious. The best thing now, Munia, is for you to stay well away from him.

~

For Zachary, the single most disorienting aspect of life at sea was the peculiar cycle of sleep that resulted from the unvarying rhythm of watch-on-watch. With four hours on and four hours off—except for the dogwatches of dawn and dusk—he often found that he had to rouse himself exactly when he was sleeping most soundly. The result of this was that he slept in the way that a glutton eats, gorging greedily when possible, and resenting every minute subtracted from the feast. While asleep, his hearing would shut out any noise that might disturb or distract—shouts and hookums, the sea and the wind. Yet, his ears would still keep count of the chimes of the ship's bell, so that even in his deepest slumber, he was never unaware of how much time was left before his next spell on deck.

That night, being off-watch till midnight, Zachary had taken to his bunk soon after dinner and had drowsed off almost at once, remaining fast asleep until the deckhouse bell began to clang. Waking instantly, he pulled on a pair of trowsers, and went racing to the stern to look for signs of the man who had fallen overboard. The vigil was a short one, for everyone knew that the silahdar's chances of survival in that choppy sea were too slim to warrant taking in the sails or bringing the ship about: by the time either manoeuvre was completed he would be long gone. But to turn your back on a drowned man was not easy, and Zachary stayed at the stern well after there was any purpose to be served by lingering.

By the time he went down to his cabin again, the offender had been roped to the mainmast, and the Captain was down in his stateroom, closeted with Bhyro Singh and his translator, Baboo Nob Kissin. An hour later, as Zachary was preparing to go on deck for his watch, Steward Pinto knocked on his door to say that the Captain had sent for him. Zachary stepped out of his cabin to find the Captain and Mr Crowle already seated around the table, with the steward hovering in the background with a tray of brandy.

Once they had all been served, the Captain dismissed Steward Pinto with a nod: 'Off with you now. And don't let me find you lurking about on the quarter-deck.'

'Sahib.'

The Captain waited for the steward to disappear before he spoke again. 'It's a bad business, gentlemen,' he said gloomily, twirling his glass. 'A bad business—worse than I thought.'

'He's a bruiser, that black bastard,' said Mr Crowle. 'I'll sleep easier after I've heard him singing the hempen croak.'

'Oh he'll hang for sure,' said the Captain. 'But be that as it may, it's not my place to sentence him. Case needs to be heard by a judge in Port Louis. And the subedar, in the meanwhile, will have to content himself with a flogging.'

'Flogged *and* hung sir?' said Zachary incredulously. 'For the same offence?'

'In the subedar's eyes,' said the Captain, 'the murder is the least of his crimes. He says that if they were at home, this man'd be cut up and fed to the dogs for what he's done.'

'What's he done, sir?' said Zachary.

'This man'—the Captain looked down at a sheet of paper, to remind himself of the name—'this Maddow Colver; he's a pariah who's run off with a woman of high caste—a relative of the subedar as it happens. That's why this Colver signed up—so he could carry the woman off to a place where she'd never be found.'

'But sir,' said Zachary, 'surely his choice of wife is not our business? And surely we can't let him be flogged for it while he is in our custody?'

'Indeed?' said the Captain, raising his eyebrows. 'I am amazed, Reid, that you of all people—an American!—should pose these questions. Why, what do you think would happen in Maryland if a white woman were to be violated by a Negro? What would you, or I, or any of us, do with a darkie who'd had his way with our wives or sisters? Why should we expect the subedar and his men to feel any less strongly than we would ourselves? And what right do we have to deny them the vengeance that we would certainly claim as our due? No sir . . .' The Captain rose from his chair and began to pace up and down the cuddy, as he continued: '. . . no sir, I will not deny these men, who have served us faithfully, the justice they seek. For this you should know, gentlemen, that there is an unspoken pact between the white man and the natives who sustain his power in Hindoosthan—it is that in matters of marriage and procreation, like must be with like, and each must keep to their own. The day the natives lose faith in us, as the guarantors of the order of castes—that will be the day, gentlemen, that will doom our rule. This is the inviolable principle on which our authority is based—it is what makes our rule different from that of such degenerate and decayed peoples as the Spanish and Portuguese. Why, sir, if you wish to see what comes of miscegenation and mongrelism, you need only visit their possessions . . .'

Here the Captain came abruptly to a stop and planted himself behind a chair: '. . . And while I am about this, let me speak plainly with both of you: gentlemen, what you do in port is your affair; I hold no jurisdiction over you onshore; whether you spend your time in bowsing-kens or cunny-warrens is none of my business. Even if you should choose to go a-buttocking in the blackest of shoreside holes, it is none of my concern. But while at sea and under my command, you should know that if any evidence of any kind of intercourse with a native, of any mould, were ever to be brought against one of my officers . . . well, gentlemen, let me just say that man could expect no mercy from me.'

Neither mate had any response to this and both averted their eyes.

'As for this Maddow Colver,' the Captain continued, 'he will be flogged tomorrow. Sixty strokes, to be administered by the subedar at noon.'

'Did you say sixty, sir?' said Zachary in awed disbelief.

'That's what the subedar's asked for,' said the Captain, 'and I have awarded it to him.'

'But might he not bleed to death, sir, the coolie?'

'That remains to be seen, Reid,' said Captain Chillingworth. 'Certainly the subedar will be none too sorry if he does.'

~

Shortly after daybreak Paulette heard her name being whispered through the air duct: Putli? Putli?

Jodu? Rising to her feet, Paulette put her eye to the duct. I want to get a good look at you, Jodu; move back.

He stepped away and she gave an involuntary gasp. In the scant light from the cracks in the bulwarks, she saw that his left arm was suspended from his neck by an improvised sling; his eyes were swollen and blackened, the whites barely visible; his wounds were still oozing blood and the fabric of his borrowed banyan was striped with stains.

Oh Jodu, Jodu! she whispered. What did they do to you?

It's only my shoulder that hurts now, he said, with an attempt at a smile. The rest looks bad but it doesn't hurt as much.

Suddenly angry, Paulette said: It's that Munia; she's such a . . .

No! Jodu broke in. You can't blame her; it's my own fault.

Paulette could not deny the truth of this. Oh Jodu, she said. What a fool you are: why did you do something so stupid?

There was nothing to it, Putli, he said offhandedly. It was just a harmless time-passing thing. That's all.

Didn't I warn you, Jodu?

Yes, you did, Putli, came the answer. And others did too. But let me ask you: didn't I warn you about trying to get on this ship? And did you listen? No—of course not. You and I, we've always been like that, both of us. We've always been able to get away with things. But I suppose some day it stops, doesn't it? And then you have to start all over again.

This alarmed Paulette, not least because introspection had always been utterly foreign to Jodu; never before had she heard him speak in this vein.

And now, Jodu? she said. What's going to happen to you now?

I don't know, he said. Some of my shipmates say the whole tamasha will be forgotten in a day or two. But others think I'll be a target for the silahdars until we get into port.

And you? What do you think?

He took his time in answering, and when he spoke it was with an effort. For myself, Putli, he said, I'm done with the *Ibis*. After being beaten like a dog in front of everyone, I would rather drown than stay afloat in this cursed ship.

There was something implacable and unfamiliar in his voice and it made her glance at him again, as if to reassure herself that it was indeed Jodu who had spoken. The sight that met her eyes offered no such comfort: with his bruises and his swollen face and bloody clothes, he looked like the chrysalis of a being new and unknown. She was reminded of a tamarind seed that she had once wrapped in layers of damp cloth: after a fortnight of watering, when a tiny shoot had poked its head through, she had undone the wrappings to look for the seed—but in vain, for nothing remained of it but tiny shell-like fragments.

What will you do then, Jodu? she said.

He came closer and put his lips to the duct. Look, Putli, he whispered, I shouldn't be telling you this—but it's possible that some of us may be able to get off this ship.

Who? And how?

In one of the boats—me, the qaidis, some others too.

Nothing's certain yet, but if it happens it'll be tonight. And there's something you may have to do for us—I don't know for sure yet, but I'll tell you when I do. In the meanwhile, not a word, to anyone.

~

*Habés-pál!*

The hookum to heave-to was called in the middle of the morning. Below, in the dabusa, everyone knew that the ship would take in her sails when it was time for Kalua's flogging, and it was the change in the sound of the canvas, as much as the slowing of the vessel, that told them the moment was imminent: with the masts stripped almost bare, the wind had begun to whistle as it tore through the rigging. The wind had held steady overnight, and the *Ibis* was still wallowing through heavy, foam-flecked swells. The sky had darkened in the meanwhile, with waves of grey cloud tumbling over each other.

Once the ship had slowed, the maistries and silahdars went about the business of mustering the migrants with a grim, almost salacious relish: the women were told to remain in the dabusa, but of the men, apart from a few who were too unwell to stand, all the rest were made to go above. The men stepped on deck expecting to find Kalua at the mast, in chains, but he was nowhere to be seen: he had been removed to the fana and would not be produced till later, when his entrance would have the greatest possible effect.

The schooner was pitching so hard that the migrants could not be kept on their feet, as at their last muster at Saugor Roads. The guards made them sit in rows, facing the quarter-deck, with their backs to the stern. As if to underline the exemplary nature of what they were about to witness, the guards and overseers were meticulous in ensuring that every man had a clear and unobstructed view of the frame-like contrivance that had been prepared for Kalua's flogging—a rectangular set of gratings that had been set against the centre of the fife-rails, with ropes tied to each corner for the shackling of his ankles and wrists.

Bhyro Singh had placed himself at the head of this assembly and he was wearing his old regimental uniform: a freshly-laundered dhoti and a maroon-coloured coattee, with a subedar's stripes on the sleeves. While the guards were organizing the migrants, he sat cross-legged on a pile of ropes, combing the strands of a leather chabuk and pausing, from time to time, to send the lash cracking through the air. He paid no attention to the migrants, but they, on the other hand, could not tear their eyes from the gleaming lash of his whip.

Presently, after administering a last test to the chabuk, the subedar rose and signalled to Steward Pinto to summon the officers to the quarter-deck. The sahibs took a few minutes to appear, the Kaptan coming first and then the two malums. All three men were seen to be armed, for they had left their coats open in such a way that the butts of the pistols in their waistbands were clearly visible.

As was the custom, the Kaptan took his stand, not at the centre of the quarter-deck, but rather at the weather end, which happened to be on the schooner's dawa side. The two malums stood guard near the centre, on either side of the frame.

All this had unfolded at a slow, ceremonial pace, to allow the migrants time to absorb every element of it: it was as though they were being primed, not merely to watch the flogging, but actually to share in the experience of the pain. The timing and the gradual accumulation of details created a kind of stupor—not so much of fear, as of collective anticipation—so that when Kalua was led through their midst, it was as if they were all, severally, being tied to the frame for the flogging.

But there was one respect in which none of them could imagine themselves to be Kalua, which was his enormous size. He was brought on deck wearing only a langot, which had been pulled tight between his legs, so as to present the lash with the widest possible expanse of flesh and skin. The white

*Amitav Ghosh*

band of the langot seemed to amplify his stature so that even before he had stepped up to the fife-rail, it was clear that his body would not fit within the chosen frame: his head rose well above it, reaching up to the top of the rails, where it was level with the malums' knees. As a result, the bindings that had been prepared for him had to be rearranged: while his ankles remained at the two lower corners of the frame, his wrists had to be tied to the fife-rails, where they were aligned with his face.

When the ropes had been tied and tested, the subedar saluted the Kaptan and announced that all was ready: *Sab taiyár sah'b*!

The Kaptan answered with a nod and gave him the signal to start: 'Chullo!'

The silence on deck was now so profound that the Kaptan's voice was clearly audible in the dabusa, as were the subedar's footsteps, when he measured out the paces for his run-up. Deeti gasped—*Hé Rám, hamré bacháo*! Paulette and the other women huddled over her, clamping their hands over their ears, in an effort to deaden the crack of the whip—in vain, as it turned out, for they could spare themselves no part of it, not the whistle of the leather as it curled through the air, nor the sickening crunch with which it bit into Kalua's skin.

Up on the quarter-deck, Zachary was the closest to Kalua, and he felt the impact of the whip through the soles of his feet. A moment later something stung him on his face; he drew the back of his hand across his cheek and saw that it was blood. He felt his gorge rise and took a backwards step.

Beside him, Mr Crowle, who had been watching with a smile, gave a chuckle: 'No goose without gravy, eh Mannikin?'

∼

The swing of his arm had brought Bhyro Singh close enough that he could watch the weal rising on Kalua's skin. In savage satisfaction, he muttered into his ear: *Kuttá*! Scavenging dog, see what you've earned for yourself? You'll be dead before I'm done with you.

Kalua heard him clearly, through the buzzing in his head, and he asked, in a whisper: Malik—what have I ever done to you?

The question—as much as the bewildered tone in which it was asked—further enraged Bhyro Singh. Done? he said. Isn't it enough that you are what you are?

These words echoed through Kalua's head as the subedar walked away, to begin his next run: Yes, what I am is enough . . . through this life and the next, it will be enough . . . this is what I will live through, again and again and again . . .

Yet, even as he was listening to the echo of Bhyro Singh's voice, in some other part of his head he was counting the subedar's paces, numbering the seconds till the next blow. When the lash dug in, the pain was so fierce, so blinding, that his head slumped sideways, towards his wrist, so that he could feel the roughness of the rope against his lips. To keep himself from biting his tongue, he clamped his teeth upon the coil, and when the lash struck again, the pain made his jaws lock so that he bit clean through one of the four turns of rope with which his wrist was tied.

Again the subedar's voice was in his ear, speaking in a mocking whisper: *Kāptí ke marlá kuchhwó dokh nahin*—To kill a deceiver is no sin . . .

These words, too, echoed through Kalua's head—*kāptí . . . ke . . . marlá . . . kuchhwó . . . dokh . . . nahin*—each of the syllables marking one of the subedar's paces, going away and then turning around to come thundering back, until the lash flamed across his back, and again he bit through another twist of rope: then it began once more, the enumeration of the syllables, the crack of the lash, and the tightening of his teeth—again, and yet again, until the bindings on his wrist were all but gone, except for a few last threads.

By this time, the drumbeat in Kalua's head had attuned itself so accurately to the subedar's paces that he knew exactly when the lash was uncoiling through the air, and he knew, too,

*Amitav Ghosh*

exactly when to pull his hand free. As the subedar came rushing forward, he torqued his torso on the fulcrum of his waist and snatched the lash out of the air as it was curling towards him. With a flick of his wrist, he sent it snaking back so that it looped itself around Bhyro Singh's ox-like neck. Then, with a single, flowing sweep of his arm, he pulled the lash tight, jerking it with such force that before anyone could take a step or utter a sound, the subedar was lying dead on the deck, his neck broken.

## twenty-two

~

Down below, in the dabusa, the women were holding their breath: so far, the charging sound of Bhyro Singh's run-up had been followed always by the flesh-splitting crack of the lash as it bit into Kalua's back. But this time the rhythm was interrupted before reaching its climax: it was as though an unseen hand had snuffed out the peal of thunder that follows upon a bolt of lightning. And when the silence was broken, it was not by a noise of the kind they had expected, but by a concerted roar, as if a wave had come crashing down upon the vessel, swamping it in chaos: screams, shouts and the thudding of feet merged and grew in volume until the individual elements could not be told apart. The dabusa became once again a giant drum, pounded on by panicked feet above and angry waves below. To the women, it sounded as if the vessel were foundering and the menfolk were fighting to get away in the ship's boats, leaving them behind to drown. Running to the ladder the women scrambled up, towards the sealed exit, but just as the first of them reached it, the hatch flew open. Expecting a wave to come crashing down, the women leapt off the ladder—but instead of a torrent of water, there came first one migrant and then another, and still another, each tumbling over the other to escape the silahdars' flailing lathis. The women pounced on them, shaking them out of their shock, demanding to know what had happened and what was going on.

. . . Kalua's killed Bhyro Singh . . .

. . . with his own chabuk . . .

. . . broke his neck . . .

. . . and now the silahdars are going to take their revenge . . .

The welter of witnessing made it hard to know what was true and what was not: one man said the silahdars had already killed Kalua, but another denied this, saying he was alive, although badly beaten. Now, as yet more men came pouring down the ladder, everyone had something new to add, something else to report, so that it was almost as if Deeti were on the main deck herself, watching the events unfold: Kalua, cut loose from the frame to which he had been tethered, was being dragged across the deck by the enraged guards. The Kaptan was on the quarter-deck, with the two malums beside him, trying to reason with the silahdars, telling them it was their right to demand justice, and they would have it too, but only through a lawful execution, properly performed, not a lynching.

But this was not enough to satisfy the maddened mob on the main deck, who began to howl: Now! Now! Hang him now!

These cries set off a sudden churning, deep inside Deeti's belly: it was as if her unborn child had taken fright and was trying to shut out the voices that were clamouring for its father's death. Clapping her hands over her ears, Deeti staggered into the arms of the other women, who half dragged and half carried her to their corner of the dabusa and laid her prostrate on the planks.

~

'Stand back y'bastards!'

An instant after the roar had erupted from Mr Crowle's lips, the air was split by a report from his pistol. On the Captain's instructions, he had aimed the shot just to the left of the starboard davits, where the silahdars had dragged Kalua's almost-senseless body, with the intention of stringing him up from an improvised noose. The sound of the gun brought them abruptly to a halt and they spun around to find themselves facing not one, but three pairs of handguns. The Captain and the two mates were standing shoulder to shoulder on the quarter-deck, with their guns drawn and cocked.

'Stand back! Stand back, I said.'

No muskets had been issued to the guards that morning, and they were armed only with spears and swords. For a minute or two, the scrape of metal on metal could be clearly heard, as they milled about on deck, fidgeting with their hilts and scabbards, trying to decide what to do next.

Later, Zachary was to remember thinking that if the silahdars had made a concerted rush upon the quarter-deck just then, there was little that they, the three officers, could have done to hold them back: they would have been defenceless after they fired their first volley. Captain Chillingworth and Mr Crowle knew this just as well as he did, but they knew also that there could be no backing down now—for if the silahdars were allowed to get away with a lynching, then there was no telling what they'd do next. That Kalua would have to hang for the killing of Bhyro Singh was clear enough—but it was clear also that the execution could not be the work of a mob. All three officers were in unspoken agreement on this: if the silahdars were of a mind to mutiny, then this was when they would have to be faced down.

It was Mr Crowle who carried the day. Squaring his shoulders, he leant over the fife-rail and wagged his guns, in invitation. 'Come on y'blackguards; don't stand there showing me yer teeth. Let's see if ye've got a pair of ballocks between the lot o'yer.'

No more than anyone else could Zachary deny that Mr Crowle made an imposing figure as he stood astride the quarter-deck, with a pistol in each hand and a stream of obscenities flowing from his lips—'. . . pack o'mollyfuckin shagbags, let's see which o'yer is going to be the first to take a bullet in yer bacon-hole . . .' In his gaze there was such a relish for bloodshed that no one could doubt that he would shoot without hesitation. The silahdars seemed to understand this, for after a minute or two, they dropped their eyes and the fight seemed to seep out of them.

Mr Crowle lost no time in pressing home his advantage. 'Stand back; stand back, I say, step away from the coolie.'

Not without some muttering, the silahdars slowly edged away from Kalua's prostrate body and gathered in the middle of the deck. They were beaten now, and they knew it, so when Mr Crowle told them to drop their armaments they made a show of obeying in proper parade-ground fashion, laying their swords and spears in a tidy heap beneath the fife-rails.

The Captain took charge now, muttering a command to Zachary. 'Reid—take those weapons abaft and see they're properly stowed. Get a couple of the lascars to lend a hand.'

'Yes, sir.'

With the help of three lascars, Zachary gathered the weapons together, carried them below and locked them safely away in the armoury. Some twenty minutes passed before he came back up, and by that time an uneasy calm had descended on the quarter-deck. Zachary stepped out of the after-companionway to find the silahdars listening in subdued silence, as the Captain launched into one of his jobations.

'I know the subedar's death has come as a great shock . . .' Here, as the gomusta translated his words, the Captain paused to wipe his streaming face. '. . . Believe me, I fully share your grief. The subedar was a fine man, and I am as determined as any of you to see justice done.' Now that a mutiny had been averted, it was clear that the Captain was disposed to be as generous as possible: 'You have my word that the murderer will be hung—but you will have to wait until tomorrow, for it would be unseemly for a hanging to follow too closely upon a funeral. Till then, you must be patient. Today you must give your attention to your subedar—and after you are finished, you must retire to your quarters.'

The officers watched in silence as the silahdars performed

the subedar's last rites. At the end of the ceremony, they joined together to herd the guards and overseers back into the midships-cabin. When the last of them had stepped through, the Captain breathed a sigh of relief. 'Best keep them down there till tomorrow. Give them time to cool off.'

The Captain's strength had been failing visibly through the day, and it was with a noticeable effort that he now mopped his face. 'Must confess I feel none too spry,' he said. 'The deck is yours, Mr Crowle.'

'Y'go ahead and rest as long as y'like,' said the first mate. 'It's all in hand, sir.'

~

Deeti was among the last to learn of the stay on Kalua's execution, and the knowledge of this—that she had wasted precious time in venting her emotions—made her furious, and with no one so much as herself. She knew full well that if she was to be of any help to her husband, she would have to try to think as he did—and she was aware also that his most valuable resource in moments of crisis was not his strength of limb but rather his coolness of head. As if by instinct, she turned to the one person she knew she could depend on: Pugli—come here, sit beside me.

Bhauji?

Deeti put an arm around Paulette's shoulders and leant towards her ear: Pugli, what's to be done, tell me? Unless there's a miracle, I'm going to be a widow tomorrow.

Paulette took hold of her fingers and gave them a squeeze: Bhauji, don't give up hope. It's not tomorrow yet. A lot could happen between now and then.

Oh? The girl had been frequenting the air duct all morning, Deeti had noticed: she sensed that she knew more than she was willing to say. What is it, Pugli? Is something going on?

Paulette hesitated before giving her a quick nod. Yes, Bhauji, but don't ask me about it. I can't talk.

Deeti gave her a shrewdly appraising glance. All right, Pugli: I won't ask what's going on. But tell me this: you think it's possible that my *jora* could get away alive? Before tomorrow?

Who can tell, Bhauji? said Paulette. All I can say is that there's a chance.

*Hé Rám*! Deeti took hold Paulette's cheeks and shook them, in gratitude. Oh Pugli, I knew I could trust you.

Don't say that, Bhauji! Paulette cried. Don't say anything yet. So much could go wrong. Let's not doom it from the start.

There was more to this protest, Deeti guessed, than mere superstition: she could feel the girl's nervousness in the tautness of her cheeks. She brought her head closer to her ear.

Tell me, Pugli, she said, are you going to have a part in it too—whatever it is that's going to happen?

Again Paulette hesitated before blurting out, in a whisper: A very small part, Bhauji. But an essential one, or so I'm told. And I'm worried that things may go wrong.

Deeti rubbed her cheeks to warm them. I'll be praying for you, Pugli . . .

~

A little after four, shortly after the start of the first dogwatch of the afternoon, Captain Chillingworth came on deck again, looking pale and feverish, and hugging an old-fashioned boat-cloak to his chest. As he emerged from the companionway, his eyes went straight to the stooped, drooping figure that was tethered to the mainmast. He turned a glance of inquiry on the first mate, who answered with a grim laugh: 'The nigger's alive all right; kill that ziggerboo ten times over and he wouldn't be dead.'

The Captain nodded, and began to shuffle to the windward side of the quarter-deck, with his head lowered and his shoulders bunched. The wind was blowing hard and steady from the east, throwing white-capped combers against the schooner's side. In deference to the weather the Captain headed not to his usual place, at the junction of the bulwark and the fife-rail, but to the protective shelter of the after-shrouds. On reaching the shrouds, he turned to look eastwards where dark scuds of cloud had tumbled together to form a dense, steel-grey mass. 'Storm-breeders if ever I saw them,' muttered the Captain. 'How bad do you think it's going to be, Mr Crowle?'

'Nothing to sweat about, sir,' said the first mate. 'Just a few scurries and sneezers. Blow itself out by dawn.'

The Captain leant back to look up at the masts, which were now bare of all canvas except for the staysails and foresails. 'None the less, gentlemen,' he said, 'we'll have her hove-to and snugged down; best to ride out the weather under a storm-staysail. No need to take any risks.'

Neither of the mates wanted to be the first to give their assent to such an excess of caution. 'Can't see as it's necessary, sir,' said Mr Crowle at last, reluctantly.

'You'll do it all the same,' said the Captain. 'Or do I have to remain on deck to see it done?'

'Don't y'worry sir,' said Mr Crowle quickly. 'I'll see to it.'

'Good,' said the Captain. 'I'll leave it to you then. And as for myself, I'm more than a little a-weather, I must confess. I would be grateful if I could be spared any interruptions tonight.'

~

That day the girmitiyas were not allowed on deck for their evening meal. The weather being as bad as it was, they were passed balties of dry rations through the hatch—stale rock-hard rotis and parched gram. Few among them cared what they were served, for none but a handful had the stomach to eat. For most of them, the events of the morning had already faded from the forefront of memory: as the weather grew steadily worse, their attention came to be wholly absorbed by the raging elements. Since all flames and lights were forbidden, they had to sit in darkness as they listened to the waves, pounding against the hull, and the wind, shrieking through the bare masts. The din was enough to confirm everything that anyone had ever thought about the Black Water: it was as if all the demons of hell were fighting to get into the dabusa.

'Miss Lambert, Miss Lambert . . .'

The whisper, barely audible above the noise, was so faint that Paulette's ears would not have picked it up, had the name not been her own. She rose to her feet, balanced herself against a beam, and turned to the air duct: all that could be seen was an eye, gleaming behind the slot, but she knew at once who it belonged to. 'Mr Halder?'

'Yes, Miss Lambert.'

Paulette went closer to the duct. 'Is there something you wish to say?'

'Only that I wish you all success for tonight: for your brother's sake and mine, and indeed for all of us.'

'I will do what I can, Mr Halder.'

'I do not doubt it for a moment, Miss Lambert. If anyone could succeed in this delicate mission it is none other than you. Your brother has told us something of your story and I confess I am amazed. You are a woman of extraordinary talent, Miss Lambert—a genius in a way. Your performance so far has been so fine, so true, as not to be an impersonation at all. I would never have thought my eye, or my ear, could have been thus deceived—and that too, by a firangin, a Frenchwoman.'

'But I am none of those things, Mr Halder,' protested Paulette. 'There is nothing untrue about the person who stands here. Is it forbidden for a human being to manifest themselves in many different aspects?'

'Evidently not. I hope very much, Miss Lambert, that we will meet again somewhere, and in happier circumstances.'

'I hope so too, Mr Halder. And when we do, I trust you will call me Paulette—or Putli, as Jodu does. But should you wish to call me Pugli, that too is not an identity that I would disown.'

'And I, Miss Paulette, would ask you to call me Neel—except that if we do meet again, I suspect I will have had to change my name. But until then, in any event, I wish you farewell. And *bon courage*.'

And to you too. *Bhalo thakben.*

Paulette had no sooner sat down than she was summoned to the air duct by Jodu: Putli, it's time; you've got to change and get ready. Mamdoo-tindal's going to let you out in a few minutes.

~

At midnight, when his watch ended, Zachary changed into a set of dry clothes and fell into his bunk fully dressed—in a blow like this one, there was no knowing when he'd be needed on deck. Apart from the single storm-sail there was not a stitch aloft on the schooner's masts, but the wind was blowing so hard that the sound of this one square of cloth was like that of a massed chorus of sail. From the violence with which his bunk was pitching under him, Zachary knew, too, that the *Ibis* was being buffeted by swells of a good twenty feet or more. The waves were no longer surging over the bulwarks, but crashing down from above, like breakers pounding a beach, and when the water ran off the decks, it was with a sucking sound, like surf retreating down a slope of sand.

Twice, as he lay on his bunk, Zachary had heard an ominous creak, like that of a spar, or a mast, about to give way, and despite his intentions of getting a good rest, his senses were at a fine pitch of alertness, listening for further signs of damage. This was why the first hint of a knock at his door made him sit up. The cabin was dark, for Zachary had put out his lamp before he lay down; as he was tumbling out of his bunk, the schooner rolled to larboard, throwing him against the door: he would have crashed into it, face first, if he hadn't turned sideways and used his shoulder to soften the impact.

As the schooner was righting itself, he called out: 'Who is it?' Receiving no answer, he pulled the door open.

Steward Pinto had left a single lamp glowing in the cuddy, and by the light of the dim, fliickering flame he saw a lascar standing at the door, with his dripping oilskins draped over his arm. He was a wiry, boyish fellow with a bandanna around his head. Zachary didn't recognize him, for his face was in shadow.

'Who're you?' he said. 'What're you doing here?'

Before Zachary could finish, the schooner listed to starboard, sending both of them stumbling into the cabin. As they were wrestling to regain their footing, the door slammed shut and the deck tilted again. All of a sudden, Zachary found himself lying on his bunk, with the lascar beside him. Then, out of the darkness, a whisper made itself heard that all but froze his blood. 'Mr Reid . . . Mr Reid . . . please . . .'

The voice was distantly familiar, but in a way that was profoundly unnerving, in the manner of something so far removed from its proper circumstance that it could only be an unnatural version of itself. Zachary's voice died in his throat and his skin began to prickle as the whispering continued. 'Mr Reid, it is I, Paulette Lambert . . .'

'What was that?' Zachary would not have been in the least surprised if the presence beside him had disappeared or dematerialized—for what else could it be but a conjuration of his own imaginings?—but this possibility was quickly dismissed, for the voice now repeated its earlier claim: 'Please Mr Reid. . . believe me, it is I, Paulette Lambert.'

'Impossible!'

'Believe me, Mr Reid,' the voice continued in the darkness. 'It is true. I pray you will not be angered, but you should know I have been aboard since the commencement of the voyage— in the 'tween-deck, among the women.'

'No!' Zachary pushed himself sideways, moving as far from her as the bunk would allow. 'I was there when the coolies boarded. I'd'a known.'

'But it is true, Mr Reid. I came aboard with the migrants. It was because of my sari that you did not reconnaisse me.'

He knew now, from her voice, that it really was Paulette—and it occurred to him that surely he ought to be glad to have her there, beside him. But no more than any other sailor did he care to be boarded in the smoke: he had never liked to be taken by surprise, and he found himself growing embarrassed as he considered how ridiculous he must have looked a minute or two ago.

'Well, Miss Lambert,' he said, stiffly. 'If it is you, you've certainly succeeded in making quite a dupe of me.'

'Such was not my intention, Mr Reid. I assure you.'

'May I ask,' he said, trying to recover his lost composure, 'which one you were—which of the women, that is?'

'Yes, for sure, Mr Reid,' she said eagerly. 'You have seen me many times, but perhaps without noticing: I was often on deck, doing the washing.' The words were no sooner out of her mouth than she sensed that she'd said too much already—but a mounting nervousness made it impossible for her to stop. 'This very shirt you are wearing now, Mr Reid, I washed it, this and all your . . .'

'. . . dirty linen? Is that what you were going to say?' Zachary was mortified now, and his cheeks began to burn. 'Pray tell me, Miss Lambert,' he said, 'what was it for, all this trickery and deceit? Just to show me up for a fool?'

Paulette was stung by the sharpness of his tone. 'You are much mistaken, Mr Reid,' she said, 'if you imagine that you are the cause of my presence on board. Believe me, it was solely for myself that I did what I have done. It was imperatif for me to leave Calcutta—you know full well the reasons. This was my only means of escape and what I did was no different from what my grand-aunt, Madame Commerson, would have done.'

'Your grand-aunt, Miss Lambert?' said Zachary acidly. 'Why, you have outdone her by far! Indeed you have proved yourself the equal of any chameleon. You have so perfected the arts of impersonation that I should not doubt they have become the very core of your soul.'

Paulette could not understand how this encounter, in which she had invested so much hope and emotion, had turned into such an ugly fencing match. But nor was she one to back down in the face of a challenge. Her response sprang from her lips before she could bite it back: 'Oh Mr Reid! You allow me more credit than is my due. If I have any equal in impersonation, surely it is none other than yourself?'

Despite the howling of the wind and the crash of the waves outside, there was a strange stillness in the cabin now. Zachary swallowed once, and then cleared his throat: 'So you know?' If his imposture had been announced from the truck of the mainmast, he could not have felt more exposed, more completely a charlatan than he did then.

'Oh forgive me!'—he could hear her choking on her words—'oh, forgive me, I did not mean . . .'

'Nor did I, Miss Lambert, mean to deceive you in the matter of my race. On the few occasions when we were able to speak to each other, I tried to indicate—no, I tried to tell you, believe me.'

'What does it matter, Mr Reid?' In a belated attempt to make amends, Paulette softened her voice. 'Are not all appearances deceptive, in the end? Whatever there is within us—whether good, or bad, or neither—its existence will continue uninterrupted, will it not, no matter what the drape of our clothes, or the colour of our skin? What if it is the world that is a duperie, Mr Reid, and we the exceptions to its lies?'

Zachary shook his head in scorn at what seemed to be merely a feeble attempt at extenuation. 'I fear, Miss Lambert, that I am too plain a man to understand these subtleties. I must ask you to be more direct. Pray tell me, why have you chosen to reveal yourself now? Why at this time? Surely it was not in order to announce our fellowship in deceit that you sought me out?'

'No, Mr Reid,' said Paulette. 'It was for wholly another

purpose. And you should know that I have come on behalf of others, our common friends . . .'

'Who, may I ask?'

'Serang Ali, for one.'

At the sound of that name, Zachary covered his eyes with his hands: if there was anything at that moment that could have made him feel any more humiliated than he did already, it was this mention of the man he had once thought to be his mentor. 'It is all clear to me now, Miss Lambert,' he said. 'I see how you have gained your intelligence in regard to my origins. But tell me, Miss Lambert, was it Serang Ali's idea, or yours, to use this information for blackmail?'

'Blackmail? Oh for shame, Mr Reid! For shame!'

~

The wind was blowing so hard, Baboo Nob Kissin dared not stand upright on the rain-lashed deck: fortunate indeed that he had moved his lodgings from the midships-cabin to the deckhouse—or else the summons to the fana would have required him to cross a much greater length of deck. Even this short distance seemed impossibly long, much too far to negotiate on his feet: instead he made his way forward on all fours, cowering in the shelter of the bulwarks as he crawled slowly towards the fana.

The hatch that led below was fastened tight against the water, but it opened at the first tap of his knuckles. There was a lamp swinging inside, illuminating the faces of Serang Ali and the lascars, lying in their jhulis, rolling with the motion of the ship, watching him as he made his way to the chokey.

The gomusta had no eyes for anyone other than the man he was seeking, no thought but for the completion of his errand. Squatting beside the bars, he held the keys out to Neel: here they are, take them, take them; may they help you find your release, your *mukti* . . .

But once he had placed the keys in Neel's palm, he would

not let go of his hand. Do you see her now? In my eyes? Ma Taramony? Is she here? Within me?

When Neel's head moved, and Baboo Nob Kissin saw that he was nodding, his joy was beyond containment. You're sure? he said. Sure she's there now? It is time?

Yes, said Neel, looking into his eyes, nodding in confirmation. Yes, she is there. I see her—a mother incarnate: her time has come . . .

The gomusta let go of Neel's hand and wrapped his arms around himself: now that the last shreds of his former being were to be discarded, he was aware of a strange affection, a tenderness for the body that had so long been his. There was no reason for him to remain here any longer: he made his way back to the main deck and took a step towards the deckhouse. His eyes fell on Kalua, and once again, he lowered himself to all fours, and crawled along the bulwarks. Pulling himself level with the drooping figure, he put an arm around him and held on as a wave surged across the deck, almost sweeping his legs out from under him.

Wait, he whispered to Kalua. Wait just a little bit longer, and you too will find your freedom; *moksha* is at hand for you too . . .

Now that Taramony's presence was fully manifest in him, it was as if he had become the key that could unlock the cages that imprisoned everyone, all these beings who were ensnared by the illusory differences of this world. It was the fullness of this insight that carried him, drenched and battered, but ecstatic in the possession of his new self, towards the after-cabins. At Zachary's door, he paused as he so often had, to listen for a flute, and caught instead the sound of whispering voices.

It was here, he remembered, in this very place, that the start of his transfiguration had been signalled, by the sound of a flute: everything had come full circle now, everything was as foretold. His hand went to his amulet and he slipped out the piece of paper that lay inside. Hugging it to his chest, he began to turn around and around; the ship was dancing with him too, the deck heaving to the rhythm of his whirling footsteps. Seized by the transcendent, blissful joy of pure ananda, he closed his eyes.

This was how Mr Crowle found him: turning around and around, with arms raised in the air. 'Pander, y'fuckin cunt-pensioner . . .!' He stopped the gomusta's dance with a slap across the face. Then his eyes went to the sheet of paper which the gomusta, now cowering, was clutching in his hands. 'What's this then? Let's have a look.'

~

Sweeping a hand across her eyes, Paulette brushed away a flurry of tears. She could never have imagined that her meeting with Zachary would take such a hostile turn, but now that it had, it was best not to make things worse than they were already. 'It is no use, Mr Reid,' she said, rising to her feet. 'It has clearly been a great meprise for us to speak with each other. I came to tell you that your friends are direly in need of you; I came to speak of my own . . . but it is no use. Everything I say seems only to deepen our misunderstandings. It is best that I leave now.'

'Wait! Miss Lambert!'

The thought of losing her panicked Zachary. Leaping to his feet, he reached blindly towards the sound of her voice, forgetting, in the darkness, how small his cabin was. Almost as soon as he raised his hand, his fingers brushed against her arm; he made as if to pull away, but his palm would not move; instead, his thumb pushed back the fabric of her shirt. She was close enough that he could hear her breathing; he could even feel the warmth of her exhalations misting on his face. His hand went along her shoulder, to the back of her neck, pausing between her collar and bandanna, to explore the patch of bare skin that had been exposed by her upswept hair. Strange how he had once been appalled by the thought of seeing her as a lascar; strange that he had wanted to keep her forever wrapped in velveteen. For even though he could not actually see her now, the very knowledge of her guise made her seem more desirable than ever, a creature so changeable and elusive as to be impossible to resist: his mouth was suddenly fastened on hers, and her lips were pressed against his.

Even though they could see nothing in the darkness of the unlit cabin, their absorption was such that they both slowly closed their eyes. When a knock sounded on the door neither of them noticed. It was only when Mr Crowle shouted—'Y'in there, Mannikin?'—that they sprang apart.

Paulette flattened herself against the bulwark as Zachary cleared his throat. 'Yes, Mr Crowle: what is it?'

'Could y'step out?'

Prising the door apart a few inches, Zachary saw that Mr Crowle was standing outside. Cowering beside him was Baboo Nob Kissin, whose neck was firmly in the first mate's grip.

'What's going on, Mr Crowle?'

'I've got something y'need to see, Mannikin,' said the first mate, with a grim smile. 'Something I got from our friend Baboon here.'

Zachary stepped quickly outside, pulling his door shut behind him. 'What is it?'

'I'll show yer, but not here. And not while I've got this Baboon on my hands. Best he cools off in yer cabin.' Before Zachary could say anything, Mr Crowle pushed the door open and kneed the gomusta in the small of his back, propelling him past Zachary, into his cabin. Without looking inside, the first mate pulled the door shut. Then he lifted an oar out of a wall-bracket and thrust the shaft through the looped handles. 'That should hold him while we're sorting this out.'

'And where are we going to do that?'

'My cabin's as good a place as any.'

~

As with a bear in its den, the reassurance of being in his own space lent an extra heft to the first mate's already formidable physique: once he and Zachary were inside, with the door closed behind them, he seemed to swell and expand, leaving Zachary very little room. The vessel was swaying wildly and they had to stretch out their arms to steady themselves against the sides of the cabin. But even then, standing spreadeagled and chest to chest, bumping against each other with the schooner's every lurch, Mr Crowle seemed intent on using his height and bulk to crowd Zachary into sitting down on his bunk. But this Zachary would not do: there was something in the first mate's demeanour that spoke of an excess of emotion that was even more disturbing than the overt aggression of the past. In order not to yield any ground to the larger man, Zachary forced himself to stay on his feet.

'Well then, Mr Crowle? What did you want to see me about?'

'Somethin ye'll thank me for, Reid.' The first mate reached into his vest and pulled out a yellowing sheet of paper. 'Got this off that gooby—Pander, innit? He was takin it t'the skipper. Ye're lucky I got a-hold o' it, Reid. Thing like this could do a cove a lot o'damage. Could'appen he'd never work on a ship again.'

'What is it?'

'It's the crew-list—for the *Ibis*, on'er run out from Baltimore.'

'And what of it?' said Zachary, frowning.

'Take a dekko, Reid.' Holding up the lamp, the mate handed him the tattered slip of paper. 'Go on—see fer y'self.'

Back when he first signed on to the *Ibis*, Zachary had known nothing of ships' papers or crew manifests, or how the filling-in of them might vary from vessel to vessel. He had walked on board the *Ibis* with his ditty-bag, shouted his name, age and birthplace to the second mate, and that was that. But he saw now that along with a few other members of the crew, there was an extra notation next to his name: he narrowed his eyes, squinting, and suddenly he froze.

'Y'see, Reid?' said Mr Crowle. 'See what I mean?'

Zachary answered by nodding mechanically, without raising

his eyes, and the first mate continued. 'Lookat, Reid,' he said, hoarsely, 'it don't mean anythin to me. Don't give a damn, I don't, if ye're a m'latter or not.'

Zachary answered, as if by rote: 'I'm not a mulatto, Mr Crowle. My mother was a quadroon and my father white. That makes me a metif.'

'Don't change nothing, Reid.' Mr Crowle's hand reached up and he brushed a knuckle against Zachary's unshaven cheek. 'Metif or m'latter, it don't change the colour o'this . . .'

Zachary, still mesmerized by the paper, made no movement, and the hand rose higher still, to flick back a curly forelock with a fingertip. '. . . And it don't change this neither. Y'are what y'are, Reid, and it don't make no difference to me. If y'ask me, it makes us two of a kind.'

Zachary looked up now, and his eyes narrowed in puzzlement. 'Don't get the gist, Mr Crowle?'

The first mate's voice sank to a low growl. 'Look'ere, Reid, we di'n't get off to a good start, there's no denyin' it. Y'made a fool o'me with yer tofficky trolly-wags and yer buncomising tongue: thought y'was way above my touch. But this'ere paper, it changes everything—I'd never'a thought I could've been so far off course.'

'What do you mean, Mr Crowle?'

'Don't y'see, Mannikin?' The first mate put his hand on Zachary's shoulder. 'We could be a team, the two o'us.' He tapped the paper and took it out of Zachary's hand. 'This thing—nobbut needs be in the know of it. Not the Captain nor anyone else. It'll stay here.' Folding the manifest, he slipped it under his vest. 'Think about it, Reid, me as skipper, and y'self as mate. Tie for tye; no lies for y'self and none for me neither: we'd have the jin o'each other, both o'us. What more could two coves like us hope for? No need for gulling, no need for lies: ton for ton and man for man. I'd be easy on yer too, Mannikin; I'm one who knows what o'clock it is and which way the bull runs. When we're in port ye'd be on the loose, free for whatever takes yer fancy: don't make no difference to me, not ashore.'

'And at sea?'

'All ye'd have to do is cross the cuddy from time to time. That in't so long a walk, is it? And if it in't t'yer taste, y'can shut yer eyes and think y'self in Jericho for all I care. Comes a day, Mannikin, when every Tar has t'learn t'work ship in headwinds and bad weather. Y'think life owes y'any different from others just cause ye're a m'latter?'

Despite the brutal roughness of the first mate's tone, Zachary could sense that he was on the verge of an inner disintegration, and he was aware of an unexpected stirring of sympathy. His eyes sought out the piece of paper that he was holding between his fingers, and he was amazed to think that something so slight, so inocuous could be invested with so much authority: that it should be able to melt away the fear, the apparent invulnerability that he, Zachary, had possessed in his guise as a 'gentleman'; that it should so change his aspect as to make him appeal to a man who could desire, evidently, only that which he held in his power; that the essence of this transformation should inhere in a single word—all of this spoke more to the delirium of the world, than to the perversity of those who had to make their way in it.

He could sense the first mate's mounting impatience for an answer, and when he spoke it was not unkindly, but with a quiet firmness. 'Look, Mr Crowle,' he said. 'I'm sorry but this deal o'yours won't work for me. It may look to you that this piece of paper has turned me inside out, but in truth it's changed nothing. I was born with my freedom and I ain't looking to give any o'it away.'

Zachary took a step towards the door but the first mate moved in front of him, blocking his way. 'Boat yer oars Mannikin,' he said, on a note of warning. 'Won't do yer no good to walk yer chalks now.'

'Listen, Mr Crowle,' said Zachary, quietly. 'Neither of us needs to remember this conversation. Once I step out this door, it's over and done with—didn't happen.'

'Too late to toss up the bunt now, Mannikin,' said the first mate. 'What's said is said and can't be forgotten.'

Zachary looked him up and down and squared his shoulders. 'What do you plan to do then, Mr Crowle? Keep me in here till I knock the door down?'

'Aren't y'forgetting something, Mannikin?' The first mate tapped his finger on the paper that was tucked into his vest. 'Wouldn't take me more'n a couple o'minutes to run this over to the skipper.'

There was a desperation, almost a pathos, in this threat of blackmail, and it made Zachary smile. 'Go ahead, Mr Crowle,' he said. 'Whatever that paper is, it's not a letter of indenture. Take it to the Captain—believe me, I'd be glad of it. And I'll wager that when he hears about the bargain you were of a mind to make, it's not because of me that he's going to be all cut up inside.'

'Stow yer magging, Reid!' The first mate's hand came flying out of the shadows to strike Zachary across the face. Then a blade flashed in the lamplight and its point came to rest on Zachary's upper lip. 'I'se done my time, Mannikin, and ye'll do it too. Ye're just a broth of a boy: I'll bring y'to yer bearings soon enough.'

'With your knife, Mr Crowle?' Now the blade began to descend, travelling downwards in a straight line, from Zachary's nose, past his chin to the base of his throat.

'I tell yer, Mannikin, ye're not nigger enough to leave Jack Crowle hangin a-cockbill; not when he's all catted and fished. I'll corpse yer before I let yer gi'me the slip.'

'Better do it then, Mr Crowle. Better do it now.'

'Oh, I'd kill yer without a thought, Mannikin,' said Mr Crowle, through his teeth. 'Don't y'doubt it. I'se done it before and I'll do it again. Wouldn't make a penn'orth o'difference to me.'

Now Zachary could feel the cold metal point pushing against his throat. 'Go on, Mr Crowle,' he said, steeling himself. 'Do it. I'm ready.'

With the tip of the knife biting into his skin, Zachary kept his eyes fixed upon the first mate's, even as he was preparing himself for the thrust. But it was Mr Crowle's gaze that wavered first, and then the knife faltered and fell away.

'God damn yer eyes, Reid!'

Throwing his head back, the first mate gave voice to a howl that welled up from the bottom of his belly. 'The devil take yer, Reid; God damn yer eyes . . .'

Just then, even as the first mate was standing in front of Zachary, staring in disbelief at the knife he had been unable to use, the door of the cabin creaked open. Framed in the doorway stood the slight, shadowy figure of the half-Chinese convict: he had a sharp-tipped handspike in his hands, Zachary saw, and he was holding it not as a sailor would, but like a swordsman, with the point extended.

Sensing his presence, the first mate spun around, with his knife at the ready. When he saw who it was, he snarled in disbelief: 'Jackin-ape?'

Ah Fatt's presence seemed to have a tonic effect on the first mate, restoring him instantly to his usual self: as if exhilarated by the prospect of violent release, he made a swinging lunge with his knife. Ah Fatt swayed easily out of the way, seeming hardly to move at all, balancing his weight on the balls of his feet. His eyes were almost closed, as if in prayer, and his handspike was no longer extended, but folded against his chest, its point tucked under his chin.

'Going to cut yer tongue out, Jackin-ape,' said Mr Crowle, in a voice that was filled with menace. 'Then I'm a-goin to make yer eat it too.'

The mate made another thrust, aiming at the belly, but Ah Fatt turned sideways, eluding the point of his blade. This time the momentum of the strike carried the mate forward, exposing his flank. Spinning on his heel, like a bullfighter, Ah Fatt thrust the handspike through his ribs, burying it almost to the hilt. He held on to his weapon as the mate dropped to the deck, and when the spike was free of his body, he turned the bloody point towards Zachary. 'Stay where you are. Or else, you too . . .'

Then, just as quickly as he had come, he was gone: slamming the door behind him, he thrust the handspike through the handles, locking Zachary into the cabin.

Zachary fell to his knees beside the pool of blood that was leaking out of the first mate's flank: 'Mr Crowle?'

He caught the sound of a choking whisper: 'Reid? Reid . . .'

Zachary lowered his head, to listen to the faltering voice.

'Y'were the one, Reid—the one I'se been lookin for. Y'were the one . . .'

His words were choked off by a surge of blood, gushing up through his mouth and nose. Then his head snapped back and his body went rigid; when Zachary put a hand under his nostrils, there was no evidence of breath. The schooner lurched and the first mate's lifeless body rolled with it. The edge of the old crew-list could be seen peering out of his vest: Zachary pulled it out and stuffed it into his own pocket. Then he rose to his feet and shoved his shoulder against the door. It gave a little, and he jiggled it gently until the handspike slipped out, falling to the deck with a thud.

~

Bursting out of the first mate's cabin, Zachary saw that his own door was already open. Without pausing to look inside, he went racing up to the quarter-deck. Rain was lashing down from the sky in knotted sheets; it was as if the schooner's sails had come unfastened and were tearing themselves apart against the hull. Instantly drenched, Zachary raised a hand to shelter his eyes from the sting of the rain. A wave of lightning surged across the sky, widening as it travelled westwards, flooding the water below with a rolling tide of radiance. In that unearthly light a longboat seemed to leap out at Zachary, from the crest of a wave: although it was already some twenty yards off the schooner's beam, the faces of the five men who were in it could be clearly seen. Serang Ali was at the rudder, and the other four were huddled in its middle—Jodu, Neel, Ah Fatt and Kalua. Serang Ali had seen Zachary too, and he was raising his hand to wave when the craft dropped behind a ridge of water and disappeared from view.

As the lightning was retreating across the sky, Zachary became aware that he was not the only one who was watching the boat: there were three others on the main deck, below, standing with their arms interlinked. Two of them he recognized immediately, Paulette and Baboo Nob Kissin—but the third was a woman in a sodden sari, who had never before uncovered her face in his presence. Now, in the fading glow of the clouds, she turned to look at him and he saw that she had piercing, grey eyes. Although it was the first time he had seen her face, he knew that he had glimpsed her somewhere, standing much as she was now, in a wet sari, hair dripping, looking at him with startled grey eyes.

# acknowledgements

~

*Sea of Poppies* owes a great debt to many 19th century scholars, dictionarists, linguists and chroniclers: most notably to Sir George Grierson, for his *Report on Colonial Emigration from the Bengal Presidency*, 1883, for his grammar of the Bhojpuri language, and for his 1884 and 1886 articles on Bhojpuri folk songs; to J.W.S. MacArthur, one-time Superintendent of the Ghazipur Opium Factory for his *Notes on an Opium Factory* (Thacker, Spink, Calcutta, 1865); to Lt. Thomas Roebuck, for his nautical lexicon, first published in Calcutta, *An English And Hindostanee Naval Dictionary Of Technical Terms And Sea Phrases As Also The Various Words Of Command Given In Working A Ship, &C. With Many Sentences Of Great Use At Sea; To Which Is Prefixed A Short Grammar Of The Hindostanee Language* (reprinted in London in 1813 by Black, Parry & Co., booksellers to the Hon. East India Company; later revised by George Small, and reissued by W.H. Allen & Co., under the title *A Laskari Dictionary Or Anglo-Indian Vocabulary Of Nautical Terms And Phrases In English And Hindustani*, London, 1882); to Sir Henry Yule and A.C. Burnell, authors of *Hobson-Jobson: A Glossary Of Colloquial Anglo-Indian Words And Phrases, And Of Kindred Terms, Etymological, Historical, Geographical And Discursive*; and to the Chief Justice of Calcutta's Supreme Court of Judicature for his verdict in the 1829 forgery trial of Prawnkissen Holdar (reprinted in Anil Chandra Das Gupta, [ed.]: *The Days of John Company: Selections from Calcutta*

*Gazette 1824–1832*, West Bengal Govt. Press, Calcutta, 1959, pp. 366–368).

This novel has been greatly enriched by the work of many contemporary and near-contemporary scholars and historians. The complete list of books, articles and essays that have contributed to my understanding of the period is too long to reproduce here, but it would be remiss of me not to acknowledge my gratitude for, and my indebtedness to, the work of the following: Clare Anderson, Robert Antony, David Arnold, Jack Beeching, Kingsley Bolton, Sarita Boodhoo, Anne Bulley, B.R. Burg, Marina Carter, Hsin-Pao Chang, Weng Eang Cheong, Tan Chung, Maurice Collis, Saloni Deerpalsingh, Guo Deyan, Jacques M. Downs, Amar Farooqui, Peter Ward Fay, Michael Fisher, Basil Greenhill, Richard H. Grove, Amalendu Guha, Edward O. Henry, Engseng Ho, Hunt Janin, Isaac Land, C.P. Liang, Brian Lubbock, Dian H. Murray, Helen Myers, Marcus Rediker, John F. Richards, Dingxu Shi, Asiya Siddiqi, Radhika Singha, Michael Sokolow, Vijaya Teelock, Madhavi Thampi and Rozina Visram.

For their support and assistance at various points in the writing of this novel, I owe many thanks to: Kanti and Champa Banymandhab, Girindre Beeharry, the late Sir Satcam Boolell and his family, Sanjay Buckory, Pushpa Burrenchobay, May Bo Ching, Careem Curreemjee, Saloni Deerpalsingh, Parmeshwar K. Dhawan, Greg Gibson, Marc Foo Kune, Surendra Ramgoolam, Vishwamitra Ramphul, Achintyarup Ray, Debashree Roy, Anthony J. Simmonds, Vijaya Teelock, Boodhun Teelock and Zhou Xiang. I owe a great debt of gratitude also to the following institutions: the National Maritime Museum, Greenwich, England; the Mahatma Gandhi Institute, Mauritius; and the Mauritius National Archives.

The lines quoted in Chapter Two (*Ág mor lágal ba . . .*) are from a song collected by Edward O. Henry (*Chant the Names of God: Music and Culture in Bhojpuri-Speaking India*, San Diego State University Press, San Diego, 1988, p. 288). The lines quoted in Chapter Three (*Majha dhára me hai bera merá . . .*) are from a song collected by Helen Myers (*Music of*

*Hindu Trinidad: Songs from the Indian Diaspora*, University of Chicago Press, Chicago, 1998, p. 307). The lines quoted in Chapter Five (*Sājh bhailé . . .*) are from Sarita Boodhoo's *Bhojpuri Traditions in Mauritius*, Mauritius Bhojpuri Institute, Port Louis, 1999, p. 63. The lines quoted in Chapter Nineteen (*Talwa jharailé . . .*) and the lines quoted in Chapter Twenty-one (. . . *uthlé há chhati ke jobanwá . . .*) are from songs collected by Sir George Grierson for his article, 'Some Bhojpuri Folksongs', *Journal of the Royal Asiatic Society*, 18, p. 207, 1886. In all these instances the translations are my own.

Without the support of Barney Karpfinger and Roland Phillips, the *Ibis* could not have crossed the Bay of Bengal; at critical moments in her journey, James Simpson and Chris Clark helped fill her sails; my children, Lila and Nayan, saw her through many a storm and my wife, Deborah Baker, was the best of malums: I, no less than this frail craft, owe them all a great debt of gratitude.

*Kolkata*                                              **Amitav Ghosh**
*2008*